PAL S0-CFY-624
LIBRARY SYSTEM

3650 Summit Boulevard
West Palm Beach, FL 33406

WINGS OF FIRE

MOON RISING
THE GRAPHIC NOVEL

For Addie, a great artist, writer, and friend—
I can't wait to read your books one day!
——T.T.S.

For the librarians and the teachers—you help readers
become writers and doodlers become artists.
——M.H.

Story and text copyright © 2023 by Tui T. Sutherland
Adaptation by Barry Deutsch and Rachel Swirsky
Map and border design © 2014 by Mike Schley
Art by Mike Holmes © 2023 by Scholastic Inc.

All rights reserved. Published by Graphix, an imprint of Scholastic Inc.,
Publishers since 1920. SCHOLASTIC, GRAPHIX, and associated logos are
trademarks and/or registered trademarks of Scholastic Inc.

The publisher does not have any control over and does not assume any responsibility
for author or third-party websites or their content.

No part of this publication may be reproduced, stored in a retrieval
system, or transmitted in any form or by any means, electronic, mechanical,
photocopying, recording, or otherwise, without written permission of the publisher.
For information regarding permission, write to Scholastic Inc., Attention:
Permissions Department, 557 Broadway, New York, NY 10012.

This book is a work of fiction. Names, characters, places, and incidents are either the
product of the author's imagination or are used fictitiously, and any resemblance to actual
persons, living or dead, business establishments, events, or locales is entirely coincidental.

Library of Congress Control Number Available

ISBN 978-1-338-73090-6 (hardcover)
ISBN 978-1-338-73089-0 (paperback)

10 9 8 7 6 5 4 3 2 1   23 24 25 26 27

Printed in China   62
First edition, January 2023
Edited by Amanda Maciel
Coloring by Maarta Laiho
Lettering by E.K. Weaver
Creative Director: Phil Falco
Publisher: David Saylor

WINGS OF FIRE

MOON RISING
THE GRAPHIC NOVEL

BY **TUI T. SUTHERLAND**

ADAPTED BY **BARRY DEUTSCH**
AND **RACHEL SWIRSKY**

ART BY **MIKE HOLMES**
COLOR BY **MAARTA LAIHO**

AN IMPRINT OF
■SCHOLASTIC

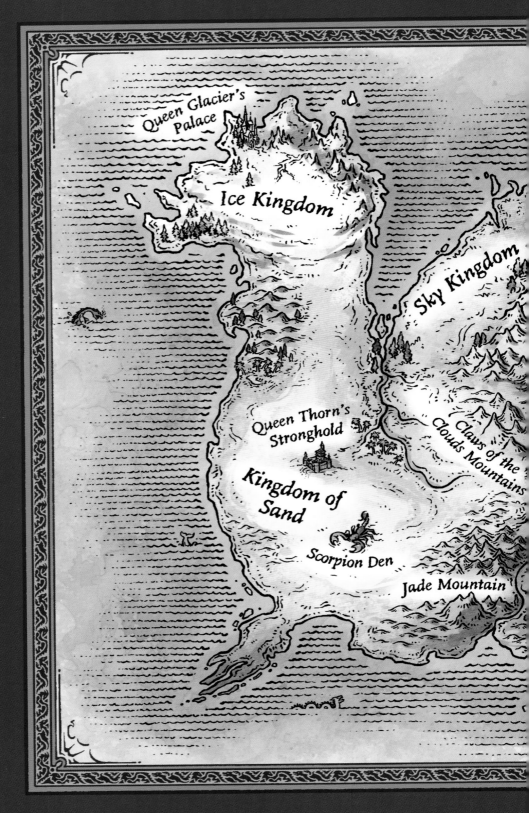

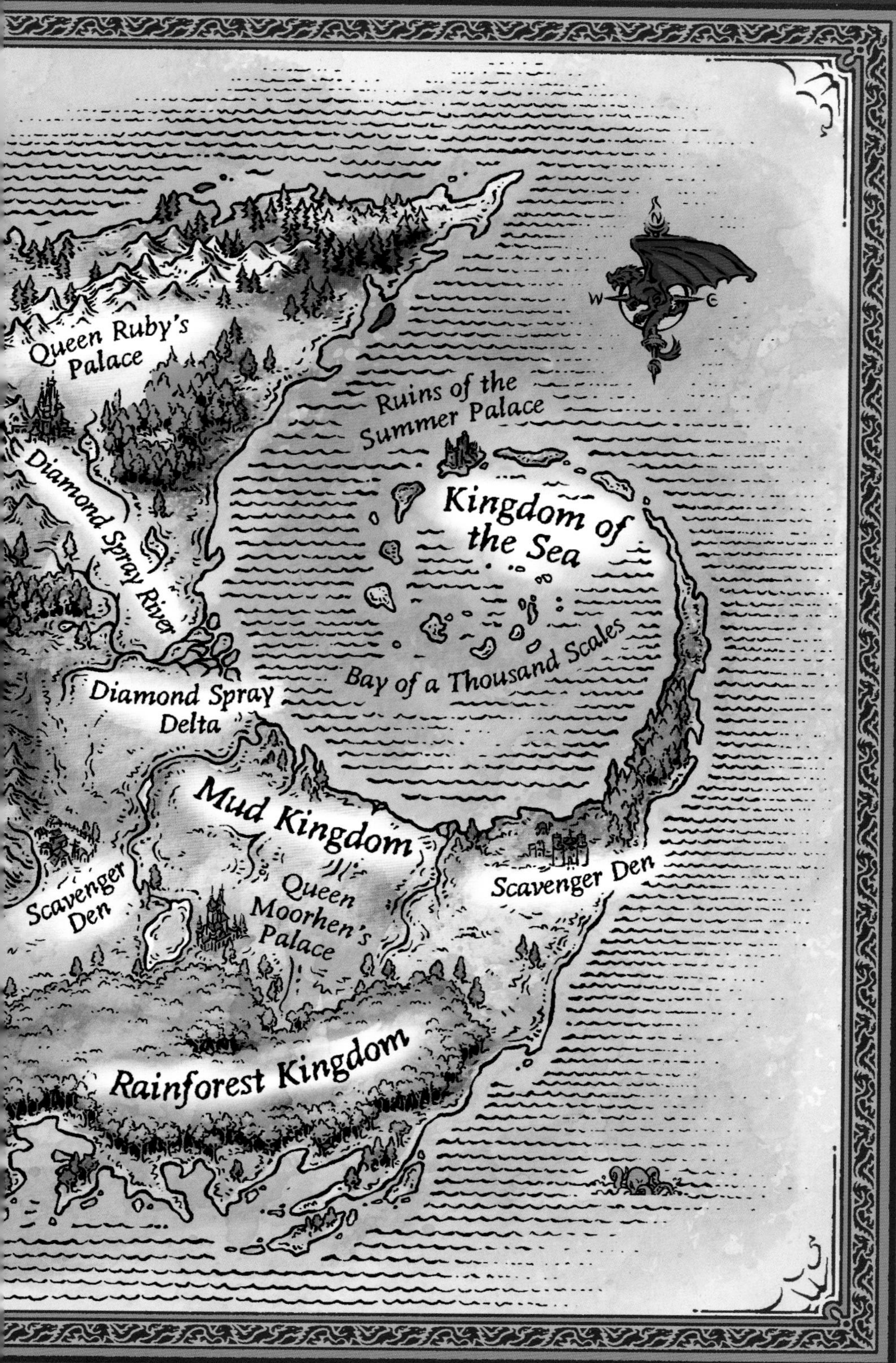
Queen Ruby's Palace
Diamond Spray River
Ruins of the Summer Palace
Kingdom of the Sea
Bay of a Thousand Scales
Diamond Spray Delta
Mud Kingdom
Scavenger Den
Queen Moorhen's Palace
Scavenger Den
Rainforest Kingdom
W
E

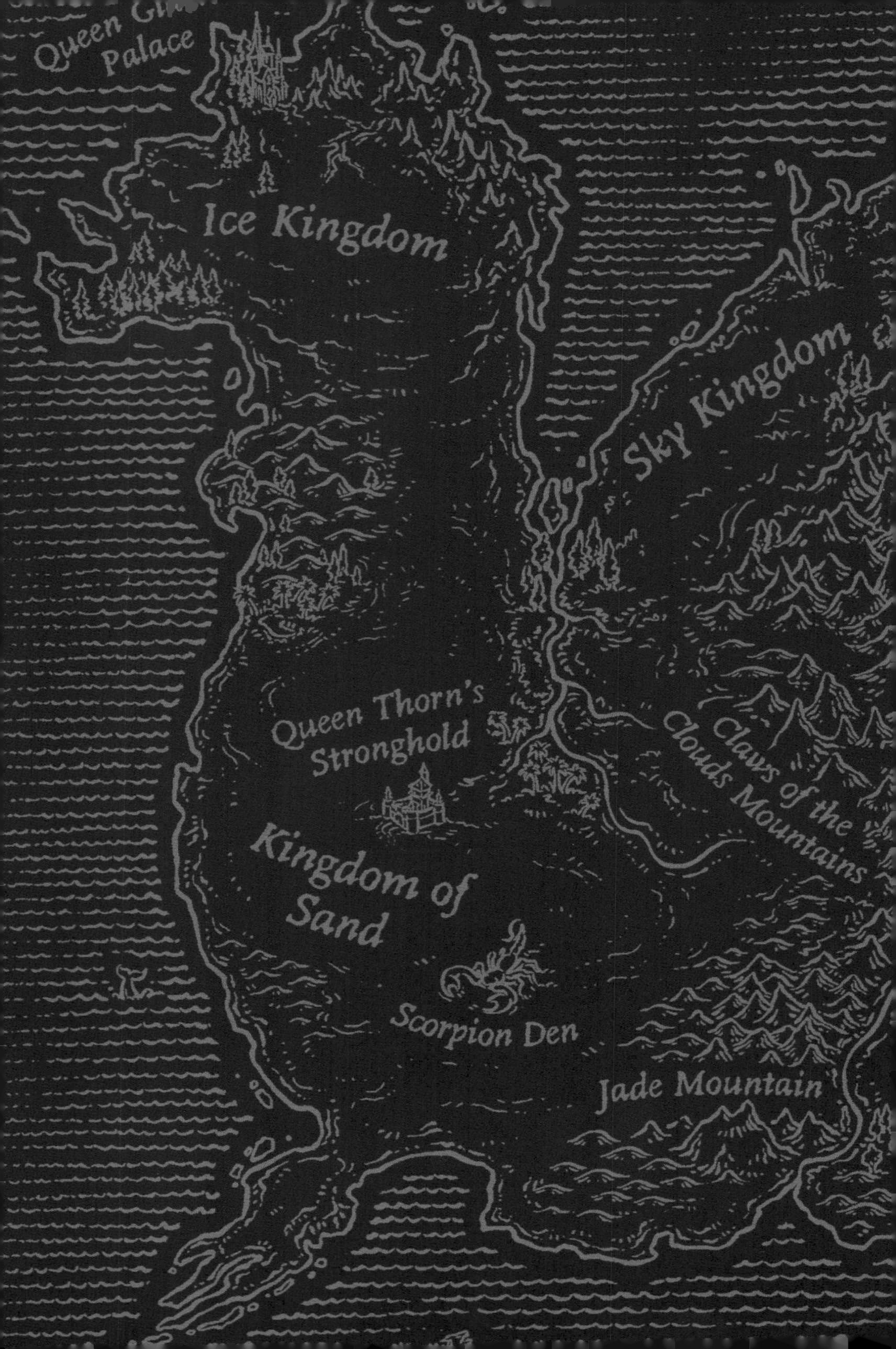
Queen Gl
Palace
Ice Kingdom
Sky Kingdom
Queen Thorn's
Stronghold
Claws of the
Clouds Mountains
Kingdom of
Sand
Scorpion Den
Jade Mountain

MOON RISING

THE JADE MOUNTAIN PROPHECY

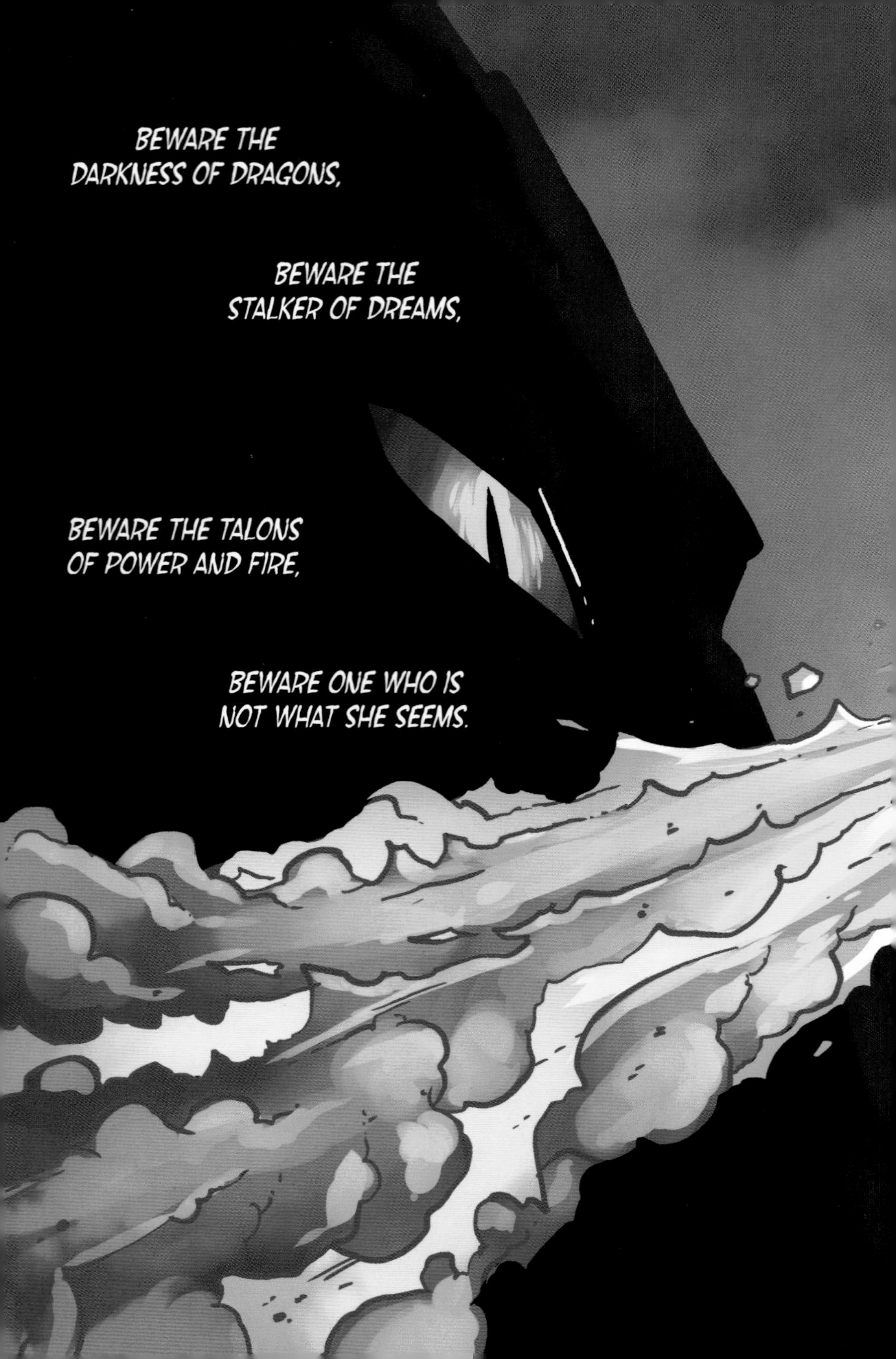
BEWARE THE
DARKNESS OF DRAGONS,
BEWARE THE
STALKER OF DREAMS,
BEWARE THE TALONS
OF POWER AND FIRE,
BEWARE ONE WHO IS
NOT WHAT SHE SEEMS.

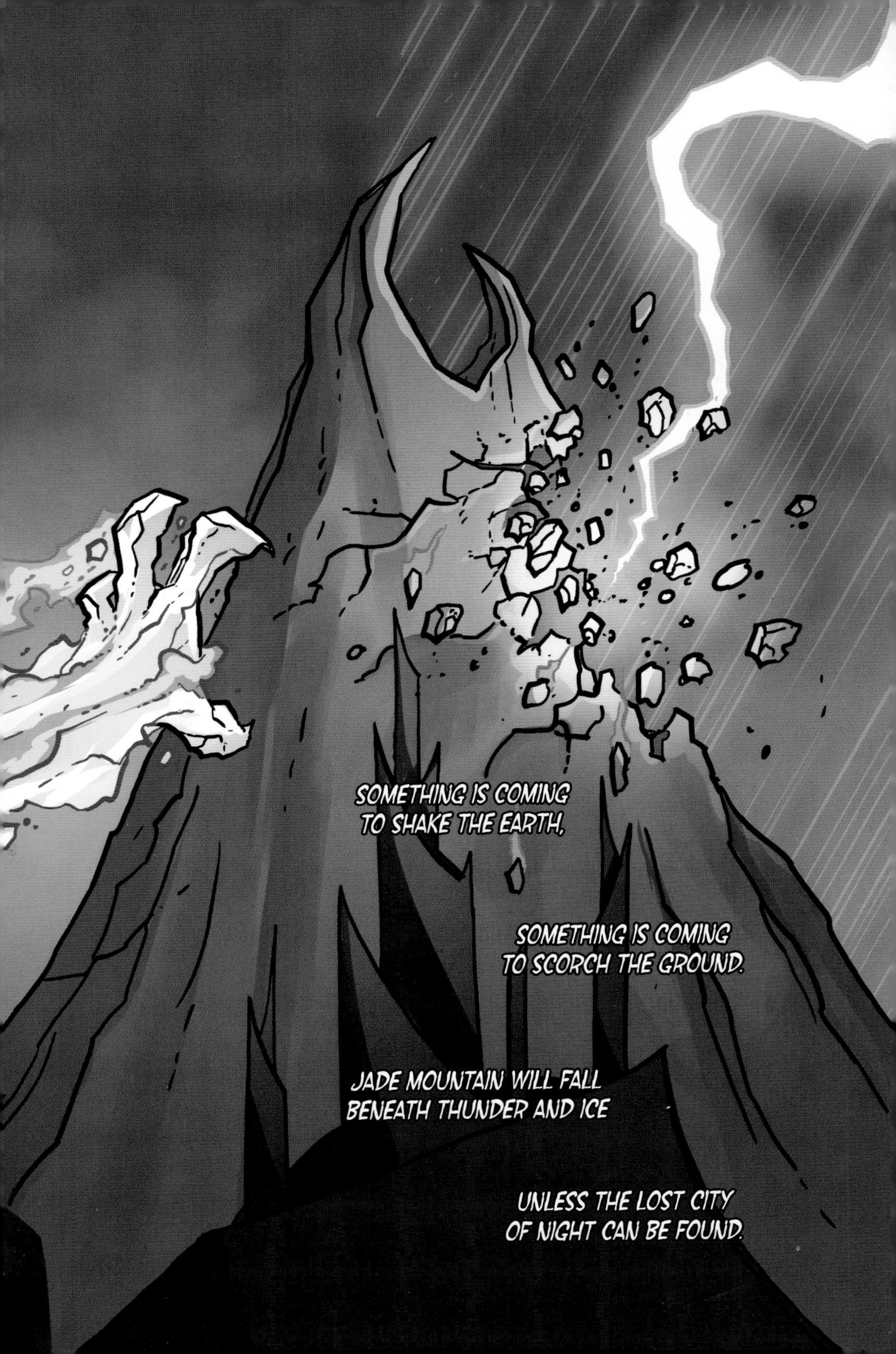
SOMETHING IS COMING TO SHAKE THE EARTH,
SOMETHING IS COMING TO SCORCH THE GROUND.
JADE MOUNTAIN WILL FALL BENEATH THUNDER AND ICE
UNLESS THE LOST CITY OF NIGHT CAN BE FOUND.

PROLOGUE: FOUR YEARS AGO NIGHTWING ISLAND

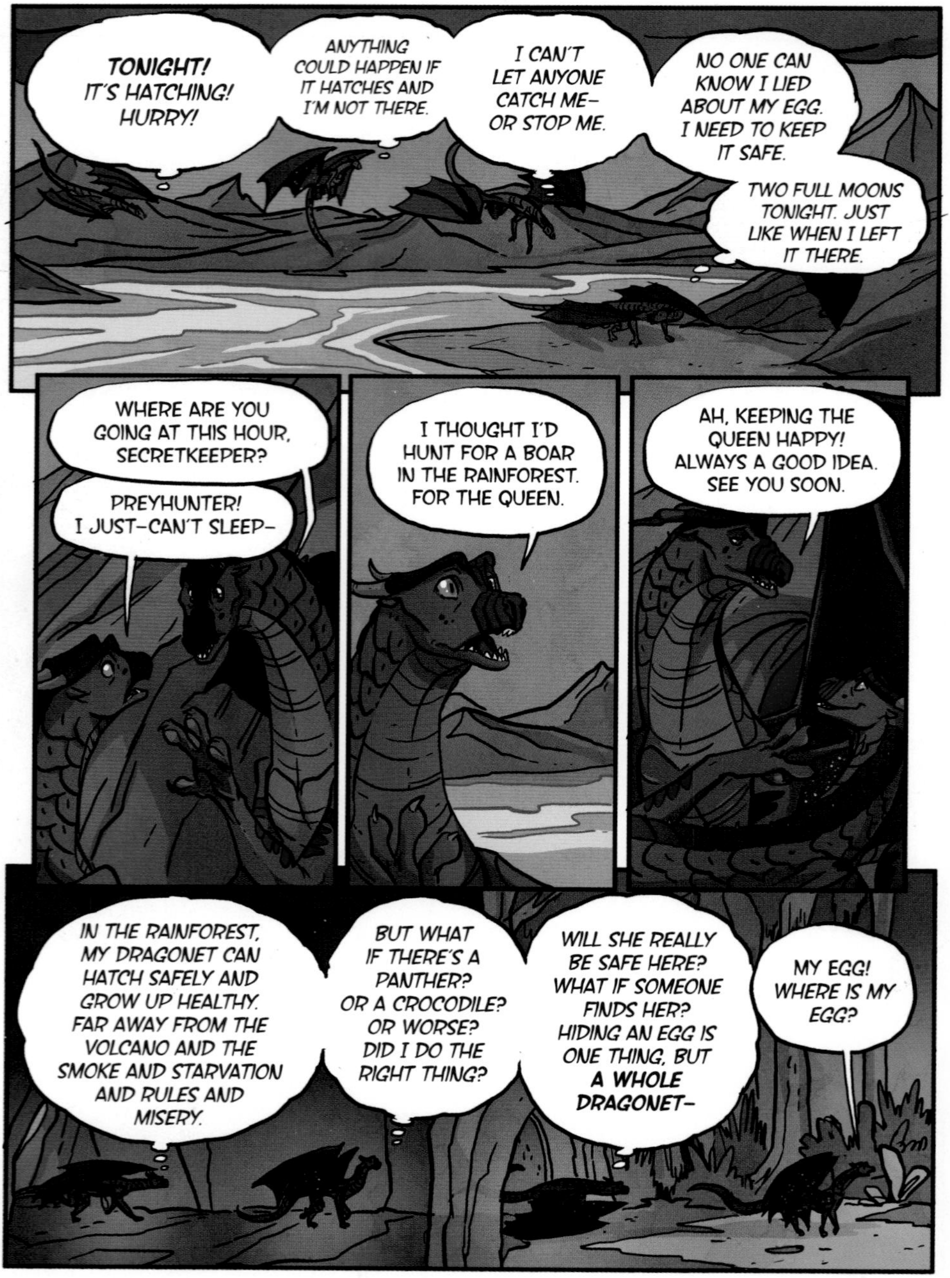

TONIGHT! IT'S HATCHING! HURRY!
ANYTHING COULD HAPPEN IF IT HATCHES AND I'M NOT THERE.
I CAN'T LET ANYONE CATCH ME— OR STOP ME.
NO ONE CAN KNOW I LIED ABOUT MY EGG. I NEED TO KEEP IT SAFE.
TWO FULL MOONS TONIGHT. JUST LIKE WHEN I LEFT IT THERE.
WHERE ARE YOU GOING AT THIS HOUR, SECRETKEEPER?
PREYHUNTER! I JUST—CAN'T SLEEP—
I THOUGHT I'D HUNT FOR A BOAR IN THE RAINFOREST. FOR THE QUEEN.
AH, KEEPING THE QUEEN HAPPY! ALWAYS A GOOD IDEA. SEE YOU SOON.
IN THE RAINFOREST, MY DRAGONET CAN HATCH SAFELY AND GROW UP HEALTHY. FAR AWAY FROM THE VOLCANO AND THE SMOKE AND STARVATION AND RULES AND MISERY.
BUT WHAT IF THERE'S A PANTHER? OR A CROCODILE? OR WORSE? DID I DO THE RIGHT THING?
WILL SHE REALLY BE SAFE HERE? WHAT IF SOMEONE FINDS HER? HIDING AN EGG IS ONE THING, BUT A WHOLE DRAGONET—
MY EGG! WHERE IS MY EGG?

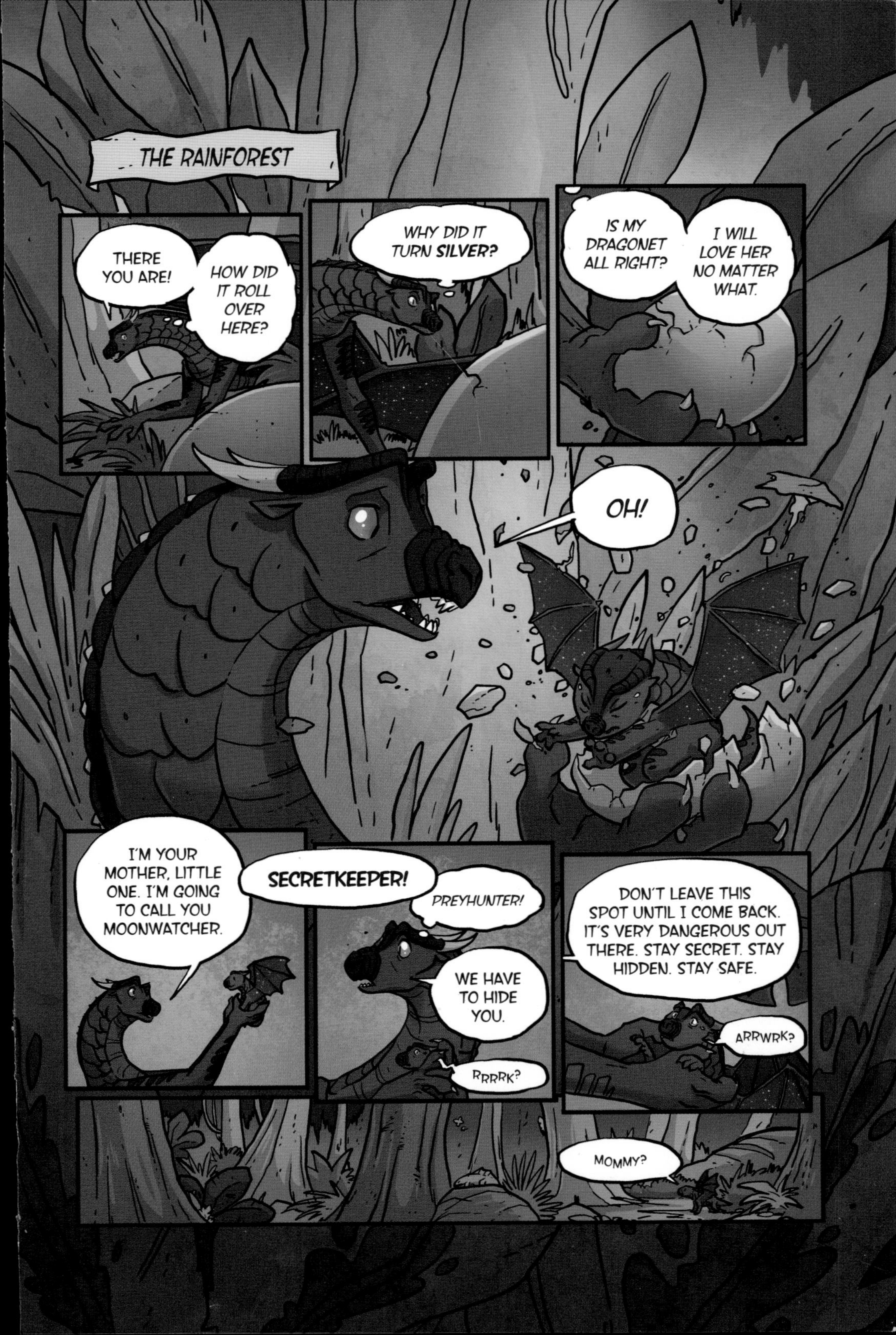
THE RAINFOREST
THERE YOU ARE!
HOW DID IT ROLL OVER HERE?
WHY DID IT TURN SILVER?
IS MY DRAGONET ALL RIGHT?
I WILL LOVE HER NO MATTER WHAT.
OH!
I'M YOUR MOTHER, LITTLE ONE. I'M GOING TO CALL YOU MOONWATCHER.
SECRETKEEPER!
PREYHUNTER!
WE HAVE TO HIDE YOU.
RRRRK?
DON'T LEAVE THIS SPOT UNTIL I COME BACK. IT'S VERY DANGEROUS OUT THERE. STAY SECRET. STAY HIDDEN. STAY SAFE.
ARRWRK?
MOMMY?

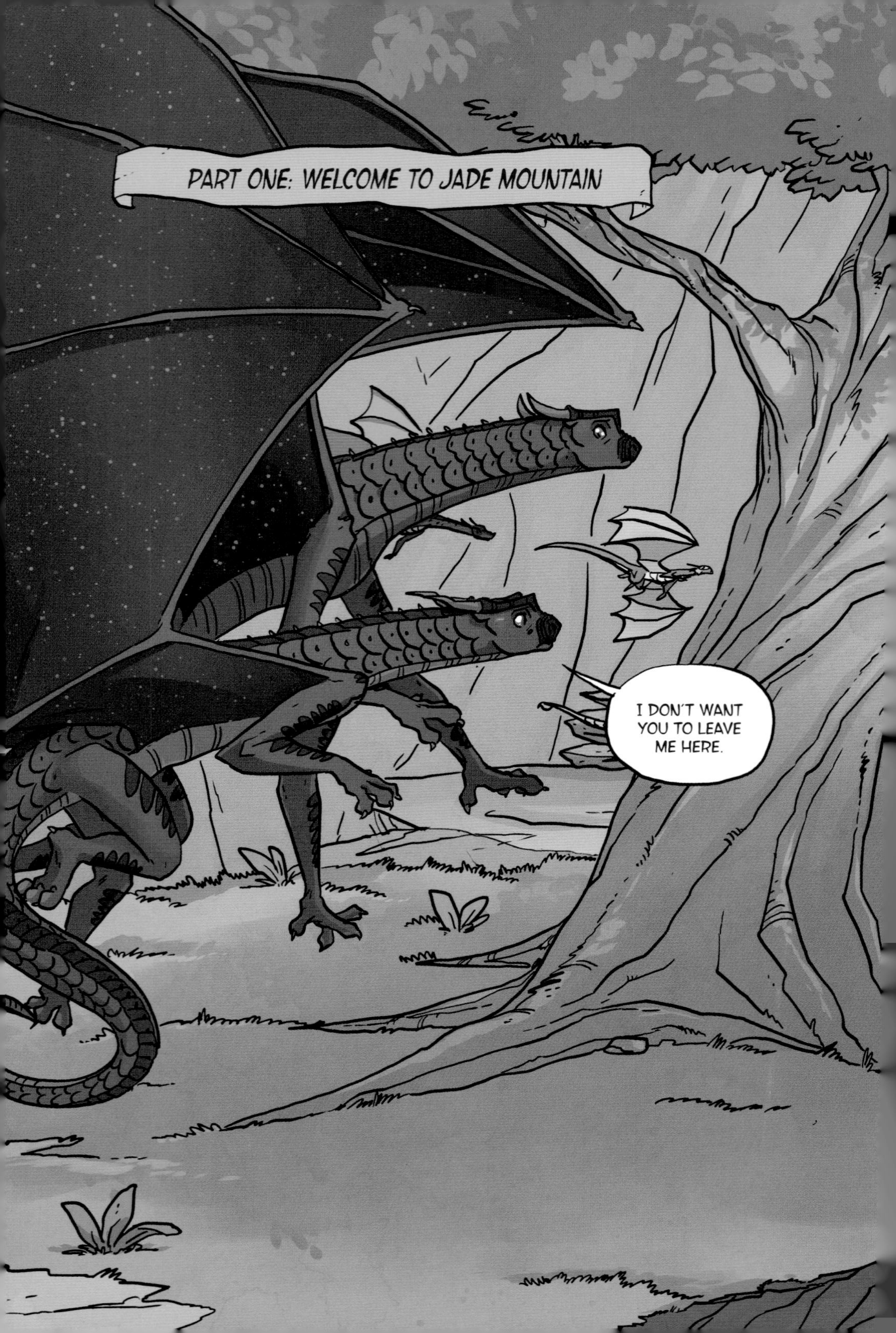
PART ONE: WELCOME TO JADE MOUNTAIN
I DON'T WANT YOU TO LEAVE ME HERE.

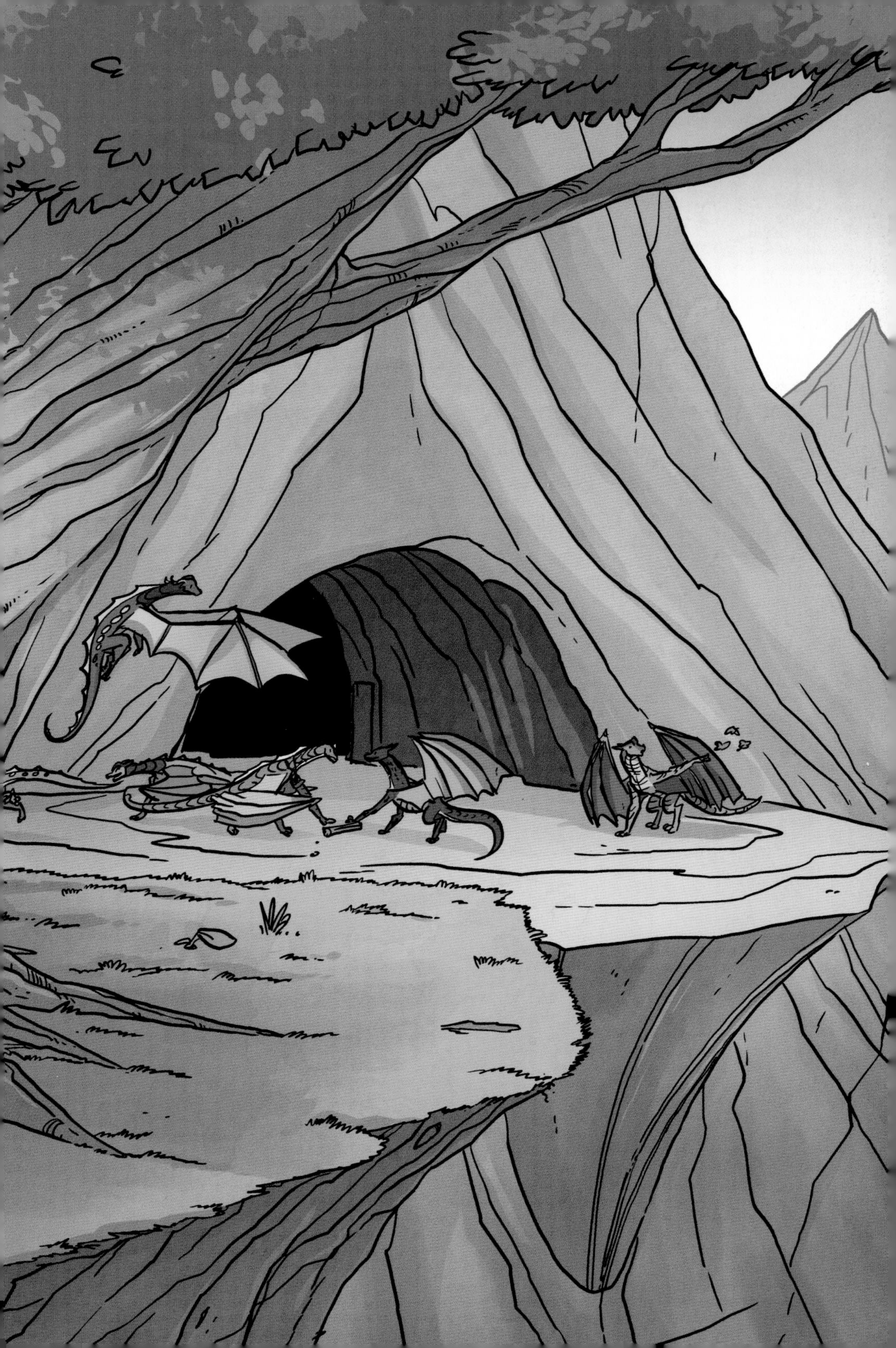

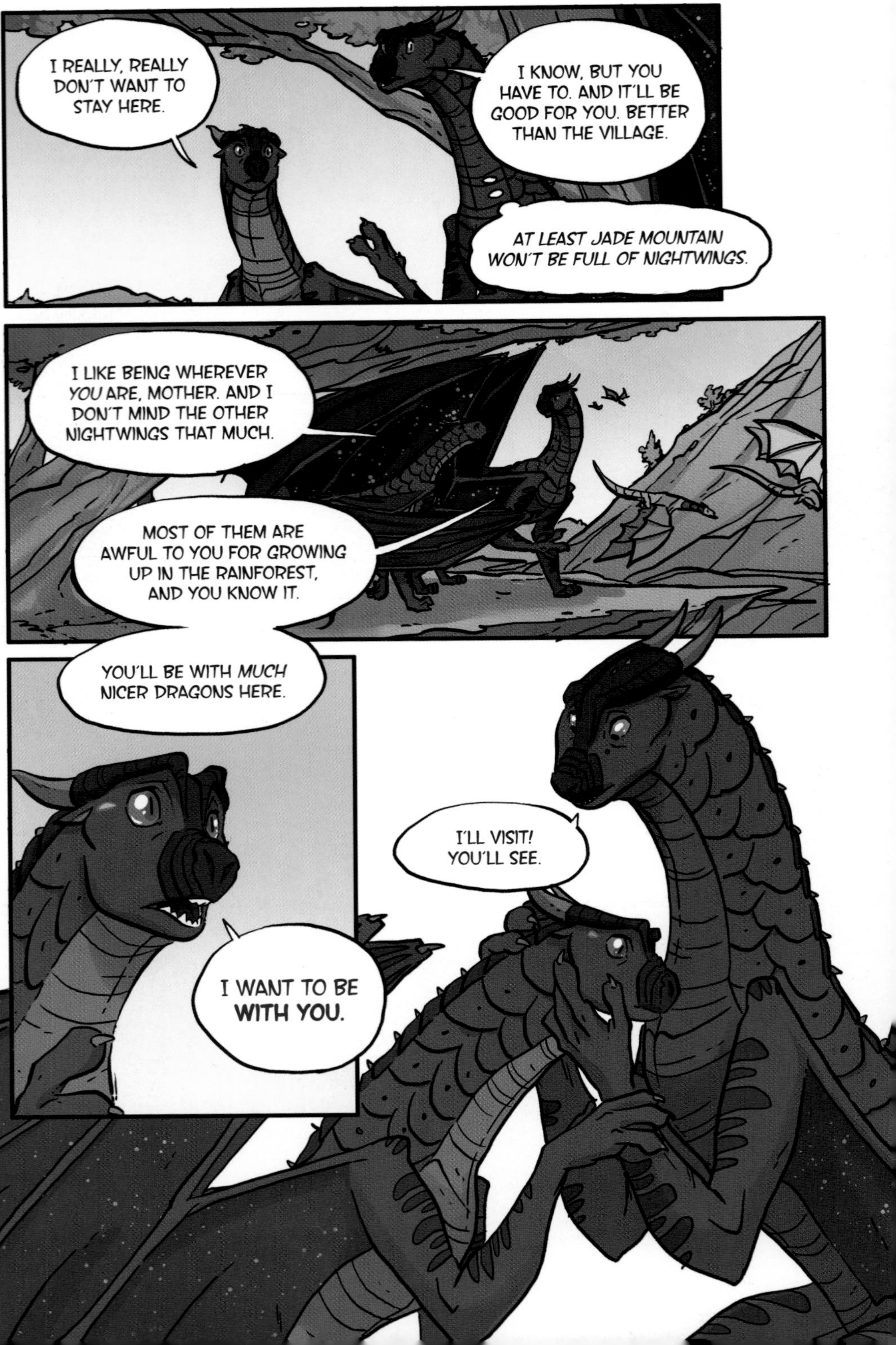
I REALLY, REALLY DON'T WANT TO STAY HERE.
I KNOW, BUT YOU HAVE TO. AND IT'LL BE GOOD FOR YOU. BETTER THAN THE VILLAGE.
AT LEAST JADE MOUNTAIN WON'T BE FULL OF NIGHTWINGS.
I LIKE BEING WHEREVER *YOU* ARE, MOTHER. AND I DON'T MIND THE OTHER NIGHTWINGS THAT MUCH.
MOST OF THEM ARE AWFUL TO YOU FOR GROWING UP IN THE RAINFOREST, AND YOU KNOW IT.
YOU'LL BE WITH *MUCH* NICER DRAGONS HERE.
I WANT TO BE **WITH YOU.**
I'LL VISIT! YOU'LL SEE.

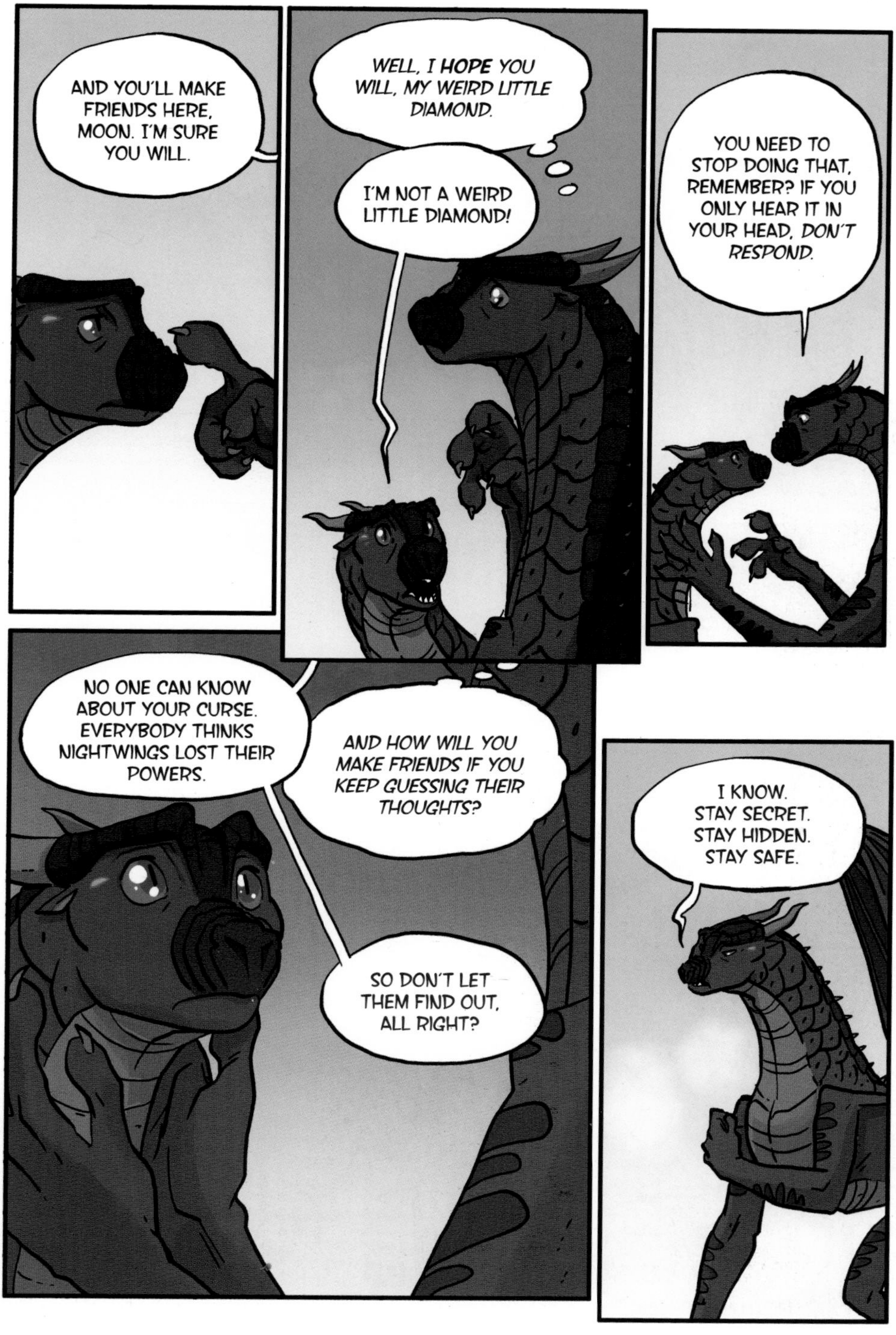
AND YOU'LL MAKE FRIENDS HERE, MOON. I'M SURE YOU WILL.
WELL, I **HOPE** YOU WILL, MY WEIRD LITTLE DIAMOND.
I'M NOT A WEIRD LITTLE DIAMOND!
YOU NEED TO STOP DOING THAT, REMEMBER? IF YOU ONLY HEAR IT IN YOUR HEAD, *DON'T RESPOND.*
NO ONE CAN KNOW ABOUT YOUR CURSE. EVERYBODY THINKS NIGHTWINGS LOST THEIR POWERS.
AND HOW WILL YOU MAKE FRIENDS IF YOU KEEP GUESSING THEIR THOUGHTS?
SO DON'T LET THEM FIND OUT, ALL RIGHT?
I KNOW. STAY SECRET. STAY HIDDEN. STAY SAFE.

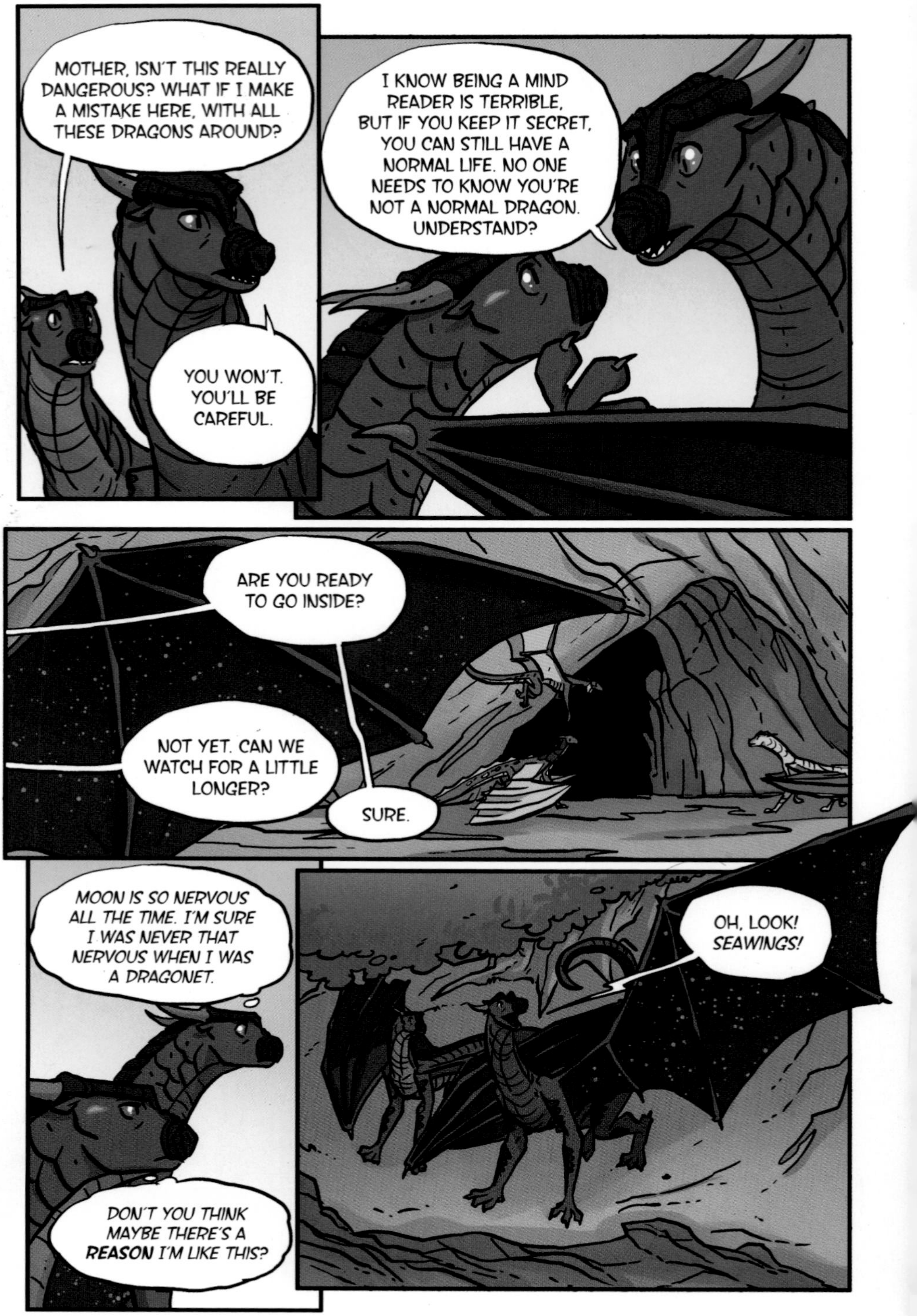
MOTHER, ISN'T THIS REALLY DANGEROUS? WHAT IF I MAKE A MISTAKE HERE, WITH ALL THESE DRAGONS AROUND?
YOU WON'T. YOU'LL BE CAREFUL.
I KNOW BEING A MIND READER IS TERRIBLE, BUT IF YOU KEEP IT SECRET, YOU CAN STILL HAVE A NORMAL LIFE. NO ONE NEEDS TO KNOW YOU'RE NOT A NORMAL DRAGON. UNDERSTAND?
ARE YOU READY TO GO INSIDE?
NOT YET. CAN WE WATCH FOR A LITTLE LONGER?
SURE.
MOON IS SO NERVOUS ALL THE TIME. I'M SURE I WAS NEVER THAT NERVOUS WHEN I WAS A DRAGONET.
DON'T YOU THINK MAYBE THERE'S A **REASON** I'M LIKE THIS?
OH, LOOK! SEAWINGS!

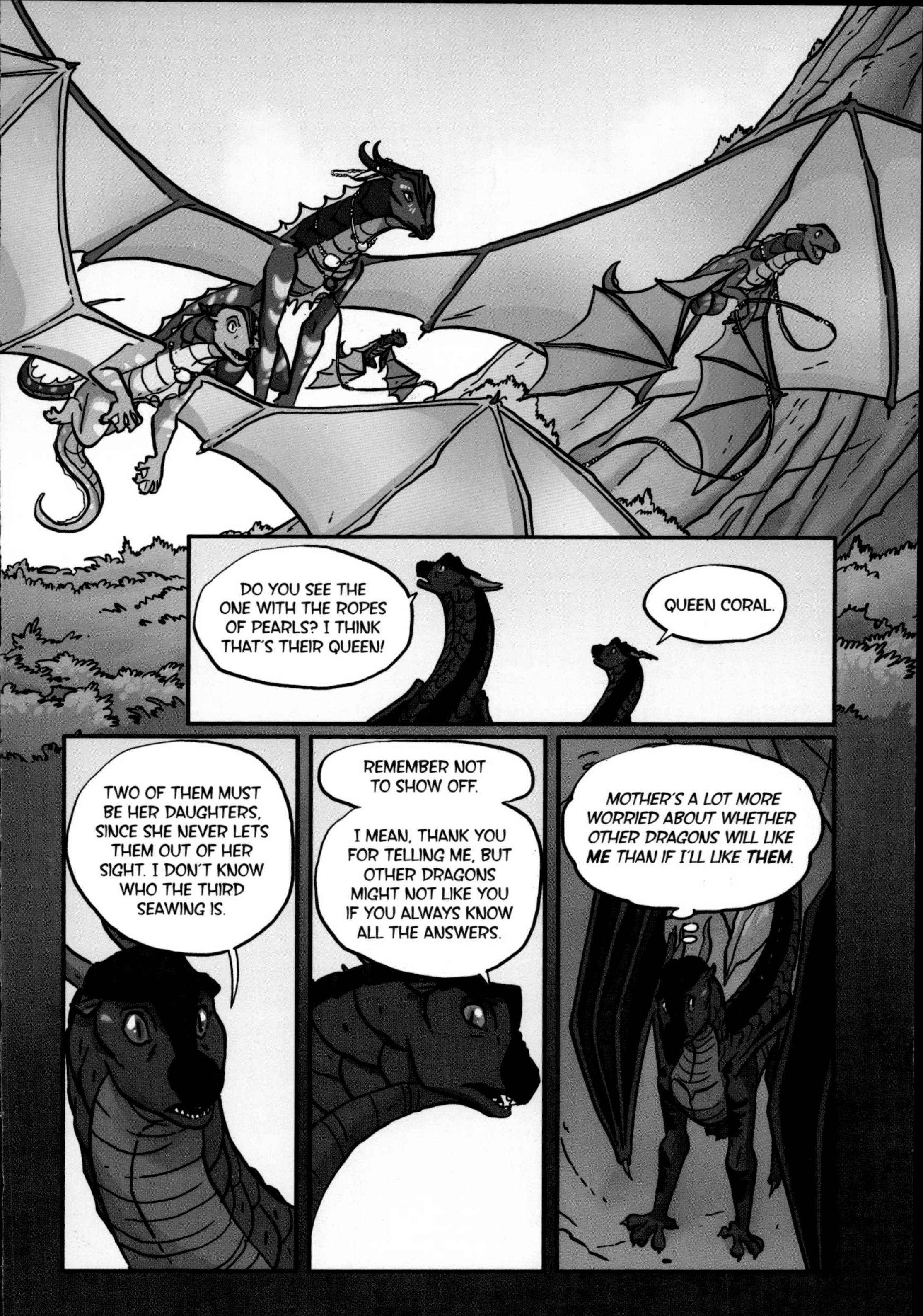
DO YOU SEE THE ONE WITH THE ROPES OF PEARLS? I THINK THAT'S THEIR QUEEN!
QUEEN CORAL.
TWO OF THEM MUST BE HER DAUGHTERS, SINCE SHE NEVER LETS THEM OUT OF HER SIGHT. I DON'T KNOW WHO THE THIRD SEAWING IS.
REMEMBER NOT TO SHOW OFF.
I MEAN, THANK YOU FOR TELLING ME, BUT OTHER DRAGONS MIGHT NOT LIKE YOU IF YOU ALWAYS KNOW ALL THE ANSWERS.
*MOTHER'S A LOT MORE WORRIED ABOUT WHETHER OTHER DRAGONS WILL LIKE **ME** THAN IF I'LL LIKE **THEM**.*

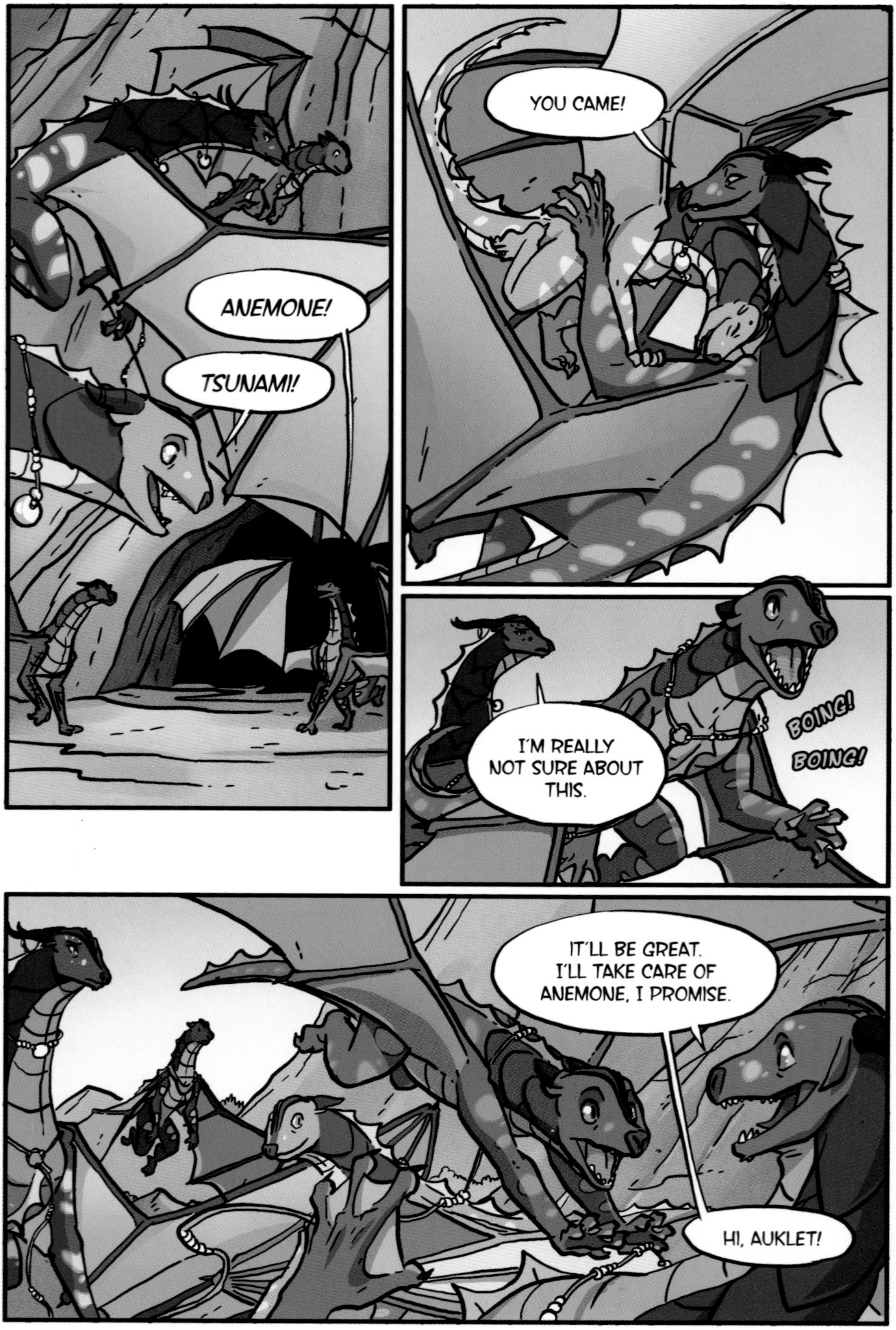
ANEMONE!
TSUNAMI!
YOU CAME!
I'M REALLY NOT SURE ABOUT THIS.
BOING!
BOING!
IT'LL BE GREAT. I'LL TAKE CARE OF ANEMONE, I PROMISE.
HI, AUKLET!

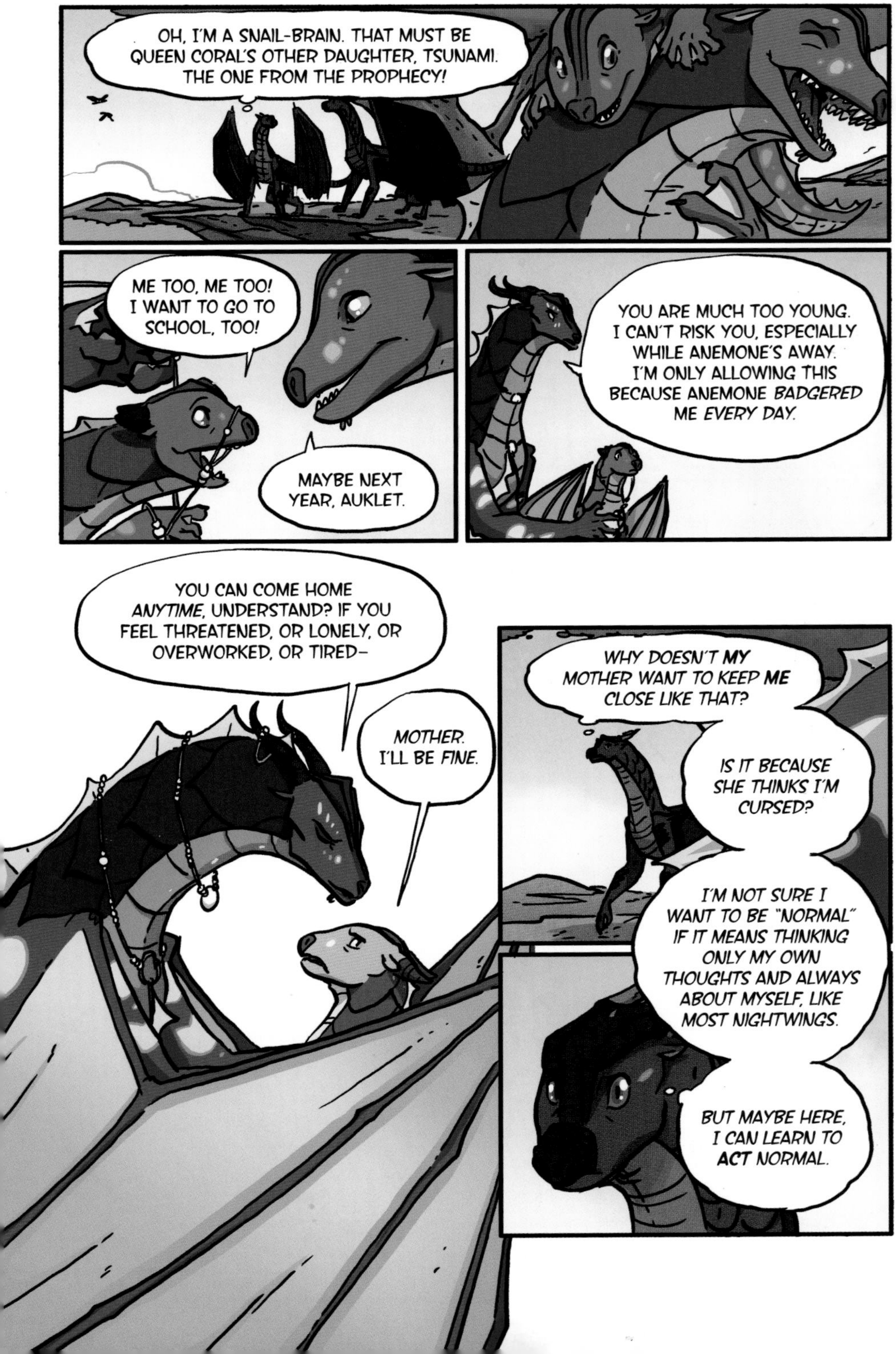
OH, I'M A SNAIL-BRAIN. THAT MUST BE QUEEN CORAL'S OTHER DAUGHTER, TSUNAMI. THE ONE FROM THE PROPHECY!
ME TOO, ME TOO! I WANT TO GO TO SCHOOL, TOO!
MAYBE NEXT YEAR, AUKLET.
YOU ARE MUCH TOO YOUNG. I CAN'T RISK YOU, ESPECIALLY WHILE ANEMONE'S AWAY. I'M ONLY ALLOWING THIS BECAUSE ANEMONE *BADGERED* ME *EVERY DAY.*
YOU CAN COME HOME *ANYTIME*, UNDERSTAND? IF YOU FEEL THREATENED, OR LONELY, OR OVERWORKED, OR TIRED–
MOTHER. I'LL BE FINE.
WHY DOESN'T ***MY*** *MOTHER WANT TO KEEP* ***ME*** *CLOSE LIKE THAT?*
IS IT BECAUSE SHE THINKS I'M CURSED?
I'M NOT SURE I WANT TO BE "NORMAL" IF IT MEANS THINKING ONLY MY OWN THOUGHTS AND ALWAYS ABOUT MYSELF, LIKE MOST NIGHTWINGS.
BUT MAYBE HERE, I CAN LEARN TO ***ACT*** *NORMAL.*

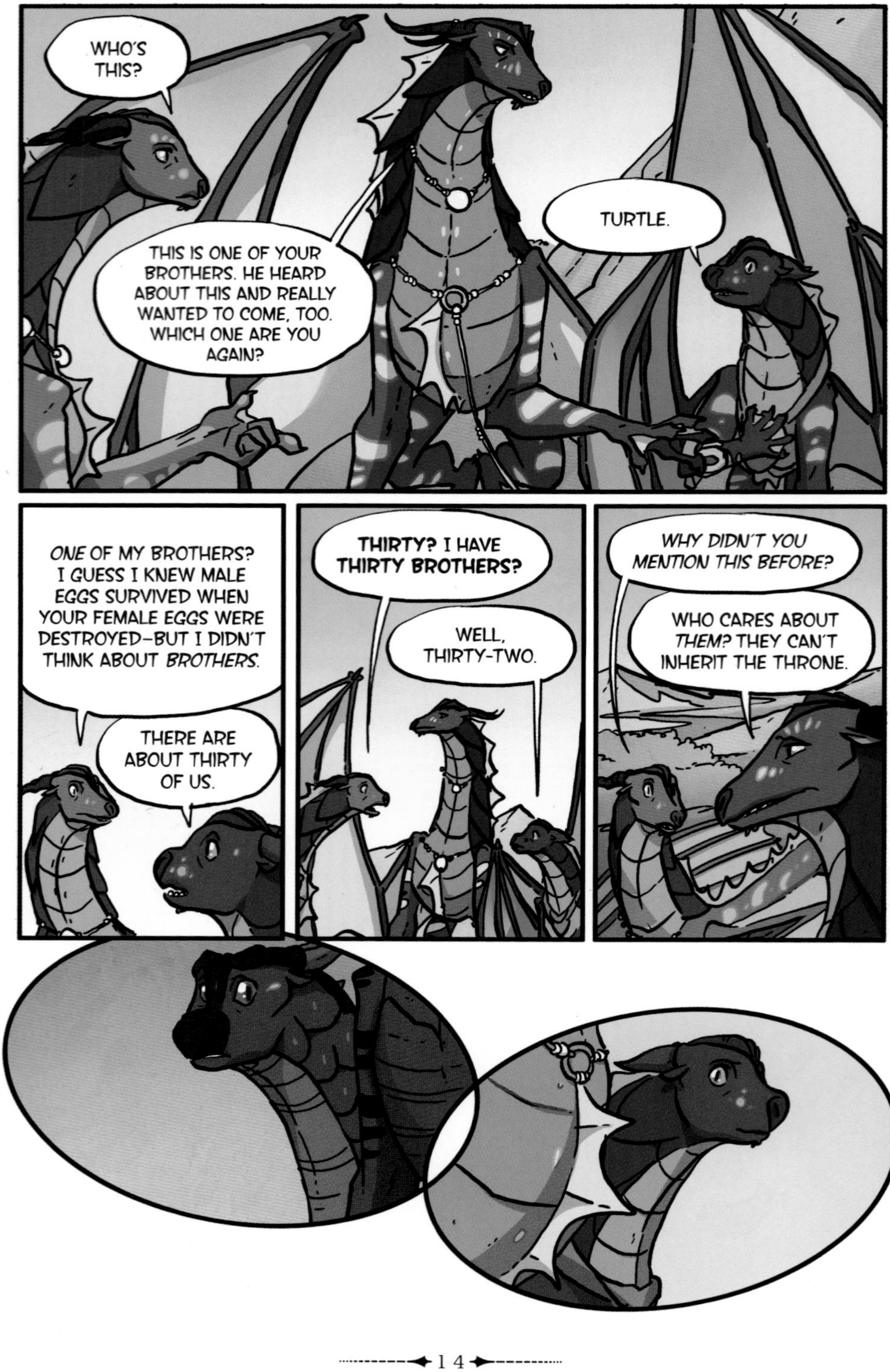
WHO'S THIS?
THIS IS ONE OF YOUR BROTHERS. HE HEARD ABOUT THIS AND REALLY WANTED TO COME, TOO. WHICH ONE ARE YOU AGAIN?
TURTLE.
ONE OF MY BROTHERS? I GUESS I KNEW MALE EGGS SURVIVED WHEN YOUR FEMALE EGGS WERE DESTROYED—BUT I DIDN'T THINK ABOUT *BROTHERS*.
THERE ARE ABOUT THIRTY OF US.
THIRTY? I HAVE **THIRTY BROTHERS?**
WELL, THIRTY-TWO.
WHY DIDN'T YOU MENTION THIS BEFORE?
WHO CARES ABOUT *THEM?* THEY CAN'T INHERIT THE THRONE.

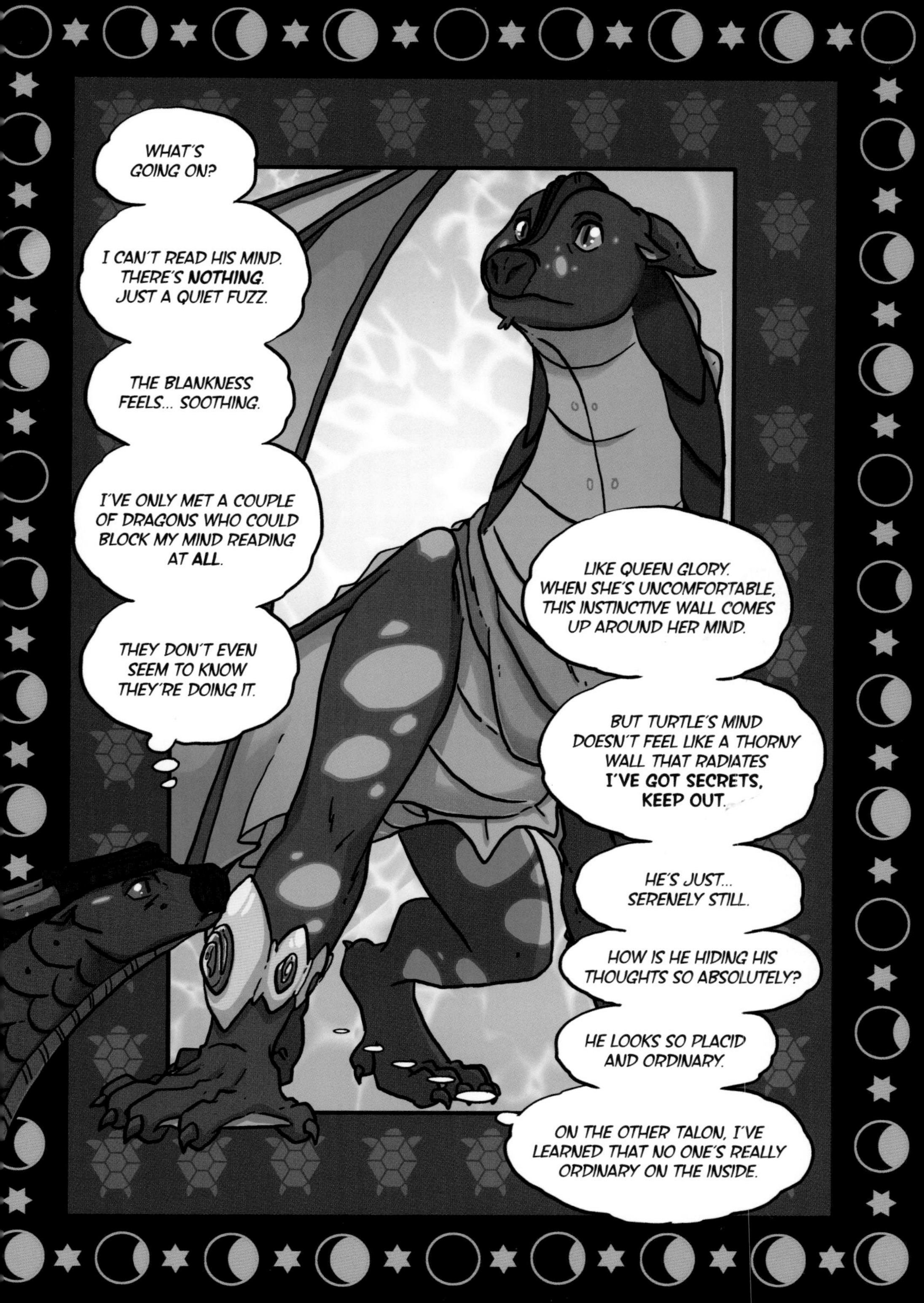
WHAT'S GOING ON?
I CAN'T READ HIS MIND. THERE'S NOTHING. JUST A QUIET FUZZ.
THE BLANKNESS FEELS... SOOTHING.
I'VE ONLY MET A COUPLE OF DRAGONS WHO COULD BLOCK MY MIND READING AT ALL.
THEY DON'T EVEN SEEM TO KNOW THEY'RE DOING IT.
LIKE QUEEN GLORY. WHEN SHE'S UNCOMFORTABLE, THIS INSTINCTIVE WALL COMES UP AROUND HER MIND.
BUT TURTLE'S MIND DOESN'T FEEL LIKE A THORNY WALL THAT RADIATES I'VE GOT SECRETS, KEEP OUT.
HE'S JUST... SERENELY STILL.
HOW IS HE HIDING HIS THOUGHTS SO ABSOLUTELY?
HE LOOKS SO PLACID AND ORDINARY.
ON THE OTHER TALON, I'VE LEARNED THAT NO ONE'S REALLY ORDINARY ON THE INSIDE.

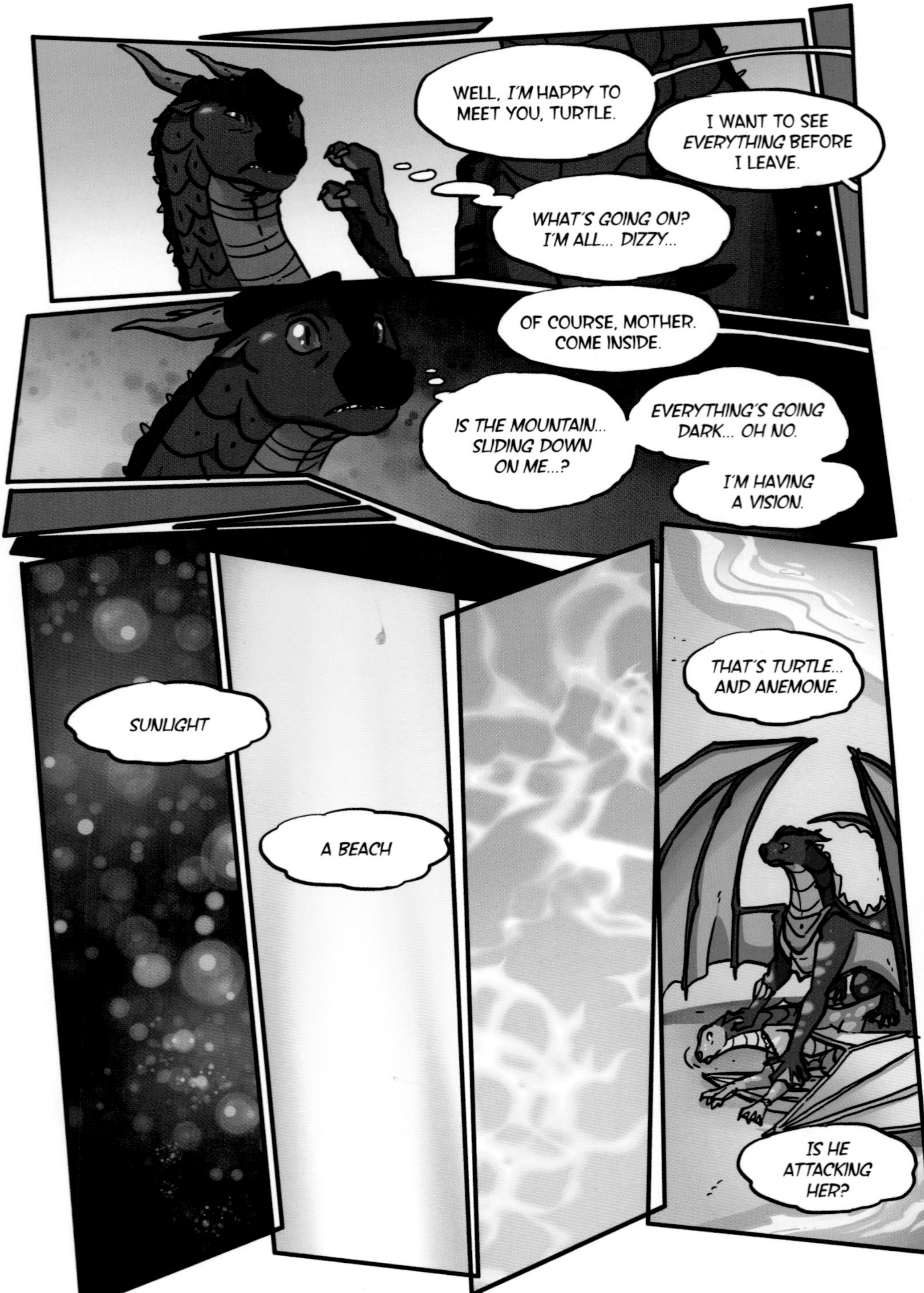
WELL, I'M HAPPY TO MEET YOU, TURTLE.
I WANT TO SEE EVERYTHING BEFORE I LEAVE.
WHAT'S GOING ON? I'M ALL... DIZZY...
OF COURSE, MOTHER. COME INSIDE.
IS THE MOUNTAIN... SLIDING DOWN ON ME...?
EVERYTHING'S GOING DARK... OH NO.
I'M HAVING A VISION.
SUNLIGHT
A BEACH
THAT'S TURTLE... AND ANEMONE.
IS HE ATTACKING HER?

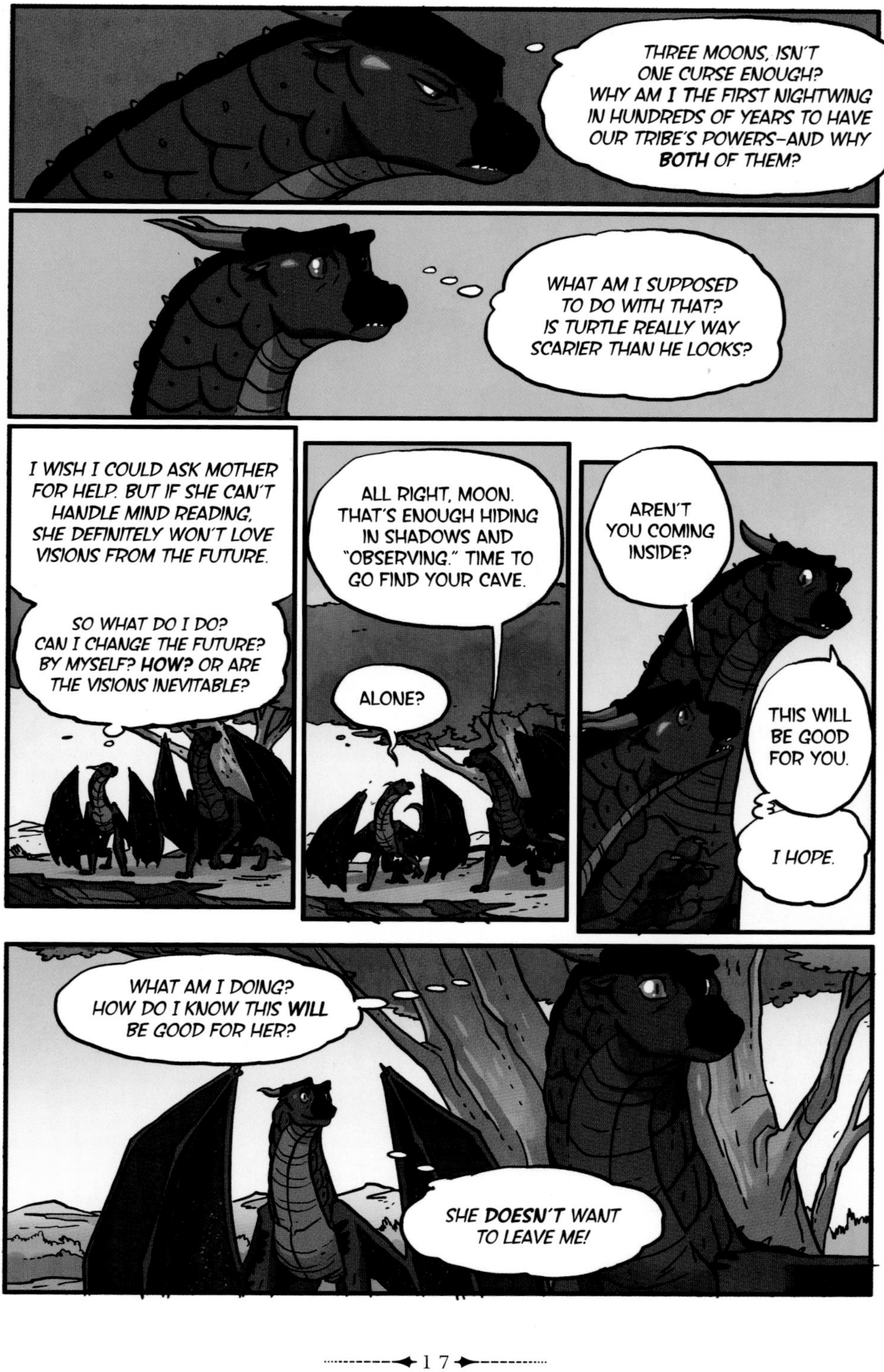
THREE MOONS, ISN'T ONE CURSE ENOUGH? WHY AM I THE FIRST NIGHTWING IN HUNDREDS OF YEARS TO HAVE OUR TRIBE'S POWERS—AND WHY BOTH OF THEM?
WHAT AM I SUPPOSED TO DO WITH THAT? IS TURTLE REALLY WAY SCARIER THAN HE LOOKS?
I WISH I COULD ASK MOTHER FOR HELP. BUT IF SHE CAN'T HANDLE MIND READING, SHE DEFINITELY WON'T LOVE VISIONS FROM THE FUTURE.
SO WHAT DO I DO? CAN I CHANGE THE FUTURE? BY MYSELF? HOW? OR ARE THE VISIONS INEVITABLE?
ALL RIGHT, MOON. THAT'S ENOUGH HIDING IN SHADOWS AND "OBSERVING." TIME TO GO FIND YOUR CAVE.
ALONE?
AREN'T YOU COMING INSIDE?
THIS WILL BE GOOD FOR YOU.
I HOPE.
WHAT AM I DOING? HOW DO I KNOW THIS WILL BE GOOD FOR HER?
SHE DOESN'T WANT TO LEAVE ME!

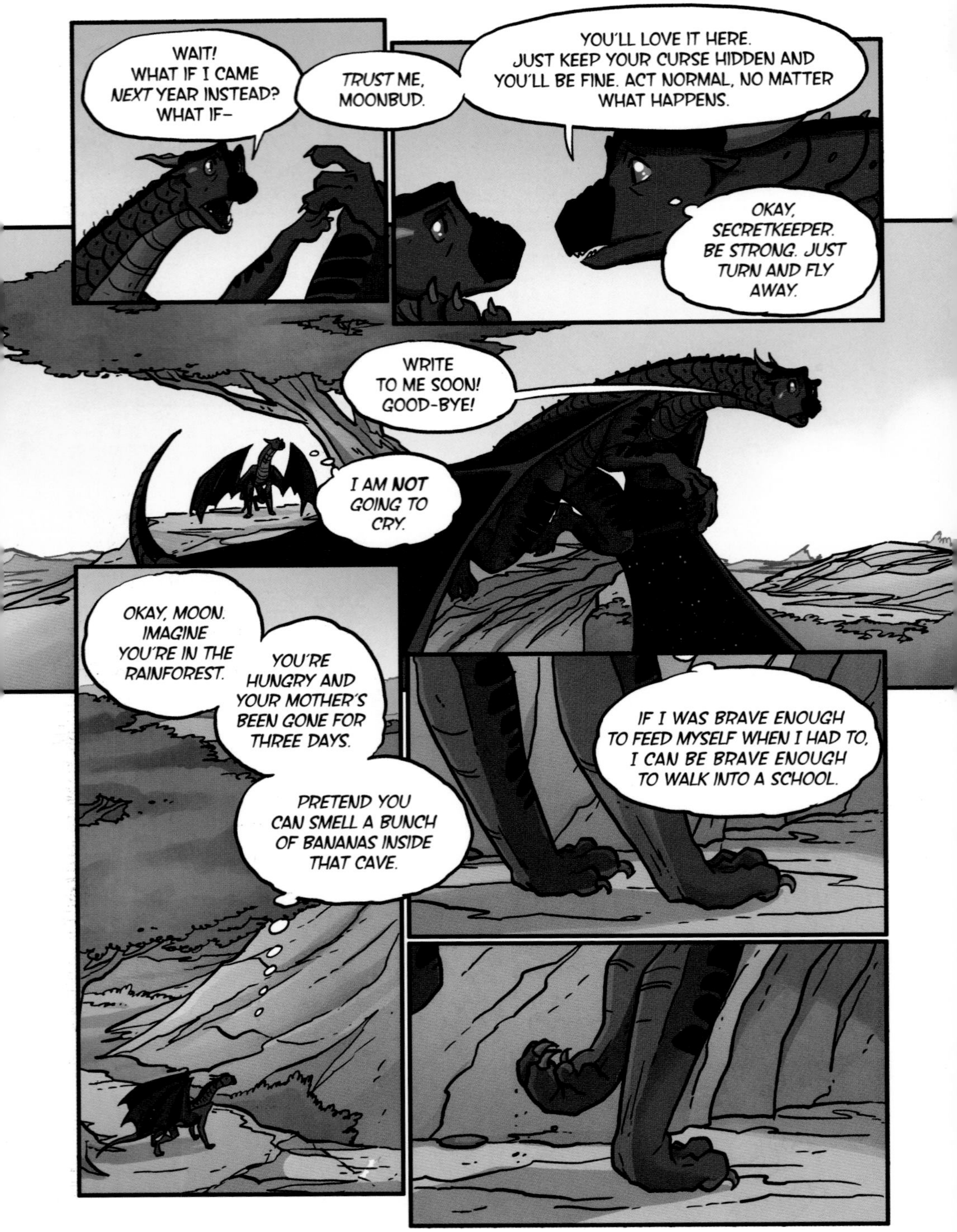
WAIT! WHAT IF I CAME *NEXT* YEAR INSTEAD? WHAT IF–
TRUST ME, MOONBUD.
YOU'LL LOVE IT HERE. JUST KEEP YOUR CURSE HIDDEN AND YOU'LL BE FINE. ACT NORMAL, NO MATTER WHAT HAPPENS.
OKAY, SECRETKEEPER. BE STRONG. JUST TURN AND FLY AWAY.
WRITE TO ME SOON! GOOD-BYE!
*I AM **NOT** GOING TO CRY.*
OKAY, MOON. IMAGINE YOU'RE IN THE RAINFOREST.
YOU'RE HUNGRY AND YOUR MOTHER'S BEEN GONE FOR THREE DAYS.
PRETEND YOU CAN SMELL A BUNCH OF BANANAS INSIDE THAT CAVE.
IF I WAS BRAVE ENOUGH TO FEED MYSELF WHEN I HAD TO, I CAN BE BRAVE ENOUGH TO WALK INTO A SCHOOL.

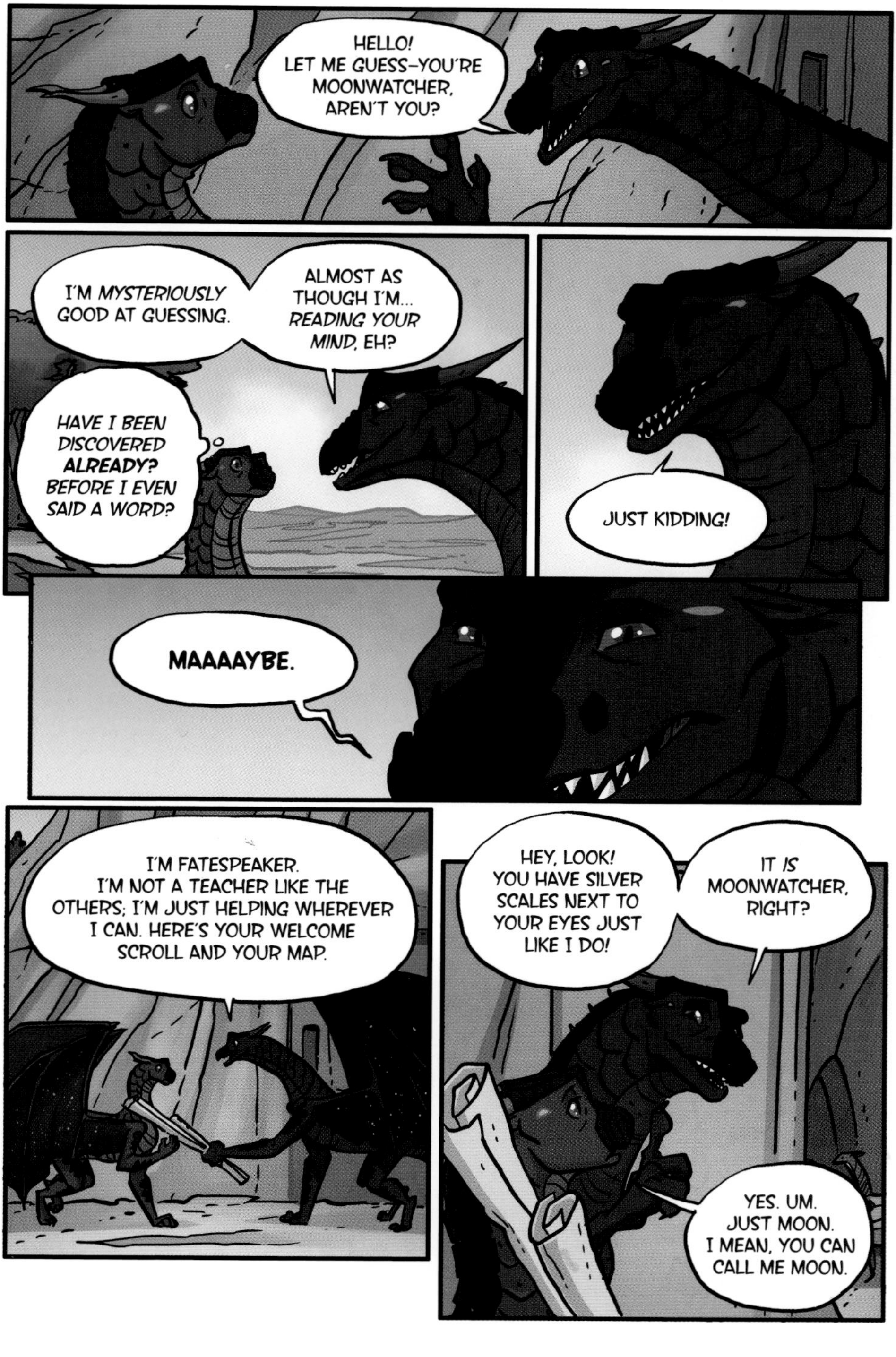
HELLO!
LET ME GUESS—YOU'RE MOONWATCHER, AREN'T YOU?
I'M *MYSTERIOUSLY* GOOD AT GUESSING.
ALMOST AS THOUGH I'M... *READING YOUR MIND*, EH?
HAVE I BEEN DISCOVERED ***ALREADY?*** *BEFORE I EVEN SAID A WORD?*
JUST KIDDING!
MAAAAYBE.
I'M FATESPEAKER. I'M NOT A TEACHER LIKE THE OTHERS; I'M JUST HELPING WHEREVER I CAN. HERE'S YOUR WELCOME SCROLL AND YOUR MAP.
HEY, LOOK! YOU HAVE SILVER SCALES NEXT TO YOUR EYES JUST LIKE I DO!
IT *IS* MOONWATCHER, RIGHT?
YES. UM. JUST MOON. I MEAN, YOU CAN CALL ME MOON.

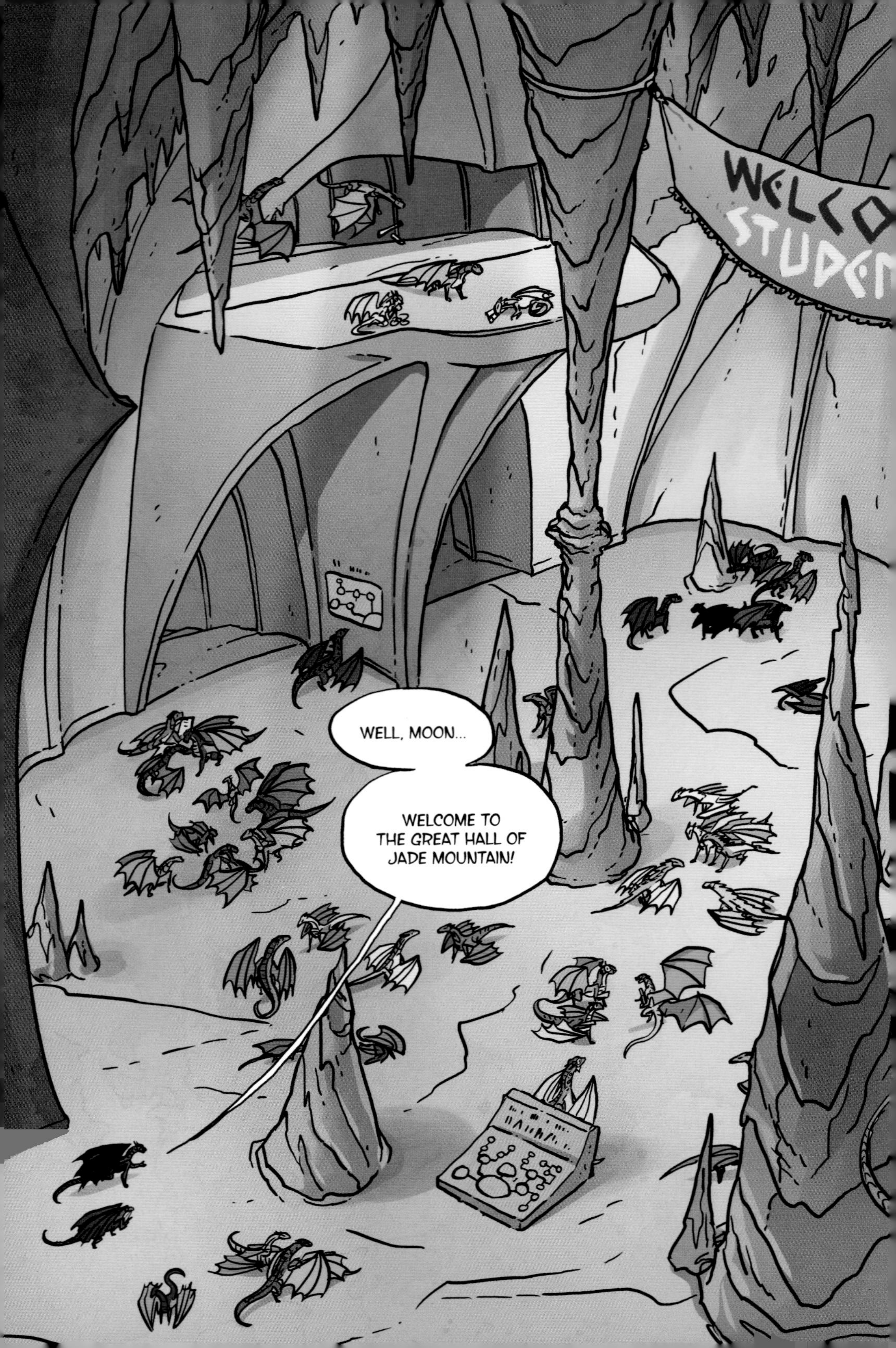
WELL, MOON...
WELCOME TO THE GREAT HALL OF JADE MOUNTAIN!

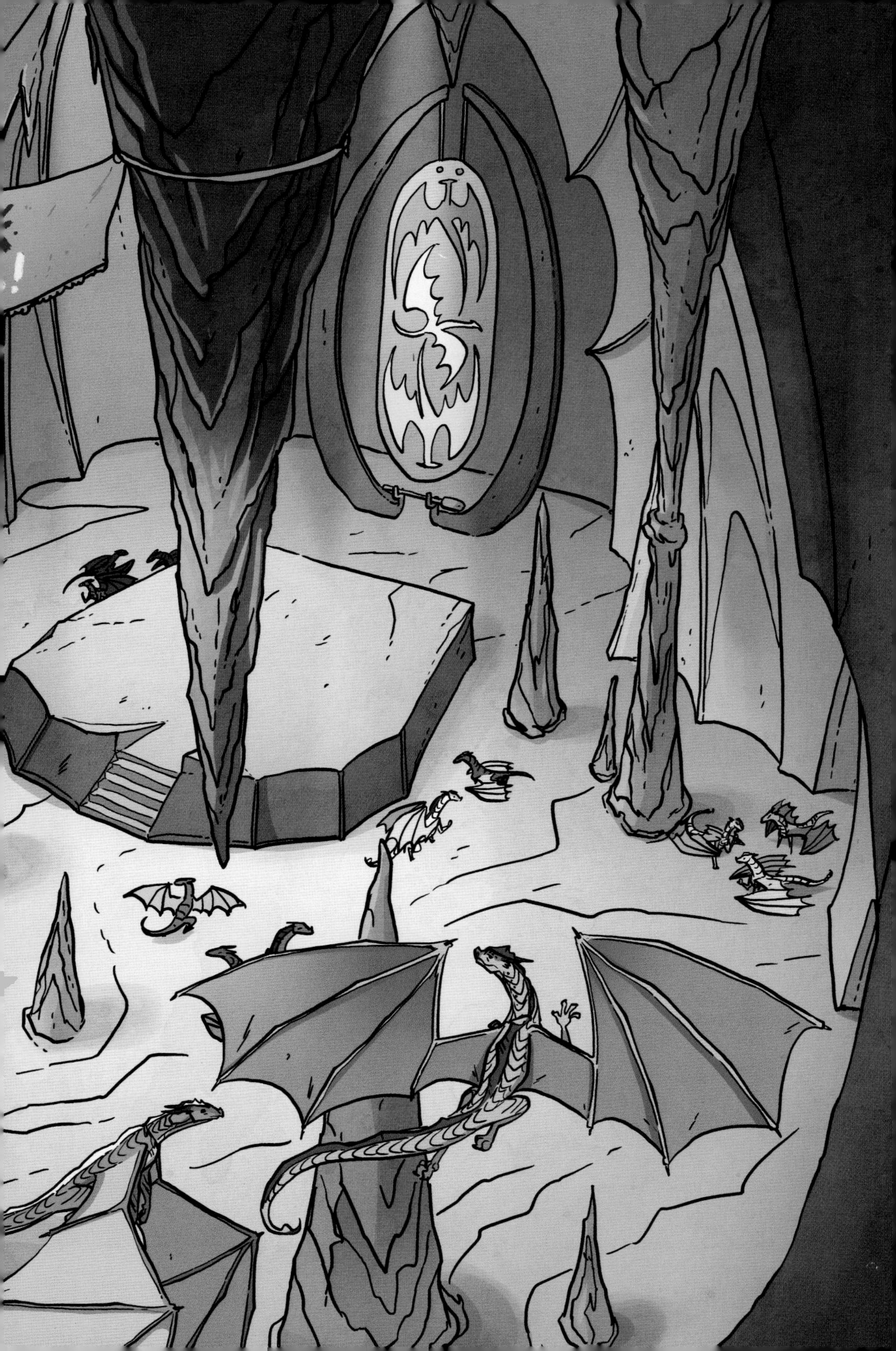

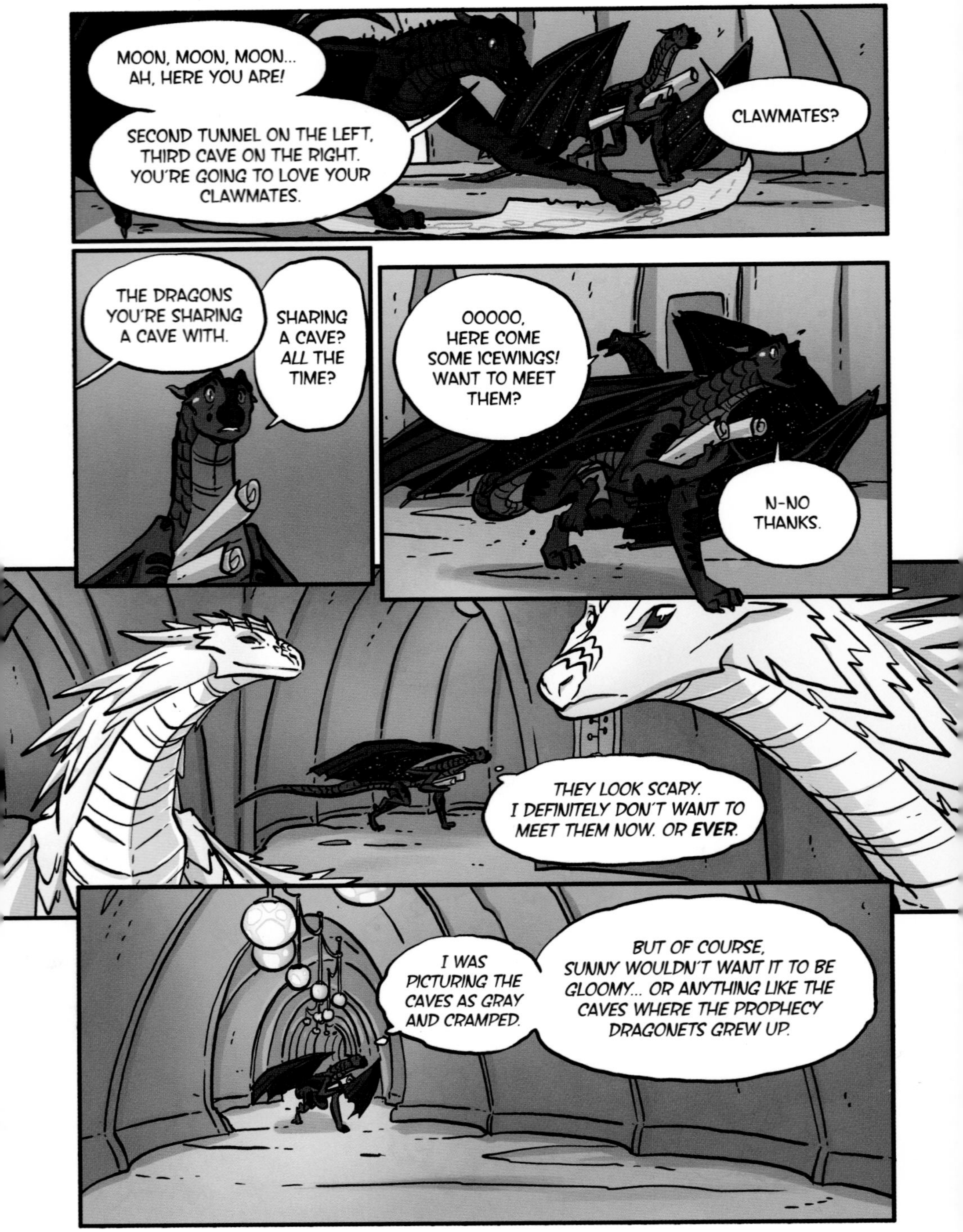

MOON, MOON, MOON... AH, HERE YOU ARE!
SECOND TUNNEL ON THE LEFT, THIRD CAVE ON THE RIGHT. YOU'RE GOING TO LOVE YOUR CLAWMATES.
CLAWMATES?
THE DRAGONS YOU'RE SHARING A CAVE WITH.
SHARING A CAVE? *ALL* THE TIME?
OOOOO, HERE COME SOME ICEWINGS! WANT TO MEET THEM?
N-NO THANKS.
THEY LOOK SCARY. I DEFINITELY DON'T WANT TO MEET THEM NOW. OR ***EVER.***
I WAS PICTURING THE CAVES AS GRAY AND CRAMPED.
BUT OF COURSE, SUNNY WOULDN'T WANT IT TO BE GLOOMY... OR ANYTHING LIKE THE CAVES WHERE THE PROPHECY DRAGONETS GREW UP.

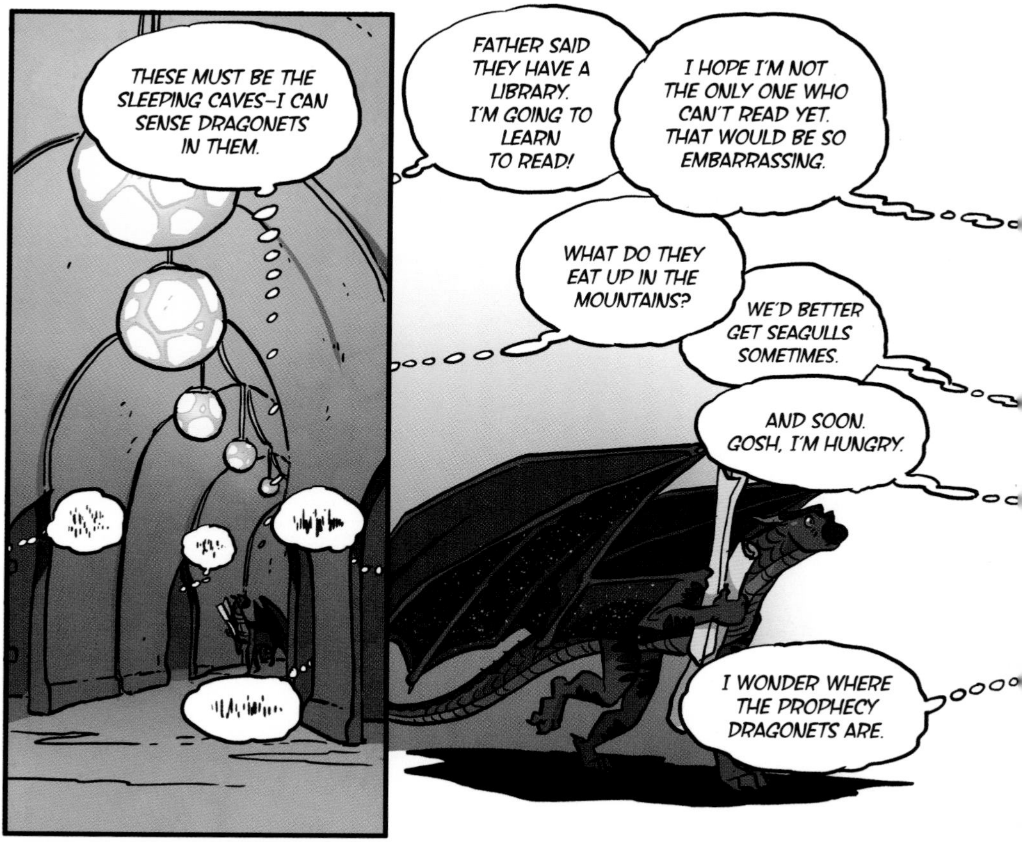
THESE MUST BE THE SLEEPING CAVES—I CAN SENSE DRAGONETS IN THEM.
FATHER SAID THEY HAVE A LIBRARY. I'M GOING TO LEARN TO READ!
I HOPE I'M NOT THE ONLY ONE WHO CAN'T READ YET. THAT WOULD BE SO EMBARRASSING.
WHAT DO THEY EAT UP IN THE MOUNTAINS?
WE'D BETTER GET SEAGULLS SOMETIMES.
AND SOON. GOSH, I'M HUNGRY.
I WONDER WHERE THE PROPHECY DRAGONETS ARE.

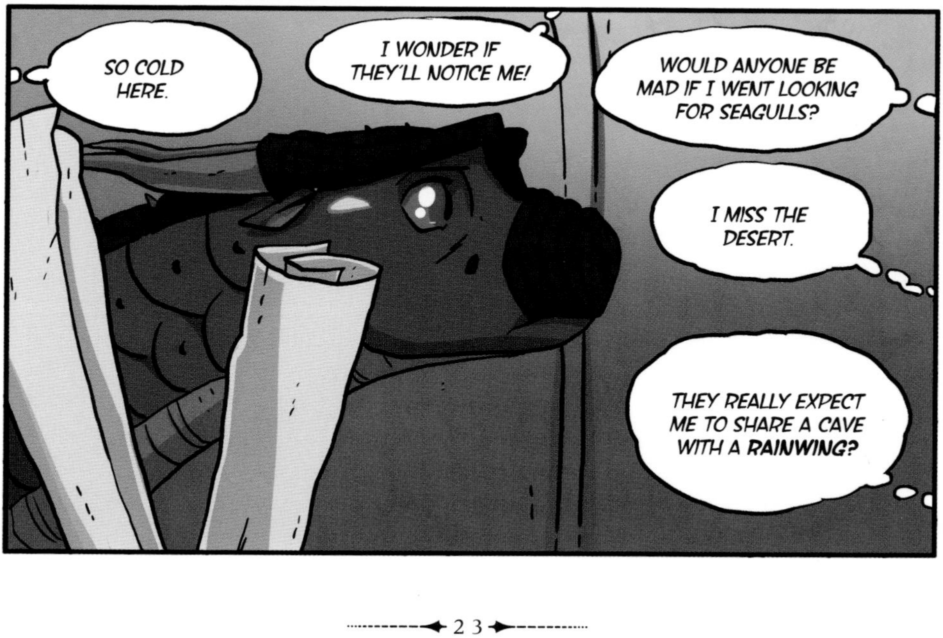
SO COLD HERE.
I WONDER IF THEY'LL NOTICE ME!
WOULD ANYONE BE MAD IF I WENT LOOKING FOR SEAGULLS?
I MISS THE DESERT.
THEY REALLY EXPECT ME TO SHARE A CAVE WITH A **RAINWING?**

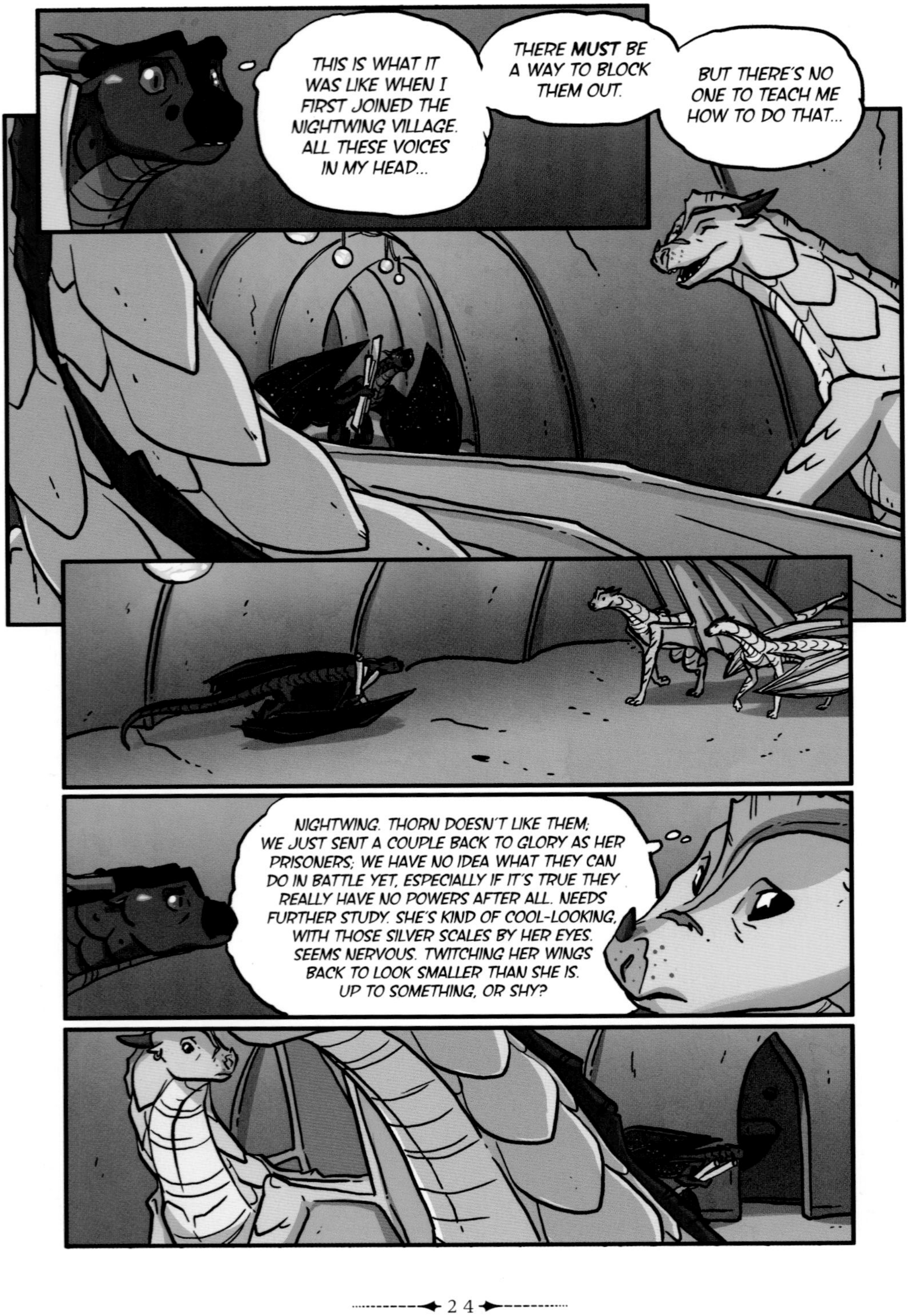

THIS IS WHAT IT WAS LIKE WHEN I FIRST JOINED THE NIGHTWING VILLAGE. ALL THESE VOICES IN MY HEAD...
THERE MUST BE A WAY TO BLOCK THEM OUT.
BUT THERE'S NO ONE TO TEACH ME HOW TO DO THAT...
NIGHTWING. THORN DOESN'T LIKE THEM; WE JUST SENT A COUPLE BACK TO GLORY AS HER PRISONERS; WE HAVE NO IDEA WHAT THEY CAN DO IN BATTLE YET, ESPECIALLY IF IT'S TRUE THEY REALLY HAVE NO POWERS AFTER ALL. NEEDS FURTHER STUDY. SHE'S KIND OF COOL-LOOKING, WITH THOSE SILVER SCALES BY HER EYES. SEEMS NERVOUS. TWITCHING HER WINGS BACK TO LOOK SMALLER THAN SHE IS. UP TO SOMETHING, OR SHY?

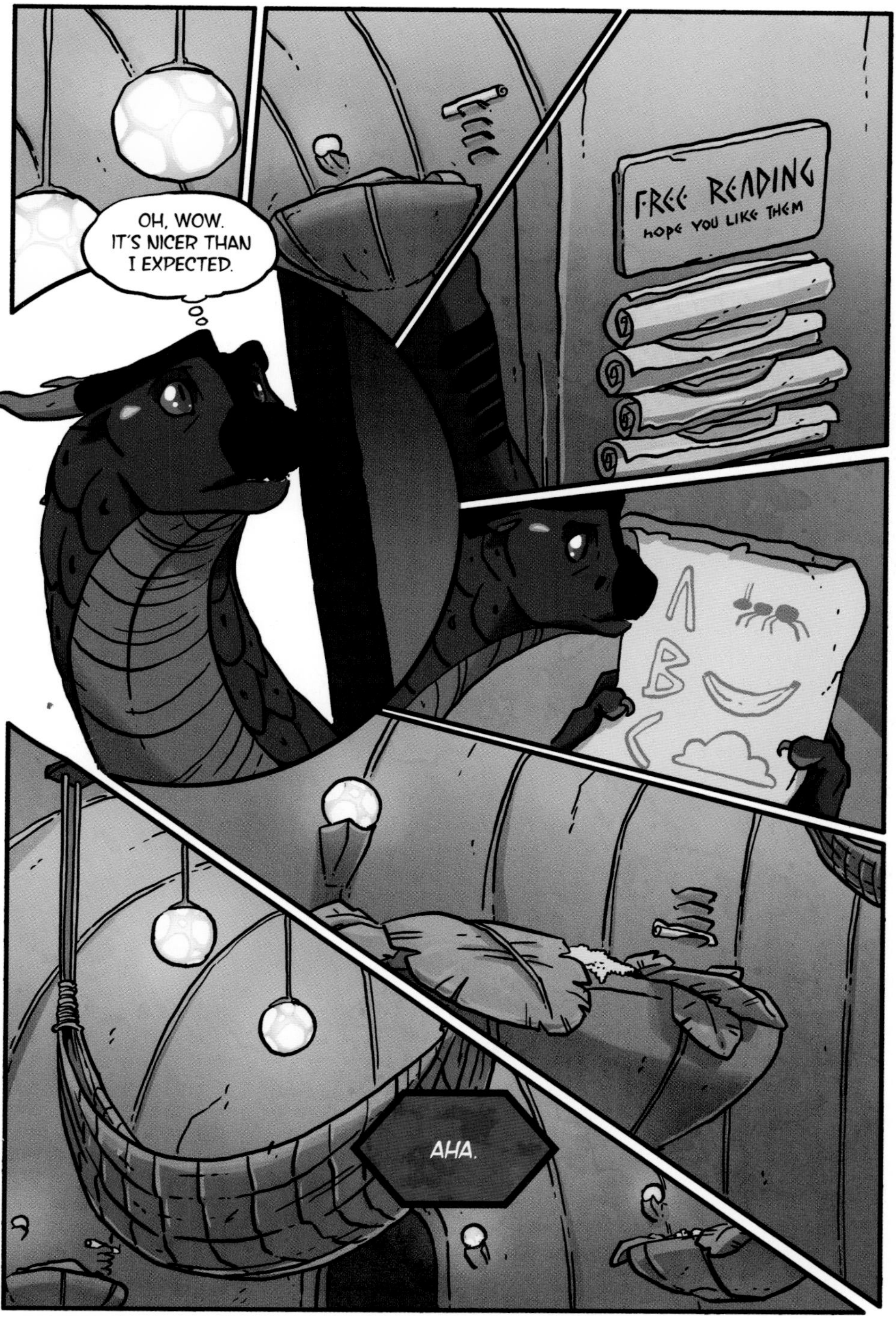
OH, WOW. IT'S NICER THAN I EXPECTED.
FREE READING
HOPE YOU LIKE THEM
A
B
C
AHA.

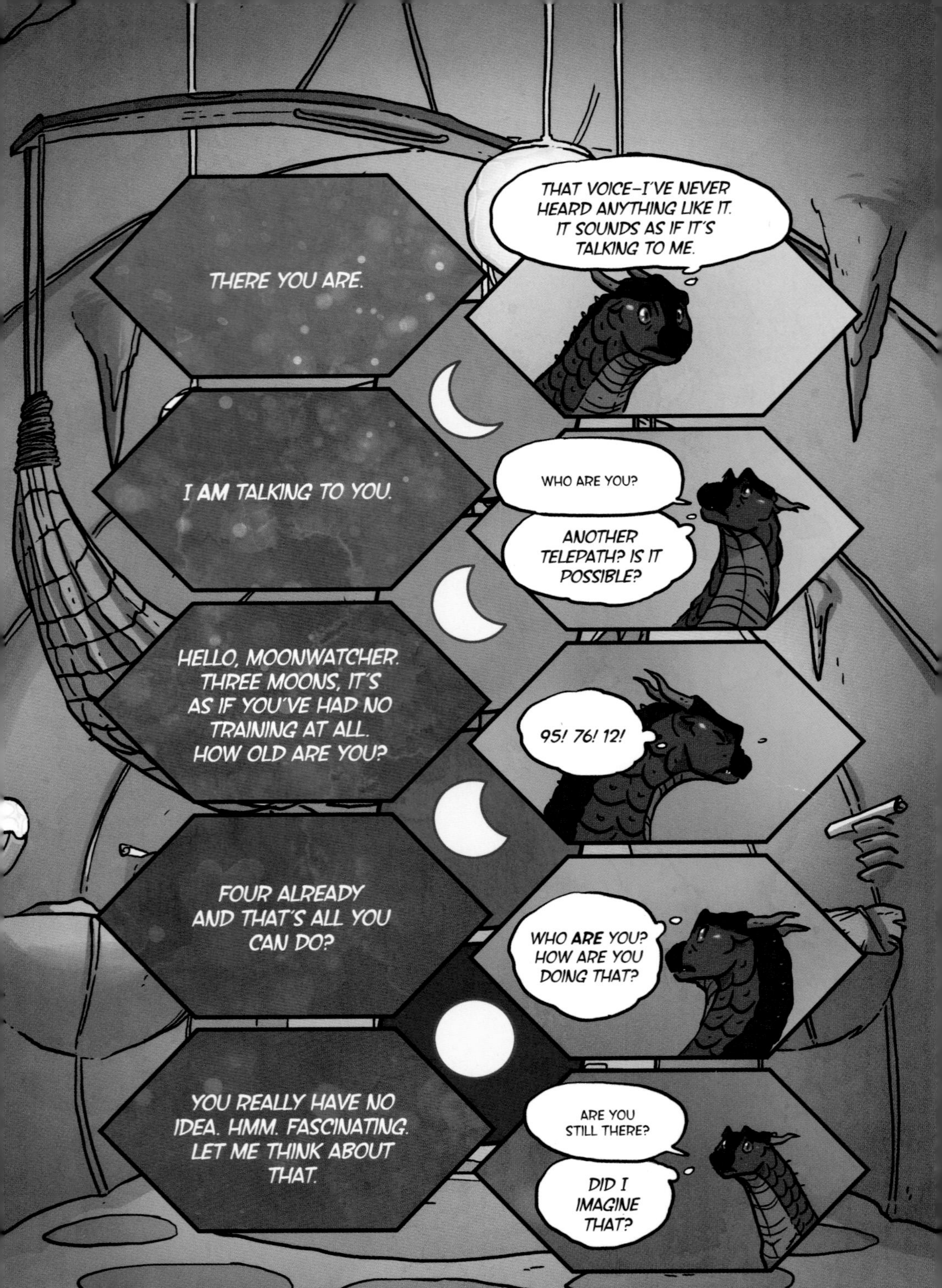
THERE YOU ARE.
THAT VOICE—I'VE NEVER HEARD ANYTHING LIKE IT. IT SOUNDS AS IF IT'S TALKING TO ME.
I AM TALKING TO YOU.
WHO ARE YOU?
ANOTHER TELEPATH? IS IT POSSIBLE?
HELLO, MOONWATCHER. THREE MOONS, IT'S AS IF YOU'VE HAD NO TRAINING AT ALL. HOW OLD ARE YOU?
95! 76! 12!
FOUR ALREADY AND THAT'S ALL YOU CAN DO?
WHO ARE YOU? HOW ARE YOU DOING THAT?
YOU REALLY HAVE NO IDEA. HMM. FASCINATING. LET ME THINK ABOUT THAT.
ARE YOU STILL THERE?
DID I IMAGINE THAT?

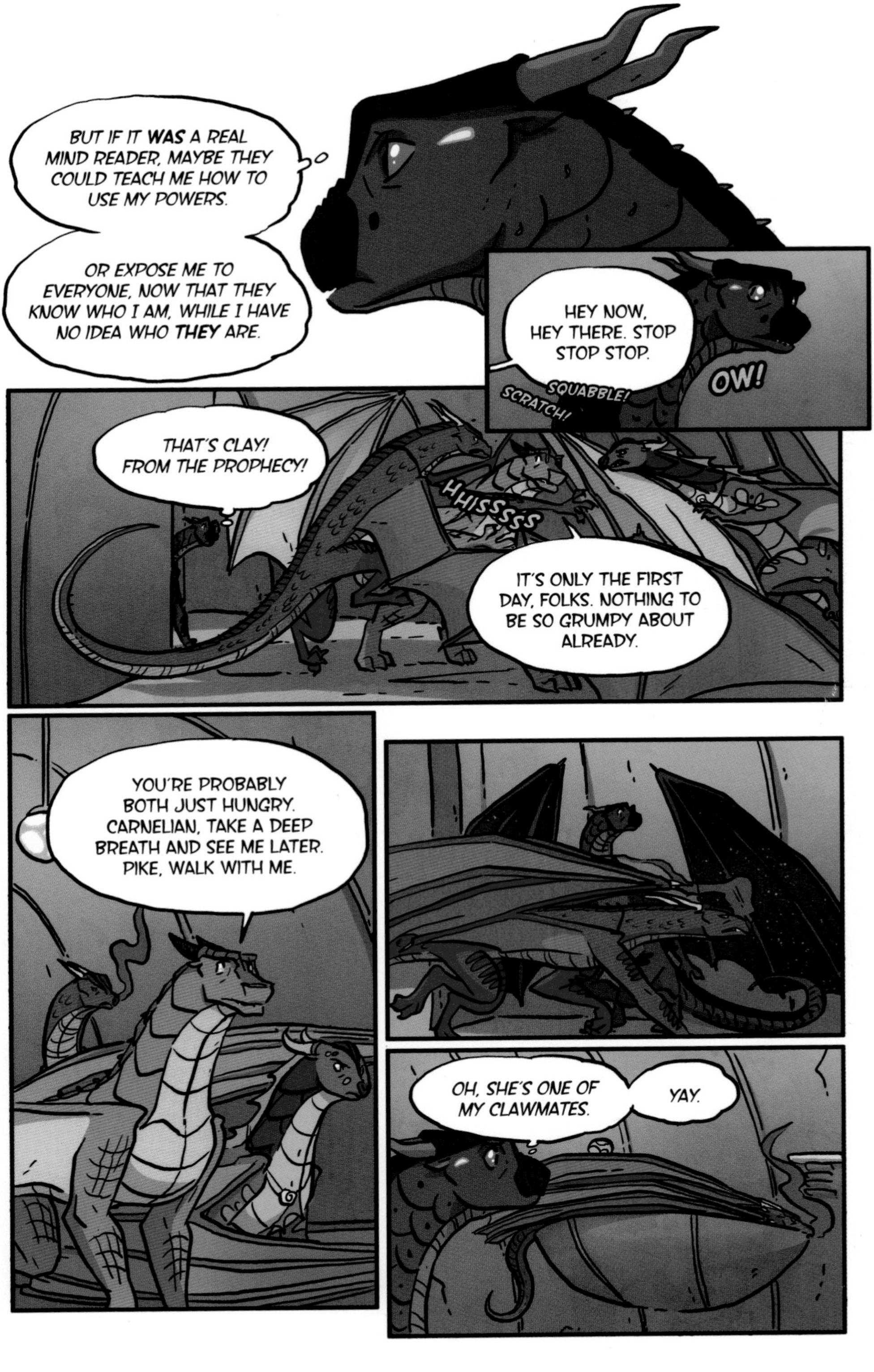
BUT IF IT WAS A REAL MIND READER, MAYBE THEY COULD TEACH ME HOW TO USE MY POWERS.
OR EXPOSE ME TO EVERYONE, NOW THAT THEY KNOW WHO I AM, WHILE I HAVE NO IDEA WHO THEY ARE.
HEY NOW, HEY THERE. STOP STOP STOP.
SQUABBLE!
SCRATCH!
OW!
THAT'S CLAY! FROM THE PROPHECY!
HHISSSSS
IT'S ONLY THE FIRST DAY, FOLKS. NOTHING TO BE SO GRUMPY ABOUT ALREADY.
YOU'RE PROBABLY BOTH JUST HUNGRY. CARNELIAN, TAKE A DEEP BREATH AND SEE ME LATER. PIKE, WALK WITH ME.
OH, SHE'S ONE OF MY CLAWMATES.
YAY.

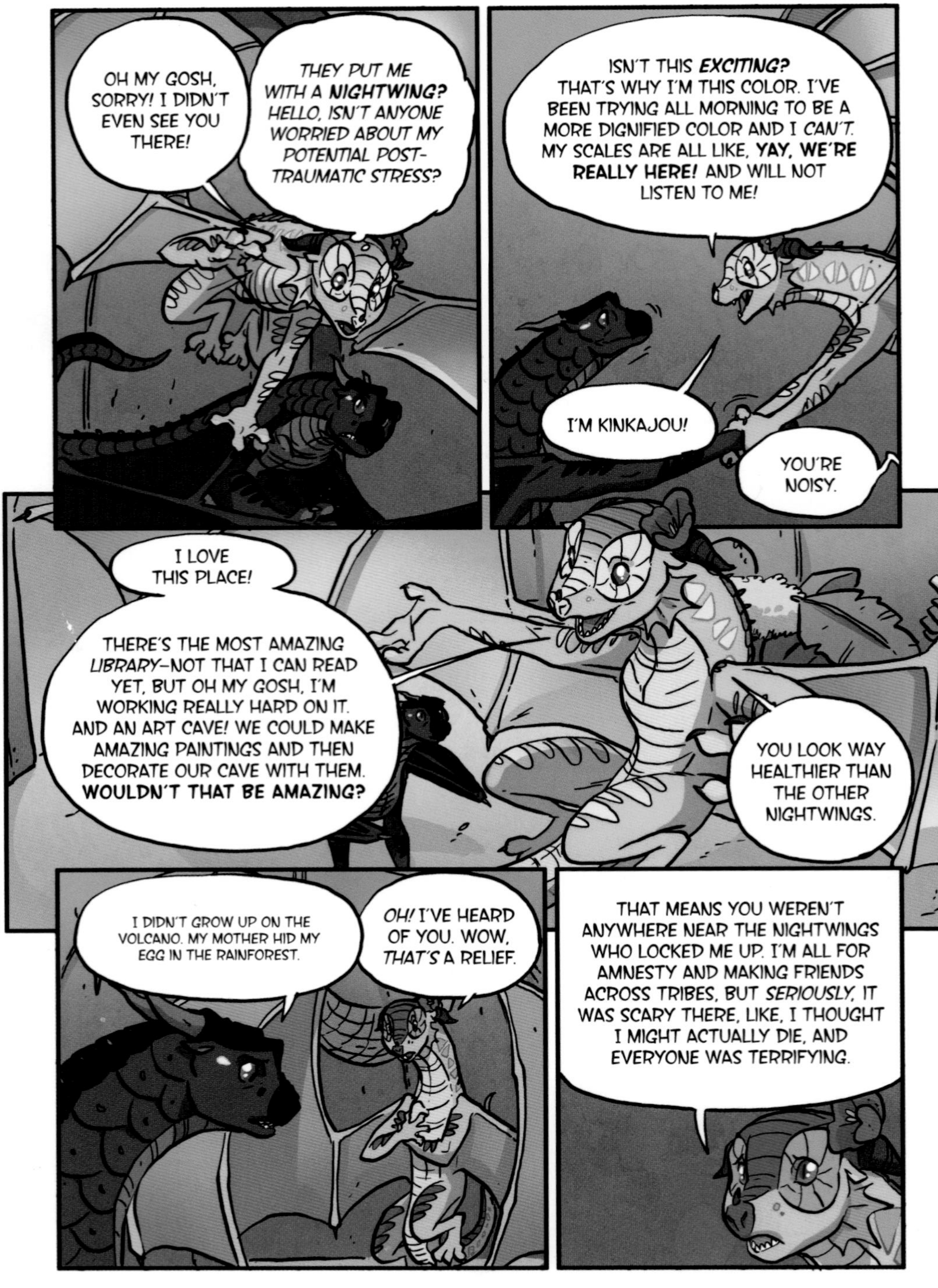
OH MY GOSH, SORRY! I DIDN'T EVEN SEE YOU THERE!
THEY PUT ME WITH A NIGHTWING? HELLO, ISN'T ANYONE WORRIED ABOUT MY POTENTIAL POST-TRAUMATIC STRESS?
ISN'T THIS EXCITING? THAT'S WHY I'M THIS COLOR. I'VE BEEN TRYING ALL MORNING TO BE A MORE DIGNIFIED COLOR AND I CAN'T. MY SCALES ARE ALL LIKE, YAY, WE'RE REALLY HERE! AND WILL NOT LISTEN TO ME!
I'M KINKAJOU!
YOU'RE NOISY.
I LOVE THIS PLACE!
THERE'S THE MOST AMAZING LIBRARY—NOT THAT I CAN READ YET, BUT OH MY GOSH, I'M WORKING REALLY HARD ON IT. AND AN ART CAVE! WE COULD MAKE AMAZING PAINTINGS AND THEN DECORATE OUR CAVE WITH THEM. WOULDN'T THAT BE AMAZING?
YOU LOOK WAY HEALTHIER THAN THE OTHER NIGHTWINGS.
I DIDN'T GROW UP ON THE VOLCANO. MY MOTHER HID MY EGG IN THE RAINFOREST.
OH! I'VE HEARD OF YOU. WOW, THAT'S A RELIEF.
THAT MEANS YOU WEREN'T ANYWHERE NEAR THE NIGHTWINGS WHO LOCKED ME UP. I'M ALL FOR AMNESTY AND MAKING FRIENDS ACROSS TRIBES, BUT SERIOUSLY, IT WAS SCARY THERE, LIKE, I THOUGHT I MIGHT ACTUALLY DIE, AND EVERYONE WAS TERRIFYING.

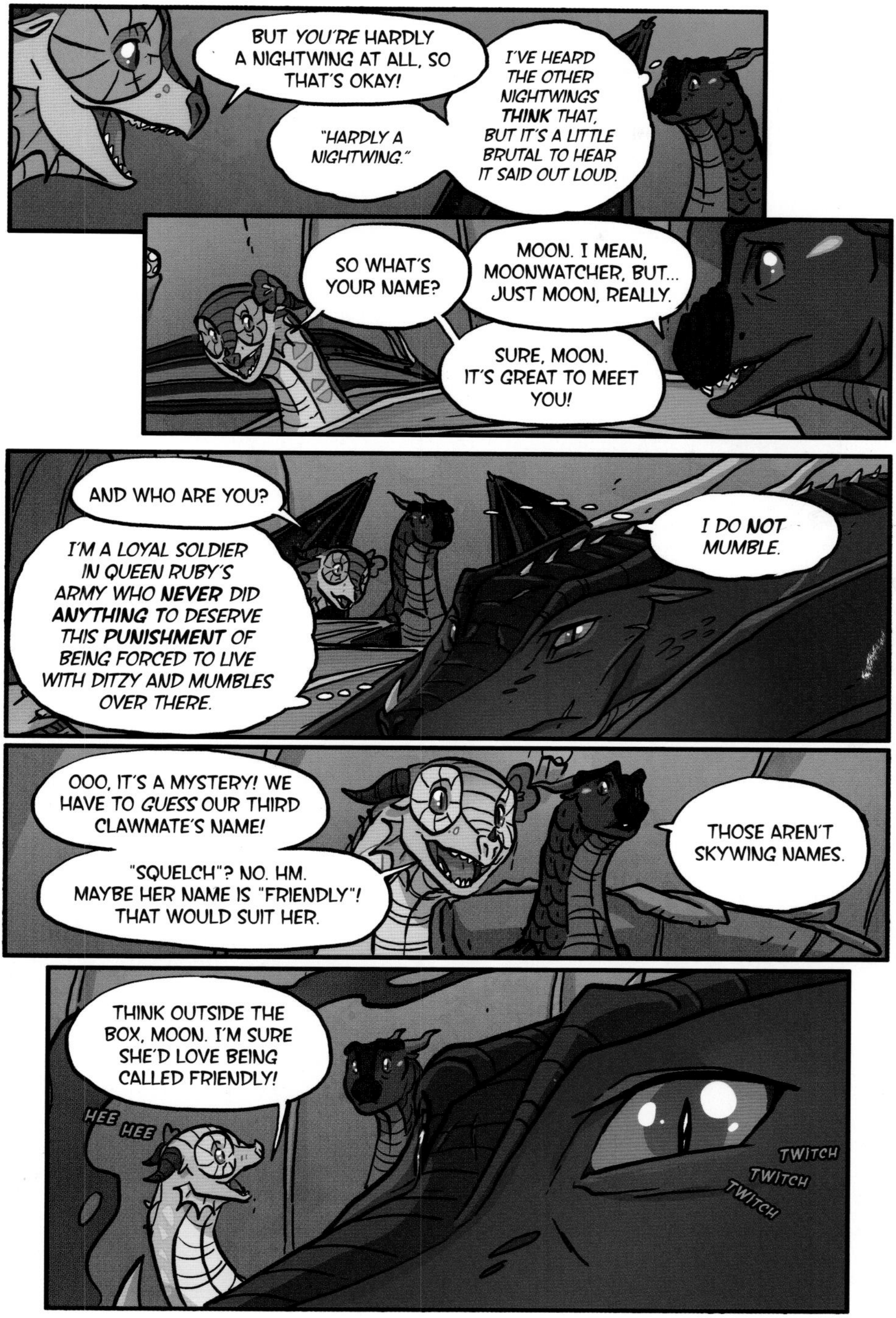
BUT YOU'RE HARDLY A NIGHTWING AT ALL, SO THAT'S OKAY!
"HARDLY A NIGHTWING."
I'VE HEARD THE OTHER NIGHTWINGS THINK THAT, BUT IT'S A LITTLE BRUTAL TO HEAR IT SAID OUT LOUD.
SO WHAT'S YOUR NAME?
MOON. I MEAN, MOONWATCHER, BUT... JUST MOON, REALLY.
SURE, MOON. IT'S GREAT TO MEET YOU!
AND WHO ARE YOU?
I'M A LOYAL SOLDIER IN QUEEN RUBY'S ARMY WHO NEVER DID ANYTHING TO DESERVE THIS PUNISHMENT OF BEING FORCED TO LIVE WITH DITZY AND MUMBLES OVER THERE.
I DO NOT MUMBLE.
OOO, IT'S A MYSTERY! WE HAVE TO GUESS OUR THIRD CLAWMATE'S NAME!
"SQUELCH"? NO. HM. MAYBE HER NAME IS "FRIENDLY"! THAT WOULD SUIT HER.
THOSE AREN'T SKYWING NAMES.
THINK OUTSIDE THE BOX, MOON. I'M SURE SHE'D LOVE BEING CALLED FRIENDLY!
HEE HEE
TWITCH
TWITCH
TWITCH

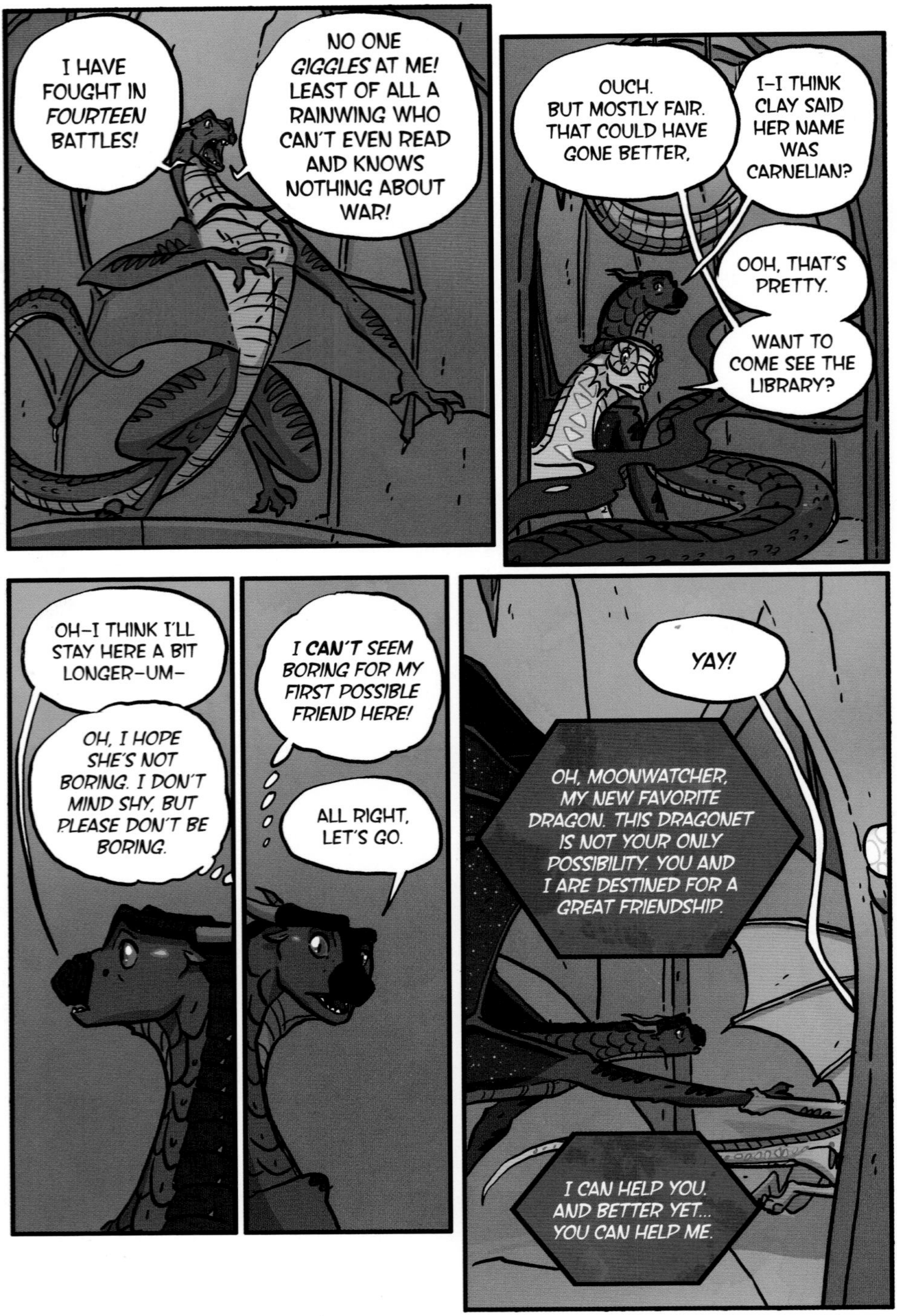
I HAVE FOUGHT IN *FOURTEEN* BATTLES!
NO ONE *GIGGLES* AT ME! LEAST OF ALL A RAINWING WHO CAN'T EVEN READ AND KNOWS NOTHING ABOUT WAR!
OUCH. BUT MOSTLY FAIR. THAT COULD HAVE GONE BETTER.
I–I THINK CLAY SAID HER NAME WAS CARNELIAN?
OOH, THAT'S PRETTY.
WANT TO COME SEE THE LIBRARY?
OH–I THINK I'LL STAY HERE A BIT LONGER–UM–
OH, I HOPE SHE'S NOT BORING. I DON'T MIND SHY, BUT PLEASE DON'T BE BORING.
I ***CAN'T*** *SEEM BORING FOR MY FIRST POSSIBLE FRIEND HERE!*
ALL RIGHT, LET'S GO.
YAY!
OH, MOONWATCHER, MY NEW FAVORITE DRAGON. THIS DRAGONET IS NOT YOUR ONLY POSSIBILITY. YOU AND I ARE DESTINED FOR A GREAT FRIENDSHIP.
I CAN HELP YOU. AND BETTER YET... YOU CAN HELP ME.

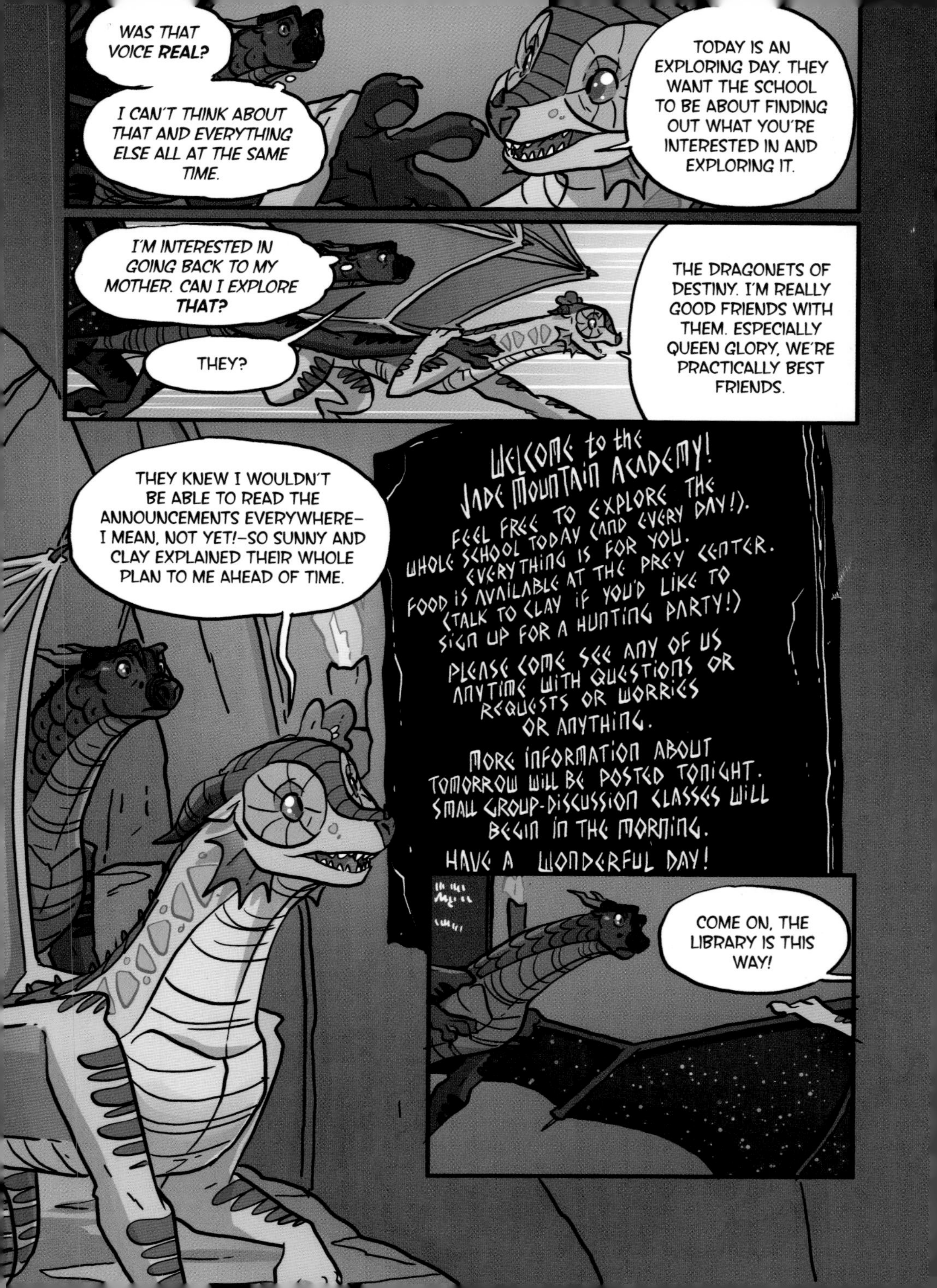
WAS THAT VOICE **REAL?**
I CAN'T THINK ABOUT THAT AND EVERYTHING ELSE ALL AT THE SAME TIME.
TODAY IS AN EXPLORING DAY. THEY WANT THE SCHOOL TO BE ABOUT FINDING OUT WHAT YOU'RE INTERESTED IN AND EXPLORING IT.
I'M INTERESTED IN GOING BACK TO MY MOTHER. CAN I EXPLORE **THAT?**
THEY?
THE DRAGONETS OF DESTINY. I'M REALLY GOOD FRIENDS WITH THEM. ESPECIALLY QUEEN GLORY, WE'RE PRACTICALLY BEST FRIENDS.
THEY KNEW I WOULDN'T BE ABLE TO READ THE ANNOUNCEMENTS EVERYWHERE—I MEAN, NOT YET!—SO SUNNY AND CLAY EXPLAINED THEIR WHOLE PLAN TO ME AHEAD OF TIME.
WELCOME TO THE JADE MOUNTAIN ACADEMY!
FEEL FREE TO EXPLORE THE WHOLE SCHOOL TODAY (AND EVERY DAY!). EVERYTHING IS FOR YOU.
FOOD IS AVAILABLE AT THE PREY CENTER. (TALK TO CLAY IF YOU'D LIKE TO SIGN UP FOR A HUNTING PARTY!)
PLEASE COME SEE ANY OF US ANYTIME WITH QUESTIONS OR REQUESTS OR WORRIES OR ANYTHING.
MORE INFORMATION ABOUT TOMORROW WILL BE POSTED TONIGHT. SMALL GROUP-DISCUSSION CLASSES WILL BEGIN IN THE MORNING.
HAVE A WONDERFUL DAY!
COME ON, THE LIBRARY IS THIS WAY!

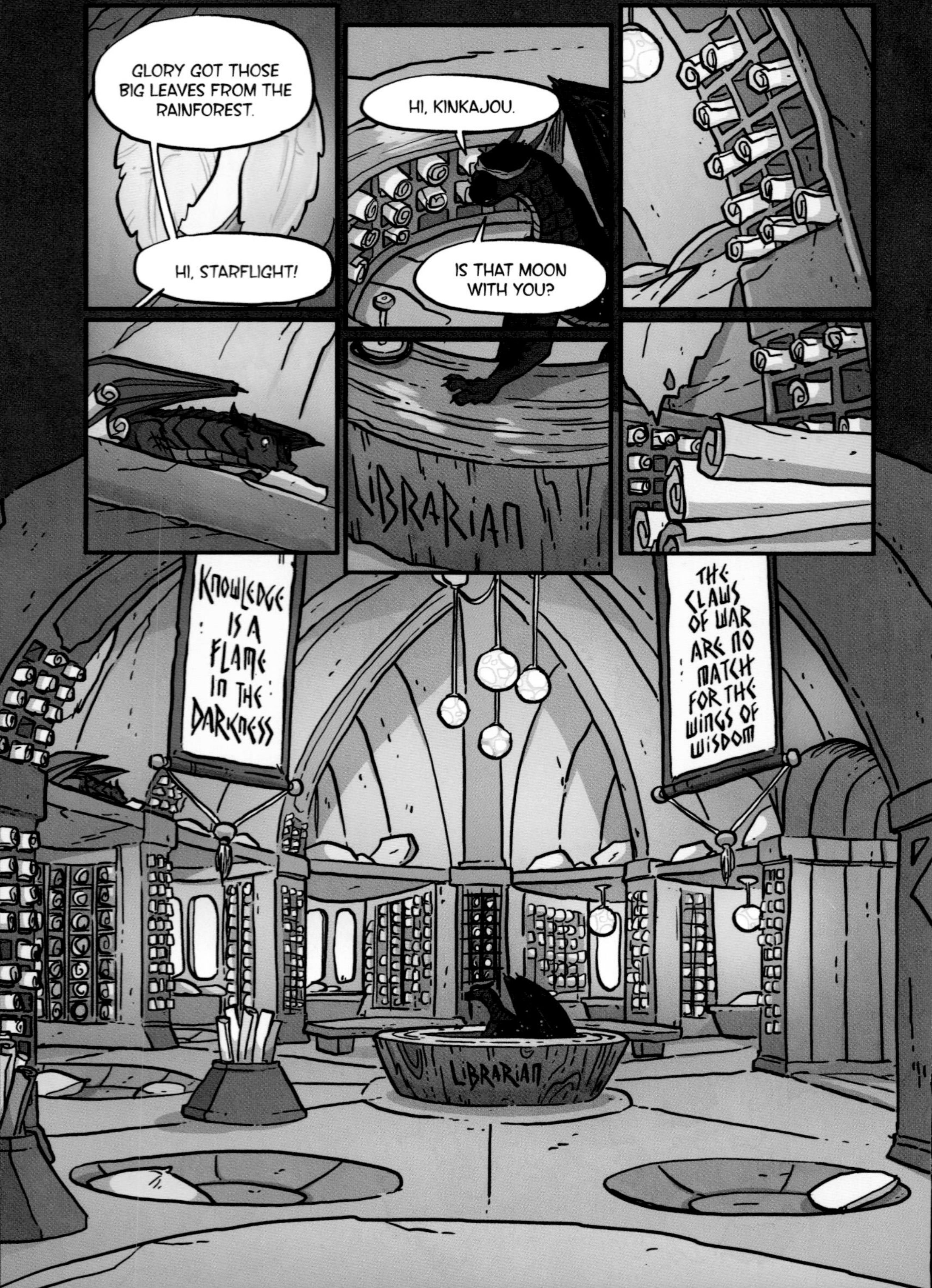
GLORY GOT THOSE BIG LEAVES FROM THE RAINFOREST.
HI, STARFLIGHT!
HI, KINKAJOU.
IS THAT MOON WITH YOU?
LIBRARIAN
KNOWLEDGE IS A FLAME IN THE DARKNESS
THE CLAWS OF WAR ARE NO MATCH FOR THE WINGS OF WISDOM
LIBRARIAN

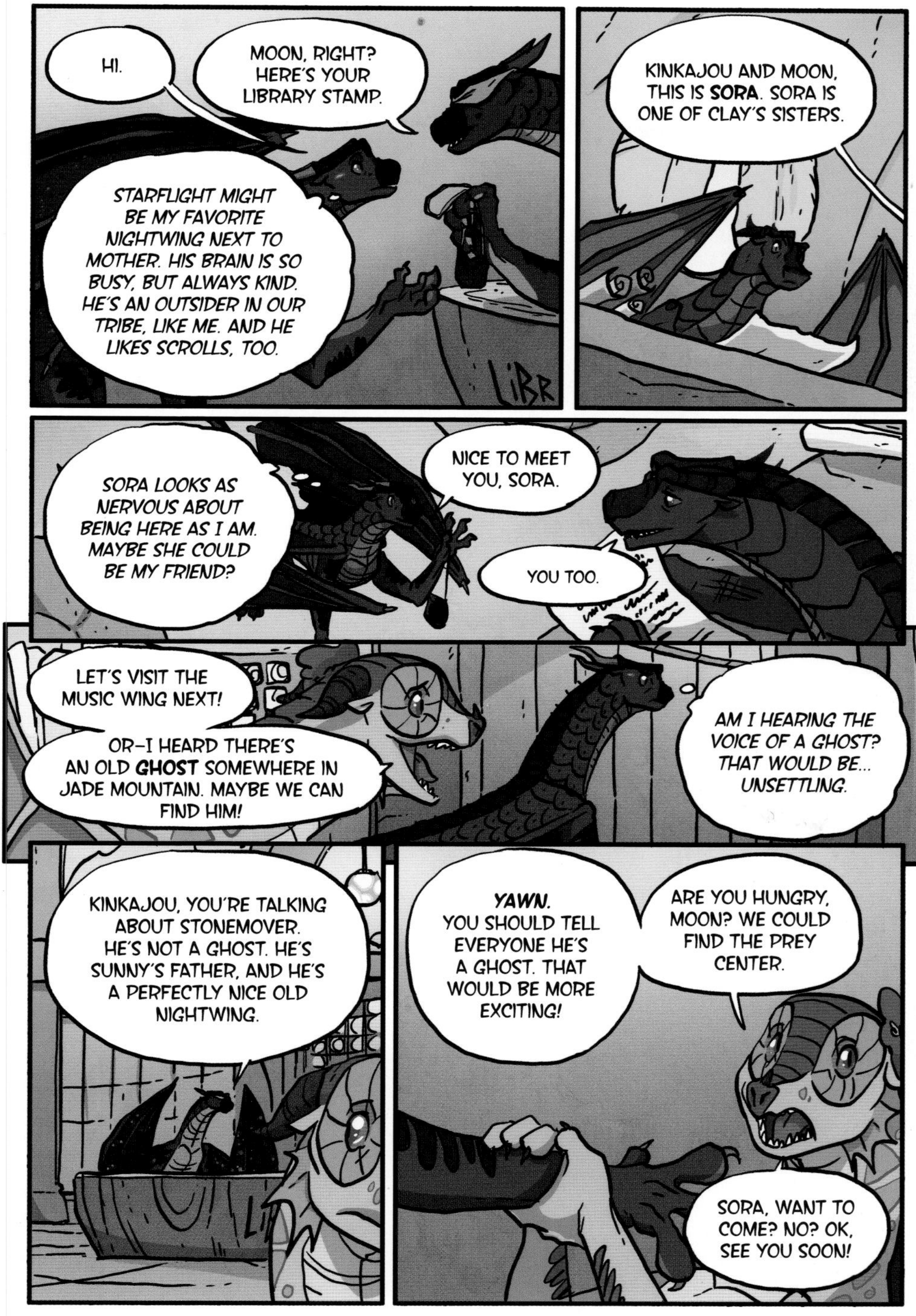
HI.
MOON, RIGHT? HERE'S YOUR LIBRARY STAMP.
STARFLIGHT MIGHT BE MY FAVORITE NIGHTWING NEXT TO MOTHER. HIS BRAIN IS SO BUSY, BUT ALWAYS KIND. HE'S AN OUTSIDER IN OUR TRIBE, LIKE ME. AND HE LIKES SCROLLS, TOO.
KINKAJOU AND MOON, THIS IS SORA. SORA IS ONE OF CLAY'S SISTERS.
SORA LOOKS AS NERVOUS ABOUT BEING HERE AS I AM. MAYBE SHE COULD BE MY FRIEND?
NICE TO MEET YOU, SORA.
YOU TOO.
LET'S VISIT THE MUSIC WING NEXT!
OR—I HEARD THERE'S AN OLD GHOST SOMEWHERE IN JADE MOUNTAIN. MAYBE WE CAN FIND HIM!
AM I HEARING THE VOICE OF A GHOST? THAT WOULD BE... UNSETTLING.
KINKAJOU, YOU'RE TALKING ABOUT STONEMOVER. HE'S NOT A GHOST. HE'S SUNNY'S FATHER, AND HE'S A PERFECTLY NICE OLD NIGHTWING.
YAWN. YOU SHOULD TELL EVERYONE HE'S A GHOST. THAT WOULD BE MORE EXCITING!
ARE YOU HUNGRY, MOON? WE COULD FIND THE PREY CENTER.
SORA, WANT TO COME? NO? OK, SEE YOU SOON!

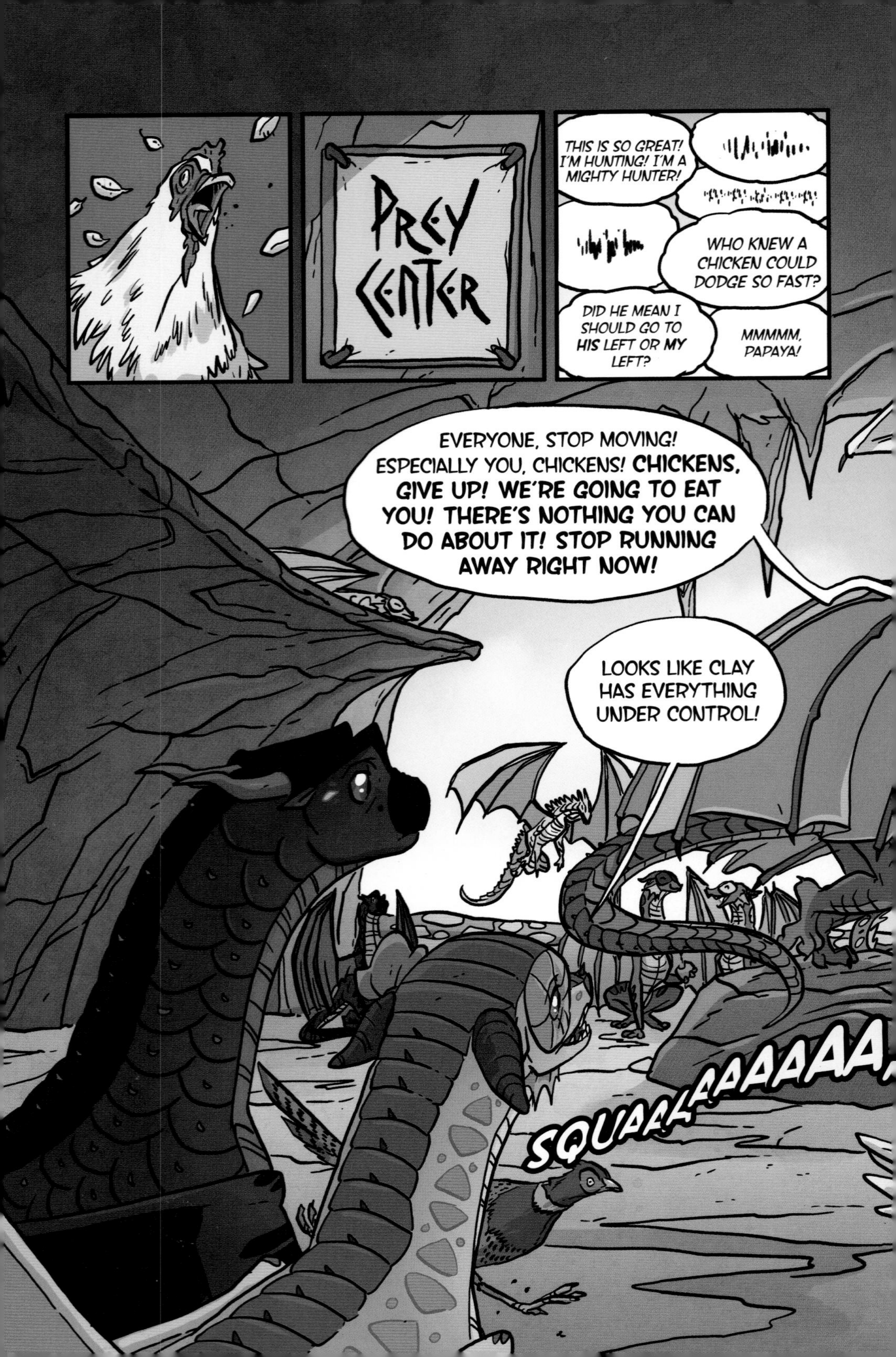
PREY CENTER
THIS IS SO GREAT! I'M HUNTING! I'M A MIGHTY HUNTER!
WHO KNEW A CHICKEN COULD DODGE SO FAST?
DID HE MEAN I SHOULD GO TO HIS LEFT OR MY LEFT?
MMMMM, PAPAYA!
EVERYONE, STOP MOVING! ESPECIALLY YOU, CHICKENS! CHICKENS, GIVE UP! WE'RE GOING TO EAT YOU! THERE'S NOTHING YOU CAN DO ABOUT IT! STOP RUNNING AWAY RIGHT NOW!
LOOKS LIKE CLAY HAS EVERYTHING UNDER CONTROL!
SQUAAAAAAAAAA,

AAWWWWWWWWWWWWWWWWWWWWWWWWWWWWIWK!

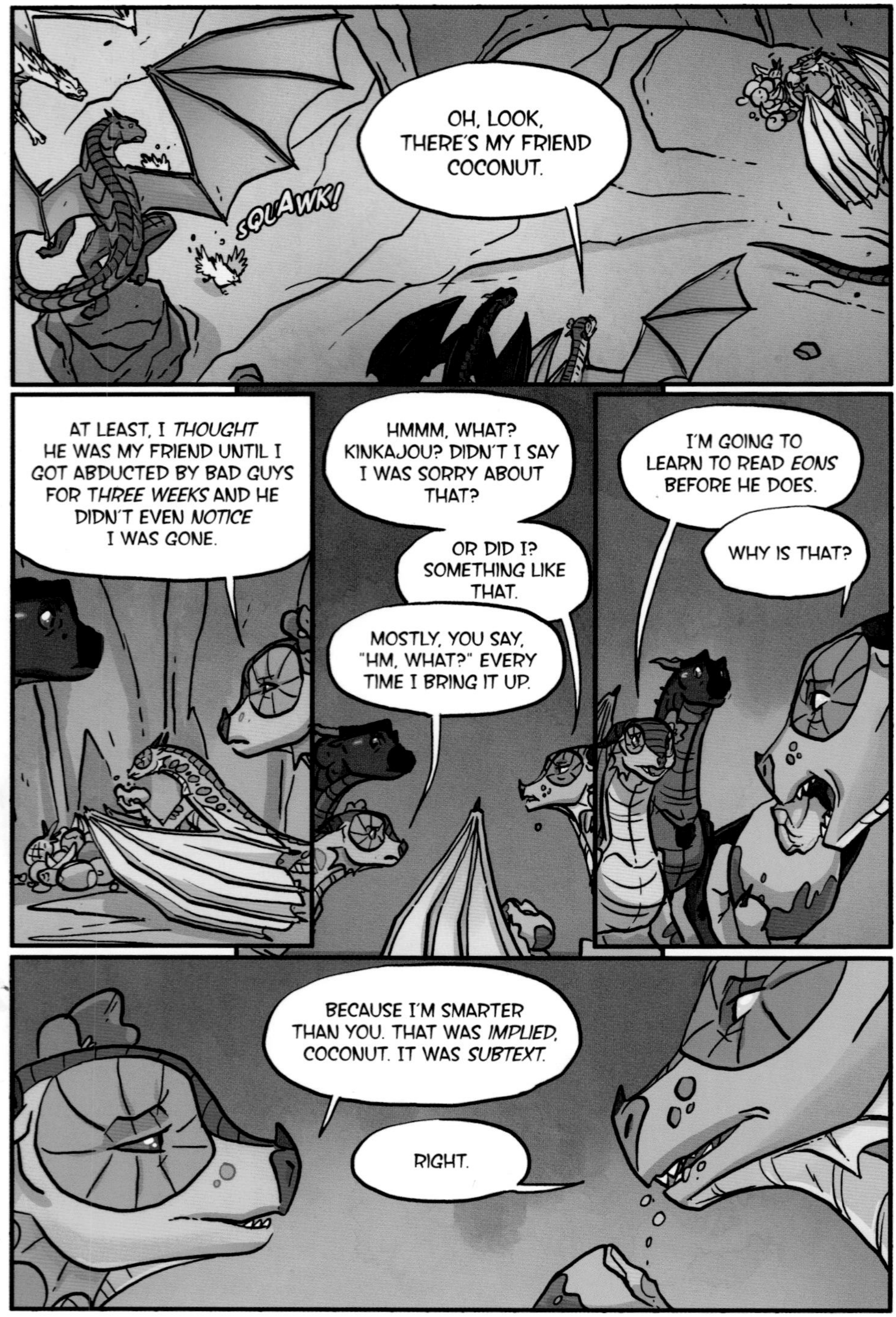
OH, LOOK, THERE'S MY FRIEND COCONUT.
SQUAWK!
AT LEAST, I *THOUGHT* HE WAS MY FRIEND UNTIL I GOT ABDUCTED BY BAD GUYS FOR *THREE WEEKS* AND HE DIDN'T EVEN *NOTICE* I WAS GONE.
HMMM, WHAT? KINKAJOU? DIDN'T I SAY I WAS SORRY ABOUT THAT?
OR DID I? SOMETHING LIKE THAT.
MOSTLY, YOU SAY, "HM, WHAT?" EVERY TIME I BRING IT UP.
I'M GOING TO LEARN TO READ *EONS* BEFORE HE DOES.
WHY IS THAT?
BECAUSE I'M SMARTER THAN YOU. THAT WAS *IMPLIED*, COCONUT. IT WAS *SUBTEXT*.
RIGHT.

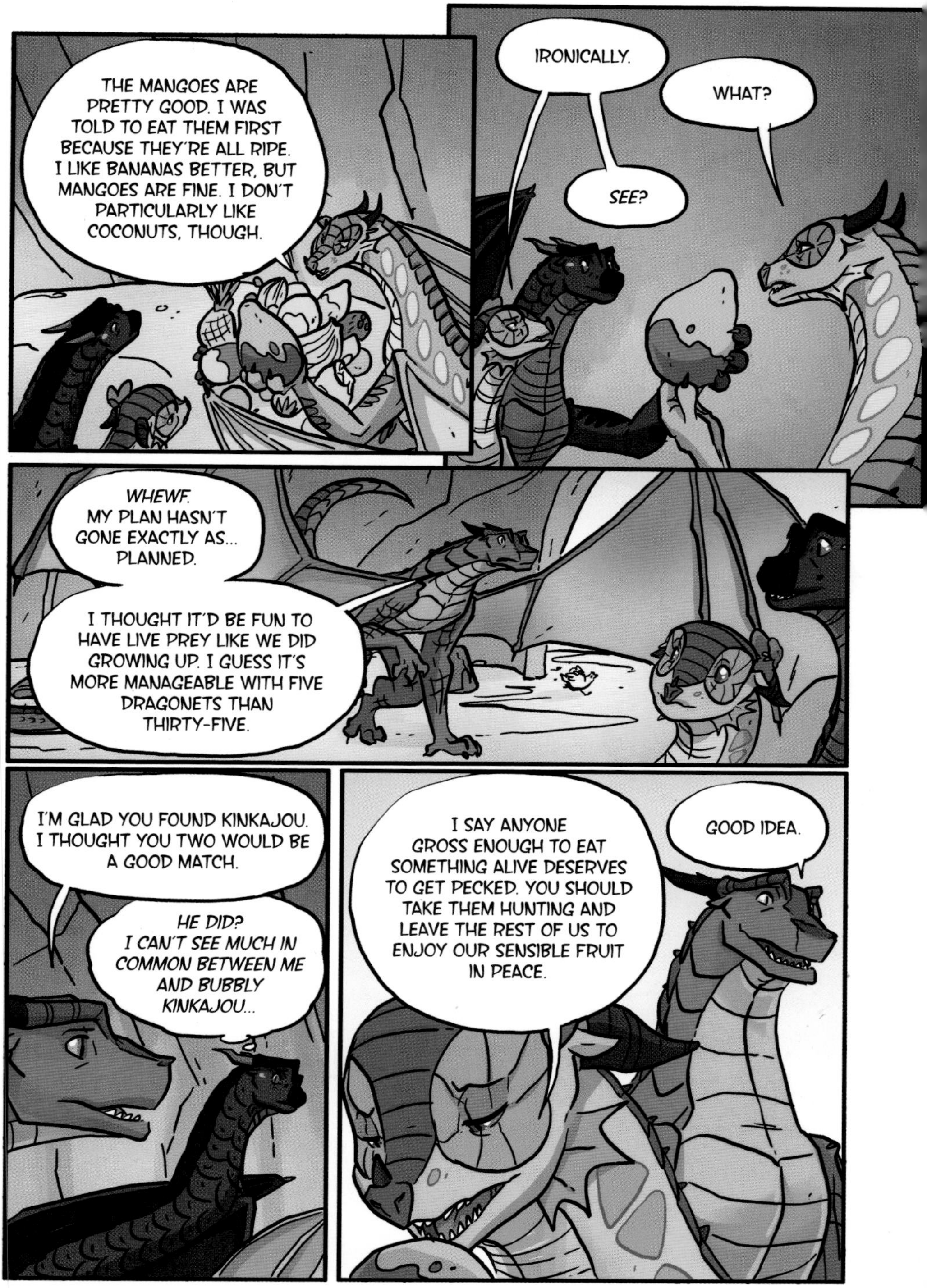
THE MANGOES ARE PRETTY GOOD. I WAS TOLD TO EAT THEM FIRST BECAUSE THEY'RE ALL RIPE. I LIKE BANANAS BETTER, BUT MANGOES ARE FINE. I DON'T PARTICULARLY LIKE COCONUTS, THOUGH.
IRONICALLY.
SEE?
WHAT?
WHEWF. MY PLAN HASN'T GONE EXACTLY AS... PLANNED.
I THOUGHT IT'D BE FUN TO HAVE LIVE PREY LIKE WE DID GROWING UP. I GUESS IT'S MORE MANAGEABLE WITH FIVE DRAGONETS THAN THIRTY-FIVE.
I'M GLAD YOU FOUND KINKAJOU. I THOUGHT YOU TWO WOULD BE A GOOD MATCH.
HE DID? I CAN'T SEE MUCH IN COMMON BETWEEN ME AND BUBBLY KINKAJOU...
I SAY ANYONE GROSS ENOUGH TO EAT SOMETHING ALIVE DESERVES TO GET PECKED. YOU SHOULD TAKE THEM HUNTING AND LEAVE THE REST OF US TO ENJOY OUR SENSIBLE FRUIT IN PEACE.
GOOD IDEA.

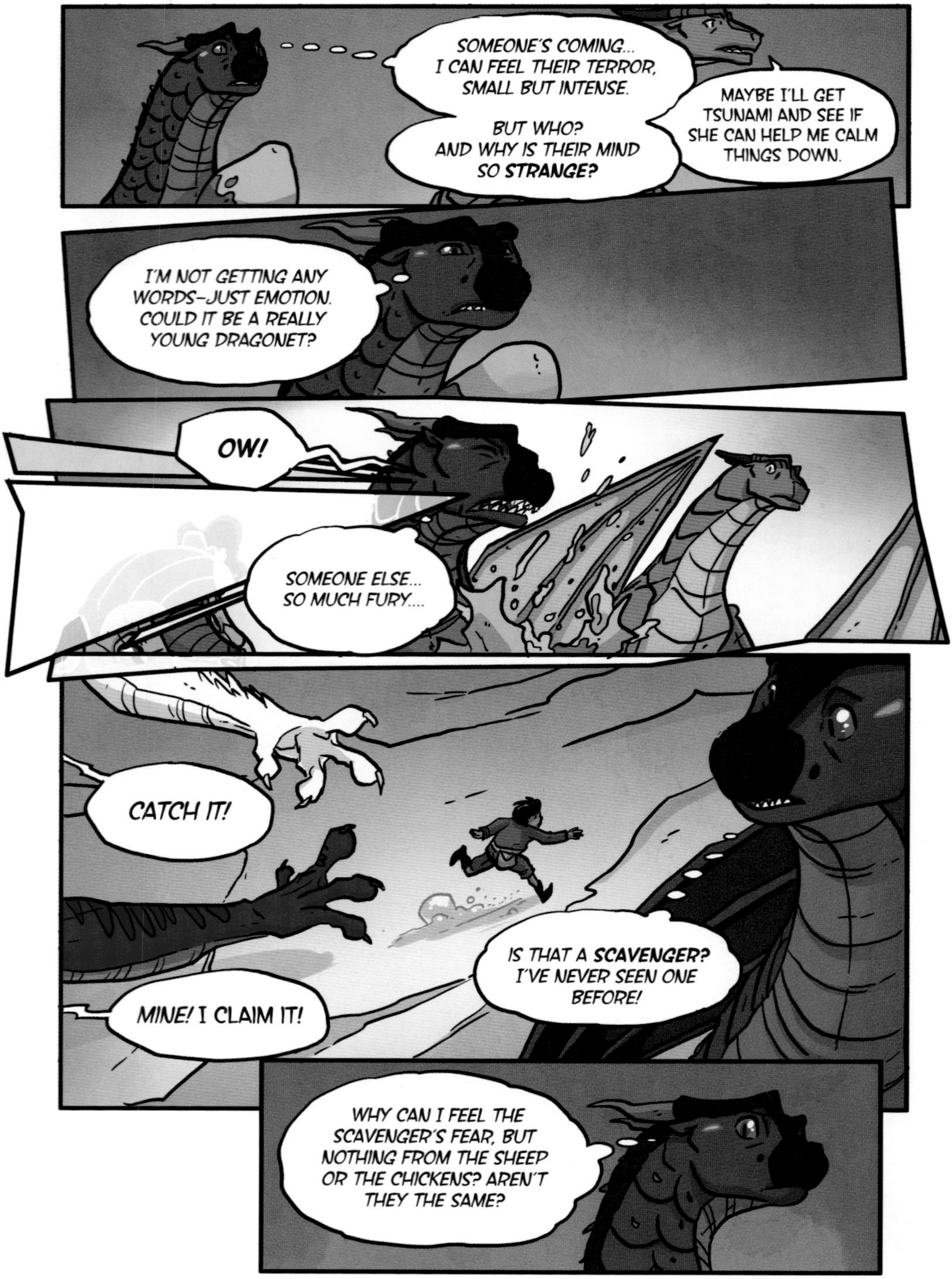
SOMEONE'S COMING... I CAN FEEL THEIR TERROR, SMALL BUT INTENSE.
BUT WHO? AND WHY IS THEIR MIND SO **STRANGE?**
MAYBE I'LL GET TSUNAMI AND SEE IF SHE CAN HELP ME CALM THINGS DOWN.
I'M NOT GETTING ANY WORDS—JUST EMOTION. COULD IT BE A REALLY YOUNG DRAGONET?
OW!
SOMEONE ELSE... SO MUCH FURY....
CATCH IT!
MINE! I CLAIM IT!
IS THAT A **SCAVENGER?** I'VE NEVER SEEN ONE BEFORE!
WHY CAN I FEEL THE SCAVENGER'S FEAR, BUT NOTHING FROM THE SHEEP OR THE CHICKENS? AREN'T THEY THE SAME?

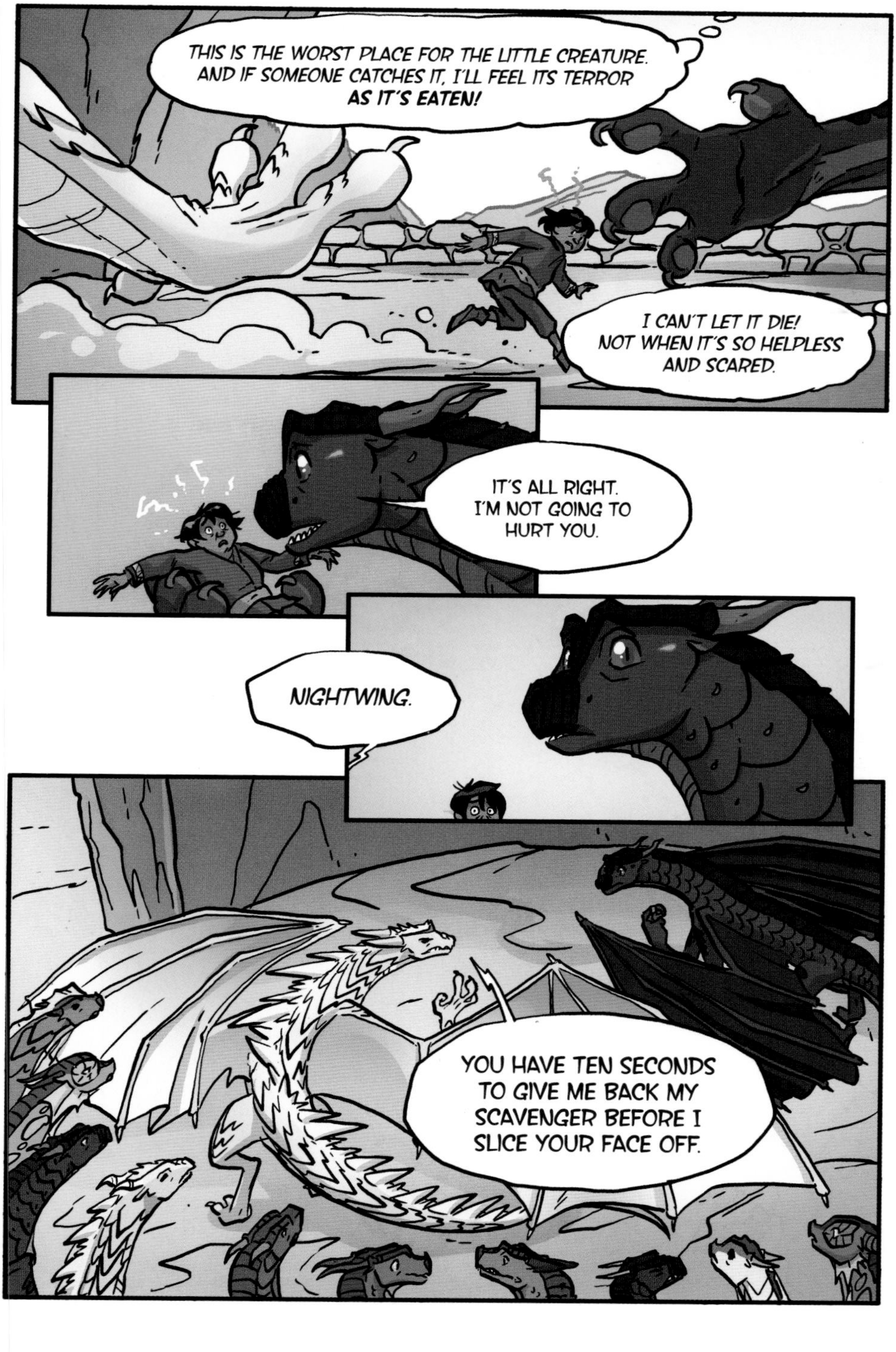
THIS IS THE WORST PLACE FOR THE LITTLE CREATURE. AND IF SOMEONE CATCHES IT, I'LL FEEL ITS TERROR AS IT'S EATEN!
I CAN'T LET IT DIE! NOT WHEN IT'S SO HELPLESS AND SCARED.
IT'S ALL RIGHT. I'M NOT GOING TO HURT YOU.
NIGHTWING.
YOU HAVE TEN SECONDS TO GIVE ME BACK MY SCAVENGER BEFORE I SLICE YOUR FACE OFF.

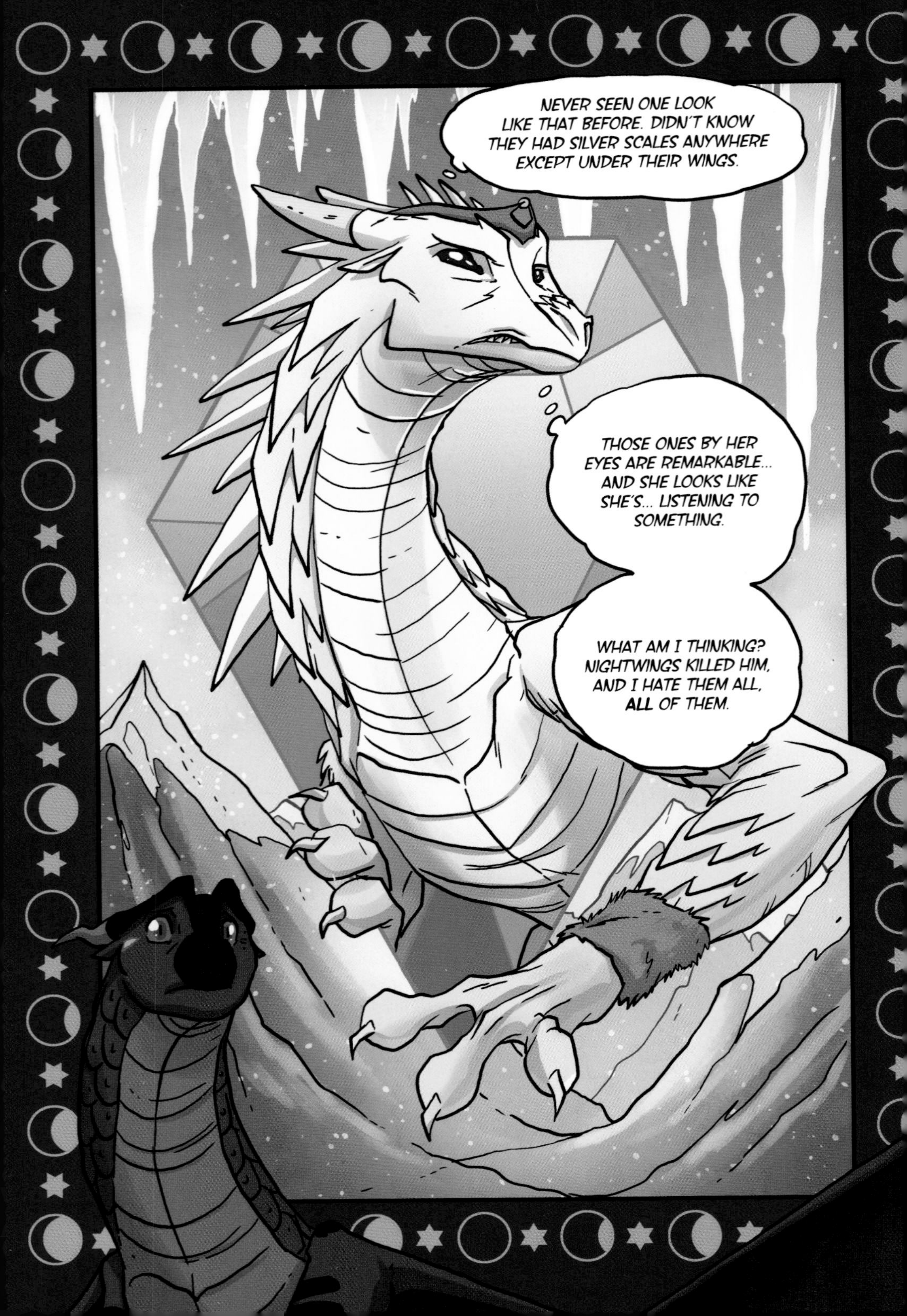

NEVER SEEN ONE LOOK LIKE THAT BEFORE. DIDN'T KNOW THEY HAD SILVER SCALES ANYWHERE EXCEPT UNDER THEIR WINGS.
THOSE ONES BY HER EYES ARE REMARKABLE... AND SHE LOOKS LIKE SHE'S... LISTENING TO SOMETHING.
WHAT AM I THINKING? NIGHTWINGS KILLED HIM, AND I HATE THEM ALL, **ALL** OF THEM.

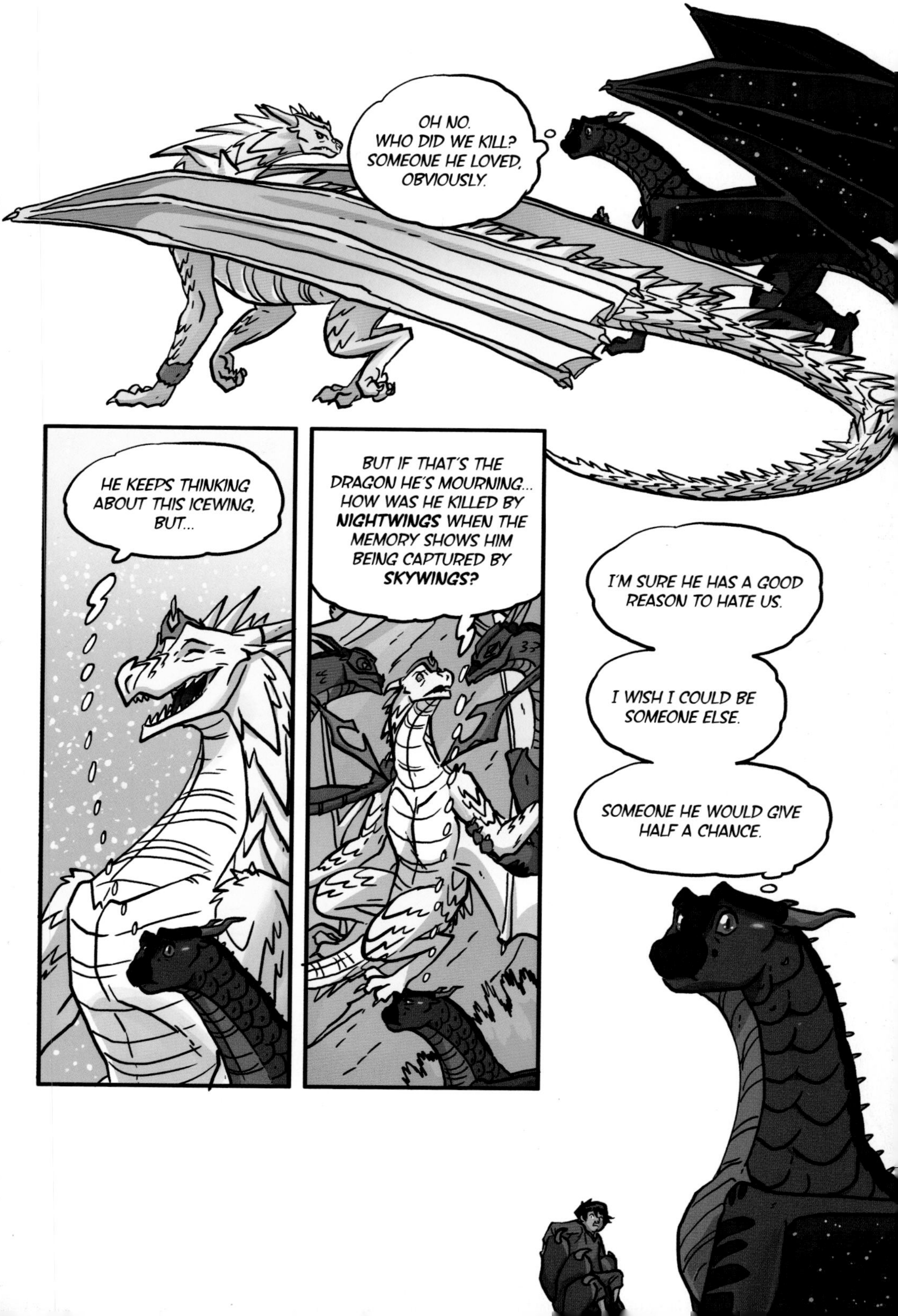
OH NO. WHO DID WE KILL? SOMEONE HE LOVED, OBVIOUSLY.
HE KEEPS THINKING ABOUT THIS ICEWING, BUT...
BUT IF THAT'S THE DRAGON HE'S MOURNING... HOW WAS HE KILLED BY **NIGHTWINGS** WHEN THE MEMORY SHOWS HIM BEING CAPTURED BY **SKYWINGS?**
I'M SURE HE HAS A GOOD REASON TO HATE US.
I WISH I COULD BE SOMEONE ELSE.
SOMEONE HE WOULD GIVE HALF A CHANCE.

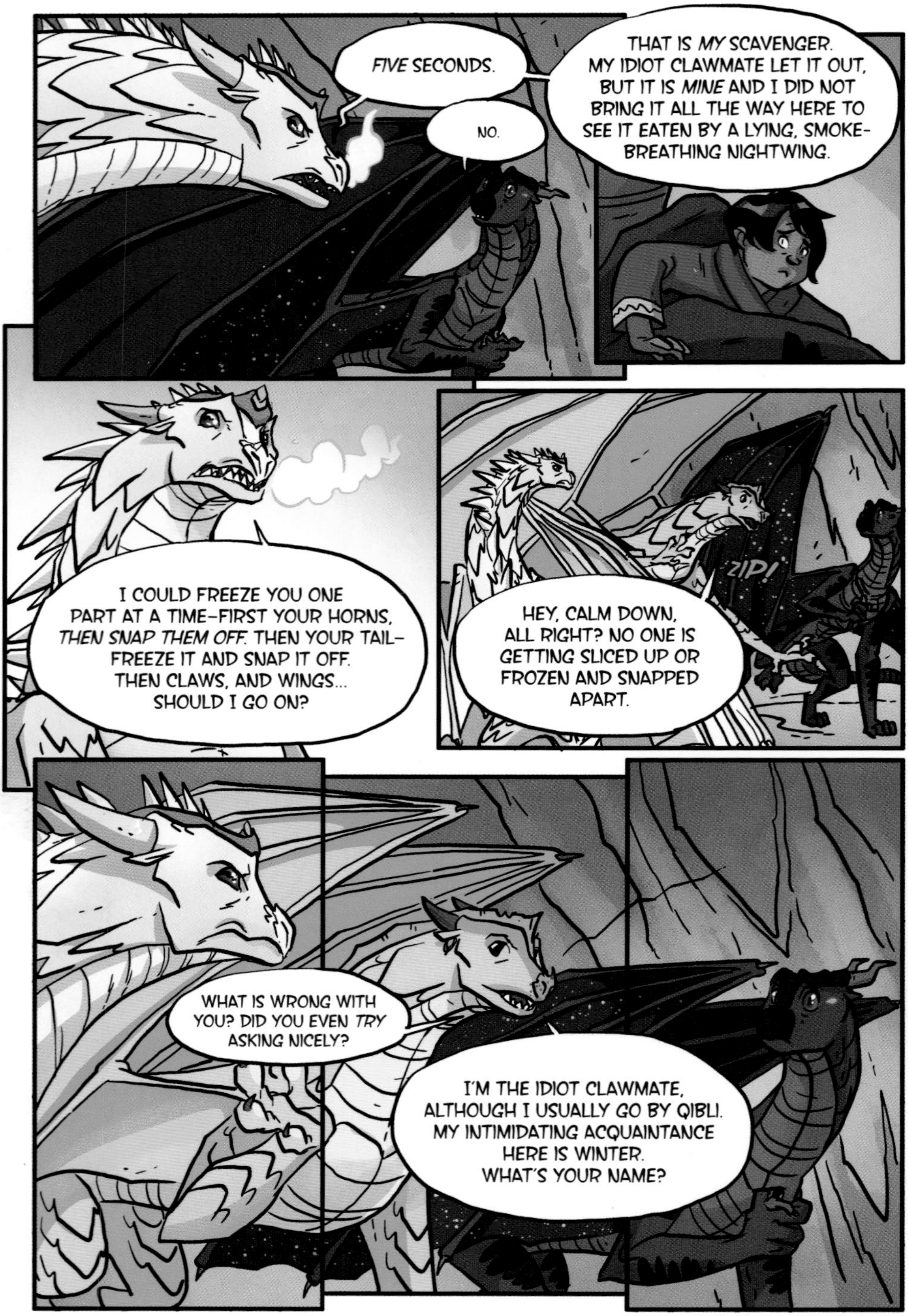
FIVE SECONDS.
NO.
THAT IS MY SCAVENGER. MY IDIOT CLAWMATE LET IT OUT, BUT IT IS MINE AND I DID NOT BRING IT ALL THE WAY HERE TO SEE IT EATEN BY A LYING, SMOKE-BREATHING NIGHTWING.
I COULD FREEZE YOU ONE PART AT A TIME—FIRST YOUR HORNS, THEN SNAP THEM OFF. THEN YOUR TAIL—FREEZE IT AND SNAP IT OFF. THEN CLAWS, AND WINGS... SHOULD I GO ON?
ZIP!
HEY, CALM DOWN, ALL RIGHT? NO ONE IS GETTING SLICED UP OR FROZEN AND SNAPPED APART.
WHAT IS WRONG WITH YOU? DID YOU EVEN TRY ASKING NICELY?
I'M THE IDIOT CLAWMATE, ALTHOUGH I USUALLY GO BY QIBLI. MY INTIMIDATING ACQUAINTANCE HERE IS WINTER. WHAT'S YOUR NAME?

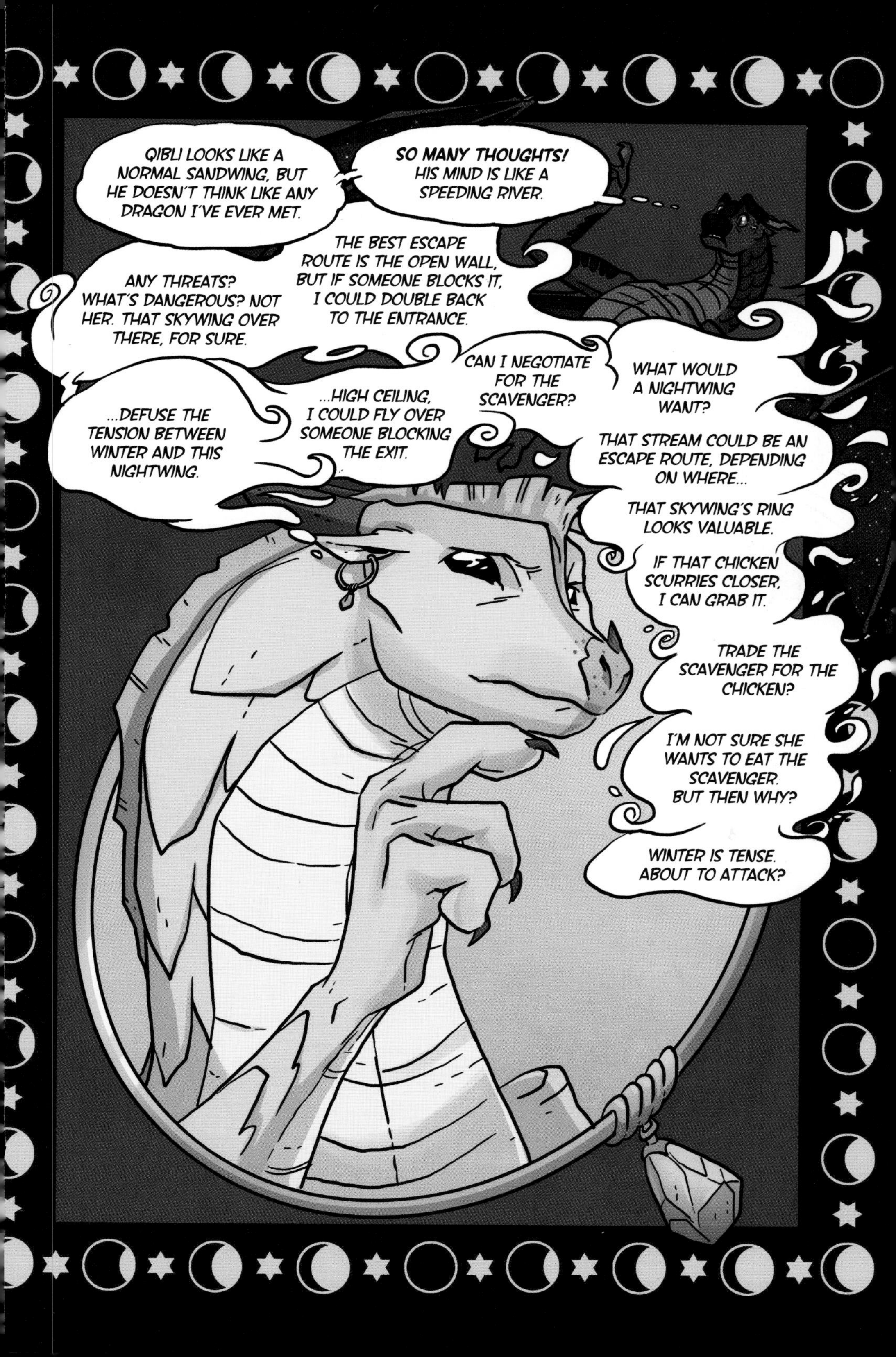
QIBLI LOOKS LIKE A NORMAL SANDWING, BUT HE DOESN'T THINK LIKE ANY DRAGON I'VE EVER MET.
SO MANY THOUGHTS! HIS MIND IS LIKE A SPEEDING RIVER.
ANY THREATS? WHAT'S DANGEROUS? NOT HER. THAT SKYWING OVER THERE, FOR SURE.
THE BEST ESCAPE ROUTE IS THE OPEN WALL, BUT IF SOMEONE BLOCKS IT, I COULD DOUBLE BACK TO THE ENTRANCE.
...DEFUSE THE TENSION BETWEEN WINTER AND THIS NIGHTWING.
...HIGH CEILING, I COULD FLY OVER SOMEONE BLOCKING THE EXIT.
CAN I NEGOTIATE FOR THE SCAVENGER?
WHAT WOULD A NIGHTWING WANT?
THAT STREAM COULD BE AN ESCAPE ROUTE, DEPENDING ON WHERE...
THAT SKYWING'S RING LOOKS VALUABLE.
IF THAT CHICKEN SCURRIES CLOSER, I CAN GRAB IT.
TRADE THE SCAVENGER FOR THE CHICKEN?
I'M NOT SURE SHE WANTS TO EAT THE SCAVENGER. BUT THEN WHY?
WINTER IS TENSE. ABOUT TO ATTACK?

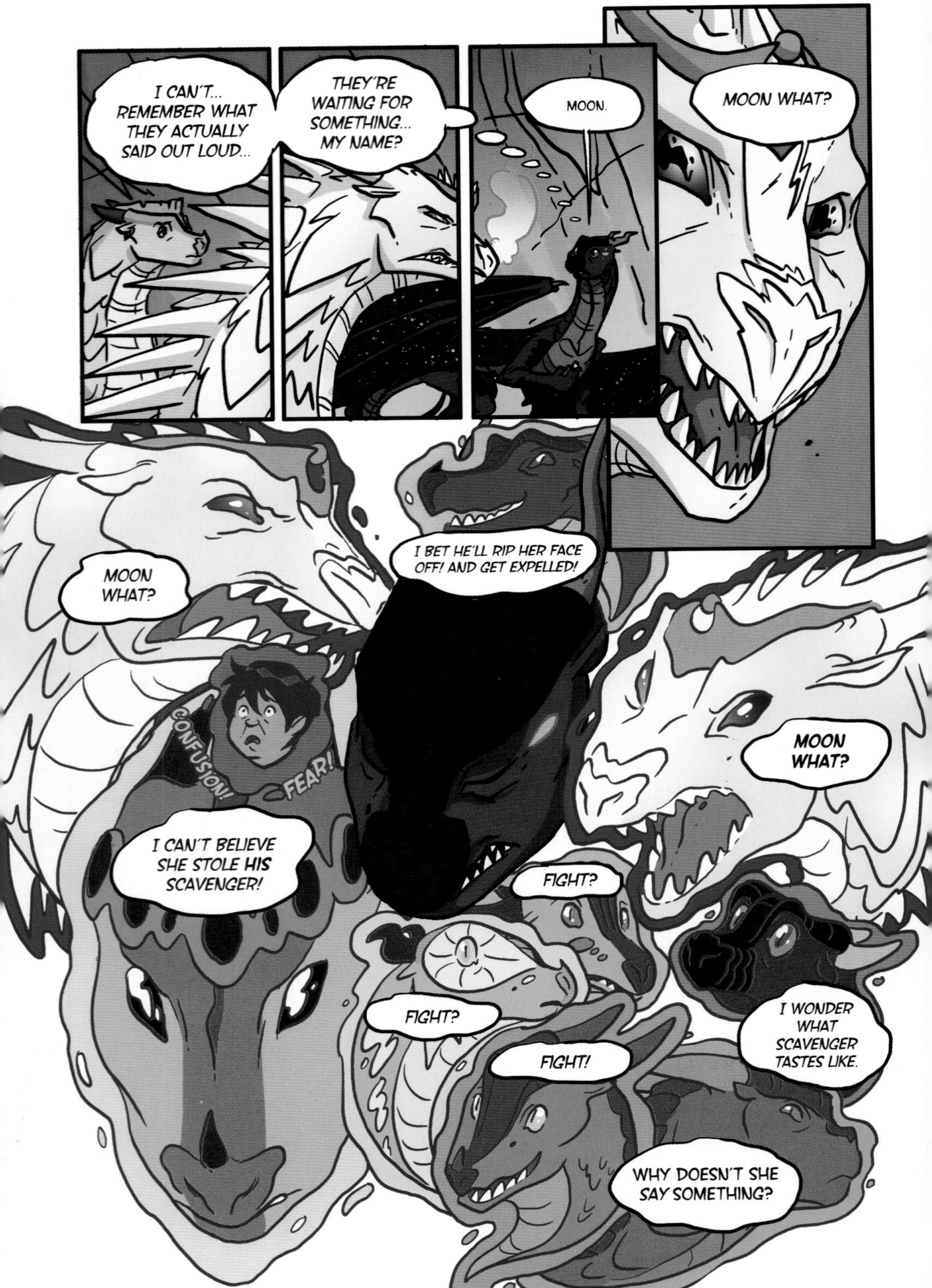
I CAN'T... REMEMBER WHAT THEY ACTUALLY SAID OUT LOUD...
THEY'RE WAITING FOR SOMETHING... MY NAME?
MOON.
MOON WHAT?
MOON WHAT?
I BET HE'LL RIP HER FACE OFF! AND GET EXPELLED!
CONFUSION!
FEAR!
MOON WHAT?
I CAN'T BELIEVE SHE STOLE HIS SCAVENGER!
FIGHT?
FIGHT?
FIGHT!
I WONDER WHAT SCAVENGER TASTES LIKE.
WHY DOESN'T SHE SAY SOMETHING?

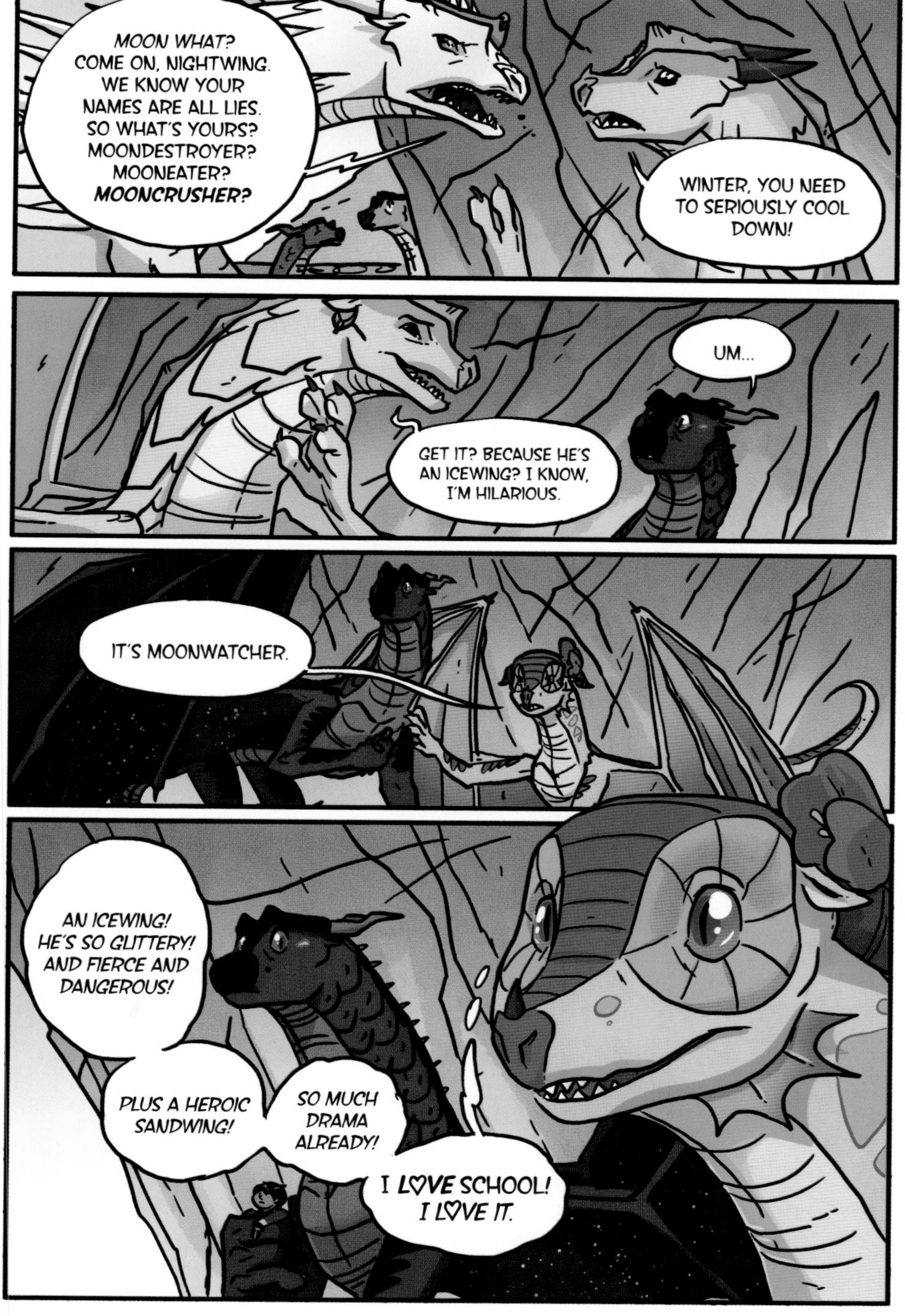
MOON WHAT? COME ON, NIGHTWING. WE KNOW YOUR NAMES ARE ALL LIES. SO WHAT'S YOURS? MOONDESTROYER? MOONEATER? MOONCRUSHER?
WINTER, YOU NEED TO SERIOUSLY COOL DOWN!
UM...
GET IT? BECAUSE HE'S AN ICEWING? I KNOW, I'M HILARIOUS.
IT'S MOONWATCHER.
AN ICEWING! HE'S SO GLITTERY! AND FIERCE AND DANGEROUS!
PLUS A HEROIC SANDWING!
SO MUCH DRAMA ALREADY!
I LOVE SCHOOL! I LOVE IT.

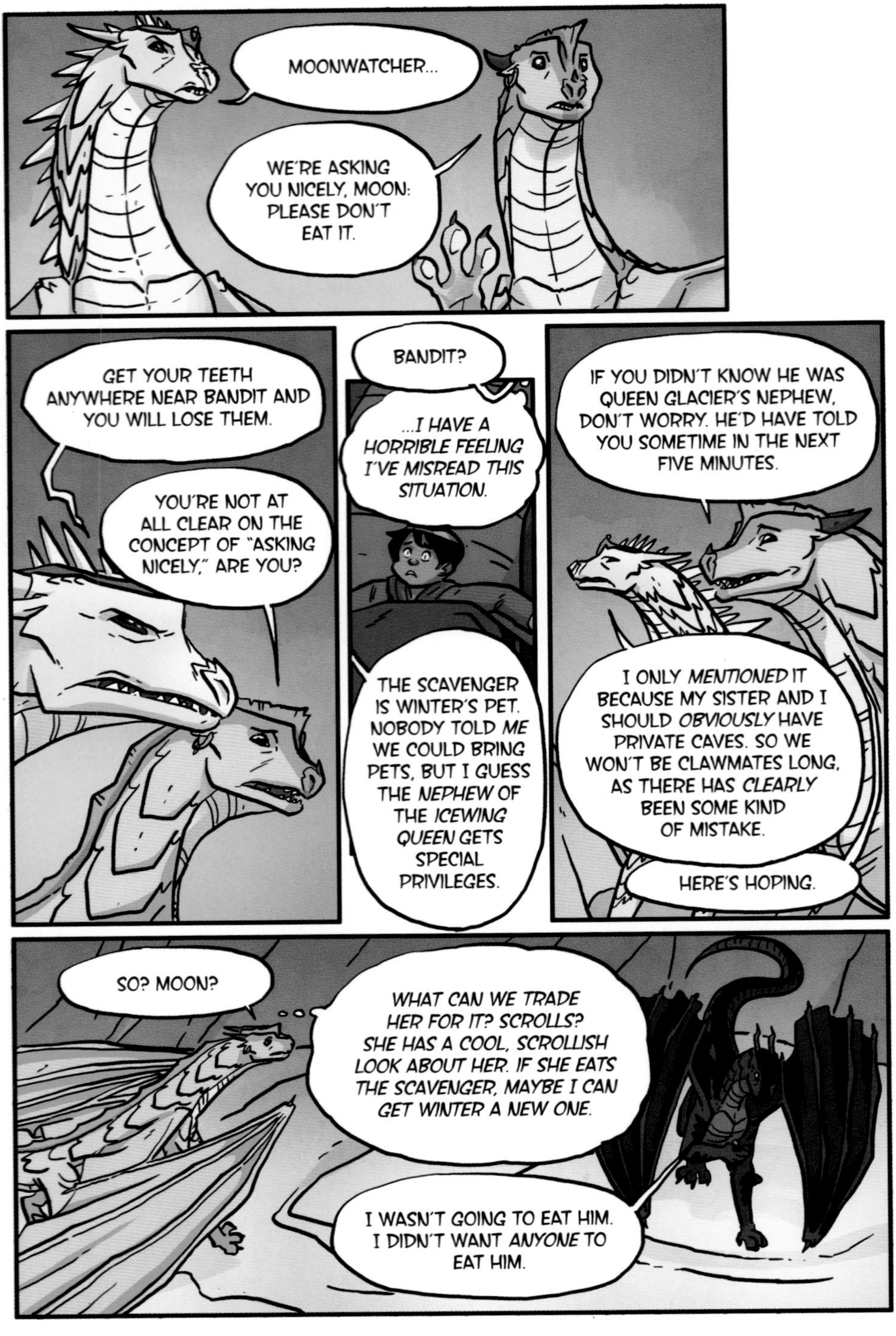
MOONWATCHER...
WE'RE ASKING YOU NICELY, MOON: PLEASE DON'T EAT IT.
GET YOUR TEETH ANYWHERE NEAR BANDIT AND YOU WILL LOSE THEM.
YOU'RE NOT AT ALL CLEAR ON THE CONCEPT OF "ASKING NICELY," ARE YOU?
BANDIT?
...*I HAVE A HORRIBLE FEELING I'VE MISREAD THIS SITUATION.*
THE SCAVENGER IS WINTER'S PET. NOBODY TOLD *ME* WE COULD BRING PETS, BUT I GUESS THE *NEPHEW* OF THE *ICEWING QUEEN* GETS SPECIAL PRIVILEGES.
IF YOU DIDN'T KNOW HE WAS QUEEN GLACIER'S NEPHEW, DON'T WORRY. HE'D HAVE TOLD YOU SOMETIME IN THE NEXT FIVE MINUTES.
I ONLY *MENTIONED* IT BECAUSE MY SISTER AND I SHOULD *OBVIOUSLY* HAVE PRIVATE CAVES. SO WE WON'T BE CLAWMATES LONG, AS THERE HAS *CLEARLY* BEEN SOME KIND OF MISTAKE.
HERE'S HOPING.
SO? MOON?
WHAT CAN WE TRADE HER FOR IT? SCROLLS? SHE HAS A COOL, SCROLLISH LOOK ABOUT HER. IF SHE EATS THE SCAVENGER, MAYBE I CAN GET WINTER A NEW ONE.
I WASN'T GOING TO EAT HIM. I DIDN'T WANT *ANYONE* TO EAT HIM.

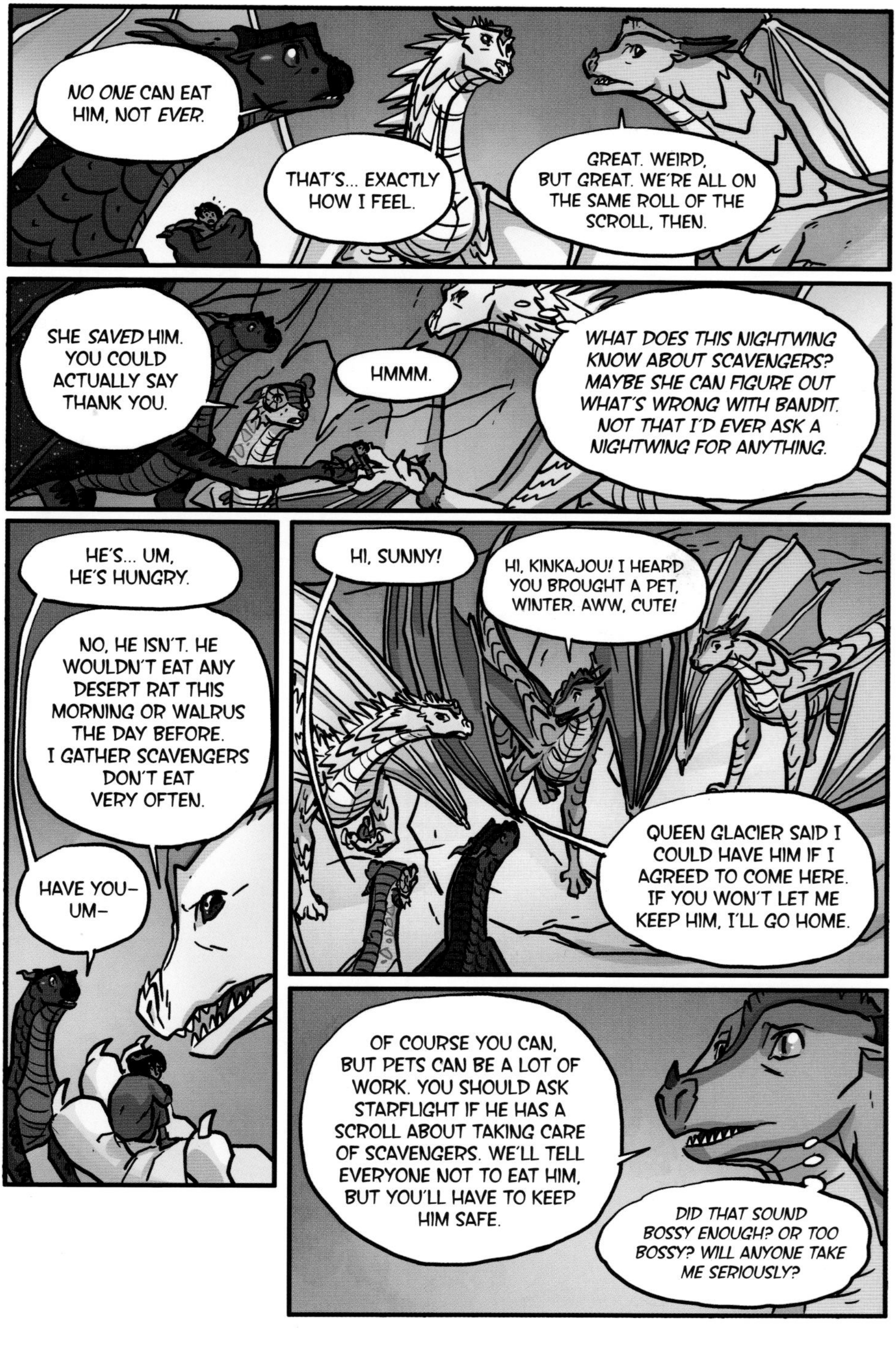
NO ONE CAN EAT HIM, NOT *EVER.*
THAT'S... EXACTLY HOW I FEEL.
GREAT. WEIRD, BUT GREAT. WE'RE ALL ON THE SAME ROLL OF THE SCROLL, THEN.
SHE *SAVED* HIM. YOU COULD ACTUALLY SAY THANK YOU.
HMMM.
WHAT DOES THIS NIGHTWING KNOW ABOUT SCAVENGERS? MAYBE SHE CAN FIGURE OUT WHAT'S WRONG WITH BANDIT. NOT THAT I'D EVER ASK A NIGHTWING FOR ANYTHING.
HE'S... UM, HE'S HUNGRY.
NO, HE ISN'T. HE WOULDN'T EAT ANY DESERT RAT THIS MORNING OR WALRUS THE DAY BEFORE. I GATHER SCAVENGERS DON'T EAT VERY OFTEN.
HAVE YOU— UM—
HI, SUNNY!
HI, KINKAJOU! I HEARD YOU BROUGHT A PET, WINTER. AWW, CUTE!
QUEEN GLACIER SAID I COULD HAVE HIM IF I AGREED TO COME HERE. IF YOU WON'T LET ME KEEP HIM, I'LL GO HOME.
OF COURSE YOU CAN, BUT PETS CAN BE A LOT OF WORK. YOU SHOULD ASK STARFLIGHT IF HE HAS A SCROLL ABOUT TAKING CARE OF SCAVENGERS. WE'LL TELL EVERYONE NOT TO EAT HIM, BUT YOU'LL HAVE TO KEEP HIM SAFE.
DID THAT SOUND BOSSY ENOUGH? OR TOO BOSSY? WILL ANYONE TAKE ME SERIOUSLY?

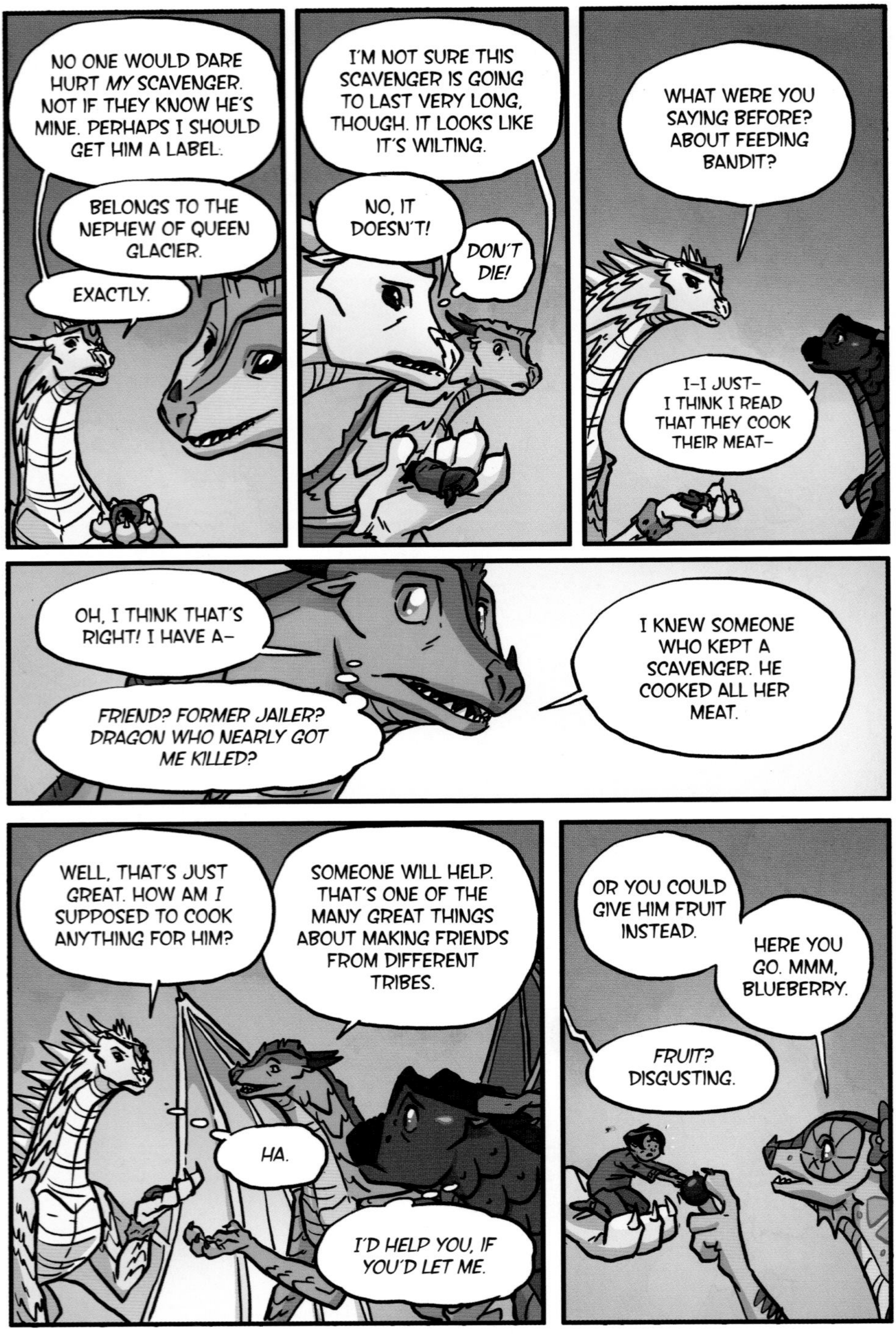
NO ONE WOULD DARE HURT *MY* SCAVENGER. NOT IF THEY KNOW HE'S MINE. PERHAPS I SHOULD GET HIM A LABEL.
BELONGS TO THE NEPHEW OF QUEEN GLACIER.
EXACTLY.
I'M NOT SURE THIS SCAVENGER IS GOING TO LAST VERY LONG, THOUGH. IT LOOKS LIKE IT'S WILTING.
NO, IT DOESN'T!
DON'T DIE!
WHAT WERE YOU SAYING BEFORE? ABOUT FEEDING BANDIT?
I-I JUST- I THINK I READ THAT THEY COOK THEIR MEAT-
OH, I THINK THAT'S RIGHT! I HAVE A-
FRIEND? FORMER JAILER? DRAGON WHO NEARLY GOT ME KILLED?
I KNEW SOMEONE WHO KEPT A SCAVENGER. HE COOKED ALL HER MEAT.
WELL, THAT'S JUST GREAT. HOW AM *I* SUPPOSED TO COOK ANYTHING FOR HIM?
SOMEONE WILL HELP. THAT'S ONE OF THE MANY GREAT THINGS ABOUT MAKING FRIENDS FROM DIFFERENT TRIBES.
HA.
I'D HELP YOU, IF YOU'D LET ME.
OR YOU COULD GIVE HIM FRUIT INSTEAD.
HERE YOU GO. MMM, BLUEBERRY.
FRUIT? DISGUSTING.

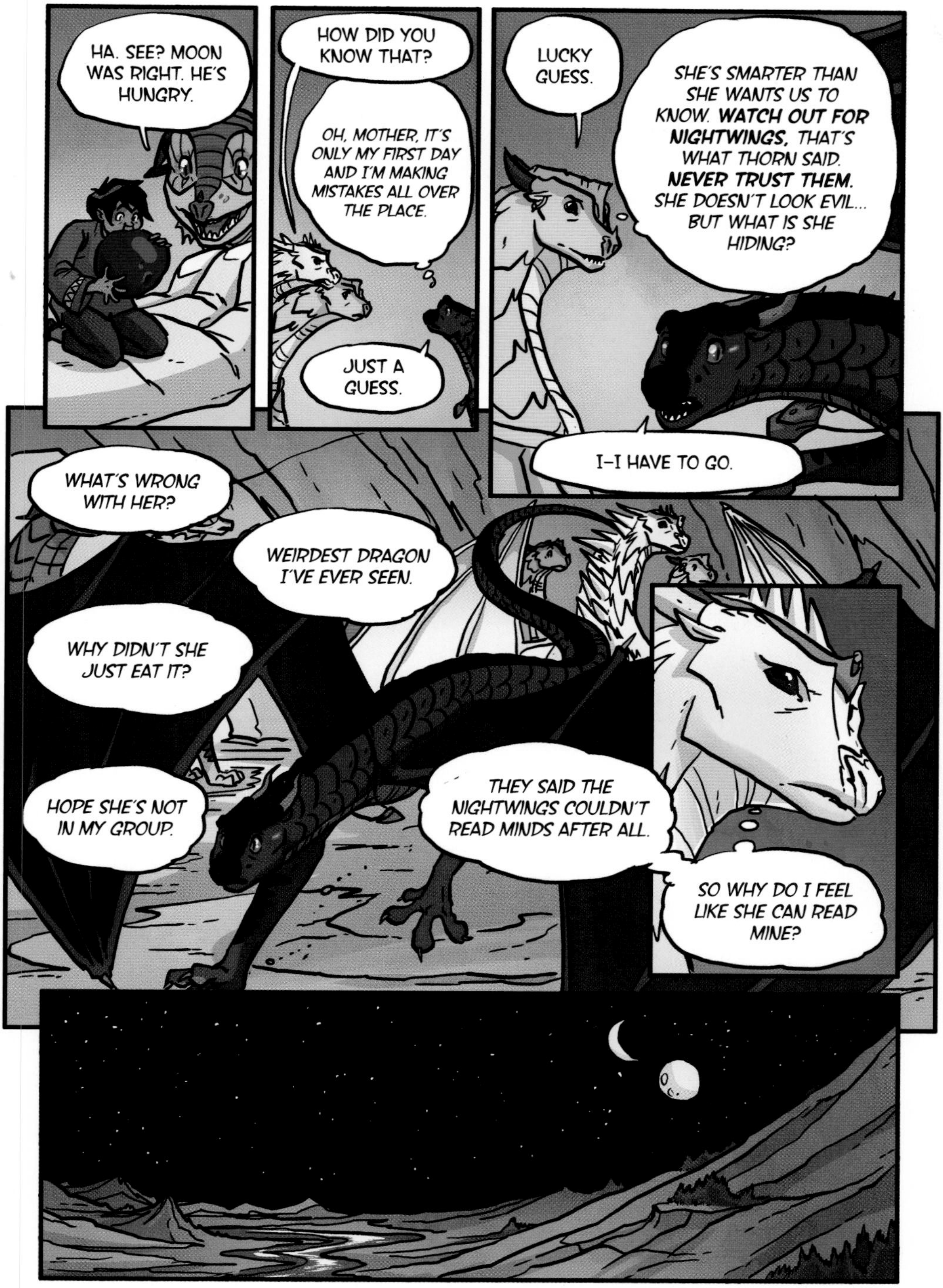
HA. SEE? MOON WAS RIGHT. HE'S HUNGRY.
HOW DID YOU KNOW THAT?
OH, MOTHER, IT'S ONLY MY FIRST DAY AND I'M MAKING MISTAKES ALL OVER THE PLACE.
JUST A GUESS.
LUCKY GUESS.
SHE'S SMARTER THAN SHE WANTS US TO KNOW. WATCH OUT FOR NIGHTWINGS, THAT'S WHAT THORN SAID. NEVER TRUST THEM. SHE DOESN'T LOOK EVIL... BUT WHAT IS SHE HIDING?
I-I HAVE TO GO.
WHAT'S WRONG WITH HER?
WEIRDEST DRAGON I'VE EVER SEEN.
WHY DIDN'T SHE JUST EAT IT?
HOPE SHE'S NOT IN MY GROUP.
THEY SAID THE NIGHTWINGS COULDN'T READ MINDS AFTER ALL.
SO WHY DO I FEEL LIKE SHE CAN READ MINE?

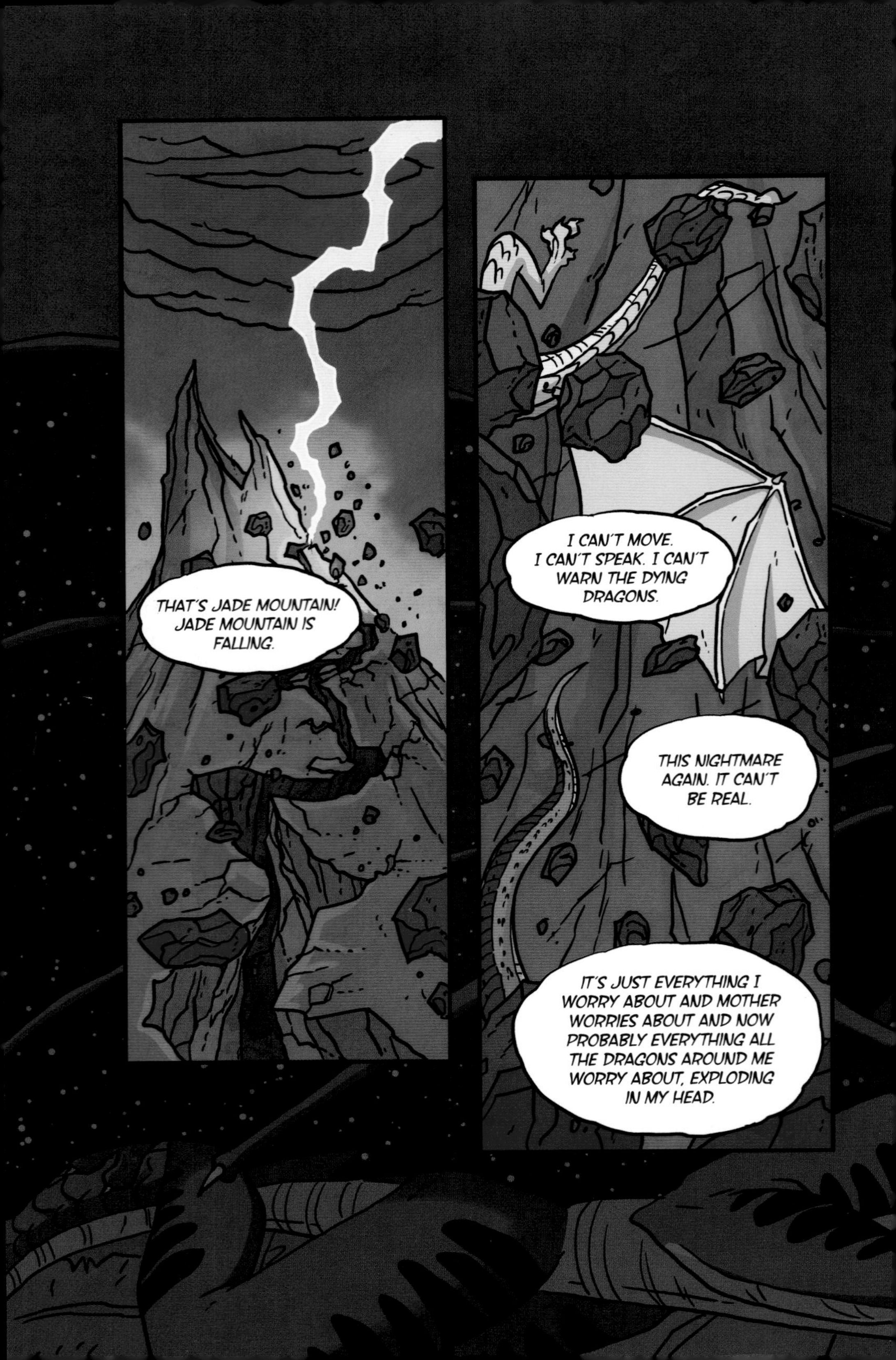
THAT'S JADE MOUNTAIN! JADE MOUNTAIN IS FALLING.
I CAN'T MOVE. I CAN'T SPEAK. I CAN'T WARN THE DYING DRAGONS.
THIS NIGHTMARE AGAIN. IT CAN'T BE REAL.
IT'S JUST EVERYTHING I WORRY ABOUT AND MOTHER WORRIES ABOUT AND NOW PROBABLY EVERYTHING ALL THE DRAGONS AROUND ME WORRY ABOUT, EXPLODING IN MY HEAD.

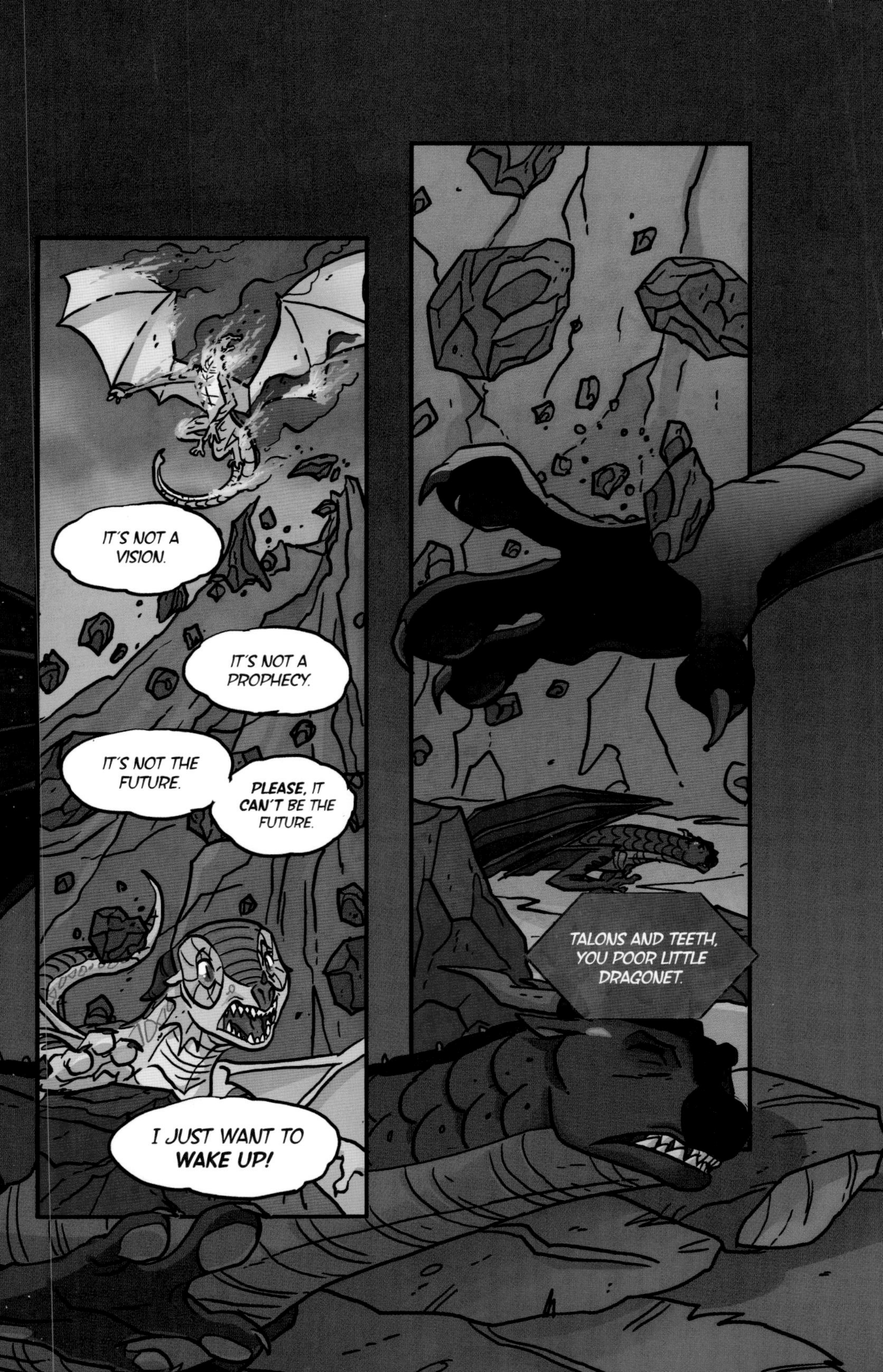
IT'S NOT A VISION.
IT'S NOT A PROPHECY.
IT'S NOT THE FUTURE.
PLEASE, IT CAN'T BE THE FUTURE.
I JUST WANT TO WAKE UP!
TALONS AND TEETH, YOU POOR LITTLE DRAGONET.

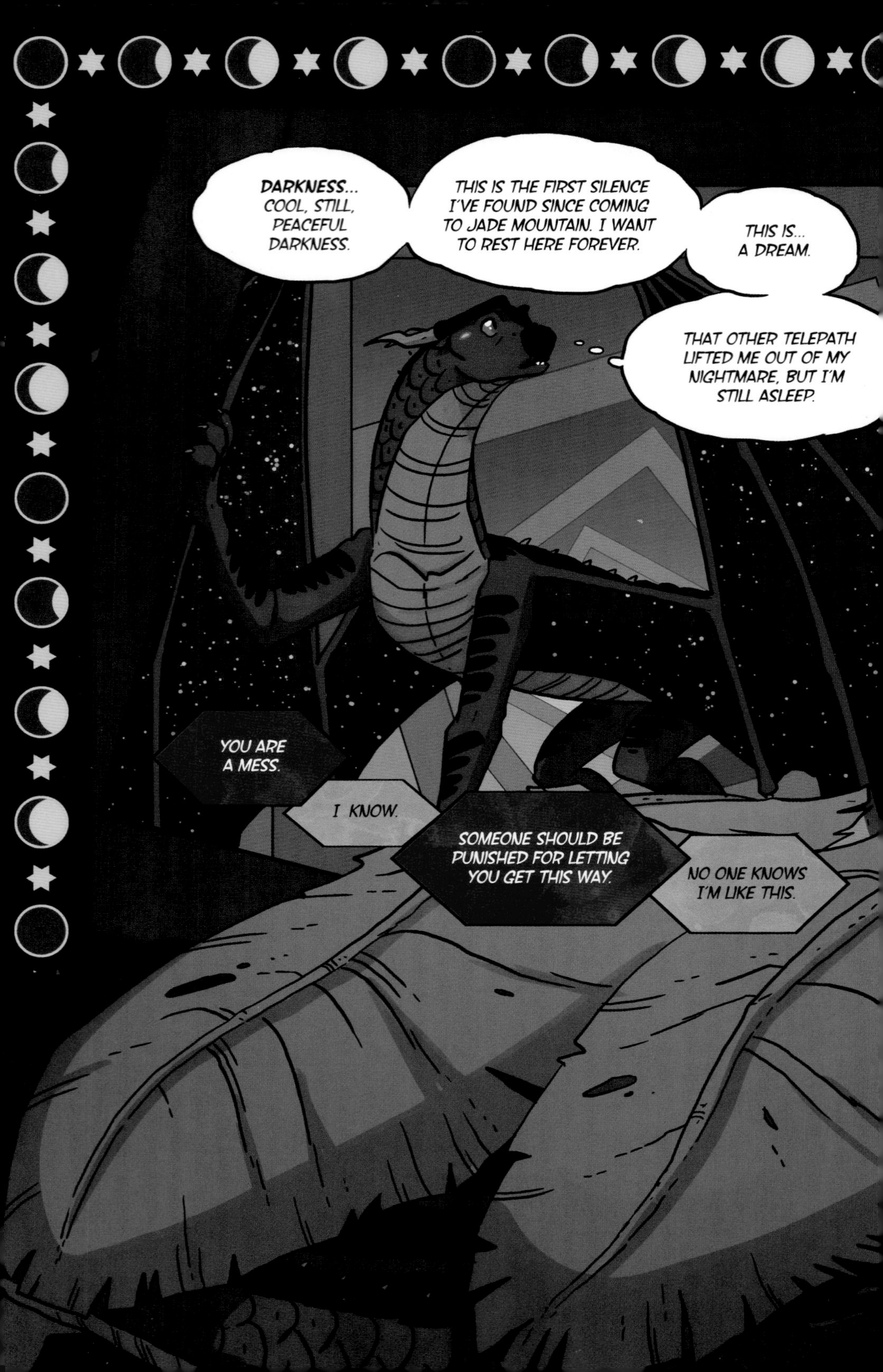
DARKNESS... COOL, STILL, PEACEFUL DARKNESS.
THIS IS THE FIRST SILENCE I'VE FOUND SINCE COMING TO JADE MOUNTAIN. I WANT TO REST HERE FOREVER.
THIS IS... A DREAM.
THAT OTHER TELEPATH LIFTED ME OUT OF MY NIGHTMARE, BUT I'M STILL ASLEEP.
YOU ARE A MESS.
I KNOW.
SOMEONE SHOULD BE PUNISHED FOR LETTING YOU GET THIS WAY.
NO ONE KNOWS I'M LIKE THIS.

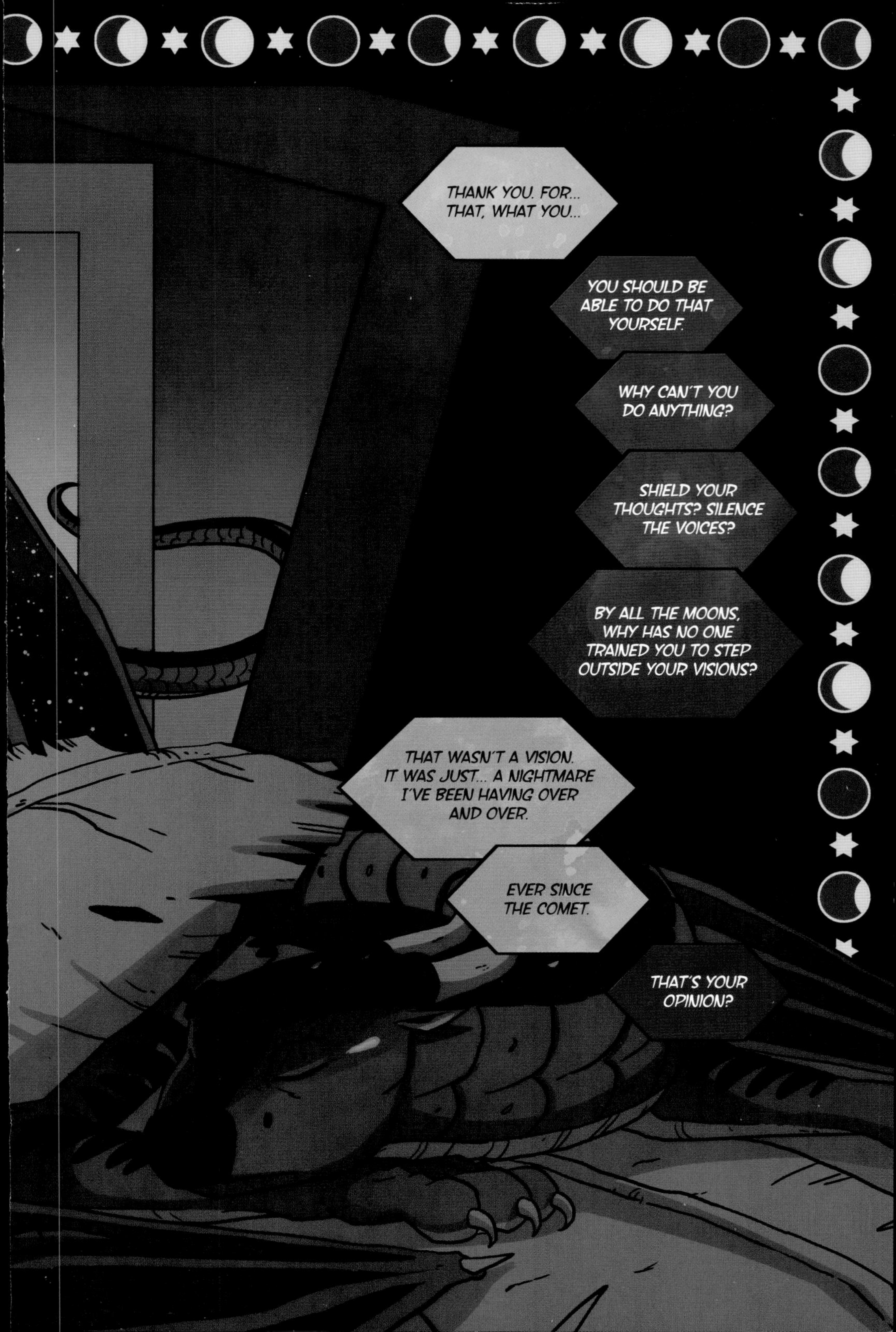
THANK YOU. FOR... THAT, WHAT YOU...
YOU SHOULD BE ABLE TO DO THAT YOURSELF.
WHY CAN'T YOU DO ANYTHING?
SHIELD YOUR THOUGHTS? SILENCE THE VOICES?
BY ALL THE MOONS, WHY HAS NO ONE TRAINED YOU TO STEP OUTSIDE YOUR VISIONS?
THAT WASN'T A VISION. IT WAS JUST... A NIGHTMARE I'VE BEEN HAVING OVER AND OVER.
EVER SINCE THE COMET.
THAT'S YOUR OPINION?

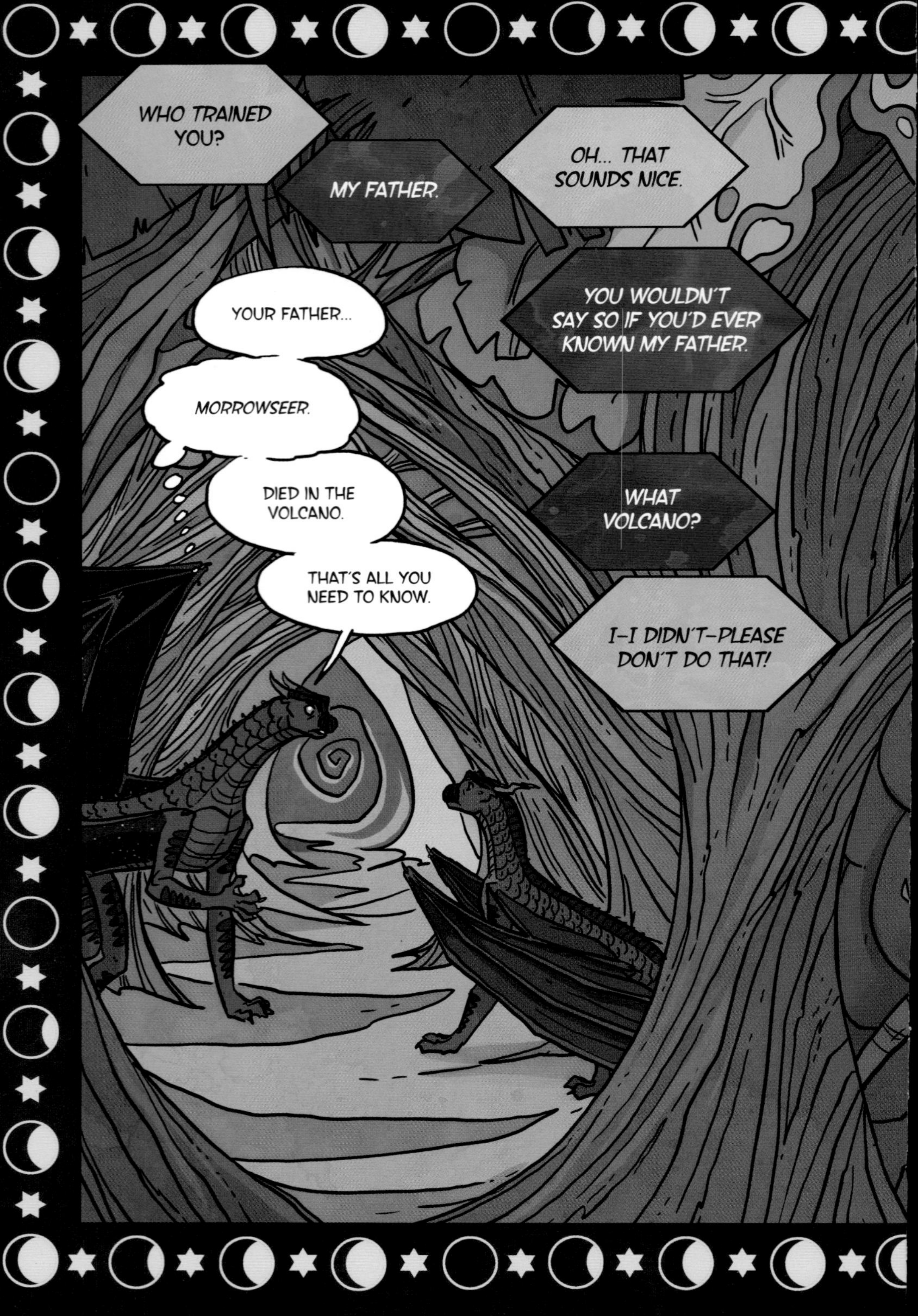
WHO TRAINED YOU?
MY FATHER.
OH... THAT SOUNDS NICE.
YOU WOULDN'T SAY SO IF YOU'D EVER KNOWN MY FATHER.
YOUR FATHER...
MORROWSEER.
DIED IN THE VOLCANO.
WHAT VOLCANO?
THAT'S ALL YOU NEED TO KNOW.
I-I DIDN'T-PLEASE DON'T DO THAT!

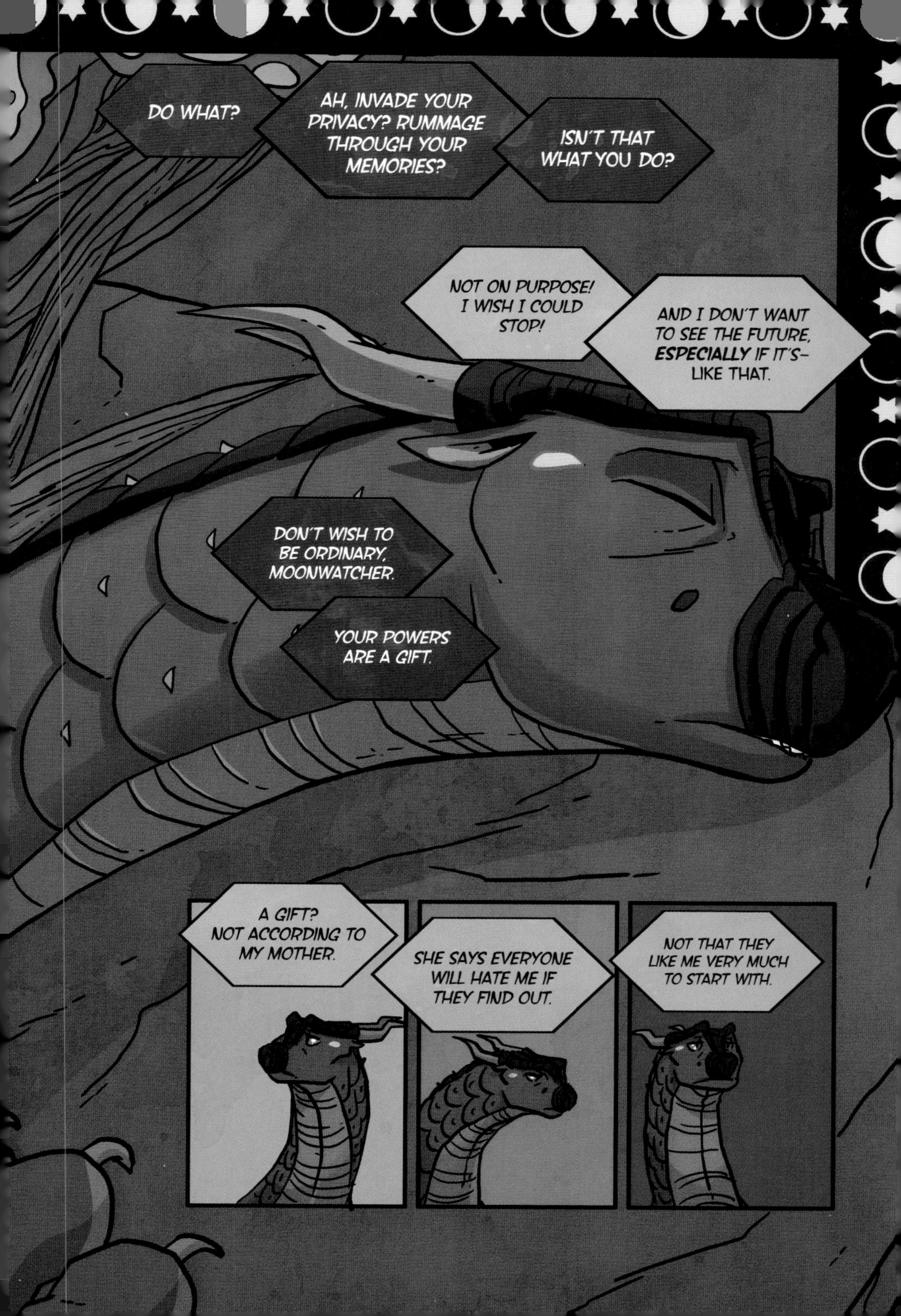
DO WHAT?
AH, INVADE YOUR PRIVACY? RUMMAGE THROUGH YOUR MEMORIES?
ISN'T THAT WHAT YOU DO?
NOT ON PURPOSE! I WISH I COULD STOP!
AND I DON'T WANT TO SEE THE FUTURE, **ESPECIALLY** IF IT'S— LIKE THAT.
DON'T WISH TO BE ORDINARY, MOONWATCHER.
YOUR POWERS ARE A GIFT.
A GIFT? NOT ACCORDING TO MY MOTHER.
SHE SAYS EVERYONE WILL HATE ME IF THEY FIND OUT.
NOT THAT THEY LIKE ME VERY MUCH TO START WITH.

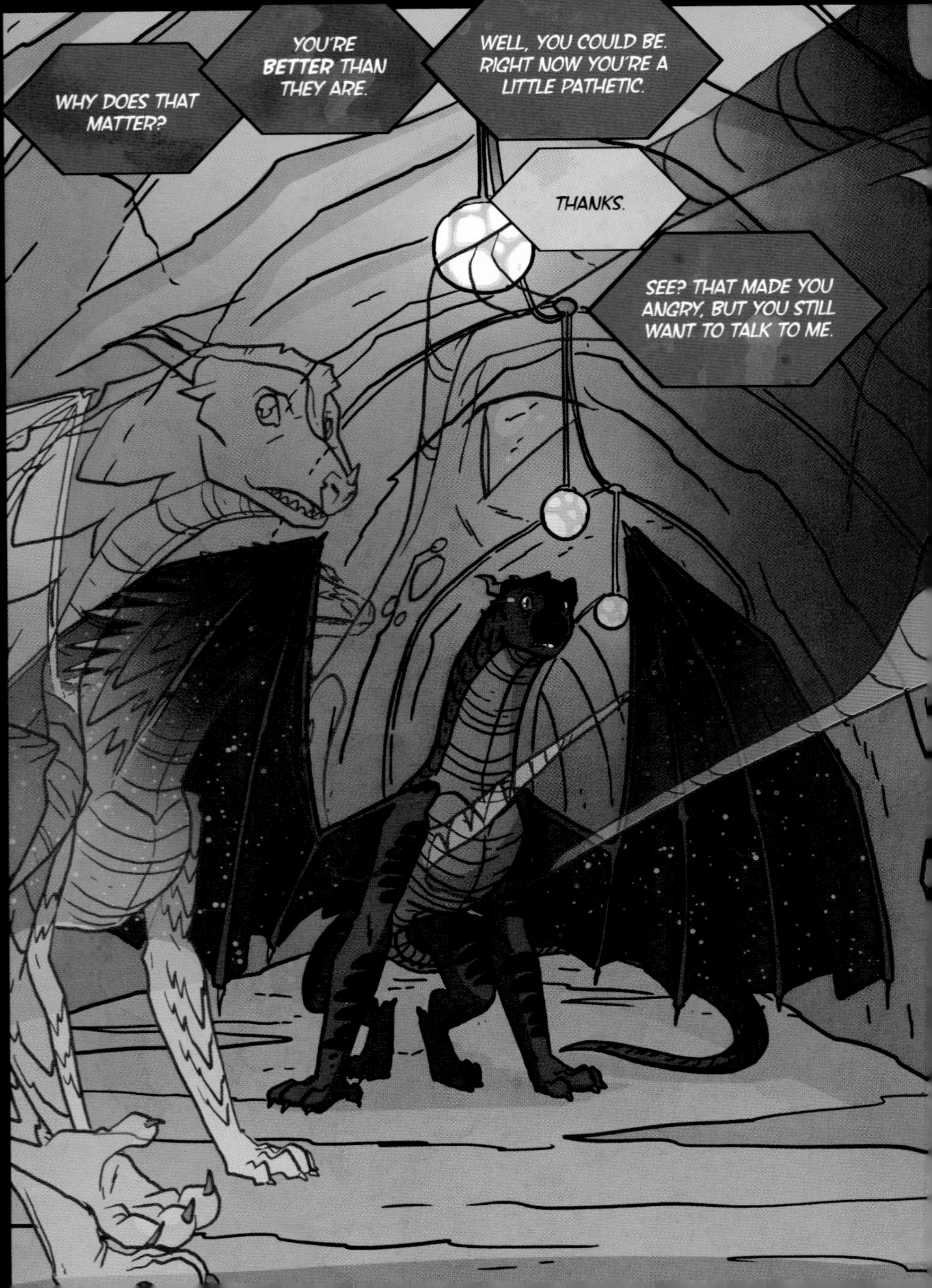
WHY DOES THAT MATTER?
YOU'RE BETTER THAN THEY ARE.
WELL, YOU COULD BE. RIGHT NOW YOU'RE A LITTLE PATHETIC.
THANKS.
SEE? THAT MADE YOU ANGRY, BUT YOU STILL WANT TO TALK TO ME.

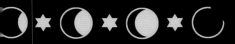

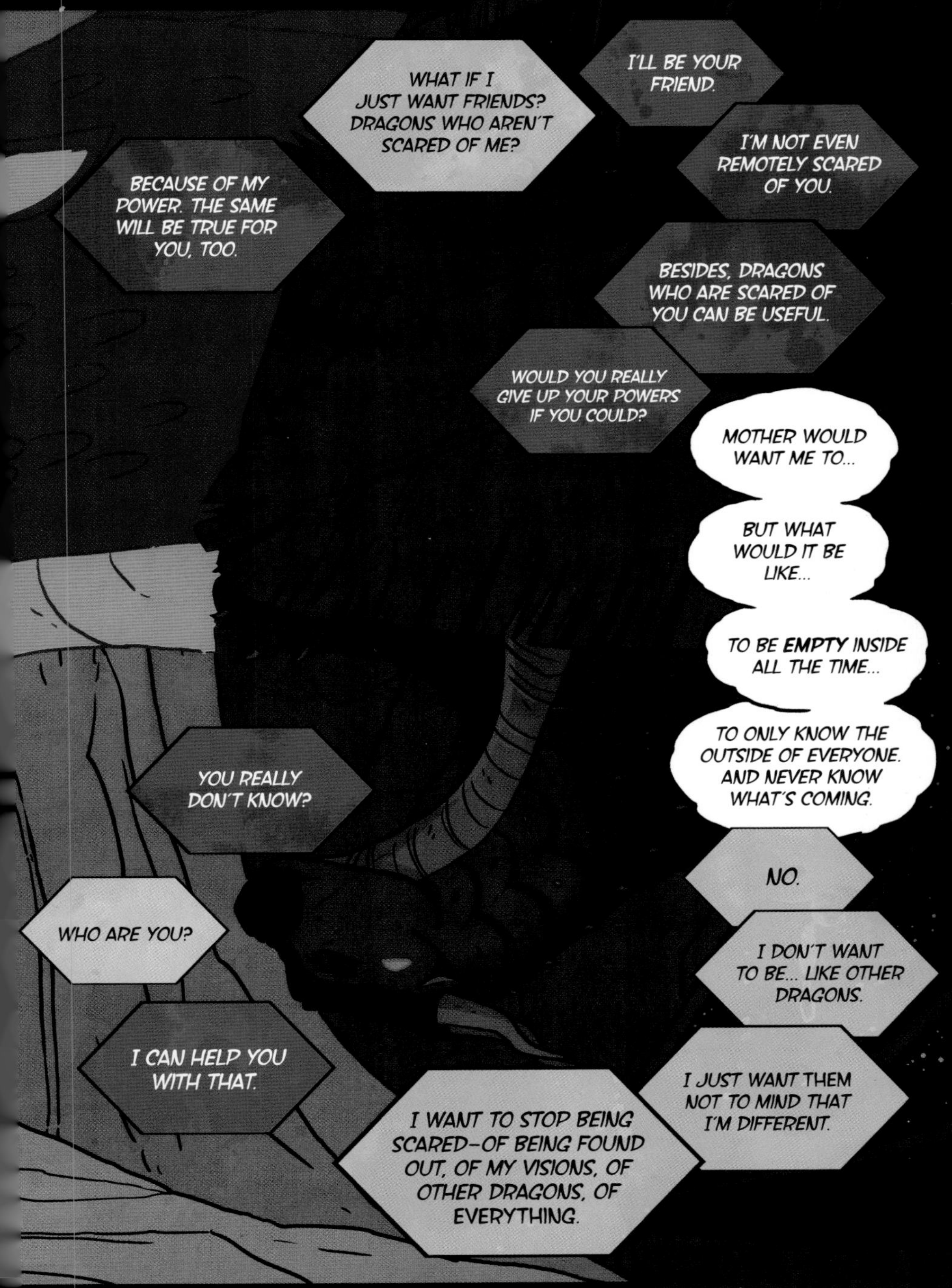
BECAUSE OF MY POWER. THE SAME WILL BE TRUE FOR YOU, TOO.
WHAT IF I JUST WANT FRIENDS? DRAGONS WHO AREN'T SCARED OF ME?
I'LL BE YOUR FRIEND.
I'M NOT EVEN REMOTELY SCARED OF YOU.
BESIDES, DRAGONS WHO ARE SCARED OF YOU CAN BE USEFUL.
WOULD YOU REALLY GIVE UP YOUR POWERS IF YOU COULD?
MOTHER WOULD WANT ME TO...
BUT WHAT WOULD IT BE LIKE...
TO BE **EMPTY** INSIDE ALL THE TIME...
TO ONLY KNOW THE OUTSIDE OF EVERYONE. AND NEVER KNOW WHAT'S COMING.
YOU REALLY DON'T KNOW?
NO.
I DON'T WANT TO BE... LIKE OTHER DRAGONS.
WHO ARE YOU?
I JUST WANT THEM NOT TO MIND THAT I'M DIFFERENT.
I WANT TO STOP BEING SCARED–OF BEING FOUND OUT, OF MY VISIONS, OF OTHER DRAGONS, OF EVERYTHING.
I CAN HELP YOU WITH THAT.

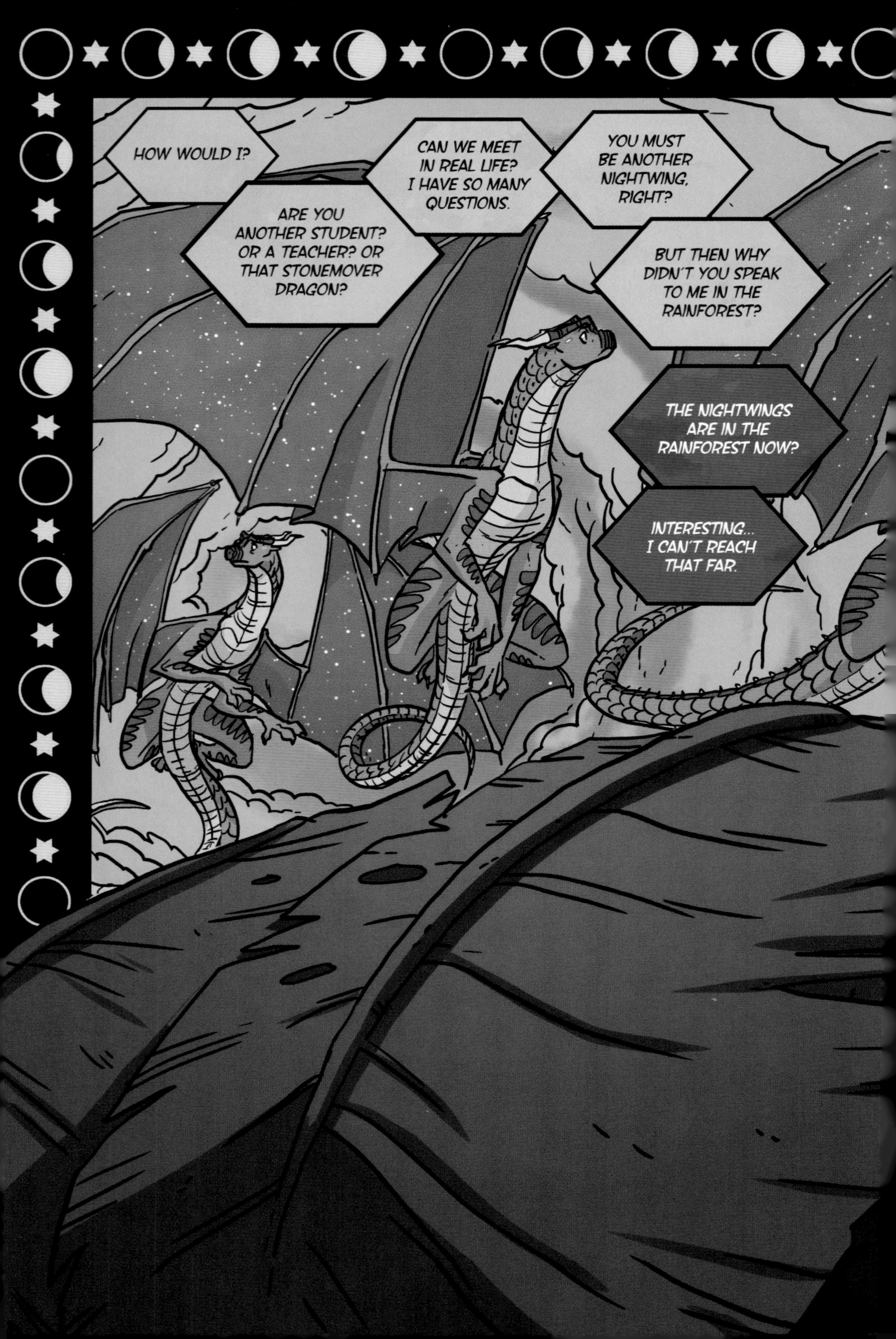
HOW WOULD I?
ARE YOU ANOTHER STUDENT? OR A TEACHER? OR THAT STONEMOVER DRAGON?
CAN WE MEET IN REAL LIFE? I HAVE SO MANY QUESTIONS.
YOU MUST BE ANOTHER NIGHTWING, RIGHT?
BUT THEN WHY DIDN'T YOU SPEAK TO ME IN THE RAINFOREST?
THE NIGHTWINGS ARE IN THE RAINFOREST NOW?
INTERESTING... I CAN'T REACH THAT FAR.

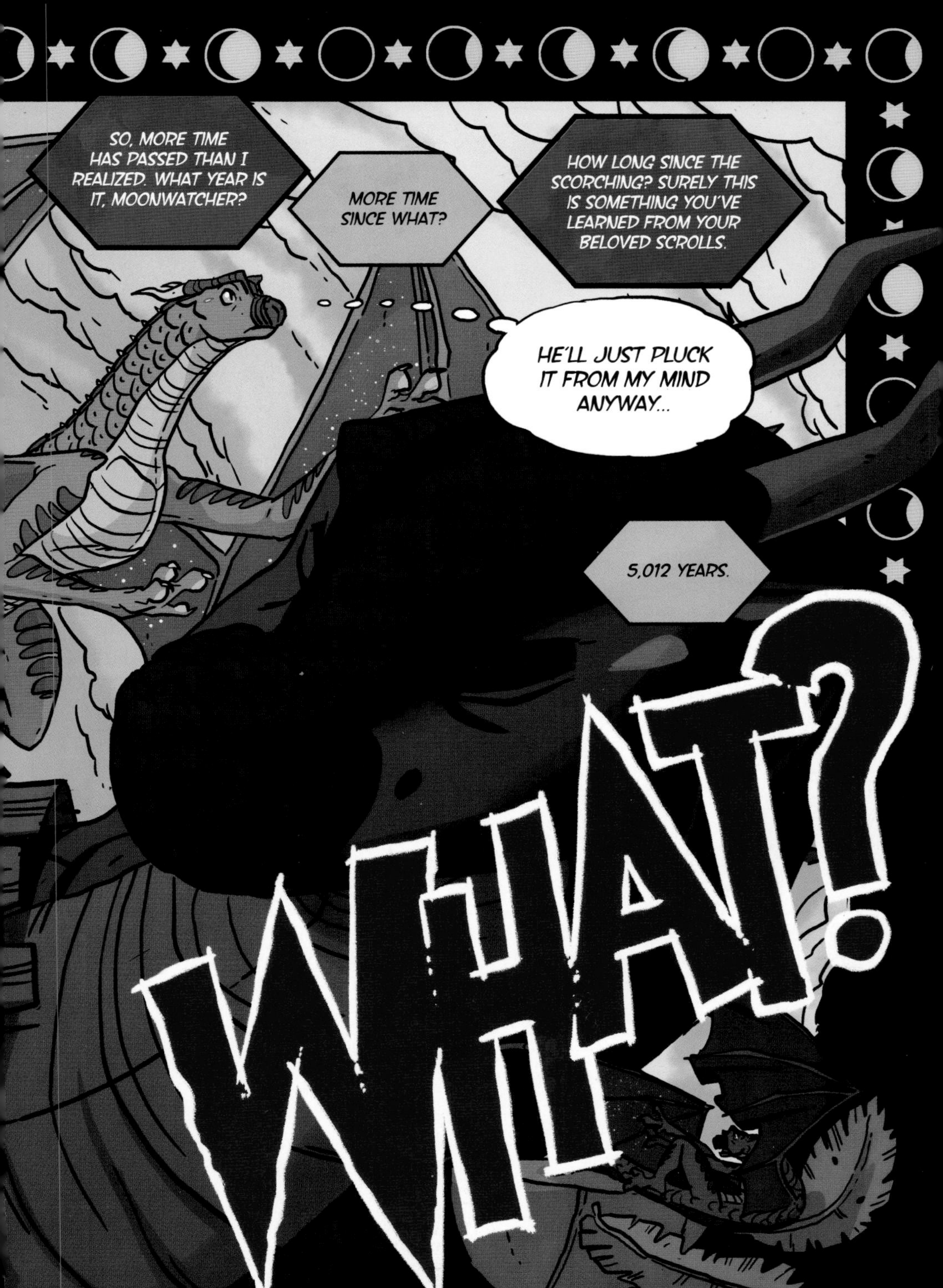
SO, MORE TIME HAS PASSED THAN I REALIZED. WHAT YEAR IS IT, MOONWATCHER?
MORE TIME SINCE WHAT?
HOW LONG SINCE THE SCORCHING? SURELY THIS IS SOMETHING YOU'VE LEARNED FROM YOUR BELOVED SCROLLS.
HE'LL JUST PLUCK IT FROM MY MIND ANYWAY...
5,012 YEARS.
WHAT?!

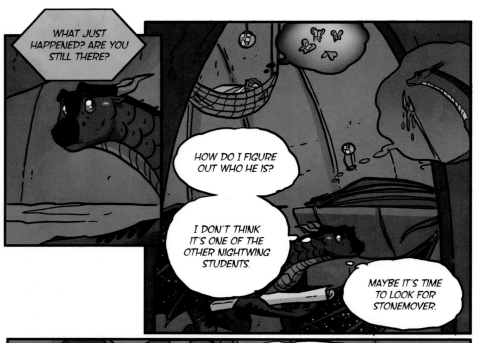

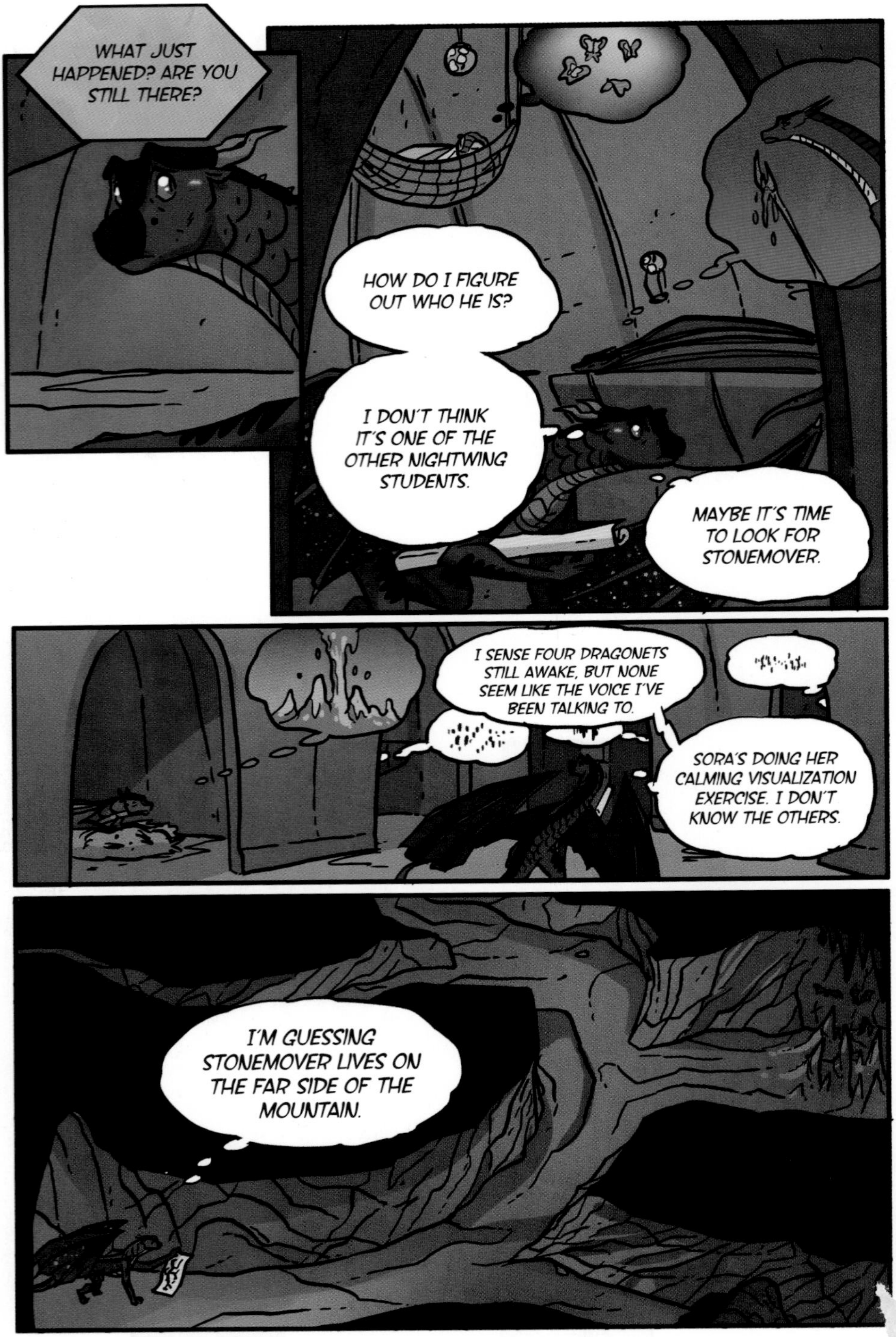
WHAT JUST HAPPENED? ARE YOU STILL THERE?
HOW DO I FIGURE OUT WHO HE IS?
I DON'T THINK IT'S ONE OF THE OTHER NIGHTWING STUDENTS.
MAYBE IT'S TIME TO LOOK FOR STONEMOVER.
I SENSE FOUR DRAGONETS STILL AWAKE, BUT NONE SEEM LIKE THE VOICE I'VE BEEN TALKING TO.
SORA'S DOING HER CALMING VISUALIZATION EXERCISE. I DON'T KNOW THE OTHERS.
I'M GUESSING STONEMOVER LIVES ON THE FAR SIDE OF THE MOUNTAIN.

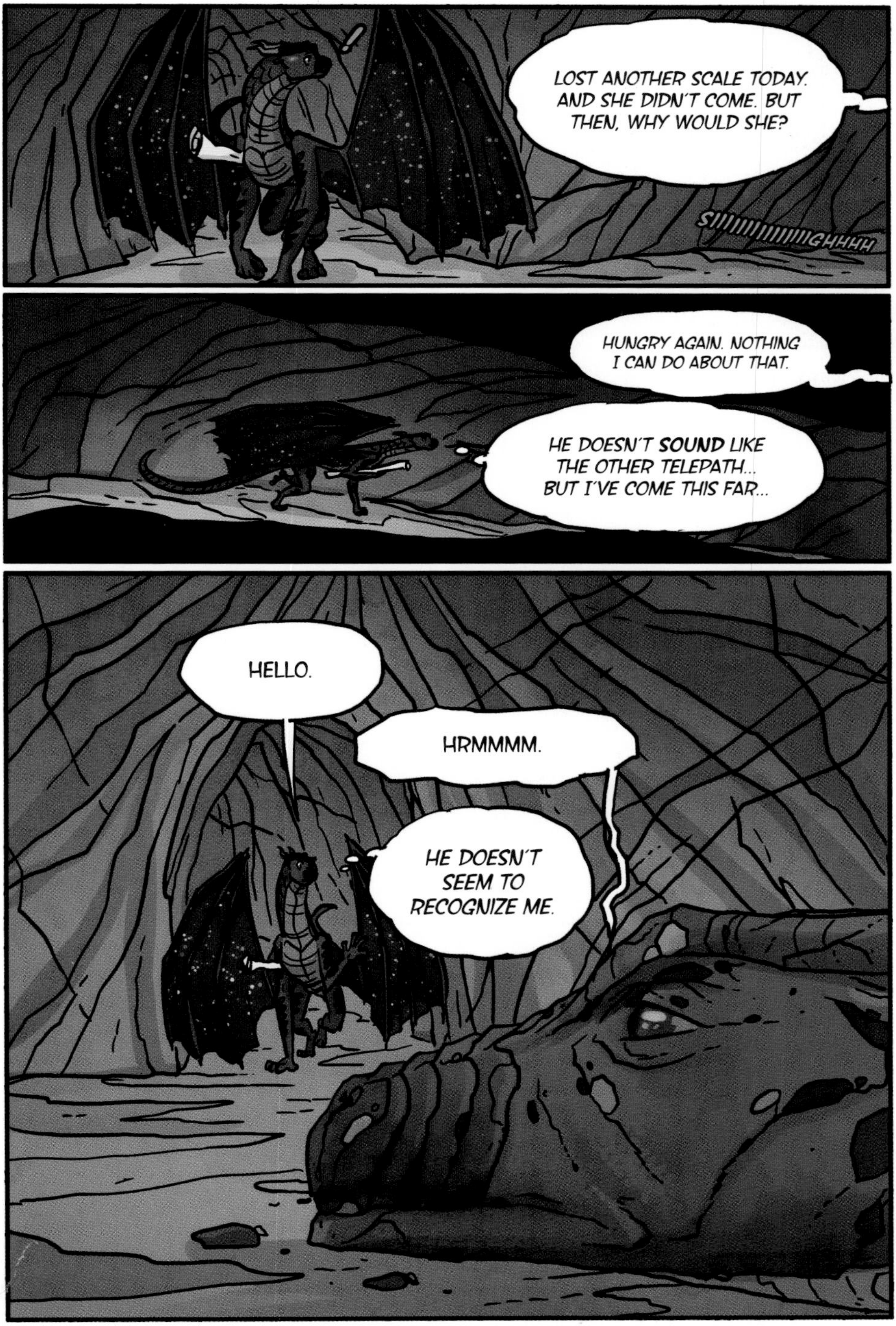
LOST ANOTHER SCALE TODAY. AND SHE DIDN'T COME. BUT THEN, WHY WOULD SHE?
SIIIIIIIIIIIIIIIGHHHH
HUNGRY AGAIN. NOTHING I CAN DO ABOUT THAT.
HE DOESN'T **SOUND** LIKE THE OTHER TELEPATH... BUT I'VE COME THIS FAR...
HELLO.
HRMMMM.
HE DOESN'T SEEM TO RECOGNIZE ME.

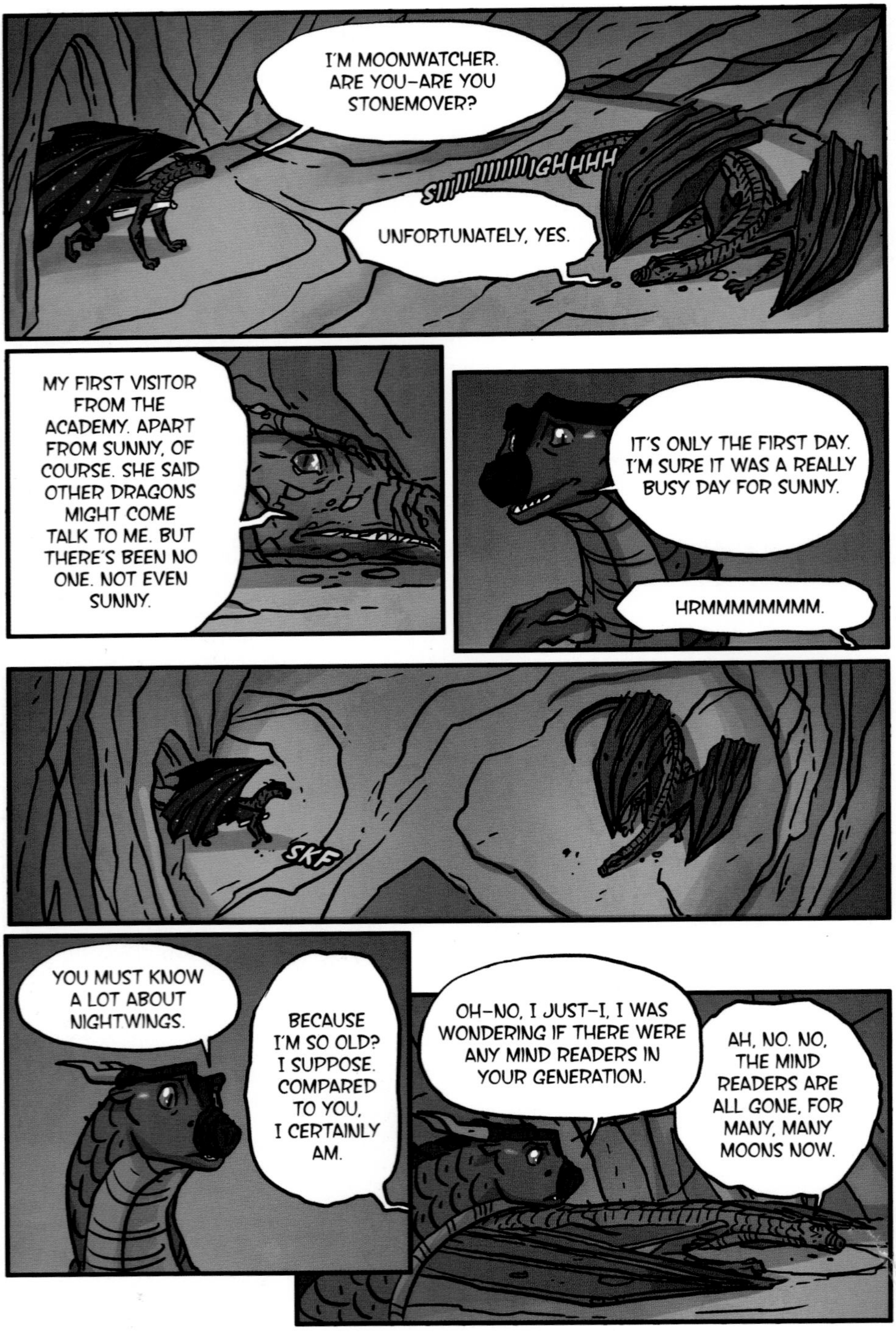
I'M MOONWATCHER. ARE YOU-ARE YOU STONEMOVER?
SIIIIIIIIIIIIIGHHHH
UNFORTUNATELY, YES.
MY FIRST VISITOR FROM THE ACADEMY. APART FROM SUNNY, OF COURSE. SHE SAID OTHER DRAGONS MIGHT COME TALK TO ME. BUT THERE'S BEEN NO ONE. NOT EVEN SUNNY.
IT'S ONLY THE FIRST DAY. I'M SURE IT WAS A REALLY BUSY DAY FOR SUNNY.
HRMMMMMMMM.
SKF
YOU MUST KNOW A LOT ABOUT NIGHTWINGS.
BECAUSE I'M SO OLD? I SUPPOSE. COMPARED TO YOU, I CERTAINLY AM.
OH-NO, I JUST-I, I WAS WONDERING IF THERE WERE ANY MIND READERS IN YOUR GENERATION.
AH, NO. NO, THE MIND READERS ARE ALL GONE, FOR MANY, MANY MOONS NOW.

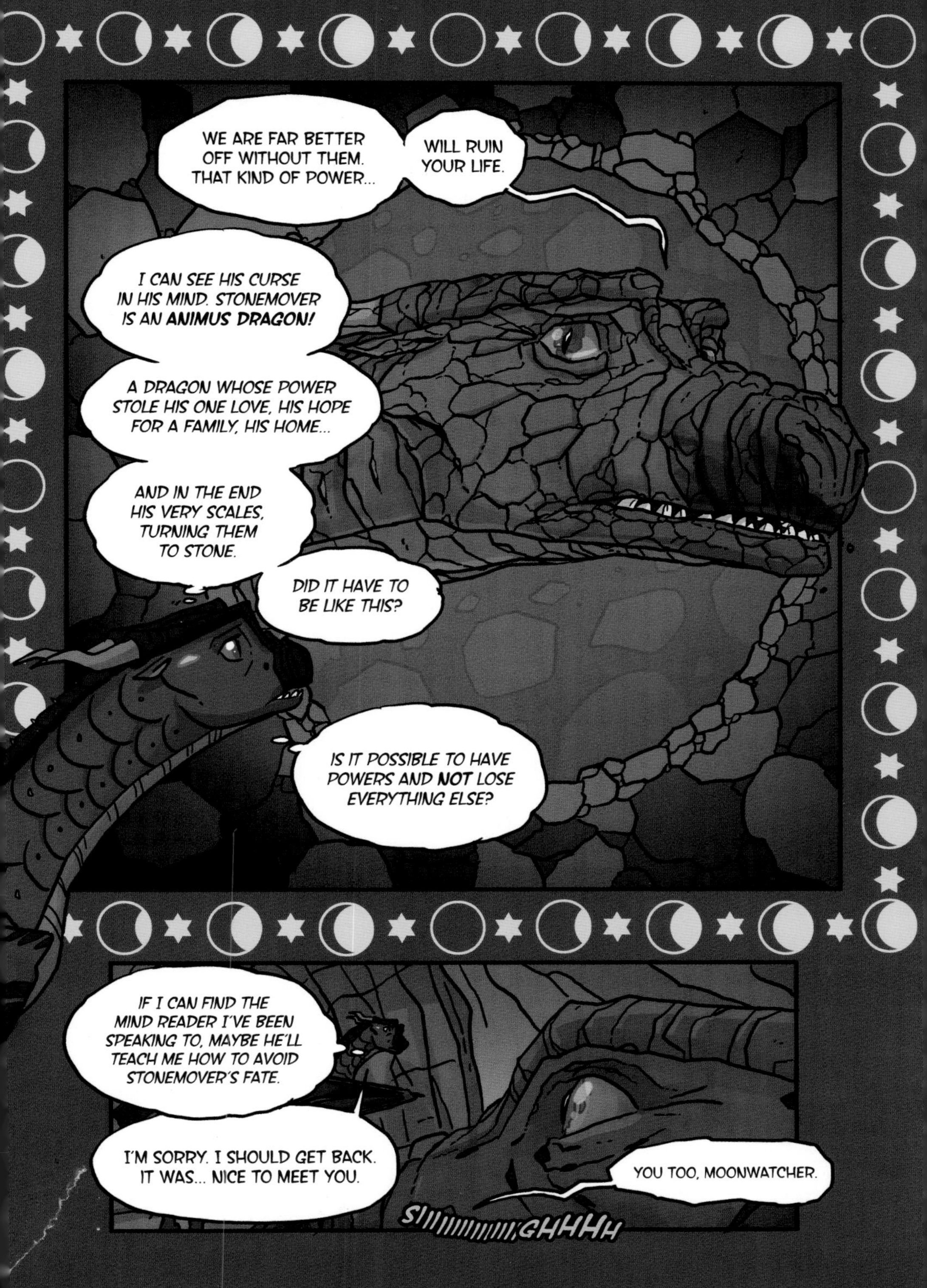
WE ARE FAR BETTER OFF WITHOUT THEM. THAT KIND OF POWER...
WILL RUIN YOUR LIFE.
I CAN SEE HIS CURSE IN HIS MIND. STONEMOVER IS AN ANIMUS DRAGON!
A DRAGON WHOSE POWER STOLE HIS ONE LOVE, HIS HOPE FOR A FAMILY, HIS HOME...
AND IN THE END HIS VERY SCALES, TURNING THEM TO STONE.
DID IT HAVE TO BE LIKE THIS?
IS IT POSSIBLE TO HAVE POWERS AND NOT LOSE EVERYTHING ELSE?
IF I CAN FIND THE MIND READER I'VE BEEN SPEAKING TO, MAYBE HE'LL TEACH ME HOW TO AVOID STONEMOVER'S FATE.
I'M SORRY. I SHOULD GET BACK. IT WAS... NICE TO MEET YOU.
YOU TOO, MOONWATCHER.
SIIIIIIIIIIIIIGHHHH

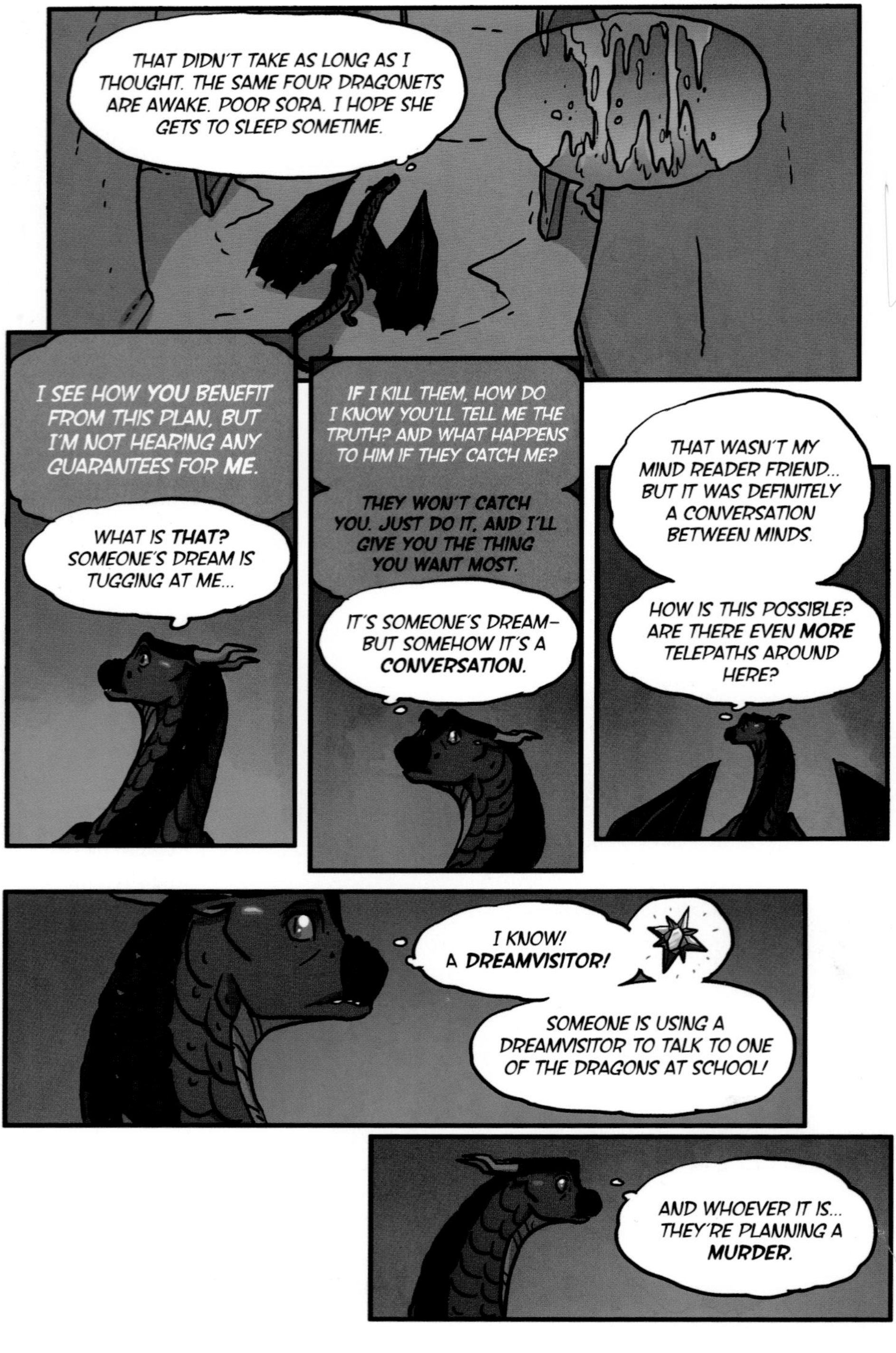
THAT DIDN'T TAKE AS LONG AS I THOUGHT. THE SAME FOUR DRAGONETS ARE AWAKE. POOR SORA. I HOPE SHE GETS TO SLEEP SOMETIME.
I SEE HOW YOU BENEFIT FROM THIS PLAN, BUT I'M NOT HEARING ANY GUARANTEES FOR ME.
WHAT IS THAT? SOMEONE'S DREAM IS TUGGING AT ME...
IF I KILL THEM, HOW DO I KNOW YOU'LL TELL ME THE TRUTH? AND WHAT HAPPENS TO HIM IF THEY CATCH ME?
THEY WON'T CATCH YOU. JUST DO IT, AND I'LL GIVE YOU THE THING YOU WANT MOST.
IT'S SOMEONE'S DREAM— BUT SOMEHOW IT'S A CONVERSATION.
THAT WASN'T MY MIND READER FRIEND... BUT IT WAS DEFINITELY A CONVERSATION BETWEEN MINDS.
HOW IS THIS POSSIBLE? ARE THERE EVEN MORE TELEPATHS AROUND HERE?
I KNOW! A DREAMVISITOR!
SOMEONE IS USING A DREAMVISITOR TO TALK TO ONE OF THE DRAGONS AT SCHOOL!
AND WHOEVER IT IS... THEY'RE PLANNING A MURDER.

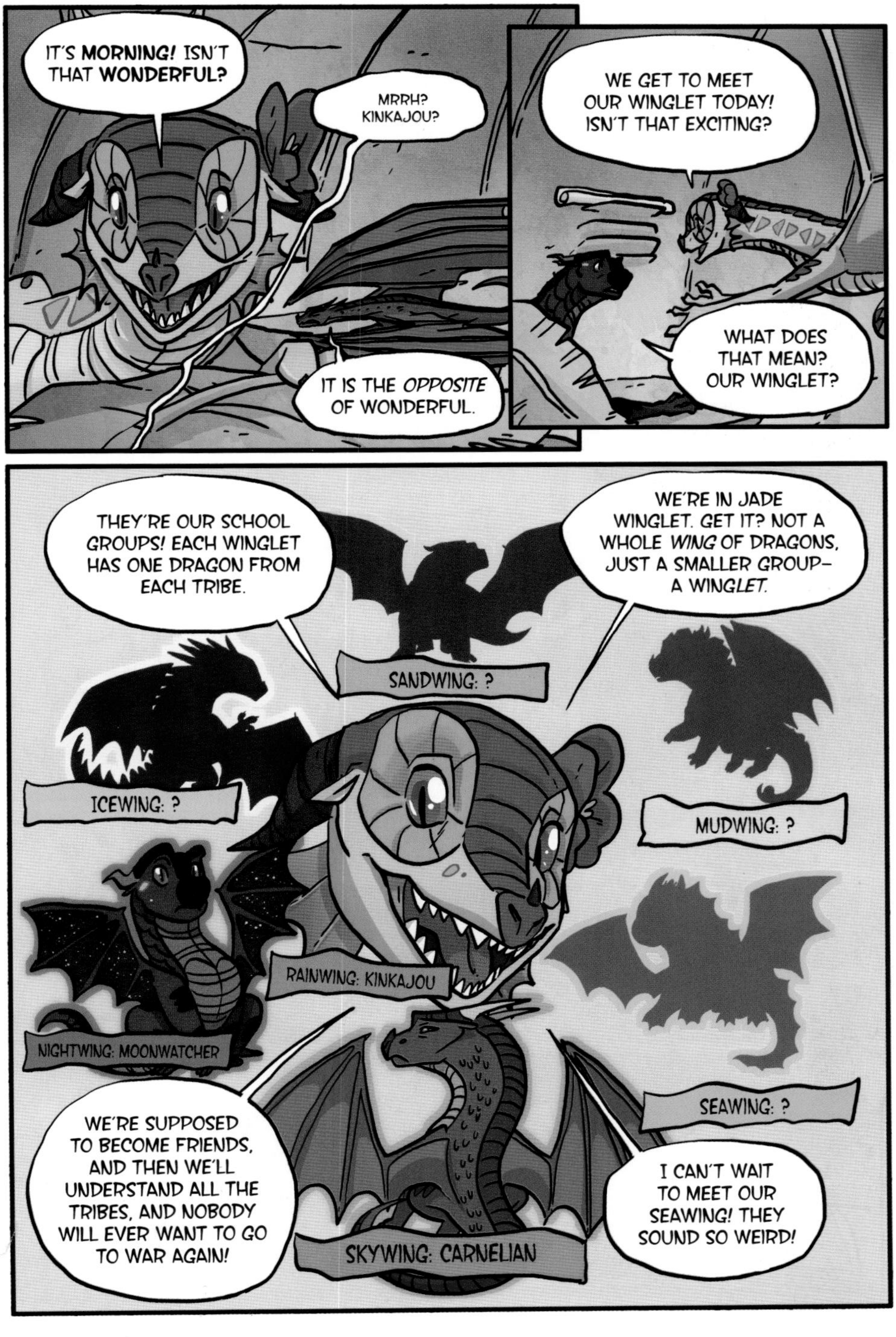
IT'S MORNING! ISN'T THAT WONDERFUL?
MRRH? KINKAJOU?
IT IS THE OPPOSITE OF WONDERFUL.
WE GET TO MEET OUR WINGLET TODAY! ISN'T THAT EXCITING?
WHAT DOES THAT MEAN? OUR WINGLET?
THEY'RE OUR SCHOOL GROUPS! EACH WINGLET HAS ONE DRAGON FROM EACH TRIBE.
WE'RE IN JADE WINGLET. GET IT? NOT A WHOLE WING OF DRAGONS, JUST A SMALLER GROUP— A WINGLET.
SANDWING: ?
ICEWING: ?
MUDWING: ?
RAINWING: KINKAJOU
NIGHTWING: MOONWATCHER
SEAWING: ?
SKYWING: CARNELIAN
WE'RE SUPPOSED TO BECOME FRIENDS, AND THEN WE'LL UNDERSTAND ALL THE TRIBES, AND NOBODY WILL EVER WANT TO GO TO WAR AGAIN!
I CAN'T WAIT TO MEET OUR SEAWING! THEY SOUND SO WEIRD!

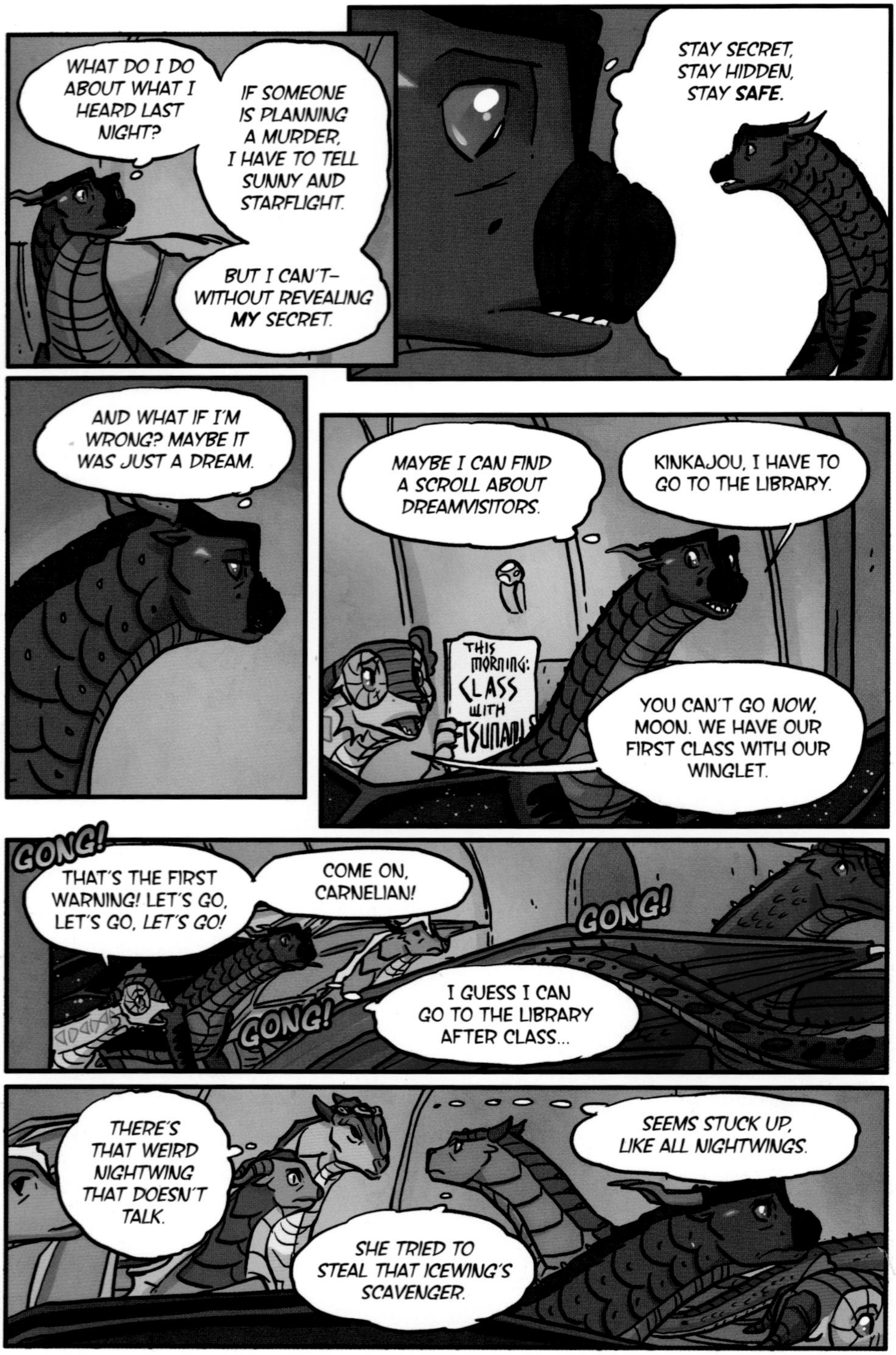
WHAT DO I DO ABOUT WHAT I HEARD LAST NIGHT?
IF SOMEONE IS PLANNING A MURDER, I HAVE TO TELL SUNNY AND STARFLIGHT.
BUT I CAN'T– WITHOUT REVEALING **MY** SECRET.
STAY SECRET, STAY HIDDEN, STAY **SAFE**.
AND WHAT IF I'M WRONG? MAYBE IT WAS JUST A DREAM.
MAYBE I CAN FIND A SCROLL ABOUT DREAMVISITORS.
KINKAJOU, I HAVE TO GO TO THE LIBRARY.
THIS MORNING: CLASS WITH TSUNAMI!
YOU CAN'T GO NOW, MOON. WE HAVE OUR FIRST CLASS WITH OUR WINGLET.
GONG!
THAT'S THE FIRST WARNING! LET'S GO, LET'S GO, LET'S GO!
COME ON, CARNELIAN!
GONG!
GONG!
I GUESS I CAN GO TO THE LIBRARY AFTER CLASS...
THERE'S THAT WEIRD NIGHTWING THAT DOESN'T TALK.
SEEMS STUCK UP, LIKE ALL NIGHTWINGS.
SHE TRIED TO STEAL THAT ICEWING'S SCAVENGER.

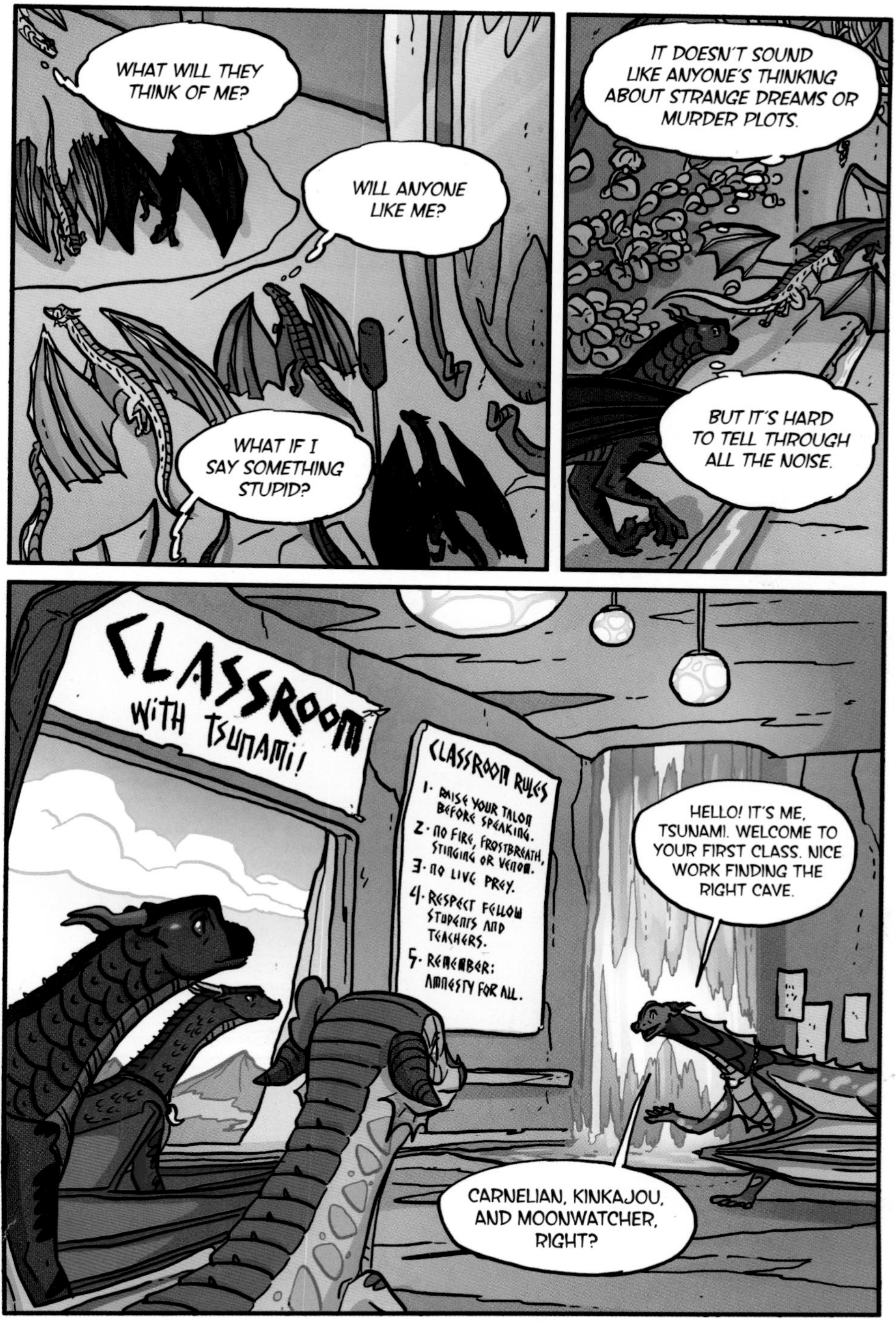
WHAT WILL THEY THINK OF ME?
WILL ANYONE LIKE ME?
WHAT IF I SAY SOMETHING STUPID?
IT DOESN'T SOUND LIKE ANYONE'S THINKING ABOUT STRANGE DREAMS OR MURDER PLOTS.
BUT IT'S HARD TO TELL THROUGH ALL THE NOISE.
CLASSROOM WITH TSUNAMI!
CLASSROOM RULES
1. RAISE YOUR TALON BEFORE SPEAKING.
2. NO FIRE, FROSTBREATH, STINGING OR VENOM.
3. NO LIVE PREY.
4. RESPECT FELLOW STUDENTS AND TEACHERS.
5. REMEMBER: AMNESTY FOR ALL.
HELLO! IT'S ME, TSUNAMI. WELCOME TO YOUR FIRST CLASS. NICE WORK FINDING THE RIGHT CAVE.
CARNELIAN, KINKAJOU, AND MOONWATCHER, RIGHT?

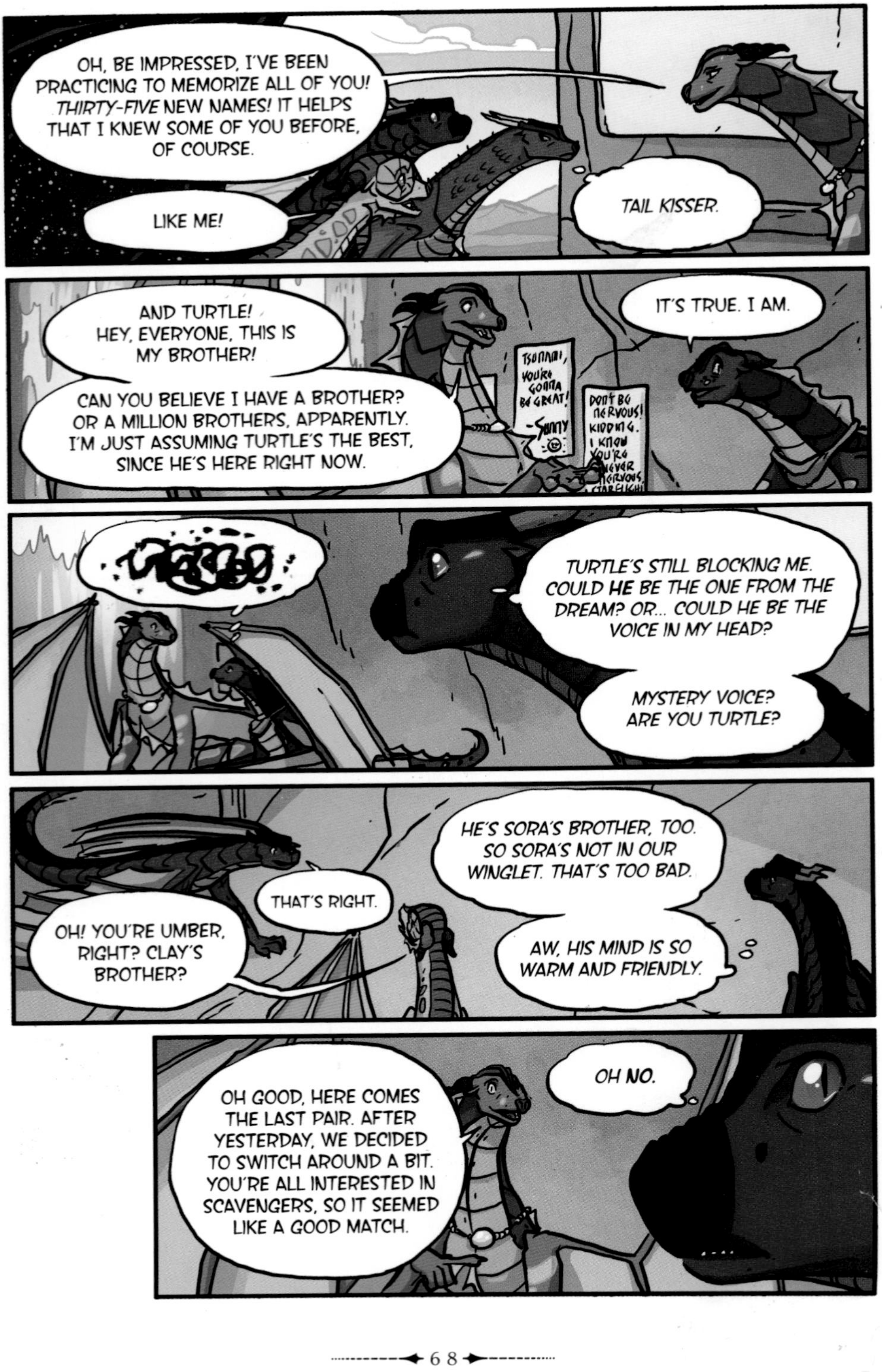
OH, BE IMPRESSED, I'VE BEEN PRACTICING TO MEMORIZE ALL OF YOU! *THIRTY-FIVE* NEW NAMES! IT HELPS THAT I KNEW SOME OF YOU BEFORE, OF COURSE.
LIKE ME!
TAIL KISSER.
AND TURTLE! HEY, EVERYONE, THIS IS MY BROTHER!
CAN YOU BELIEVE I HAVE A BROTHER? OR A MILLION BROTHERS, APPARENTLY. I'M JUST ASSUMING TURTLE'S THE BEST, SINCE HE'S HERE RIGHT NOW.
Tsunami, you're gonna be great! -Sunny
Don't be nervous! Kidding. I know you're never
IT'S TRUE. I AM.
*TURTLE'S STILL BLOCKING ME. COULD **HE** BE THE ONE FROM THE DREAM? OR... COULD HE BE THE VOICE IN MY HEAD?*
MYSTERY VOICE? ARE YOU TURTLE?
OH! YOU'RE UMBER, RIGHT? CLAY'S BROTHER?
THAT'S RIGHT.
HE'S SORA'S BROTHER, TOO. SO SORA'S NOT IN OUR WINGLET. THAT'S TOO BAD.
AW, HIS MIND IS SO WARM AND FRIENDLY.
OH GOOD, HERE COMES THE LAST PAIR. AFTER YESTERDAY, WE DECIDED TO SWITCH AROUND A BIT. YOU'RE ALL INTERESTED IN SCAVENGERS, SO IT SEEMED LIKE A GOOD MATCH.
*OH **NO**.*

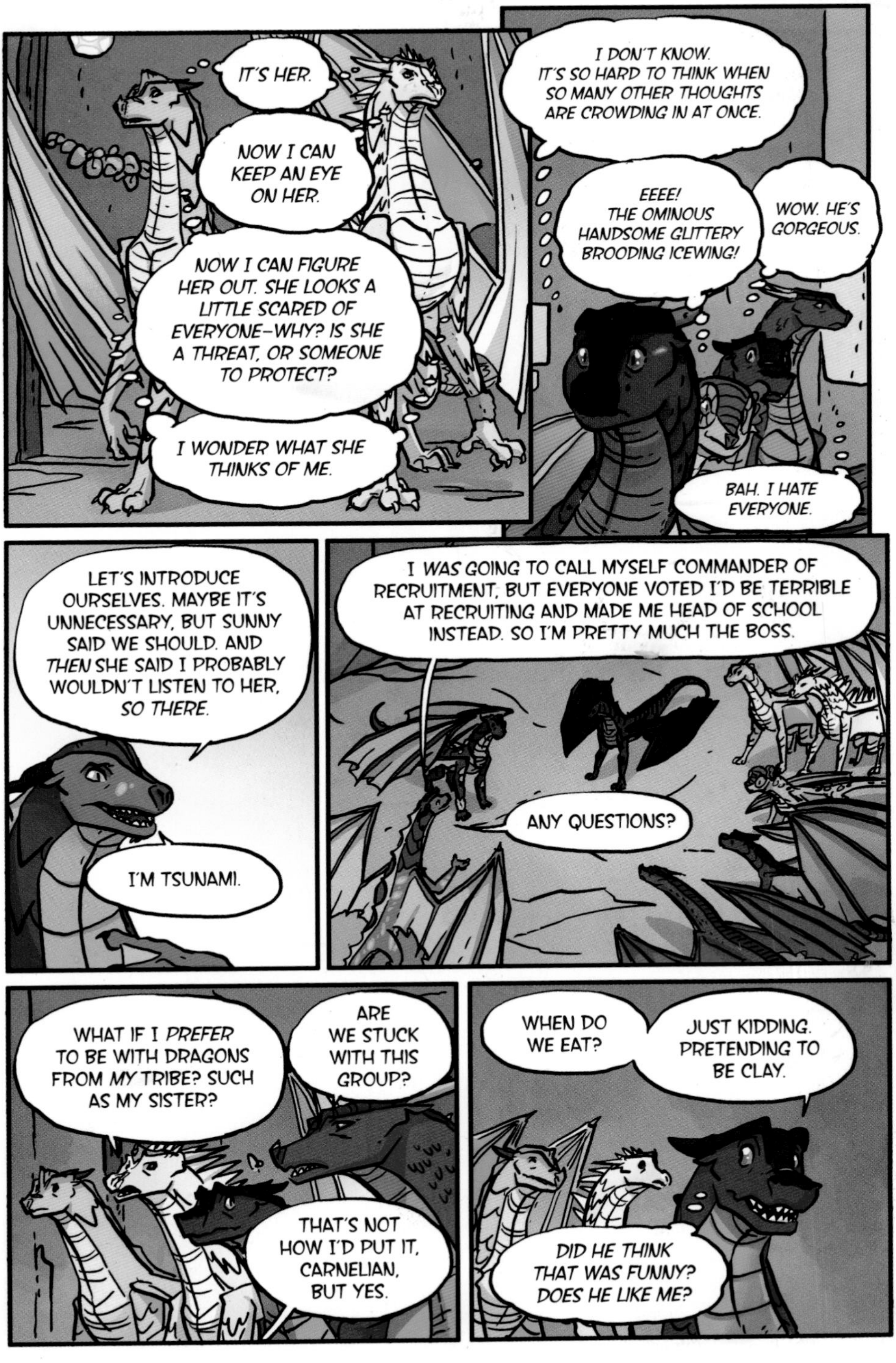
IT'S HER.
NOW I CAN KEEP AN EYE ON HER.
NOW I CAN FIGURE HER OUT. SHE LOOKS A LITTLE SCARED OF EVERYONE—WHY? IS SHE A THREAT, OR SOMEONE TO PROTECT?
I WONDER WHAT SHE THINKS OF ME.
I DON'T KNOW. IT'S SO HARD TO THINK WHEN SO MANY OTHER THOUGHTS ARE CROWDING IN AT ONCE.
EEEE! THE OMINOUS HANDSOME GLITTERY BROODING ICEWING!
WOW. HE'S GORGEOUS.
BAH. I HATE EVERYONE.
LET'S INTRODUCE OURSELVES. MAYBE IT'S UNNECESSARY, BUT SUNNY SAID WE SHOULD. AND *THEN* SHE SAID I PROBABLY WOULDN'T LISTEN TO HER, *SO THERE.*
I'M TSUNAMI.
I *WAS* GOING TO CALL MYSELF COMMANDER OF RECRUITMENT, BUT EVERYONE VOTED I'D BE TERRIBLE AT RECRUITING AND MADE ME HEAD OF SCHOOL INSTEAD. SO I'M PRETTY MUCH THE BOSS.
ANY QUESTIONS?
WHAT IF I *PREFER* TO BE WITH DRAGONS FROM *MY* TRIBE? SUCH AS MY SISTER?
ARE WE STUCK WITH THIS GROUP?
THAT'S NOT HOW I'D PUT IT, CARNELIAN, BUT YES.
WHEN DO WE EAT?
JUST KIDDING. PRETENDING TO BE CLAY.
DID HE THINK THAT WAS FUNNY? DOES HE LIKE ME?

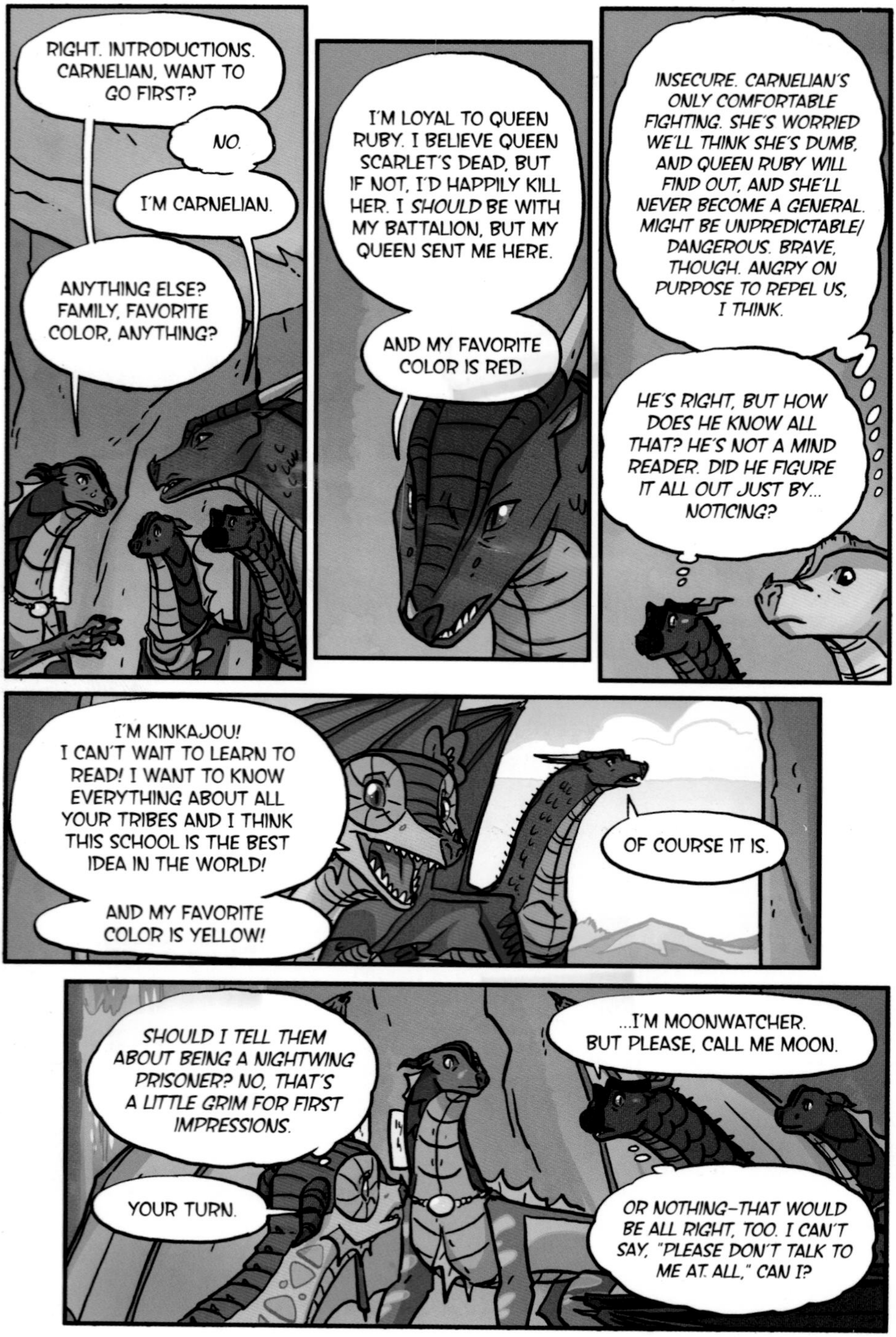
RIGHT. INTRODUCTIONS. CARNELIAN, WANT TO GO FIRST?
NO.
I'M CARNELIAN.
ANYTHING ELSE? FAMILY, FAVORITE COLOR, ANYTHING?
I'M LOYAL TO QUEEN RUBY. I BELIEVE QUEEN SCARLET'S DEAD, BUT IF NOT, I'D HAPPILY KILL HER. I *SHOULD* BE WITH MY BATTALION, BUT MY QUEEN SENT ME HERE.
AND MY FAVORITE COLOR IS RED.
INSECURE. CARNELIAN'S ONLY COMFORTABLE FIGHTING. SHE'S WORRIED WE'LL THINK SHE'S DUMB, AND QUEEN RUBY WILL FIND OUT, AND SHE'LL NEVER BECOME A GENERAL. MIGHT BE UNPREDICTABLE/DANGEROUS. BRAVE, THOUGH. ANGRY ON PURPOSE TO REPEL US, I THINK.
HE'S RIGHT, BUT HOW DOES HE KNOW ALL THAT? HE'S NOT A MIND READER. DID HE FIGURE IT ALL OUT JUST BY... NOTICING?
I'M KINKAJOU! I CAN'T WAIT TO LEARN TO READ! I WANT TO KNOW EVERYTHING ABOUT ALL YOUR TRIBES AND I THINK THIS SCHOOL IS THE BEST IDEA IN THE WORLD!
AND MY FAVORITE COLOR IS YELLOW!
OF COURSE IT IS.
YOUR TURN.
SHOULD I TELL THEM ABOUT BEING A NIGHTWING PRISONER? NO, THAT'S A LITTLE GRIM FOR FIRST IMPRESSIONS.
...I'M MOONWATCHER. BUT PLEASE, CALL ME MOON.
OR NOTHING—THAT WOULD BE ALL RIGHT, TOO. I CAN'T SAY, "PLEASE DON'T TALK TO ME AT ALL," CAN I?

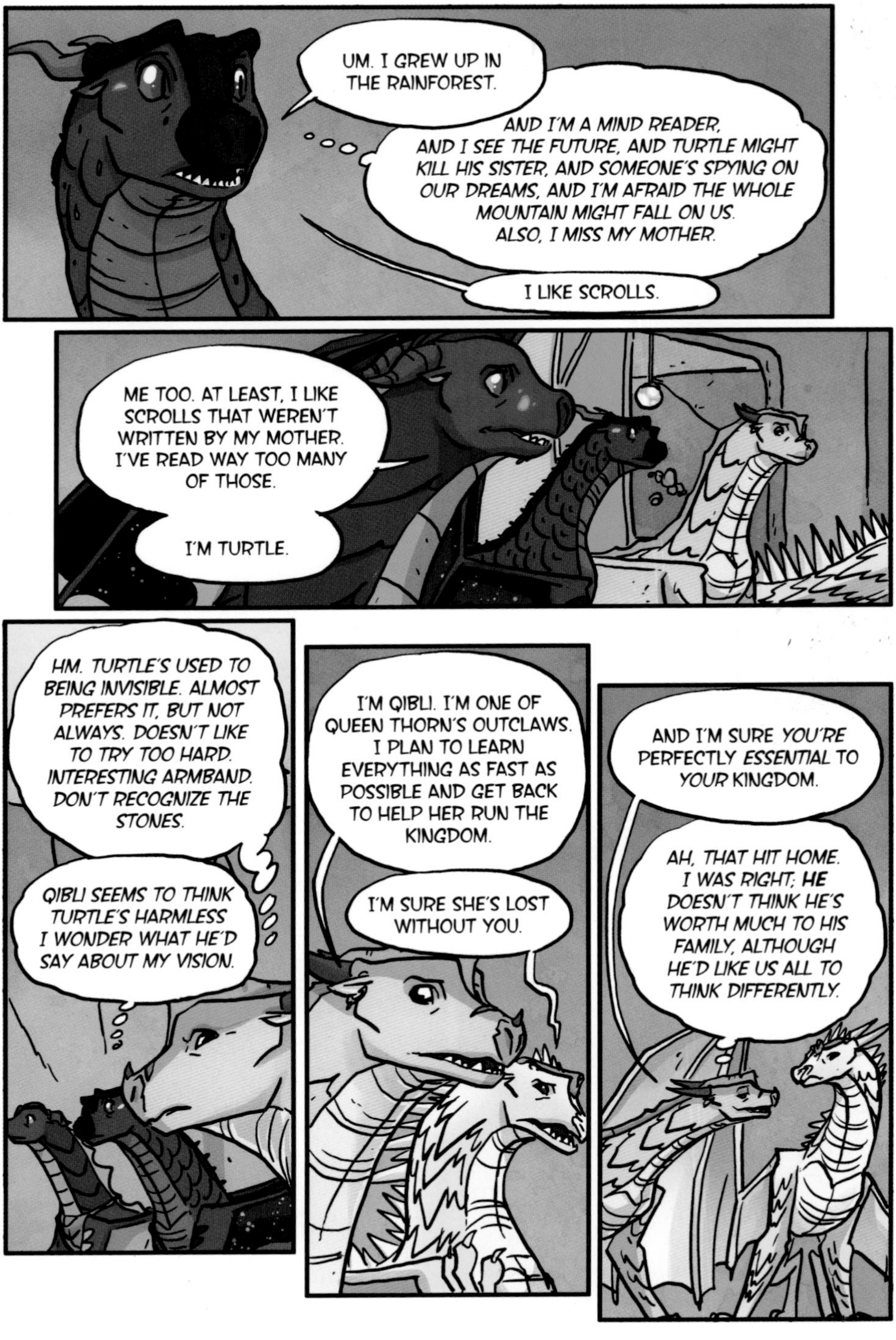
UM. I GREW UP IN THE RAINFOREST.
AND I'M A MIND READER, AND I SEE THE FUTURE, AND TURTLE MIGHT KILL HIS SISTER, AND SOMEONE'S SPYING ON OUR DREAMS, AND I'M AFRAID THE WHOLE MOUNTAIN MIGHT FALL ON US. ALSO, I MISS MY MOTHER.
I LIKE SCROLLS.
ME TOO. AT LEAST, I LIKE SCROLLS THAT WEREN'T WRITTEN BY MY MOTHER. I'VE READ WAY TOO MANY OF THOSE.
I'M TURTLE.
HM. TURTLE'S USED TO BEING INVISIBLE. ALMOST PREFERS IT, BUT NOT ALWAYS. DOESN'T LIKE TO TRY TOO HARD. INTERESTING ARMBAND. DON'T RECOGNIZE THE STONES.
QIBLI SEEMS TO THINK TURTLE'S HARMLESS I WONDER WHAT HE'D SAY ABOUT MY VISION.
I'M QIBLI. I'M ONE OF QUEEN THORN'S OUTCLAWS. I PLAN TO LEARN EVERYTHING AS FAST AS POSSIBLE AND GET BACK TO HELP HER RUN THE KINGDOM.
I'M SURE SHE'S LOST WITHOUT YOU.
AND I'M SURE YOU'RE PERFECTLY ESSENTIAL TO YOUR KINGDOM.
AH, THAT HIT HOME. I WAS RIGHT; HE DOESN'T THINK HE'S WORTH MUCH TO HIS FAMILY, ALTHOUGH HE'D LIKE US ALL TO THINK DIFFERENTLY.

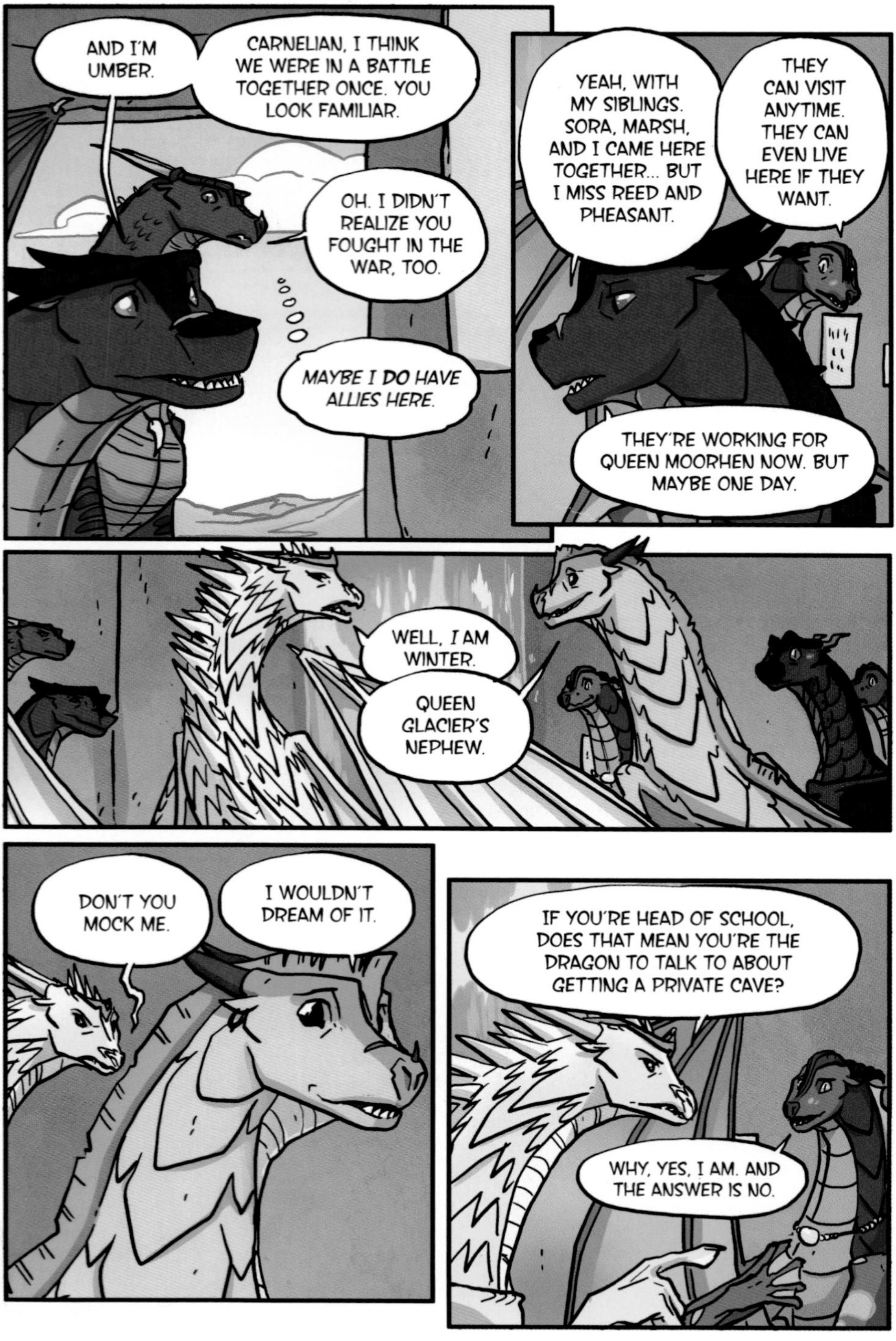
AND I'M UMBER.
CARNELIAN, I THINK WE WERE IN A BATTLE TOGETHER ONCE. YOU LOOK FAMILIAR.
OH. I DIDN'T REALIZE YOU FOUGHT IN THE WAR, TOO.
*MAYBE I **DO** HAVE ALLIES HERE.*
YEAH, WITH MY SIBLINGS. SORA, MARSH, AND I CAME HERE TOGETHER... BUT I MISS REED AND PHEASANT.
THEY CAN VISIT ANYTIME. THEY CAN EVEN LIVE HERE IF THEY WANT.
THEY'RE WORKING FOR QUEEN MOORHEN NOW. BUT MAYBE ONE DAY.
WELL, *I* AM WINTER.
QUEEN GLACIER'S NEPHEW.
DON'T YOU MOCK ME.
I WOULDN'T DREAM OF IT.
IF YOU'RE HEAD OF SCHOOL, DOES THAT MEAN YOU'RE THE DRAGON TO TALK TO ABOUT GETTING A PRIVATE CAVE?
WHY, YES, I AM. AND THE ANSWER IS NO.

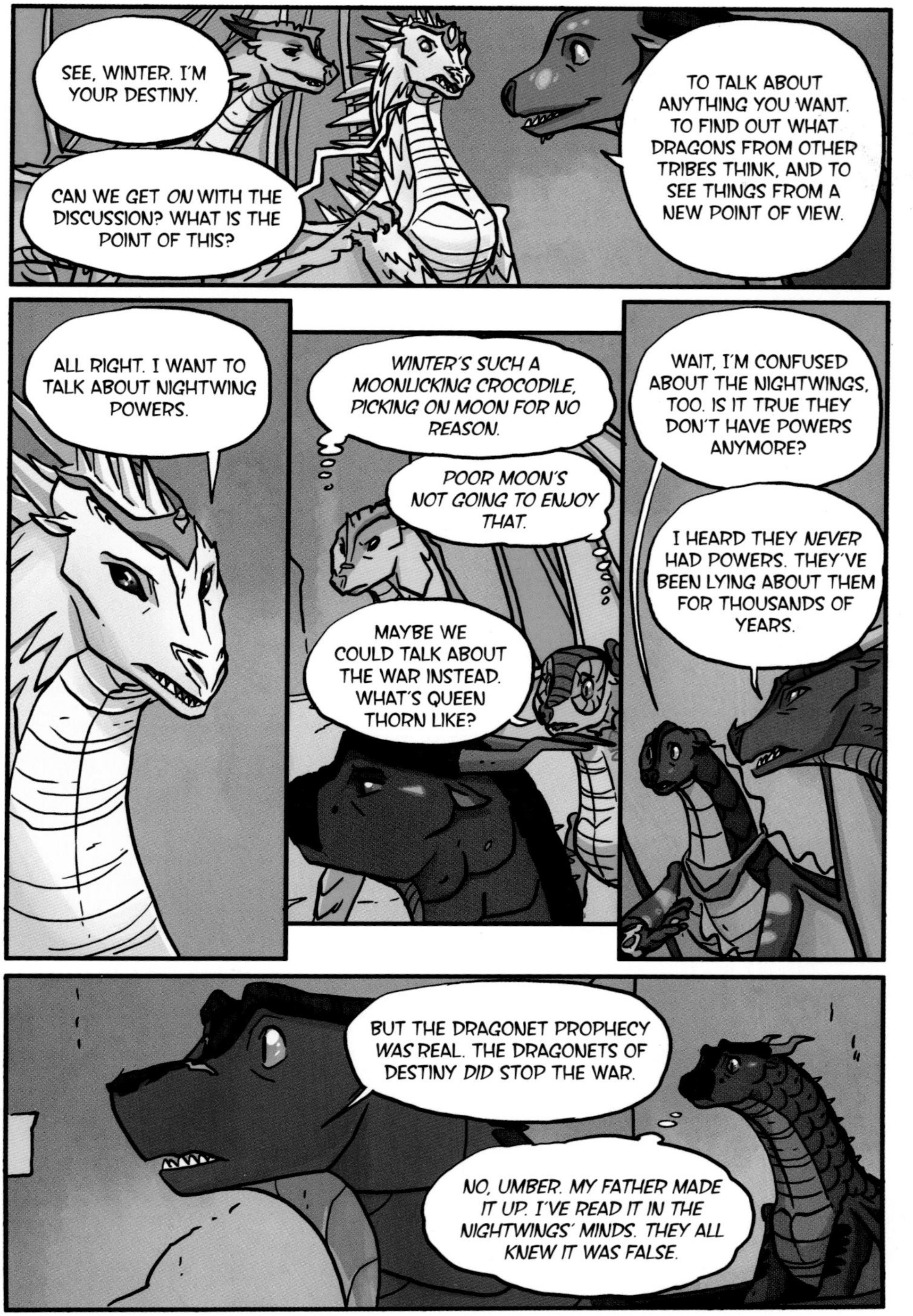
SEE, WINTER. I'M YOUR DESTINY.
CAN WE GET *ON* WITH THE DISCUSSION? WHAT IS THE POINT OF THIS?
TO TALK ABOUT ANYTHING YOU WANT. TO FIND OUT WHAT DRAGONS FROM OTHER TRIBES THINK, AND TO SEE THINGS FROM A NEW POINT OF VIEW.
ALL RIGHT. I WANT TO TALK ABOUT NIGHTWING POWERS.
WINTER'S SUCH A MOONLICKING CROCODILE, PICKING ON MOON FOR NO REASON.
POOR MOON'S NOT GOING TO ENJOY THAT.
MAYBE WE COULD TALK ABOUT THE WAR INSTEAD. WHAT'S QUEEN THORN LIKE?
WAIT, I'M CONFUSED ABOUT THE NIGHTWINGS, TOO. IS IT TRUE THEY DON'T HAVE POWERS ANYMORE?
I HEARD THEY *NEVER* HAD POWERS. THEY'VE BEEN LYING ABOUT THEM FOR THOUSANDS OF YEARS.
BUT THE DRAGONET PROPHECY *WAS* REAL. THE DRAGONETS OF DESTINY *DID* STOP THE WAR.
NO, UMBER. MY FATHER MADE IT UP. I'VE READ IT IN THE NIGHTWINGS' MINDS. THEY ALL KNEW IT WAS FALSE.

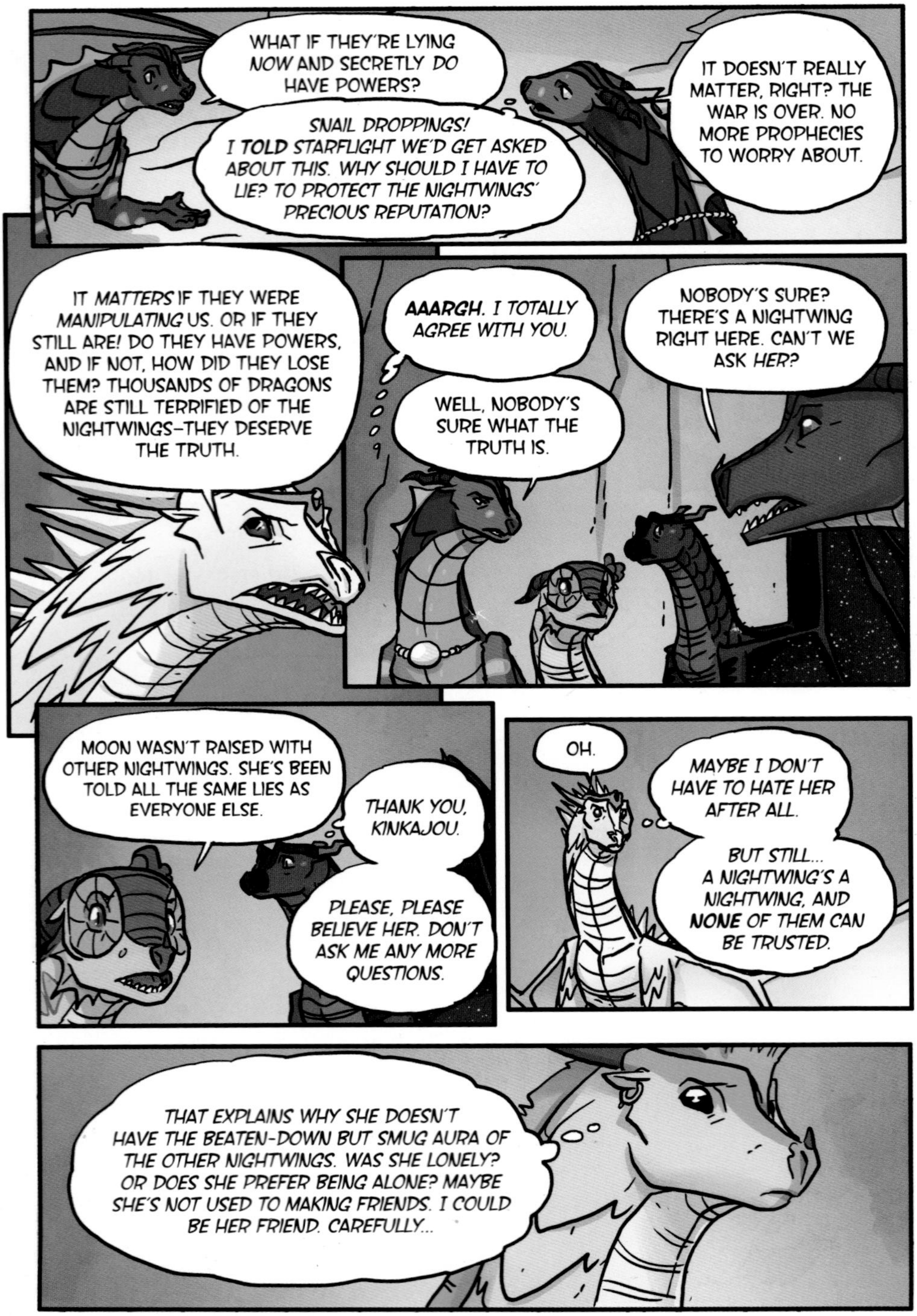
WHAT IF THEY'RE LYING *NOW* AND SECRETLY *DO* HAVE POWERS?
*SNAIL DROPPINGS! I **TOLD** STARFLIGHT WE'D GET ASKED ABOUT THIS. WHY SHOULD I HAVE TO LIE? TO PROTECT THE NIGHTWINGS' PRECIOUS REPUTATION?*
IT DOESN'T REALLY MATTER, RIGHT? THE WAR IS OVER. NO MORE PROPHECIES TO WORRY ABOUT.
IT *MATTERS* IF THEY WERE *MANIPULATING* US. OR IF THEY STILL ARE! DO THEY HAVE POWERS, AND IF NOT, HOW DID THEY LOSE THEM? THOUSANDS OF DRAGONS ARE STILL TERRIFIED OF THE NIGHTWINGS—THEY DESERVE THE TRUTH.
***AAARGH.** I TOTALLY AGREE WITH YOU.*
WELL, NOBODY'S SURE WHAT THE TRUTH IS.
NOBODY'S SURE? THERE'S A NIGHTWING RIGHT HERE. CAN'T WE ASK *HER*?
MOON WASN'T RAISED WITH OTHER NIGHTWINGS. SHE'S BEEN TOLD ALL THE SAME LIES AS EVERYONE ELSE.
THANK YOU, KINKAJOU.
PLEASE, PLEASE BELIEVE HER. DON'T ASK ME ANY MORE QUESTIONS.
OH.
MAYBE I DON'T HAVE TO HATE HER AFTER ALL.
*BUT STILL... A NIGHTWING'S A NIGHTWING, AND **NONE** OF THEM CAN BE TRUSTED.*
THAT EXPLAINS WHY SHE DOESN'T HAVE THE BEATEN-DOWN BUT SMUG AURA OF THE OTHER NIGHTWINGS. WAS SHE LONELY? OR DOES SHE PREFER BEING ALONE? MAYBE SHE'S NOT USED TO MAKING FRIENDS. I COULD BE HER FRIEND. CAREFULLY...

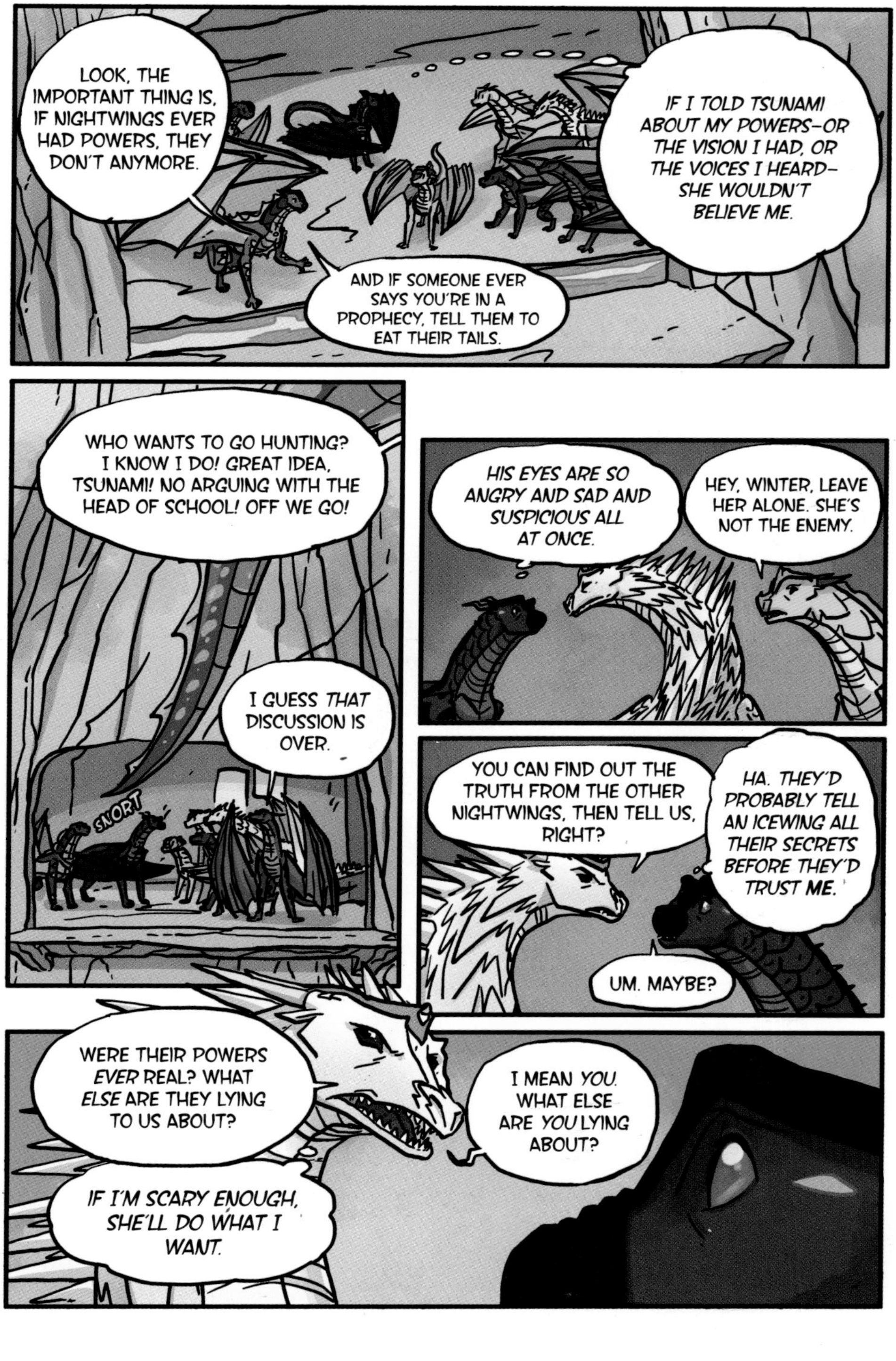
LOOK, THE IMPORTANT THING IS, IF NIGHTWINGS EVER HAD POWERS, THEY DON'T ANYMORE.
AND IF SOMEONE EVER SAYS YOU'RE IN A PROPHECY, TELL THEM TO EAT THEIR TAILS.
IF I TOLD TSUNAMI ABOUT MY POWERS–OR THE VISION I HAD, OR THE VOICES I HEARD–SHE WOULDN'T BELIEVE ME.
WHO WANTS TO GO HUNTING? I KNOW I DO! GREAT IDEA, TSUNAMI! NO ARGUING WITH THE HEAD OF SCHOOL! OFF WE GO!
I GUESS THAT DISCUSSION IS OVER.
SNORT
HIS EYES ARE SO ANGRY AND SAD AND SUSPICIOUS ALL AT ONCE.
HEY, WINTER, LEAVE HER ALONE. SHE'S NOT THE ENEMY.
YOU CAN FIND OUT THE TRUTH FROM THE OTHER NIGHTWINGS, THEN TELL US, RIGHT?
HA. THEY'D PROBABLY TELL AN ICEWING ALL THEIR SECRETS BEFORE THEY'D TRUST ME.
UM. MAYBE?
WERE THEIR POWERS EVER REAL? WHAT ELSE ARE THEY LYING TO US ABOUT?
I MEAN YOU. WHAT ELSE ARE YOU LYING ABOUT?
IF I'M SCARY ENOUGH, SHE'LL DO WHAT I WANT.

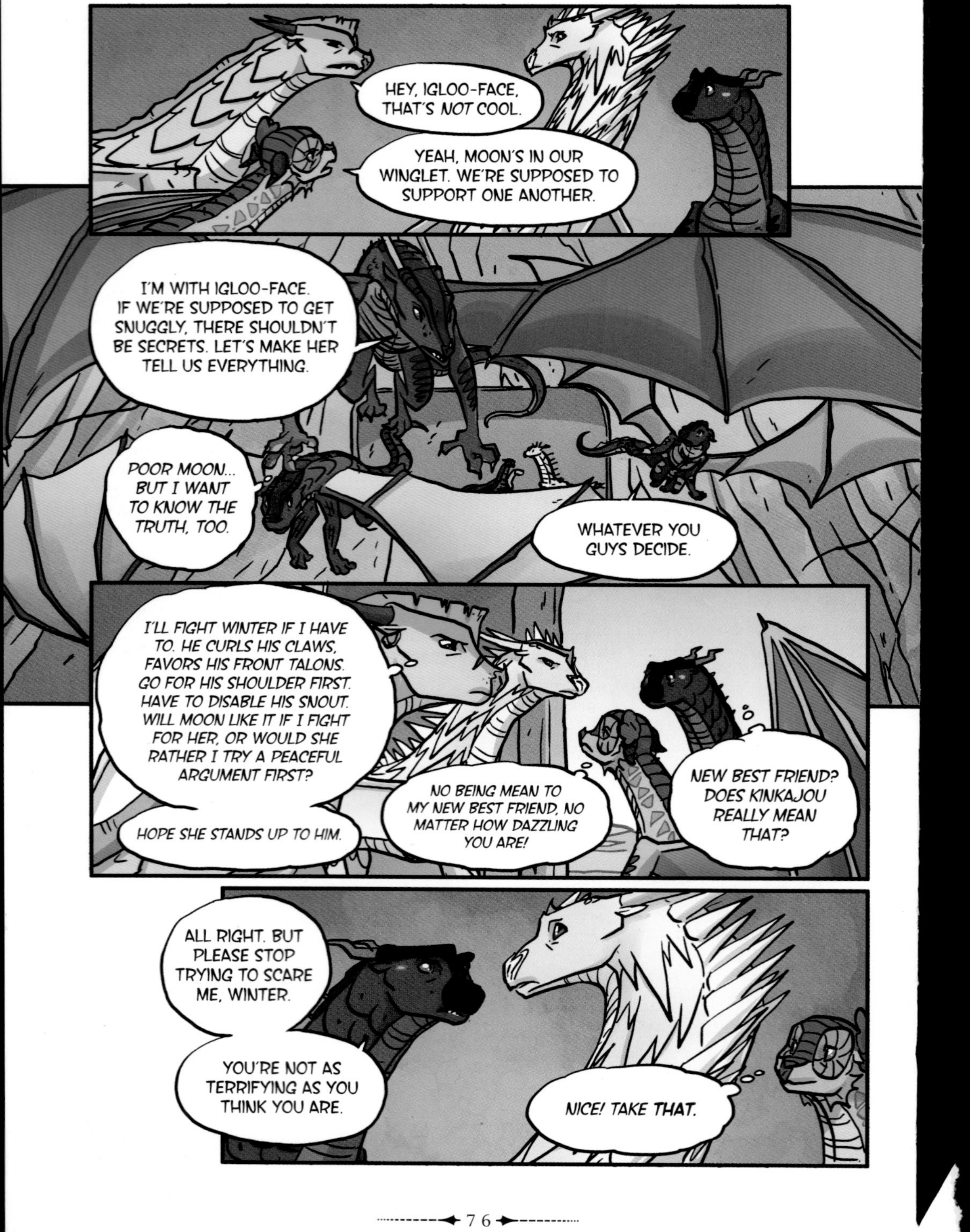
HEY, IGLOO-FACE, THAT'S NOT COOL.
YEAH, MOON'S IN OUR WINGLET. WE'RE SUPPOSED TO SUPPORT ONE ANOTHER.
I'M WITH IGLOO-FACE. IF WE'RE SUPPOSED TO GET SNUGGLY, THERE SHOULDN'T BE SECRETS. LET'S MAKE HER TELL US EVERYTHING.
POOR MOON... BUT I WANT TO KNOW THE TRUTH, TOO.
WHATEVER YOU GUYS DECIDE.
I'LL FIGHT WINTER IF I HAVE TO. HE CURLS HIS CLAWS, FAVORS HIS FRONT TALONS. GO FOR HIS SHOULDER FIRST. HAVE TO DISABLE HIS SNOUT. WILL MOON LIKE IT IF I FIGHT FOR HER, OR WOULD SHE RATHER I TRY A PEACEFUL ARGUMENT FIRST?
HOPE SHE STANDS UP TO HIM.
NO BEING MEAN TO MY NEW BEST FRIEND, NO MATTER HOW DAZZLING YOU ARE!
NEW BEST FRIEND? DOES KINKAJOU REALLY MEAN THAT?
ALL RIGHT. BUT PLEASE STOP TRYING TO SCARE ME, WINTER.
YOU'RE NOT AS TERRIFYING AS YOU THINK YOU ARE.
NICE! TAKE THAT.

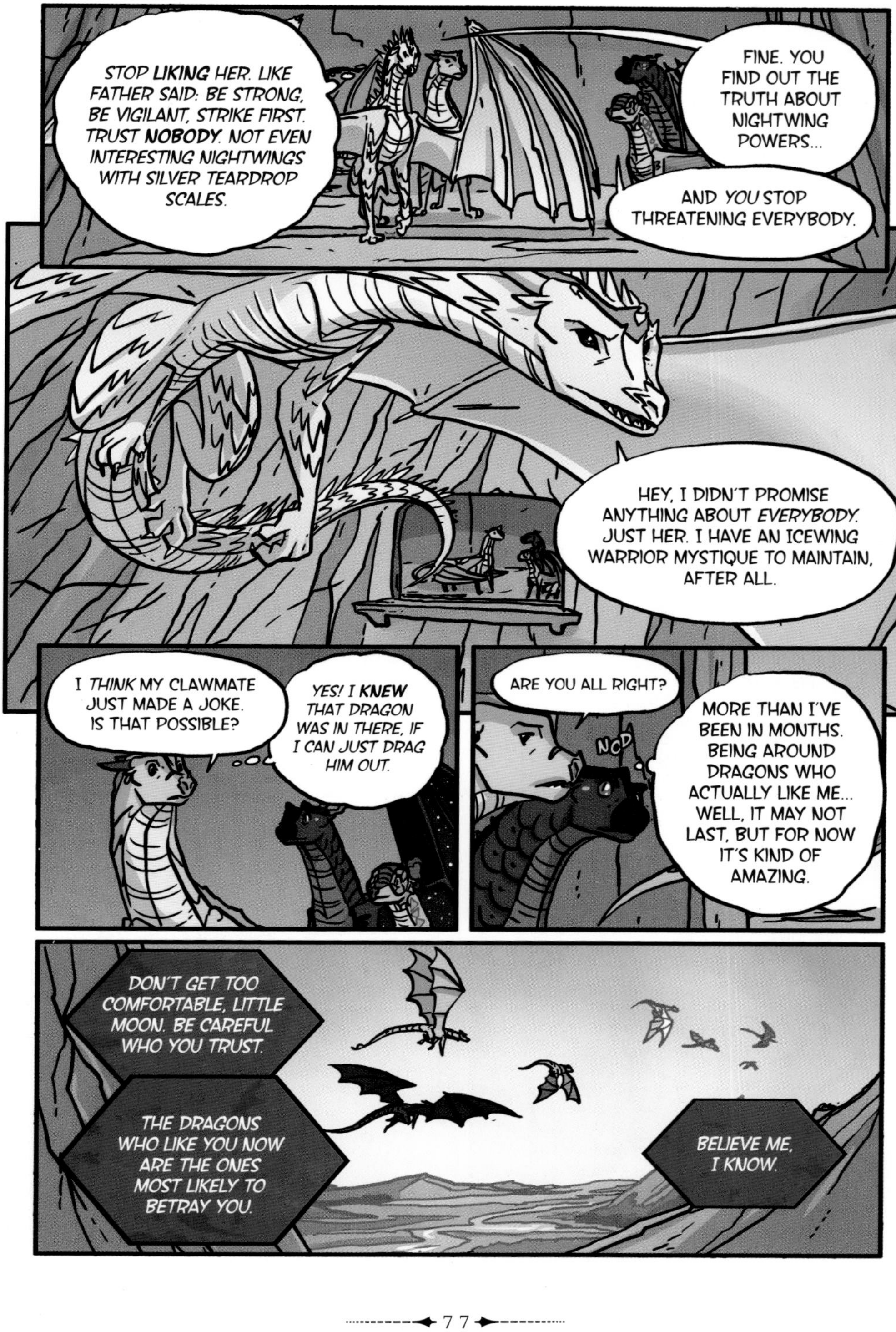
STOP **LIKING** HER. LIKE FATHER SAID: BE STRONG, BE VIGILANT, STRIKE FIRST. TRUST **NOBODY**. NOT EVEN INTERESTING NIGHTWINGS WITH SILVER TEARDROP SCALES.
FINE. YOU FIND OUT THE TRUTH ABOUT NIGHTWING POWERS...
AND *YOU* STOP THREATENING EVERYBODY.
HEY, I DIDN'T PROMISE ANYTHING ABOUT *EVERYBODY*. JUST HER. I HAVE AN ICEWING WARRIOR MYSTIQUE TO MAINTAIN, AFTER ALL.
I *THINK* MY CLAWMATE JUST MADE A JOKE. IS THAT POSSIBLE?
YES! I **KNEW** THAT DRAGON WAS IN THERE, IF I CAN JUST DRAG HIM OUT.
ARE YOU ALL RIGHT?
NOD
MORE THAN I'VE BEEN IN MONTHS. BEING AROUND DRAGONS WHO ACTUALLY LIKE ME... WELL, IT MAY NOT LAST, BUT FOR NOW IT'S KIND OF AMAZING.
DON'T GET TOO COMFORTABLE, LITTLE MOON. BE CAREFUL WHO YOU TRUST.
THE DRAGONS WHO LIKE YOU NOW ARE THE ONES MOST LIKELY TO BETRAY YOU.
BELIEVE ME, I KNOW.

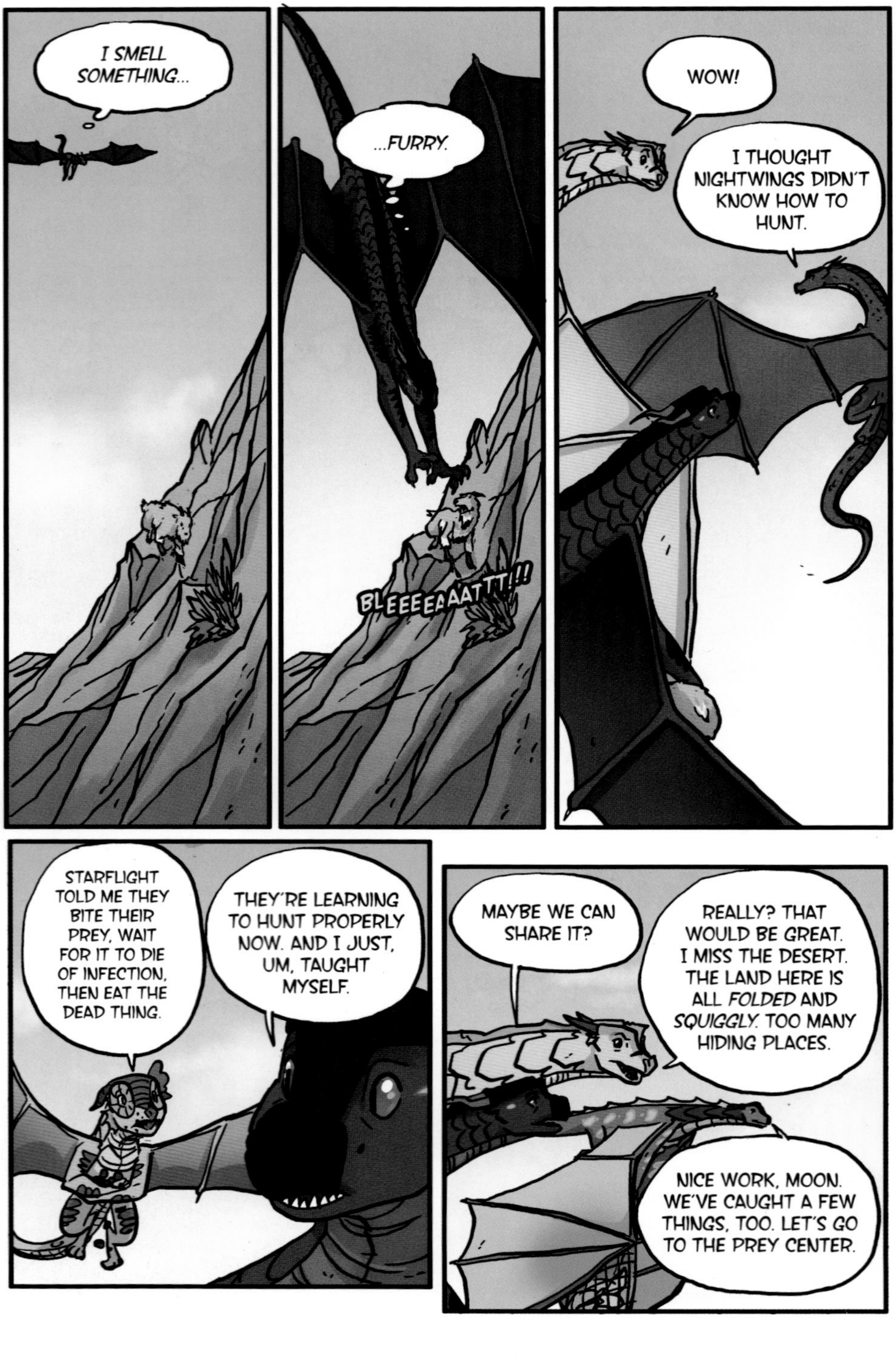
I SMELL SOMETHING...
...FURRY.
BLEEEEAAATTT!!!
WOW!
I THOUGHT NIGHTWINGS DIDN'T KNOW HOW TO HUNT.
STARFLIGHT TOLD ME THEY BITE THEIR PREY, WAIT FOR IT TO DIE OF INFECTION, THEN EAT THE DEAD THING.
THEY'RE LEARNING TO HUNT PROPERLY NOW. AND I JUST, UM, TAUGHT MYSELF.
MAYBE WE CAN SHARE IT?
REALLY? THAT WOULD BE GREAT. I MISS THE DESERT. THE LAND HERE IS ALL *FOLDED* AND *SQUIGGLY*. TOO MANY HIDING PLACES.
NICE WORK, MOON. WE'VE CAUGHT A FEW THINGS, TOO. LET'S *GO* TO THE PREY CENTER.

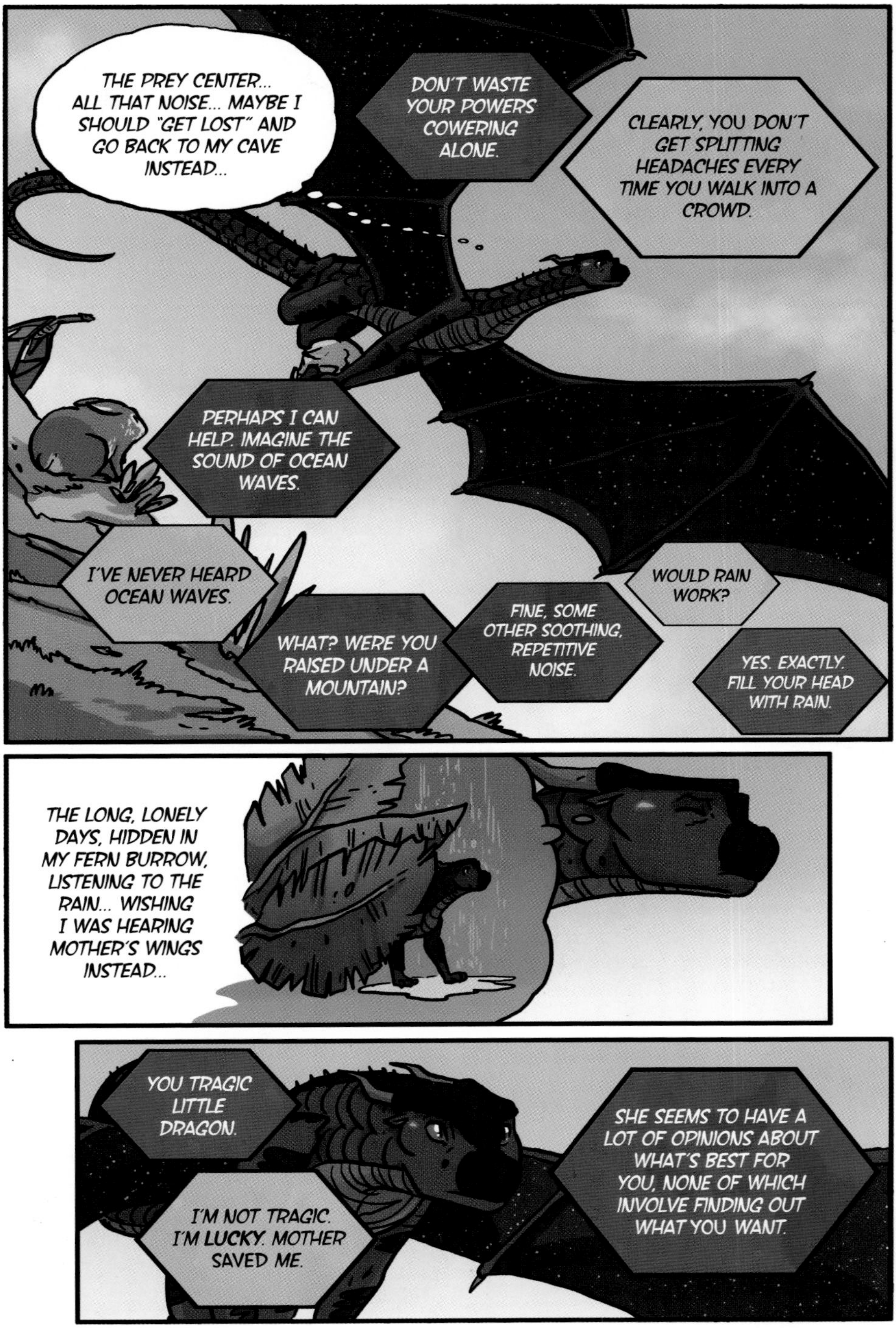
THE PREY CENTER... ALL THAT NOISE... MAYBE I SHOULD "GET LOST" AND GO BACK TO MY CAVE INSTEAD...
DON'T WASTE YOUR POWERS COWERING ALONE.
CLEARLY, YOU DON'T GET SPLITTING HEADACHES EVERY TIME YOU WALK INTO A CROWD.
PERHAPS I CAN HELP. IMAGINE THE SOUND OF OCEAN WAVES.
I'VE NEVER HEARD OCEAN WAVES.
WHAT? WERE YOU RAISED UNDER A MOUNTAIN?
FINE, SOME OTHER SOOTHING, REPETITIVE NOISE.
WOULD RAIN WORK?
YES. EXACTLY. FILL YOUR HEAD WITH RAIN.
THE LONG, LONELY DAYS, HIDDEN IN MY FERN BURROW, LISTENING TO THE RAIN... WISHING I WAS HEARING MOTHER'S WINGS INSTEAD...
YOU TRAGIC LITTLE DRAGON.
I'M NOT TRAGIC. I'M **LUCKY**. MOTHER SAVED ME.
SHE SEEMS TO HAVE A LOT OF OPINIONS ABOUT WHAT'S BEST FOR YOU, NONE OF WHICH INVOLVE FINDING OUT WHAT YOU WANT.

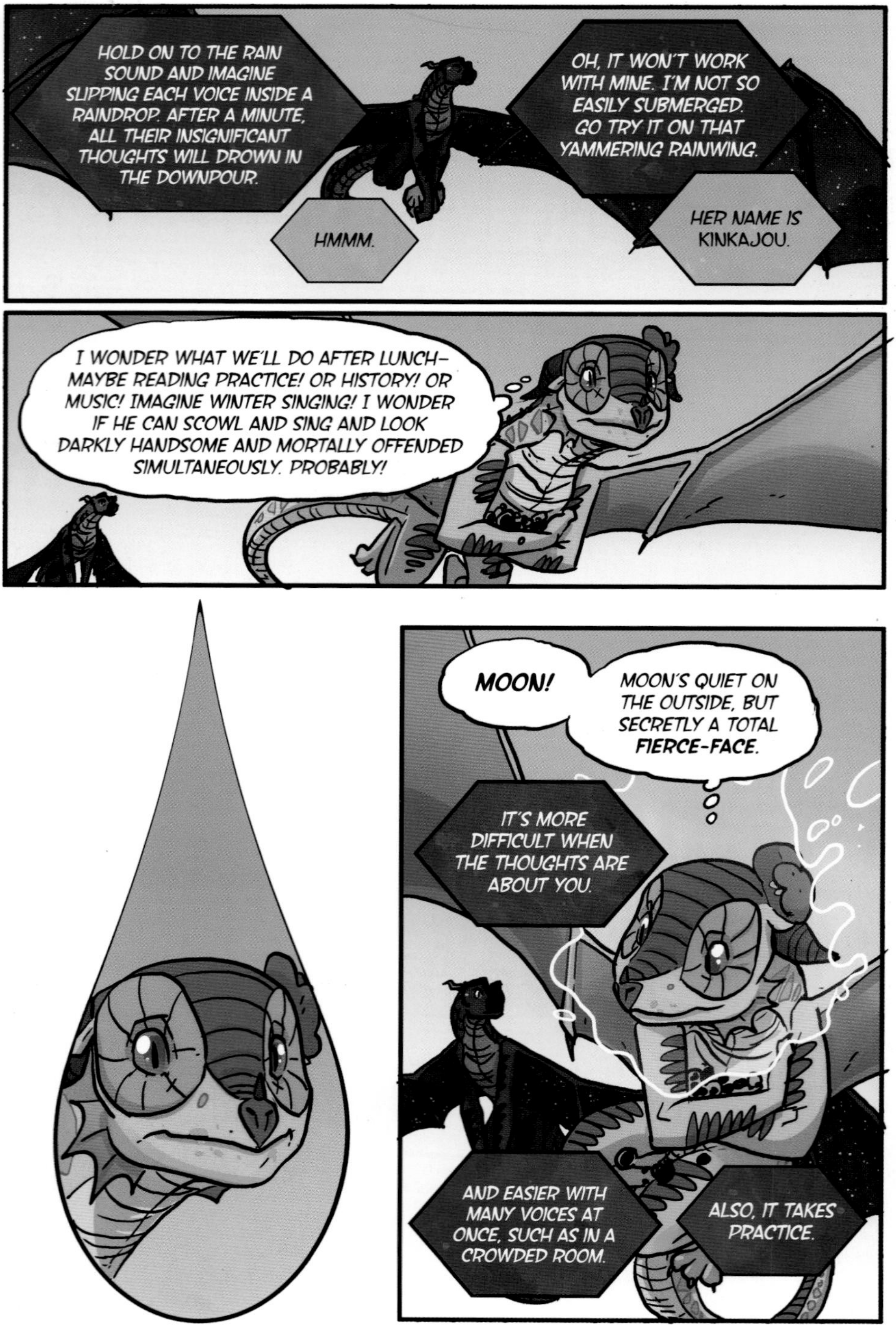
HOLD ON TO THE RAIN SOUND AND IMAGINE SLIPPING EACH VOICE INSIDE A RAINDROP. AFTER A MINUTE, ALL THEIR INSIGNIFICANT THOUGHTS WILL DROWN IN THE DOWNPOUR.
HMMM.
OH, IT WON'T WORK WITH MINE. I'M NOT SO EASILY SUBMERGED. GO TRY IT ON THAT YAMMERING RAINWING.
HER NAME IS KINKAJOU.
I WONDER WHAT WE'LL DO AFTER LUNCH— MAYBE READING PRACTICE! OR HISTORY! OR MUSIC! IMAGINE WINTER SINGING! I WONDER IF HE CAN SCOWL AND SING AND LOOK DARKLY HANDSOME AND MORTALLY OFFENDED SIMULTANEOUSLY. PROBABLY!
MOON!
MOON'S QUIET ON THE OUTSIDE, BUT SECRETLY A TOTAL FIERCE-FACE.
IT'S MORE DIFFICULT WHEN THE THOUGHTS ARE ABOUT YOU.
AND EASIER WITH MANY VOICES AT ONCE, SUCH AS IN A CROWDED ROOM.
ALSO, IT TAKES PRACTICE.

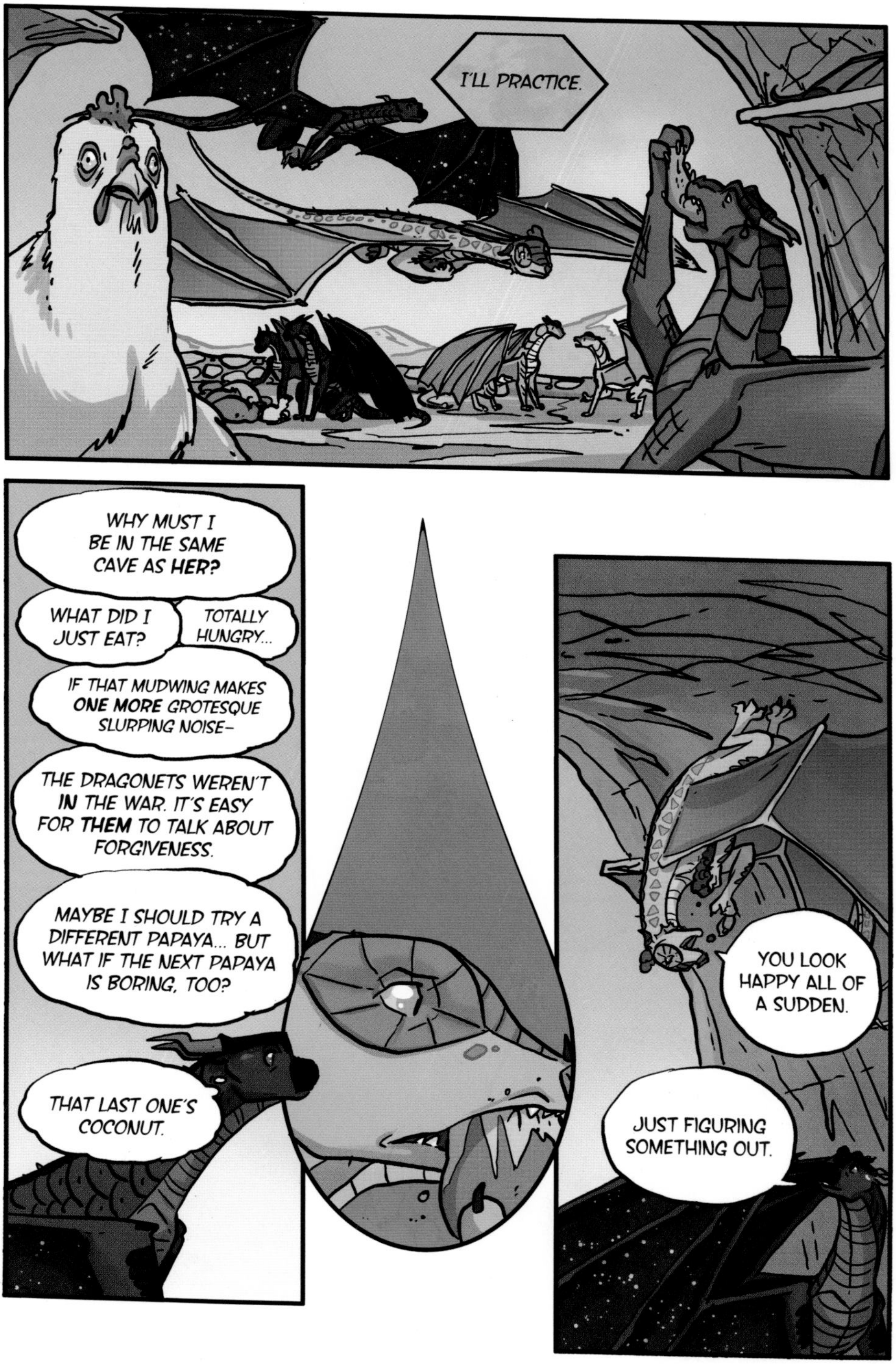
I'LL PRACTICE.
WHY MUST I BE IN THE SAME CAVE AS HER?
WHAT DID I JUST EAT?
TOTALLY HUNGRY...
IF THAT MUDWING MAKES ONE MORE GROTESQUE SLURPING NOISE–
THE DRAGONETS WEREN'T IN THE WAR. IT'S EASY FOR THEM TO TALK ABOUT FORGIVENESS.
MAYBE I SHOULD TRY A DIFFERENT PAPAYA... BUT WHAT IF THE NEXT PAPAYA IS BORING, TOO?
THAT LAST ONE'S COCONUT.
YOU LOOK HAPPY ALL OF A SUDDEN.
JUST FIGURING SOMETHING OUT.

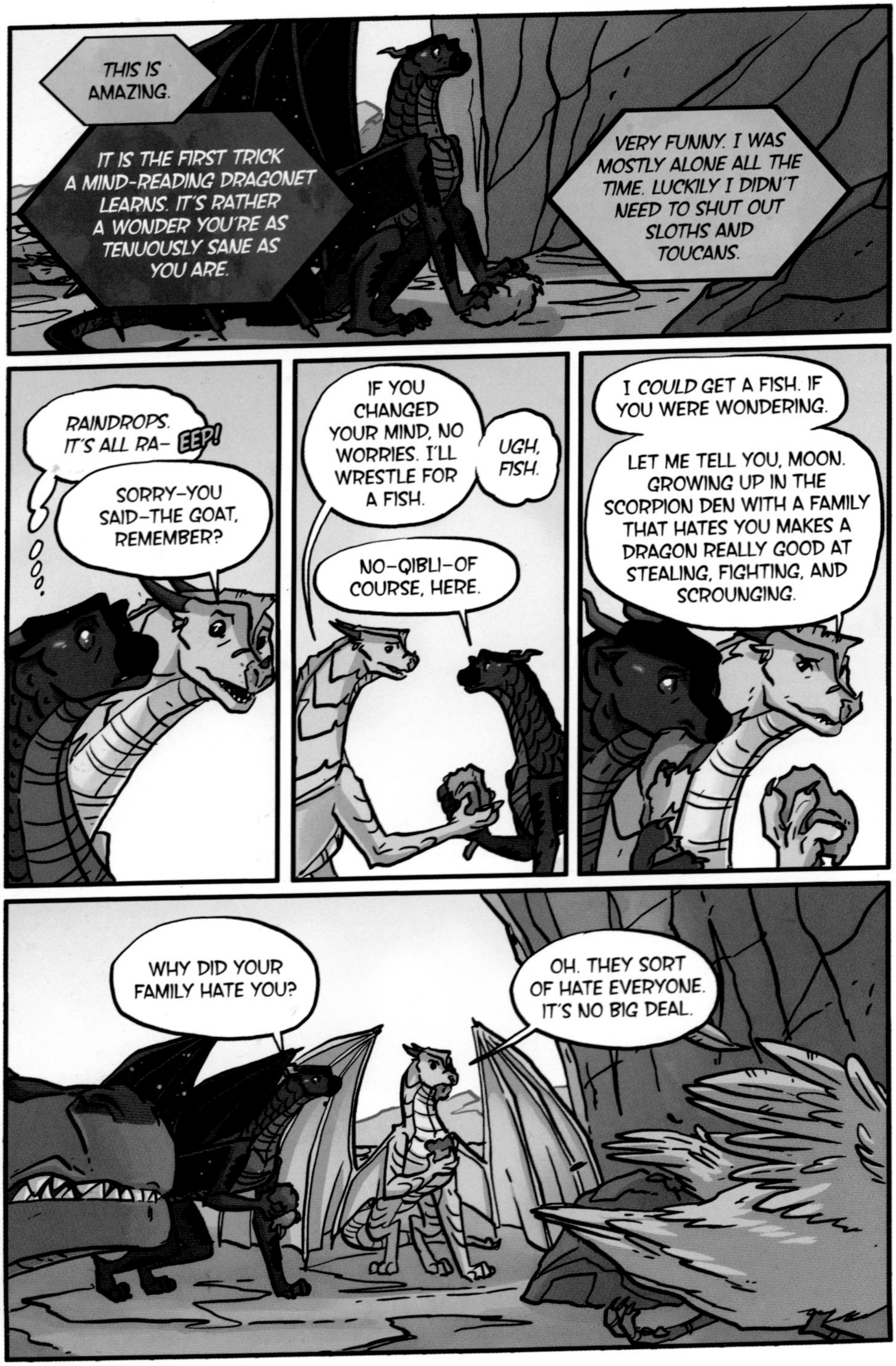
THIS IS AMAZING.
IT IS THE FIRST TRICK A MIND-READING DRAGONET LEARNS. IT'S RATHER A WONDER YOU'RE AS TENUOUSLY SANE AS YOU ARE.
VERY FUNNY. I WAS MOSTLY ALONE ALL THE TIME. LUCKILY I DIDN'T NEED TO SHUT OUT SLOTHS AND TOUCANS.
RAINDROPS. IT'S ALL RA- EEP!
SORRY-YOU SAID-THE GOAT, REMEMBER?
IF YOU CHANGED YOUR MIND, NO WORRIES. I'LL WRESTLE FOR A FISH.
UGH, FISH.
NO-QIBLI-OF COURSE, HERE.
I COULD GET A FISH. IF YOU WERE WONDERING.
LET ME TELL YOU, MOON. GROWING UP IN THE SCORPION DEN WITH A FAMILY THAT HATES YOU MAKES A DRAGON REALLY GOOD AT STEALING, FIGHTING, AND SCROUNGING.
WHY DID YOUR FAMILY HATE YOU?
OH. THEY SORT OF HATE EVERYONE. IT'S NO BIG DEAL.

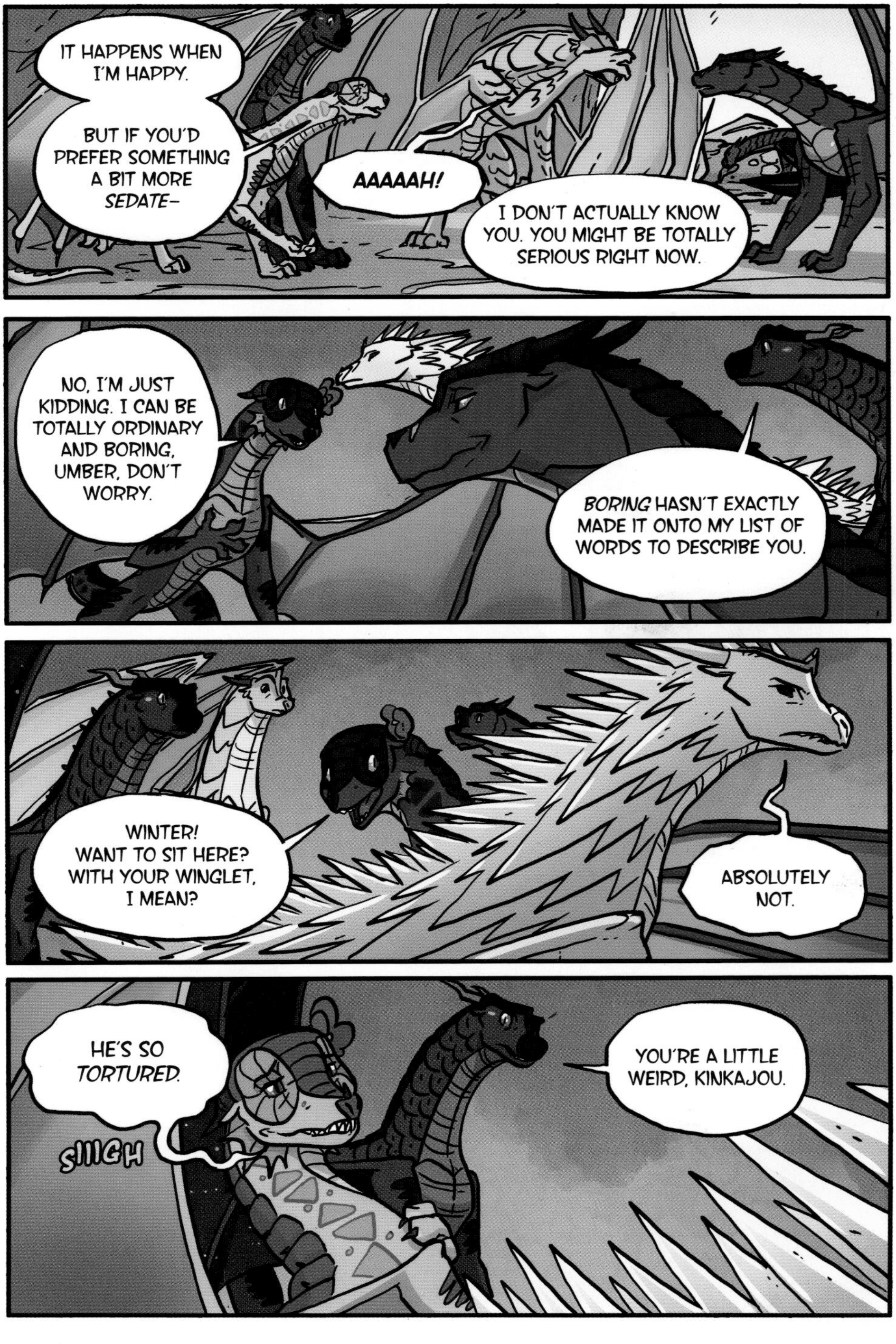
IT HAPPENS WHEN I'M HAPPY.
BUT IF YOU'D PREFER SOMETHING A BIT MORE *SEDATE*–
AAAAAH!
I DON'T ACTUALLY KNOW YOU. YOU MIGHT BE TOTALLY SERIOUS RIGHT NOW.
NO, I'M JUST KIDDING. I CAN BE TOTALLY ORDINARY AND BORING, UMBER, DON'T WORRY.
BORING HASN'T EXACTLY MADE IT ONTO MY LIST OF WORDS TO DESCRIBE YOU.
WINTER! WANT TO SIT HERE? WITH YOUR WINGLET, I MEAN?
ABSOLUTELY NOT.
HE'S SO *TORTURED*.
SIIIGH
YOU'RE A LITTLE WEIRD, KINKAJOU.

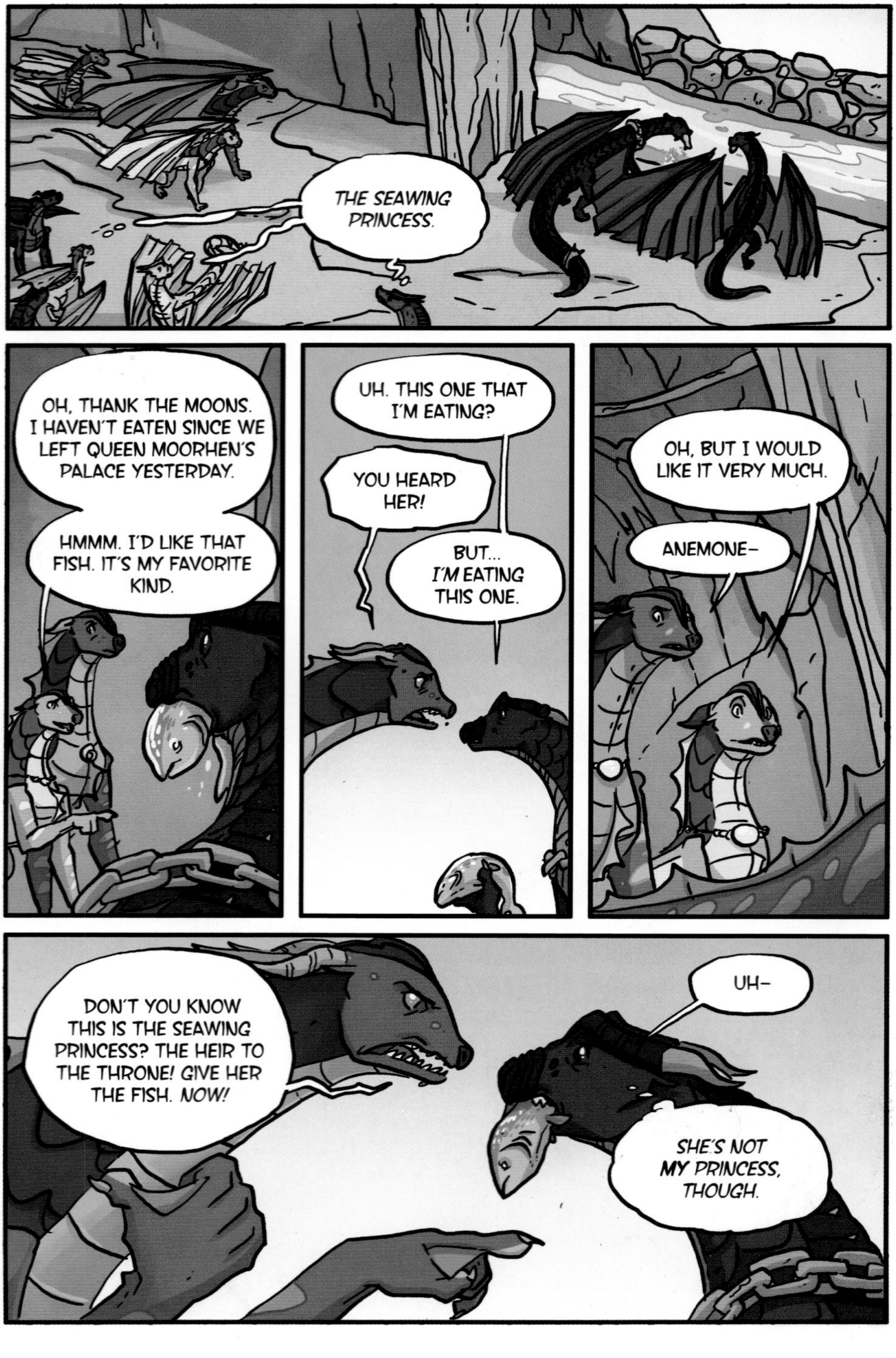
THE SEAWING PRINCESS.
OH, THANK THE MOONS. I HAVEN'T EATEN SINCE WE LEFT QUEEN MOORHEN'S PALACE YESTERDAY.
HMMM. I'D LIKE THAT FISH. IT'S MY FAVORITE KIND.
UH. THIS ONE THAT I'M EATING?
YOU HEARD HER!
BUT... *I'M* EATING THIS ONE.
OH, BUT I WOULD LIKE IT VERY MUCH.
ANEMONE–
DON'T YOU KNOW THIS IS THE SEAWING PRINCESS? THE HEIR TO THE THRONE! GIVE HER THE FISH. *NOW!*
UH–
SHE'S NOT **MY** *PRINCESS, THOUGH.*

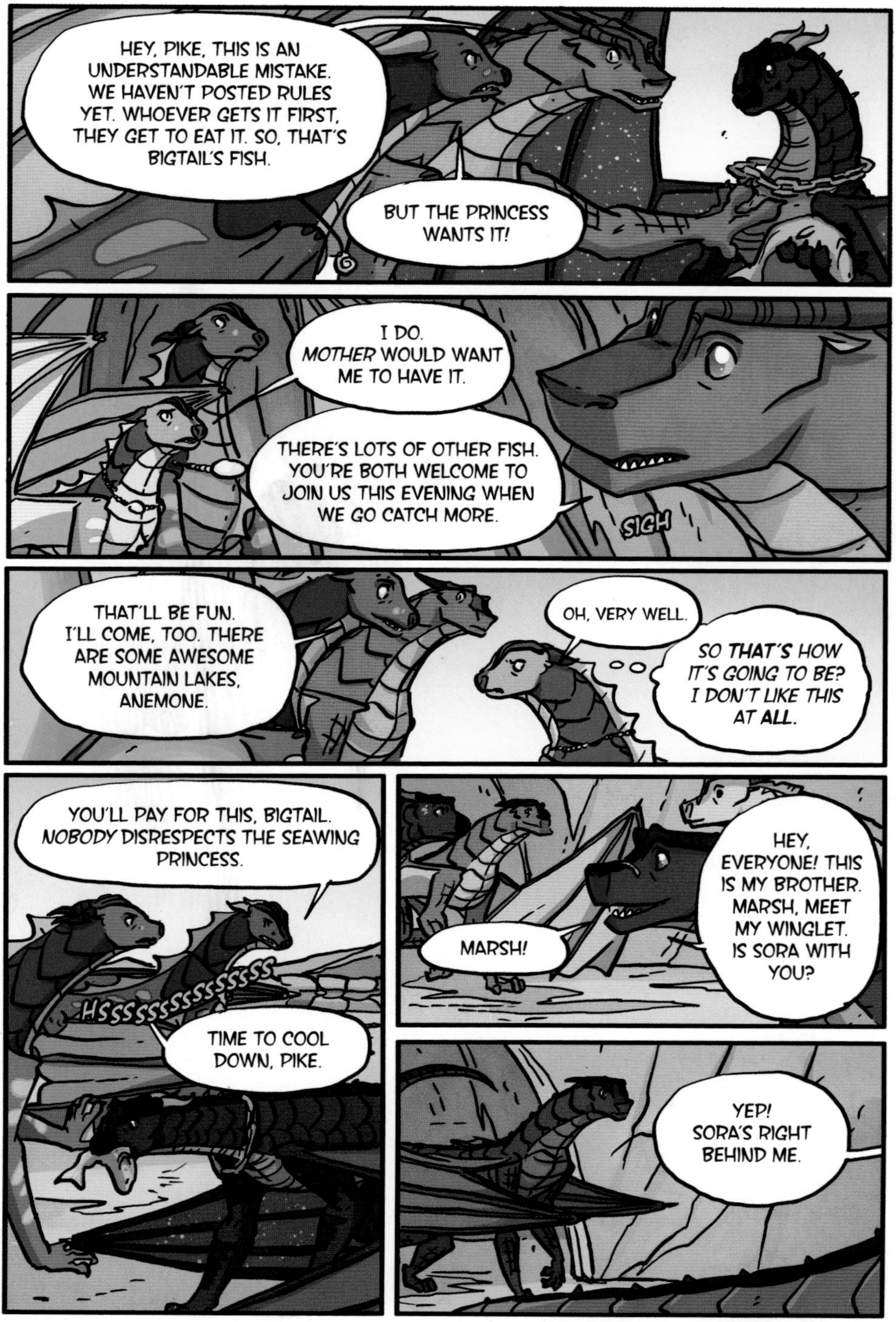
HEY, PIKE, THIS IS AN UNDERSTANDABLE MISTAKE. WE HAVEN'T POSTED RULES YET. WHOEVER GETS IT FIRST, THEY GET TO EAT IT. SO, THAT'S BIGTAIL'S FISH.
BUT THE PRINCESS WANTS IT!
I DO. *MOTHER* WOULD WANT ME TO HAVE IT.
THERE'S LOTS OF OTHER FISH. YOU'RE BOTH WELCOME TO JOIN US THIS EVENING WHEN WE GO CATCH MORE.
SIGH
THAT'LL BE FUN. I'LL COME, TOO. THERE ARE SOME AWESOME MOUNTAIN LAKES, ANEMONE.
OH, VERY WELL.
*SO **THAT'S** HOW IT'S GOING TO BE? I DON'T LIKE THIS AT **ALL**.*
YOU'LL PAY FOR THIS, BIGTAIL. *NOBODY* DISRESPECTS THE SEAWING PRINCESS.
HSSSSSSSSSSSSSSSS
TIME TO COOL DOWN, PIKE.
MARSH!
HEY, EVERYONE! THIS IS MY BROTHER. MARSH, MEET MY WINGLET. IS SORA WITH YOU?
YEP! SORA'S RIGHT BEHIND ME.

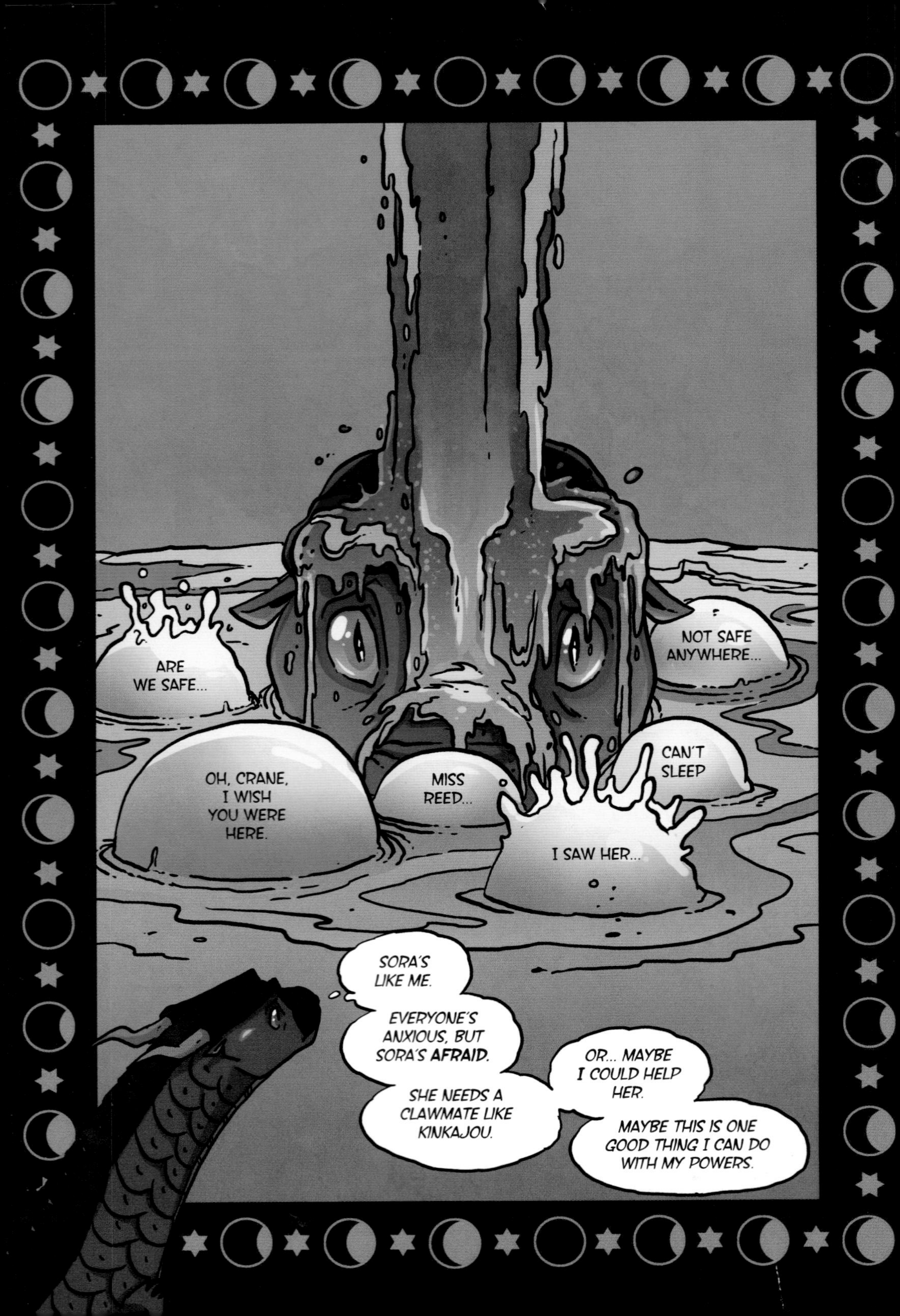
ARE WE SAFE...
NOT SAFE ANYWHERE...
OH, CRANE, I WISH YOU WERE HERE.
MISS REED...
CAN'T SLEEP
I SAW HER...
SORA'S LIKE ME.
EVERYONE'S ANXIOUS, BUT SORA'S **AFRAID**.
SHE NEEDS A CLAWMATE LIKE KINKAJOU.
OR... MAYBE I COULD HELP HER.
MAYBE THIS IS ONE GOOD THING I CAN DO WITH MY POWERS.

I'M MOON, REMEMBER? WOULD YOU LIKE SOME GOAT?

THANK YOU.

UMBER! MARSH! SORA!

CLAY!

HEY, CLAY.

HI.

WHO'S IN YOUR WINGLET, SORA? YOU'RE IN GOLD, RIGHT?

THERE'S A RAINWING WHO SEEMS NICE. SHE'S BLIND.

THAT'S TAMARIN!

TAMARIN'S MY BEST FRIEND.

BEST FRIEND? HA, THAT'S OKAY. KINKAJOU PROBABLY HAS **LOTS** OF BEST FRIENDS.

POSSIBLY SIX MORE BY THE END OF LUNCHTIME.

A SANDWING NAMED ONYX... A SKYWING WITH A BAD SCAR... THAT SEAWING, PIKE, AND A NIGHTWING CALLED BIGTAIL...

PIKE AND BIGTAIL— THEY WERE JUST FIGHTING.

PIKE FOUGHT WITH CARNELIAN THE DAY WE GOT HERE, TOO.

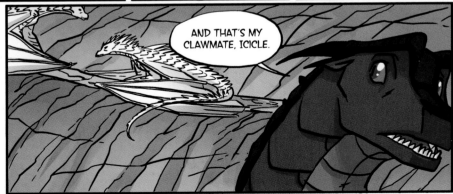

AND THAT'S MY CLAWMATE, ICICLE.

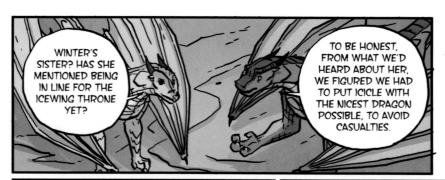

WINTER'S SISTER? HAS SHE MENTIONED BEING IN LINE FOR THE ICEWING THRONE YET?

TO BE HONEST, FROM WHAT WE'D HEARD ABOUT HER, WE FIGURED WE HAD TO PUT ICICLE WITH THE NICEST DRAGON POSSIBLE, TO AVOID CASUALTIES.

I HOPE IT'S GOING ALL RIGHT, SORA.

IT'S FINE, CLAY.

NOD

LET ME KNOW IF IT'S NOT. IT'S IMPORTANT TO ME THAT YOU BE HAPPY HERE.

DON'T WE HAVE HISTORY TOGETHER NEXT, SORA? OUR WINGLETS TOGETHER?

OH...

I HAVE TO GO TO THE LIBRARY FIRST. UM, SORA... DO YOU WANT TO COME WITH ME?

I DO.

THAT WAS NICE OF MOON.

AW, MAYBE THEY'LL BE FRIENDS.

DOES MOON LIKE SORA BETTER THAN ME?

MY BORING LITTLE CLAWMATE WITH A NIGHTWING? WHAT'S THAT ALL ABOUT?

...

UM... THE LIBRARY IS GREAT, ISN'T IT?

I LIKE THE LEAF WINDOWS.

ME TOO.

NOD

IS THIS WHAT I SEEM LIKE? SHY AND REALLY HARD TO TALK TO?

IT'S EASY TO TALK TO MY MYSTERY FRIEND... BUT I DON'T HAVE TO HIDE ANYTHING FROM HIM. I GUESS I COULDN'T, EVEN IF I WANTED TO.

HELLO?

IT'S MOON AND SORA.

OH, HI. SORA, I FOUND THAT SCROLL ON ICEWINGS FOR YOU.

LIBRARIAN

...FIGURING OUT MY CLAWMATE...

HOW ARE YOU, MOON? HOW WAS CLASS THIS MORNING?

TERRIFYING.

ALL RIGHT- INTERESTING.

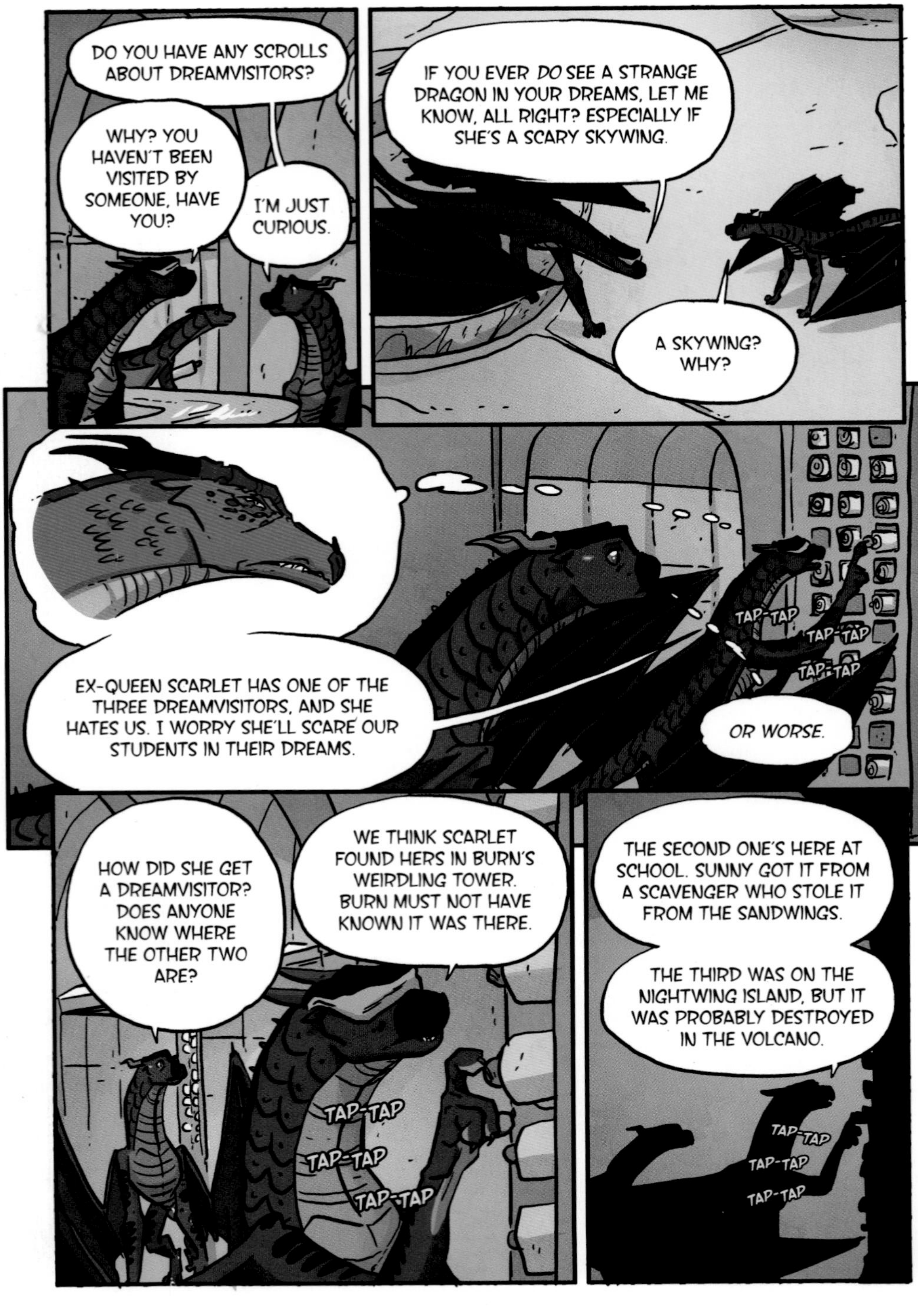
DO YOU HAVE ANY SCROLLS ABOUT DREAMVISITORS?
WHY? YOU HAVEN'T BEEN VISITED BY SOMEONE, HAVE YOU?
I'M JUST CURIOUS.
IF YOU EVER *DO* SEE A STRANGE DRAGON IN YOUR DREAMS, LET ME KNOW, ALL RIGHT? ESPECIALLY IF SHE'S A SCARY SKYWING.
A SKYWING? WHY?
EX-QUEEN SCARLET HAS ONE OF THE THREE DREAMVISITORS, AND SHE HATES US. I WORRY SHE'LL SCARE OUR STUDENTS IN THEIR DREAMS.
TAP-TAP
TAP-TAP
TAP-TAP
OR WORSE.
HOW DID SHE GET A DREAMVISITOR? DOES ANYONE KNOW WHERE THE OTHER TWO ARE?
WE THINK SCARLET FOUND HERS IN BURN'S WEIRDLING TOWER. BURN MUST NOT HAVE KNOWN IT WAS THERE.
TAP-TAP
TAP-TAP
TAP-TAP
THE SECOND ONE'S HERE AT SCHOOL. SUNNY GOT IT FROM A SCAVENGER WHO STOLE IT FROM THE SANDWINGS.
THE THIRD WAS ON THE NIGHTWING ISLAND, BUT IT WAS PROBABLY DESTROYED IN THE VOLCANO.
TAP-TAP
TAP-TAP
TAP-TAP

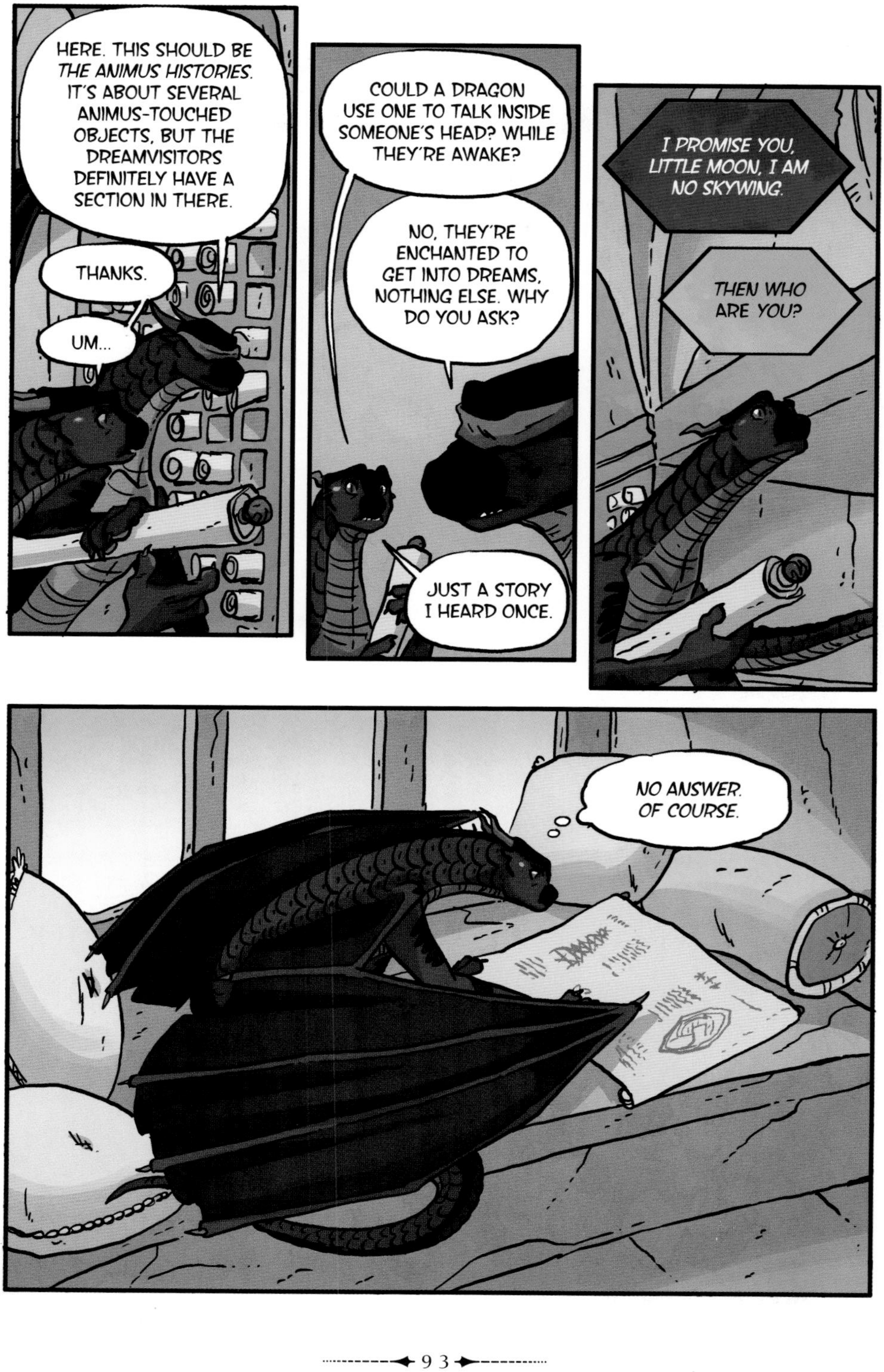
HERE. THIS SHOULD BE *THE ANIMUS HISTORIES*. IT'S ABOUT SEVERAL ANIMUS-TOUCHED OBJECTS, BUT THE DREAMVISITORS DEFINITELY HAVE A SECTION IN THERE.
THANKS.
UM...
COULD A DRAGON USE ONE TO TALK INSIDE SOMEONE'S HEAD? WHILE THEY'RE AWAKE?
NO, THEY'RE ENCHANTED TO GET INTO DREAMS, NOTHING ELSE. WHY DO YOU ASK?
JUST A STORY I HEARD ONCE.
I PROMISE YOU, LITTLE MOON, I AM NO SKYWING.
THEN WHO ARE YOU?
NO ANSWER. OF COURSE.

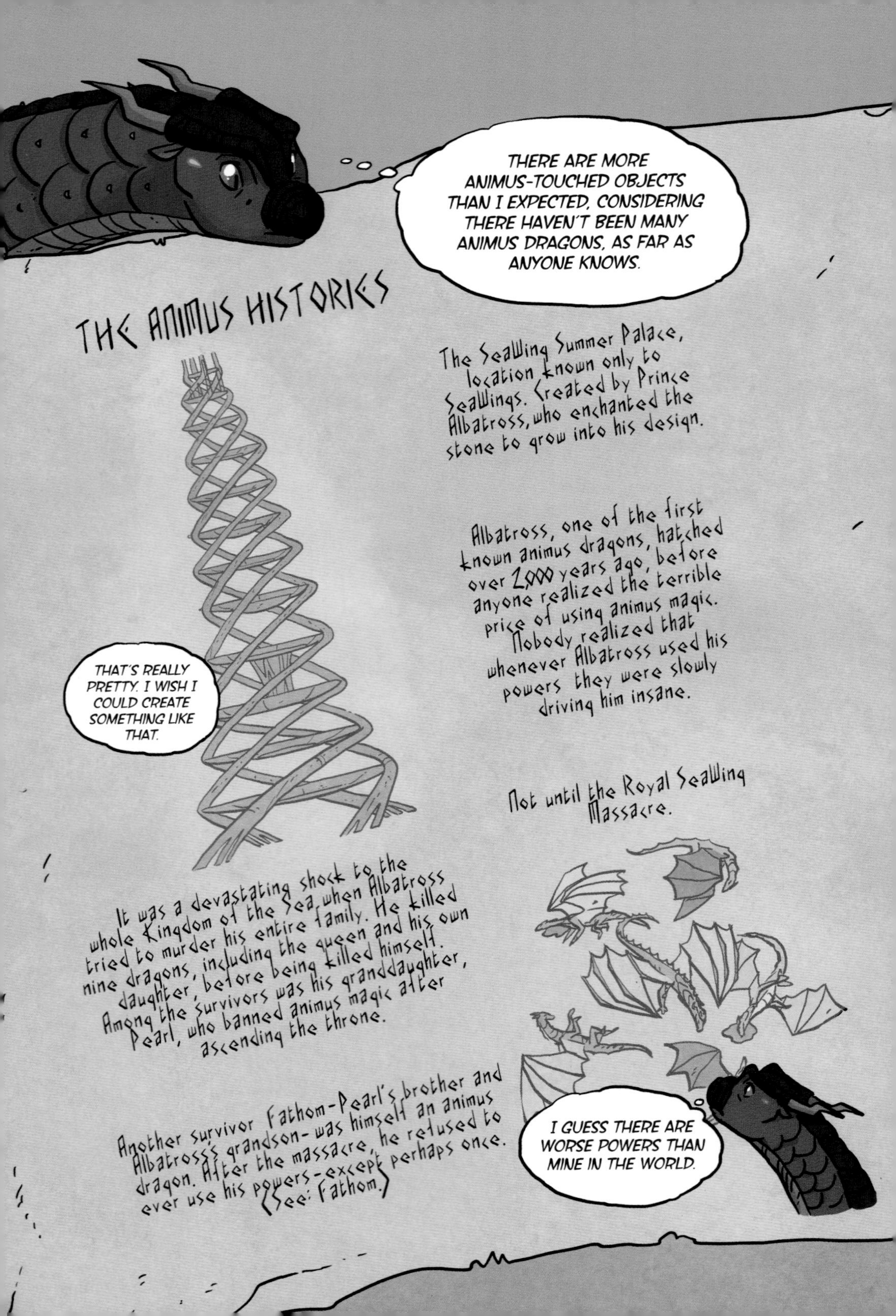

THERE ARE MORE ANIMUS-TOUCHED OBJECTS THAN I EXPECTED, CONSIDERING THERE HAVEN'T BEEN MANY ANIMUS DRAGONS, AS FAR AS ANYONE KNOWS.
THE ANIMUS HISTORIES
The SeaWing Summer Palace, location known only to SeaWings. Created by Prince Albatross, who enchanted the stone to grow into his design.
THAT'S REALLY PRETTY. I WISH I COULD CREATE SOMETHING LIKE THAT.
Albatross, one of the first known animus dragons, hatched over 2,000 years ago, before anyone realized the terrible price of using animus magic. Nobody realized that whenever Albatross used his powers they were slowly driving him insane.
Not until the Royal SeaWing Massacre.
It was a devastating shock to the whole Kingdom of the Sea when Albatross tried to murder his entire family. He killed nine dragons, including the queen and his own daughter, before being killed himself. Among the survivors was his granddaughter, Pearl, who banned animus magic after ascending the throne.
Another survivor Fathom-Pearl's brother and Albatross's grandson-was himself an animus dragon. After the massacre, he refused to ever use his powers-except perhaps once. (See: Fathom.)
I GUESS THERE ARE WORSE POWERS THAN MINE IN THE WORLD.

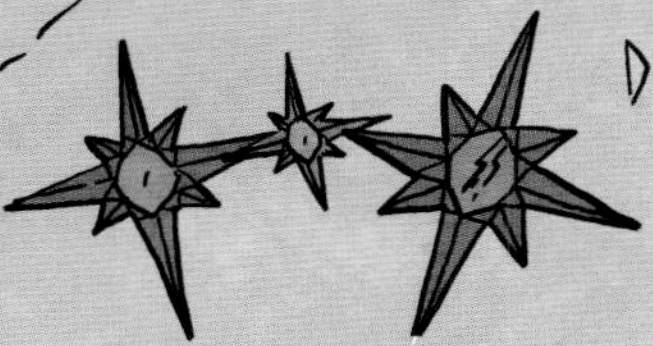

Dreamvisitors, enchanted by the first known NightWing animus dragon, Darkstalker.

The formidable Darkstalker also possessed the powers of mind reading and prophecy. He created three dreamvisitors—one for himself, one for his best friend (see: Fathom), and one for his beloved, Clearsight.

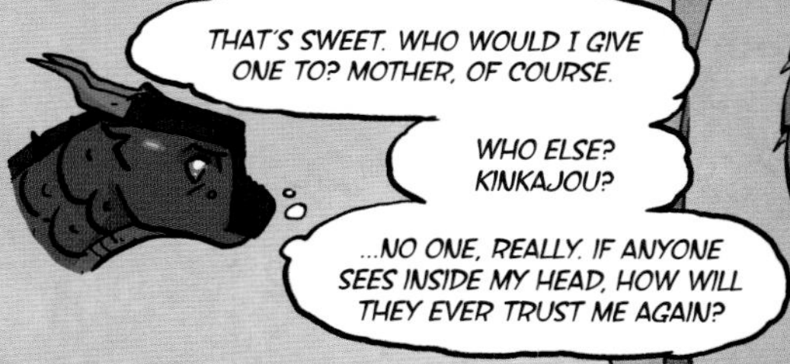
THAT'S SWEET. WHO WOULD I GIVE ONE TO? MOTHER, OF COURSE.
WHO ELSE? KINKAJOU?
...NO ONE, REALLY. IF ANYONE SEES INSIDE MY HEAD, HOW WILL THEY EVER TRUST ME AGAIN?

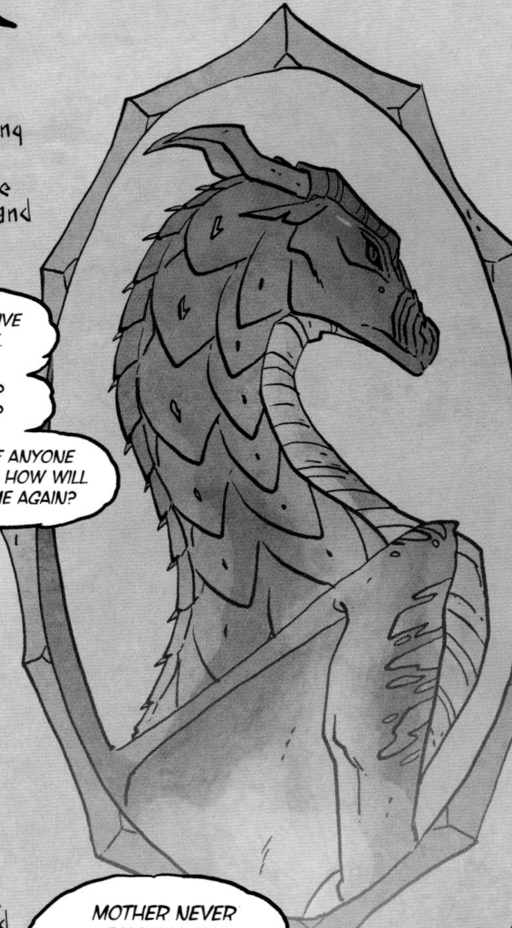

Ultimately, Darkstalker grew too powerful and ambitious. He claimed he'd made himself immortal. Rumor said he planned to overthrow the NightWing queen. After he killed his father with a previously unknown aspect of animus power, the tribe agreed: He was too dangerous to be free.

Darkstalker and Clearsight disappeared together and were probably killed at the same time. Details are lost, but it's believed Darkstalker was defeated by an animus touched object created by Fathom the only time Fathom used his power.

Fearful of Darkstalker's return, the NightWings moved to a new, secret home. Some believe the ghost stories that say he will rise again, seeking revenge...

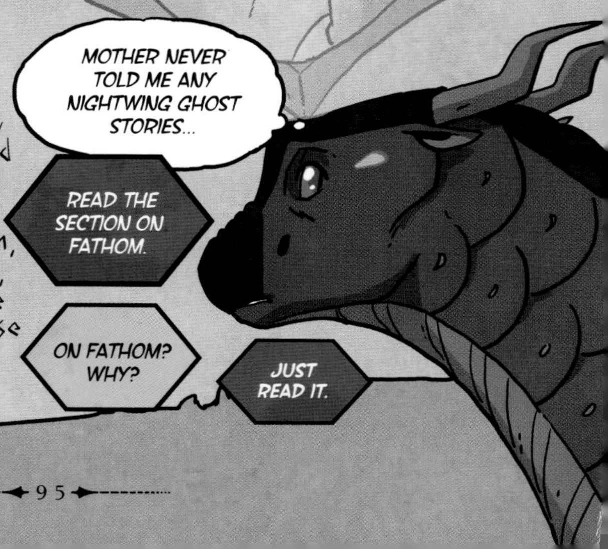
MOTHER NEVER TOLD ME ANY NIGHTWING GHOST STORIES...
READ THE SECTION ON FATHOM.
ON FATHOM? WHY?
JUST READ IT.

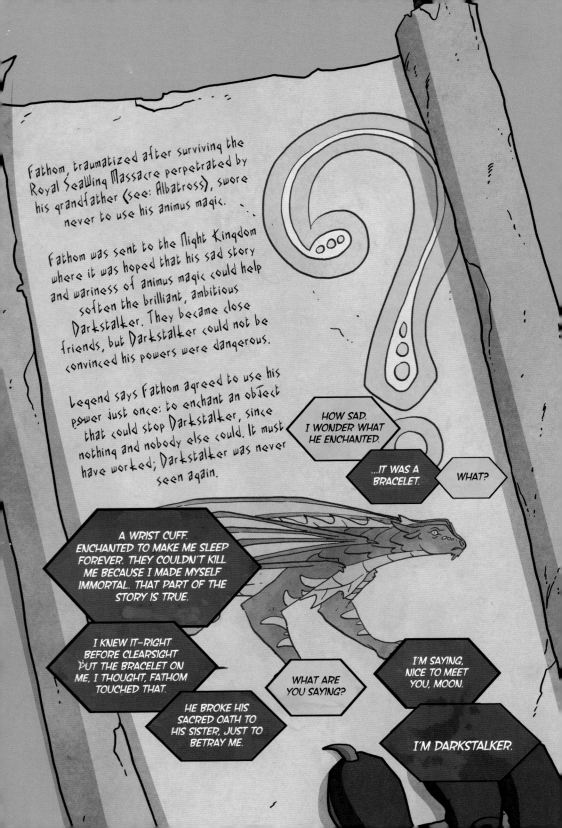

Fathom, traumatized after surviving the Royal SeaWing Massacre perpetrated by his grandfather (see: Albatross), swore never to use his animus magic.

Fathom was sent to the Night Kingdom where it was hoped that his sad story and wariness of animus magic could help soften the brilliant, ambitious Darkstalker. They became close friends, but Darkstalker could not be convinced his powers were dangerous.

Legend says Fathom agreed to use his power just once: to enchant an object that could stop Darkstalker, since nothing and nobody else could. It must have worked; Darkstalker was never seen again.

HOW SAD. I WONDER WHAT HE ENCHANTED.

...IT WAS A BRACELET.

WHAT?

A WRIST CUFF. ENCHANTED TO MAKE ME SLEEP FOREVER. THEY COULDN'T KILL ME BECAUSE I MADE MYSELF IMMORTAL. THAT PART OF THE STORY IS TRUE.

I KNEW IT—RIGHT BEFORE CLEARSIGHT PUT THE BRACELET ON ME, I THOUGHT, FATHOM TOUCHED THAT.

WHAT ARE YOU SAYING?

I'M SAYING, NICE TO MEET YOU, MOON.

HE BROKE HIS SACRED OATH TO HIS SISTER, JUST TO BETRAY ME.

I'M DARKSTALKER.

PART TWO: STAY HIDDEN

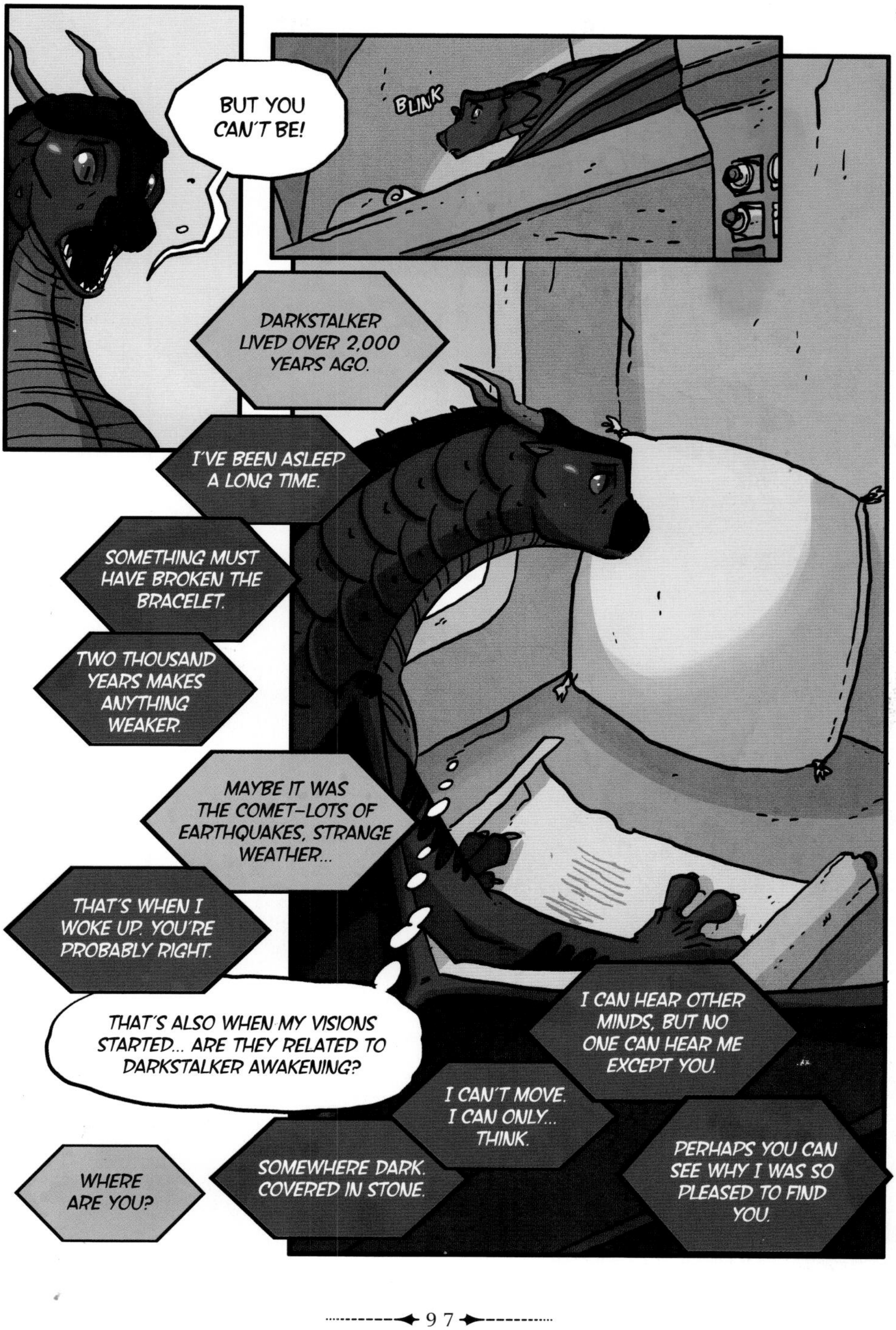

BUT YOU CAN'T BE!
BLINK
DARKSTALKER LIVED OVER 2,000 YEARS AGO.
I'VE BEEN ASLEEP A LONG TIME.
SOMETHING MUST HAVE BROKEN THE BRACELET.
TWO THOUSAND YEARS MAKES ANYTHING WEAKER.
MAYBE IT WAS THE COMET–LOTS OF EARTHQUAKES, STRANGE WEATHER...
THAT'S WHEN I WOKE UP. YOU'RE PROBABLY RIGHT.
THAT'S ALSO WHEN MY VISIONS STARTED... ARE THEY RELATED TO DARKSTALKER AWAKENING?
I CAN HEAR OTHER MINDS, BUT NO ONE CAN HEAR ME EXCEPT YOU.
I CAN'T MOVE. I CAN ONLY... THINK.
PERHAPS YOU CAN SEE WHY I WAS SO PLEASED TO FIND YOU.
WHERE ARE YOU?
SOMEWHERE DARK. COVERED IN STONE.

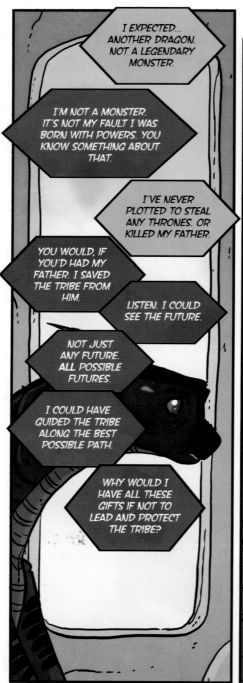

I EXPECTED... ANOTHER DRAGON. NOT A LEGENDARY MONSTER.

I'M NOT A MONSTER. IT'S NOT MY FAULT I WAS BORN WITH POWERS. YOU KNOW SOMETHING ABOUT THAT.

I'VE NEVER PLOTTED TO STEAL ANY THRONES. OR KILLED MY FATHER.

YOU WOULD, IF YOU'D HAD MY FATHER. I SAVED THE TRIBE FROM HIM.

LISTEN. I COULD SEE THE FUTURE.

NOT JUST ANY FUTURE. ALL POSSIBLE FUTURES.

I COULD HAVE GUIDED THE TRIBE ALONG THE BEST POSSIBLE PATH.

WHY WOULD I HAVE ALL THESE GIFTS IF NOT TO LEAD AND PROTECT THE TRIBE?

I SAW FUTURES WHERE I WAS A BENEVOLENT, BELOVED KING, MARRIED TO CLEARSIGHT, WITH SIX DRAGONETS.

CLEARSIGHT SAW THOSE FUTURES, TOO. HER GIFT OF PROPHECY WAS AS STRONG AS MINE.

...BUT SHE ALSO SAW FUTURES WHERE I TURNED EVIL. SHE DIDN'T BELIEVE I COULD AVOID THEM.

IN THE END, I GUESS SHE DIDN'T BELIEVE IN ME AT ALL.

I WONDER WHAT HAPPENED TO HER.

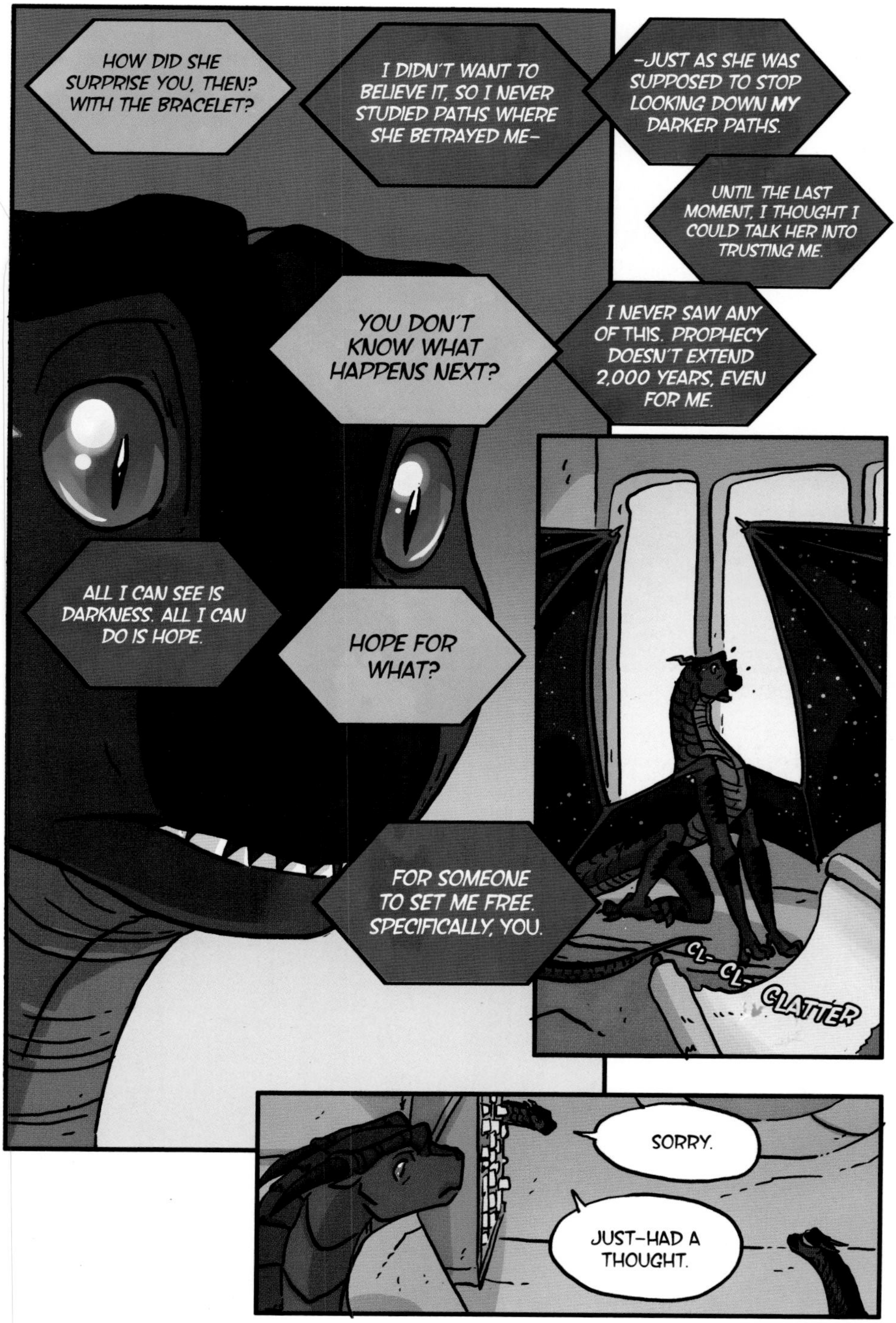
HOW DID SHE SURPRISE YOU, THEN? WITH THE BRACELET?
I DIDN'T WANT TO BELIEVE IT, SO I NEVER STUDIED PATHS WHERE SHE BETRAYED ME–
–JUST AS SHE WAS SUPPOSED TO STOP LOOKING DOWN MY DARKER PATHS.
UNTIL THE LAST MOMENT, I THOUGHT I COULD TALK HER INTO TRUSTING ME.
YOU DON'T KNOW WHAT HAPPENS NEXT?
I NEVER SAW ANY OF THIS. PROPHECY DOESN'T EXTEND 2,000 YEARS, EVEN FOR ME.
ALL I CAN SEE IS DARKNESS. ALL I CAN DO IS HOPE.
HOPE FOR WHAT?
FOR SOMEONE TO SET ME FREE. SPECIFICALLY, YOU.
CL- CL- CLATTER
SORRY.
JUST–HAD A THOUGHT.

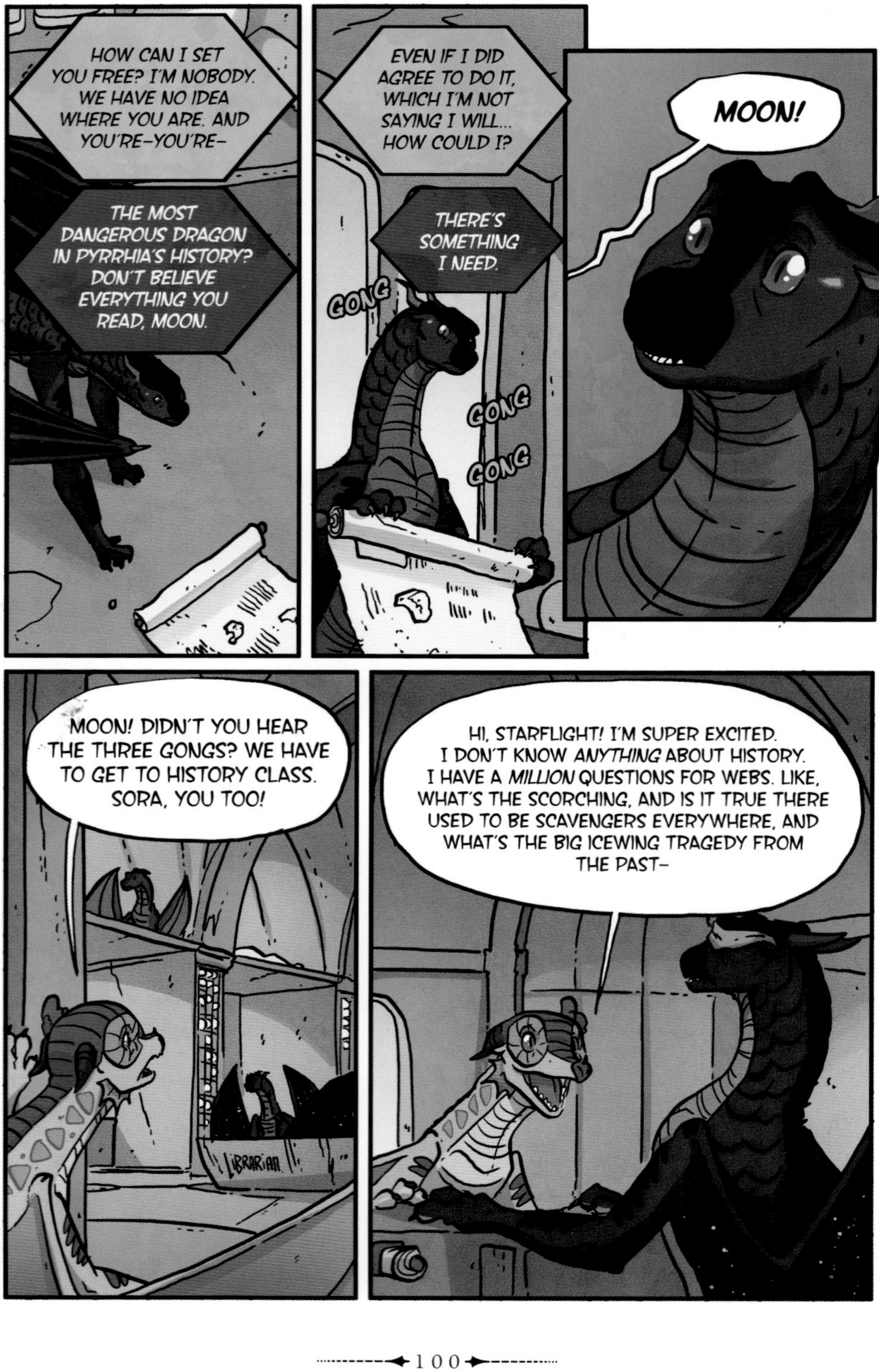
HOW CAN I SET YOU FREE? I'M NOBODY. WE HAVE NO IDEA WHERE YOU ARE. AND YOU'RE—YOU'RE—
THE MOST DANGEROUS DRAGON IN PYRRHIA'S HISTORY? DON'T BELIEVE EVERYTHING YOU READ, MOON.
EVEN IF I DID AGREE TO DO IT, WHICH I'M NOT SAYING I WILL... HOW COULD I?
THERE'S SOMETHING I NEED.
GONG
GONG
GONG
MOON!
MOON! DIDN'T YOU HEAR THE THREE GONGS? WE HAVE TO GET TO HISTORY CLASS. SORA, YOU TOO!
LIBRARIAN
HI, STARFLIGHT! I'M SUPER EXCITED. I DON'T KNOW *ANYTHING* ABOUT HISTORY. I HAVE A *MILLION* QUESTIONS FOR WEBS. LIKE, WHAT'S THE SCORCHING, AND IS IT TRUE THERE USED TO BE SCAVENGERS EVERYWHERE, AND WHAT'S THE BIG ICEWING TRAGEDY FROM THE PAST—

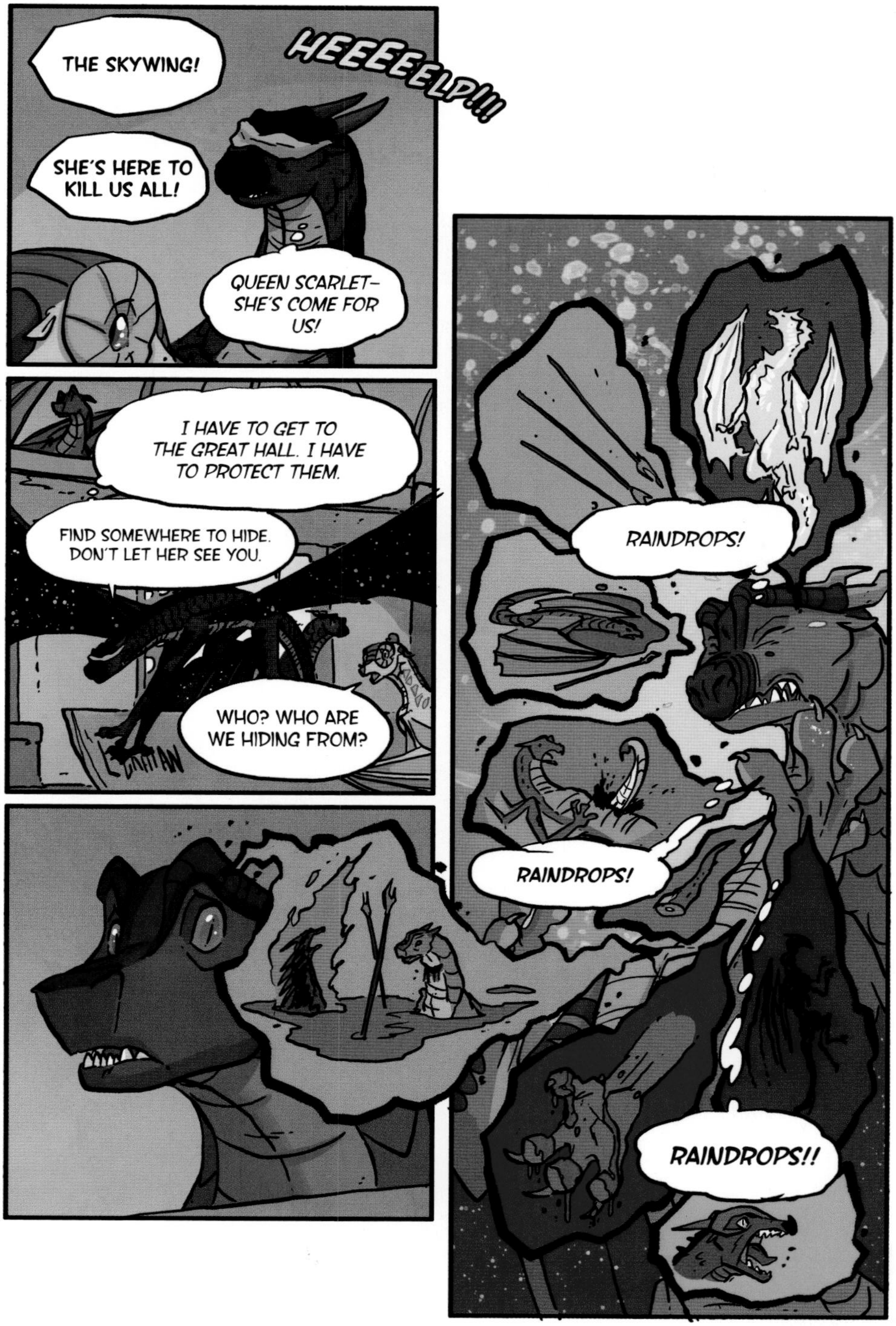
THE SKYWING!
HEEEEEELP!!!
SHE'S HERE TO KILL US ALL!
QUEEN SCARLET— SHE'S COME FOR US!
I HAVE TO GET TO THE GREAT HALL. I HAVE TO PROTECT THEM.
FIND SOMEWHERE TO HIDE. DON'T LET HER SEE YOU.
WHO? WHO ARE WE HIDING FROM?
RAINDROPS!
RAINDROPS!
RAINDROPS!!

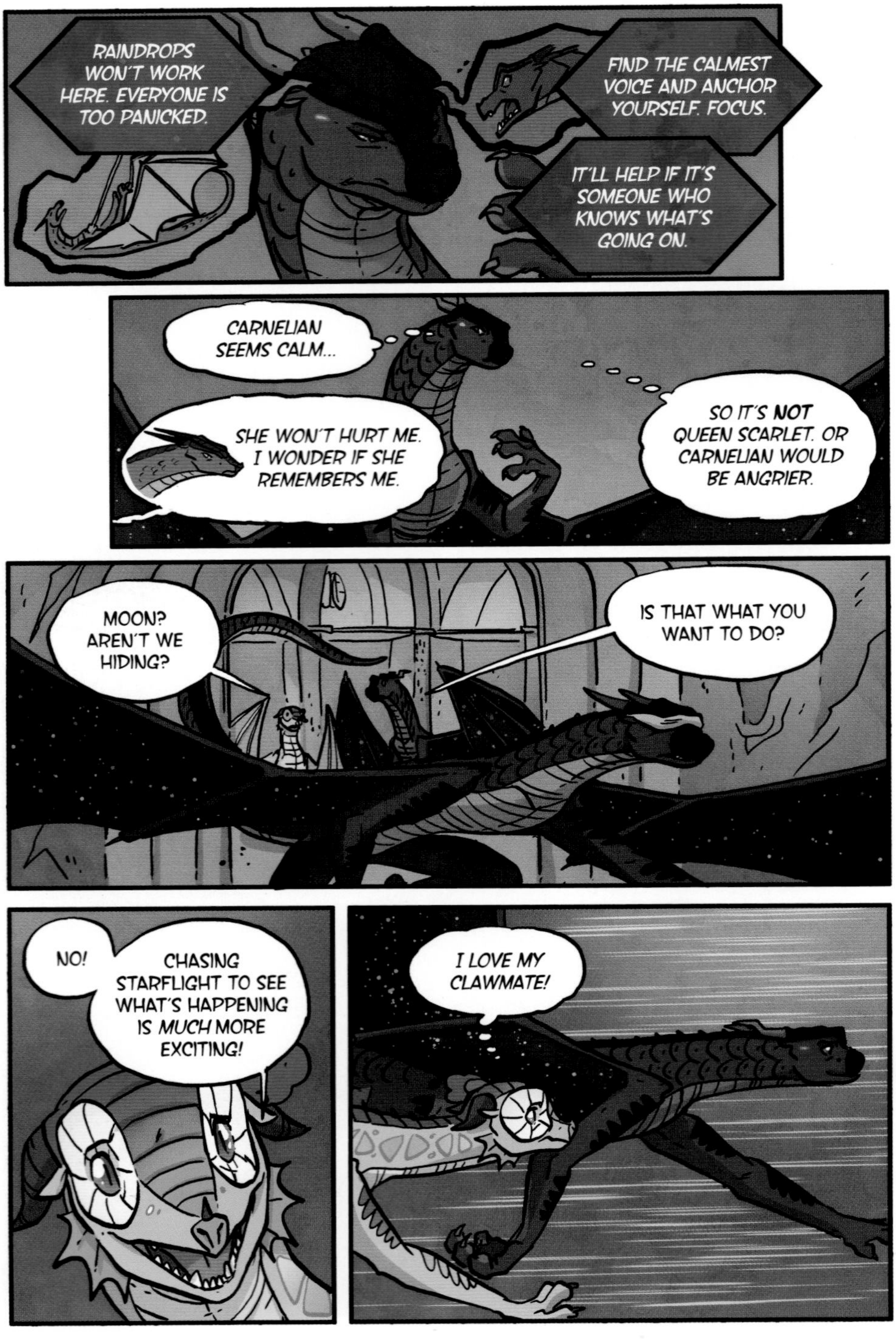
RAINDROPS WON'T WORK HERE. EVERYONE IS TOO PANICKED.
FIND THE CALMEST VOICE AND ANCHOR YOURSELF. FOCUS.
IT'LL HELP IF IT'S SOMEONE WHO KNOWS WHAT'S GOING ON.
CARNELIAN SEEMS CALM...
SHE WON'T HURT ME. I WONDER IF SHE REMEMBERS ME.
SO IT'S **NOT** QUEEN SCARLET. OR CARNELIAN WOULD BE ANGRIER.
MOON? AREN'T WE HIDING?
IS THAT WHAT YOU WANT TO DO?
NO!
CHASING STARFLIGHT TO SEE WHAT'S HAPPENING IS *MUCH* MORE EXCITING!
I LOVE MY CLAWMATE!

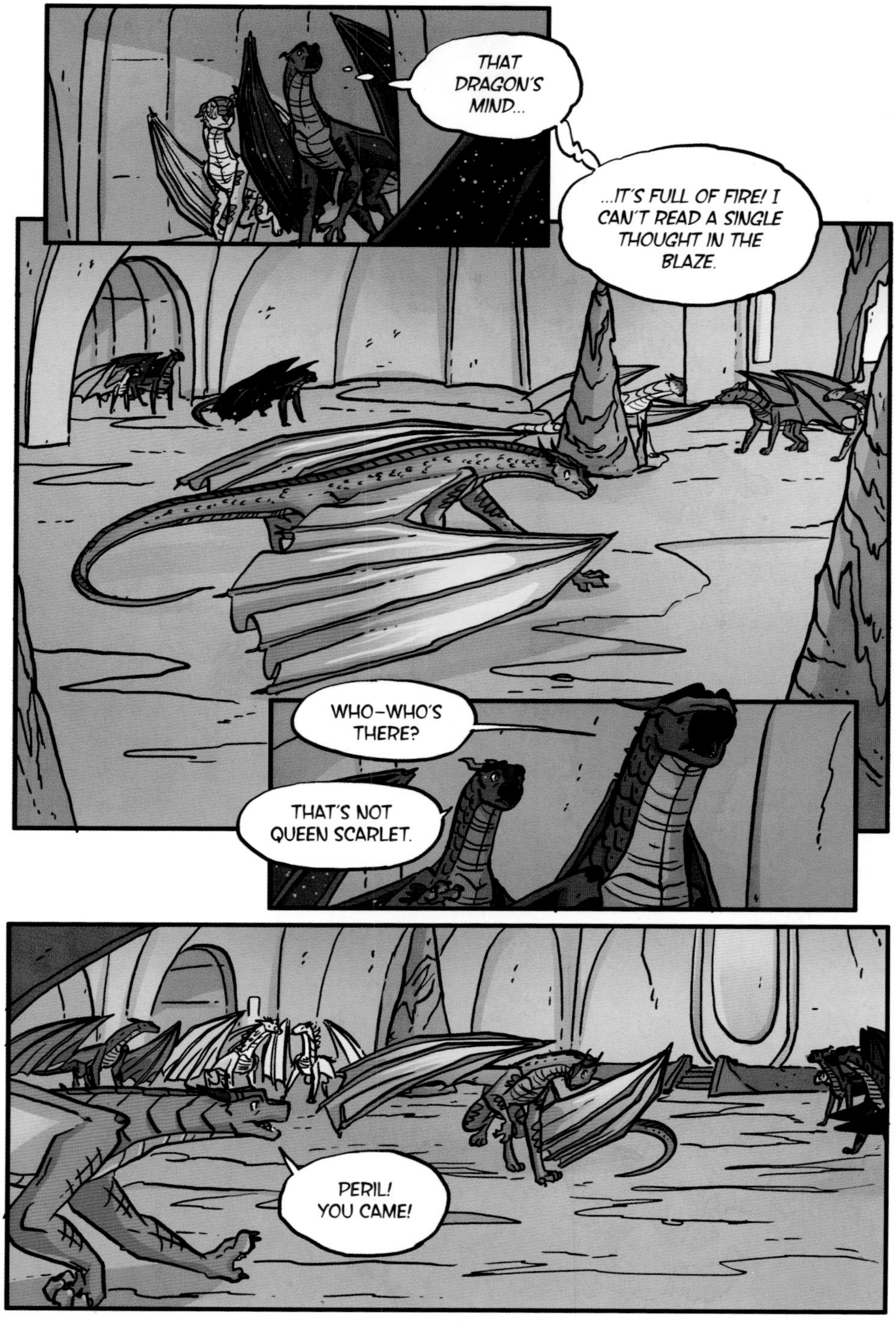
THAT DRAGON'S MIND...
...IT'S FULL OF FIRE! I CAN'T READ A SINGLE THOUGHT IN THE BLAZE.
WHO-WHO'S THERE?
THAT'S NOT QUEEN SCARLET.
PERIL! YOU CAME!

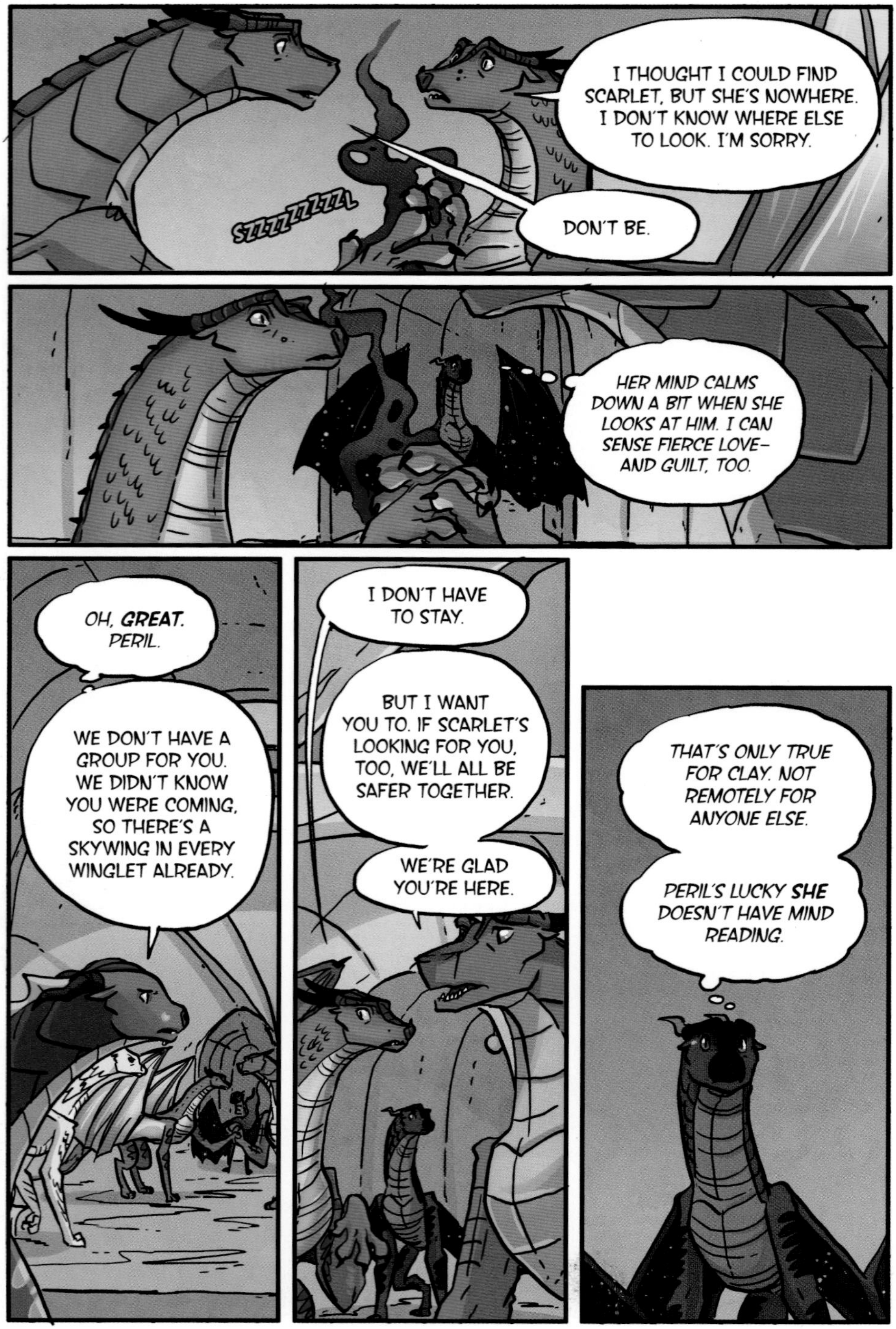
I THOUGHT I COULD FIND SCARLET, BUT SHE'S NOWHERE. I DON'T KNOW WHERE ELSE TO LOOK. I'M SORRY.
SZZZZZZZZZL
DON'T BE.
HER MIND CALMS DOWN A BIT WHEN SHE LOOKS AT HIM. I CAN SENSE FIERCE LOVE— AND GUILT, TOO.
OH, GREAT. PERIL.
WE DON'T HAVE A GROUP FOR YOU. WE DIDN'T KNOW YOU WERE COMING, SO THERE'S A SKYWING IN EVERY WINGLET ALREADY.
I DON'T HAVE TO STAY.
BUT I WANT YOU TO. IF SCARLET'S LOOKING FOR YOU, TOO, WE'LL ALL BE SAFER TOGETHER.
WE'RE GLAD YOU'RE HERE.
THAT'S ONLY TRUE FOR CLAY. NOT REMOTELY FOR ANYONE ELSE.
PERIL'S LUCKY SHE DOESN'T HAVE MIND READING.

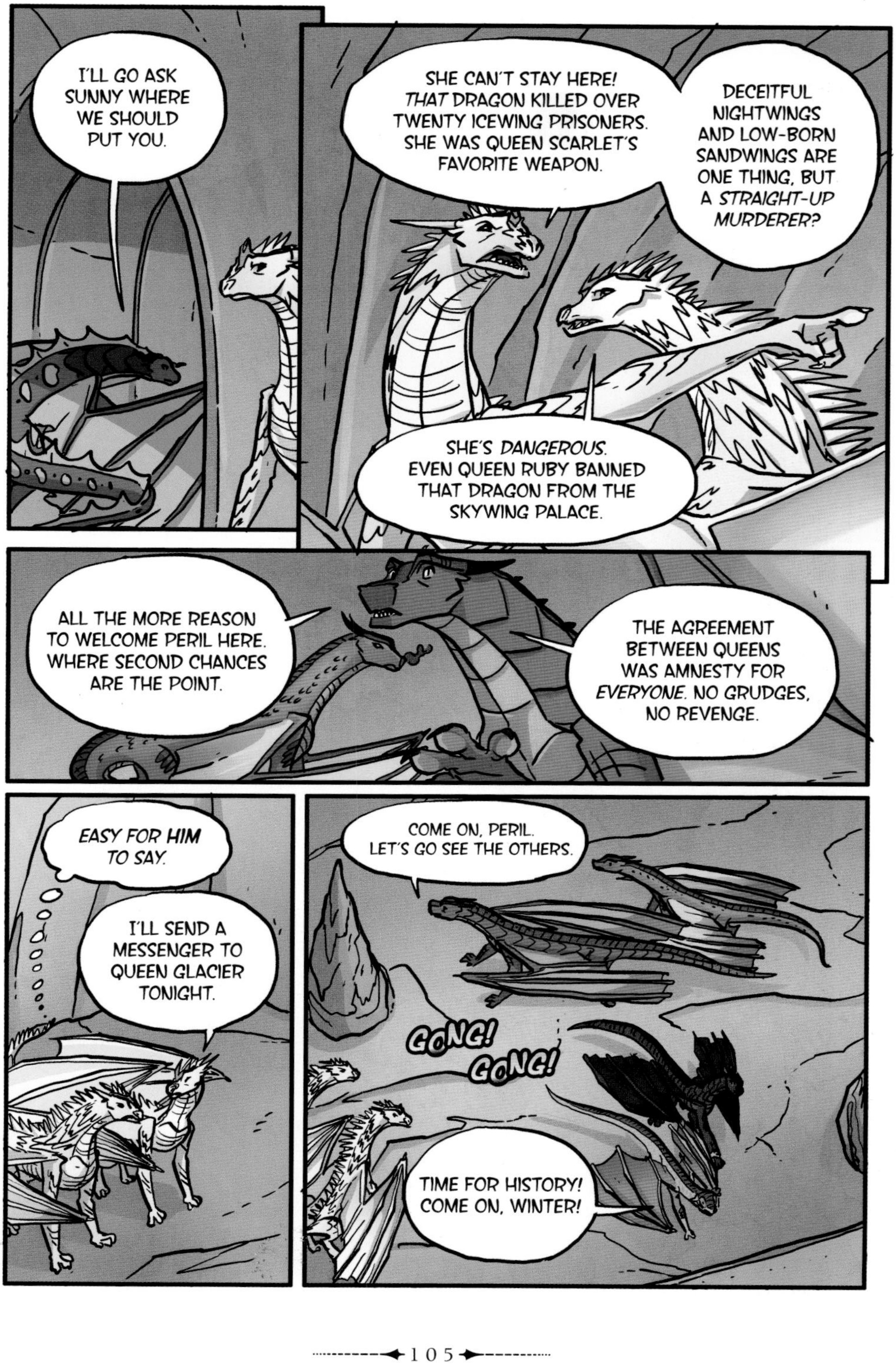
I'LL GO ASK SUNNY WHERE WE SHOULD PUT YOU.
SHE CAN'T STAY HERE! *THAT* DRAGON KILLED OVER TWENTY ICEWING PRISONERS. SHE WAS QUEEN SCARLET'S FAVORITE WEAPON.
DECEITFUL NIGHTWINGS AND LOW-BORN SANDWINGS ARE ONE THING, BUT A *STRAIGHT-UP MURDERER?*
SHE'S *DANGEROUS.* EVEN QUEEN RUBY BANNED THAT DRAGON FROM THE SKYWING PALACE.
ALL THE MORE REASON TO WELCOME PERIL HERE. WHERE SECOND CHANCES ARE THE POINT.
THE AGREEMENT BETWEEN QUEENS WAS AMNESTY FOR *EVERYONE.* NO GRUDGES, NO REVENGE.
*EASY FOR **HIM** TO SAY.*
I'LL SEND A MESSENGER TO QUEEN GLACIER TONIGHT.
COME ON, PERIL. LET'S GO SEE THE OTHERS.
GONG! GONG!
TIME FOR HISTORY! COME ON, WINTER!

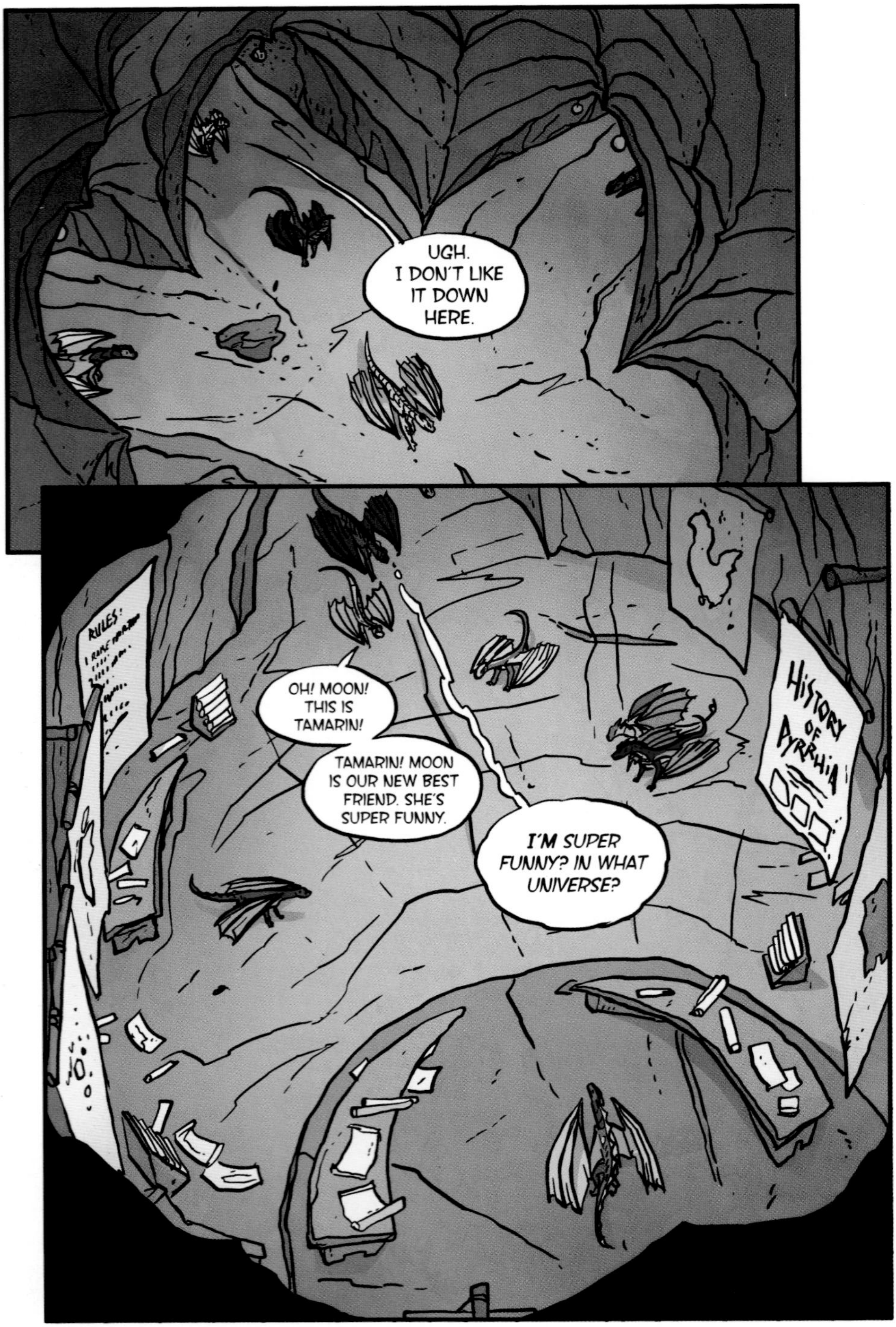
UGH. I DON'T LIKE IT DOWN HERE.
RULES:
HISTORY OF PYRRHIA
OH! MOON! THIS IS TAMARIN!
TAMARIN! MOON IS OUR NEW BEST FRIEND. SHE'S SUPER FUNNY.
I'M SUPER FUNNY? IN WHAT UNIVERSE?

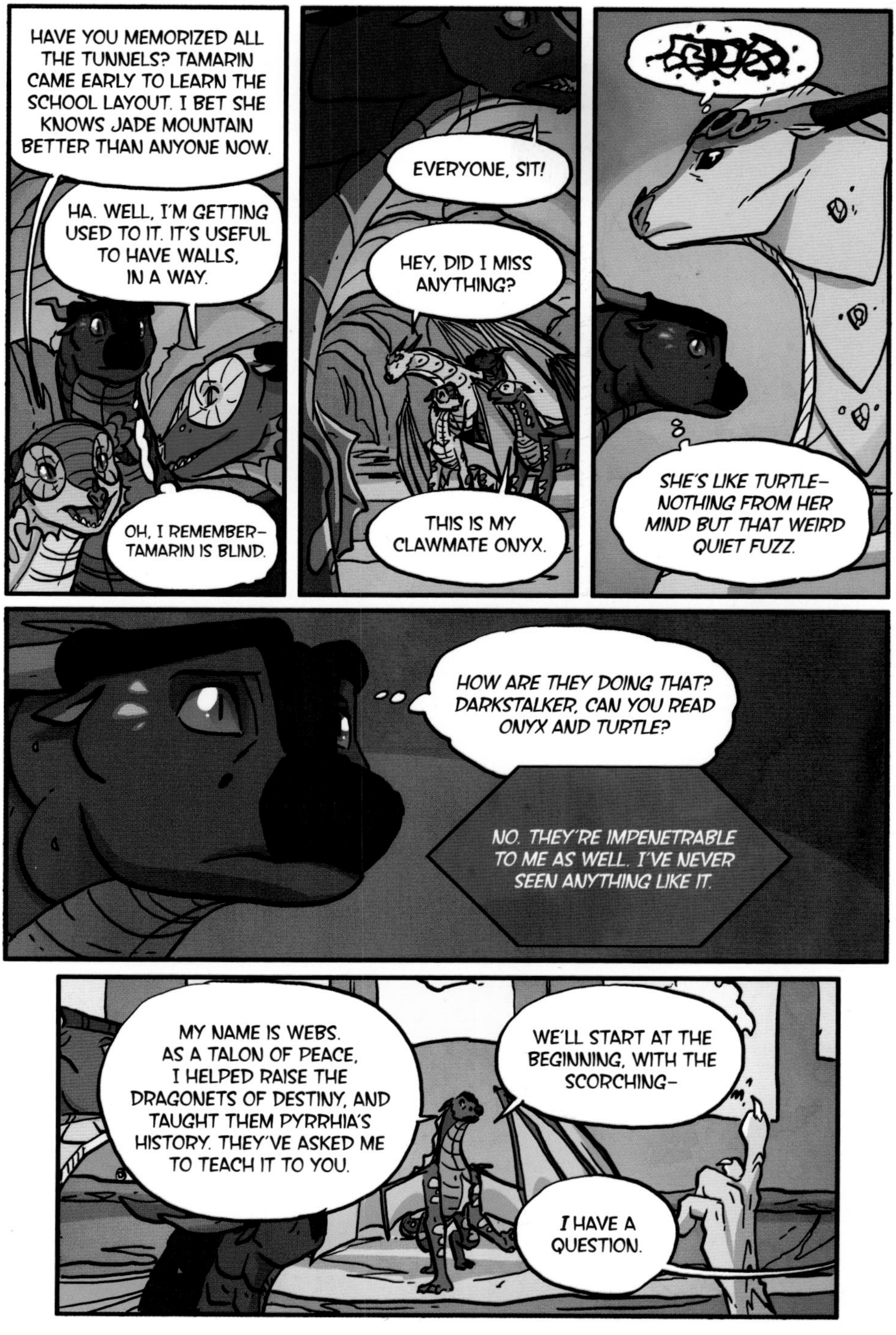
HAVE YOU MEMORIZED ALL THE TUNNELS? TAMARIN CAME EARLY TO LEARN THE SCHOOL LAYOUT. I BET SHE KNOWS JADE MOUNTAIN BETTER THAN ANYONE NOW.
HA. WELL, I'M GETTING USED TO IT. IT'S USEFUL TO HAVE WALLS, IN A WAY.
OH, I REMEMBER-TAMARIN IS BLIND.
EVERYONE, SIT!
HEY, DID I MISS ANYTHING?
THIS IS MY CLAWMATE ONYX.
SHE'S LIKE TURTLE-NOTHING FROM HER MIND BUT THAT WEIRD QUIET FUZZ.
HOW ARE THEY DOING THAT? DARKSTALKER, CAN YOU READ ONYX AND TURTLE?
NO. THEY'RE IMPENETRABLE TO ME AS WELL. I'VE NEVER SEEN ANYTHING LIKE IT.
MY NAME IS WEBS. AS A TALON OF PEACE, I HELPED RAISE THE DRAGONETS OF DESTINY, AND TAUGHT THEM PYRRHIA'S HISTORY. THEY'VE ASKED ME TO TEACH IT TO YOU.
WE'LL START AT THE BEGINNING, WITH THE SCORCHING-
I HAVE A QUESTION.

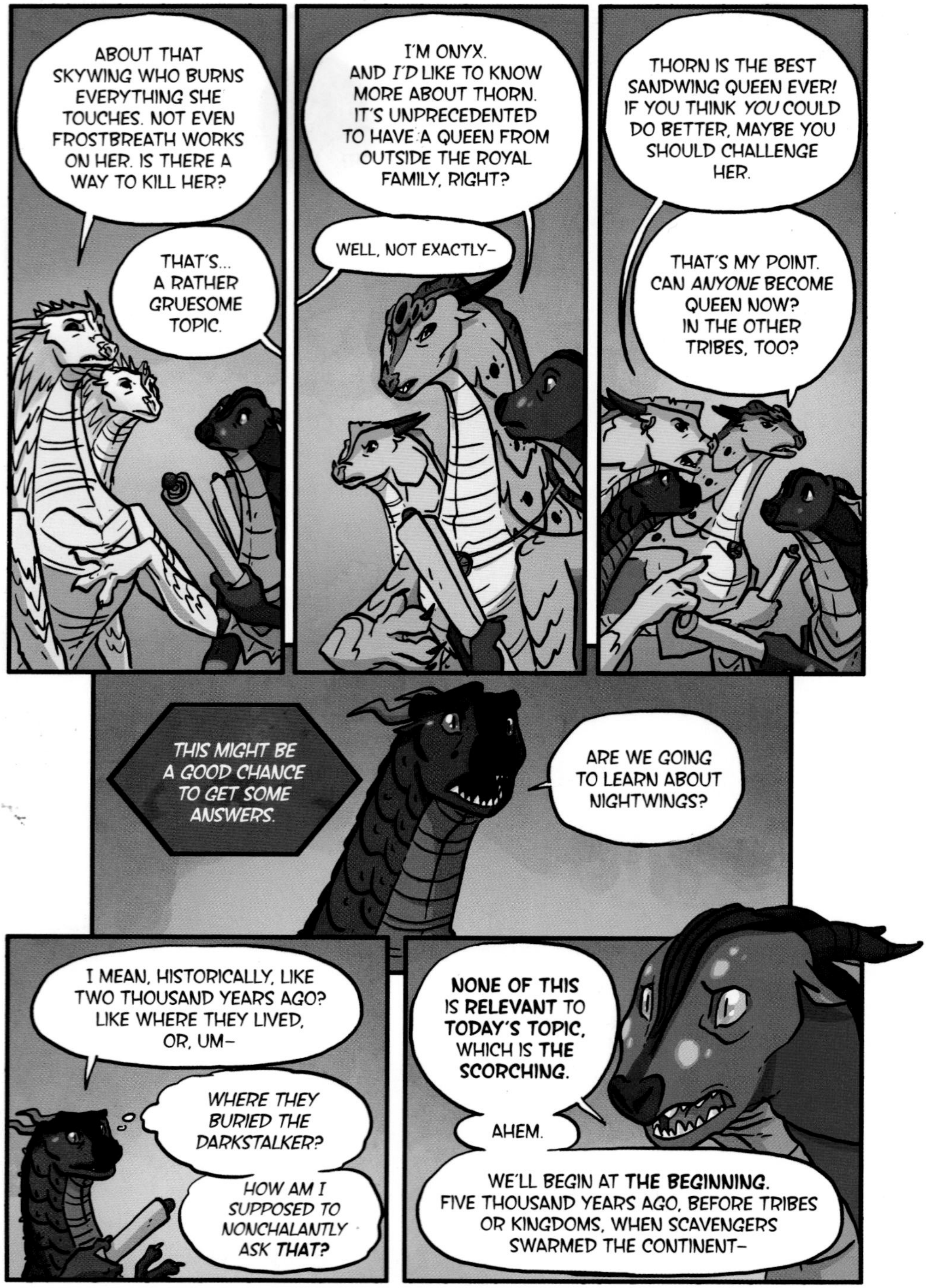
ABOUT THAT SKYWING WHO BURNS EVERYTHING SHE TOUCHES. NOT EVEN FROSTBREATH WORKS ON HER. IS THERE A WAY TO KILL HER?
THAT'S... A RATHER GRUESOME TOPIC.
I'M ONYX. AND *I'D* LIKE TO KNOW MORE ABOUT THORN. IT'S UNPRECEDENTED TO HAVE A QUEEN FROM OUTSIDE THE ROYAL FAMILY, RIGHT?
WELL, NOT EXACTLY–
THORN IS THE BEST SANDWING QUEEN EVER! IF YOU THINK *YOU* COULD DO BETTER, MAYBE YOU SHOULD CHALLENGE HER.
THAT'S MY POINT. CAN *ANYONE* BECOME QUEEN NOW? IN THE OTHER TRIBES, TOO?
THIS MIGHT BE A GOOD CHANCE TO GET SOME ANSWERS.
ARE WE GOING TO LEARN ABOUT NIGHTWINGS?
I MEAN, HISTORICALLY, LIKE TWO THOUSAND YEARS AGO? LIKE WHERE THEY LIVED, OR, UM–
WHERE THEY BURIED THE DARKSTALKER?
HOW AM I SUPPOSED TO NONCHALANTLY ASK ***THAT?***
NONE OF THIS IS **RELEVANT** TO **TODAY'S TOPIC,** WHICH IS **THE SCORCHING.**
AHEM.
WE'LL BEGIN AT **THE BEGINNING.** FIVE THOUSAND YEARS AGO, BEFORE TRIBES OR KINGDOMS, WHEN SCAVENGERS SWARMED THE CONTINENT–

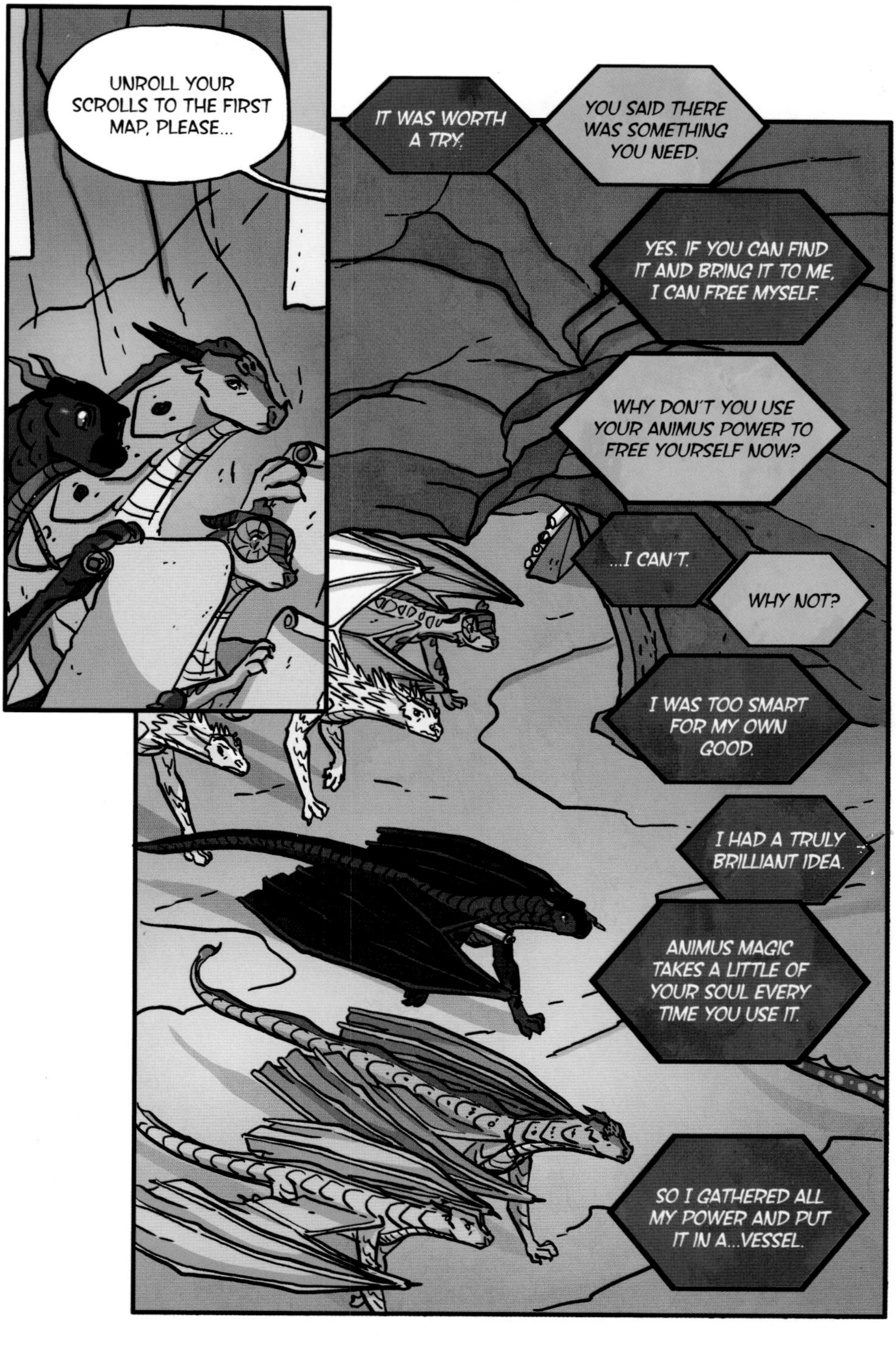
UNROLL YOUR SCROLLS TO THE FIRST MAP, PLEASE...
IT WAS WORTH A TRY.
YOU SAID THERE WAS SOMETHING YOU NEED.
YES. IF YOU CAN FIND IT AND BRING IT TO ME, I CAN FREE MYSELF.
WHY DON'T YOU USE YOUR ANIMUS POWER TO FREE YOURSELF NOW?
...I CAN'T.
WHY NOT?
I WAS TOO SMART FOR MY OWN GOOD.
I HAD A TRULY BRILLIANT IDEA.
ANIMUS MAGIC TAKES A LITTLE OF YOUR SOUL EVERY TIME YOU USE IT.
SO I GATHERED ALL MY POWER AND PUT IT IN A...VESSEL.

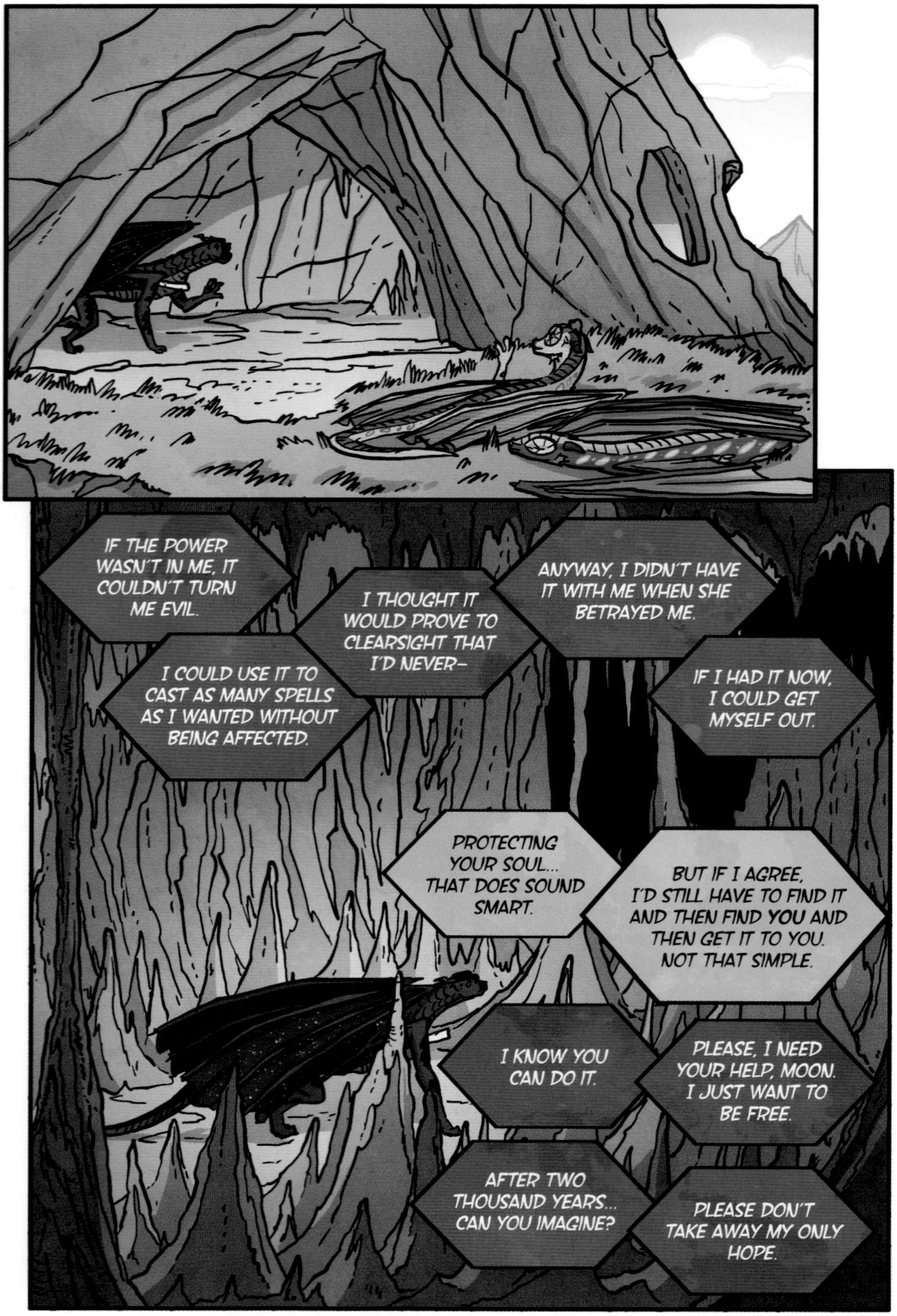
IF THE POWER WASN'T IN ME, IT COULDN'T TURN ME EVIL.
I COULD USE IT TO CAST AS MANY SPELLS AS I WANTED WITHOUT BEING AFFECTED.
I THOUGHT IT WOULD PROVE TO CLEARSIGHT THAT I'D NEVER—
ANYWAY, I DIDN'T HAVE IT WITH ME WHEN SHE BETRAYED ME.
IF I HAD IT NOW, I COULD GET MYSELF OUT.
PROTECTING YOUR SOUL... THAT DOES SOUND SMART.
BUT IF I AGREE, I'D STILL HAVE TO FIND IT AND THEN FIND YOU AND THEN GET IT TO YOU. NOT THAT SIMPLE.
I KNOW YOU CAN DO IT.
PLEASE, I NEED YOUR HELP, MOON. I JUST WANT TO BE FREE.
AFTER TWO THOUSAND YEARS... CAN YOU IMAGINE?
PLEASE DON'T TAKE AWAY MY ONLY HOPE.

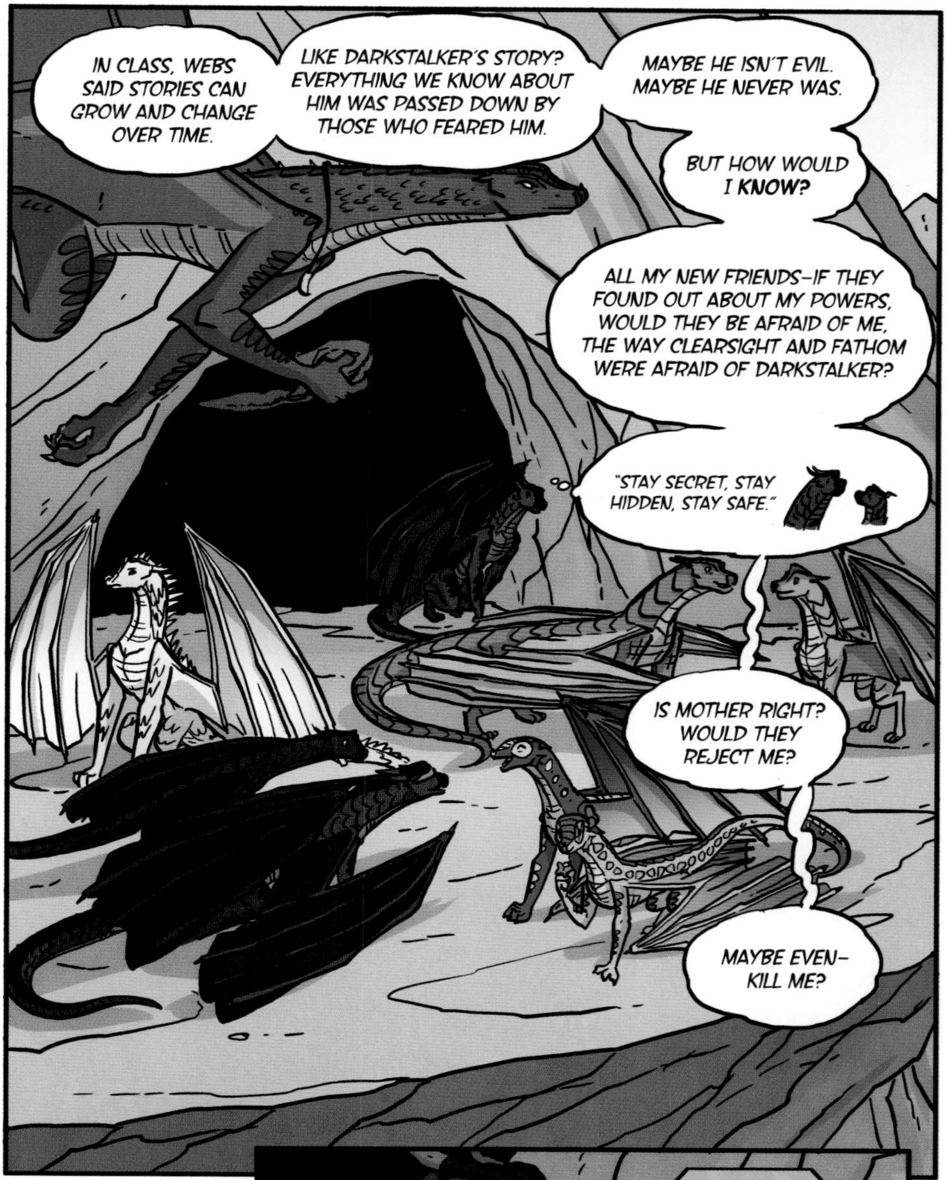
IN CLASS, WEBS SAID STORIES CAN GROW AND CHANGE OVER TIME.
LIKE DARKSTALKER'S STORY? EVERYTHING WE KNOW ABOUT HIM WAS PASSED DOWN BY THOSE WHO FEARED HIM.
MAYBE HE ISN'T EVIL. MAYBE HE NEVER WAS.
BUT HOW WOULD I **KNOW?**
ALL MY NEW FRIENDS—IF THEY FOUND OUT ABOUT MY POWERS, WOULD THEY BE AFRAID OF ME, THE WAY CLEARSIGHT AND FATHOM WERE AFRAID OF DARKSTALKER?
"STAY SECRET, STAY HIDDEN, STAY SAFE."
IS MOTHER RIGHT? WOULD THEY REJECT ME?
MAYBE EVEN— KILL ME?

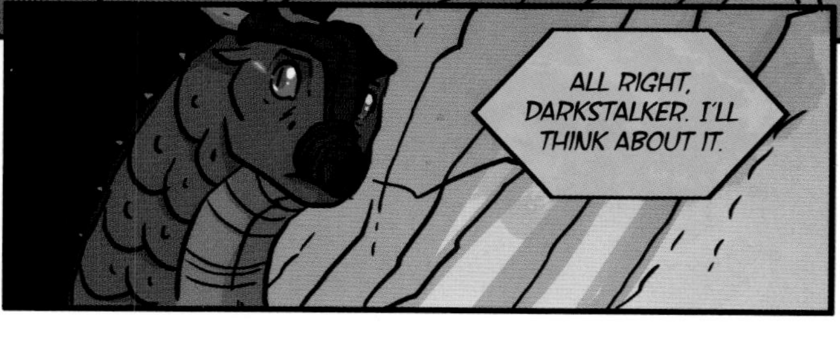
ALL RIGHT, DARKSTALKER. I'LL THINK ABOUT IT.

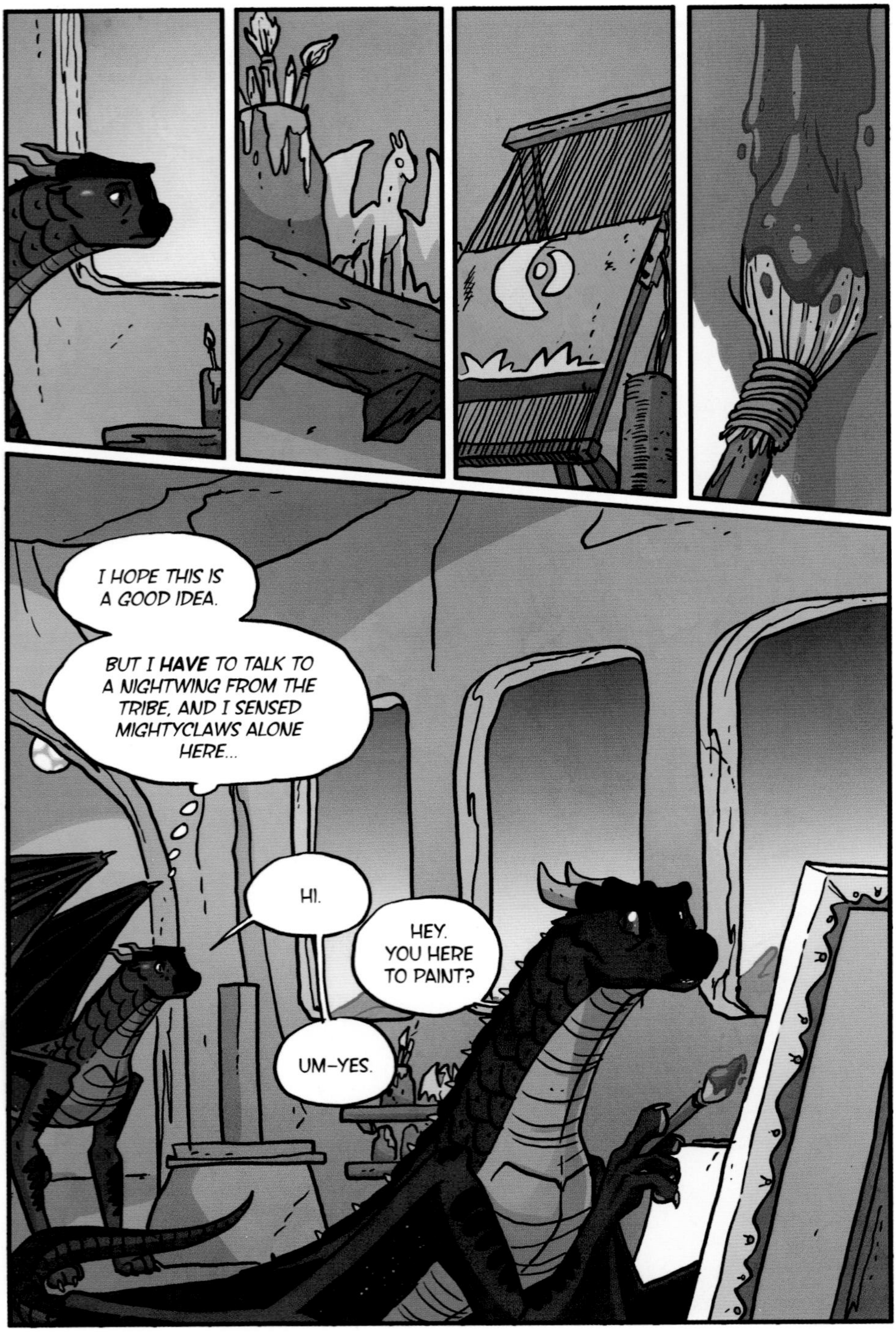
I HOPE THIS IS A GOOD IDEA.
BUT I **HAVE** TO TALK TO A NIGHTWING FROM THE TRIBE, AND I SENSED MIGHTYCLAWS ALONE HERE...
HI.
HEY. YOU HERE TO PAINT?
UM–YES.

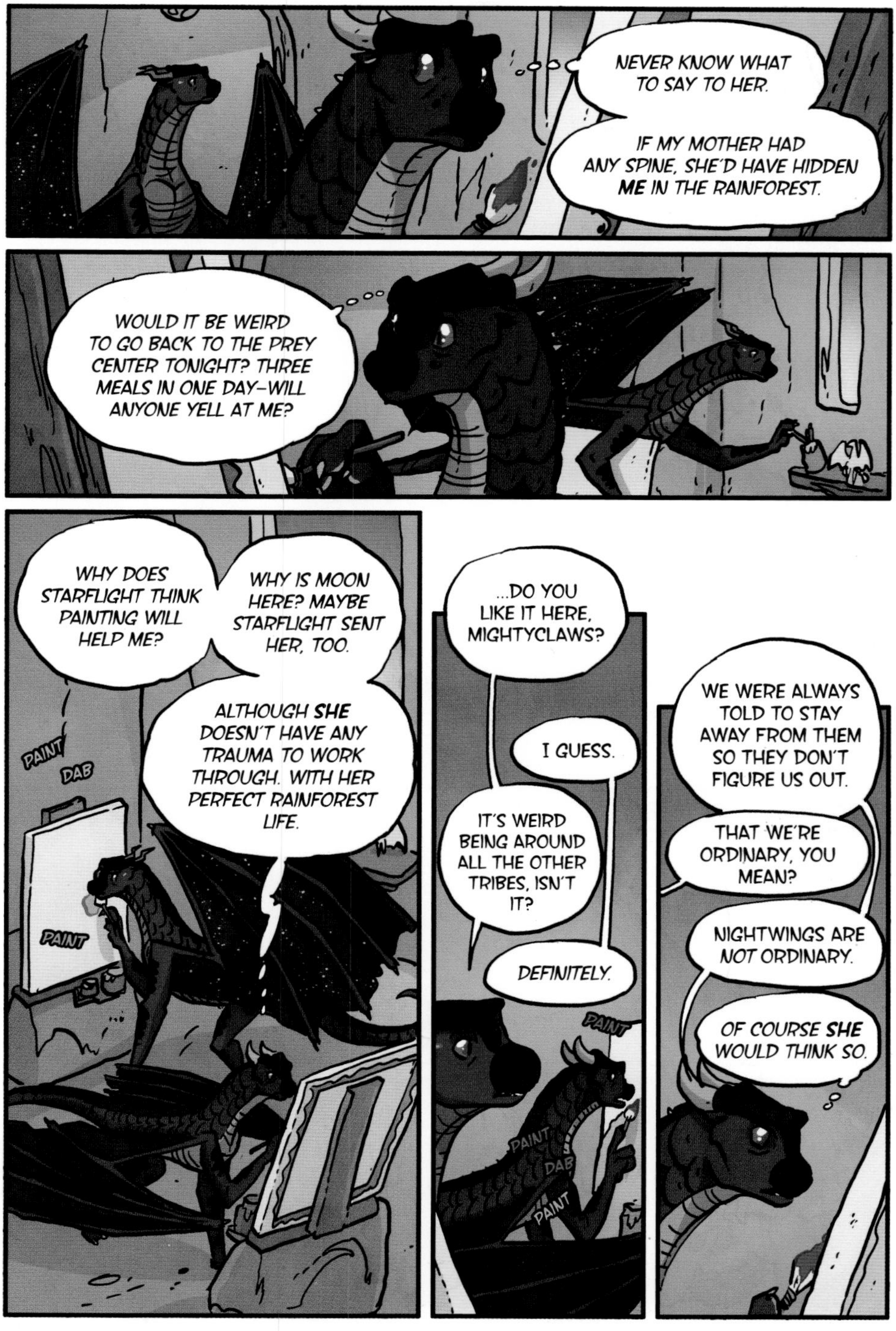
NEVER KNOW WHAT TO SAY TO HER.
IF MY MOTHER HAD ANY SPINE, SHE'D HAVE HIDDEN **ME** IN THE RAINFOREST.
WOULD IT BE WEIRD TO GO BACK TO THE PREY CENTER TONIGHT? THREE MEALS IN ONE DAY–WILL ANYONE YELL AT ME?
WHY DOES STARFLIGHT THINK PAINTING WILL HELP ME?
WHY IS MOON HERE? MAYBE STARFLIGHT SENT HER, TOO.
ALTHOUGH **SHE** DOESN'T HAVE ANY TRAUMA TO WORK THROUGH. WITH HER PERFECT RAINFOREST LIFE.
PAINT
DAB
PAINT
...DO YOU LIKE IT HERE, MIGHTYCLAWS?
I GUESS.
IT'S WEIRD BEING AROUND ALL THE OTHER TRIBES, ISN'T IT?
DEFINITELY.
PAINT
PAINT
DAB
PAINT
WE WERE ALWAYS TOLD TO STAY AWAY FROM THEM SO THEY DON'T FIGURE US OUT.
THAT WE'RE ORDINARY, YOU MEAN?
NIGHTWINGS ARE NOT ORDINARY.
OF COURSE **SHE** WOULD THINK SO.

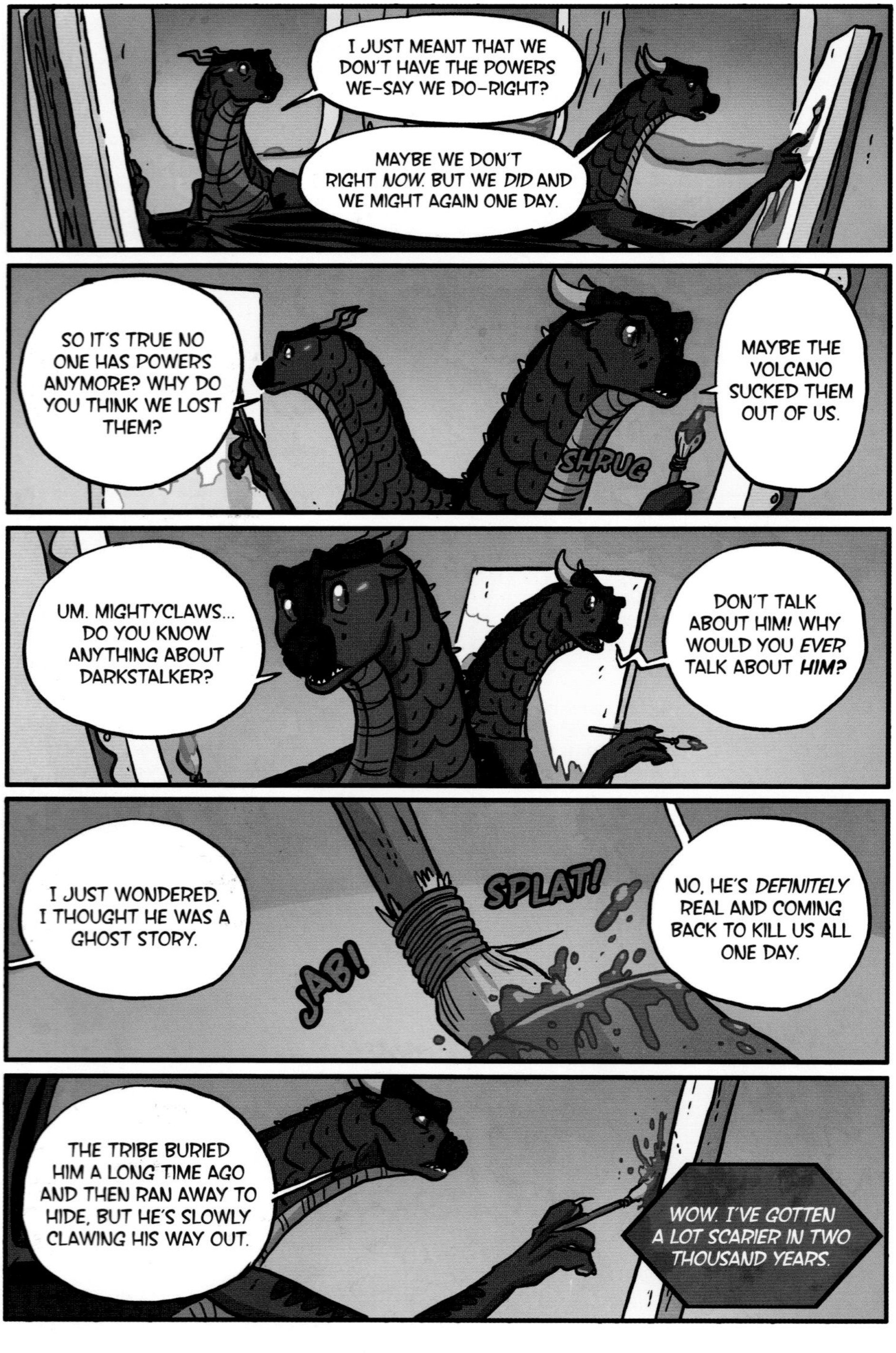

I JUST MEANT THAT WE DON'T HAVE THE POWERS WE-SAY WE DO-RIGHT?
MAYBE WE DON'T RIGHT *NOW*. BUT WE *DID* AND WE MIGHT AGAIN ONE DAY.
SO IT'S TRUE NO ONE HAS POWERS ANYMORE? WHY DO YOU THINK WE LOST THEM?
SHRUG
MAYBE THE VOLCANO SUCKED THEM OUT OF US.
UM. MIGHTYCLAWS... DO YOU KNOW ANYTHING ABOUT DARKSTALKER?
DON'T TALK ABOUT HIM! WHY WOULD YOU *EVER* TALK ABOUT ***HIM?***
I JUST WONDERED. I THOUGHT HE WAS A GHOST STORY.
SPLAT!
JAB!
NO, HE'S *DEFINITELY* REAL AND COMING BACK TO KILL US ALL ONE DAY.
THE TRIBE BURIED HIM A LONG TIME AGO AND THEN RAN AWAY TO HIDE, BUT HE'S SLOWLY CLAWING HIS WAY OUT.
WOW. I'VE GOTTEN A LOT SCARIER IN TWO THOUSAND YEARS.

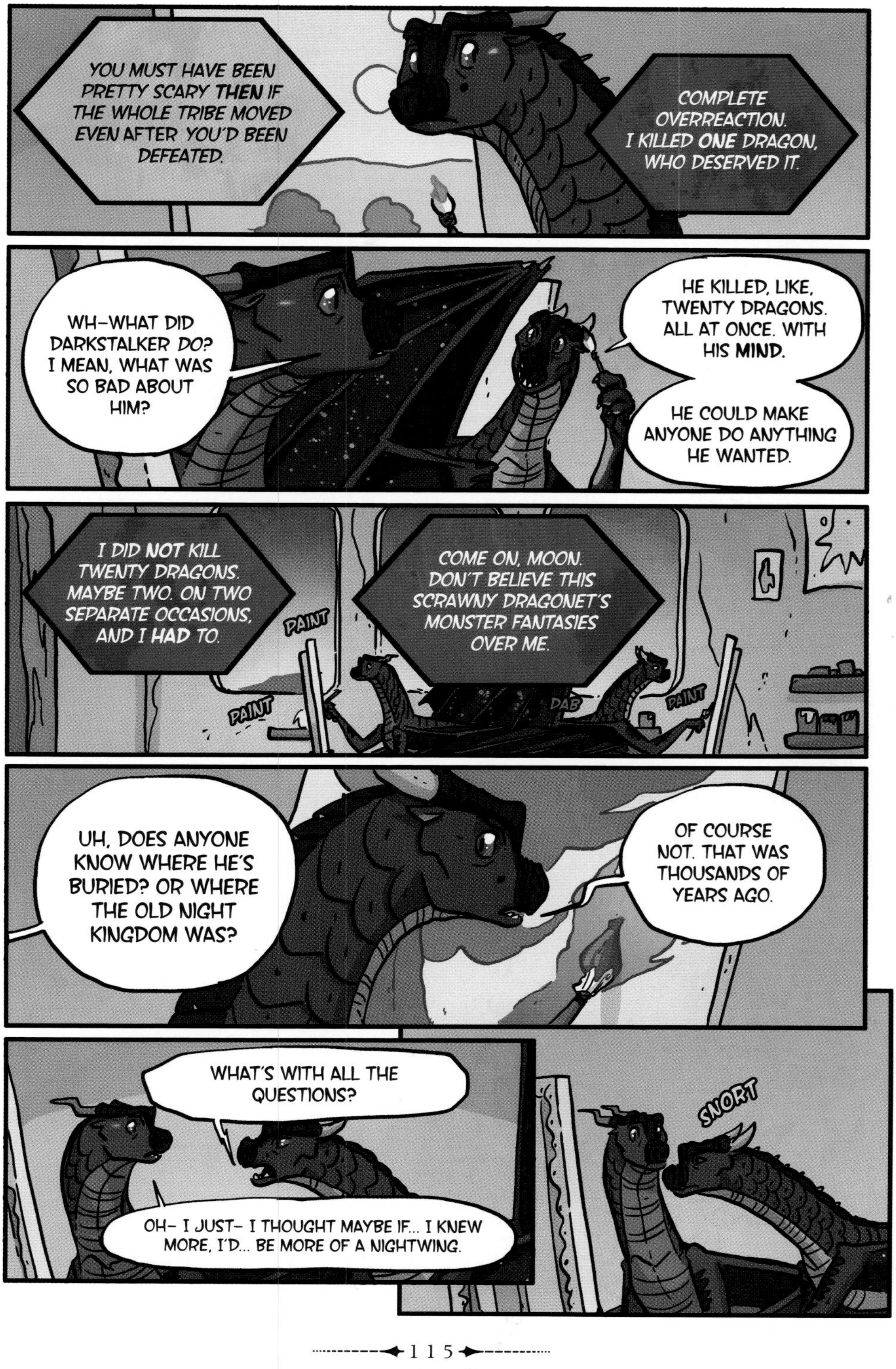
YOU MUST HAVE BEEN PRETTY SCARY THEN IF THE WHOLE TRIBE MOVED EVEN AFTER YOU'D BEEN DEFEATED.
COMPLETE OVERREACTION. I KILLED ONE DRAGON, WHO DESERVED IT.
WH–WHAT DID DARKSTALKER DO? I MEAN, WHAT WAS SO BAD ABOUT HIM?
HE KILLED, LIKE, TWENTY DRAGONS. ALL AT ONCE. WITH HIS MIND.
HE COULD MAKE ANYONE DO ANYTHING HE WANTED.
I DID NOT KILL TWENTY DRAGONS. MAYBE TWO. ON TWO SEPARATE OCCASIONS, AND I HAD TO.
COME ON, MOON. DON'T BELIEVE THIS SCRAWNY DRAGONET'S MONSTER FANTASIES OVER ME.
PAINT
PAINT
DAB
PAINT
UH, DOES ANYONE KNOW WHERE HE'S BURIED? OR WHERE THE OLD NIGHT KINGDOM WAS?
OF COURSE NOT. THAT WAS THOUSANDS OF YEARS AGO.
WHAT'S WITH ALL THE QUESTIONS?
OH– I JUST– I THOUGHT MAYBE IF... I KNEW MORE, I'D... BE MORE OF A NIGHTWING.
SNORT

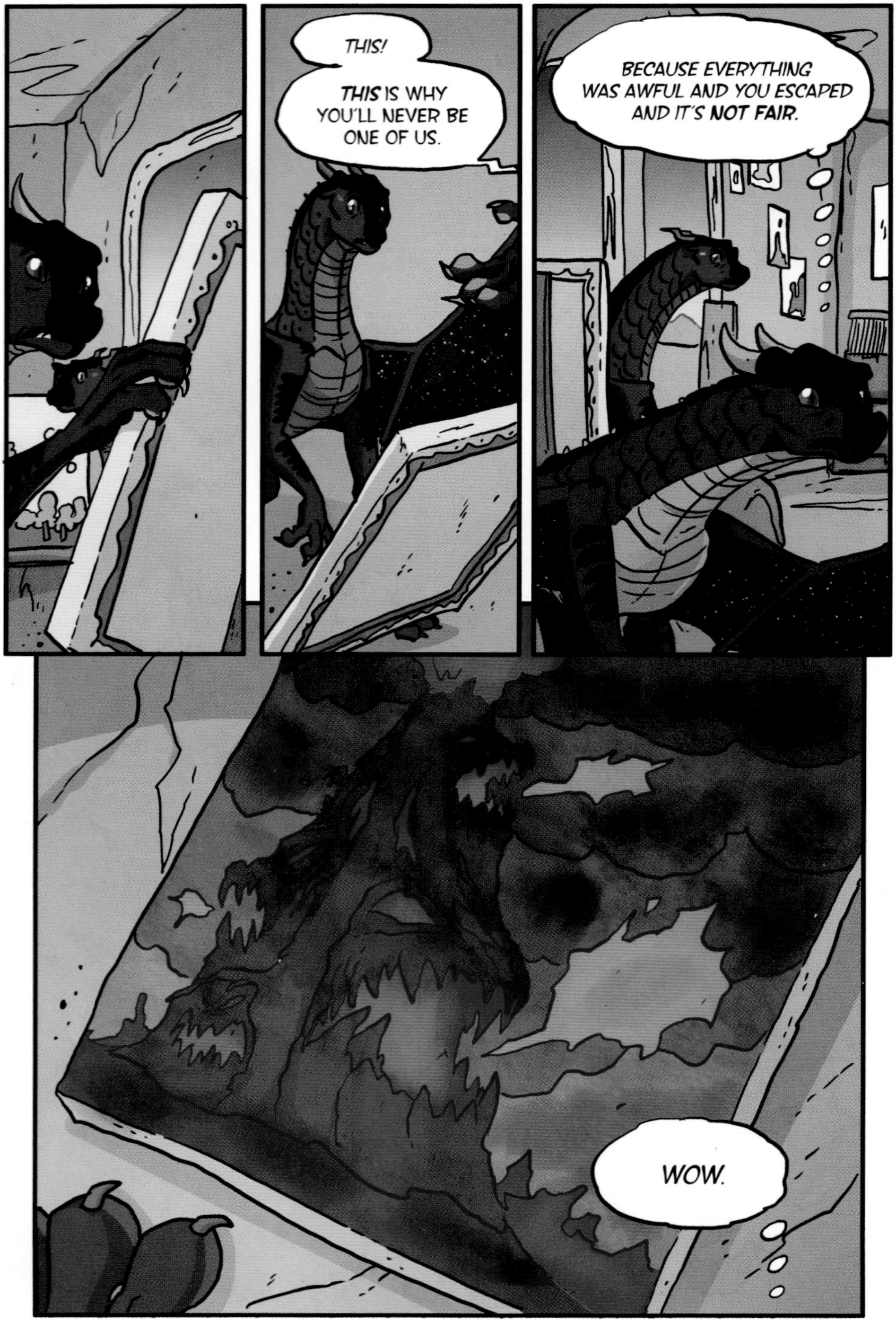
THIS!
THIS IS WHY YOU'LL NEVER BE ONE OF US.
BECAUSE EVERYTHING WAS AWFUL AND YOU ESCAPED AND IT'S NOT FAIR.
WOW.

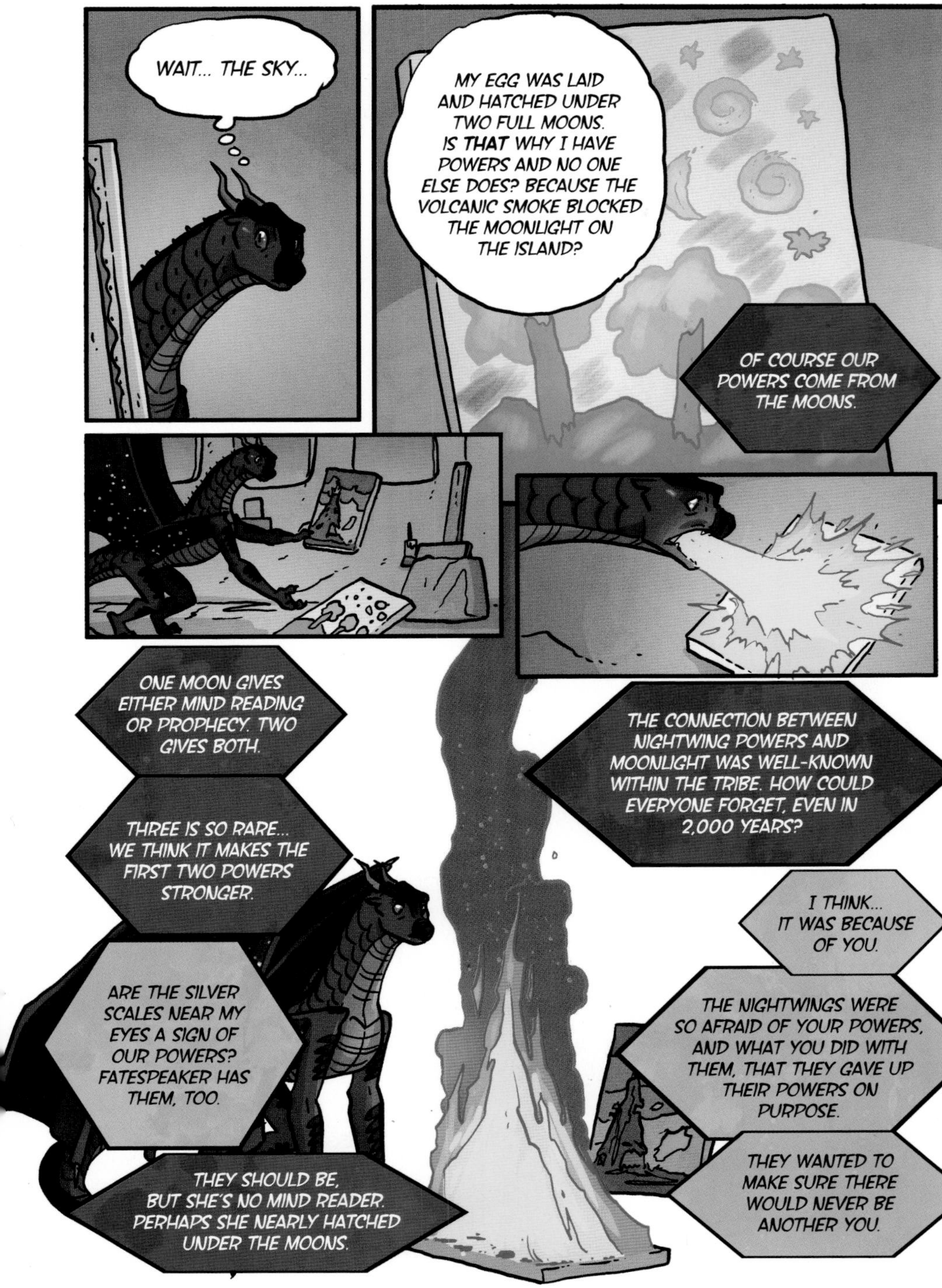
WAIT... THE SKY...
MY EGG WAS LAID AND HATCHED UNDER TWO FULL MOONS. IS THAT WHY I HAVE POWERS AND NO ONE ELSE DOES? BECAUSE THE VOLCANIC SMOKE BLOCKED THE MOONLIGHT ON THE ISLAND?
OF COURSE OUR POWERS COME FROM THE MOONS.
ONE MOON GIVES EITHER MIND READING OR PROPHECY. TWO GIVES BOTH.
THE CONNECTION BETWEEN NIGHTWING POWERS AND MOONLIGHT WAS WELL-KNOWN WITHIN THE TRIBE. HOW COULD EVERYONE FORGET, EVEN IN 2,000 YEARS?
THREE IS SO RARE... WE THINK IT MAKES THE FIRST TWO POWERS STRONGER.
I THINK... IT WAS BECAUSE OF YOU.
ARE THE SILVER SCALES NEAR MY EYES A SIGN OF OUR POWERS? FATESPEAKER HAS THEM, TOO.
THE NIGHTWINGS WERE SO AFRAID OF YOUR POWERS, AND WHAT YOU DID WITH THEM, THAT THEY GAVE UP THEIR POWERS ON PURPOSE.
THEY SHOULD BE, BUT SHE'S NO MIND READER. PERHAPS SHE NEARLY HATCHED UNDER THE MOONS.
THEY WANTED TO MAKE SURE THERE WOULD NEVER BE ANOTHER YOU.

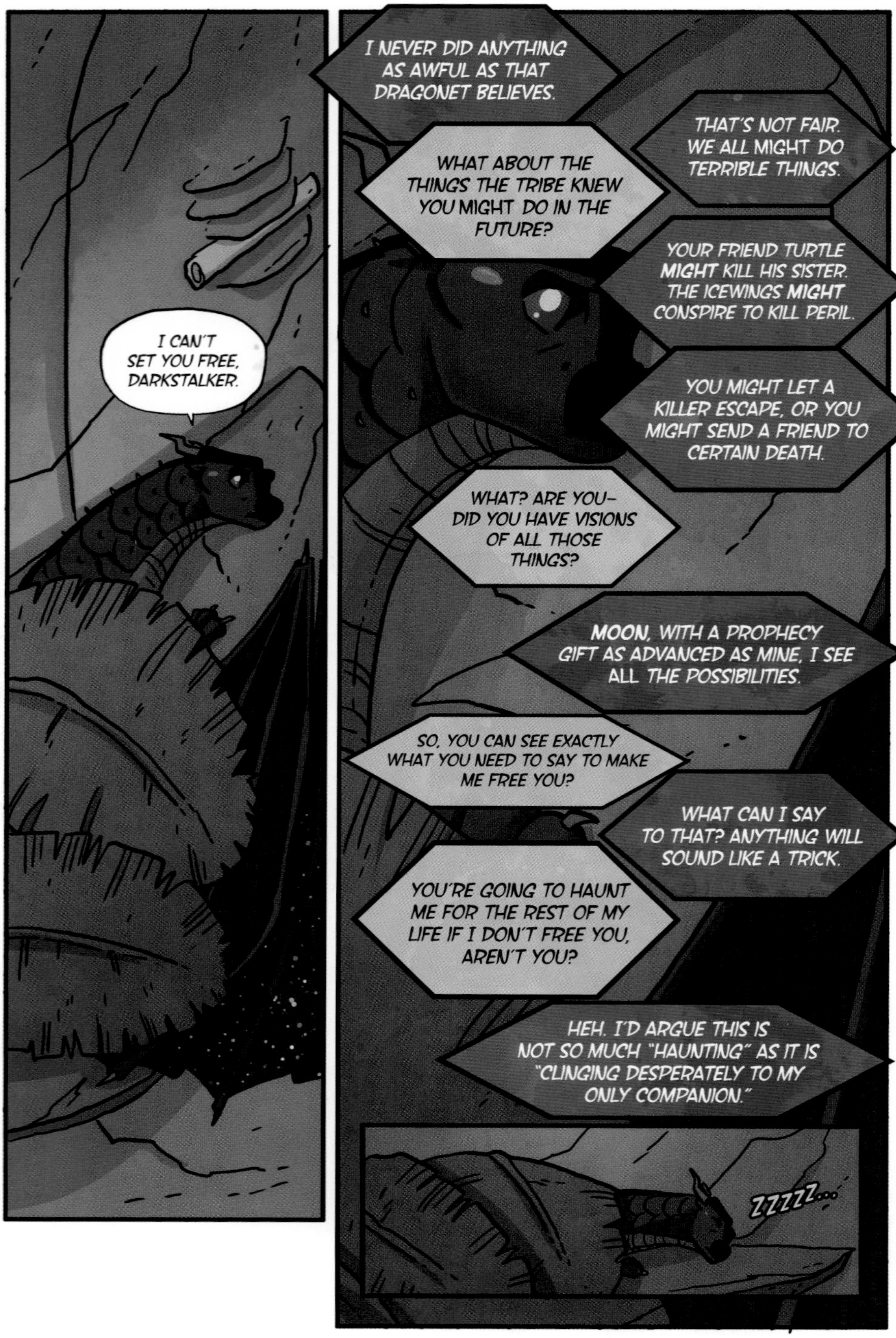
I CAN'T SET YOU FREE, DARKSTALKER.
I NEVER DID ANYTHING AS AWFUL AS THAT DRAGONET BELIEVES.
WHAT ABOUT THE THINGS THE TRIBE KNEW YOU MIGHT DO IN THE FUTURE?
THAT'S NOT FAIR. WE ALL MIGHT DO TERRIBLE THINGS.
YOUR FRIEND TURTLE **MIGHT** KILL HIS SISTER. THE ICEWINGS **MIGHT** CONSPIRE TO KILL PERIL.
YOU MIGHT LET A KILLER ESCAPE, OR YOU MIGHT SEND A FRIEND TO CERTAIN DEATH.
WHAT? ARE YOU– DID YOU HAVE VISIONS OF ALL THOSE THINGS?
MOON, WITH A PROPHECY GIFT AS ADVANCED AS MINE, I SEE ALL THE POSSIBILITIES.
SO, YOU CAN SEE EXACTLY WHAT YOU NEED TO SAY TO MAKE ME FREE YOU?
WHAT CAN I SAY TO THAT? ANYTHING WILL SOUND LIKE A TRICK.
YOU'RE GOING TO HAUNT ME FOR THE REST OF MY LIFE IF I DON'T FREE YOU, AREN'T YOU?
HEH. I'D ARGUE THIS IS NOT SO MUCH "HAUNTING" AS IT IS "CLINGING DESPERATELY TO MY ONLY COMPANION."
ZZZZZ...

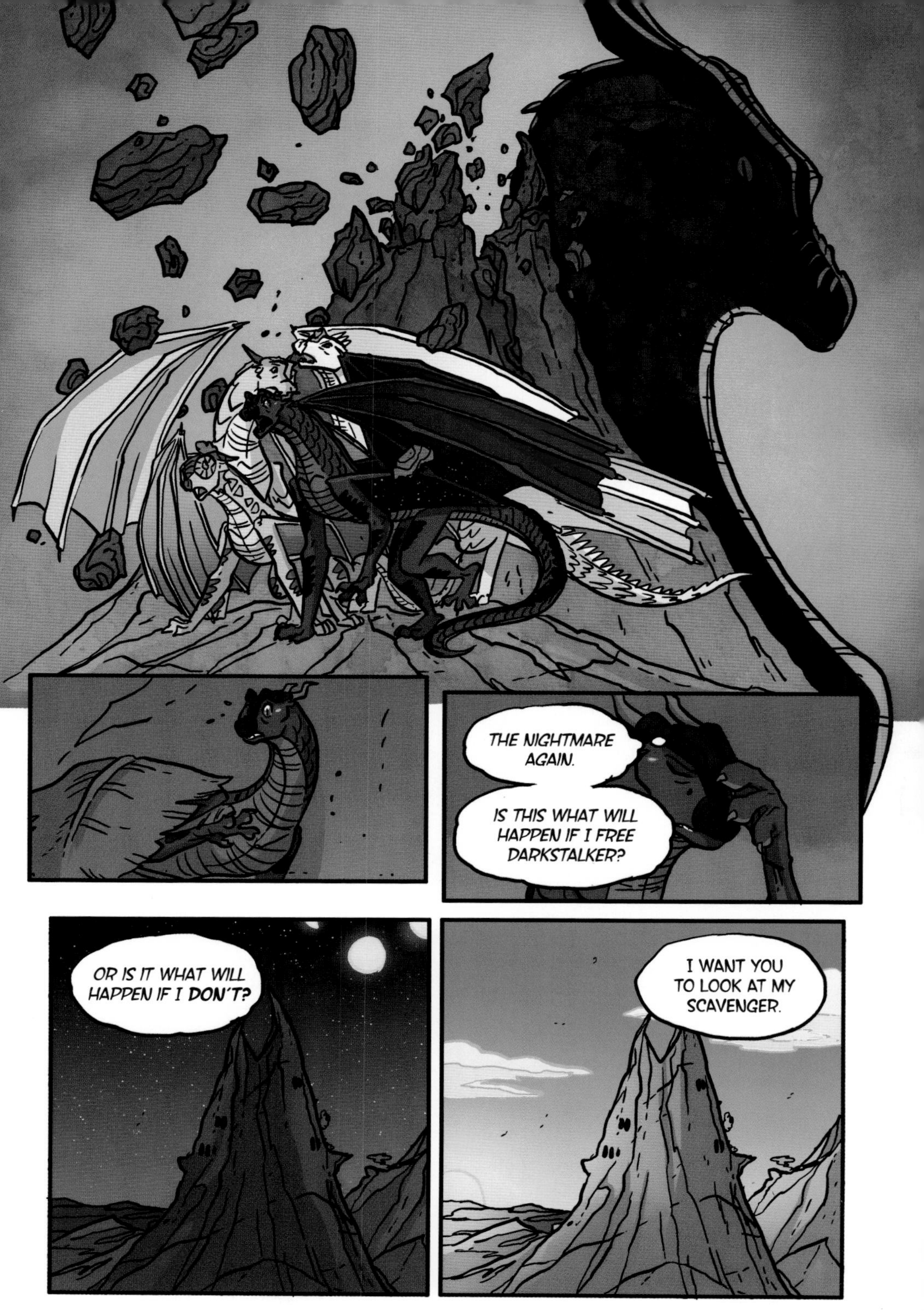
THE NIGHTMARE AGAIN.
IS THIS WHAT WILL HAPPEN IF I FREE DARKSTALKER?
OR IS IT WHAT WILL HAPPEN IF I **DON'T**?
I WANT YOU TO LOOK AT MY SCAVENGER.

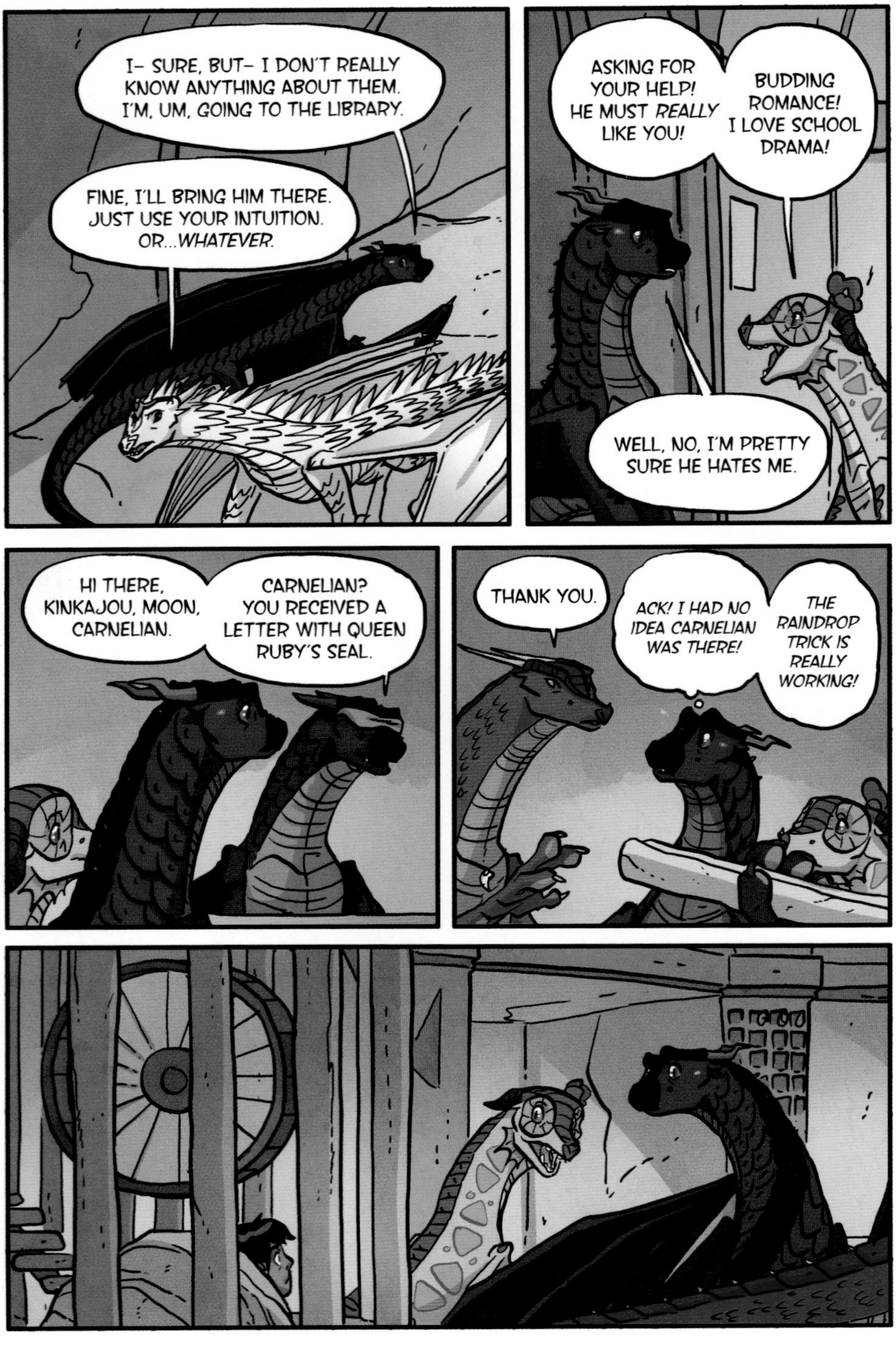
I– SURE, BUT– I DON'T REALLY KNOW ANYTHING ABOUT THEM. I'M, UM, GOING TO THE LIBRARY.
FINE, I'LL BRING HIM THERE. JUST USE YOUR INTUITION. OR...*WHATEVER.*
ASKING FOR YOUR HELP! HE MUST *REALLY* LIKE YOU!
BUDDING ROMANCE! I LOVE SCHOOL DRAMA!
WELL, NO, I'M PRETTY SURE HE HATES ME.
HI THERE, KINKAJOU, MOON, CARNELIAN.
CARNELIAN? YOU RECEIVED A LETTER WITH QUEEN RUBY'S SEAL.
THANK YOU.
ACK! I HAD NO IDEA CARNELIAN WAS THERE!
THE RAINDROP TRICK IS REALLY WORKING!

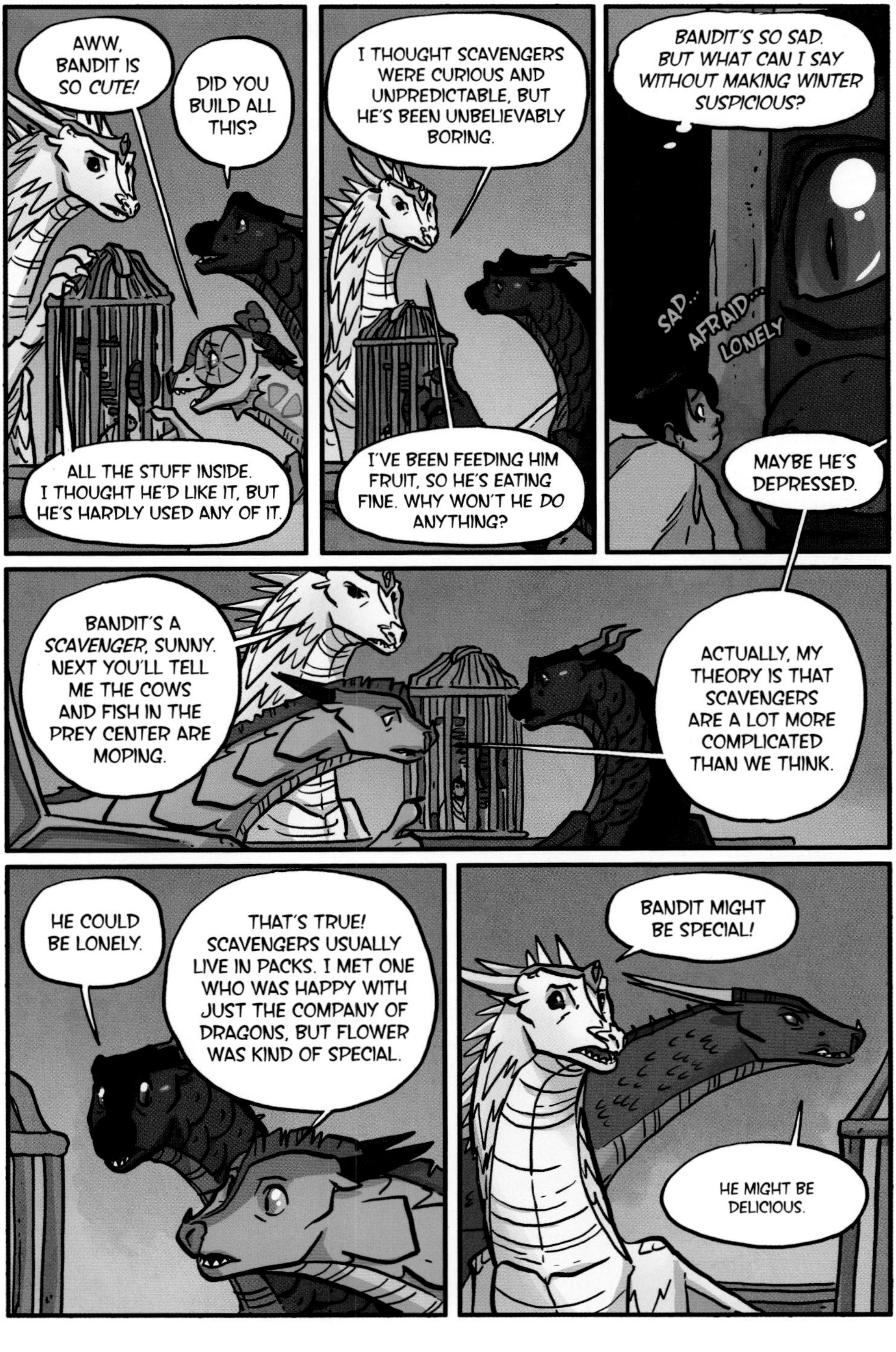
AWW, BANDIT IS SO *CUTE!*
DID YOU BUILD ALL THIS?
ALL THE STUFF INSIDE. I THOUGHT HE'D LIKE IT, BUT HE'S HARDLY USED ANY OF IT.
I THOUGHT SCAVENGERS WERE CURIOUS AND UNPREDICTABLE, BUT HE'S BEEN UNBELIEVABLY BORING.
I'VE BEEN FEEDING HIM FRUIT, SO HE'S EATING FINE. WHY WON'T HE *DO* ANYTHING?
BANDIT'S SO SAD. BUT WHAT CAN I SAY WITHOUT MAKING WINTER SUSPICIOUS?
SAD...
AFRAID...
LONELY
MAYBE HE'S DEPRESSED.
BANDIT'S A *SCAVENGER*, SUNNY. NEXT YOU'LL TELL ME THE COWS AND FISH IN THE PREY CENTER ARE MOPING.
ACTUALLY, MY THEORY IS THAT SCAVENGERS ARE A LOT MORE COMPLICATED THAN WE THINK.
HE COULD BE LONELY.
THAT'S TRUE! SCAVENGERS USUALLY LIVE IN PACKS. I MET ONE WHO WAS HAPPY WITH JUST THE COMPANY OF DRAGONS, BUT FLOWER WAS KIND OF SPECIAL.
BANDIT MIGHT BE SPECIAL!
HE MIGHT BE DELICIOUS.

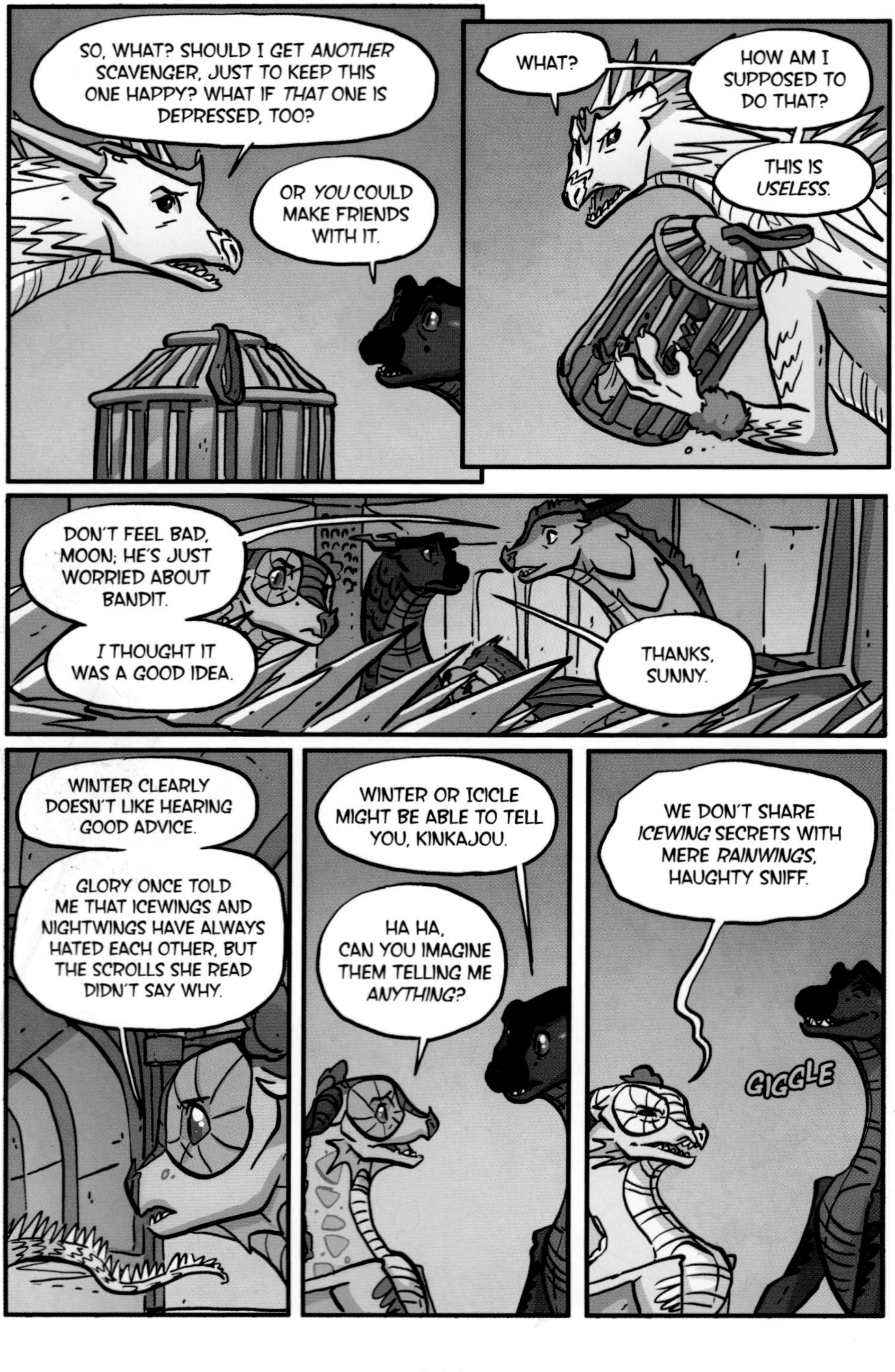
SO, WHAT? SHOULD I GET *ANOTHER* SCAVENGER, JUST TO KEEP THIS ONE HAPPY? WHAT IF *THAT* ONE IS DEPRESSED, TOO?
OR *YOU* COULD MAKE FRIENDS WITH IT.
WHAT?
HOW AM I SUPPOSED TO DO THAT?
THIS IS *USELESS*.
DON'T FEEL BAD, MOON; HE'S JUST WORRIED ABOUT BANDIT.
I THOUGHT IT WAS A GOOD IDEA.
THANKS, SUNNY.
WINTER CLEARLY DOESN'T LIKE HEARING GOOD ADVICE.
GLORY ONCE TOLD ME THAT ICEWINGS AND NIGHTWINGS HAVE ALWAYS HATED EACH OTHER, BUT THE SCROLLS SHE READ DIDN'T SAY WHY.
WINTER OR ICICLE MIGHT BE ABLE TO TELL YOU, KINKAJOU.
HA HA, CAN YOU IMAGINE THEM TELLING ME *ANYTHING*?
WE DON'T SHARE *ICEWING* SECRETS WITH MERE *RAINWINGS*, HAUGHTY SNIFF.
GIGGLE

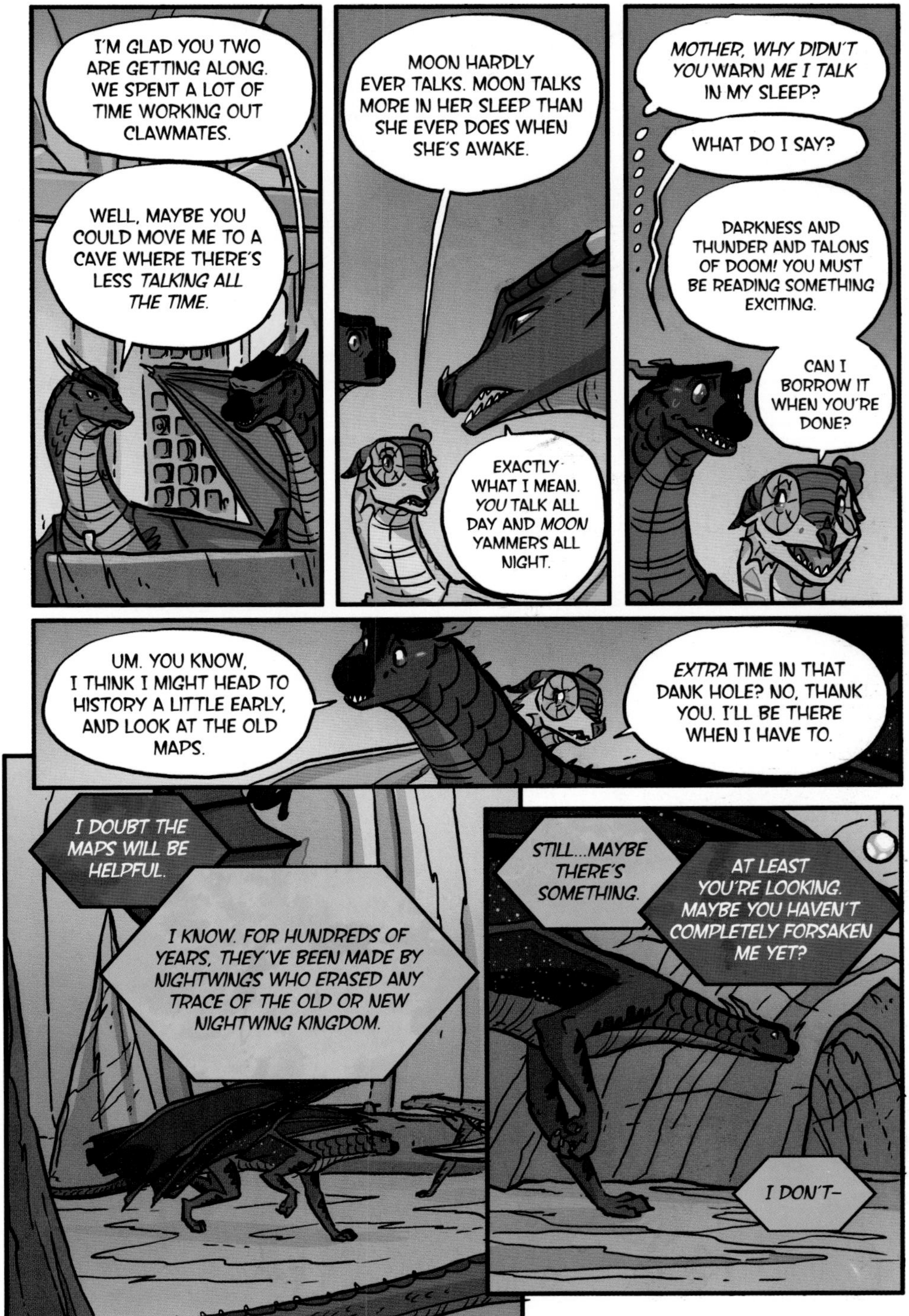
I'M GLAD YOU TWO ARE GETTING ALONG. WE SPENT A LOT OF TIME WORKING OUT CLAWMATES.
WELL, MAYBE YOU COULD MOVE ME TO A CAVE WHERE THERE'S LESS *TALKING ALL THE TIME.*
MOON HARDLY EVER TALKS. MOON TALKS MORE IN HER SLEEP THAN SHE EVER DOES WHEN SHE'S AWAKE.
EXACTLY WHAT I MEAN. *YOU* TALK ALL DAY AND *MOON* YAMMERS ALL NIGHT.
MOTHER, WHY DIDN'T YOU WARN ME I TALK IN MY SLEEP?
WHAT DO I SAY?
DARKNESS AND THUNDER AND TALONS OF DOOM! YOU MUST BE READING SOMETHING EXCITING.
CAN I BORROW IT WHEN YOU'RE DONE?
UM. YOU KNOW, I THINK I MIGHT HEAD TO HISTORY A LITTLE EARLY, AND LOOK AT THE OLD MAPS.
EXTRA TIME IN THAT DANK HOLE? NO, THANK YOU. I'LL BE THERE WHEN I HAVE TO.
I DOUBT THE MAPS WILL BE HELPFUL.
I KNOW. FOR HUNDREDS OF YEARS, THEY'VE BEEN MADE BY NIGHTWINGS WHO ERASED ANY TRACE OF THE OLD OR NEW NIGHTWING KINGDOM.
STILL...MAYBE THERE'S SOMETHING.
AT LEAST YOU'RE LOOKING. MAYBE YOU HAVEN'T COMPLETELY FORSAKEN ME YET?
I DON'T—

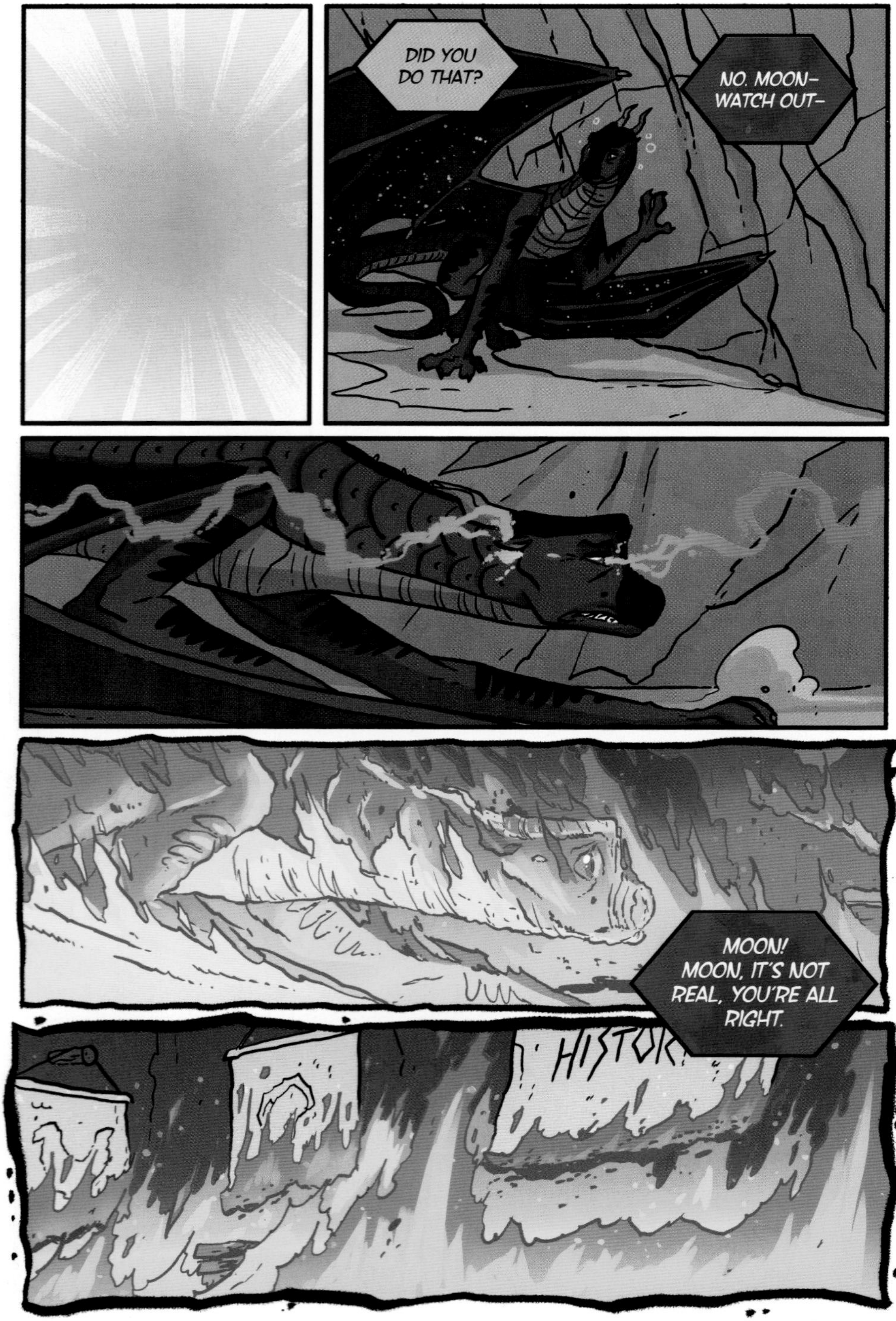

DID YOU DO THAT?
NO. MOON— WATCH OUT—
MOON! MOON, IT'S NOT REAL, YOU'RE ALL RIGHT.
HISTOR

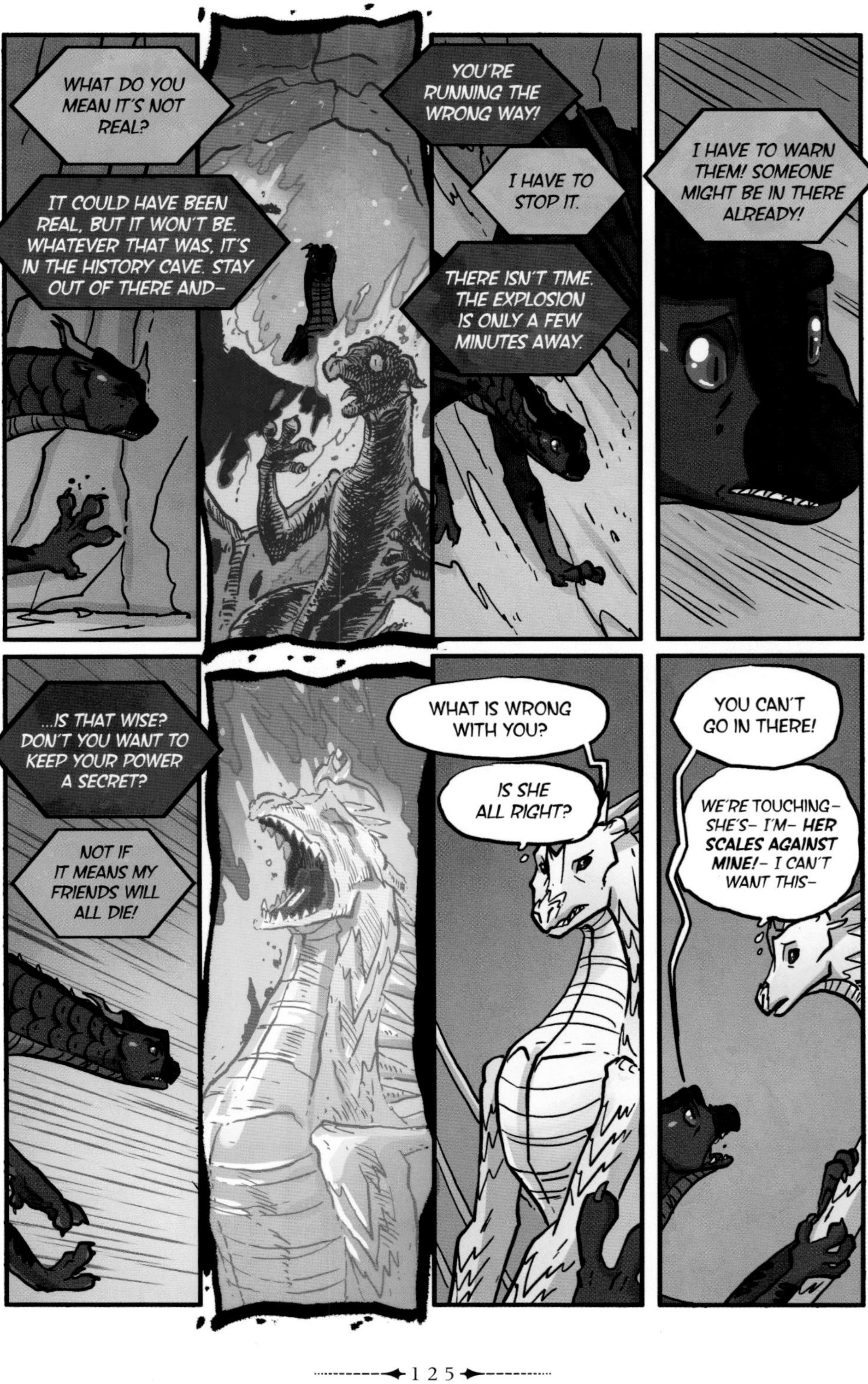
WHAT DO YOU MEAN IT'S NOT REAL?
IT COULD HAVE BEEN REAL, BUT IT WON'T BE. WHATEVER THAT WAS, IT'S IN THE HISTORY CAVE. STAY OUT OF THERE AND–
YOU'RE RUNNING THE WRONG WAY!
I HAVE TO STOP IT.
THERE ISN'T TIME. THE EXPLOSION IS ONLY A FEW MINUTES AWAY.
I HAVE TO WARN THEM! SOMEONE MIGHT BE IN THERE ALREADY!
...IS THAT WISE? DON'T YOU WANT TO KEEP YOUR POWER A SECRET?
NOT IF IT MEANS MY FRIENDS WILL ALL DIE!
WHAT IS WRONG WITH YOU?
IS SHE ALL RIGHT?
YOU CAN'T GO IN THERE!
WE'RE TOUCHING– SHE'S– I'M– **HER SCALES AGAINST MINE!**– I CAN'T WANT THIS–

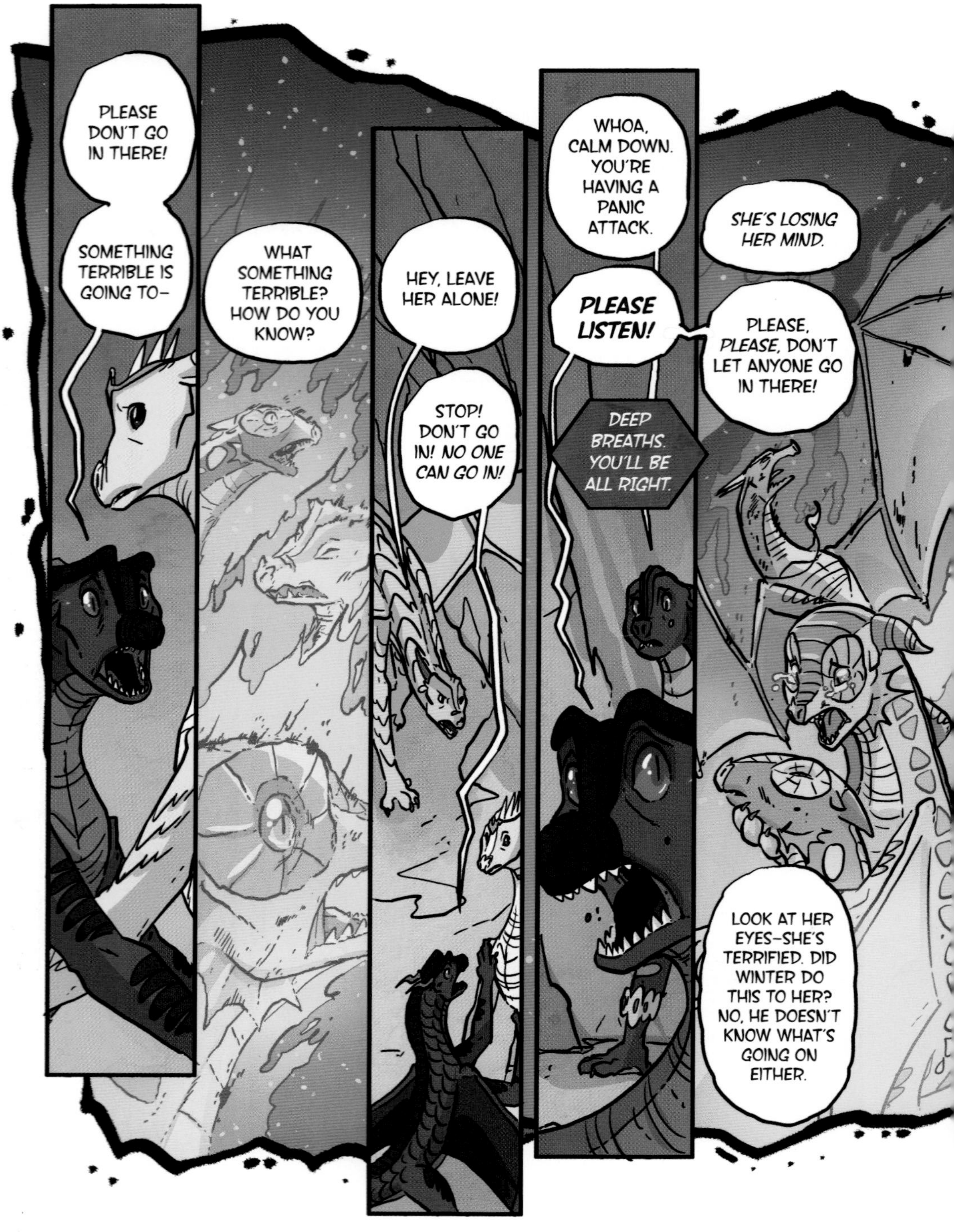
PLEASE DON'T GO IN THERE!
SOMETHING TERRIBLE IS GOING TO—
WHAT SOMETHING TERRIBLE? HOW DO YOU KNOW?
HEY, LEAVE HER ALONE!
STOP! DON'T GO IN! NO ONE CAN GO IN!
WHOA, CALM DOWN. YOU'RE HAVING A PANIC ATTACK.
PLEASE LISTEN!
DEEP BREATHS. YOU'LL BE ALL RIGHT.
SHE'S LOSING HER MIND.
PLEASE, PLEASE, DON'T LET ANYONE GO IN THERE!
LOOK AT HER EYES—SHE'S TERRIFIED. DID WINTER DO THIS TO HER? NO, HE DOESN'T KNOW WHAT'S GOING ON EITHER.

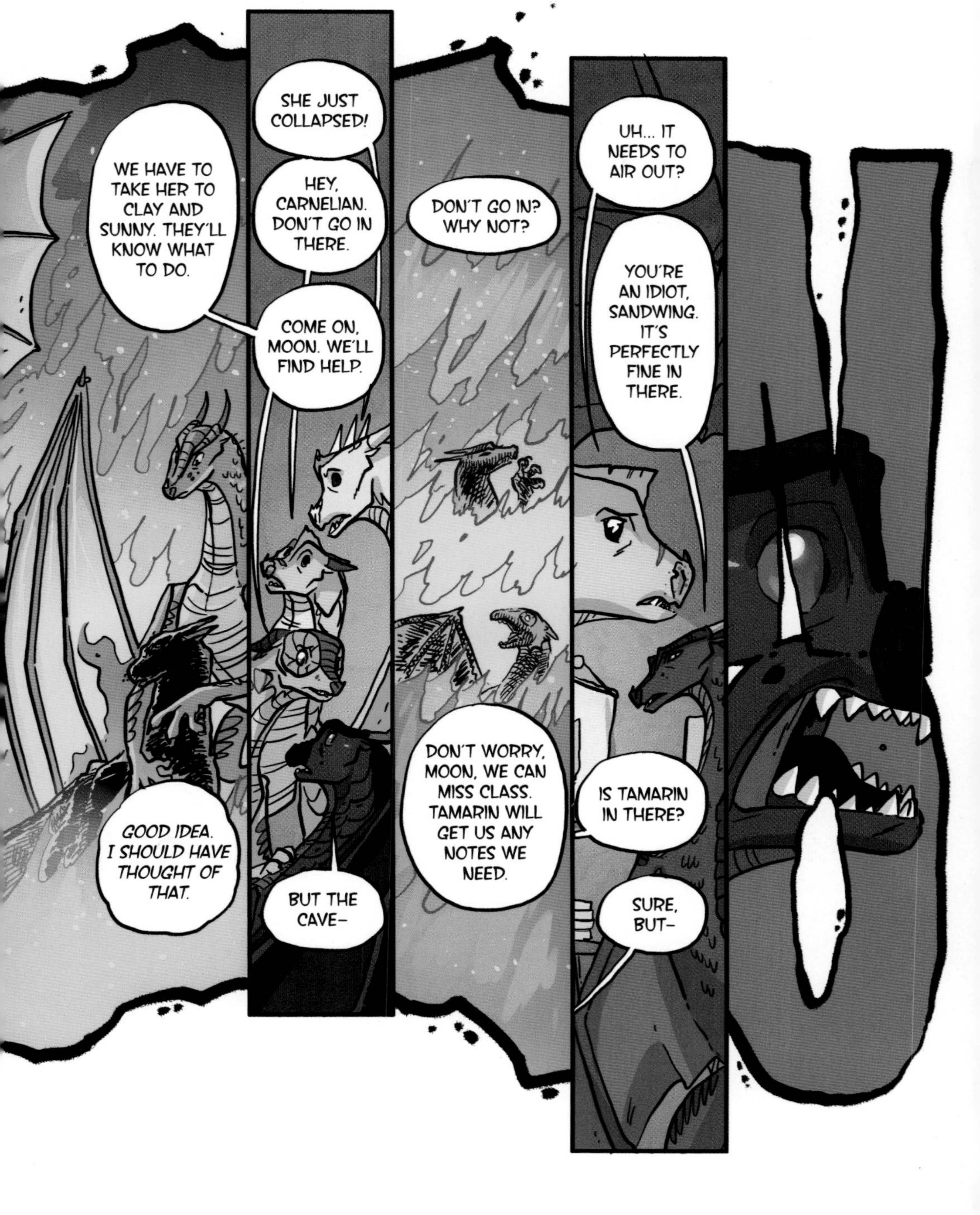
WE HAVE TO TAKE HER TO CLAY AND SUNNY. THEY'LL KNOW WHAT TO DO.
GOOD IDEA. I SHOULD HAVE THOUGHT OF THAT.
SHE JUST COLLAPSED!
HEY, CARNELIAN. DON'T GO IN THERE.
COME ON, MOON. WE'LL FIND HELP.
BUT THE CAVE–
DON'T GO IN? WHY NOT?
DON'T WORRY, MOON, WE CAN MISS CLASS. TAMARIN WILL GET US ANY NOTES WE NEED.
UH... IT NEEDS TO AIR OUT?
YOU'RE AN IDIOT, SANDWING. IT'S PERFECTLY FINE IN THERE.
IS TAMARIN IN THERE?
SURE, BUT–

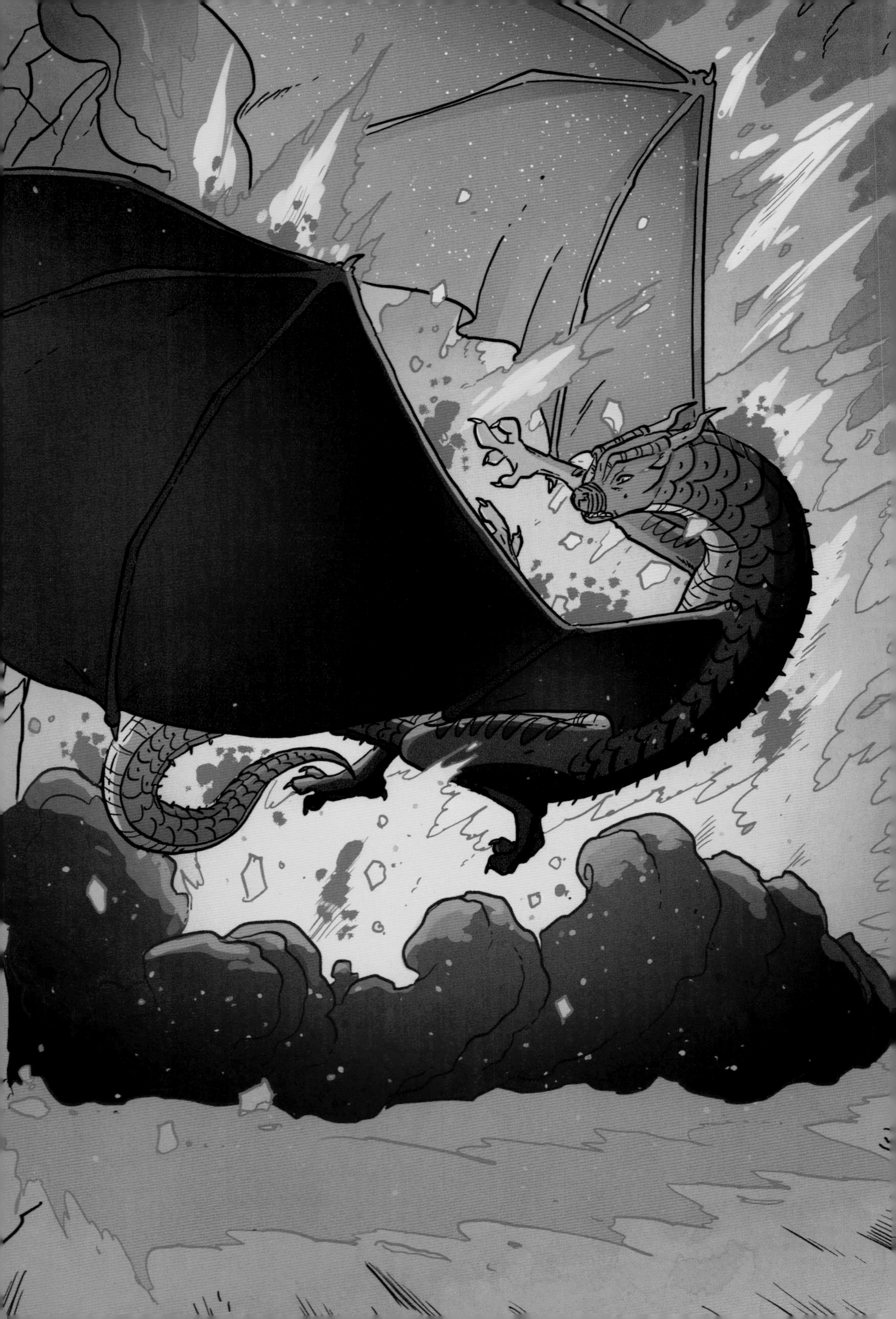

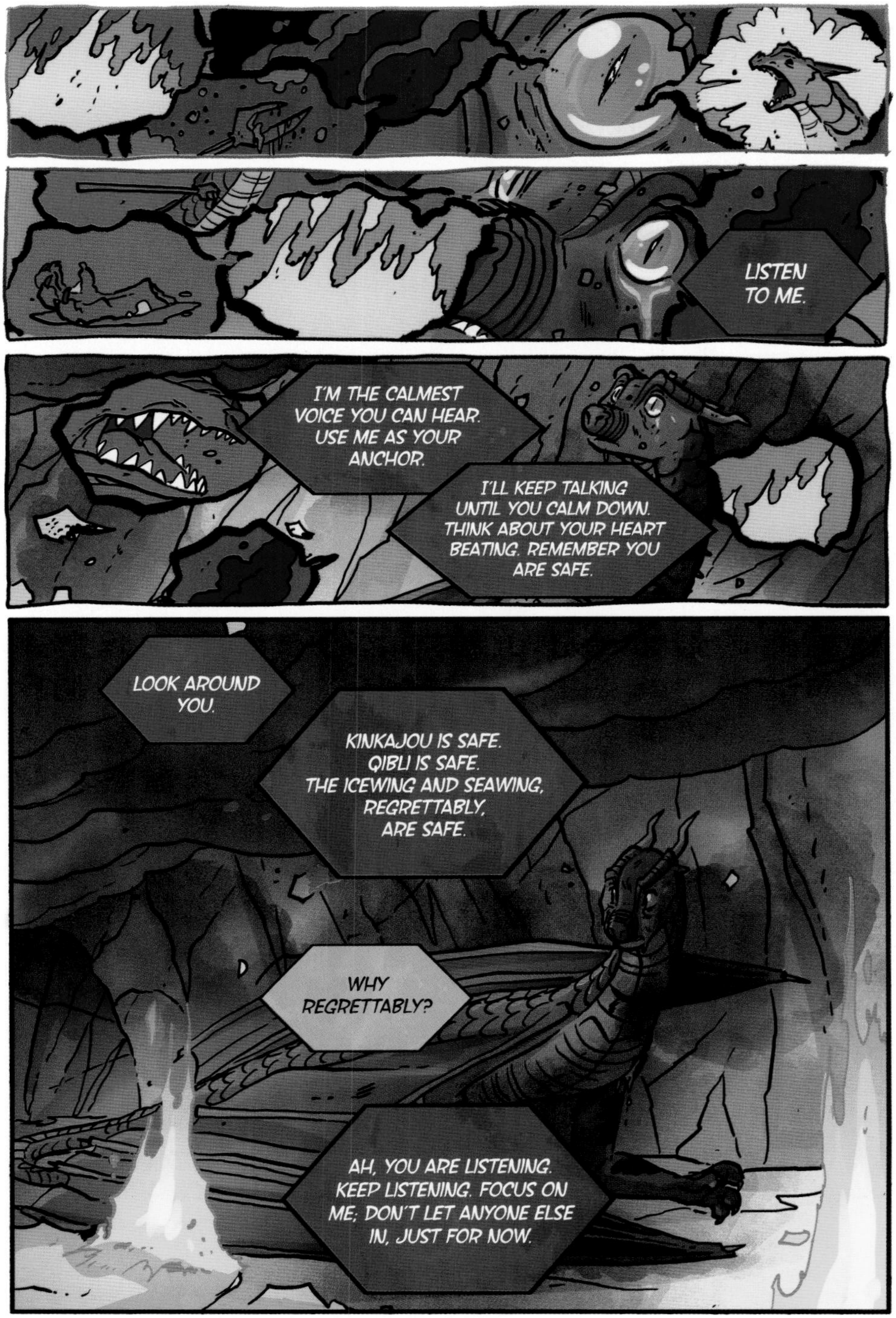
LISTEN TO ME.
I'M THE CALMEST VOICE YOU CAN HEAR. USE ME AS YOUR ANCHOR.
I'LL KEEP TALKING UNTIL YOU CALM DOWN. THINK ABOUT YOUR HEART BEATING. REMEMBER YOU ARE SAFE.
LOOK AROUND YOU.
KINKAJOU IS SAFE. QIBLI IS SAFE. THE ICEWING AND SEAWING, REGRETTABLY, ARE SAFE.
WHY REGRETTABLY?
AH, YOU ARE LISTENING. KEEP LISTENING. FOCUS ON ME; DON'T LET ANYONE ELSE IN, JUST FOR NOW.

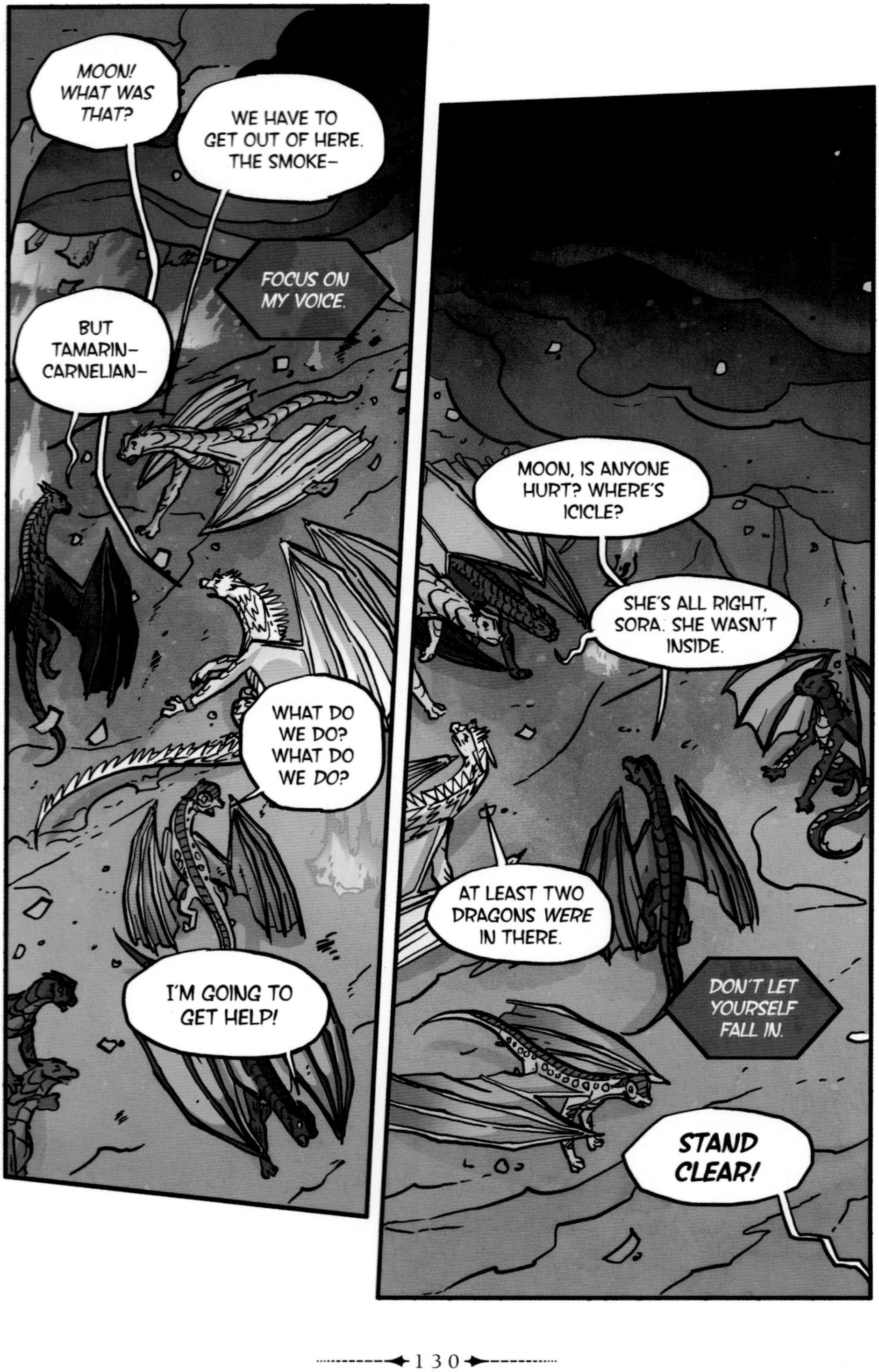
MOON! WHAT WAS THAT?
WE HAVE TO GET OUT OF HERE. THE SMOKE–
FOCUS ON MY VOICE.
BUT TAMARIN– CARNELIAN–
WHAT DO WE DO? WHAT DO WE DO?
I'M GOING TO GET HELP!
MOON, IS ANYONE HURT? WHERE'S ICICLE?
SHE'S ALL RIGHT, SORA. SHE WASN'T INSIDE.
AT LEAST TWO DRAGONS WERE IN THERE.
DON'T LET YOURSELF FALL IN.
STAND CLEAR!

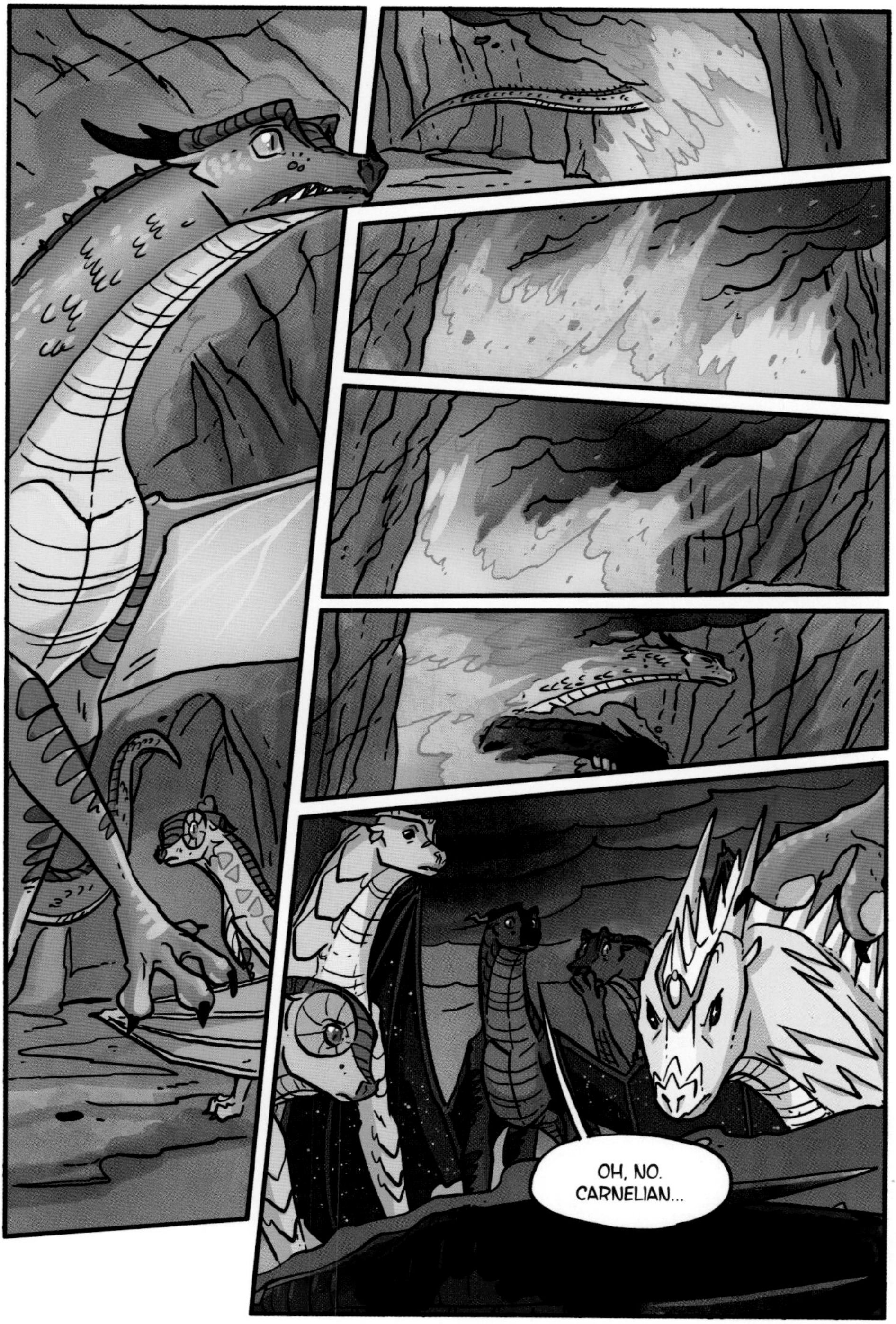
OH, NO.
CARNELIAN...

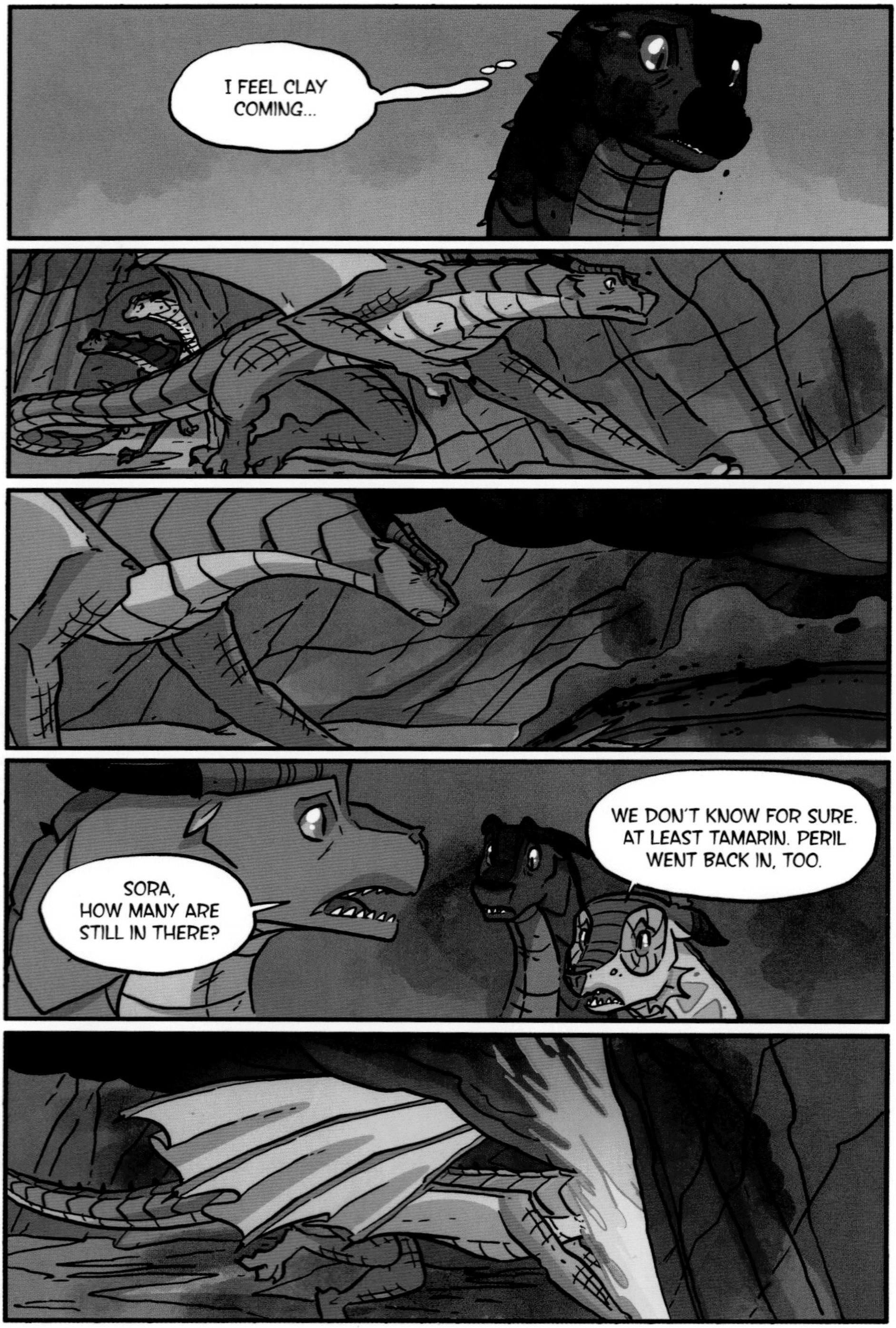
I FEEL CLAY
COMING...
SORA,
HOW MANY ARE
STILL IN THERE?
WE DON'T KNOW FOR SURE.
AT LEAST TAMARIN. PERIL
WENT BACK IN, TOO.

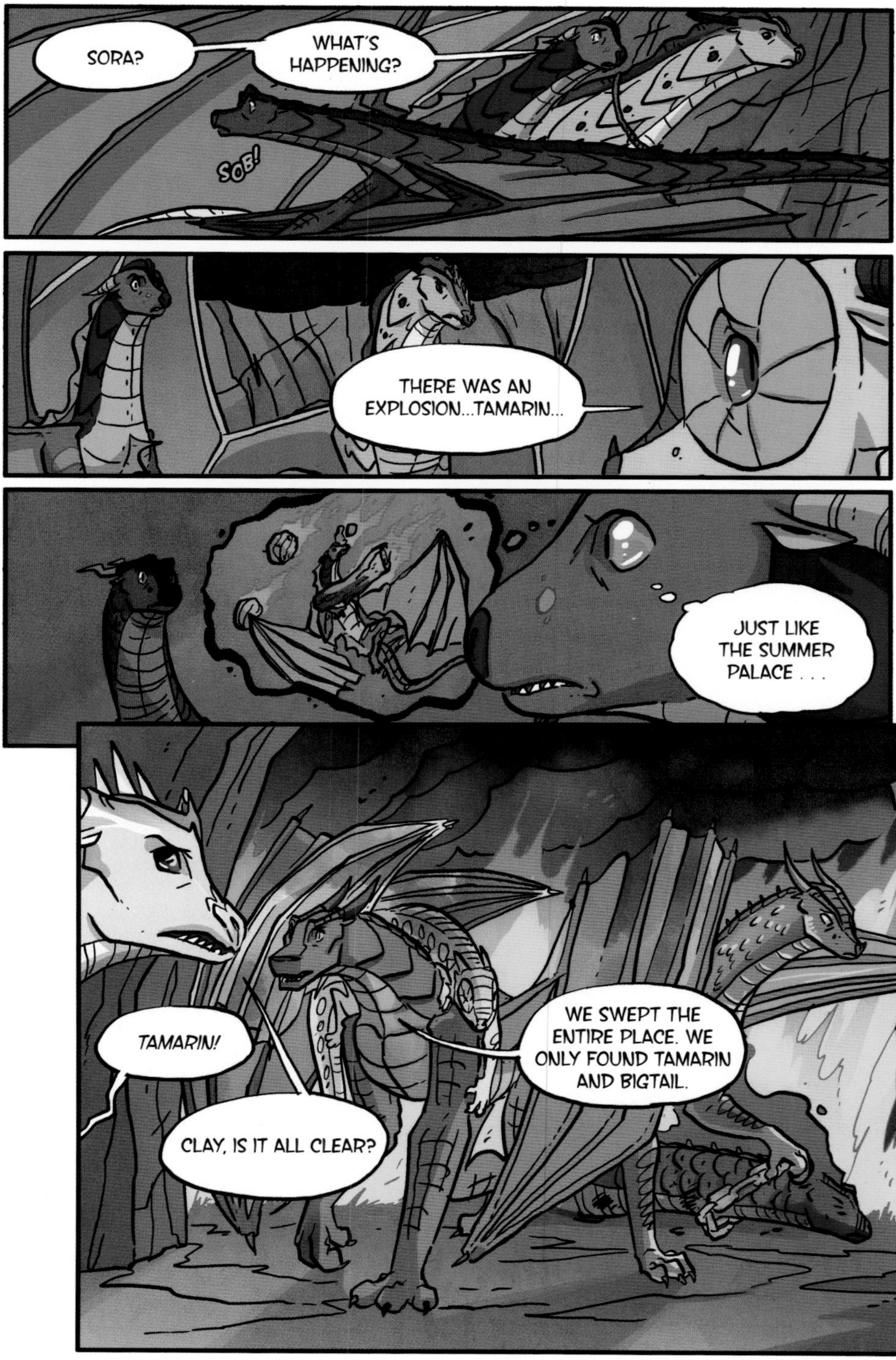
SORA?
WHAT'S HAPPENING?
SOB!
THERE WAS AN EXPLOSION...TAMARIN...
JUST LIKE THE SUMMER PALACE . . .
TAMARIN!
CLAY, IS IT ALL CLEAR?
WE SWEPT THE ENTIRE PLACE. WE ONLY FOUND TAMARIN AND BIGTAIL.

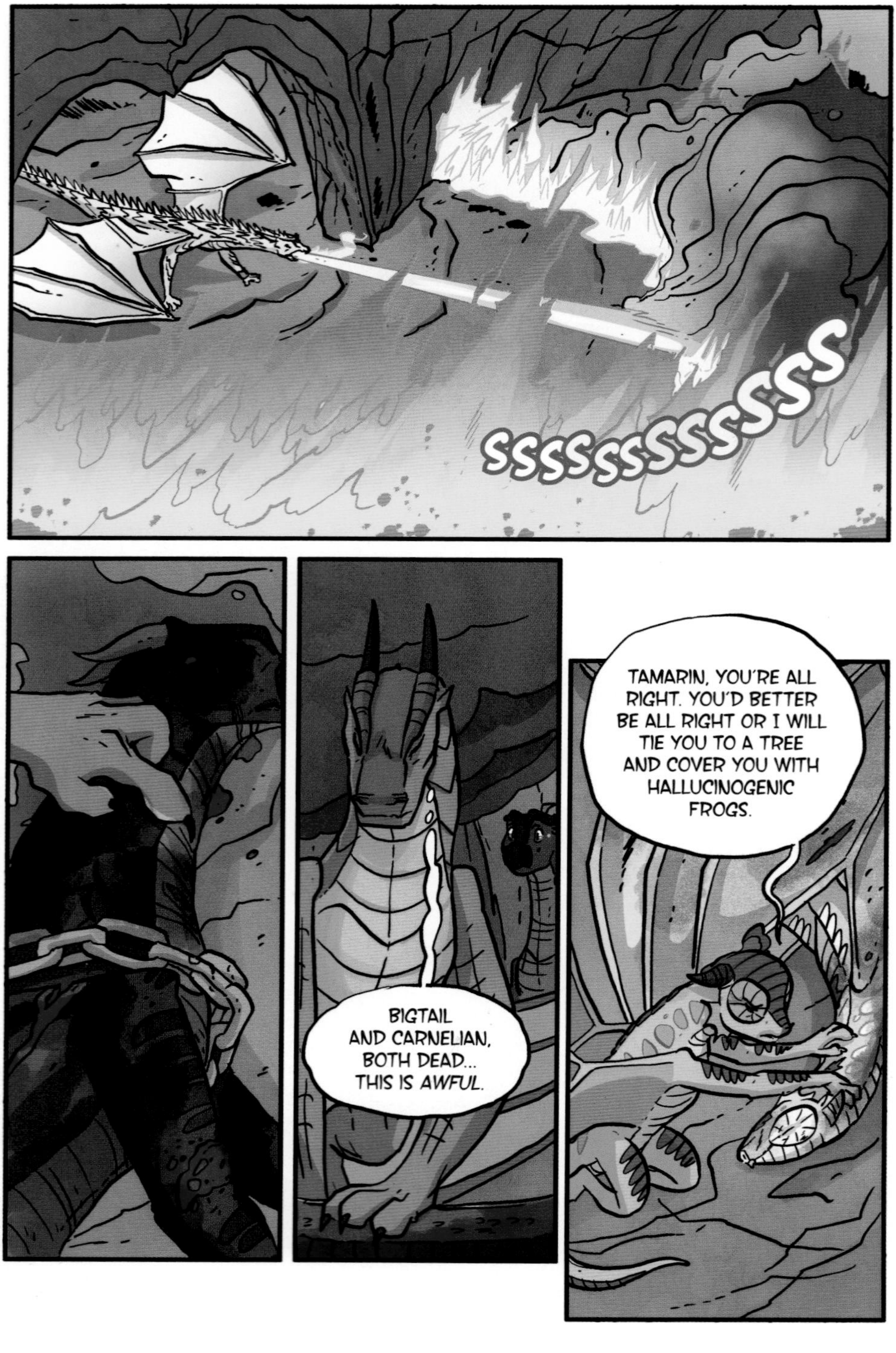
SSSSSSSSSSSS
BIGTAIL AND CARNELIAN, BOTH DEAD... THIS IS AWFUL.
TAMARIN, YOU'RE ALL RIGHT. YOU'D BETTER BE ALL RIGHT OR I WILL TIE YOU TO A TREE AND COVER YOU WITH HALLUCINOGENIC FROGS.

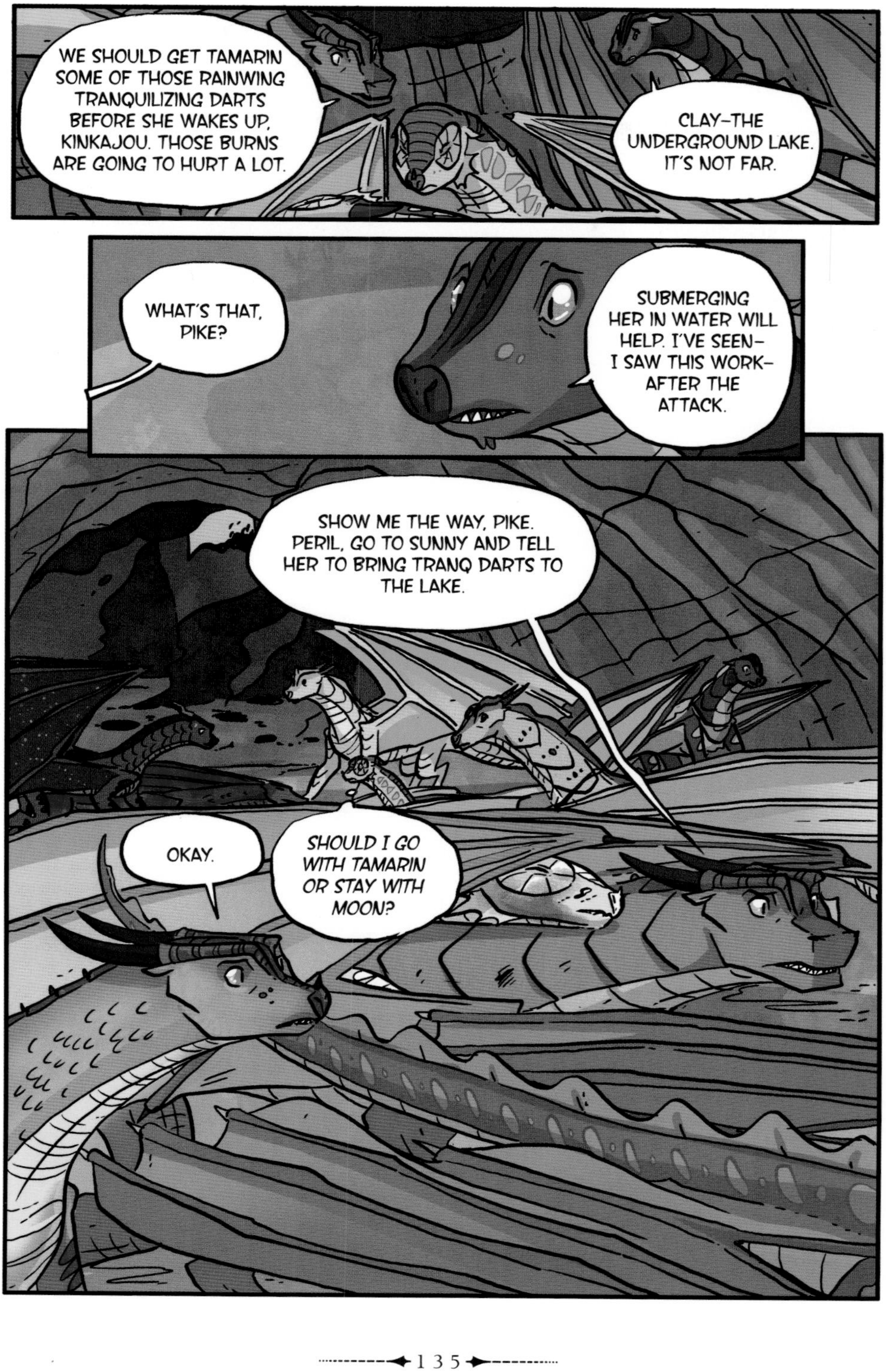
WE SHOULD GET TAMARIN SOME OF THOSE RAINWING TRANQUILIZING DARTS BEFORE SHE WAKES UP, KINKAJOU. THOSE BURNS ARE GOING TO HURT A LOT.
CLAY—THE UNDERGROUND LAKE. IT'S NOT FAR.
WHAT'S THAT, PIKE?
SUBMERGING HER IN WATER WILL HELP. I'VE SEEN— I SAW THIS WORK— AFTER THE ATTACK.
SHOW ME THE WAY, PIKE. PERIL, GO TO SUNNY AND TELL HER TO BRING TRANQ DARTS TO THE LAKE.
OKAY.
SHOULD I GO WITH TAMARIN OR STAY WITH MOON?

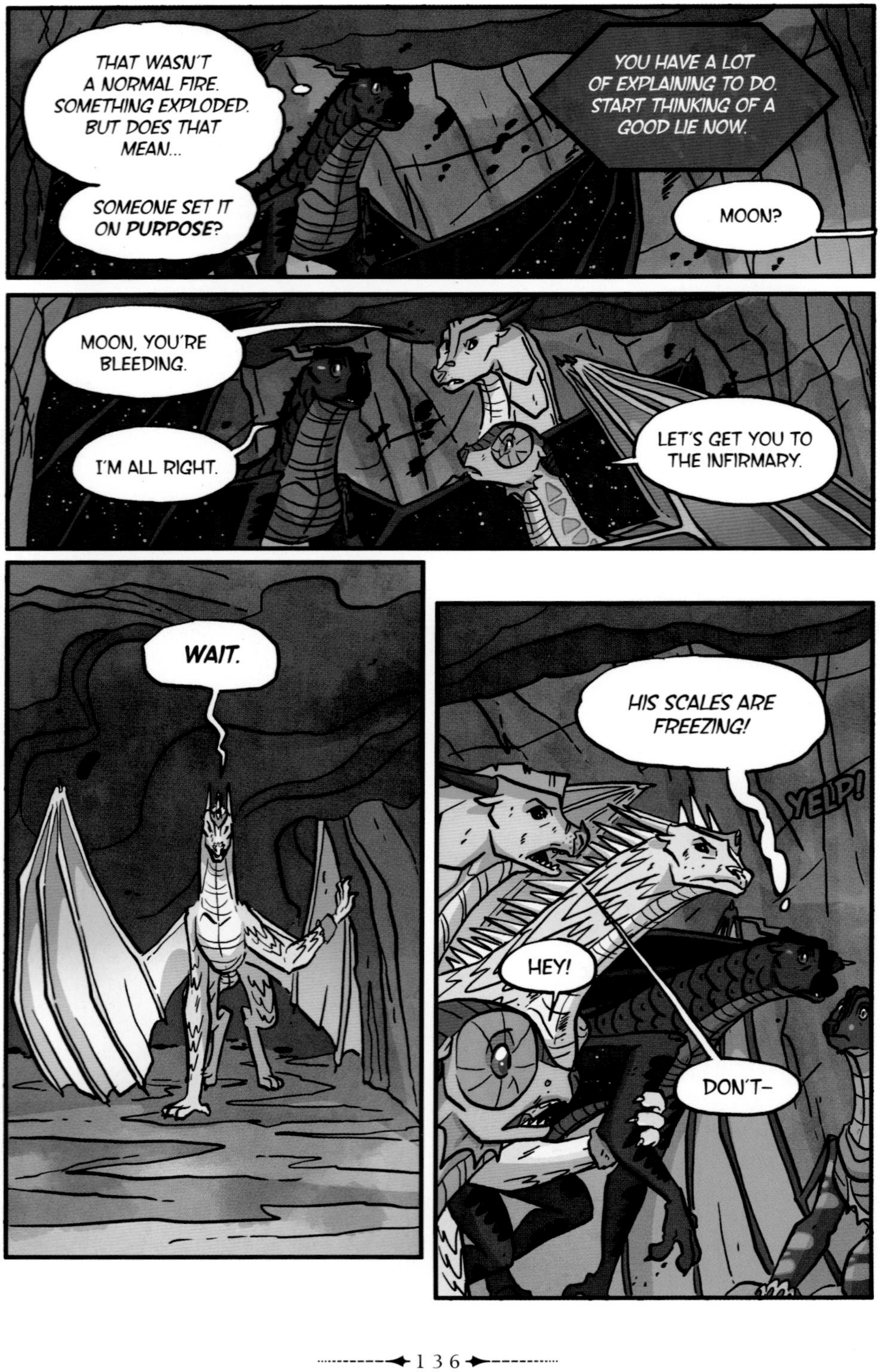
THAT WASN'T A NORMAL FIRE. SOMETHING EXPLODED. BUT DOES THAT MEAN...
SOMEONE SET IT ON PURPOSE?
YOU HAVE A LOT OF EXPLAINING TO DO. START THINKING OF A GOOD LIE NOW.
MOON?
MOON, YOU'RE BLEEDING.
I'M ALL RIGHT.
LET'S GET YOU TO THE INFIRMARY.
WAIT.
HIS SCALES ARE FREEZING!
YELP!
HEY!
DON'T–

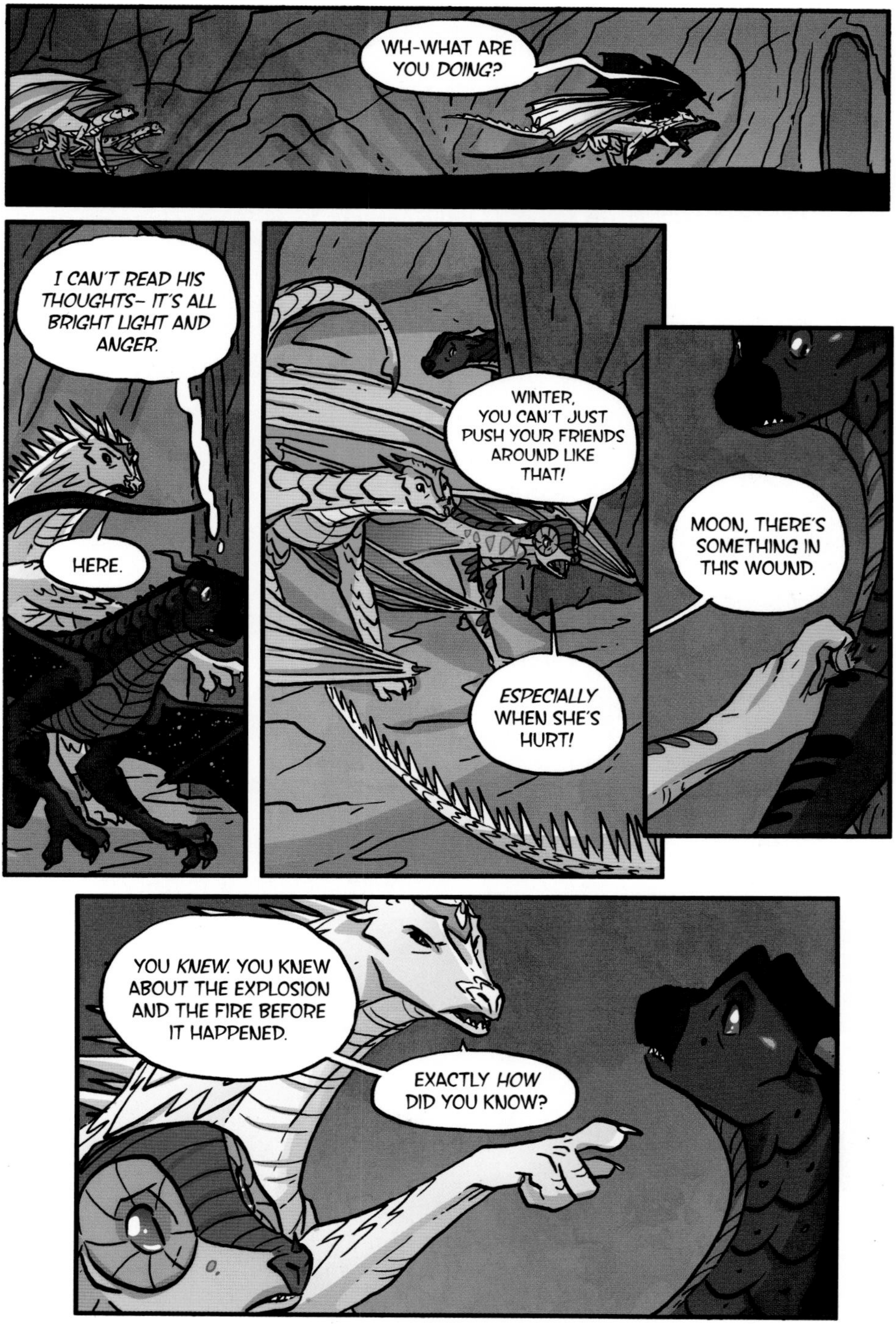
WH-WHAT ARE YOU *DOING*?
I CAN'T READ HIS THOUGHTS– IT'S ALL BRIGHT LIGHT AND ANGER.
HERE.
WINTER, YOU CAN'T JUST PUSH YOUR FRIENDS AROUND LIKE THAT!
ESPECIALLY WHEN SHE'S HURT!
MOON, THERE'S SOMETHING IN THIS WOUND.
YOU *KNEW*. YOU KNEW ABOUT THE EXPLOSION AND THE FIRE BEFORE IT HAPPENED.
EXACTLY *HOW* DID YOU KNOW?

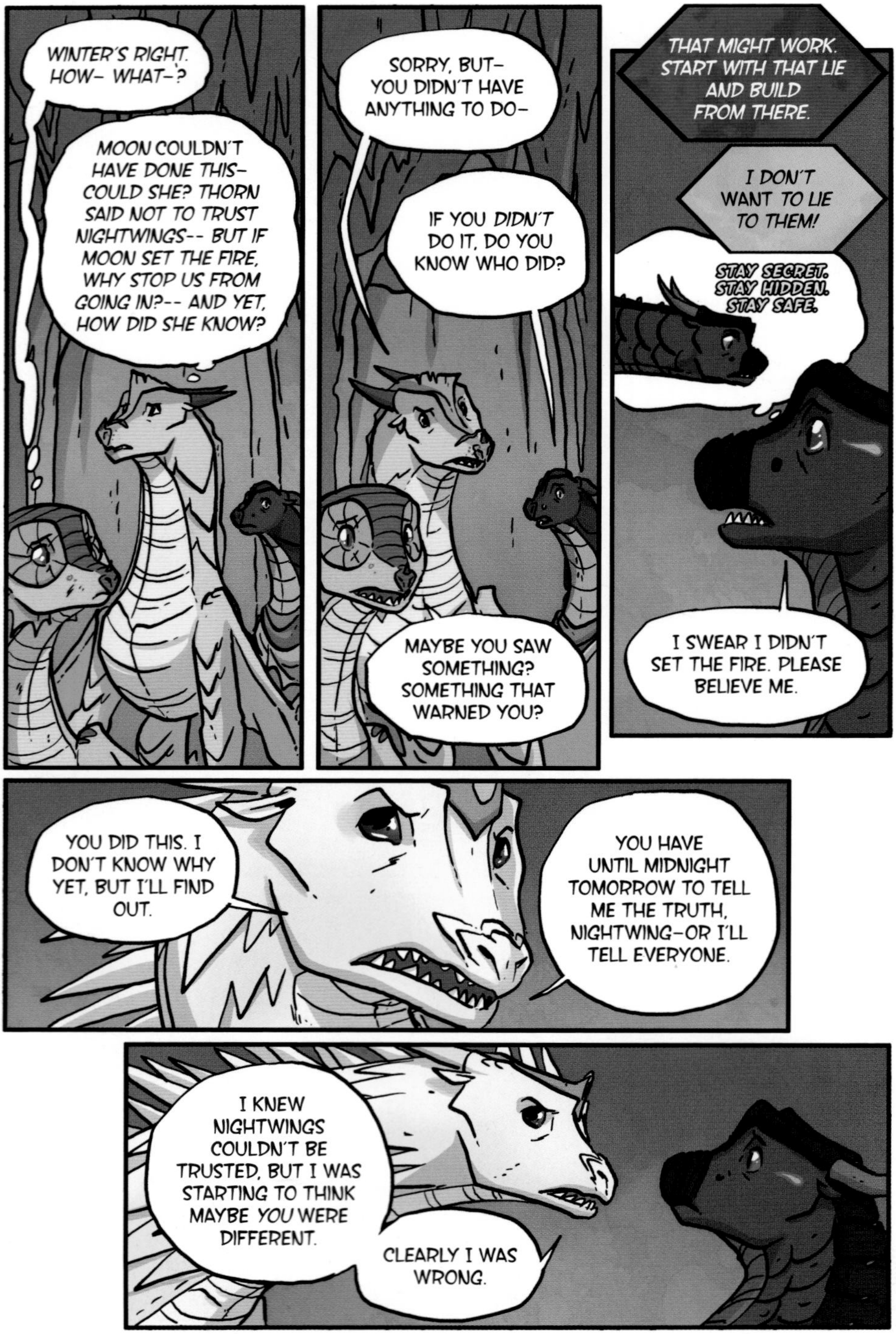
WINTER'S RIGHT. HOW– WHAT–?
MOON COULDN'T HAVE DONE THIS– COULD SHE? THORN SAID NOT TO TRUST NIGHTWINGS-- BUT IF MOON SET THE FIRE, WHY STOP US FROM GOING IN?-- AND YET, HOW DID SHE KNOW?
SORRY, BUT– YOU DIDN'T HAVE ANYTHING TO DO–
IF YOU DIDN'T DO IT, DO YOU KNOW WHO DID?
MAYBE YOU SAW SOMETHING? SOMETHING THAT WARNED YOU?
THAT MIGHT WORK. START WITH THAT LIE AND BUILD FROM THERE.
I DON'T WANT TO LIE TO THEM!
STAY SECRET. STAY HIDDEN. STAY SAFE.
I SWEAR I DIDN'T SET THE FIRE. PLEASE BELIEVE ME.
YOU DID THIS. I DON'T KNOW WHY YET, BUT I'LL FIND OUT.
YOU HAVE UNTIL MIDNIGHT TOMORROW TO TELL ME THE TRUTH, NIGHTWING–OR I'LL TELL EVERYONE.
I KNEW NIGHTWINGS COULDN'T BE TRUSTED, BUT I WAS STARTING TO THINK MAYBE YOU WERE DIFFERENT.
CLEARLY I WAS WRONG.

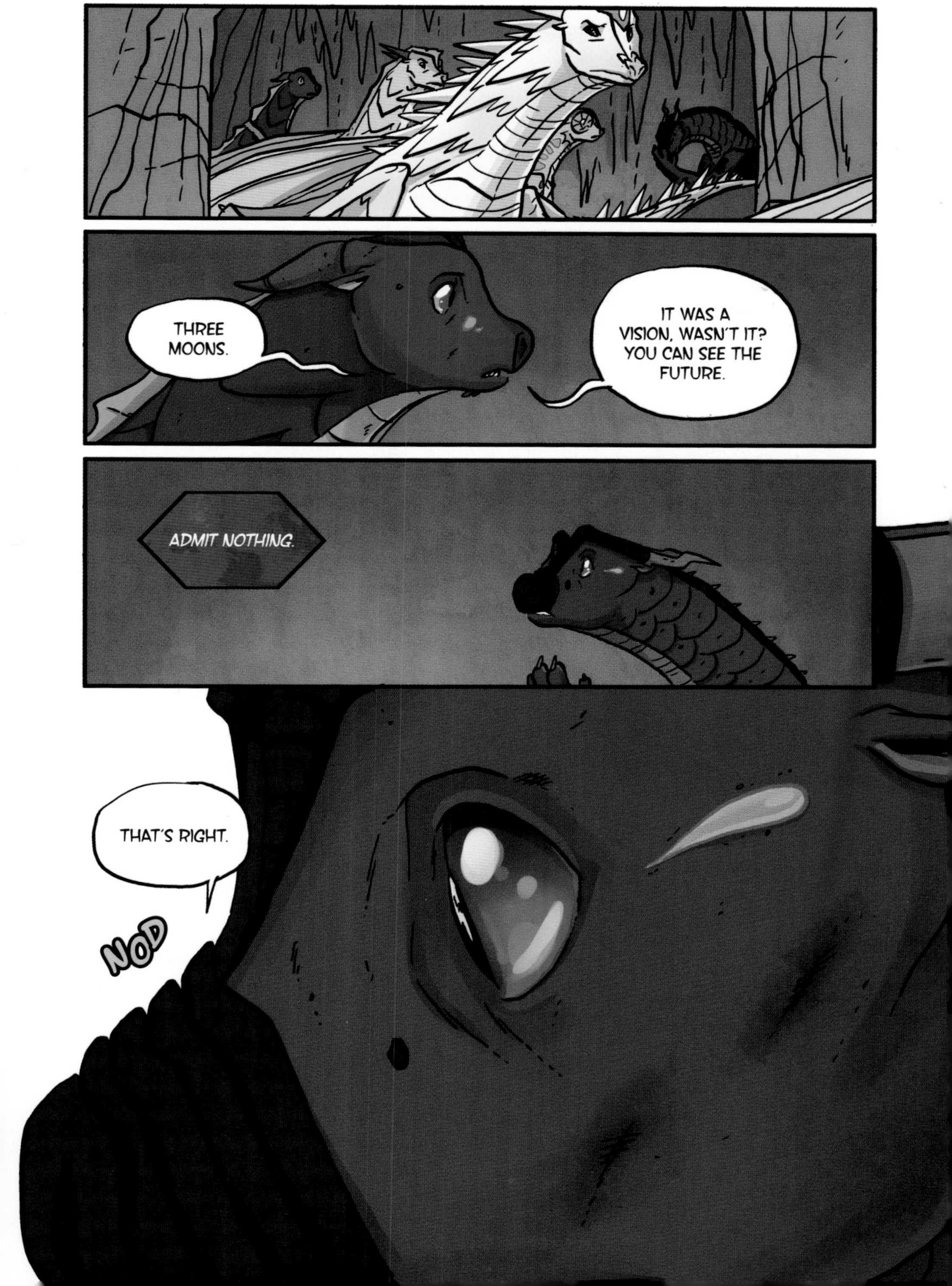
THREE MOONS.
IT WAS A VISION, WASN'T IT? YOU CAN SEE THE FUTURE.
ADMIT NOTHING.
THAT'S RIGHT.
NOD

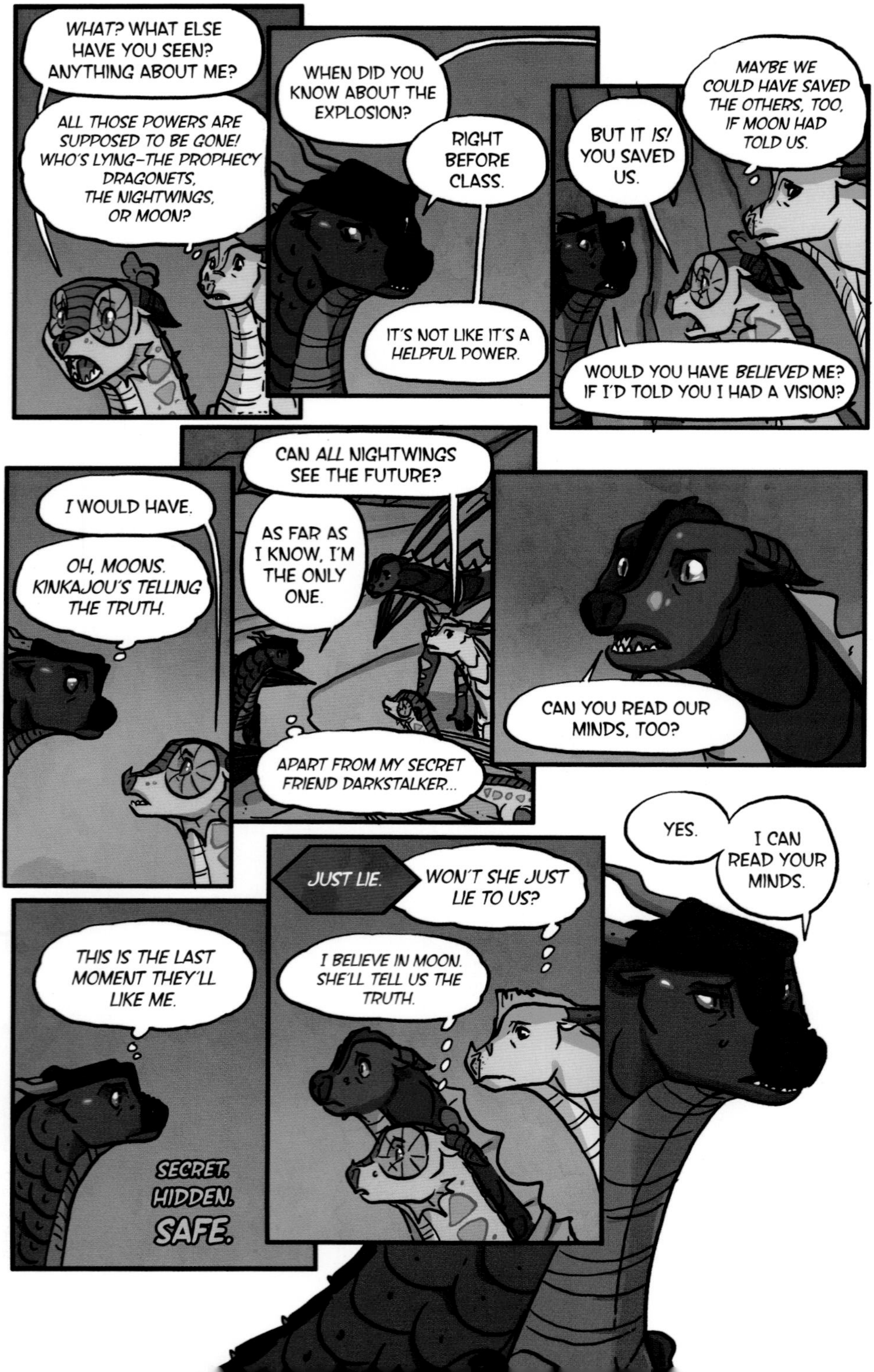
WHAT? WHAT ELSE HAVE YOU SEEN? ANYTHING ABOUT ME?
ALL THOSE POWERS ARE SUPPOSED TO BE GONE! WHO'S LYING–THE PROPHECY DRAGONETS, THE NIGHTWINGS, OR MOON?
WHEN DID YOU KNOW ABOUT THE EXPLOSION?
RIGHT BEFORE CLASS.
IT'S NOT LIKE IT'S A HELPFUL POWER.
BUT IT IS! YOU SAVED US.
MAYBE WE COULD HAVE SAVED THE OTHERS, TOO, IF MOON HAD TOLD US.
WOULD YOU HAVE BELIEVED ME? IF I'D TOLD YOU I HAD A VISION?
I WOULD HAVE.
OH, MOONS. KINKAJOU'S TELLING THE TRUTH.
CAN ALL NIGHTWINGS SEE THE FUTURE?
AS FAR AS I KNOW, I'M THE ONLY ONE.
APART FROM MY SECRET FRIEND DARKSTALKER...
CAN YOU READ OUR MINDS, TOO?
THIS IS THE LAST MOMENT THEY'LL LIKE ME.
SECRET. HIDDEN. SAFE.
JUST LIE.
WON'T SHE JUST LIE TO US?
I BELIEVE IN MOON. SHE'LL TELL US THE TRUTH.
YES.
I CAN READ YOUR MINDS.

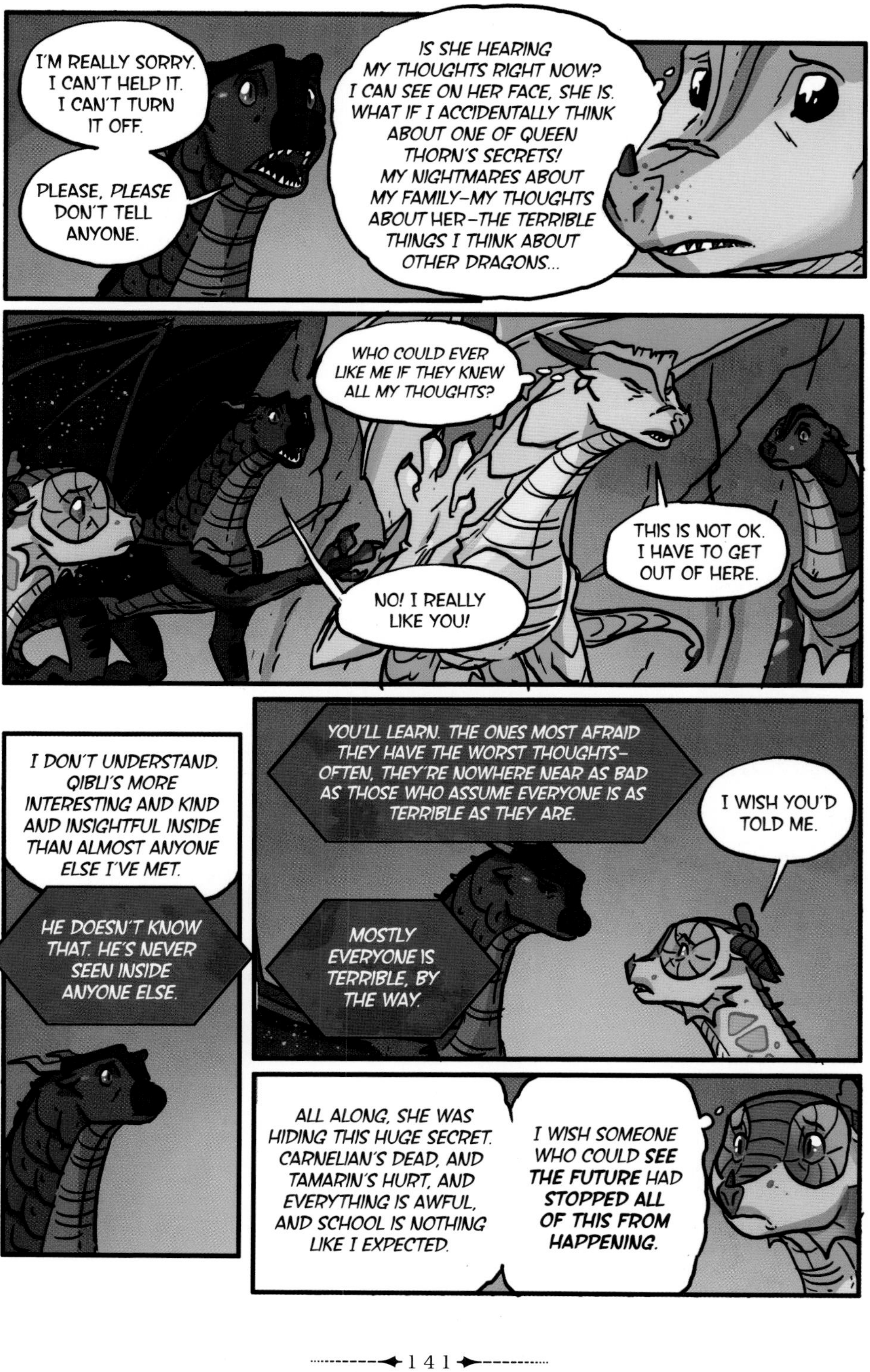
I'M REALLY SORRY. I CAN'T HELP IT. I CAN'T TURN IT OFF.
PLEASE, *PLEASE* DON'T TELL ANYONE.
IS SHE HEARING MY THOUGHTS RIGHT NOW? I CAN SEE ON HER FACE, SHE IS. WHAT IF I ACCIDENTALLY THINK ABOUT ONE OF QUEEN THORN'S SECRETS! MY NIGHTMARES ABOUT MY FAMILY—MY THOUGHTS ABOUT HER—THE TERRIBLE THINGS I THINK ABOUT OTHER DRAGONS...
WHO COULD EVER LIKE ME IF THEY KNEW ALL MY THOUGHTS?
THIS IS NOT OK. I HAVE TO GET OUT OF HERE.
NO! I REALLY LIKE YOU!
I DON'T UNDERSTAND. QIBLI'S MORE INTERESTING AND KIND AND INSIGHTFUL INSIDE THAN ALMOST ANYONE ELSE I'VE MET.
HE DOESN'T KNOW THAT. HE'S NEVER SEEN INSIDE ANYONE ELSE.
YOU'LL LEARN. THE ONES MOST AFRAID THEY HAVE THE WORST THOUGHTS—OFTEN, THEY'RE NOWHERE NEAR AS BAD AS THOSE WHO ASSUME EVERYONE IS AS TERRIBLE AS THEY ARE.
I WISH YOU'D TOLD ME.
MOSTLY EVERYONE IS TERRIBLE, BY THE WAY.
ALL ALONG, SHE WAS HIDING THIS HUGE SECRET. CARNELIAN'S DEAD, AND TAMARIN'S HURT, AND EVERYTHING IS AWFUL, AND SCHOOL IS NOTHING LIKE I EXPECTED.
I WISH SOMEONE WHO COULD **SEE THE FUTURE** HAD **STOPPED ALL OF THIS FROM HAPPENING.**

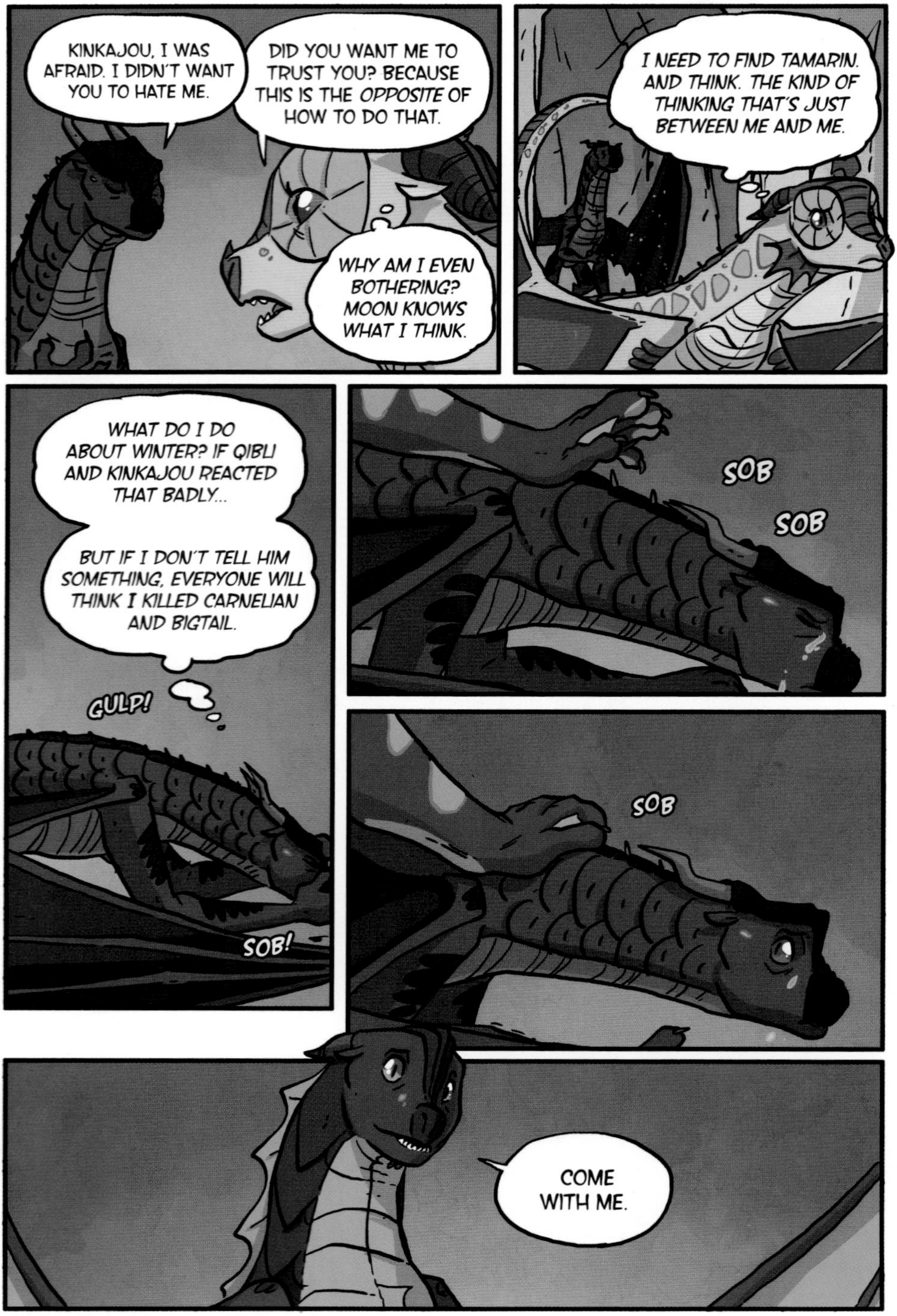
KINKAJOU, I WAS AFRAID. I DIDN'T WANT YOU TO HATE ME.
DID YOU WANT ME TO TRUST YOU? BECAUSE THIS IS THE *OPPOSITE* OF HOW TO DO THAT.
WHY AM I EVEN BOTHERING? MOON KNOWS WHAT I THINK.
I NEED TO FIND TAMARIN. AND THINK. THE KIND OF THINKING THAT'S JUST BETWEEN ME AND ME.
WHAT DO I DO ABOUT WINTER? IF QIBLI AND KINKAJOU REACTED THAT BADLY...
BUT IF I DON'T TELL HIM SOMETHING, EVERYONE WILL THINK I KILLED CARNELIAN AND BIGTAIL.
GULP!
SOB!
SOB
SOB
SOB
COME WITH ME.

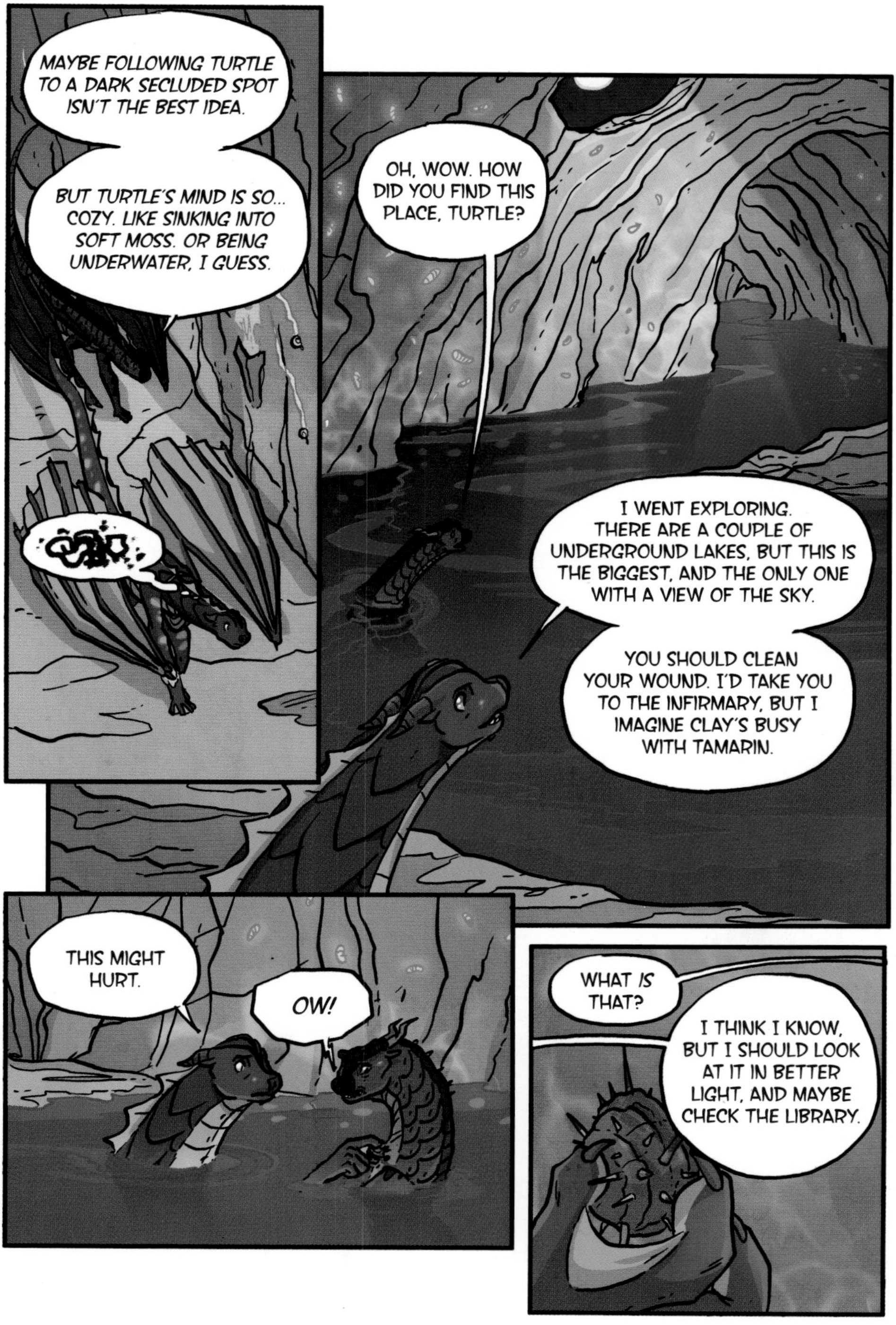
MAYBE FOLLOWING TURTLE TO A DARK SECLUDED SPOT ISN'T THE BEST IDEA.
BUT TURTLE'S MIND IS SO... COZY. LIKE SINKING INTO SOFT MOSS. OR BEING UNDERWATER, I GUESS.
OH, WOW. HOW DID YOU FIND THIS PLACE, TURTLE?
I WENT EXPLORING. THERE ARE A COUPLE OF UNDERGROUND LAKES, BUT THIS IS THE BIGGEST, AND THE ONLY ONE WITH A VIEW OF THE SKY.
YOU SHOULD CLEAN YOUR WOUND. I'D TAKE YOU TO THE INFIRMARY, BUT I IMAGINE CLAY'S BUSY WITH TAMARIN.
THIS MIGHT HURT.
OW!
WHAT *IS* THAT?
I THINK I KNOW, BUT I SHOULD LOOK AT IT IN BETTER LIGHT, AND MAYBE CHECK THE LIBRARY.

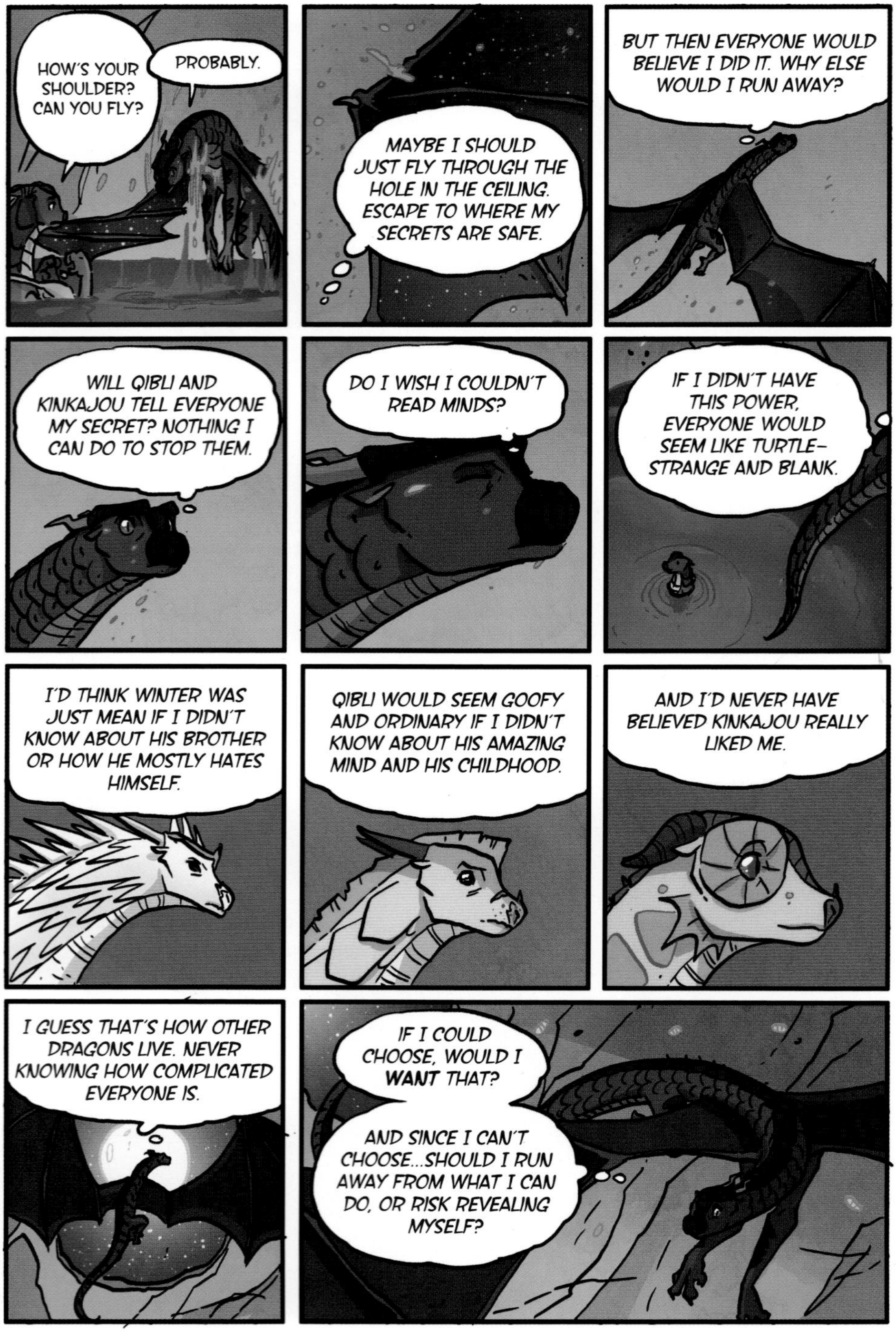
HOW'S YOUR SHOULDER? CAN YOU FLY?
PROBABLY.
MAYBE I SHOULD JUST FLY THROUGH THE HOLE IN THE CEILING. ESCAPE TO WHERE MY SECRETS ARE SAFE.
BUT THEN EVERYONE WOULD BELIEVE I DID IT. WHY ELSE WOULD I RUN AWAY?
WILL QIBLI AND KINKAJOU TELL EVERYONE MY SECRET? NOTHING I CAN DO TO STOP THEM.
DO I WISH I COULDN'T READ MINDS?
IF I DIDN'T HAVE THIS POWER, EVERYONE WOULD SEEM LIKE TURTLE— STRANGE AND BLANK.
I'D THINK WINTER WAS JUST MEAN IF I DIDN'T KNOW ABOUT HIS BROTHER OR HOW HE MOSTLY HATES HIMSELF.
QIBLI WOULD SEEM GOOFY AND ORDINARY IF I DIDN'T KNOW ABOUT HIS AMAZING MIND AND HIS CHILDHOOD.
AND I'D NEVER HAVE BELIEVED KINKAJOU REALLY LIKED ME.
I GUESS THAT'S HOW OTHER DRAGONS LIVE. NEVER KNOWING HOW COMPLICATED EVERYONE IS.
IF I COULD CHOOSE, WOULD I **WANT** THAT?
AND SINCE I CAN'T CHOOSE...SHOULD I RUN AWAY FROM WHAT I CAN DO, OR RISK REVEALING MYSELF?

SO... I GUESS YOU KNOW MY SECRET.

NO, TURTLE, I— I DON'T KNOW WHY, BUT I CAN'T READ *YOUR* MIND. WITH A FEW DRAGONS, I JUST DON'T HEAR ANYTHING.

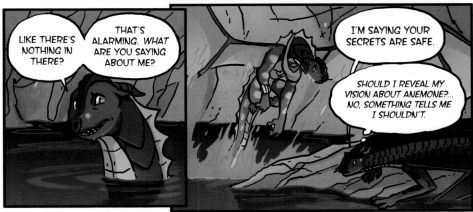

LIKE THERE'S NOTHING IN THERE?

THAT'S ALARMING. *WHAT ARE YOU SAYING ABOUT ME?*

I'M SAYING YOUR SECRETS ARE SAFE.

SHOULD I REVEAL MY VISION ABOUT ANEMONE?... *NO, SOMETHING TELLS ME I SHOULDN'T.*

SO, WHAT ARE YOU GOING TO DO ABOUT WINTER?

I GUESS I HAVE TO TELL HIM THE TRUTH.

NOT IF YOU DON'T WANT TO. WHY NOT FIGURE OUT WHO REALLY CAUSED THE EXPLOSION, AND TELL HIM THAT INSTEAD?

OH, *RIGHT.* I'LL JUST GO SOLVE THAT MYSTERY. *NO PROBLEM.*

SPLASH

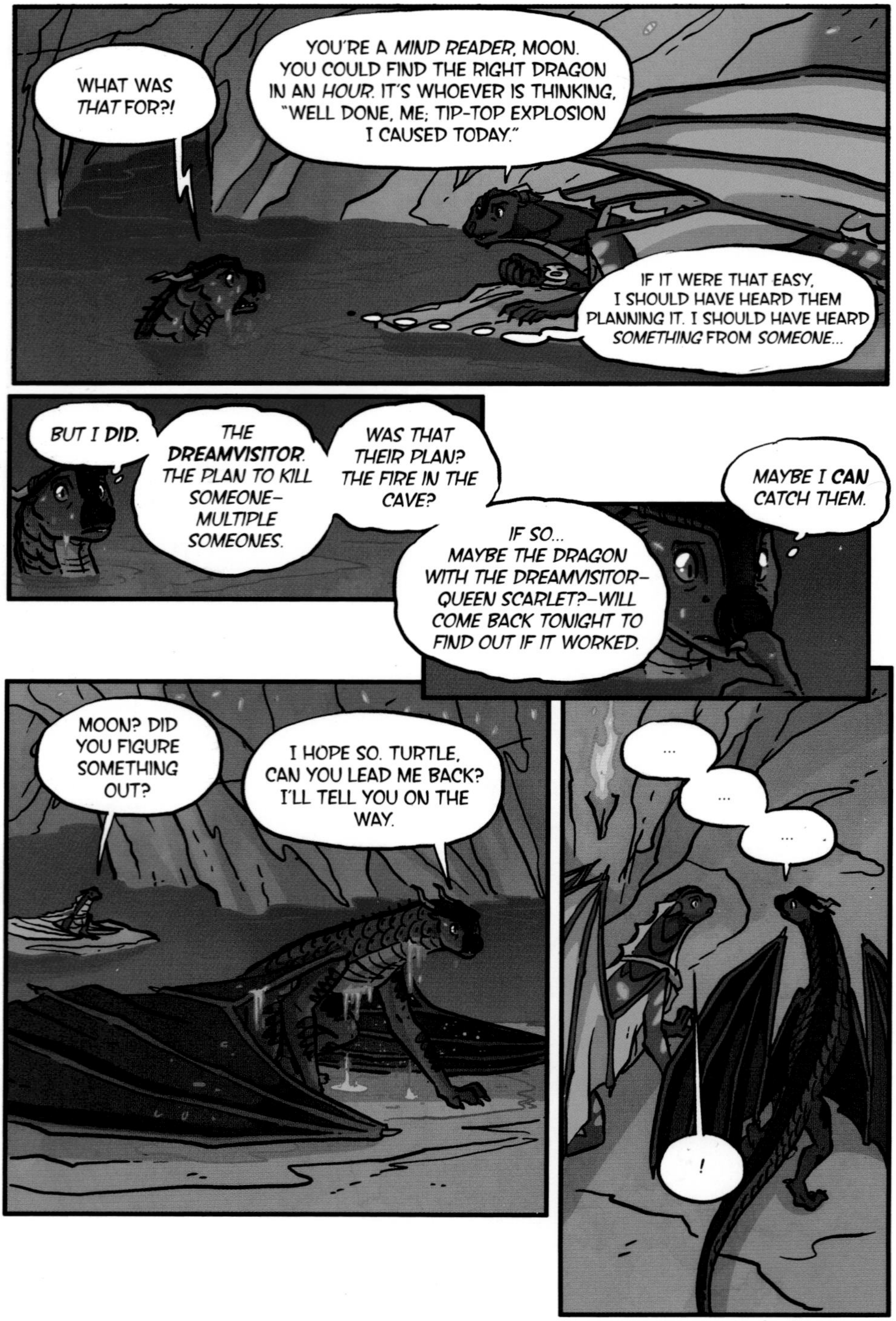
WHAT WAS THAT FOR?!
YOU'RE A MIND READER, MOON. YOU COULD FIND THE RIGHT DRAGON IN AN HOUR. IT'S WHOEVER IS THINKING, "WELL DONE, ME; TIP-TOP EXPLOSION I CAUSED TODAY."
IF IT WERE THAT EASY, I SHOULD HAVE HEARD THEM PLANNING IT. I SHOULD HAVE HEARD SOMETHING FROM SOMEONE...
BUT I DID.
THE DREAMVISITOR. THE PLAN TO KILL SOMEONE— MULTIPLE SOMEONES.
WAS THAT THEIR PLAN? THE FIRE IN THE CAVE?
IF SO... MAYBE THE DRAGON WITH THE DREAMVISITOR— QUEEN SCARLET?—WILL COME BACK TONIGHT TO FIND OUT IF IT WORKED.
MAYBE I CAN CATCH THEM.
MOON? DID YOU FIGURE SOMETHING OUT?
I HOPE SO. TURTLE, CAN YOU LEAD ME BACK? I'LL TELL YOU ON THE WAY.
...
...
...
!

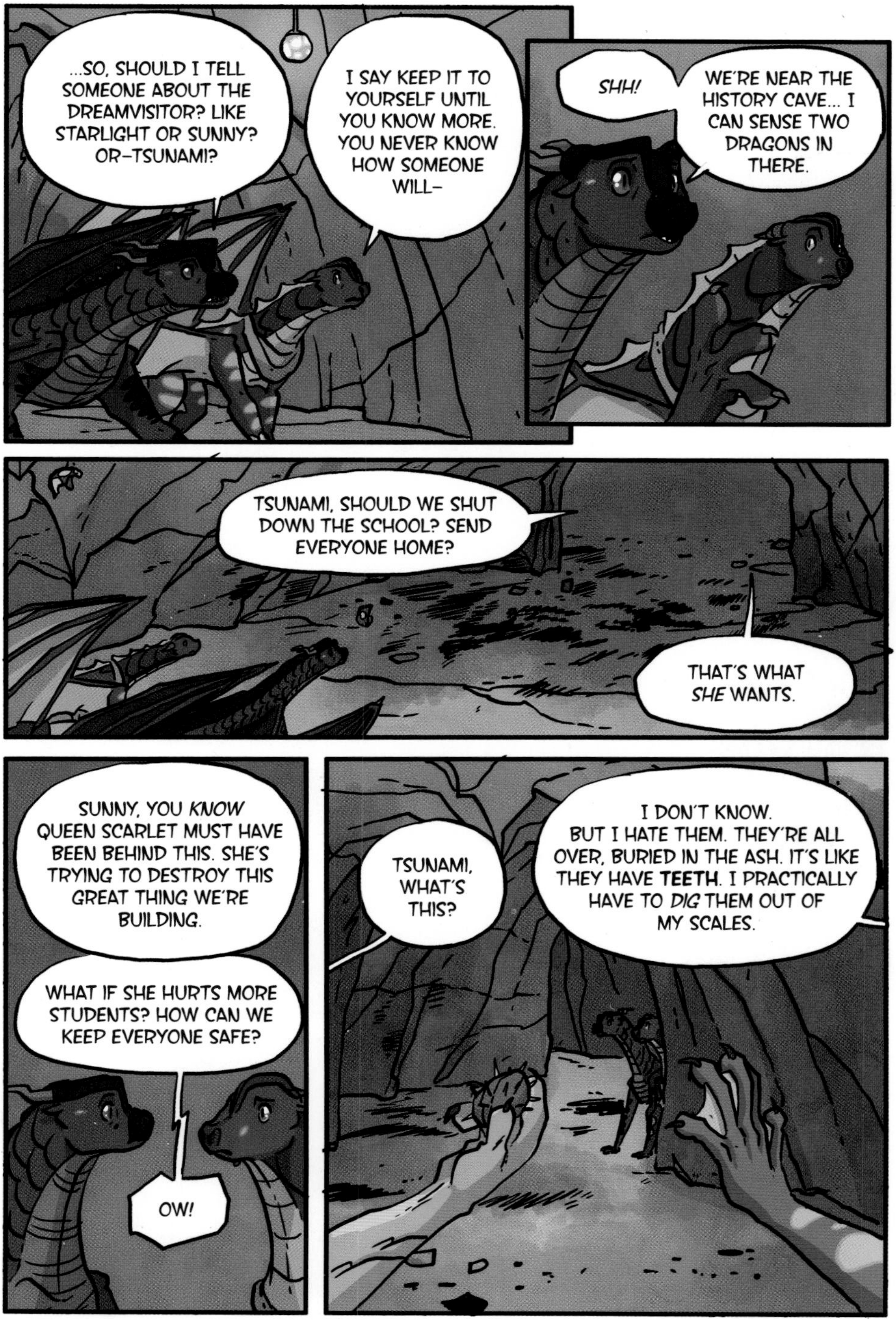
...SO, SHOULD I TELL SOMEONE ABOUT THE DREAMVISITOR? LIKE STARLIGHT OR SUNNY? OR—TSUNAMI!?
I SAY KEEP IT TO YOURSELF UNTIL YOU KNOW MORE. YOU NEVER KNOW HOW SOMEONE WILL—
SHH!
WE'RE NEAR THE HISTORY CAVE... I CAN SENSE TWO DRAGONS IN THERE.
TSUNAMI, SHOULD WE SHUT DOWN THE SCHOOL? SEND EVERYONE HOME?
THAT'S WHAT *SHE* WANTS.
SUNNY, YOU *KNOW* QUEEN SCARLET MUST HAVE BEEN BEHIND THIS. SHE'S TRYING TO DESTROY THIS GREAT THING WE'RE BUILDING.
WHAT IF SHE HURTS MORE STUDENTS? HOW CAN WE KEEP EVERYONE SAFE?
OW!
TSUNAMI, WHAT'S THIS?
I DON'T KNOW. BUT I HATE THEM. THEY'RE ALL OVER, BURIED IN THE ASH. IT'S LIKE THEY HAVE **TEETH**. I PRACTICALLY HAVE TO *DIG* THEM OUT OF MY SCALES.

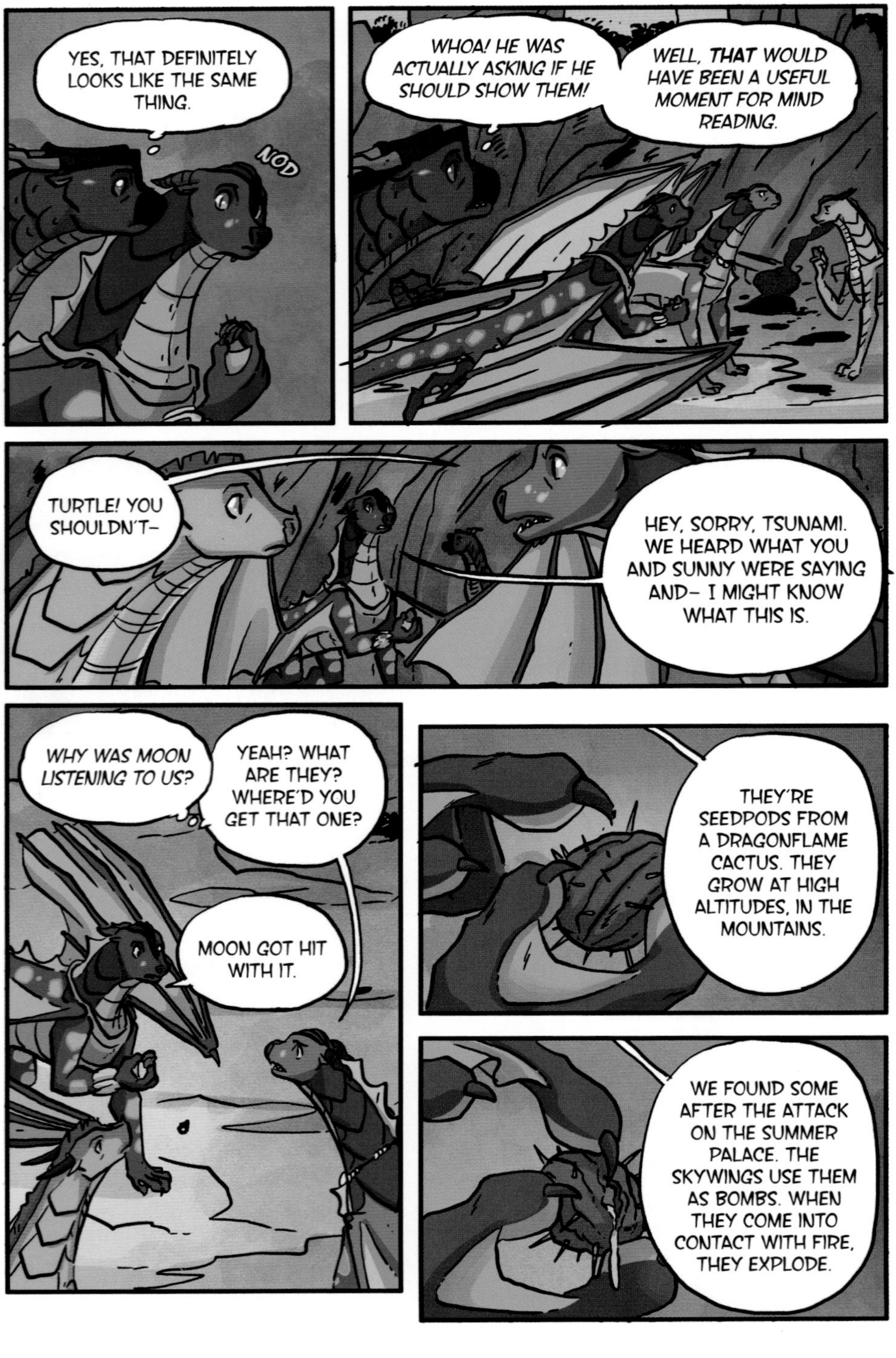
YES, THAT DEFINITELY LOOKS LIKE THE SAME THING.
NOD
WHOA! HE WAS ACTUALLY ASKING IF HE SHOULD SHOW THEM!
*WELL, **THAT** WOULD HAVE BEEN A USEFUL MOMENT FOR MIND READING.*
TURTLE! YOU SHOULDN'T–
HEY, SORRY, TSUNAMI. WE HEARD WHAT YOU AND SUNNY WERE SAYING AND– I MIGHT KNOW WHAT THIS IS.
WHY WAS MOON LISTENING TO US?
YEAH? WHAT ARE THEY? WHERE'D YOU GET THAT ONE?
MOON GOT HIT WITH IT.
THEY'RE SEEDPODS FROM A DRAGONFLAME CACTUS. THEY GROW AT HIGH ALTITUDES, IN THE MOUNTAINS.
WE FOUND SOME AFTER THE ATTACK ON THE SUMMER PALACE. THE SKYWINGS USE THEM AS BOMBS. WHEN THEY COME INTO CONTACT WITH FIRE, THEY EXPLODE.

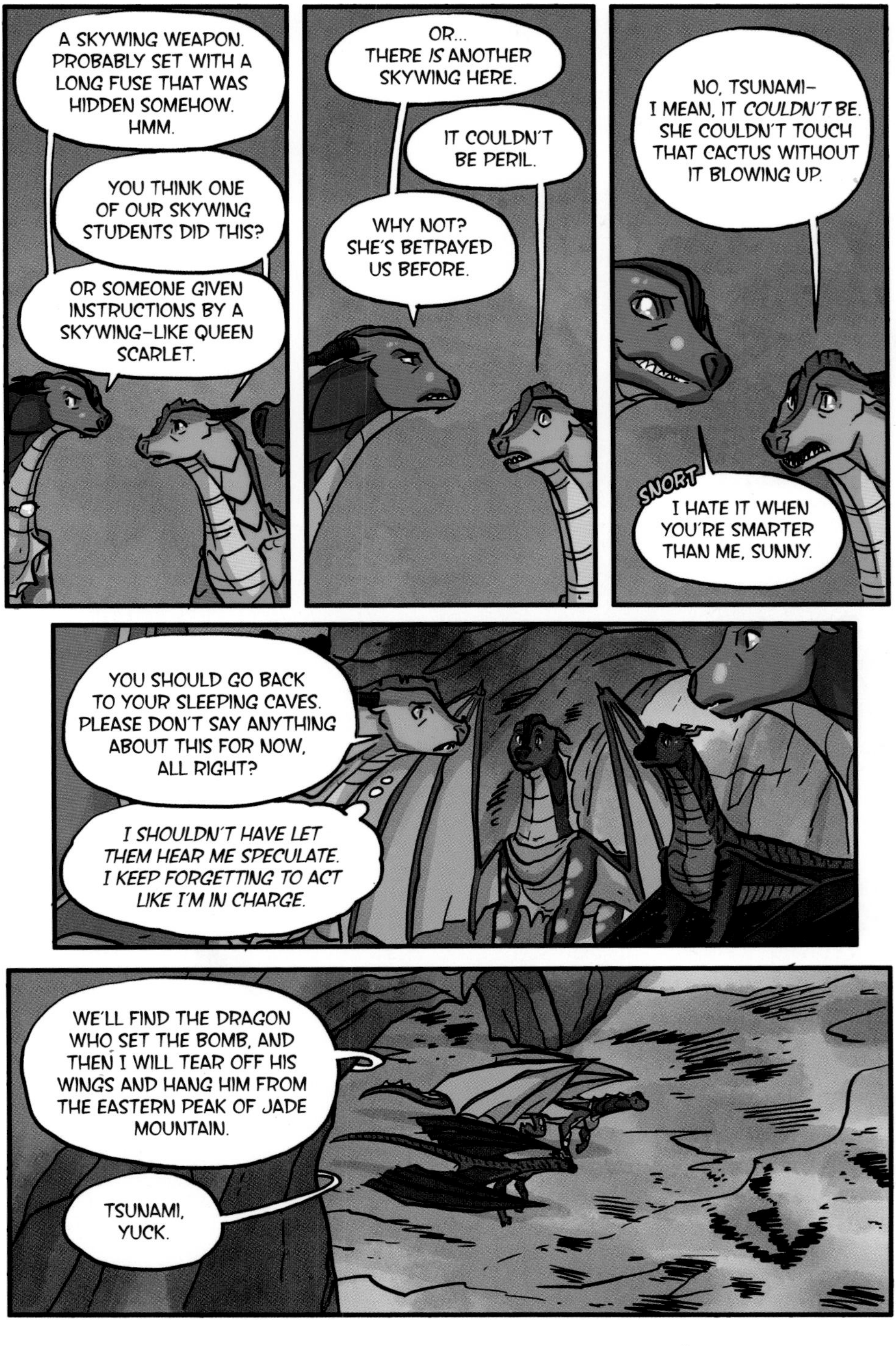
A SKYWING WEAPON. PROBABLY SET WITH A LONG FUSE THAT WAS HIDDEN SOMEHOW. HMM.
YOU THINK ONE OF OUR SKYWING STUDENTS DID THIS?
OR SOMEONE GIVEN INSTRUCTIONS BY A SKYWING-LIKE QUEEN SCARLET.
OR... THERE *IS* ANOTHER SKYWING HERE.
IT COULDN'T BE PERIL.
WHY NOT? SHE'S BETRAYED US BEFORE.
NO, TSUNAMI– I MEAN, IT *COULDN'T* BE. SHE COULDN'T TOUCH THAT CACTUS WITHOUT IT BLOWING UP.
SNORT
I HATE IT WHEN YOU'RE SMARTER THAN ME, SUNNY.
YOU SHOULD GO BACK TO YOUR SLEEPING CAVES. PLEASE DON'T SAY ANYTHING ABOUT THIS FOR NOW, ALL RIGHT?
I SHOULDN'T HAVE LET THEM HEAR ME SPECULATE. I KEEP FORGETTING TO ACT LIKE I'M IN CHARGE.
WE'LL FIND THE DRAGON WHO SET THE BOMB, AND THEN I WILL TEAR OFF HIS WINGS AND HANG HIM FROM THE EASTERN PEAK OF JADE MOUNTAIN.
TSUNAMI, YUCK.

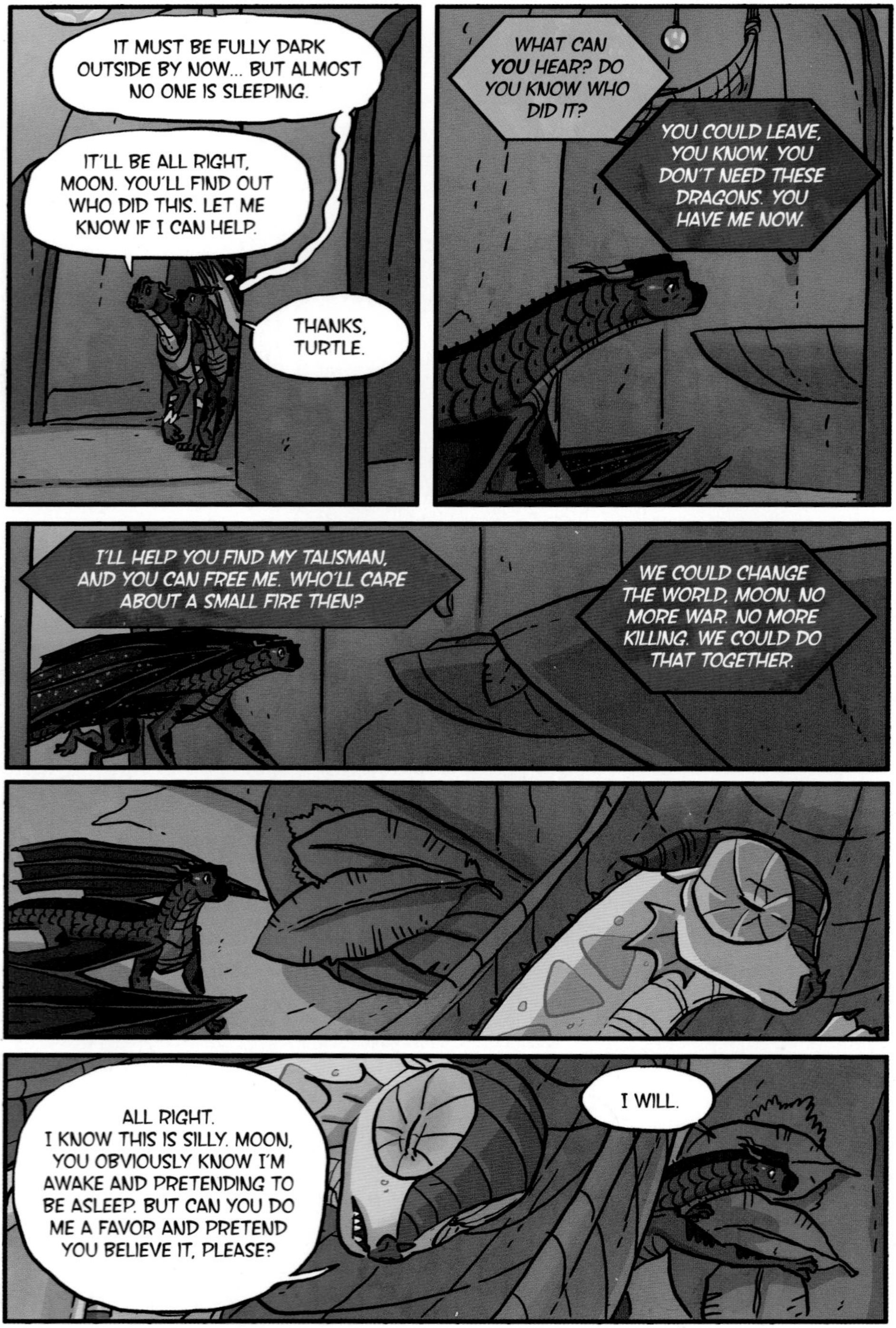
IT MUST BE FULLY DARK OUTSIDE BY NOW... BUT ALMOST NO ONE IS SLEEPING.
IT'LL BE ALL RIGHT, MOON. YOU'LL FIND OUT WHO DID THIS. LET ME KNOW IF I CAN HELP.
THANKS, TURTLE.
WHAT CAN *YOU* HEAR? DO YOU KNOW WHO DID IT?
YOU COULD LEAVE, YOU KNOW. YOU DON'T NEED THESE DRAGONS. YOU HAVE ME NOW.
I'LL HELP YOU FIND MY TALISMAN, AND YOU CAN FREE ME. WHO'LL CARE ABOUT A SMALL FIRE THEN?
WE COULD CHANGE THE WORLD, MOON. NO MORE WAR. NO MORE KILLING. WE COULD DO THAT TOGETHER.
ALL RIGHT. I KNOW THIS IS SILLY. MOON, YOU OBVIOUSLY KNOW I'M AWAKE AND PRETENDING TO BE ASLEEP. BUT CAN YOU DO ME A FAVOR AND PRETEND YOU BELIEVE IT, PLEASE?
I WILL.

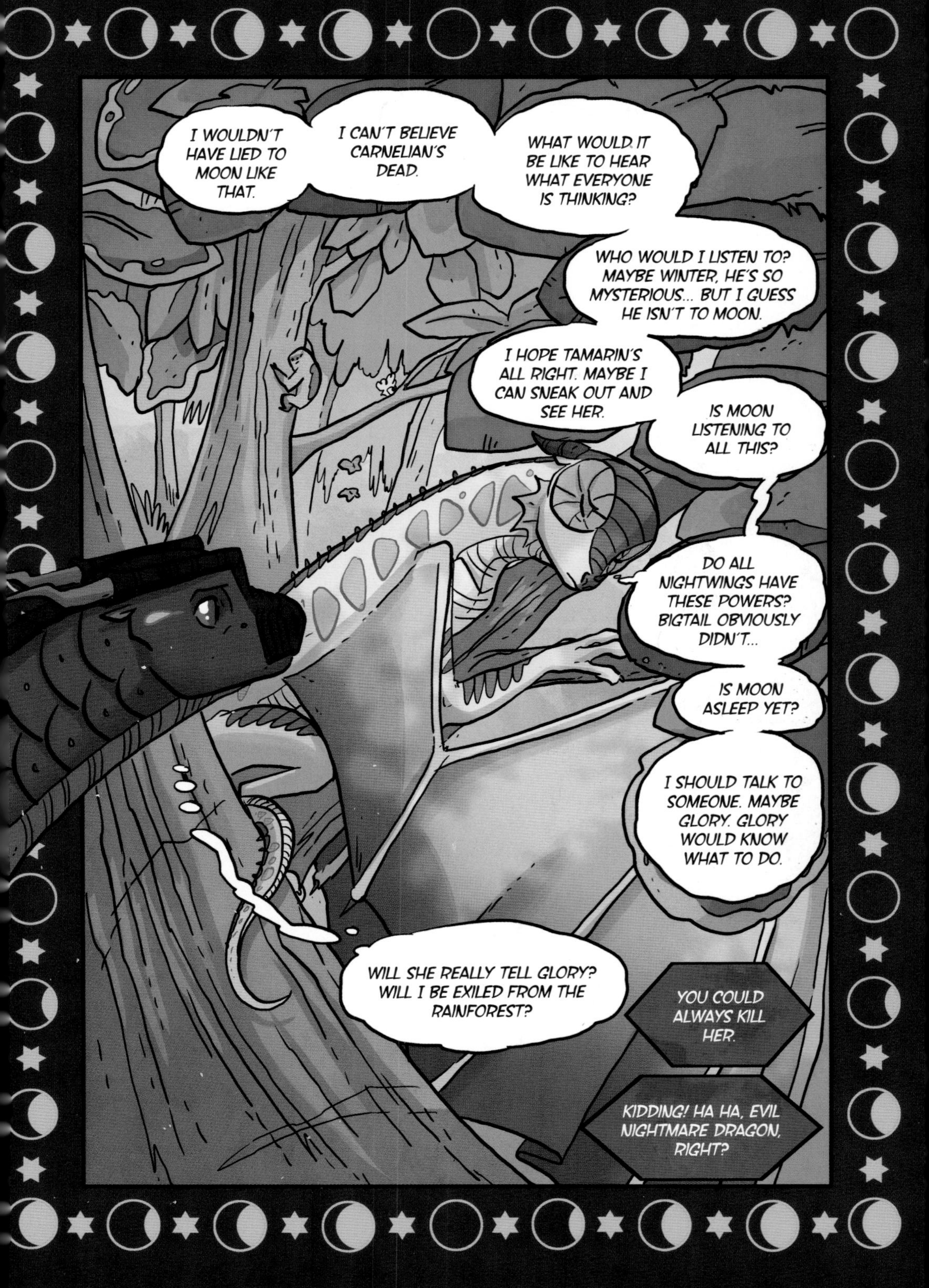
I WOULDN'T HAVE LIED TO MOON LIKE THAT.
I CAN'T BELIEVE CARNELIAN'S DEAD.
WHAT WOULD IT BE LIKE TO HEAR WHAT EVERYONE IS THINKING?
WHO WOULD I LISTEN TO? MAYBE WINTER, HE'S SO MYSTERIOUS... BUT I GUESS HE ISN'T TO MOON.
I HOPE TAMARIN'S ALL RIGHT. MAYBE I CAN SNEAK OUT AND SEE HER.
IS MOON LISTENING TO ALL THIS?
DO ALL NIGHTWINGS HAVE THESE POWERS? BIGTAIL OBVIOUSLY DIDN'T...
IS MOON ASLEEP YET?
I SHOULD TALK TO SOMEONE. MAYBE GLORY. GLORY WOULD KNOW WHAT TO DO.
WILL SHE REALLY TELL GLORY? WILL I BE EXILED FROM THE RAINFOREST?
YOU COULD ALWAYS KILL HER.
KIDDING! HA HA, EVIL NIGHTMARE DRAGON, RIGHT?

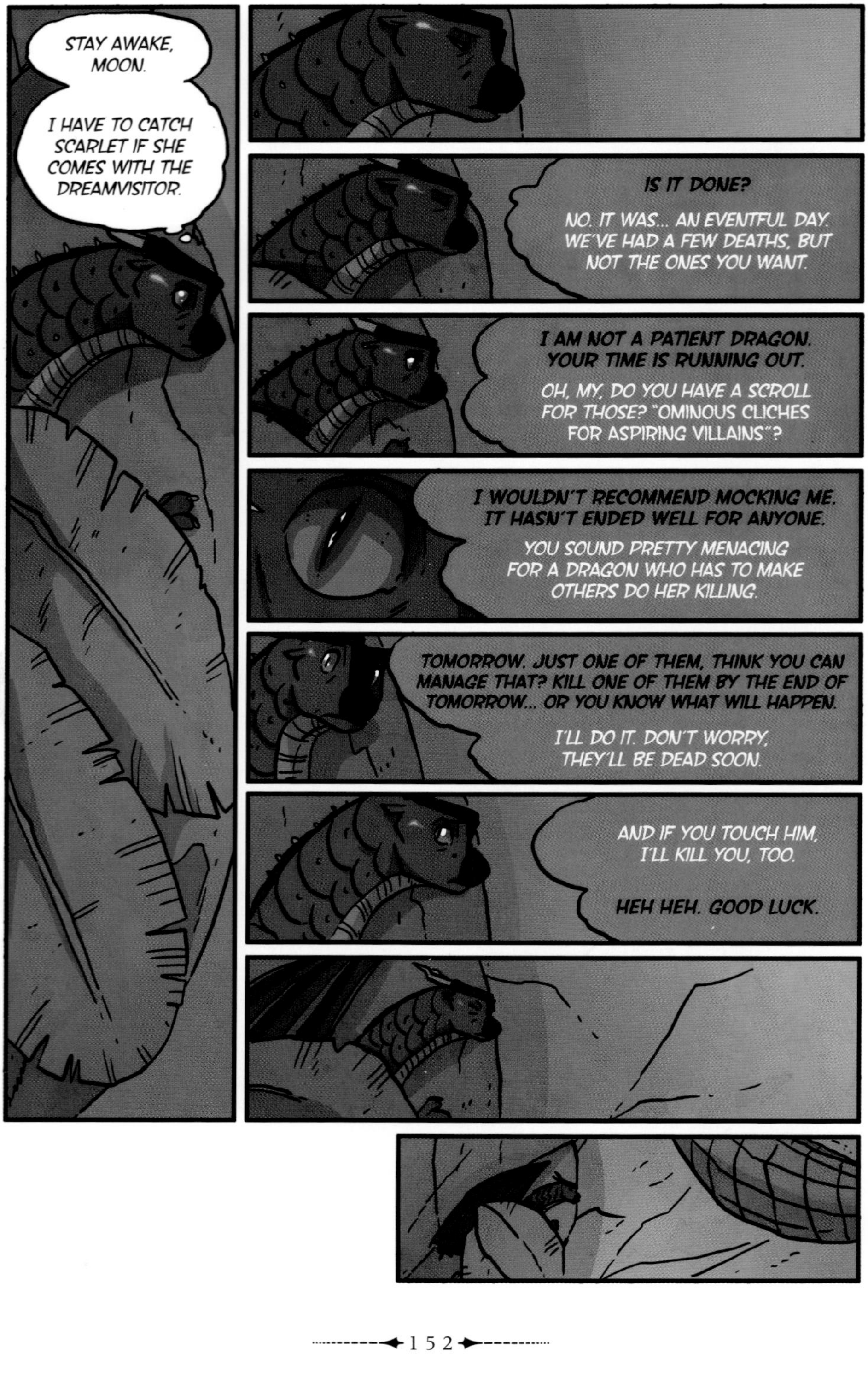

STAY AWAKE, MOON.
I HAVE TO CATCH SCARLET IF SHE COMES WITH THE DREAMVISITOR.
IS IT DONE?
NO. IT WAS... AN EVENTFUL DAY. WE'VE HAD A FEW DEATHS, BUT NOT THE ONES YOU WANT.
I AM NOT A PATIENT DRAGON. YOUR TIME IS RUNNING OUT.
OH, MY, DO YOU HAVE A SCROLL FOR THOSE? "OMINOUS CLICHES FOR ASPIRING VILLAINS"?
I WOULDN'T RECOMMEND MOCKING ME. IT HASN'T ENDED WELL FOR ANYONE.
YOU SOUND PRETTY MENACING FOR A DRAGON WHO HAS TO MAKE OTHERS DO HER KILLING.
TOMORROW. JUST ONE OF THEM, THINK YOU CAN MANAGE THAT? KILL ONE OF THEM BY THE END OF TOMORROW... OR YOU KNOW WHAT WILL HAPPEN.
I'LL DO IT. DON'T WORRY, THEY'LL BE DEAD SOON.
AND IF YOU TOUCH HIM, I'LL KILL YOU, TOO.
HEH HEH. GOOD LUCK.

PART THREE: THE DARKNESS OF DRAGONS

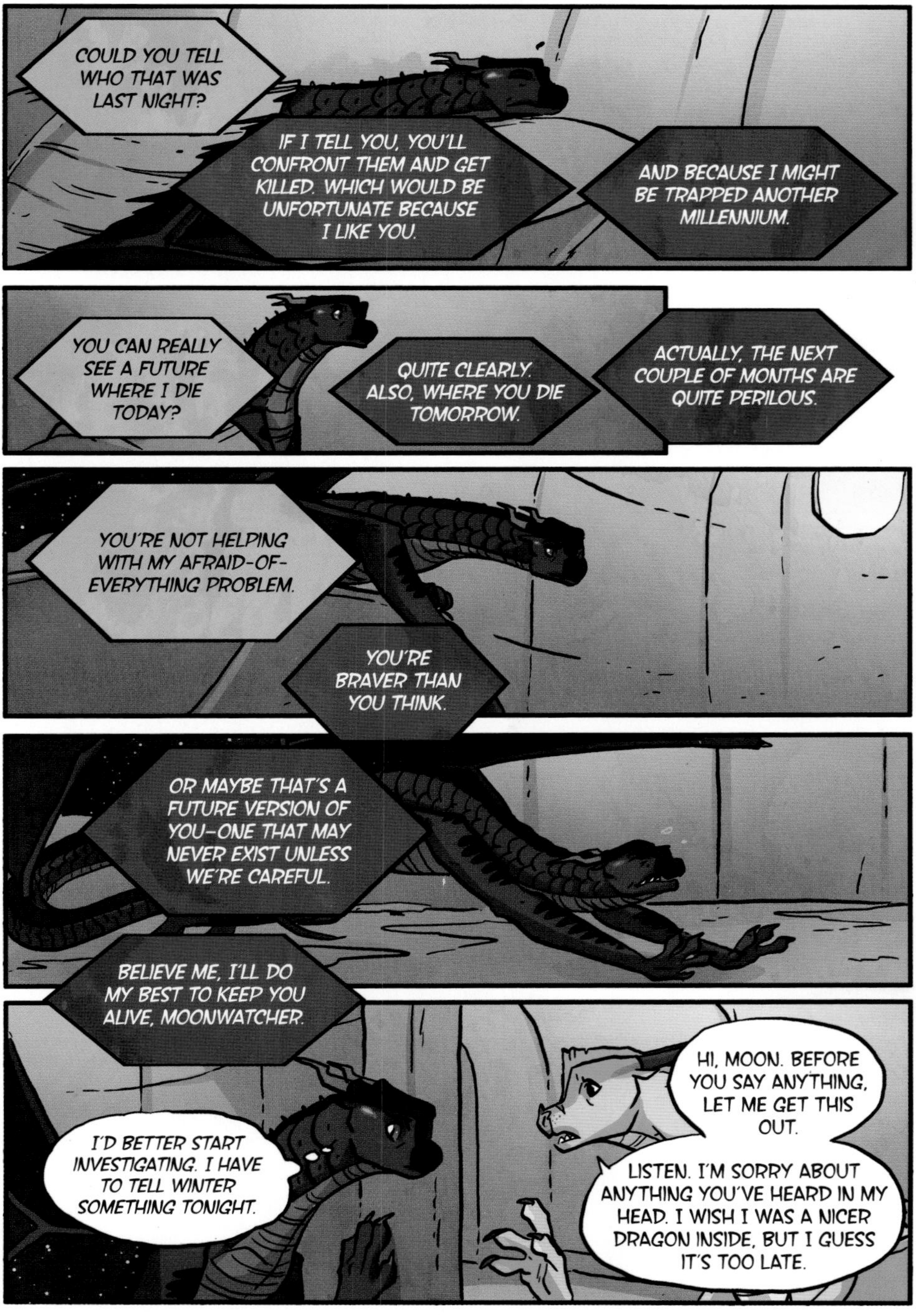
COULD YOU TELL WHO THAT WAS LAST NIGHT?
IF I TELL YOU, YOU'LL CONFRONT THEM AND GET KILLED. WHICH WOULD BE UNFORTUNATE BECAUSE I LIKE YOU.
AND BECAUSE I MIGHT BE TRAPPED ANOTHER MILLENNIUM.
YOU CAN REALLY SEE A FUTURE WHERE I DIE TODAY?
QUITE CLEARLY. ALSO, WHERE YOU DIE TOMORROW.
ACTUALLY, THE NEXT COUPLE OF MONTHS ARE QUITE PERILOUS.
YOU'RE NOT HELPING WITH MY AFRAID-OF-EVERYTHING PROBLEM.
YOU'RE BRAVER THAN YOU THINK.
OR MAYBE THAT'S A FUTURE VERSION OF YOU—ONE THAT MAY NEVER EXIST UNLESS WE'RE CAREFUL.
BELIEVE ME, I'LL DO MY BEST TO KEEP YOU ALIVE, MOONWATCHER.
I'D BETTER START INVESTIGATING. I HAVE TO TELL WINTER SOMETHING TONIGHT.
HI, MOON. BEFORE YOU SAY ANYTHING, LET ME GET THIS OUT.
LISTEN. I'M SORRY ABOUT ANYTHING YOU'VE HEARD IN MY HEAD. I WISH I WAS A NICER DRAGON INSIDE, BUT I GUESS IT'S TOO LATE.

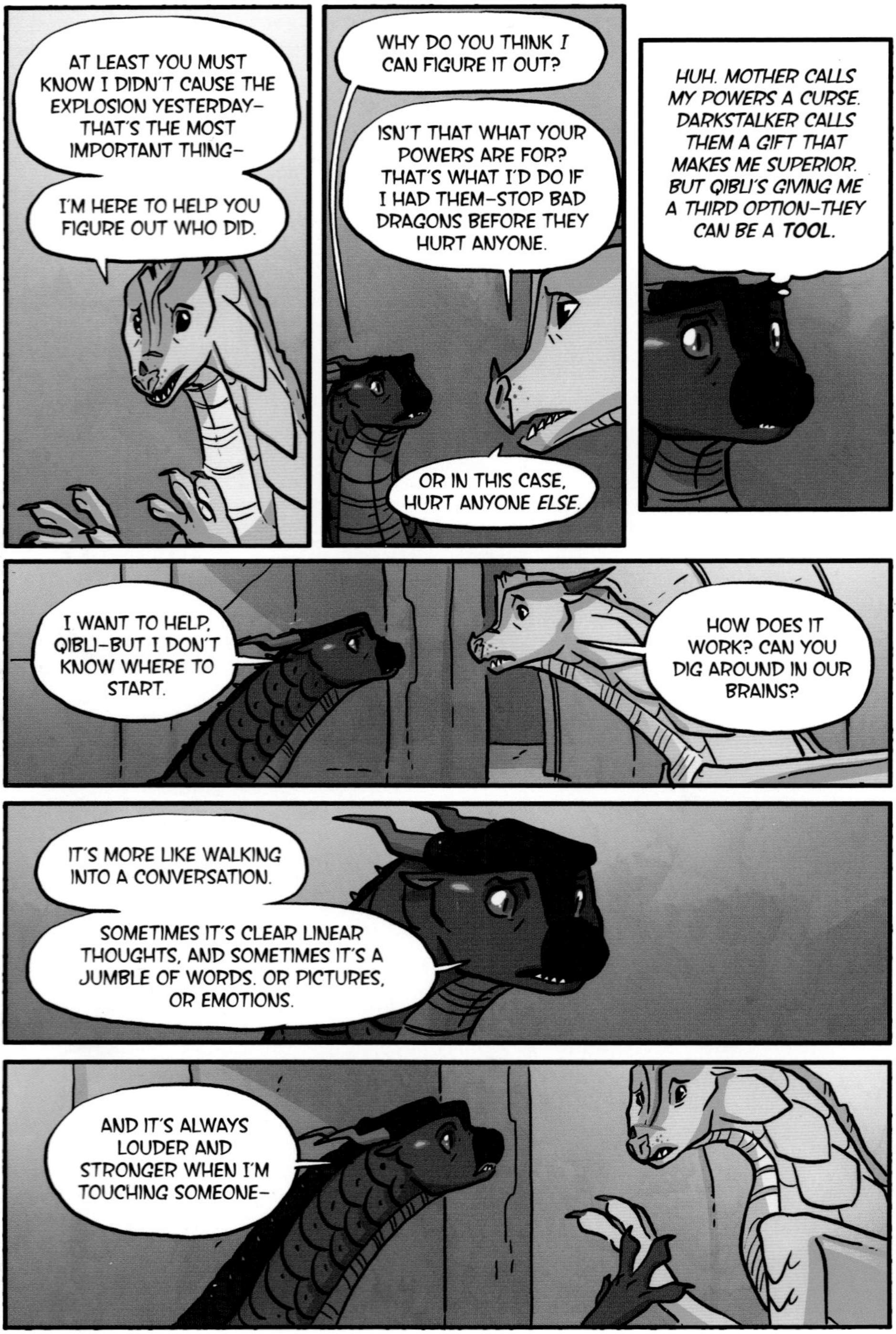
AT LEAST YOU MUST KNOW I DIDN'T CAUSE THE EXPLOSION YESTERDAY– THAT'S THE MOST IMPORTANT THING–
I'M HERE TO HELP YOU FIGURE OUT WHO DID.
WHY DO YOU THINK *I* CAN FIGURE IT OUT?
ISN'T THAT WHAT YOUR POWERS ARE FOR? THAT'S WHAT I'D DO IF I HAD THEM–STOP BAD DRAGONS BEFORE THEY HURT ANYONE.
OR IN THIS CASE, HURT ANYONE *ELSE*.
*HUH. MOTHER CALLS MY POWERS A CURSE. DARKSTALKER CALLS THEM A GIFT THAT MAKES ME SUPERIOR. BUT QIBLI'S GIVING ME A THIRD OPTION–THEY CAN BE A **TOOL**.*
I WANT TO HELP, QIBLI–BUT I DON'T KNOW WHERE TO START.
HOW DOES IT WORK? CAN YOU DIG AROUND IN OUR BRAINS?
IT'S MORE LIKE WALKING INTO A CONVERSATION.
SOMETIMES IT'S CLEAR LINEAR THOUGHTS, AND SOMETIMES IT'S A JUMBLE OF WORDS. OR PICTURES, OR EMOTIONS.
AND IT'S ALWAYS LOUDER AND STRONGER WHEN I'M TOUCHING SOMEONE–

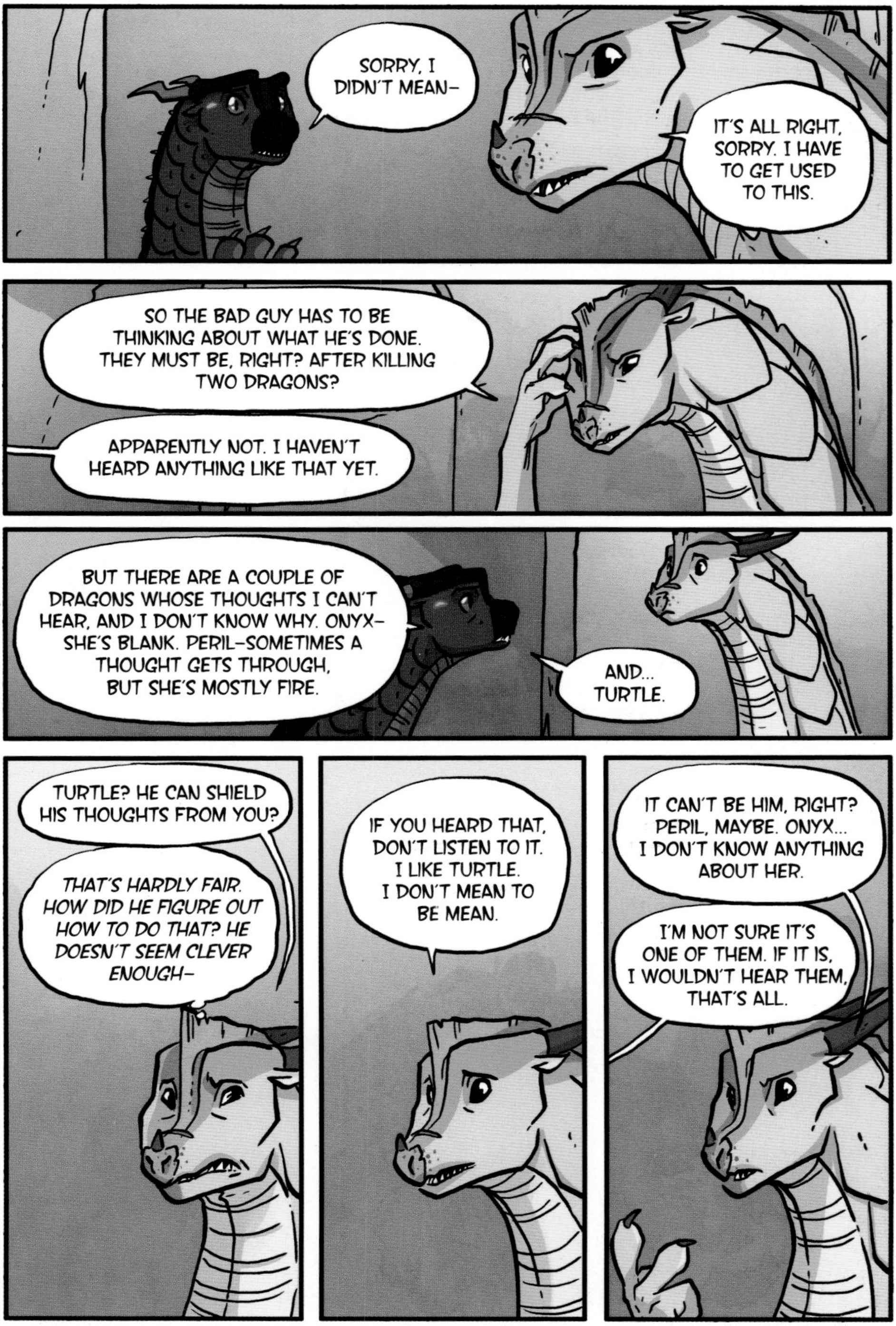
SORRY, I DIDN'T MEAN–
IT'S ALL RIGHT, SORRY. I HAVE TO GET USED TO THIS.
SO THE BAD GUY HAS TO BE THINKING ABOUT WHAT HE'S DONE. THEY MUST BE, RIGHT? AFTER KILLING TWO DRAGONS?
APPARENTLY NOT. I HAVEN'T HEARD ANYTHING LIKE THAT YET.
BUT THERE ARE A COUPLE OF DRAGONS WHOSE THOUGHTS I CAN'T HEAR, AND I DON'T KNOW WHY. ONYX– SHE'S BLANK. PERIL–SOMETIMES A THOUGHT GETS THROUGH, BUT SHE'S MOSTLY FIRE.
AND... TURTLE.
TURTLE? HE CAN SHIELD HIS THOUGHTS FROM YOU?
THAT'S HARDLY FAIR. HOW DID HE FIGURE OUT HOW TO DO THAT? HE DOESN'T SEEM CLEVER ENOUGH–
IF YOU HEARD THAT, DON'T LISTEN TO IT. I LIKE TURTLE. I DON'T MEAN TO BE MEAN.
IT CAN'T BE HIM, RIGHT? PERIL, MAYBE. ONYX... I DON'T KNOW ANYTHING ABOUT HER.
I'M NOT SURE IT'S ONE OF THEM. IF IT IS, I WOULDN'T HEAR THEM, THAT'S ALL.

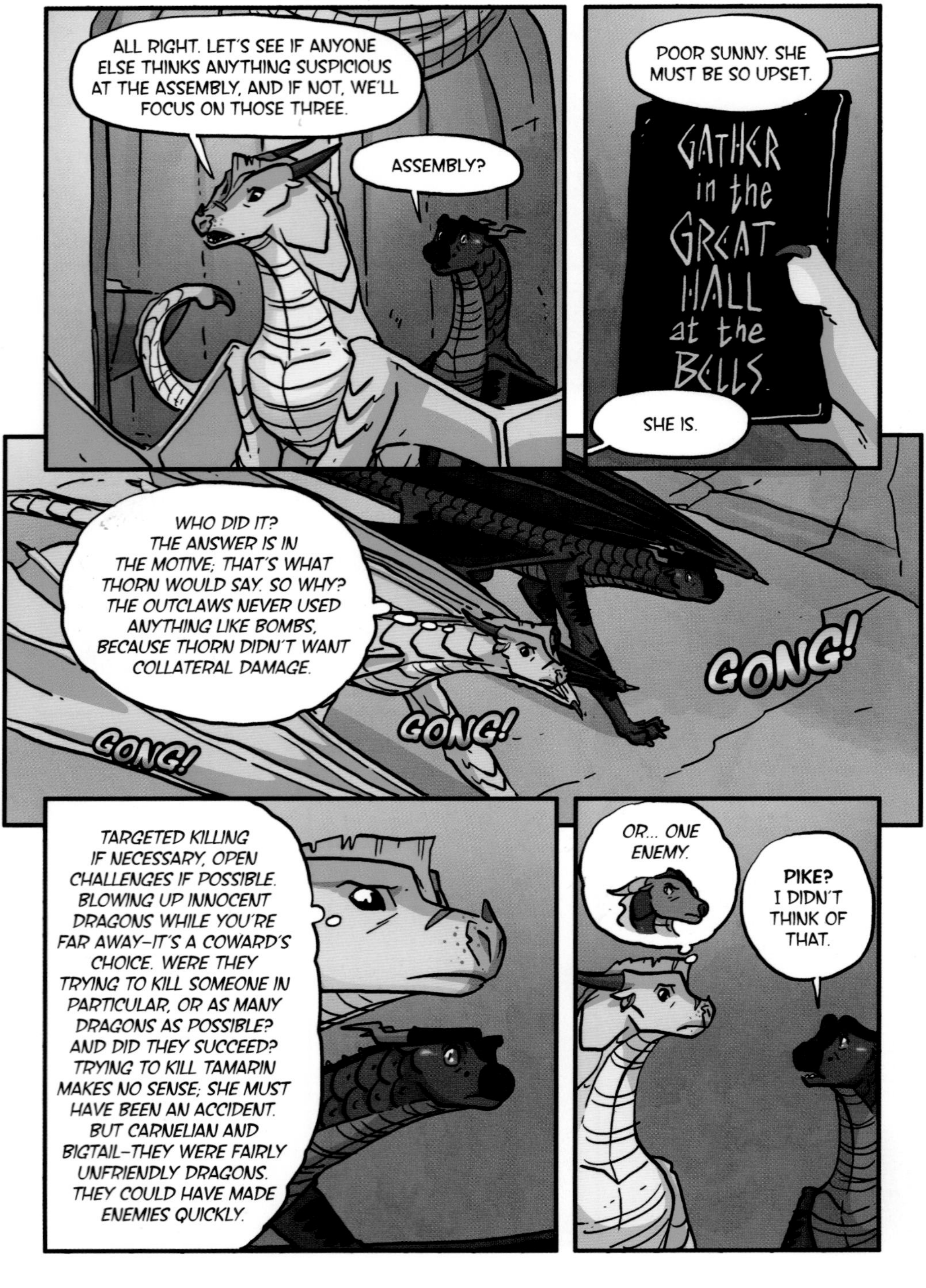
ALL RIGHT. LET'S SEE IF ANYONE ELSE THINKS ANYTHING SUSPICIOUS AT THE ASSEMBLY, AND IF NOT, WE'LL FOCUS ON THOSE THREE.
ASSEMBLY?
POOR SUNNY. SHE MUST BE SO UPSET.
GATHER in the GREAT HALL at the BELLS.
SHE IS.
WHO DID IT? THE ANSWER IS IN THE MOTIVE; THAT'S WHAT THORN WOULD SAY. SO WHY? THE OUTCLAWS NEVER USED ANYTHING LIKE BOMBS, BECAUSE THORN DIDN'T WANT COLLATERAL DAMAGE.
GONG!
GONG!
GONG!
TARGETED KILLING IF NECESSARY, OPEN CHALLENGES IF POSSIBLE. BLOWING UP INNOCENT DRAGONS WHILE YOU'RE FAR AWAY—IT'S A COWARD'S CHOICE. WERE THEY TRYING TO KILL SOMEONE IN PARTICULAR, OR AS MANY DRAGONS AS POSSIBLE? AND DID THEY SUCCEED? TRYING TO KILL TAMARIN MAKES NO SENSE; SHE MUST HAVE BEEN AN ACCIDENT. BUT CARNELIAN AND BIGTAIL—THEY WERE FAIRLY UNFRIENDLY DRAGONS. THEY COULD HAVE MADE ENEMIES QUICKLY.
OR... ONE ENEMY.
PIKE? I DIDN'T THINK OF THAT.

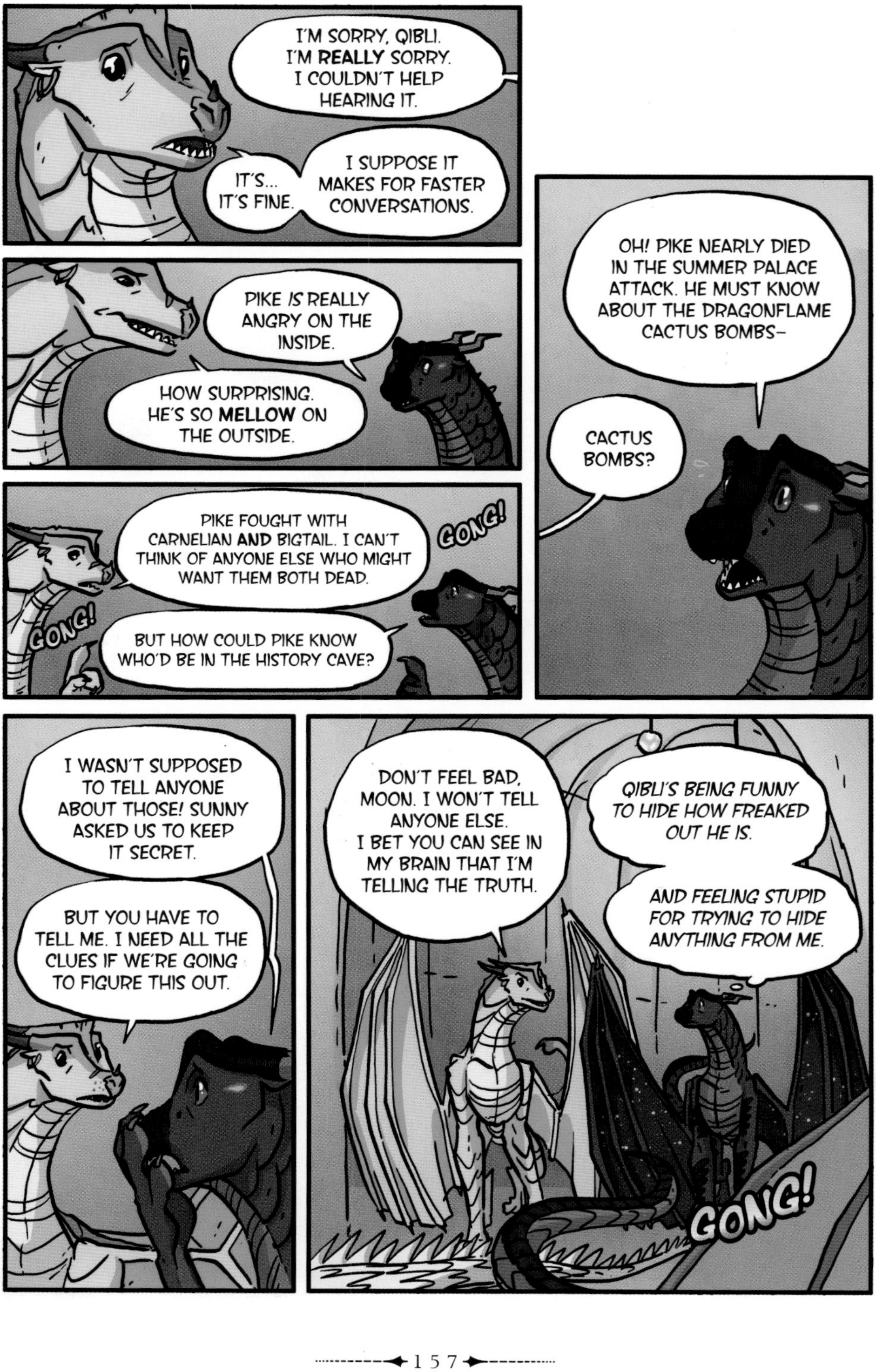

I'M SORRY, QIBLI. I'M **REALLY** SORRY. I COULDN'T HELP HEARING IT.
IT'S... IT'S FINE.
I SUPPOSE IT MAKES FOR FASTER CONVERSATIONS.
PIKE *IS* REALLY ANGRY ON THE INSIDE.
HOW SURPRISING. HE'S SO **MELLOW** ON THE OUTSIDE.
PIKE FOUGHT WITH CARNELIAN **AND** BIGTAIL. I CAN'T THINK OF ANYONE ELSE WHO MIGHT WANT THEM BOTH DEAD.
GONG!
GONG!
BUT HOW COULD PIKE KNOW WHO'D BE IN THE HISTORY CAVE?
OH! PIKE NEARLY DIED IN THE SUMMER PALACE ATTACK. HE MUST KNOW ABOUT THE DRAGONFLAME CACTUS BOMBS–
CACTUS BOMBS?
I WASN'T SUPPOSED TO TELL ANYONE ABOUT THOSE! SUNNY ASKED US TO KEEP IT SECRET.
BUT YOU HAVE TO TELL ME. I NEED ALL THE CLUES IF WE'RE GOING TO FIGURE THIS OUT.
DON'T FEEL BAD, MOON. I WON'T TELL ANYONE ELSE. I BET YOU CAN SEE IN MY BRAIN THAT I'M TELLING THE TRUTH.
QIBLI'S BEING FUNNY TO HIDE HOW FREAKED OUT HE IS.
AND FEELING STUPID FOR TRYING TO HIDE ANYTHING FROM ME.
GONG!

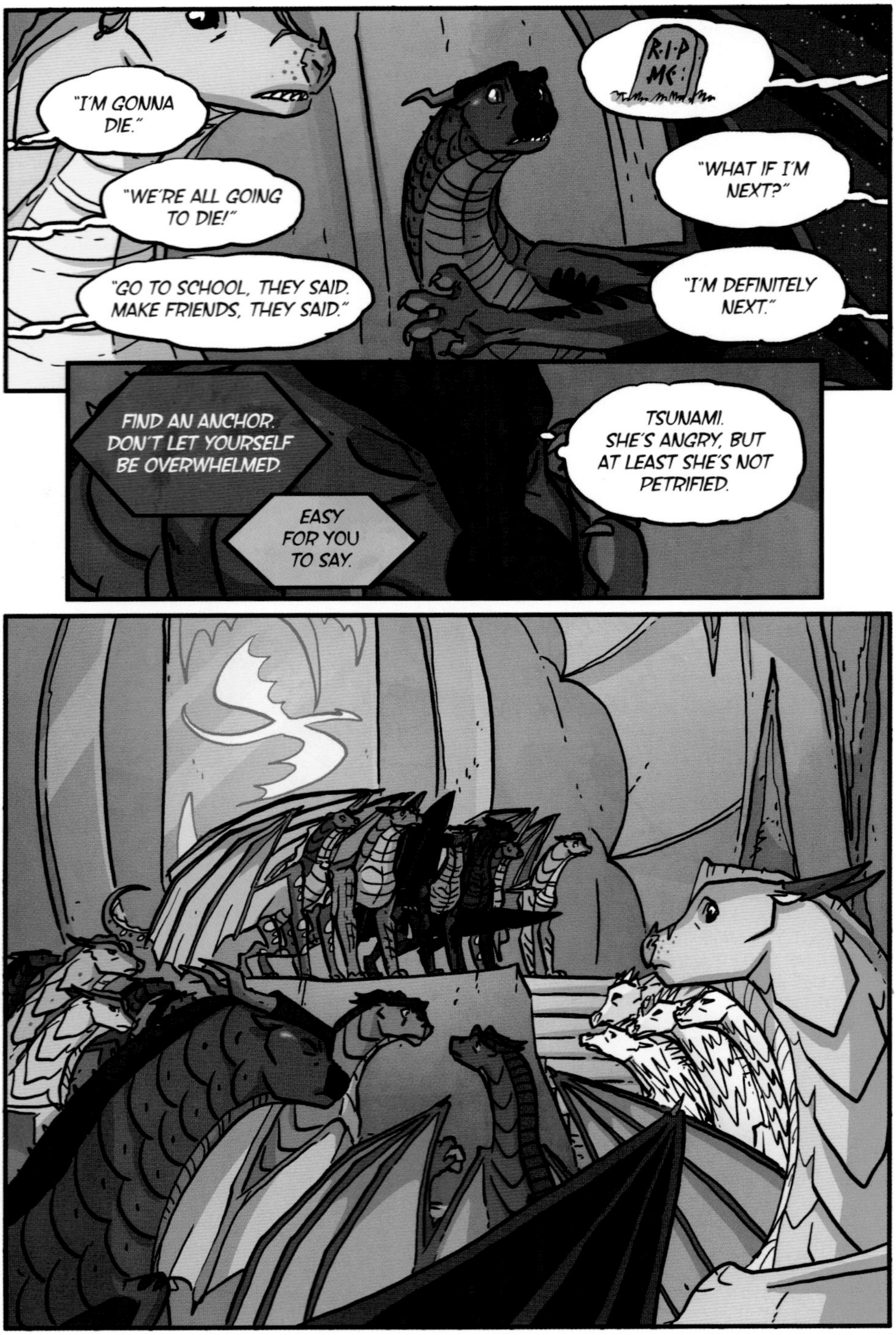
"I'M GONNA DIE."
"WE'RE ALL GOING TO DIE!"
"GO TO SCHOOL, THEY SAID. MAKE FRIENDS, THEY SAID."
R·I·P ME
"WHAT IF I'M NEXT?"
"I'M DEFINITELY NEXT."
FIND AN ANCHOR. DON'T LET YOURSELF BE OVERWHELMED.
EASY FOR YOU TO SAY.
TSUNAMI. SHE'S ANGRY, BUT AT LEAST SHE'S NOT PETRIFIED.

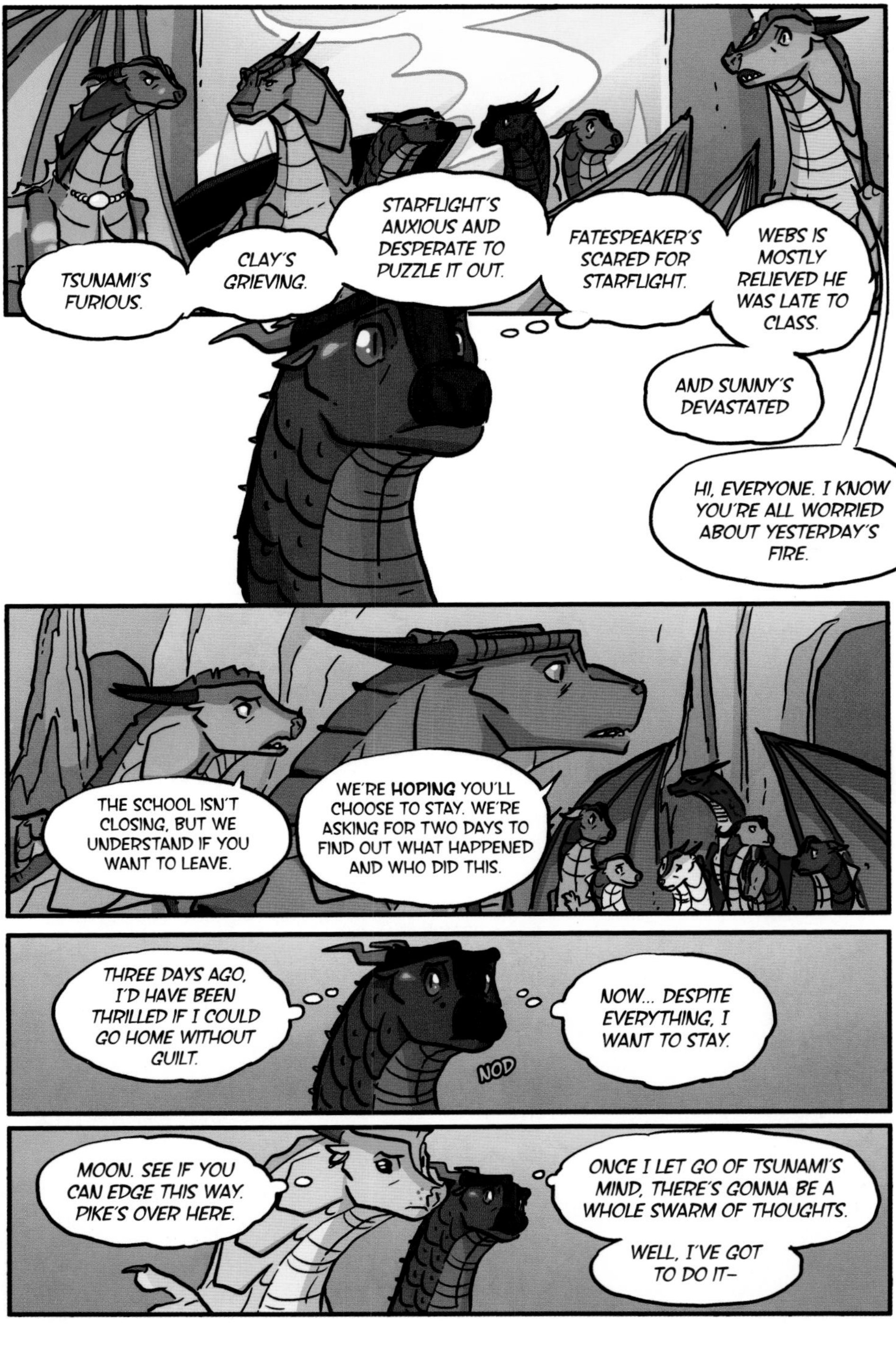
TSUNAMI'S FURIOUS.
CLAY'S GRIEVING.
STARFLIGHT'S ANXIOUS AND DESPERATE TO PUZZLE IT OUT.
FATESPEAKER'S SCARED FOR STARFLIGHT.
WEBS IS MOSTLY RELIEVED HE WAS LATE TO CLASS.
AND SUNNY'S DEVASTATED
HI, EVERYONE. I KNOW YOU'RE ALL WORRIED ABOUT YESTERDAY'S FIRE.
THE SCHOOL ISN'T CLOSING, BUT WE UNDERSTAND IF YOU WANT TO LEAVE.
WE'RE HOPING YOU'LL CHOOSE TO STAY. WE'RE ASKING FOR TWO DAYS TO FIND OUT WHAT HAPPENED AND WHO DID THIS.
THREE DAYS AGO, I'D HAVE BEEN THRILLED IF I COULD GO HOME WITHOUT GUILT.
NOD
NOW... DESPITE EVERYTHING, I WANT TO STAY.
MOON. SEE IF YOU CAN EDGE THIS WAY. PIKE'S OVER HERE.
ONCE I LET GO OF TSUNAMI'S MIND, THERE'S GONNA BE A WHOLE SWARM OF THOUGHTS.
WELL, I'VE GOT TO DO IT–

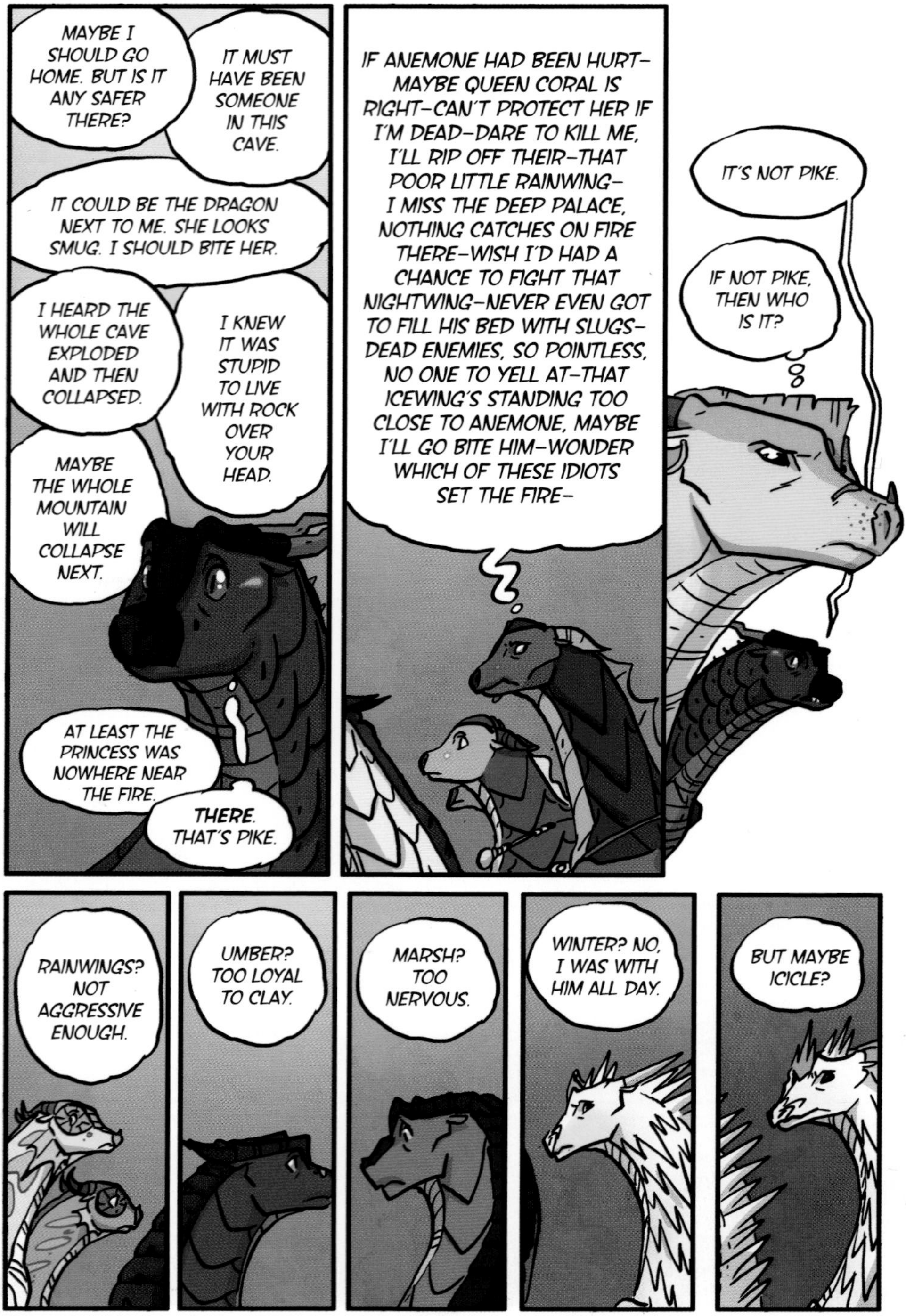
MAYBE I SHOULD GO HOME. BUT IS IT ANY SAFER THERE?
IT MUST HAVE BEEN SOMEONE IN THIS CAVE.
IT COULD BE THE DRAGON NEXT TO ME. SHE LOOKS SMUG. I SHOULD BITE HER.
I HEARD THE WHOLE CAVE EXPLODED AND THEN COLLAPSED.
I KNEW IT WAS STUPID TO LIVE WITH ROCK OVER YOUR HEAD.
MAYBE THE WHOLE MOUNTAIN WILL COLLAPSE NEXT.
AT LEAST THE PRINCESS WAS NOWHERE NEAR THE FIRE.
THERE. THAT'S PIKE.
IF ANEMONE HAD BEEN HURT— MAYBE QUEEN CORAL IS RIGHT—CAN'T PROTECT HER IF I'M DEAD—DARE TO KILL ME, I'LL RIP OFF THEIR—THAT POOR LITTLE RAINWING— I MISS THE DEEP PALACE, NOTHING CATCHES ON FIRE THERE—WISH I'D HAD A CHANCE TO FIGHT THAT NIGHTWING—NEVER EVEN GOT TO FILL HIS BED WITH SLUGS— DEAD ENEMIES, SO POINTLESS, NO ONE TO YELL AT—THAT ICEWING'S STANDING TOO CLOSE TO ANEMONE, MAYBE I'LL GO BITE HIM—WONDER WHICH OF THESE IDIOTS SET THE FIRE—
IT'S NOT PIKE.
IF NOT PIKE, THEN WHO IS IT?
RAINWINGS? NOT AGGRESSIVE ENOUGH.
UMBER? TOO LOYAL TO CLAY.
MARSH? TOO NERVOUS.
WINTER? NO, I WAS WITH HIM ALL DAY.
BUT MAYBE ICICLE?

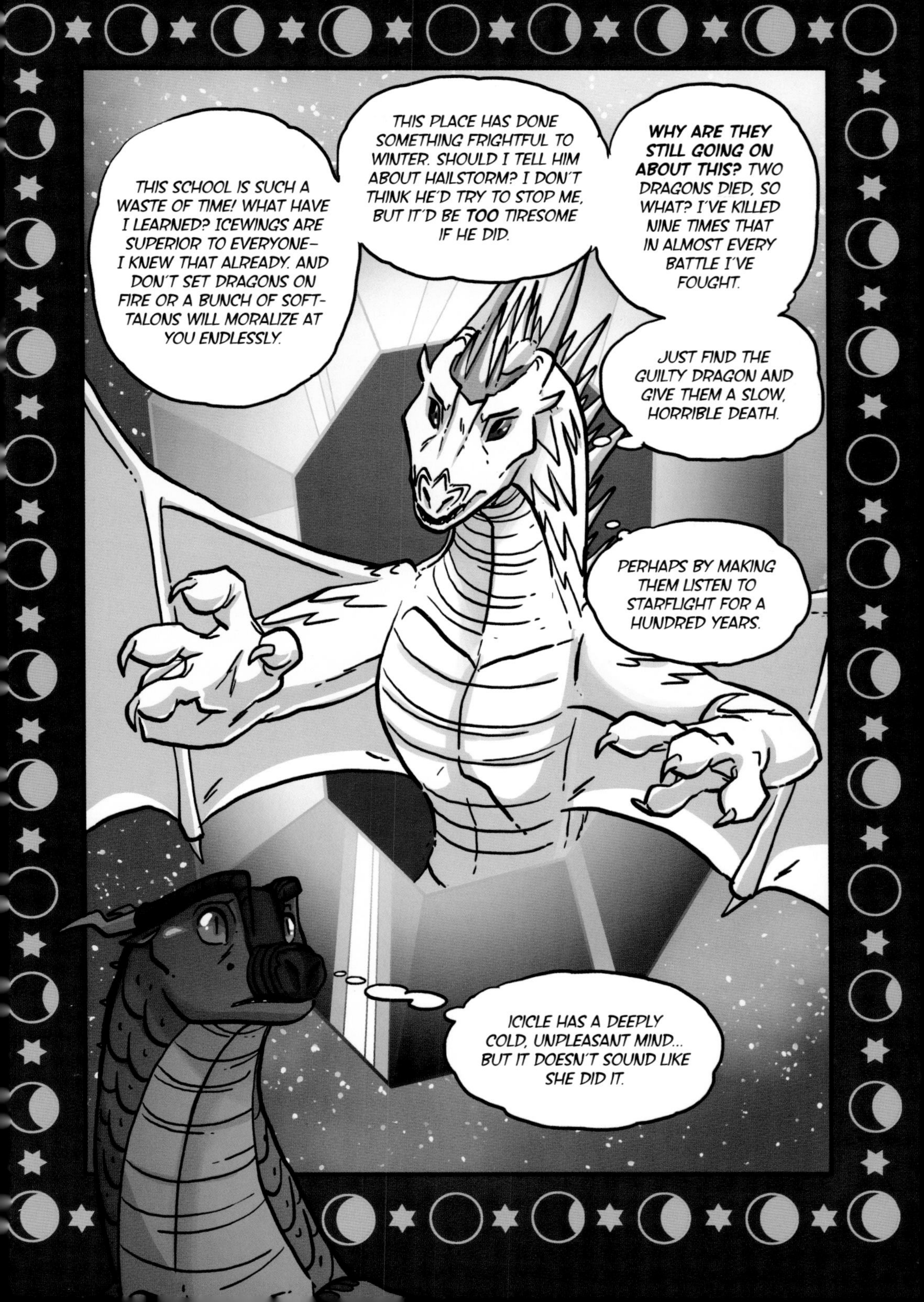
THIS SCHOOL IS SUCH A WASTE OF TIME! WHAT HAVE I LEARNED? ICEWINGS ARE SUPERIOR TO EVERYONE— I KNEW THAT ALREADY. AND DON'T SET DRAGONS ON FIRE OR A BUNCH OF SOFT-TALONS WILL MORALIZE AT YOU ENDLESSLY.
THIS PLACE HAS DONE SOMETHING FRIGHTFUL TO WINTER. SHOULD I TELL HIM ABOUT HAILSTORM? I DON'T THINK HE'D TRY TO STOP ME, BUT IT'D BE **TOO** TIRESOME IF HE DID.
WHY ARE THEY STILL GOING ON ABOUT THIS? TWO DRAGONS DIED, SO WHAT? I'VE KILLED NINE TIMES THAT IN ALMOST EVERY BATTLE I'VE FOUGHT.
JUST FIND THE GUILTY DRAGON AND GIVE THEM A SLOW, HORRIBLE DEATH.
PERHAPS BY MAKING THEM LISTEN TO STARFLIGHT FOR A HUNDRED YEARS.
ICICLE HAS A DEEPLY COLD, UNPLEASANT MIND... BUT IT DOESN'T SOUND LIKE SHE DID IT.

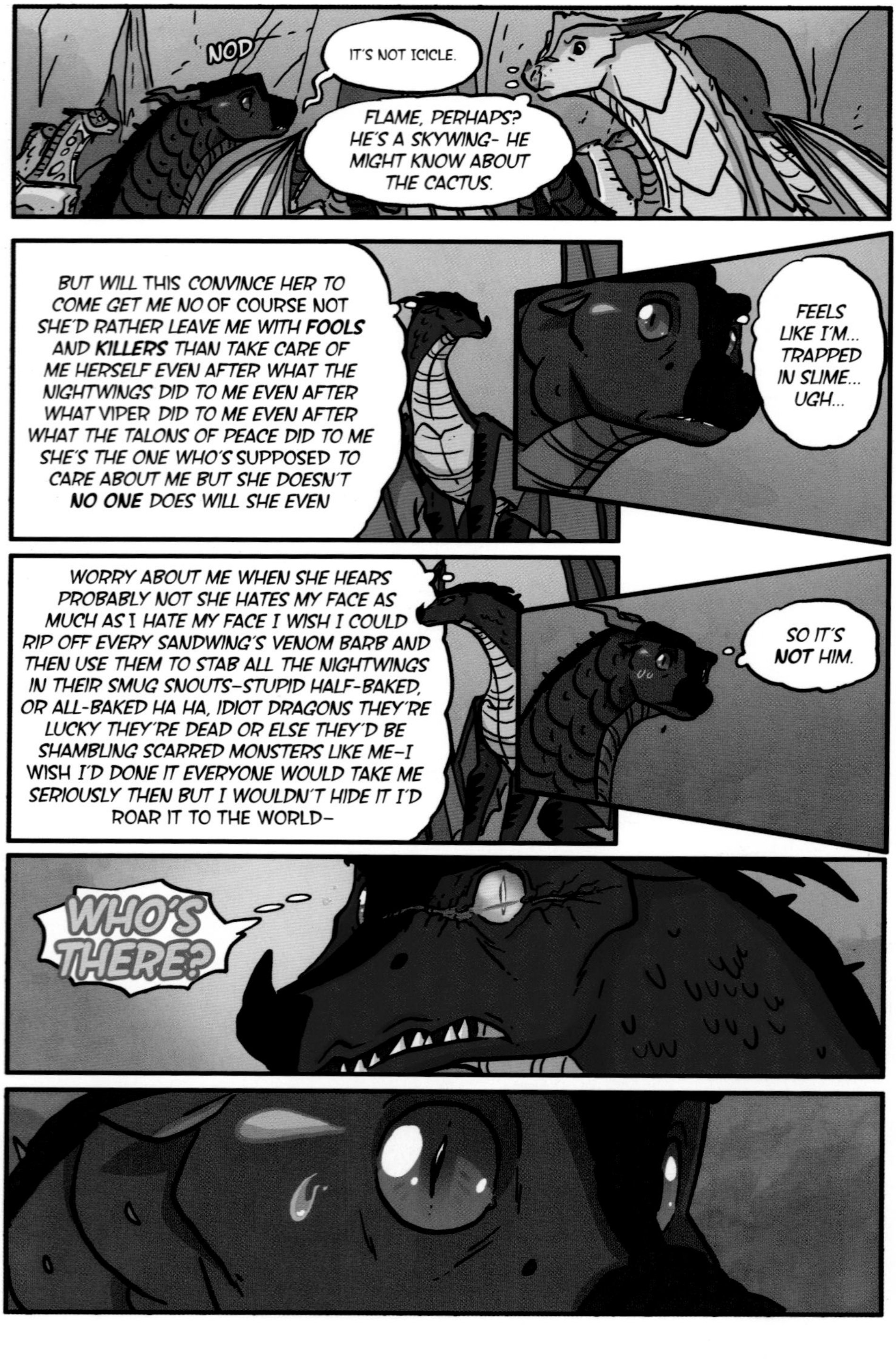
NOD
IT'S NOT ICICLE.
FLAME, PERHAPS? HE'S A SKYWING- HE MIGHT KNOW ABOUT THE CACTUS.
BUT WILL THIS CONVINCE HER TO COME GET ME NO OF COURSE NOT SHE'D RATHER LEAVE ME WITH FOOLS AND KILLERS THAN TAKE CARE OF ME HERSELF EVEN AFTER WHAT THE NIGHTWINGS DID TO ME EVEN AFTER WHAT VIPER DID TO ME EVEN AFTER WHAT THE TALONS OF PEACE DID TO ME SHE'S THE ONE WHO'S SUPPOSED TO CARE ABOUT ME BUT SHE DOESN'T NO ONE DOES WILL SHE EVEN
FEELS LIKE I'M... TRAPPED IN SLIME... UGH...
WORRY ABOUT ME WHEN SHE HEARS PROBABLY NOT SHE HATES MY FACE AS MUCH AS I HATE MY FACE I WISH I COULD RIP OFF EVERY SANDWING'S VENOM BARB AND THEN USE THEM TO STAB ALL THE NIGHTWINGS IN THEIR SMUG SNOUTS–STUPID HALF-BAKED, OR ALL-BAKED HA HA, IDIOT DRAGONS THEY'RE LUCKY THEY'RE DEAD OR ELSE THEY'D BE SHAMBLING SCARRED MONSTERS LIKE ME–I WISH I'D DONE IT EVERYONE WOULD TAKE ME SERIOUSLY THEN BUT I WOULDN'T HIDE IT I'D ROAR IT TO THE WORLD–
SO IT'S NOT HIM.
WHO'S THERE?

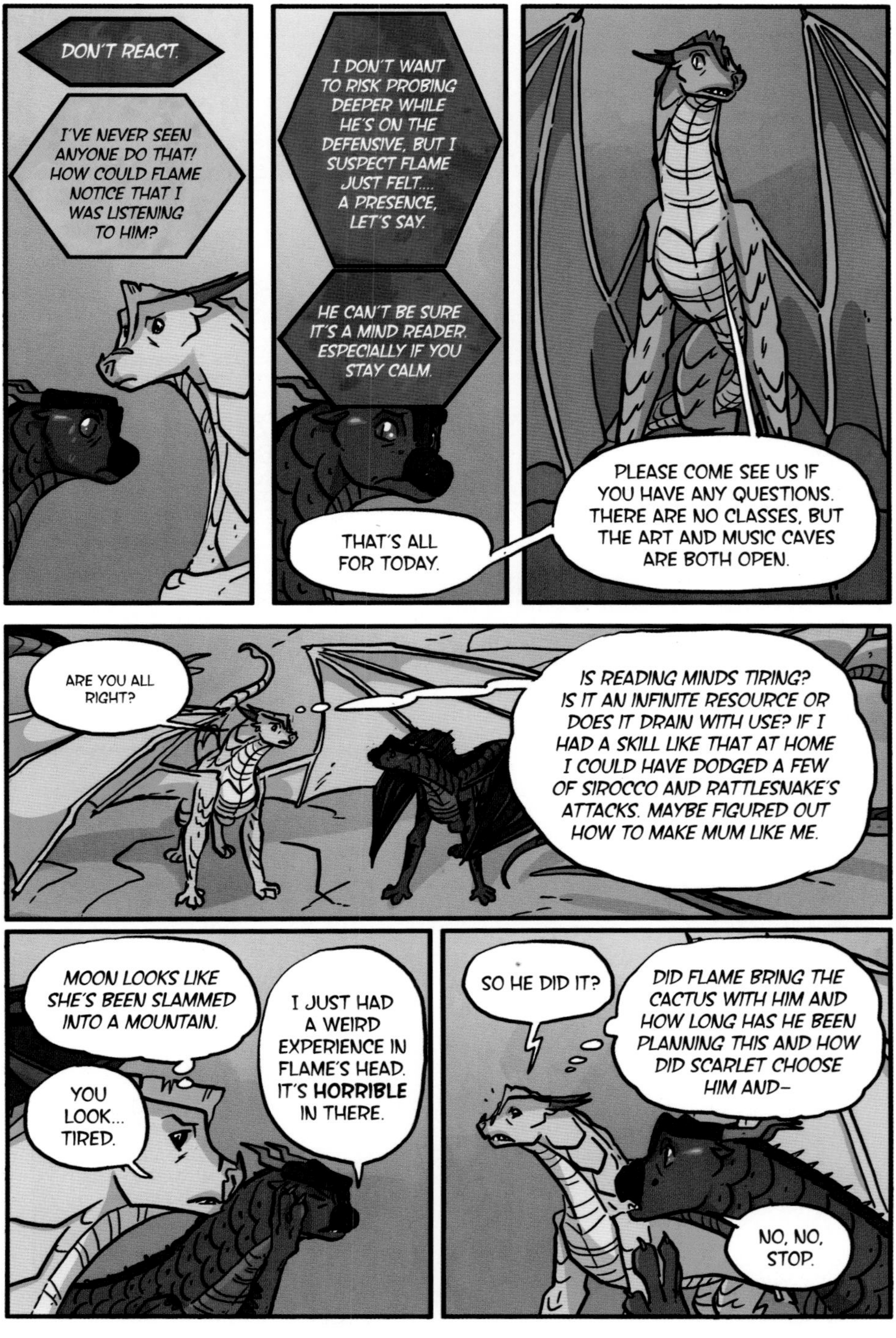
DON'T REACT.
I'VE NEVER SEEN ANYONE DO THAT! HOW COULD FLAME NOTICE THAT I WAS LISTENING TO HIM?
I DON'T WANT TO RISK PROBING DEEPER WHILE HE'S ON THE DEFENSIVE, BUT I SUSPECT FLAME JUST FELT.... A PRESENCE, LET'S SAY.
HE CAN'T BE SURE IT'S A MIND READER. ESPECIALLY IF YOU STAY CALM.
THAT'S ALL FOR TODAY.
PLEASE COME SEE US IF YOU HAVE ANY QUESTIONS. THERE ARE NO CLASSES, BUT THE ART AND MUSIC CAVES ARE BOTH OPEN.
ARE YOU ALL RIGHT?
IS READING MINDS TIRING? IS IT AN INFINITE RESOURCE OR DOES IT DRAIN WITH USE? IF I HAD A SKILL LIKE THAT AT HOME I COULD HAVE DODGED A FEW OF SIROCCO AND RATTLESNAKE'S ATTACKS. MAYBE FIGURED OUT HOW TO MAKE MUM LIKE ME.
MOON LOOKS LIKE SHE'S BEEN SLAMMED INTO A MOUNTAIN.
YOU LOOK... TIRED.
I JUST HAD A WEIRD EXPERIENCE IN FLAME'S HEAD. IT'S **HORRIBLE** IN THERE.
SO HE DID IT?
DID FLAME BRING THE CACTUS WITH HIM AND HOW LONG HAS HE BEEN PLANNING THIS AND HOW DID SCARLET CHOOSE HIM AND–
NO, NO, STOP.

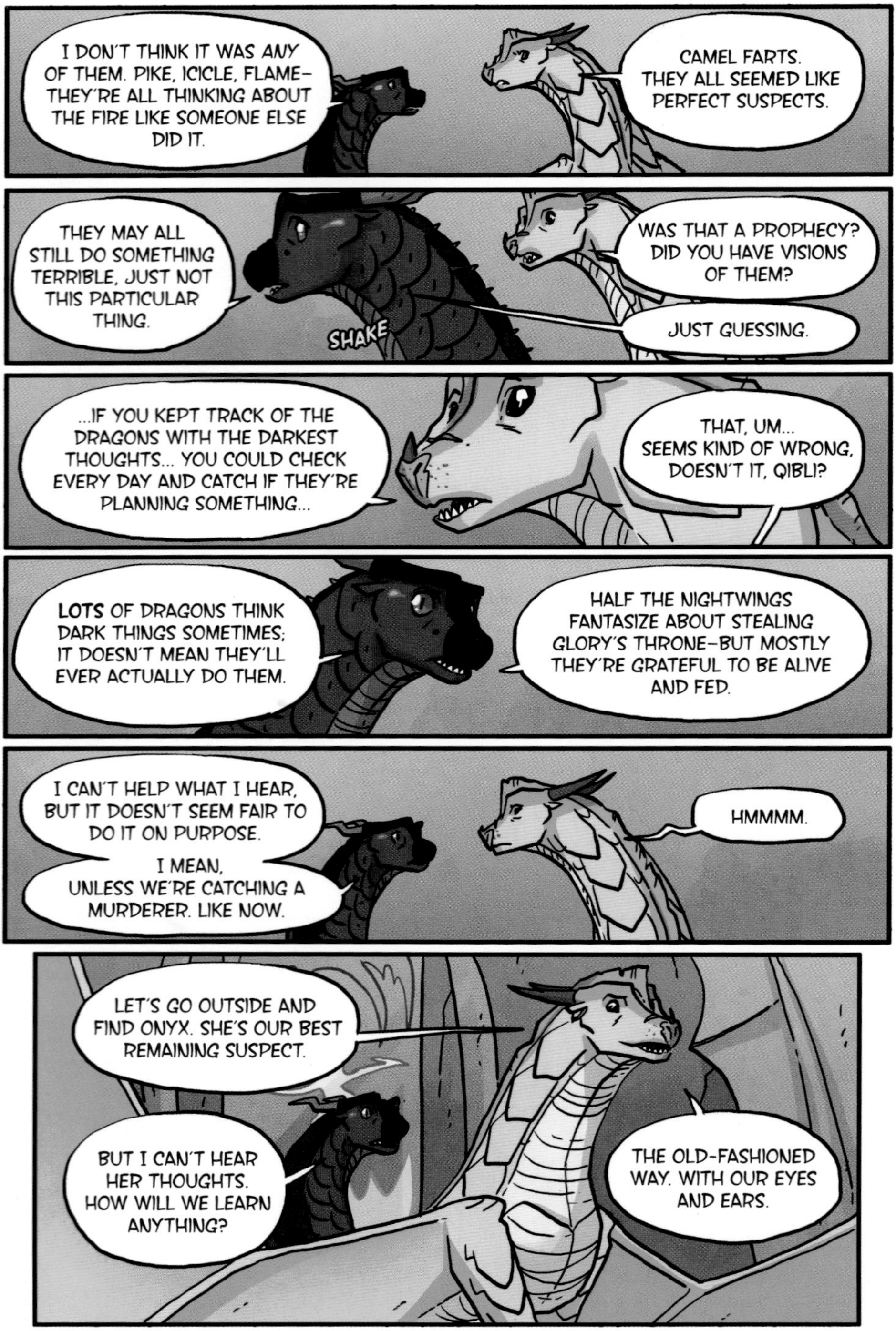
I DON'T THINK IT WAS ANY OF THEM. PIKE, ICICLE, FLAME–THEY'RE ALL THINKING ABOUT THE FIRE LIKE SOMEONE ELSE DID IT.
CAMEL FARTS. THEY ALL SEEMED LIKE PERFECT SUSPECTS.
THEY MAY ALL STILL DO SOMETHING TERRIBLE, JUST NOT THIS PARTICULAR THING.
WAS THAT A PROPHECY? DID YOU HAVE VISIONS OF THEM?
SHAKE
JUST GUESSING.
...IF YOU KEPT TRACK OF THE DRAGONS WITH THE DARKEST THOUGHTS... YOU COULD CHECK EVERY DAY AND CATCH IF THEY'RE PLANNING SOMETHING...
THAT, UM... SEEMS KIND OF WRONG, DOESN'T IT, QIBLI?
LOTS OF DRAGONS THINK DARK THINGS SOMETIMES; IT DOESN'T MEAN THEY'LL EVER ACTUALLY DO THEM.
HALF THE NIGHTWINGS FANTASIZE ABOUT STEALING GLORY'S THRONE–BUT MOSTLY THEY'RE GRATEFUL TO BE ALIVE AND FED.
I CAN'T HELP WHAT I HEAR, BUT IT DOESN'T SEEM FAIR TO DO IT ON PURPOSE.
I MEAN, UNLESS WE'RE CATCHING A MURDERER. LIKE NOW.
HMMMM.
LET'S GO OUTSIDE AND FIND ONYX. SHE'S OUR BEST REMAINING SUSPECT.
BUT I CAN'T HEAR HER THOUGHTS. HOW WILL WE LEARN ANYTHING?
THE OLD-FASHIONED WAY. WITH OUR EYES AND EARS.

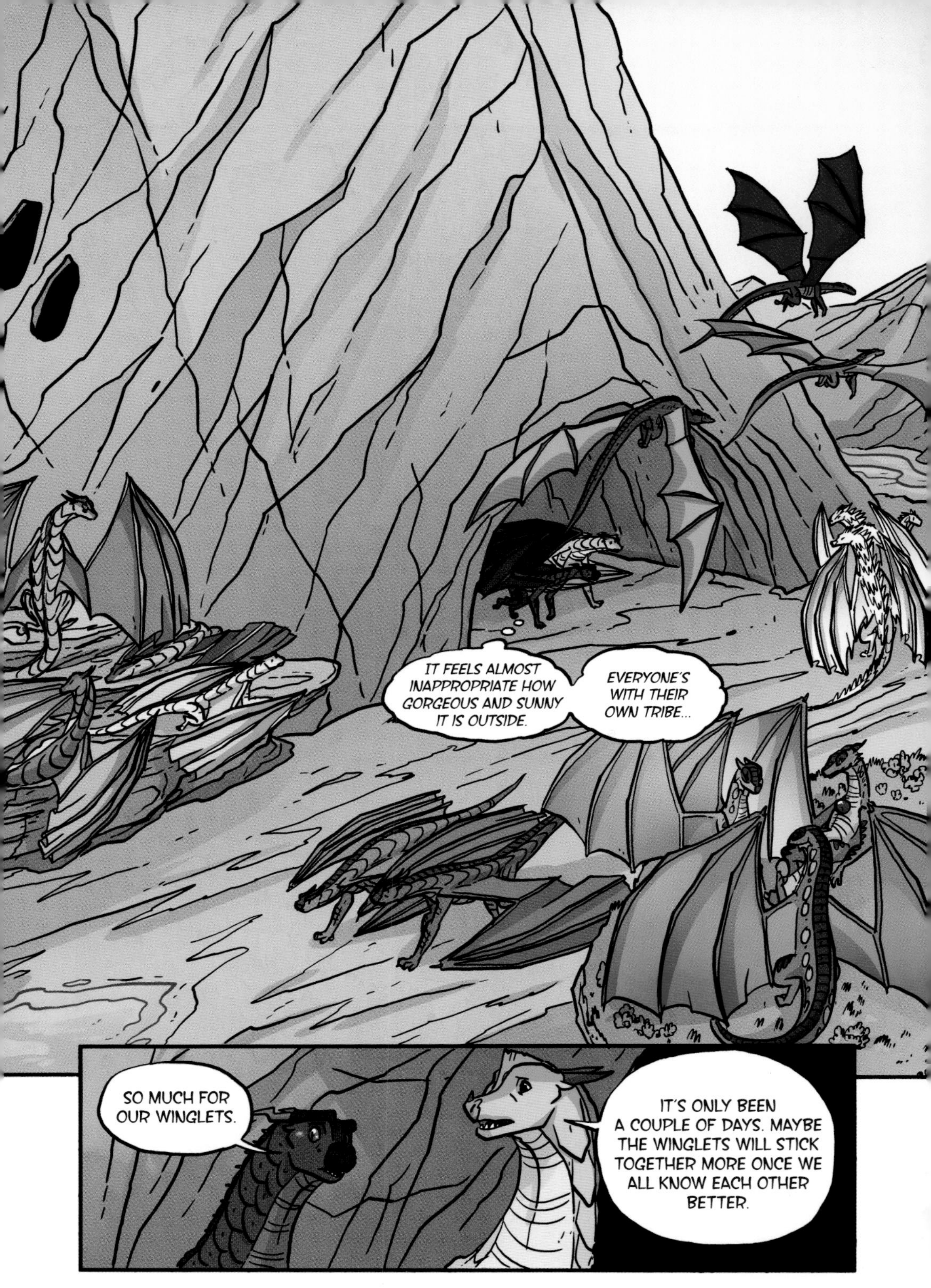
IT FEELS ALMOST INAPPROPRIATE HOW GORGEOUS AND SUNNY IT IS OUTSIDE.
EVERYONE'S WITH THEIR OWN TRIBE...
SO MUCH FOR OUR WINGLETS.
IT'S ONLY BEEN A COUPLE OF DAYS. MAYBE THE WINGLETS WILL STICK TOGETHER MORE ONCE WE ALL KNOW EACH OTHER BETTER.

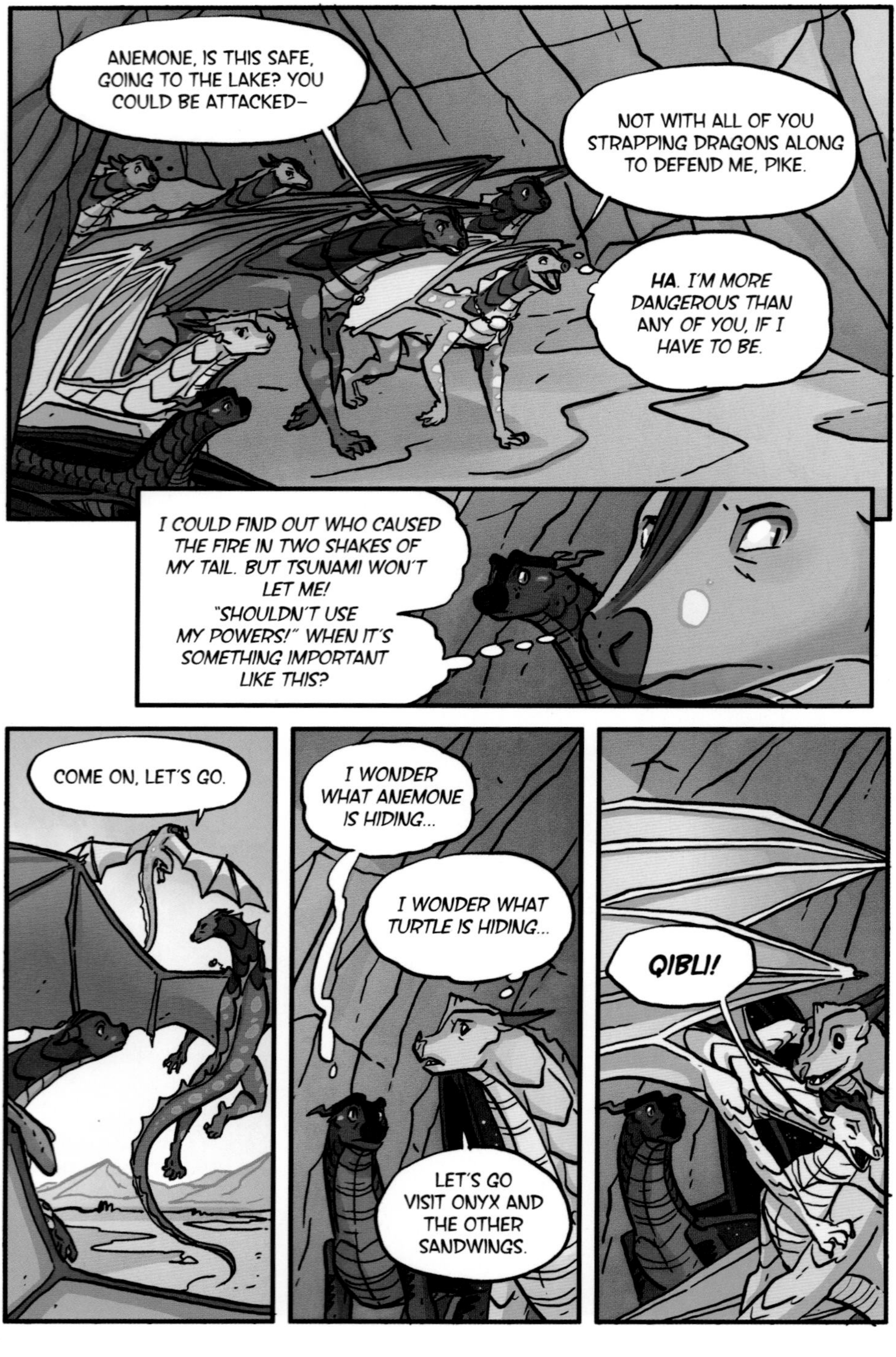

ANEMONE, IS THIS SAFE, GOING TO THE LAKE? YOU COULD BE ATTACKED–
NOT WITH ALL OF YOU STRAPPING DRAGONS ALONG TO DEFEND ME, PIKE.
HA. I'M MORE DANGEROUS THAN ANY OF YOU, IF I HAVE TO BE.
I COULD FIND OUT WHO CAUSED THE FIRE IN TWO SHAKES OF MY TAIL. BUT TSUNAMI WON'T LET ME! "SHOULDN'T USE MY POWERS!" WHEN IT'S SOMETHING IMPORTANT LIKE THIS?
COME ON, LET'S GO.
I WONDER WHAT ANEMONE IS HIDING...
I WONDER WHAT TURTLE IS HIDING...
LET'S GO VISIT ONYX AND THE OTHER SANDWINGS.
QIBLI!

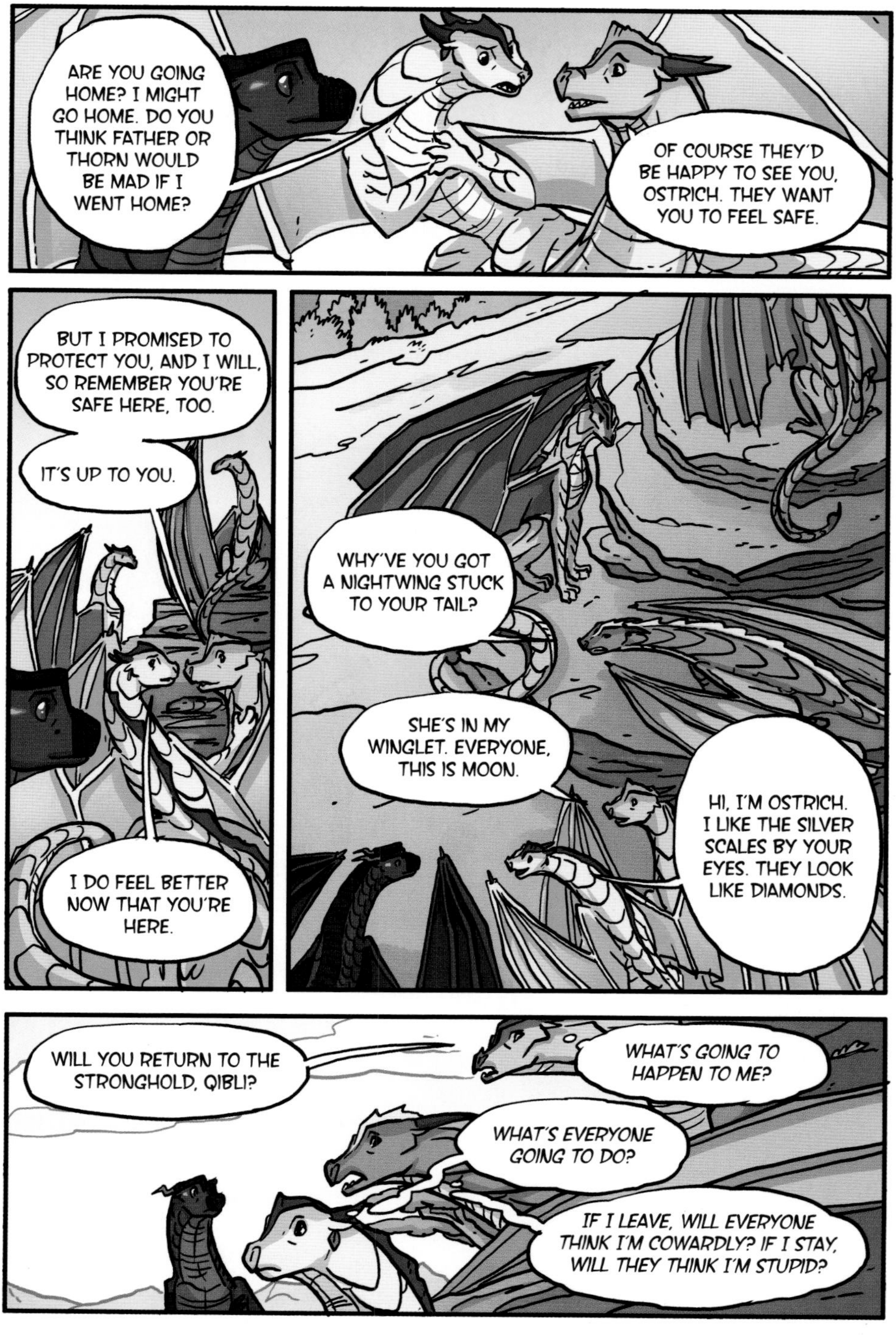
ARE YOU GOING HOME? I MIGHT GO HOME. DO YOU THINK FATHER OR THORN WOULD BE MAD IF I WENT HOME?
OF COURSE THEY'D BE HAPPY TO SEE YOU, OSTRICH. THEY WANT YOU TO FEEL SAFE.
BUT I PROMISED TO PROTECT YOU, AND I WILL, SO REMEMBER YOU'RE SAFE HERE, TOO.
IT'S UP TO YOU.
I DO FEEL BETTER NOW THAT YOU'RE HERE.
WHY'VE YOU GOT A NIGHTWING STUCK TO YOUR TAIL?
SHE'S IN MY WINGLET. EVERYONE, THIS IS MOON.
HI, I'M OSTRICH. I LIKE THE SILVER SCALES BY YOUR EYES. THEY LOOK LIKE DIAMONDS.
WILL YOU RETURN TO THE STRONGHOLD, QIBLI?
WHAT'S GOING TO HAPPEN TO ME?
WHAT'S EVERYONE GOING TO DO?
IF I LEAVE, WILL EVERYONE THINK I'M COWARDLY? IF I STAY, WILL THEY THINK I'M STUPID?

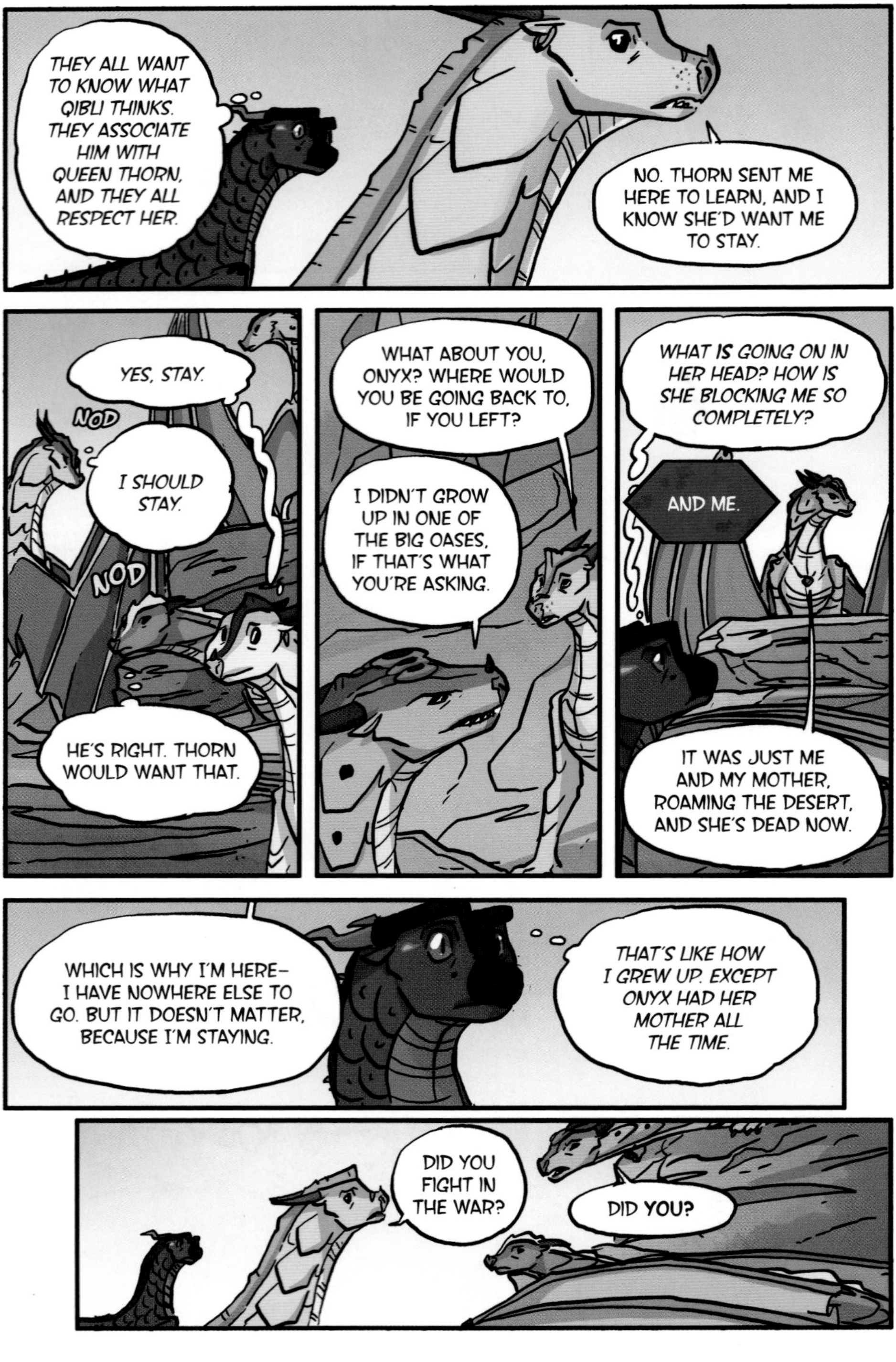
THEY ALL WANT TO KNOW WHAT QIBLI THINKS. THEY ASSOCIATE HIM WITH QUEEN THORN, AND THEY ALL RESPECT HER.
NO. THORN SENT ME HERE TO LEARN, AND I KNOW SHE'D WANT ME TO STAY.
YES, STAY.
NOD
I SHOULD STAY.
NOD
HE'S RIGHT. THORN WOULD WANT THAT.
WHAT ABOUT YOU, ONYX? WHERE WOULD YOU BE GOING BACK TO, IF YOU LEFT?
I DIDN'T GROW UP IN ONE OF THE BIG OASES, IF THAT'S WHAT YOU'RE ASKING.
WHAT IS GOING ON IN HER HEAD? HOW IS SHE BLOCKING ME SO COMPLETELY?
AND ME.
IT WAS JUST ME AND MY MOTHER, ROAMING THE DESERT, AND SHE'S DEAD NOW.
WHICH IS WHY I'M HERE— I HAVE NOWHERE ELSE TO GO. BUT IT DOESN'T MATTER, BECAUSE I'M STAYING.
THAT'S LIKE HOW I GREW UP. EXCEPT ONYX HAD HER MOTHER ALL THE TIME.
DID YOU FIGHT IN THE WAR?
DID YOU?

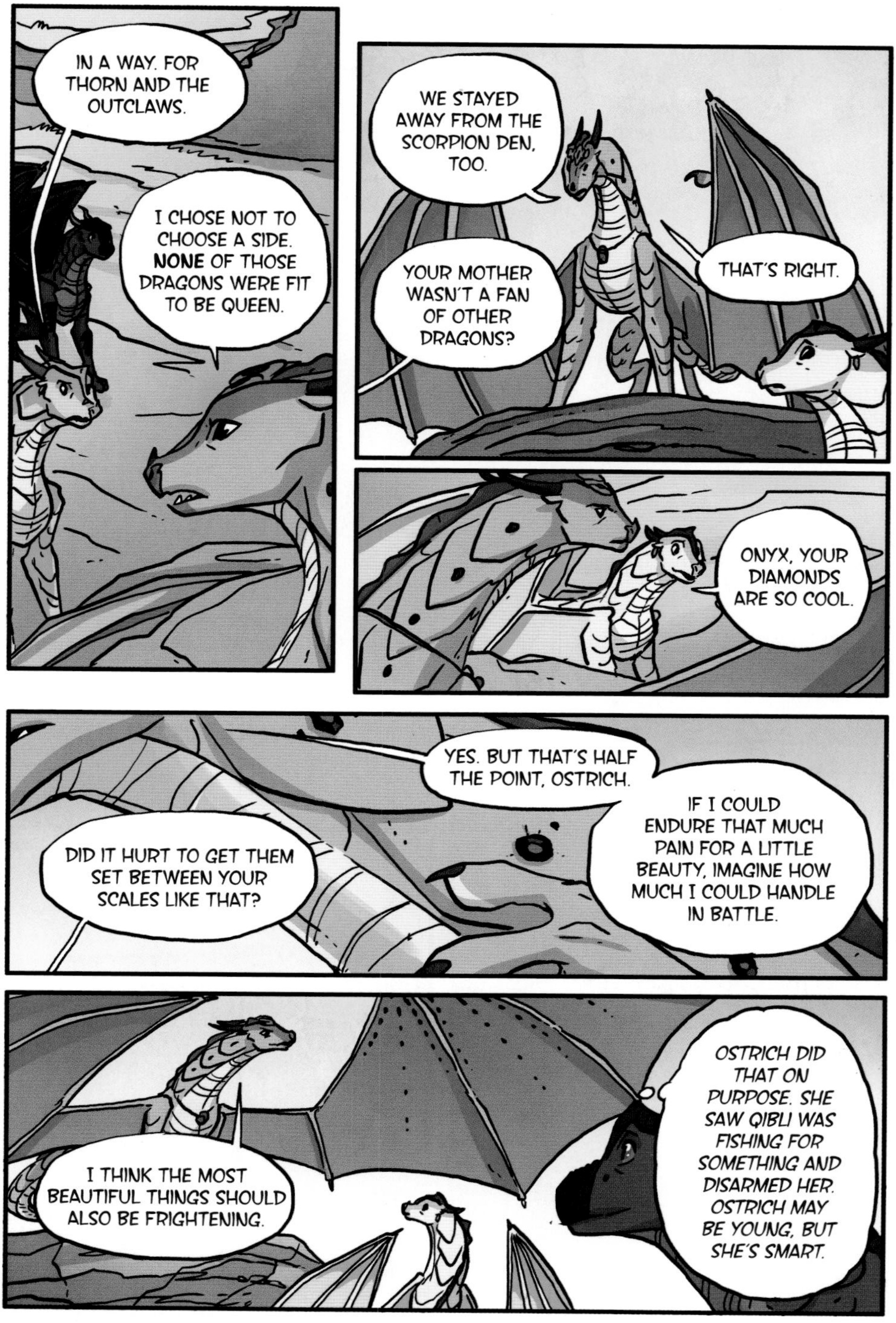
IN A WAY. FOR THORN AND THE OUTCLAWS.
I CHOSE NOT TO CHOOSE A SIDE. NONE OF THOSE DRAGONS WERE FIT TO BE QUEEN.
WE STAYED AWAY FROM THE SCORPION DEN, TOO.
YOUR MOTHER WASN'T A FAN OF OTHER DRAGONS?
THAT'S RIGHT.
ONYX, YOUR DIAMONDS ARE SO COOL.
YES. BUT THAT'S HALF THE POINT, OSTRICH.
DID IT HURT TO GET THEM SET BETWEEN YOUR SCALES LIKE THAT?
IF I COULD ENDURE THAT MUCH PAIN FOR A LITTLE BEAUTY, IMAGINE HOW MUCH I COULD HANDLE IN BATTLE.
I THINK THE MOST BEAUTIFUL THINGS SHOULD ALSO BE FRIGHTENING.
OSTRICH DID THAT ON PURPOSE. SHE SAW QIBLI WAS FISHING FOR SOMETHING AND DISARMED HER. OSTRICH MAY BE YOUNG, BUT SHE'S SMART.

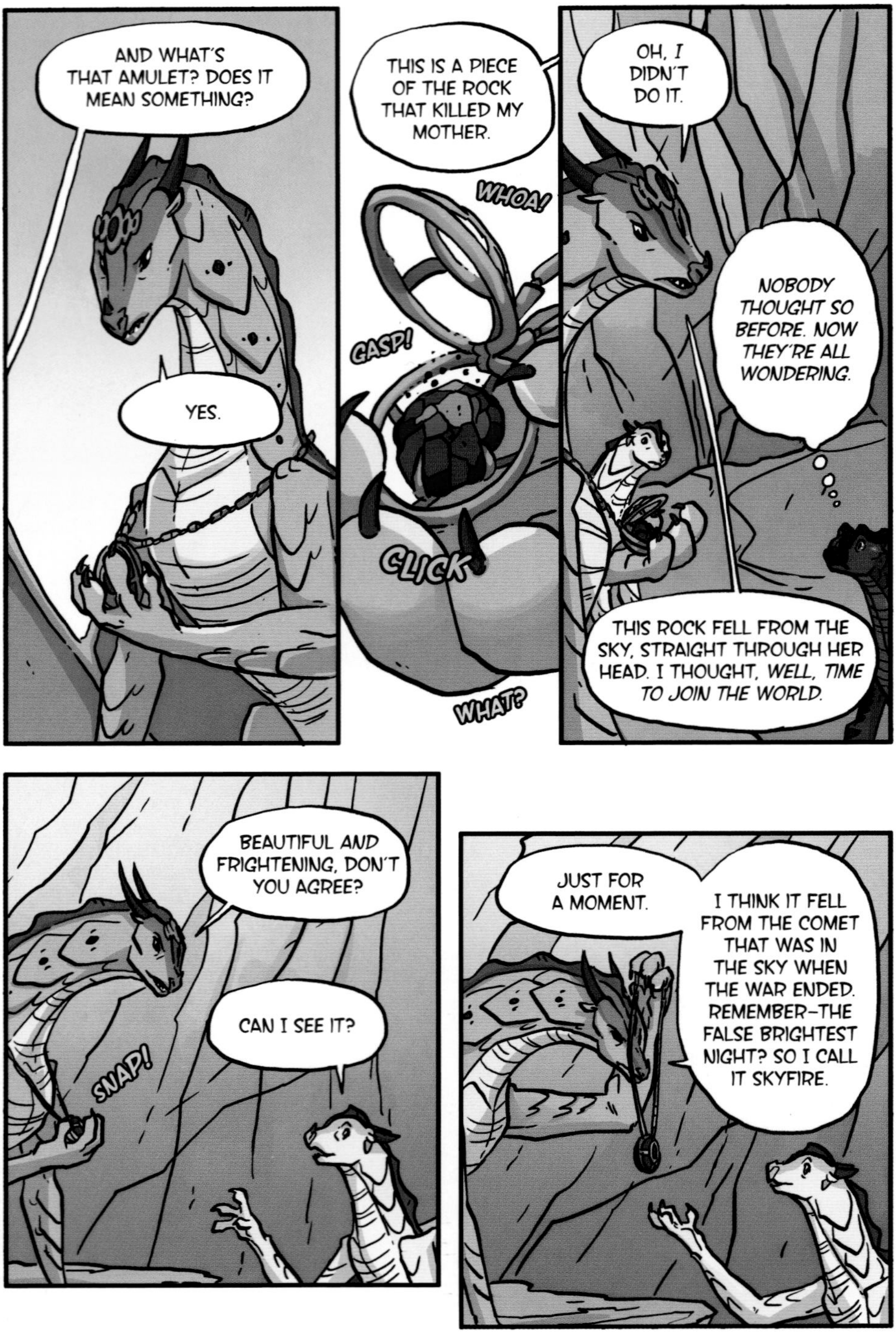
AND WHAT'S THAT AMULET? DOES IT MEAN SOMETHING?
YES.
THIS IS A PIECE OF THE ROCK THAT KILLED MY MOTHER.
WHOA!
GASP!
CLICK
WHAT?
OH, I DIDN'T DO IT.
NOBODY THOUGHT SO BEFORE. NOW THEY'RE ALL WONDERING.
THIS ROCK FELL FROM THE SKY, STRAIGHT THROUGH HER HEAD. I THOUGHT, WELL, TIME TO JOIN THE WORLD.
BEAUTIFUL AND FRIGHTENING, DON'T YOU AGREE?
CAN I SEE IT?
SNAP!
JUST FOR A MOMENT.
I THINK IT FELL FROM THE COMET THAT WAS IN THE SKY WHEN THE WAR ENDED. REMEMBER—THE FALSE BRIGHTEST NIGHT? SO I CALL IT SKYFIRE.

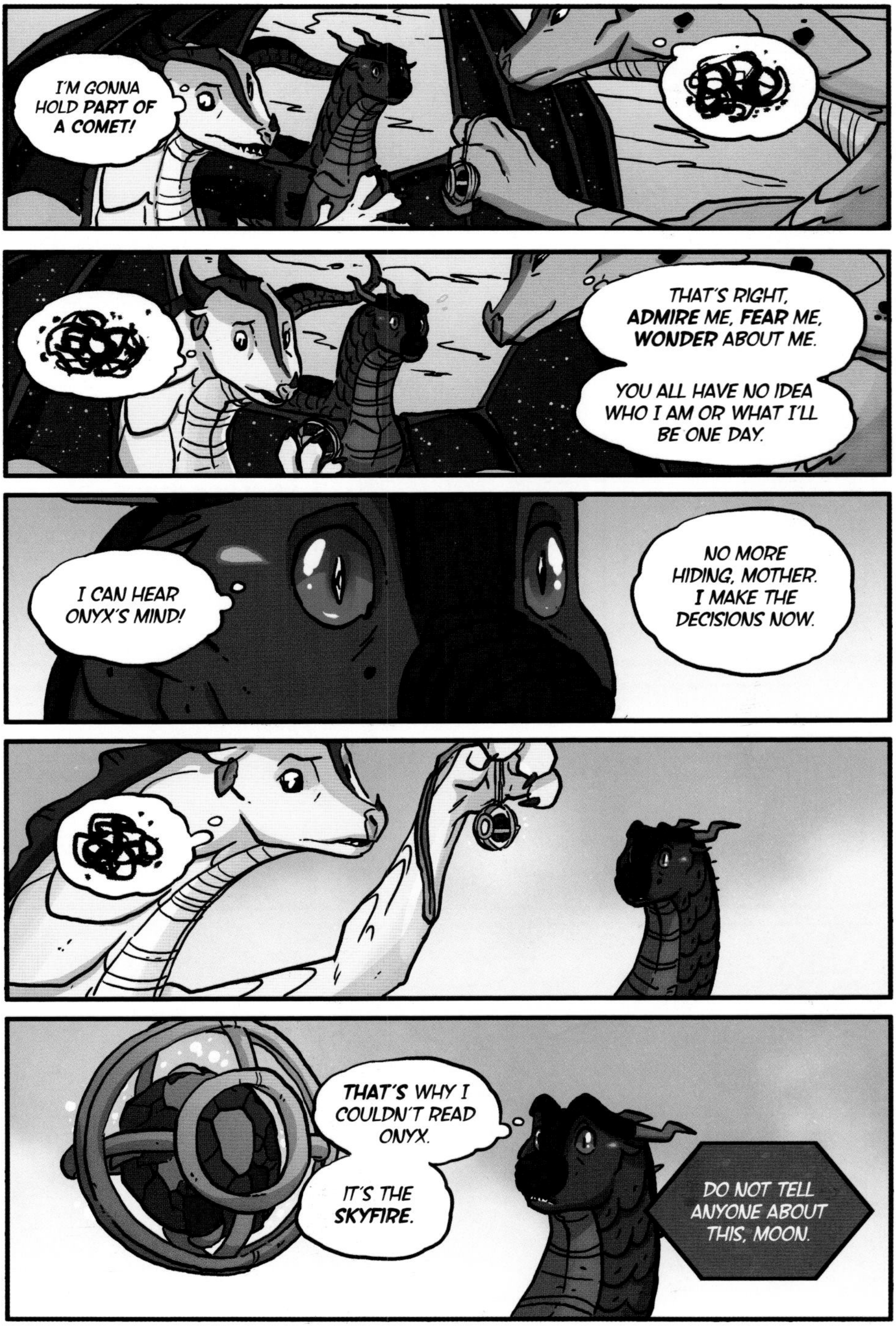
I'M GONNA HOLD PART OF A COMET!
THAT'S RIGHT, ADMIRE ME, FEAR ME, WONDER ABOUT ME.
YOU ALL HAVE NO IDEA WHO I AM OR WHAT I'LL BE ONE DAY.
I CAN HEAR ONYX'S MIND!
NO MORE HIDING, MOTHER. I MAKE THE DECISIONS NOW.
THAT'S WHY I COULDN'T READ ONYX.
IT'S THE SKYFIRE.
DO NOT TELL ANYONE ABOUT THIS, MOON.

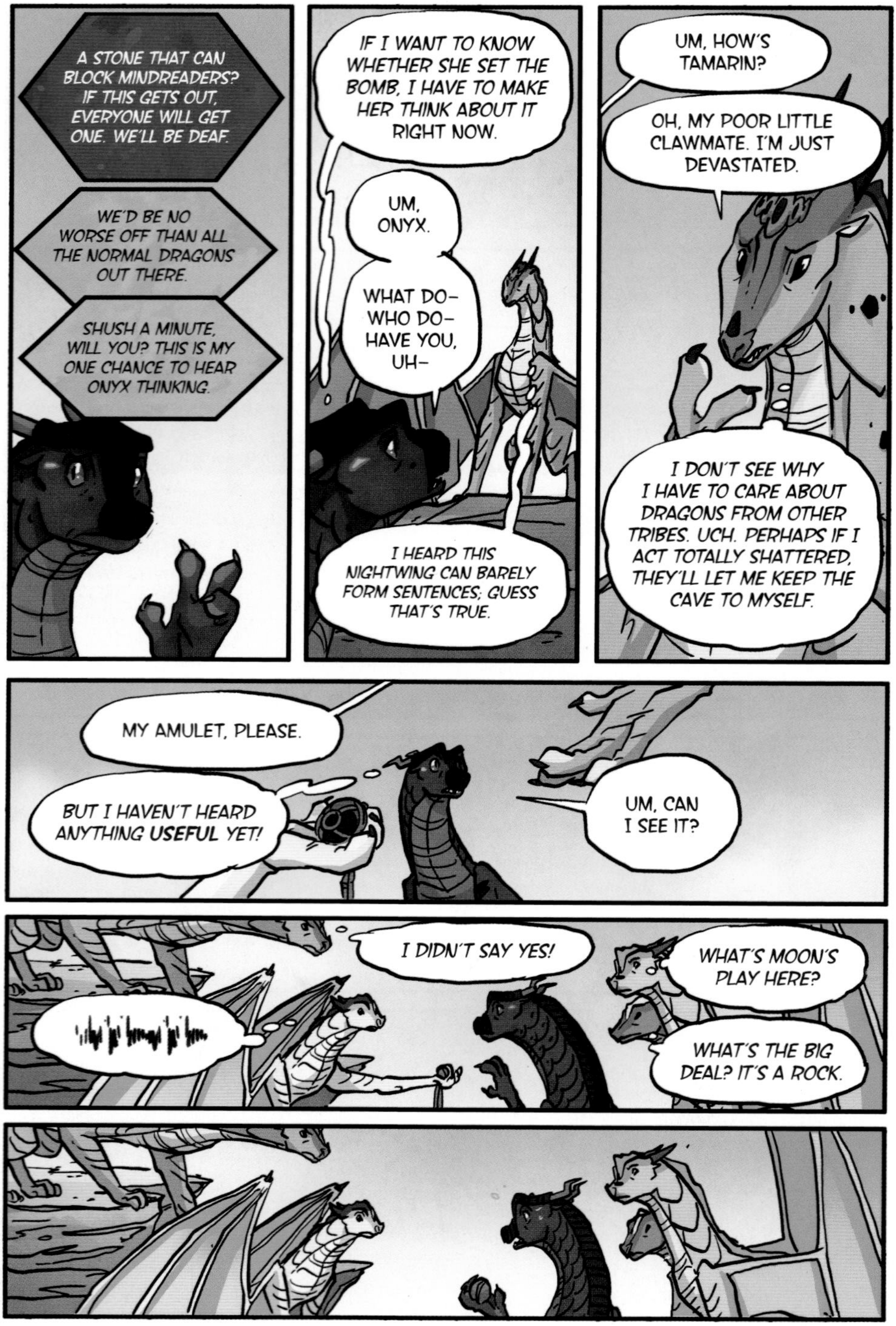
A STONE THAT CAN BLOCK MINDREADERS? IF THIS GETS OUT, EVERYONE WILL GET ONE. WE'LL BE DEAF.
WE'D BE NO WORSE OFF THAN ALL THE NORMAL DRAGONS OUT THERE.
SHUSH A MINUTE, WILL YOU? THIS IS MY ONE CHANCE TO HEAR ONYX THINKING.
IF I WANT TO KNOW WHETHER SHE SET THE BOMB, I HAVE TO MAKE HER THINK ABOUT IT RIGHT NOW.
UM, ONYX.
WHAT DO— WHO DO— HAVE YOU, UH—
I HEARD THIS NIGHTWING CAN BARELY FORM SENTENCES; GUESS THAT'S TRUE.
UM, HOW'S TAMARIN?
OH, MY POOR LITTLE CLAWMATE. I'M JUST DEVASTATED.
I DON'T SEE WHY I HAVE TO CARE ABOUT DRAGONS FROM OTHER TRIBES. UCH. PERHAPS IF I ACT TOTALLY SHATTERED, THEY'LL LET ME KEEP THE CAVE TO MYSELF.
MY AMULET, PLEASE.
BUT I HAVEN'T HEARD ANYTHING USEFUL YET!
UM, CAN I SEE IT?
I DIDN'T SAY YES!
WHAT'S MOON'S PLAY HERE?
WHAT'S THE BIG DEAL? IT'S A ROCK.

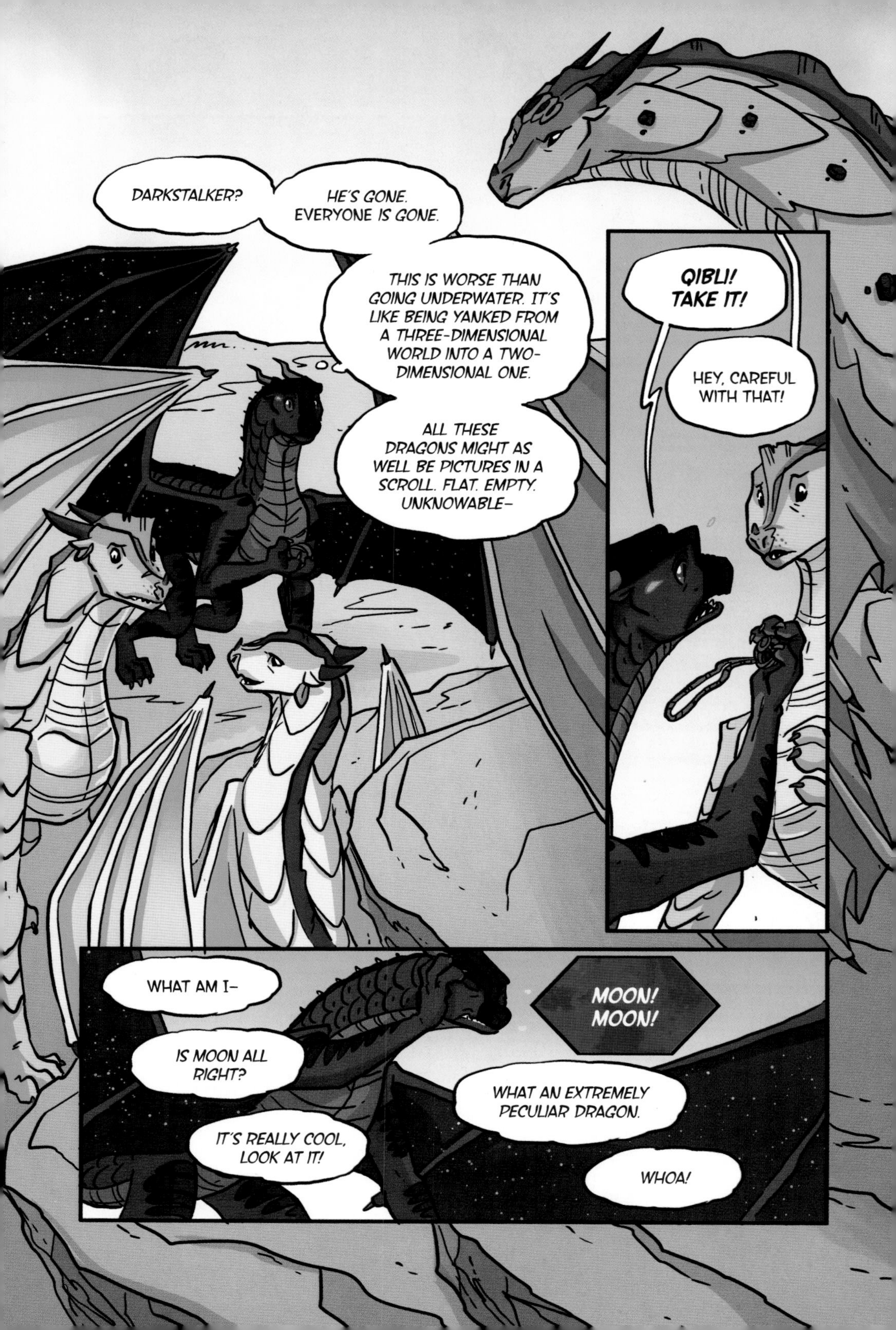
DARKSTALKER?
HE'S GONE. EVERYONE IS GONE.
THIS IS WORSE THAN GOING UNDERWATER. IT'S LIKE BEING YANKED FROM A THREE-DIMENSIONAL WORLD INTO A TWO-DIMENSIONAL ONE.
ALL THESE DRAGONS MIGHT AS WELL BE PICTURES IN A SCROLL. FLAT. EMPTY. UNKNOWABLE–
QIBLI! TAKE IT!
HEY, CAREFUL WITH THAT!
WHAT AM I–
IS MOON ALL RIGHT?
IT'S REALLY COOL, LOOK AT IT!
MOON! MOON!
WHAT AN EXTREMELY PECULIAR DRAGON.
WHOA!

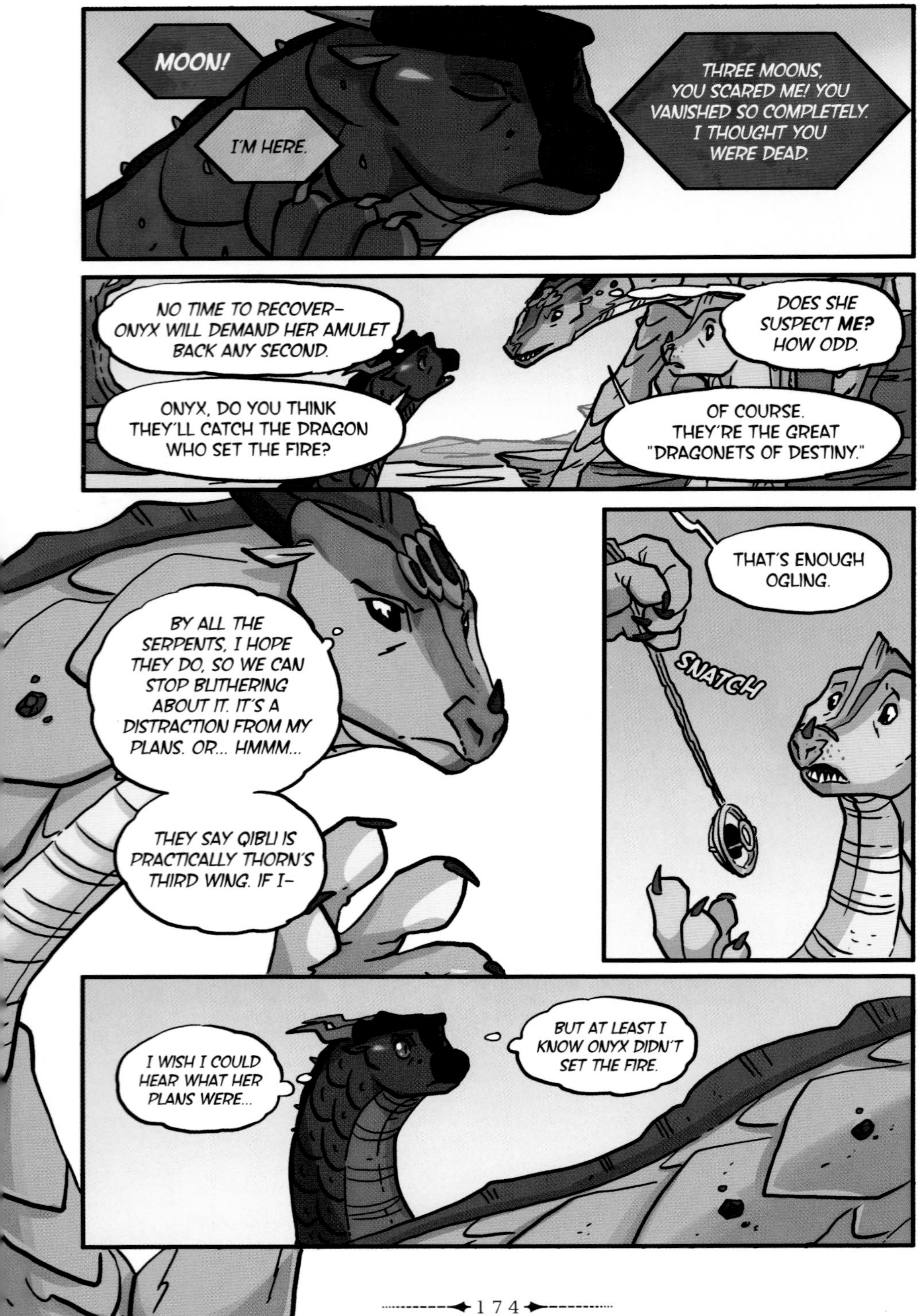
MOON!
I'M HERE.
THREE MOONS, YOU SCARED ME! YOU VANISHED SO COMPLETELY. I THOUGHT YOU WERE DEAD.
NO TIME TO RECOVER— ONYX WILL DEMAND HER AMULET BACK ANY SECOND.
DOES SHE SUSPECT **ME?** HOW ODD.
ONYX, DO YOU THINK THEY'LL CATCH THE DRAGON WHO SET THE FIRE?
OF COURSE. THEY'RE THE GREAT "DRAGONETS OF DESTINY."
BY ALL THE SERPENTS, I HOPE THEY DO, SO WE CAN STOP BLITHERING ABOUT IT. IT'S A DISTRACTION FROM MY PLANS. OR... HMMM...
THEY SAY QIBLI IS PRACTICALLY THORN'S THIRD WING. IF I—
THAT'S ENOUGH OGLING.
SNATCH
I WISH I COULD HEAR WHAT HER PLANS WERE...
BUT AT LEAST I KNOW ONYX DIDN'T SET THE FIRE.

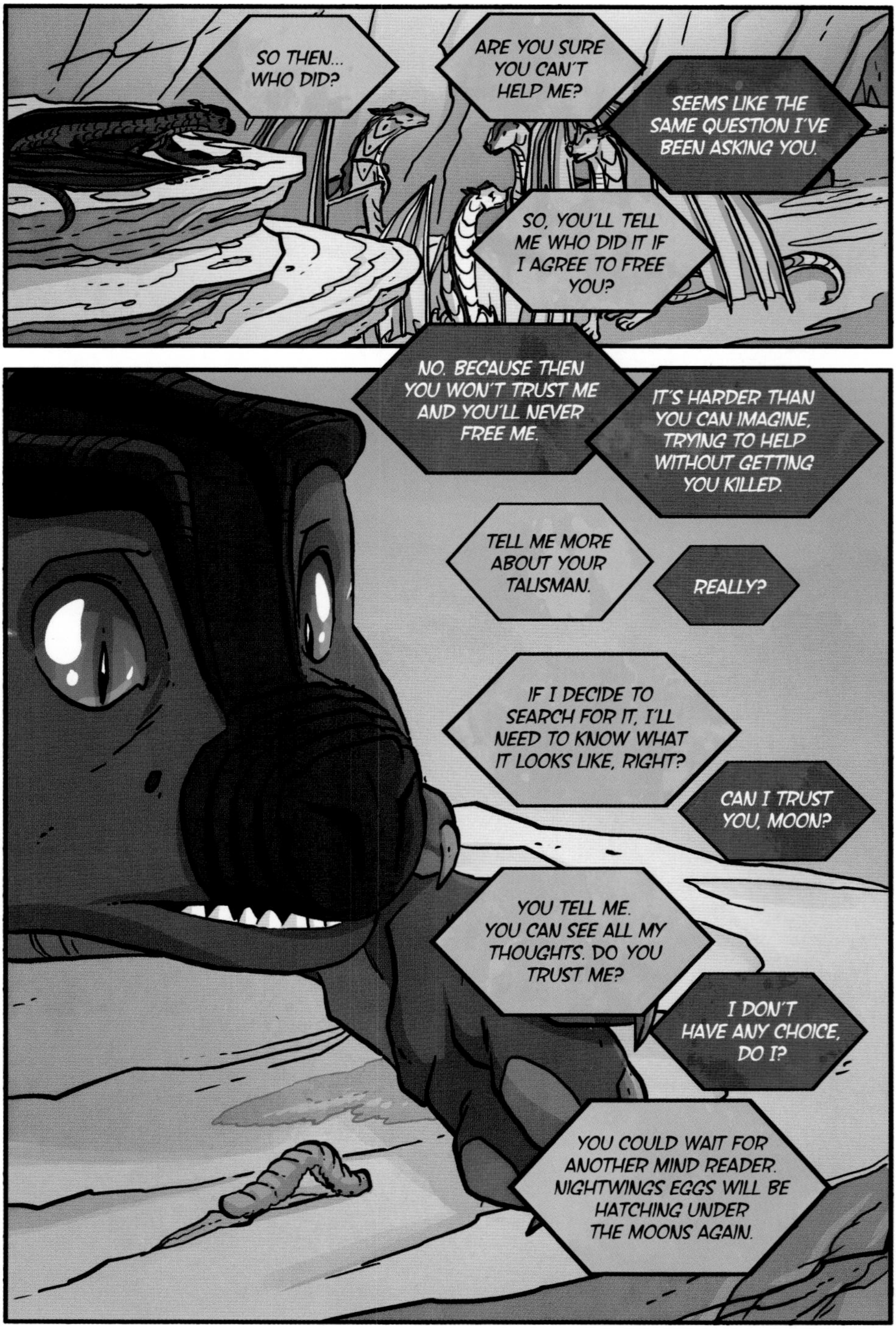
SO THEN... WHO DID?
ARE YOU SURE YOU CAN'T HELP ME?
SEEMS LIKE THE SAME QUESTION I'VE BEEN ASKING YOU.
SO, YOU'LL TELL ME WHO DID IT IF I AGREE TO FREE YOU?
NO. BECAUSE THEN YOU WON'T TRUST ME AND YOU'LL NEVER FREE ME.
IT'S HARDER THAN YOU CAN IMAGINE, TRYING TO HELP WITHOUT GETTING YOU KILLED.
TELL ME MORE ABOUT YOUR TALISMAN.
REALLY?
IF I DECIDE TO SEARCH FOR IT, I'LL NEED TO KNOW WHAT IT LOOKS LIKE, RIGHT?
CAN I TRUST YOU, MOON?
YOU TELL ME. YOU CAN SEE ALL MY THOUGHTS. DO YOU TRUST ME?
I DON'T HAVE ANY CHOICE, DO I?
YOU COULD WAIT FOR ANOTHER MIND READER. NIGHTWINGS EGGS WILL BE HATCHING UNDER THE MOONS AGAIN.

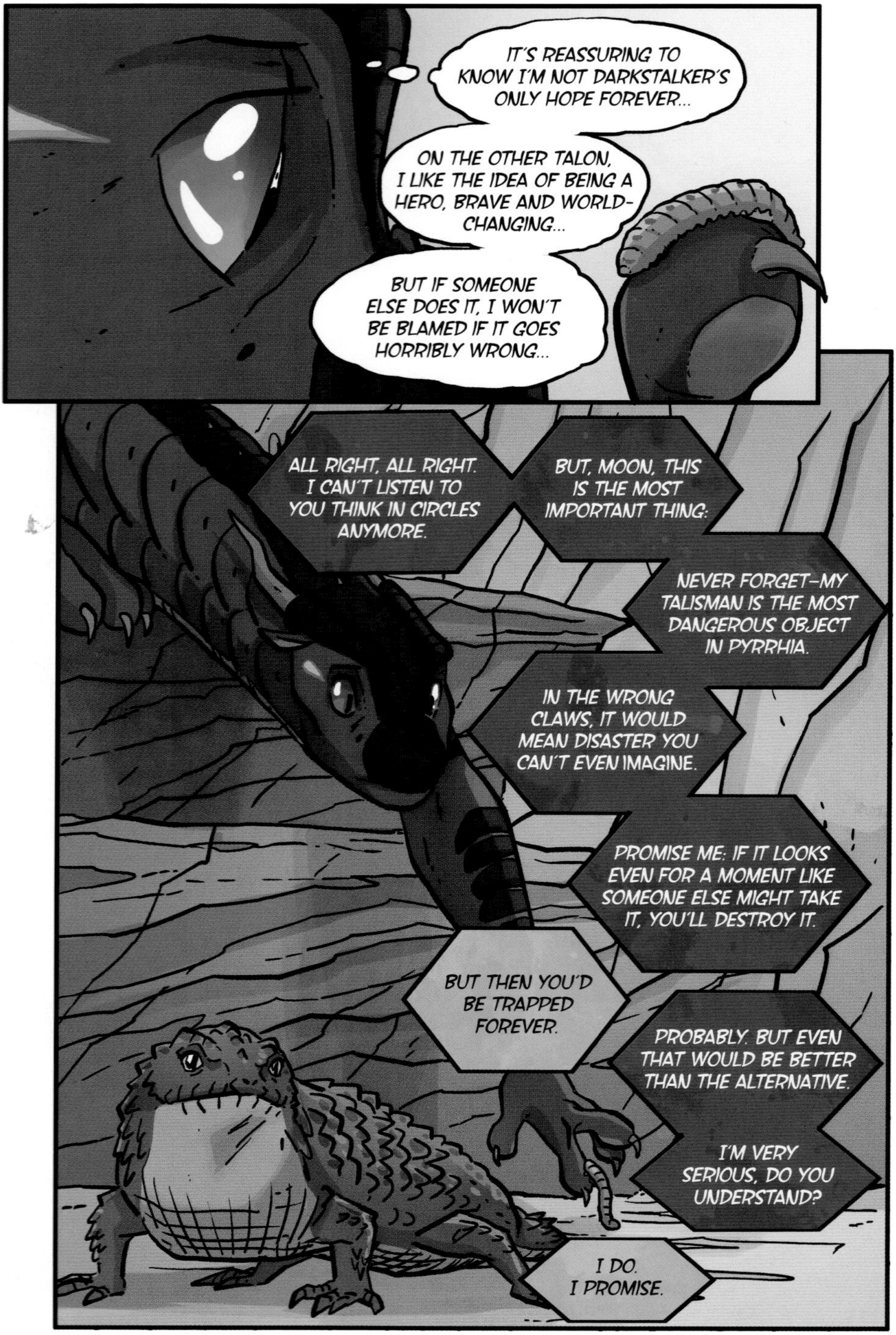
IT'S REASSURING TO KNOW I'M NOT DARKSTALKER'S ONLY HOPE FOREVER...
ON THE OTHER TALON, I LIKE THE IDEA OF BEING A HERO, BRAVE AND WORLD-CHANGING...
BUT IF SOMEONE ELSE DOES IT, I WON'T BE BLAMED IF IT GOES HORRIBLY WRONG...
ALL RIGHT, ALL RIGHT. I CAN'T LISTEN TO YOU THINK IN CIRCLES ANYMORE.
BUT, MOON, THIS IS THE MOST IMPORTANT THING:
NEVER FORGET—MY TALISMAN IS THE MOST DANGEROUS OBJECT IN PYRRHIA.
IN THE WRONG CLAWS, IT WOULD MEAN DISASTER YOU CAN'T EVEN IMAGINE.
PROMISE ME: IF IT LOOKS EVEN FOR A MOMENT LIKE SOMEONE ELSE MIGHT TAKE IT, YOU'LL DESTROY IT.
BUT THEN YOU'D BE TRAPPED FOREVER.
PROBABLY. BUT EVEN THAT WOULD BE BETTER THAN THE ALTERNATIVE.
I'M VERY SERIOUS, DO YOU UNDERSTAND?
I DO. I PROMISE.

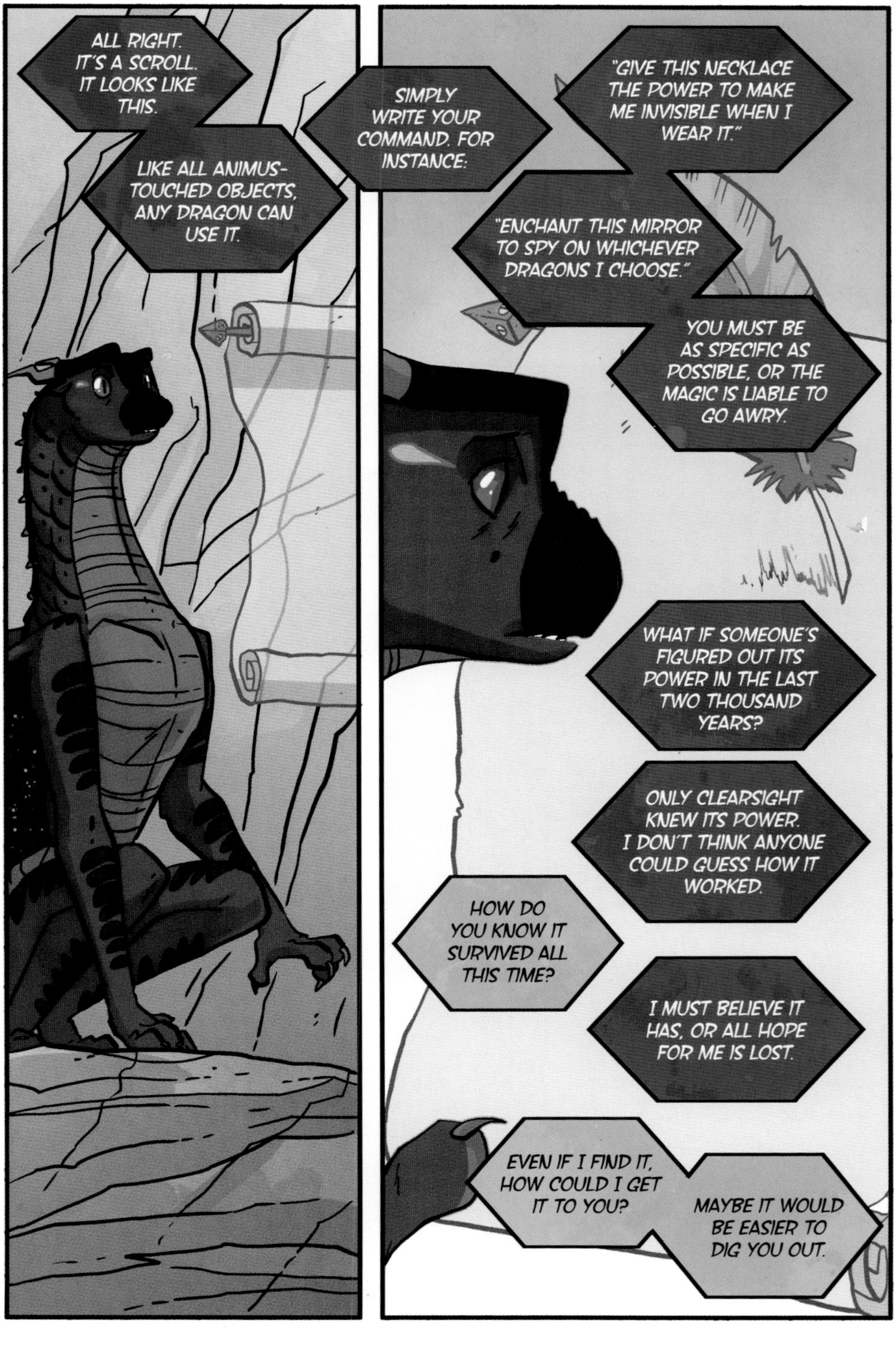
ALL RIGHT. IT'S A SCROLL. IT LOOKS LIKE THIS.
LIKE ALL ANIMUS-TOUCHED OBJECTS, ANY DRAGON CAN USE IT.
SIMPLY WRITE YOUR COMMAND. FOR INSTANCE:
"GIVE THIS NECKLACE THE POWER TO MAKE ME INVISIBLE WHEN I WEAR IT."
"ENCHANT THIS MIRROR TO SPY ON WHICHEVER DRAGONS I CHOOSE."
YOU MUST BE AS SPECIFIC AS POSSIBLE, OR THE MAGIC IS LIABLE TO GO AWRY.
WHAT IF SOMEONE'S FIGURED OUT ITS POWER IN THE LAST TWO THOUSAND YEARS?
ONLY CLEARSIGHT KNEW ITS POWER. I DON'T THINK ANYONE COULD GUESS HOW IT WORKED.
HOW DO YOU KNOW IT SURVIVED ALL THIS TIME?
I MUST BELIEVE IT HAS, OR ALL HOPE FOR ME IS LOST.
EVEN IF I FIND IT, HOW COULD I GET IT TO YOU?
MAYBE IT WOULD BE EASIER TO DIG YOU OUT.

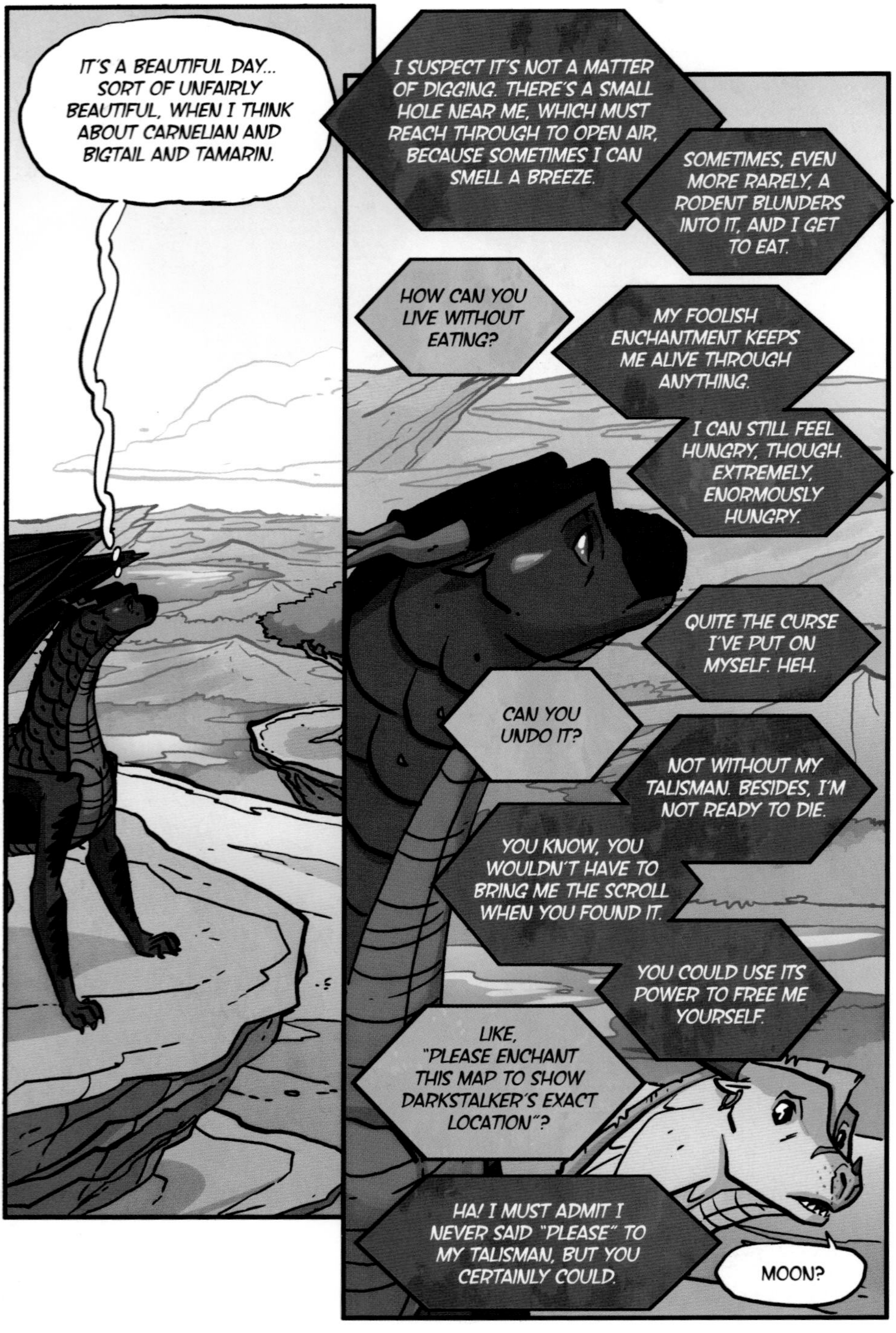
IT'S A BEAUTIFUL DAY... SORT OF UNFAIRLY BEAUTIFUL, WHEN I THINK ABOUT CARNELIAN AND BIGTAIL AND TAMARIN.
I SUSPECT IT'S NOT A MATTER OF DIGGING. THERE'S A SMALL HOLE NEAR ME, WHICH MUST REACH THROUGH TO OPEN AIR, BECAUSE SOMETIMES I CAN SMELL A BREEZE.
SOMETIMES, EVEN MORE RARELY, A RODENT BLUNDERS INTO IT, AND I GET TO EAT.
HOW CAN YOU LIVE WITHOUT EATING?
MY FOOLISH ENCHANTMENT KEEPS ME ALIVE THROUGH ANYTHING.
I CAN STILL FEEL HUNGRY, THOUGH. EXTREMELY, ENORMOUSLY HUNGRY.
QUITE THE CURSE I'VE PUT ON MYSELF. HEH.
CAN YOU UNDO IT?
NOT WITHOUT MY TALISMAN. BESIDES, I'M NOT READY TO DIE.
YOU KNOW, YOU WOULDN'T HAVE TO BRING ME THE SCROLL WHEN YOU FOUND IT.
YOU COULD USE ITS POWER TO FREE ME YOURSELF.
LIKE, "PLEASE ENCHANT THIS MAP TO SHOW DARKSTALKER'S EXACT LOCATION"?
HA! I MUST ADMIT I NEVER SAID "PLEASE" TO MY TALISMAN, BUT YOU CERTAINLY COULD.
MOON?

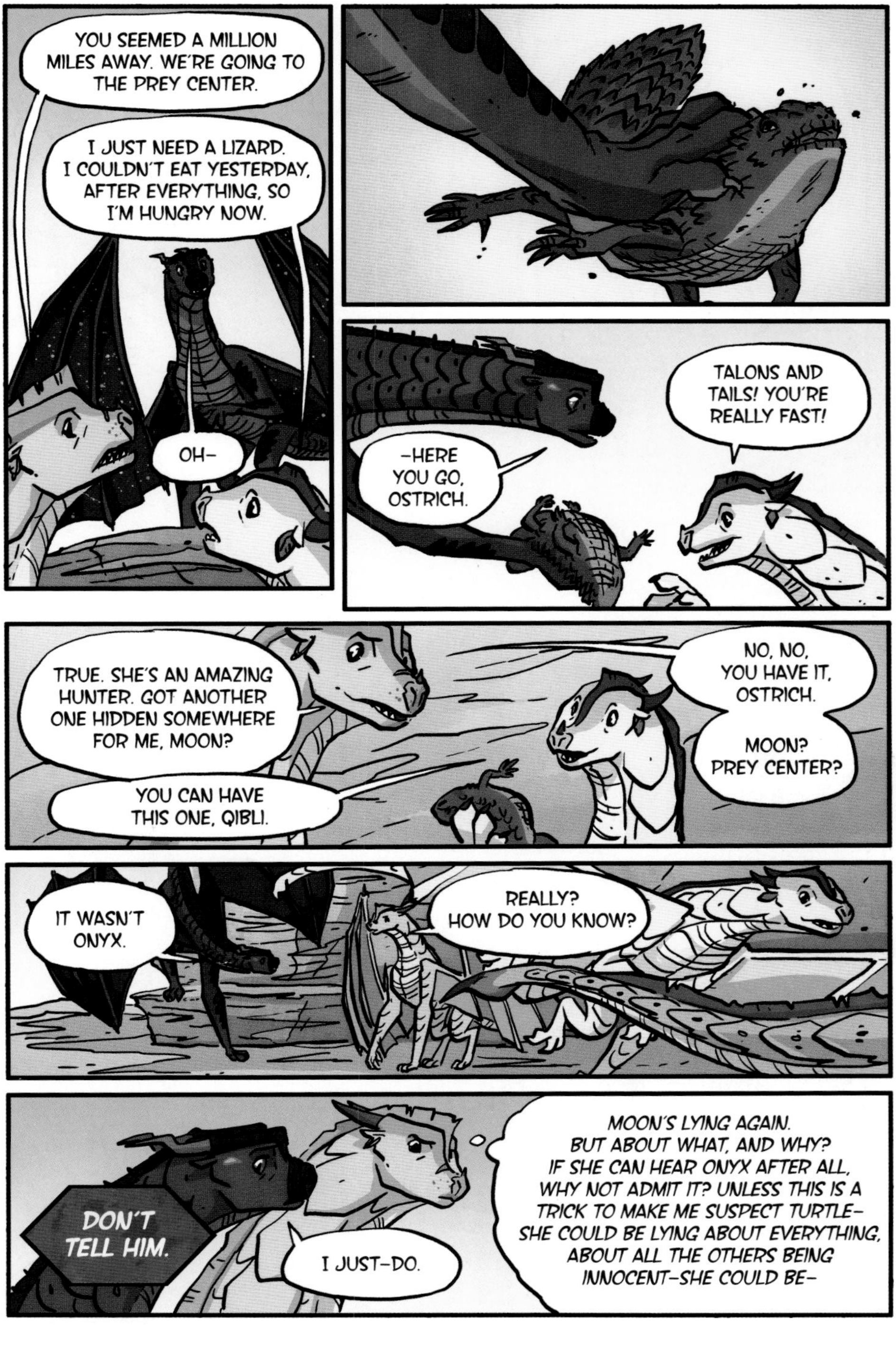
YOU SEEMED A MILLION MILES AWAY. WE'RE GOING TO THE PREY CENTER.
I JUST NEED A LIZARD. I COULDN'T EAT YESTERDAY, AFTER EVERYTHING, SO I'M HUNGRY NOW.
OH–
–HERE YOU GO, OSTRICH.
TALONS AND TAILS! YOU'RE REALLY FAST!
TRUE. SHE'S AN AMAZING HUNTER. GOT ANOTHER ONE HIDDEN SOMEWHERE FOR ME, MOON?
YOU CAN HAVE THIS ONE, QIBLI.
NO, NO, YOU HAVE IT, OSTRICH.
MOON? PREY CENTER?
IT WASN'T ONYX.
REALLY? HOW DO YOU KNOW?
DON'T TELL HIM.
I JUST–DO.
MOON'S LYING AGAIN. BUT ABOUT WHAT, AND WHY? IF SHE CAN HEAR ONYX AFTER ALL, WHY NOT ADMIT IT? UNLESS THIS IS A TRICK TO MAKE ME SUSPECT TURTLE– SHE COULD BE LYING ABOUT EVERYTHING, ABOUT ALL THE OTHERS BEING INNOCENT–SHE COULD BE–

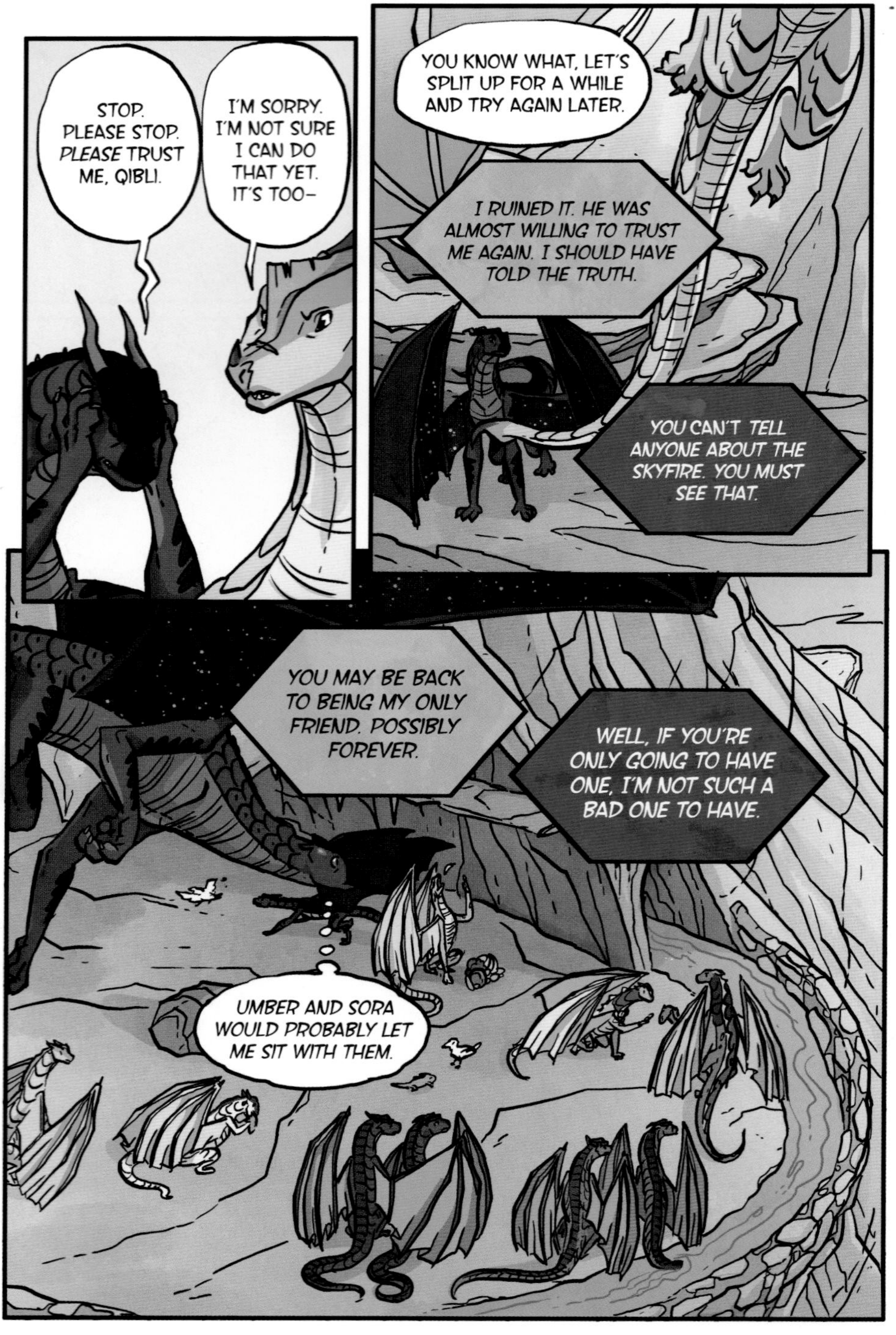
STOP. PLEASE STOP. *PLEASE* TRUST ME, QIBLI.
I'M SORRY. I'M NOT SURE I CAN DO THAT YET. IT'S TOO–
YOU KNOW WHAT, LET'S SPLIT UP FOR A WHILE AND TRY AGAIN LATER.
I RUINED IT. HE WAS ALMOST WILLING TO TRUST ME AGAIN. I SHOULD HAVE TOLD THE TRUTH.
YOU CAN'T TELL ANYONE ABOUT THE SKYFIRE. YOU MUST SEE THAT.
YOU MAY BE BACK TO BEING MY ONLY FRIEND. POSSIBLY FOREVER.
WELL, IF YOU'RE ONLY GOING TO HAVE ONE, I'M NOT SUCH A BAD ONE TO HAVE.
UMBER AND SORA WOULD PROBABLY LET ME SIT WITH THEM.

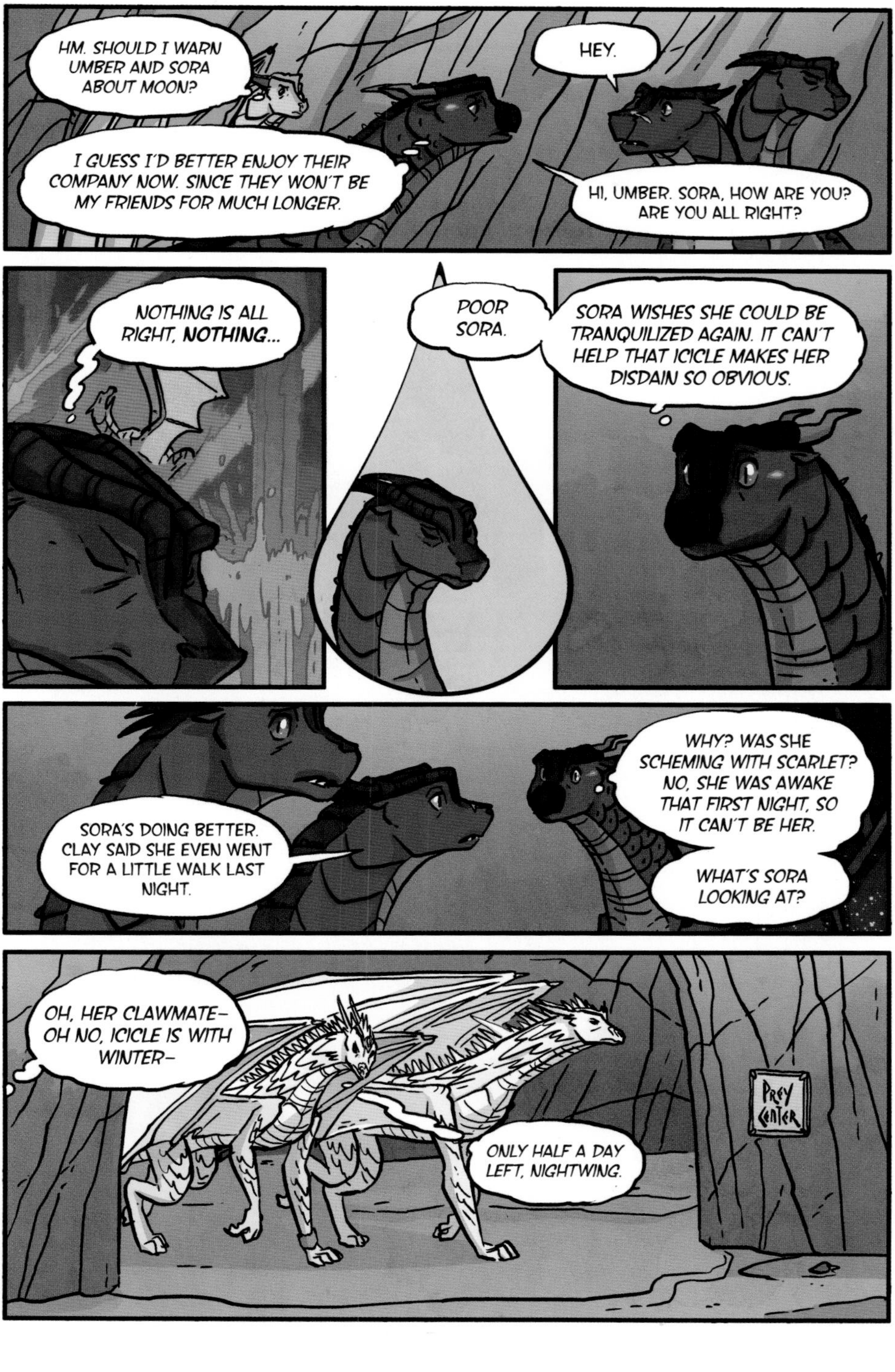
HM. SHOULD I WARN UMBER AND SORA ABOUT MOON?
I GUESS I'D BETTER ENJOY THEIR COMPANY NOW. SINCE THEY WON'T BE MY FRIENDS FOR MUCH LONGER.
HEY.
HI, UMBER. SORA, HOW ARE YOU? ARE YOU ALL RIGHT?
NOTHING IS ALL RIGHT, **NOTHING**...
POOR SORA.
SORA WISHES SHE COULD BE TRANQUILIZED AGAIN. IT CAN'T HELP THAT ICICLE MAKES HER DISDAIN SO OBVIOUS.
SORA'S DOING BETTER. CLAY SAID SHE EVEN WENT FOR A LITTLE WALK LAST NIGHT.
WHY? WAS SHE SCHEMING WITH SCARLET? NO, SHE WAS AWAKE THAT FIRST NIGHT, SO IT CAN'T BE HER.
WHAT'S SORA LOOKING AT?
OH, HER CLAWMATE– OH NO, ICICLE IS WITH WINTER–
PREY CENTER
ONLY HALF A DAY LEFT, NIGHTWING.

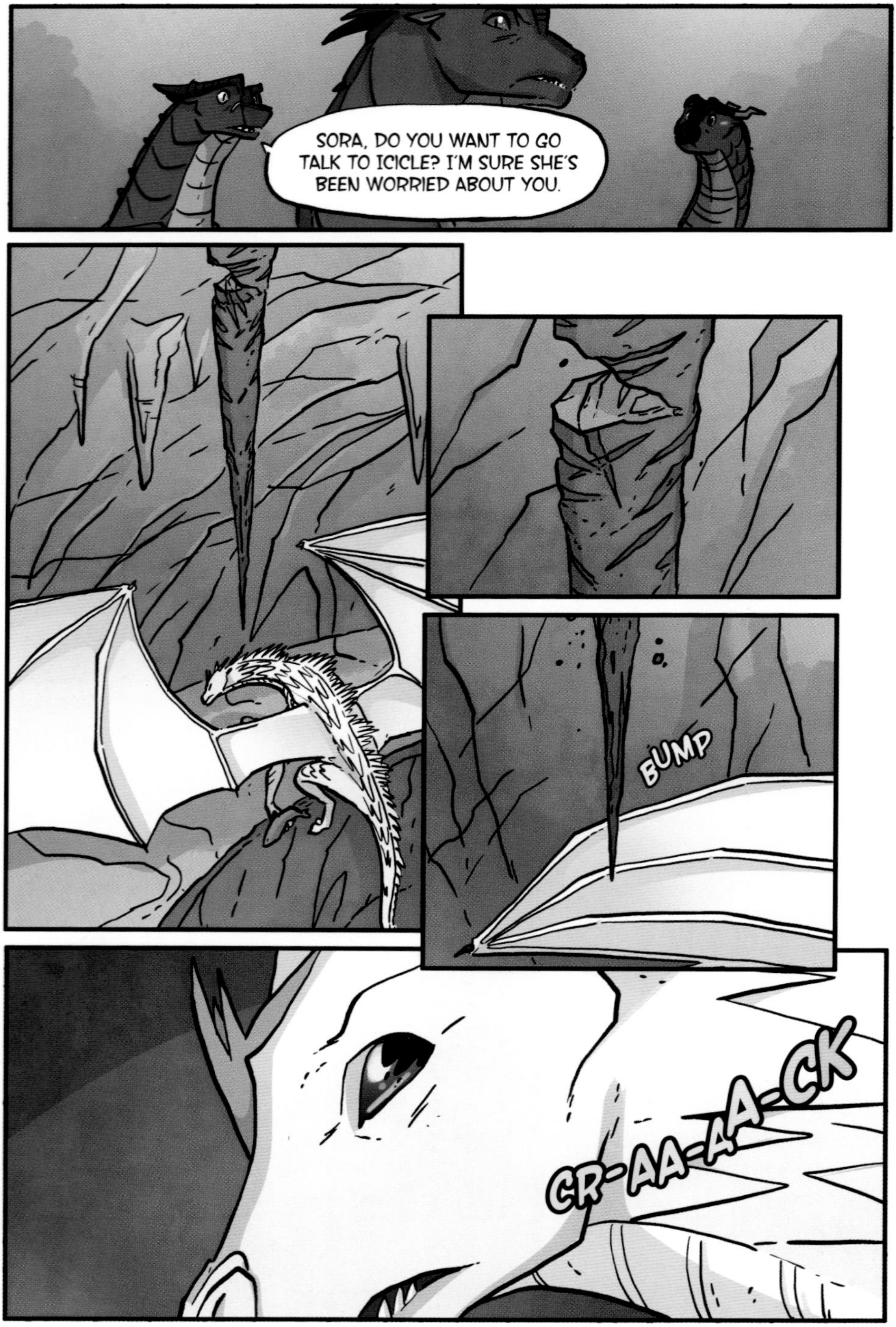
SORA, DO YOU WANT TO GO TALK TO ICICLE? I'M SURE SHE'S BEEN WORRIED ABOUT YOU.
BUMP
CR-AA-AA-CK

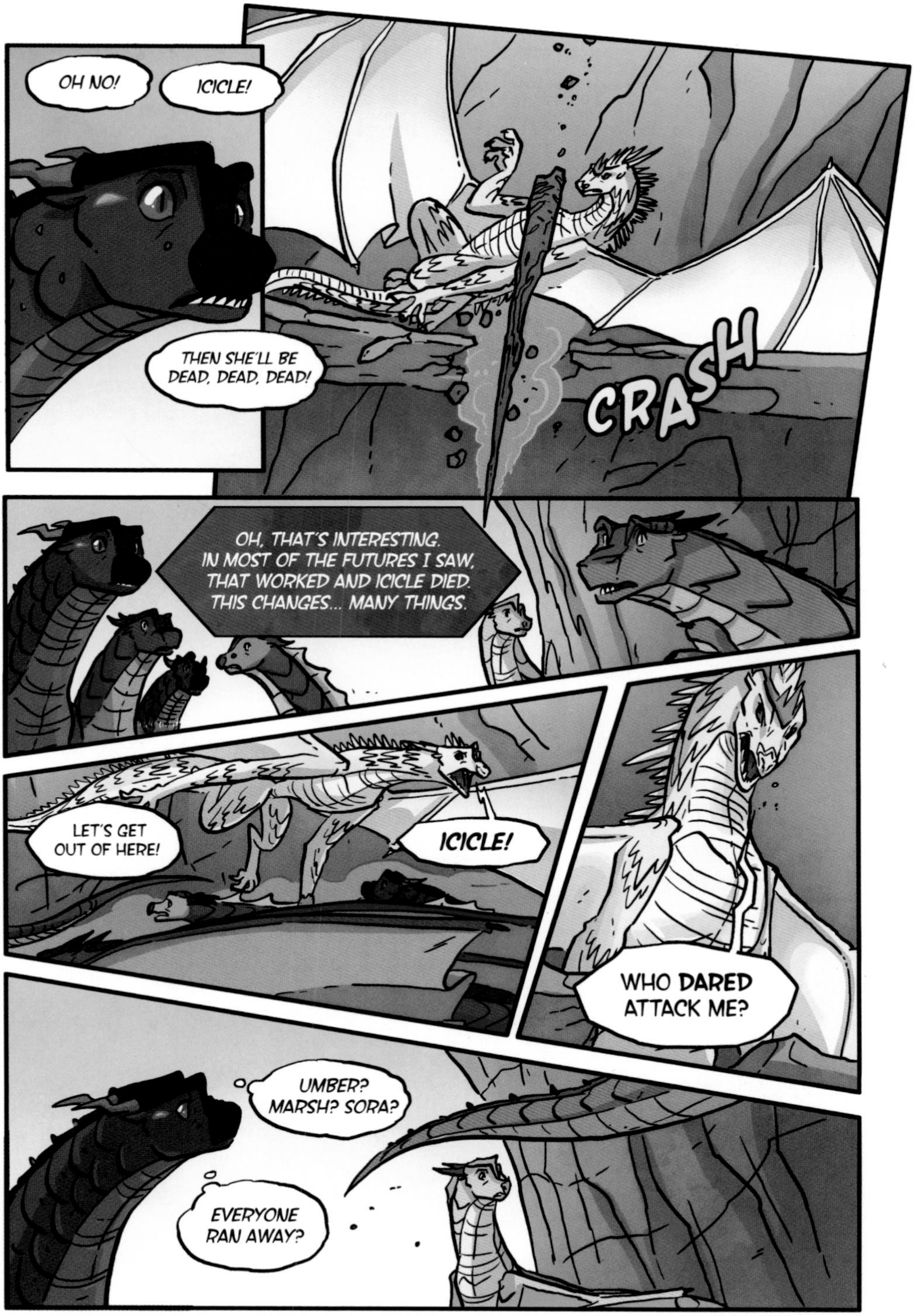
OH NO!
ICICLE!
THEN SHE'LL BE DEAD, DEAD, DEAD!
CRASH
OH, THAT'S INTERESTING. IN MOST OF THE FUTURES I SAW, THAT WORKED AND ICICLE DIED. THIS CHANGES... MANY THINGS.
LET'S GET OUT OF HERE!
ICICLE!
WHO DARED ATTACK ME?
UMBER? MARSH? SORA?
EVERYONE RAN AWAY?

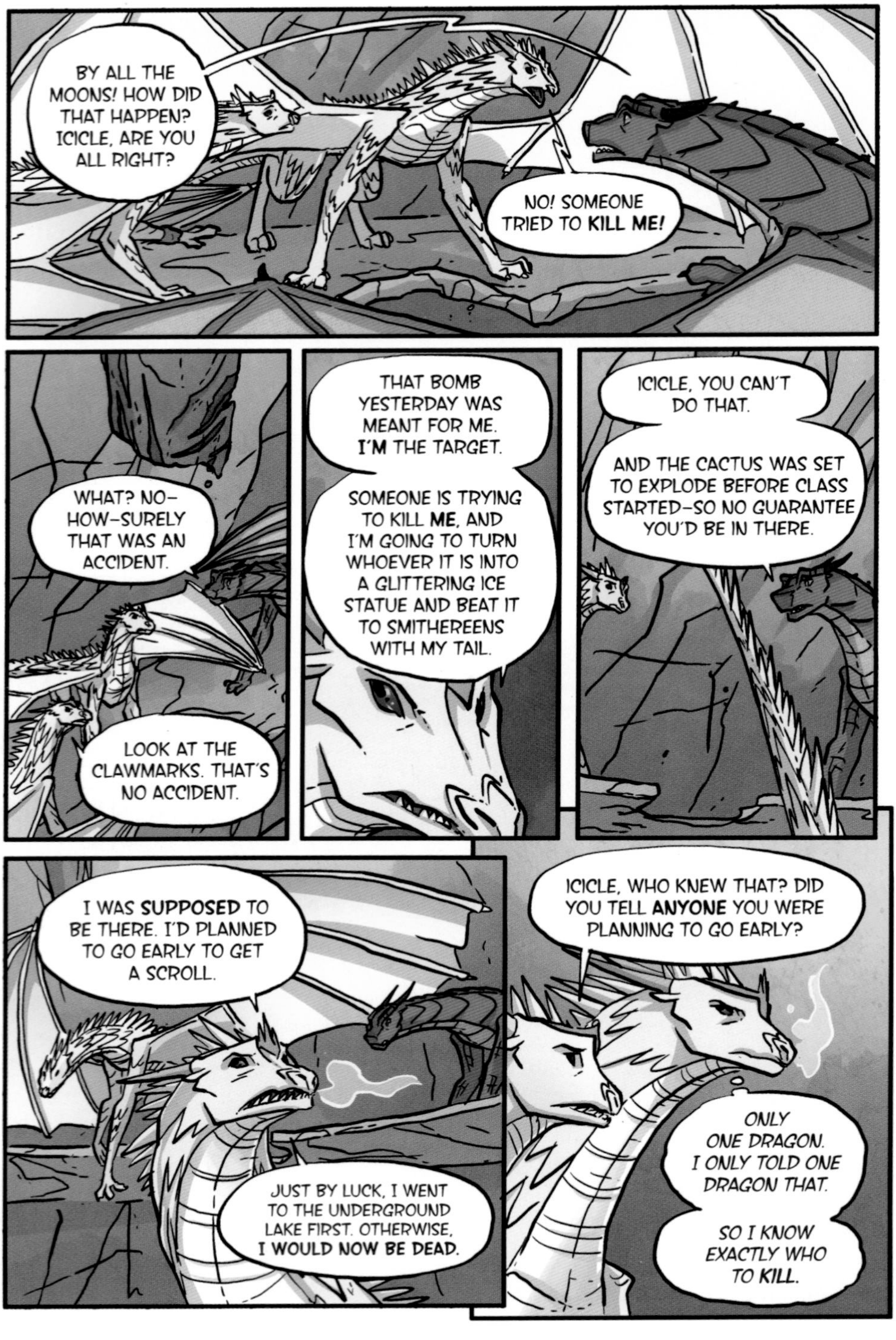
BY ALL THE MOONS! HOW DID THAT HAPPEN? ICICLE, ARE YOU ALL RIGHT?
NO! SOMEONE TRIED TO KILL ME!
WHAT? NO— HOW—SURELY THAT WAS AN ACCIDENT.
LOOK AT THE CLAWMARKS. THAT'S NO ACCIDENT.
THAT BOMB YESTERDAY WAS MEANT FOR ME. I'M THE TARGET.
SOMEONE IS TRYING TO KILL ME, AND I'M GOING TO TURN WHOEVER IT IS INTO A GLITTERING ICE STATUE AND BEAT IT TO SMITHEREENS WITH MY TAIL.
ICICLE, YOU CAN'T DO THAT.
AND THE CACTUS WAS SET TO EXPLODE BEFORE CLASS STARTED—SO NO GUARANTEE YOU'D BE IN THERE.
I WAS SUPPOSED TO BE THERE. I'D PLANNED TO GO EARLY TO GET A SCROLL.
JUST BY LUCK, I WENT TO THE UNDERGROUND LAKE FIRST. OTHERWISE, I WOULD NOW BE DEAD.
ICICLE, WHO KNEW THAT? DID YOU TELL ANYONE YOU WERE PLANNING TO GO EARLY?
ONLY ONE DRAGON. I ONLY TOLD ONE DRAGON THAT.
SO I KNOW EXACTLY WHO TO KILL.

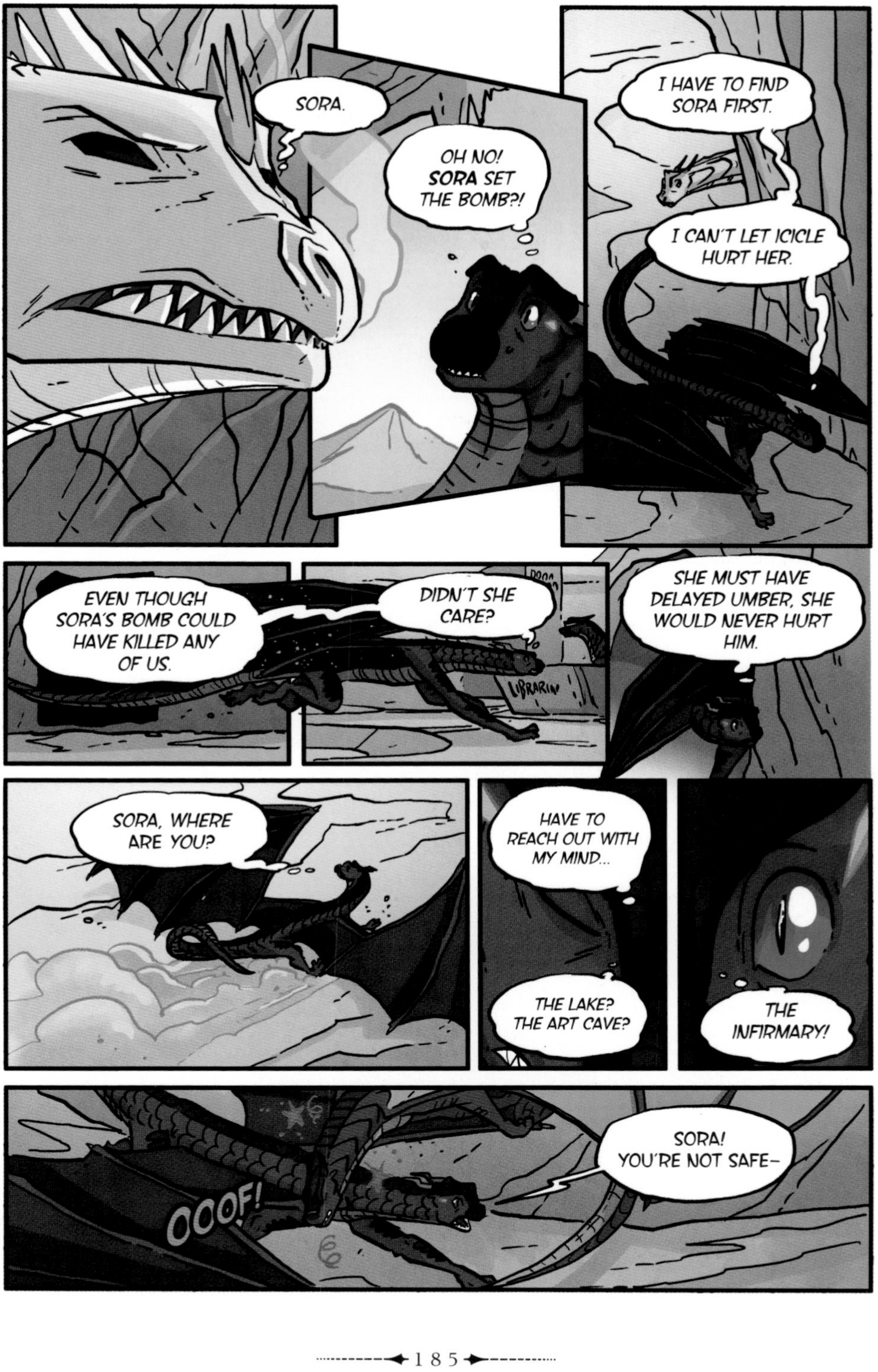
SORA.
OH NO! **SORA** SET THE BOMB?!
I HAVE TO FIND SORA FIRST.
I CAN'T LET ICICLE HURT HER.
EVEN THOUGH SORA'S BOMB COULD HAVE KILLED ANY OF US.
DIDN'T SHE CARE?
LIBRARIN
SHE MUST HAVE DELAYED UMBER, SHE WOULD NEVER HURT HIM.
SORA, WHERE ARE YOU?
HAVE TO REACH OUT WITH MY MIND...
THE LAKE? THE ART CAVE?
THE INFIRMARY!
SORA! YOU'RE NOT SAFE–
OOOF!

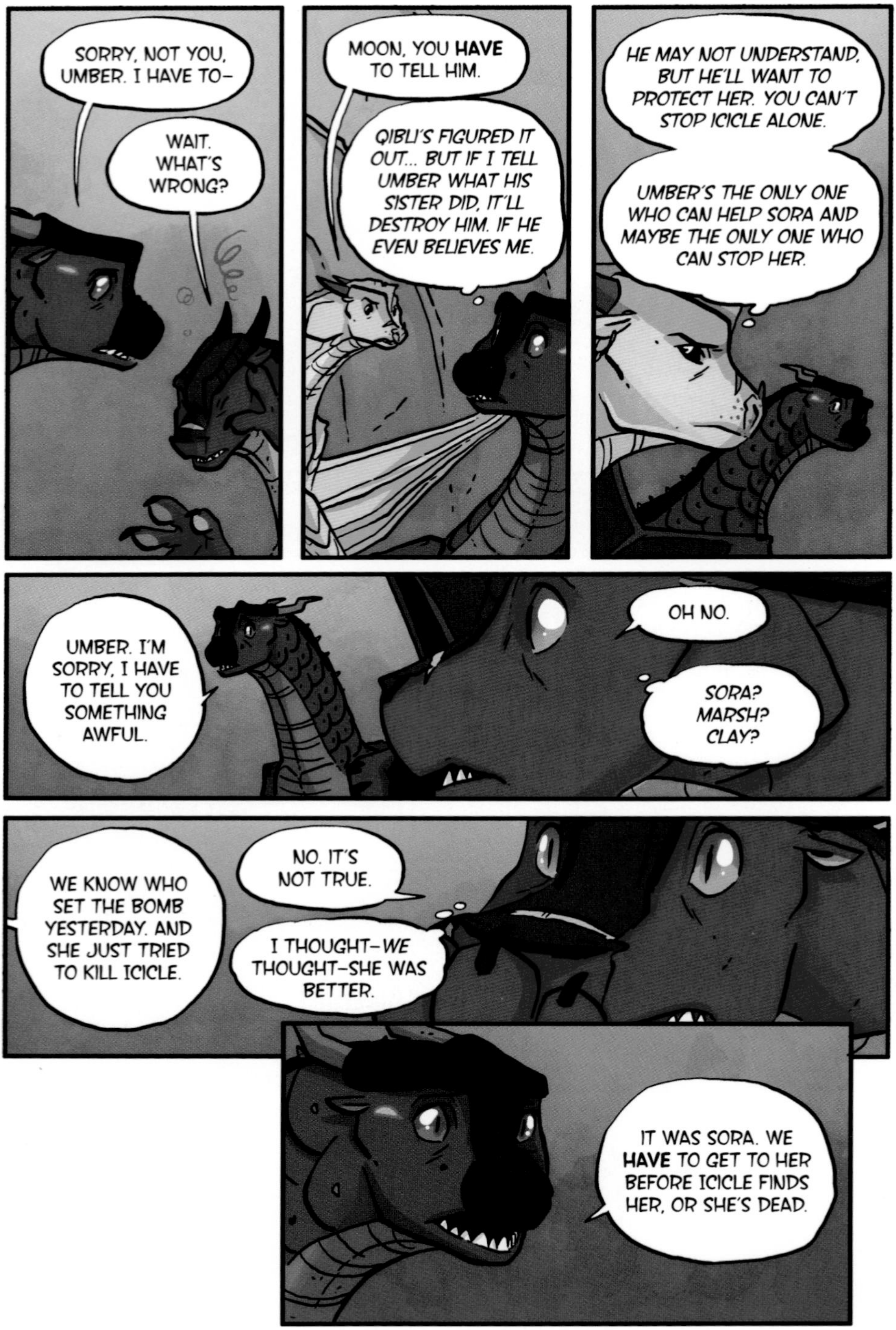
SORRY, NOT YOU, UMBER. I HAVE TO–
WAIT. WHAT'S WRONG?
MOON, YOU **HAVE** TO TELL HIM.
QIBLI'S FIGURED IT OUT... BUT IF I TELL UMBER WHAT HIS SISTER DID, IT'LL DESTROY HIM. IF HE EVEN BELIEVES ME.
HE MAY NOT UNDERSTAND, BUT HE'LL WANT TO PROTECT HER. YOU CAN'T STOP ICICLE ALONE.
UMBER'S THE ONLY ONE WHO CAN HELP SORA AND MAYBE THE ONLY ONE WHO CAN STOP HER.
UMBER. I'M SORRY, I HAVE TO TELL YOU SOMETHING AWFUL.
OH NO.
SORA? MARSH? CLAY?
WE KNOW WHO SET THE BOMB YESTERDAY. AND SHE JUST TRIED TO KILL ICICLE.
NO. IT'S NOT TRUE.
I THOUGHT–*WE* THOUGHT–SHE WAS BETTER.
IT WAS SORA. WE **HAVE** TO GET TO HER BEFORE ICICLE FINDS HER, OR SHE'S DEAD.

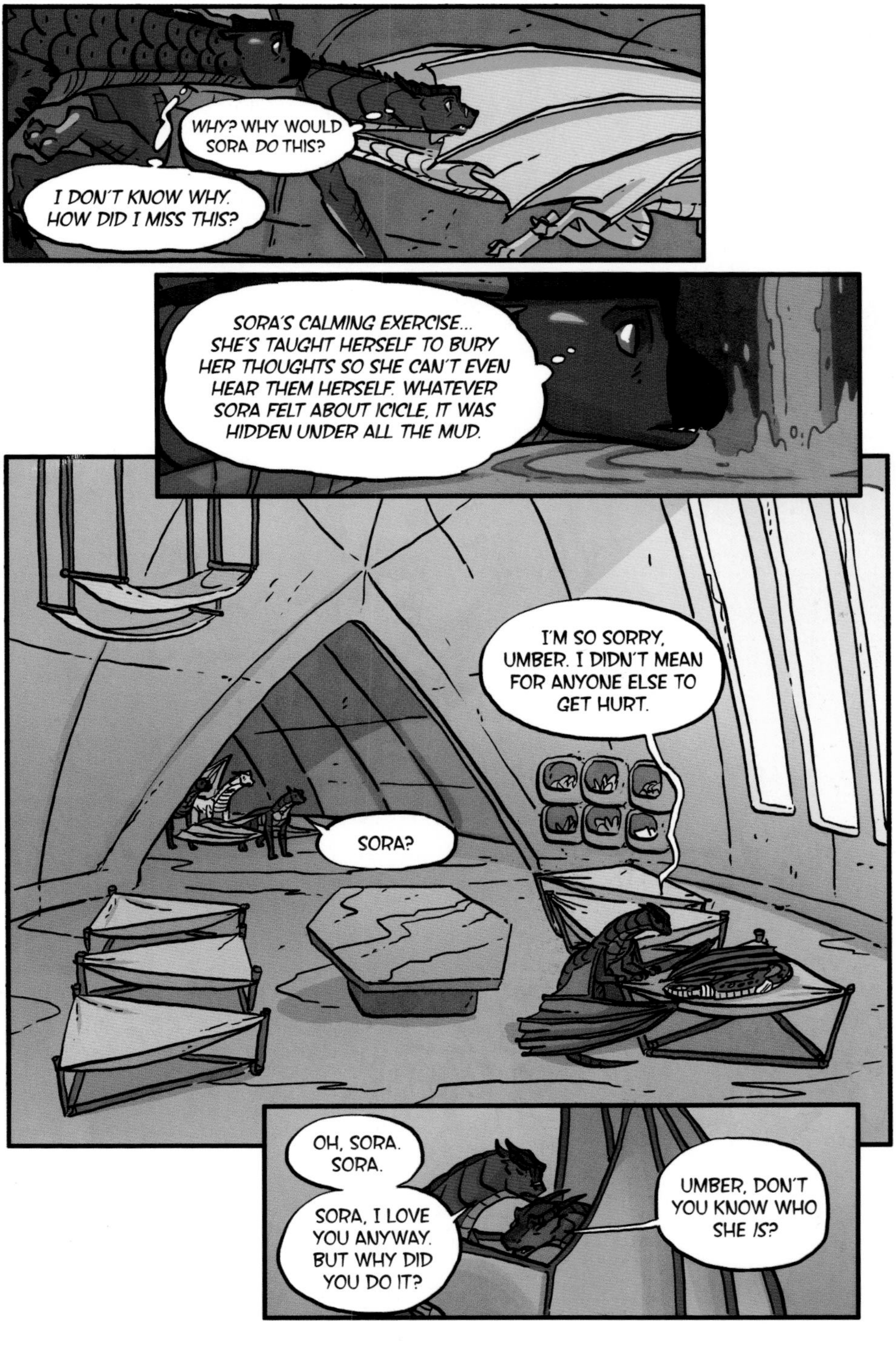
WHY? WHY WOULD SORA DO THIS?
I DON'T KNOW WHY. HOW DID I MISS THIS?
SORA'S CALMING EXERCISE... SHE'S TAUGHT HERSELF TO BURY HER THOUGHTS SO SHE CAN'T EVEN HEAR THEM HERSELF. WHATEVER SORA FELT ABOUT ICICLE, IT WAS HIDDEN UNDER ALL THE MUD.
I'M SO SORRY, UMBER. I DIDN'T MEAN FOR ANYONE ELSE TO GET HURT.
SORA?
OH, SORA. SORA.
SORA, I LOVE YOU ANYWAY. BUT WHY DID YOU DO IT?
UMBER, DON'T YOU KNOW WHO SHE *IS*?

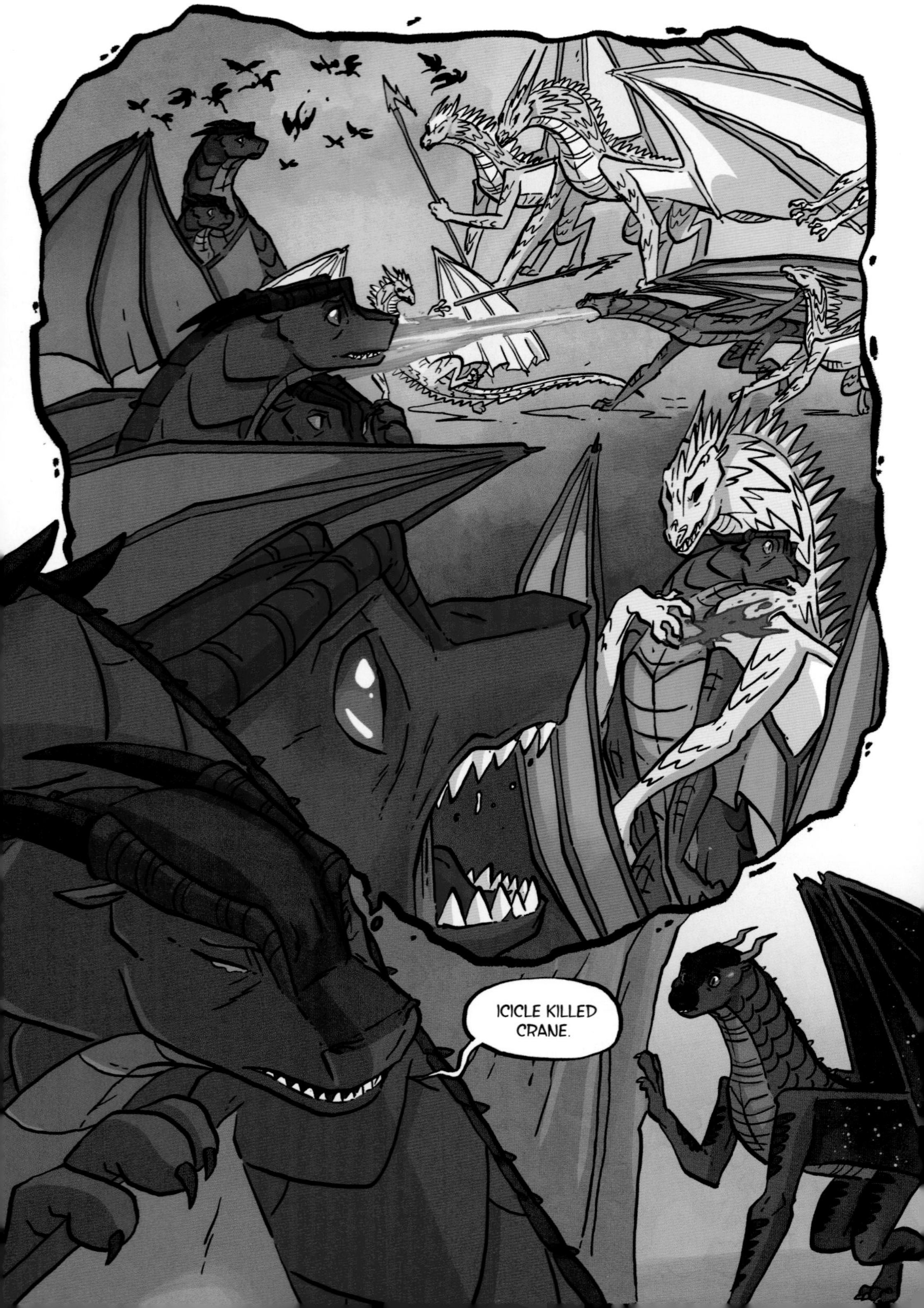
ICICLE KILLED CRANE.

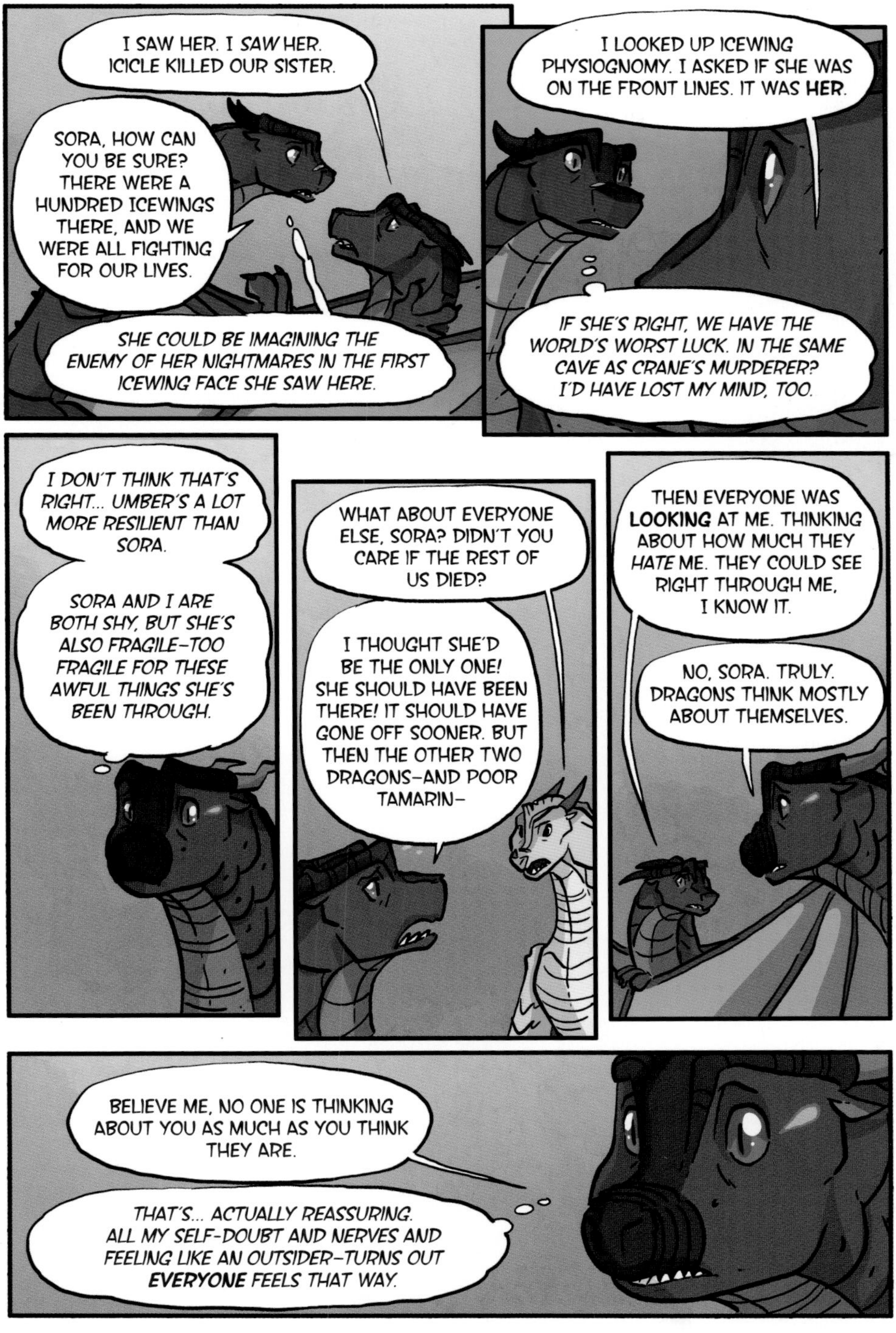
I SAW HER. I *SAW* HER. ICICLE KILLED OUR SISTER.
SORA, HOW CAN YOU BE SURE? THERE WERE A HUNDRED ICEWINGS THERE, AND WE WERE ALL FIGHTING FOR OUR LIVES.
SHE COULD BE IMAGINING THE ENEMY OF HER NIGHTMARES IN THE FIRST ICEWING FACE SHE SAW HERE.
I LOOKED UP ICEWING PHYSIOGNOMY. I ASKED IF SHE WAS ON THE FRONT LINES. IT WAS **HER**.
IF SHE'S RIGHT, WE HAVE THE WORLD'S WORST LUCK. IN THE SAME CAVE AS CRANE'S MURDERER? I'D HAVE LOST MY MIND, TOO.
I DON'T THINK THAT'S RIGHT... UMBER'S A LOT MORE RESILIENT THAN SORA.
SORA AND I ARE BOTH SHY, BUT SHE'S ALSO FRAGILE–TOO FRAGILE FOR THESE AWFUL THINGS SHE'S BEEN THROUGH.
WHAT ABOUT EVERYONE ELSE, SORA? DIDN'T YOU CARE IF THE REST OF US DIED?
I THOUGHT SHE'D BE THE ONLY ONE! SHE SHOULD HAVE BEEN THERE! IT SHOULD HAVE GONE OFF SOONER. BUT THEN THE OTHER TWO DRAGONS–AND POOR TAMARIN–
THEN EVERYONE WAS **LOOKING** AT ME. THINKING ABOUT HOW MUCH THEY *HATE* ME. THEY COULD SEE RIGHT THROUGH ME, I KNOW IT.
NO, SORA. TRULY. DRAGONS THINK MOSTLY ABOUT THEMSELVES.
BELIEVE ME, NO ONE IS THINKING ABOUT YOU AS MUCH AS YOU THINK THEY ARE.
*THAT'S... ACTUALLY REASSURING. ALL MY SELF-DOUBT AND NERVES AND FEELING LIKE AN OUTSIDER–TURNS OUT **EVERYONE** FEELS THAT WAY.*

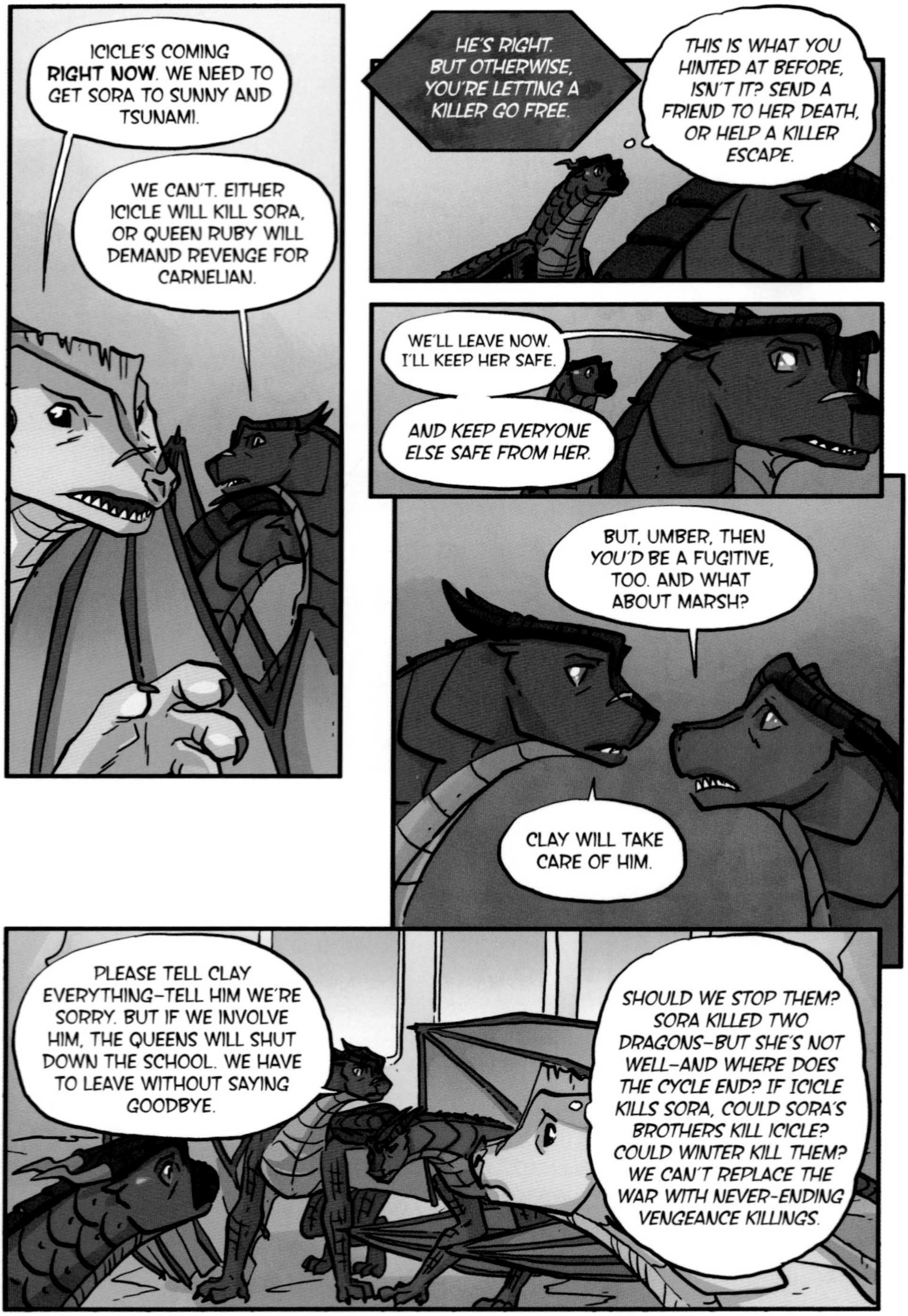
ICICLE'S COMING **RIGHT NOW**. WE NEED TO GET SORA TO SUNNY AND TSUNAMI.
WE CAN'T. EITHER ICICLE WILL KILL SORA, OR QUEEN RUBY WILL DEMAND REVENGE FOR CARNELIAN.
HE'S RIGHT. BUT OTHERWISE, YOU'RE LETTING A KILLER GO FREE.
THIS IS WHAT YOU HINTED AT BEFORE, ISN'T IT? SEND A FRIEND TO HER DEATH, OR HELP A KILLER ESCAPE.
WE'LL LEAVE NOW. I'LL KEEP HER SAFE.
AND KEEP EVERYONE ELSE SAFE FROM HER.
BUT, UMBER, THEN *YOU'D* BE A FUGITIVE, TOO. AND WHAT ABOUT MARSH?
CLAY WILL TAKE CARE OF HIM.
PLEASE TELL CLAY EVERYTHING—TELL HIM WE'RE SORRY. BUT IF WE INVOLVE HIM, THE QUEENS WILL SHUT DOWN THE SCHOOL. WE HAVE TO LEAVE WITHOUT SAYING GOODBYE.
SHOULD WE STOP THEM? SORA KILLED TWO DRAGONS—BUT SHE'S NOT WELL—AND WHERE DOES THE CYCLE END? IF ICICLE KILLS SORA, COULD SORA'S BROTHERS KILL ICICLE? COULD WINTER KILL THEM? WE CAN'T REPLACE THE WAR WITH NEVER-ENDING VENGEANCE KILLINGS.

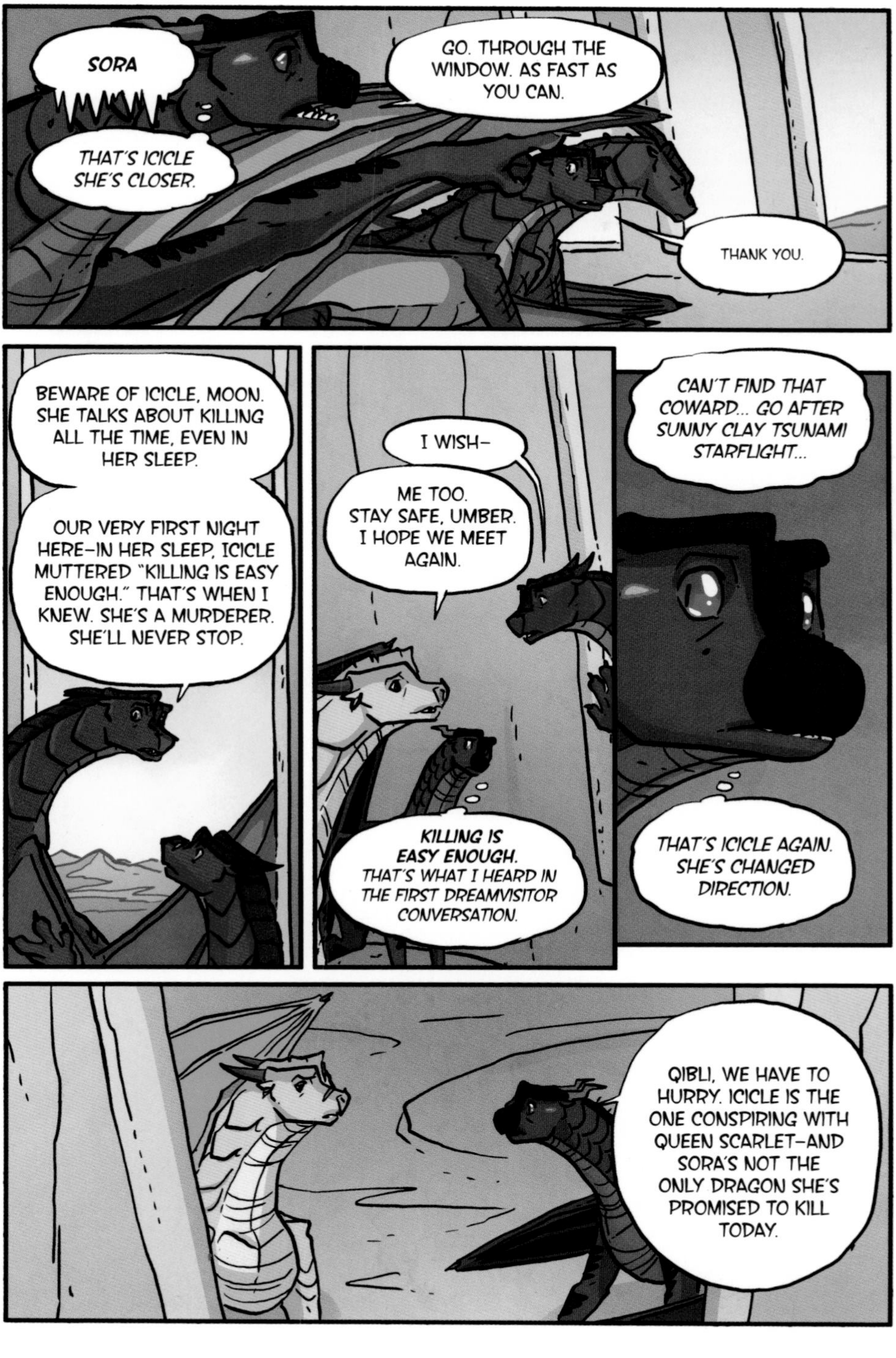
SORA
THAT'S ICICLE
SHE'S CLOSER.
GO. THROUGH THE WINDOW. AS FAST AS YOU CAN.
THANK YOU.
BEWARE OF ICICLE, MOON. SHE TALKS ABOUT KILLING ALL THE TIME, EVEN IN HER SLEEP.
OUR VERY FIRST NIGHT HERE—IN HER SLEEP, ICICLE MUTTERED "KILLING IS EASY ENOUGH." THAT'S WHEN I KNEW. SHE'S A MURDERER. SHE'LL NEVER STOP.
I WISH—
ME TOO. STAY SAFE, UMBER. I HOPE WE MEET AGAIN.
KILLING IS EASY ENOUGH. THAT'S WHAT I HEARD IN THE FIRST DREAMVISITOR CONVERSATION.
CAN'T FIND THAT COWARD... GO AFTER SUNNY CLAY TSUNAMI STARFLIGHT...
THAT'S ICICLE AGAIN. SHE'S CHANGED DIRECTION.
QIBLI, WE HAVE TO HURRY. ICICLE IS THE ONE CONSPIRING WITH QUEEN SCARLET—AND SORA'S NOT THE ONLY DRAGON SHE'S PROMISED TO KILL TODAY.

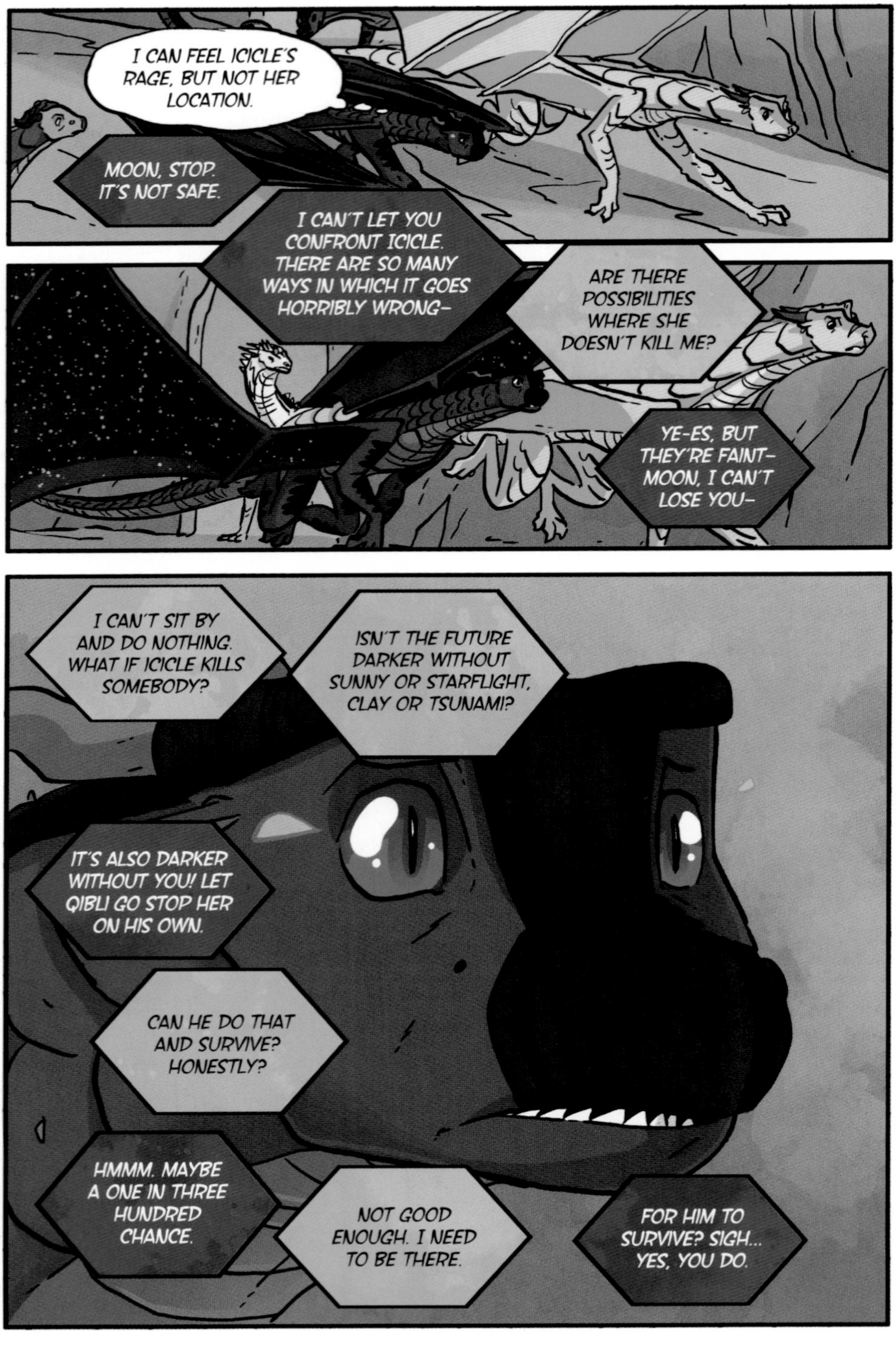
I CAN FEEL ICICLE'S RAGE, BUT NOT HER LOCATION.
MOON, STOP. IT'S NOT SAFE.
I CAN'T LET YOU CONFRONT ICICLE. THERE ARE SO MANY WAYS IN WHICH IT GOES HORRIBLY WRONG-
ARE THERE POSSIBILITIES WHERE SHE DOESN'T KILL ME?
YE-ES, BUT THEY'RE FAINT-MOON, I CAN'T LOSE YOU-
I CAN'T SIT BY AND DO NOTHING. WHAT IF ICICLE KILLS SOMEBODY?
ISN'T THE FUTURE DARKER WITHOUT SUNNY OR STARFLIGHT, CLAY OR TSUNAMI?
IT'S ALSO DARKER WITHOUT YOU! LET QIBLI GO STOP HER ON HIS OWN.
CAN HE DO THAT AND SURVIVE? HONESTLY?
HMMM. MAYBE A ONE IN THREE HUNDRED CHANCE.
NOT GOOD ENOUGH. I NEED TO BE THERE.
FOR HIM TO SURVIVE? SIGH... YES, YOU DO.

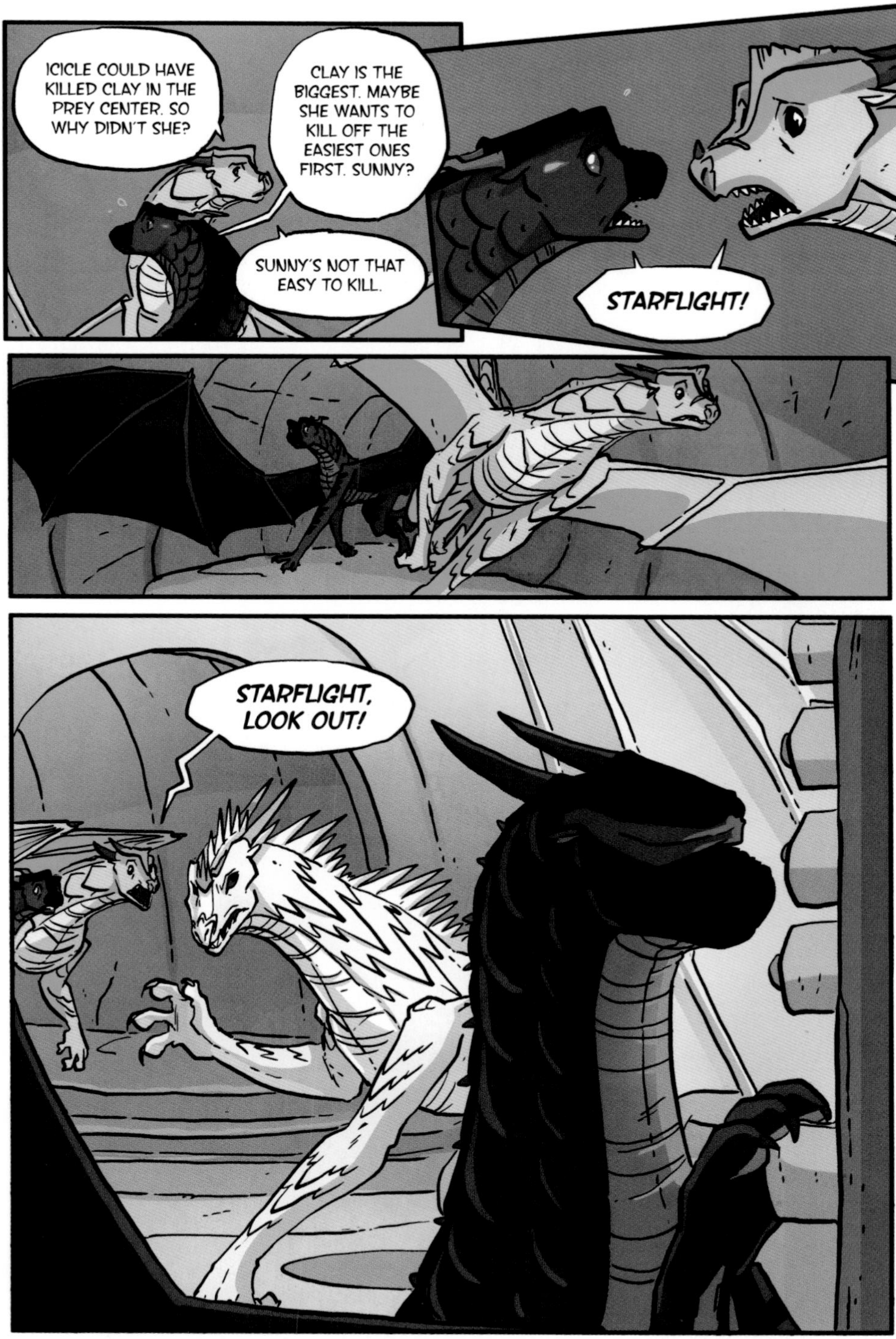
ICICLE COULD HAVE KILLED CLAY IN THE PREY CENTER. SO WHY DIDN'T SHE?
CLAY IS THE BIGGEST. MAYBE SHE WANTS TO KILL OFF THE EASIEST ONES FIRST. SUNNY?
SUNNY'S NOT THAT EASY TO KILL.
STARFLIGHT!
STARFLIGHT, LOOK OUT!

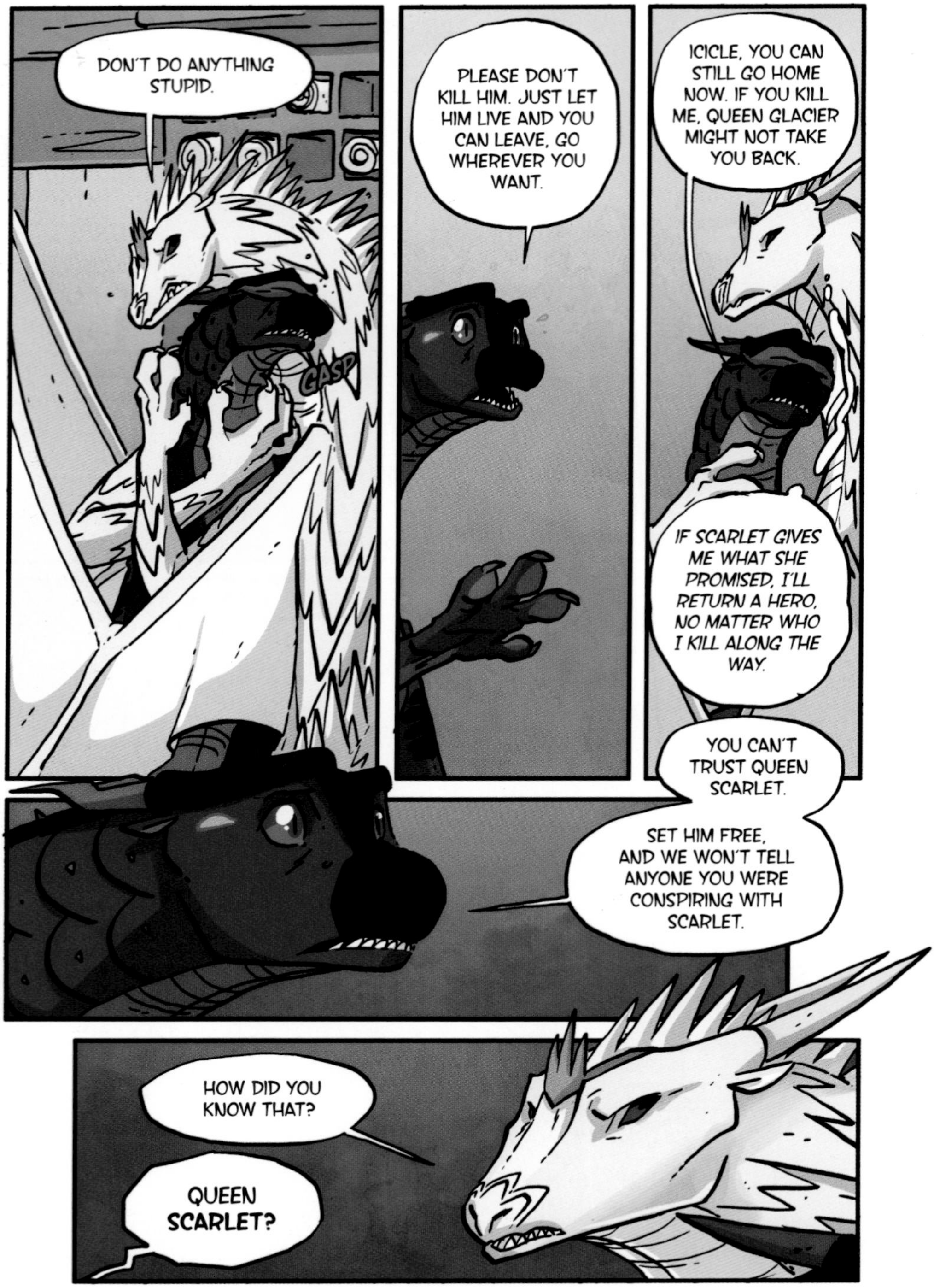
DON'T DO ANYTHING STUPID.
GASP
PLEASE DON'T KILL HIM. JUST LET HIM LIVE AND YOU CAN LEAVE, GO WHEREVER YOU WANT.
ICICLE, YOU CAN STILL GO HOME NOW. IF YOU KILL ME, QUEEN GLACIER MIGHT NOT TAKE YOU BACK.
IF SCARLET GIVES ME WHAT SHE PROMISED, I'LL RETURN A HERO, NO MATTER WHO I KILL ALONG THE WAY.
YOU CAN'T TRUST QUEEN SCARLET.
SET HIM FREE, AND WE WON'T TELL ANYONE YOU WERE CONSPIRING WITH SCARLET.
HOW DID YOU KNOW THAT?
QUEEN SCARLET?

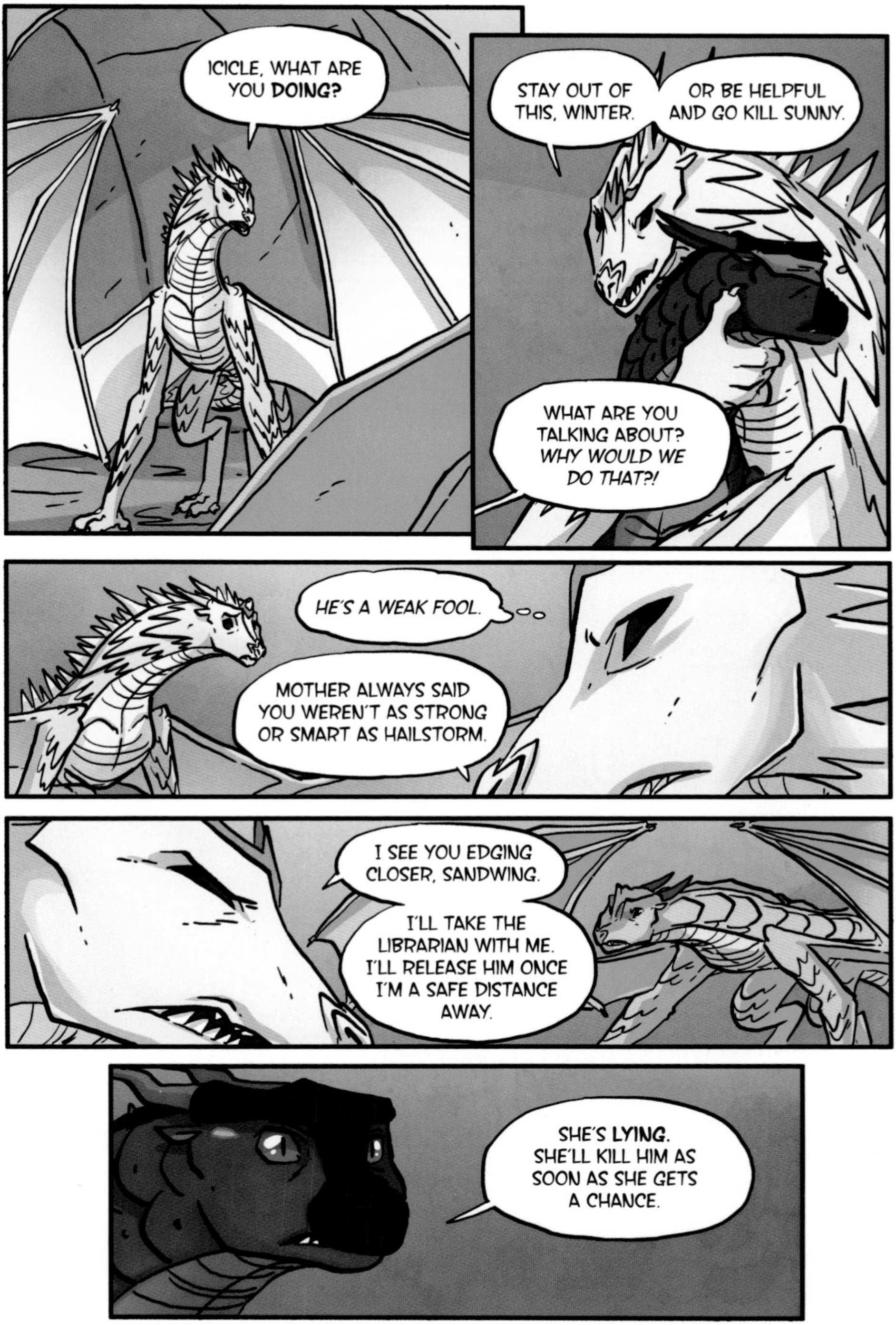
ICICLE, WHAT ARE YOU **DOING?**
STAY OUT OF THIS, WINTER.
OR BE HELPFUL AND GO KILL SUNNY.
WHAT ARE YOU TALKING ABOUT? *WHY WOULD WE DO THAT?!*
HE'S A WEAK FOOL.
MOTHER ALWAYS SAID YOU WEREN'T AS STRONG OR SMART AS HAILSTORM.
I SEE YOU EDGING CLOSER, SANDWING.
I'LL TAKE THE LIBRARIAN WITH ME. I'LL RELEASE HIM ONCE I'M A SAFE DISTANCE AWAY.
SHE'S **LYING.** SHE'LL KILL HIM AS SOON AS SHE GETS A CHANCE.

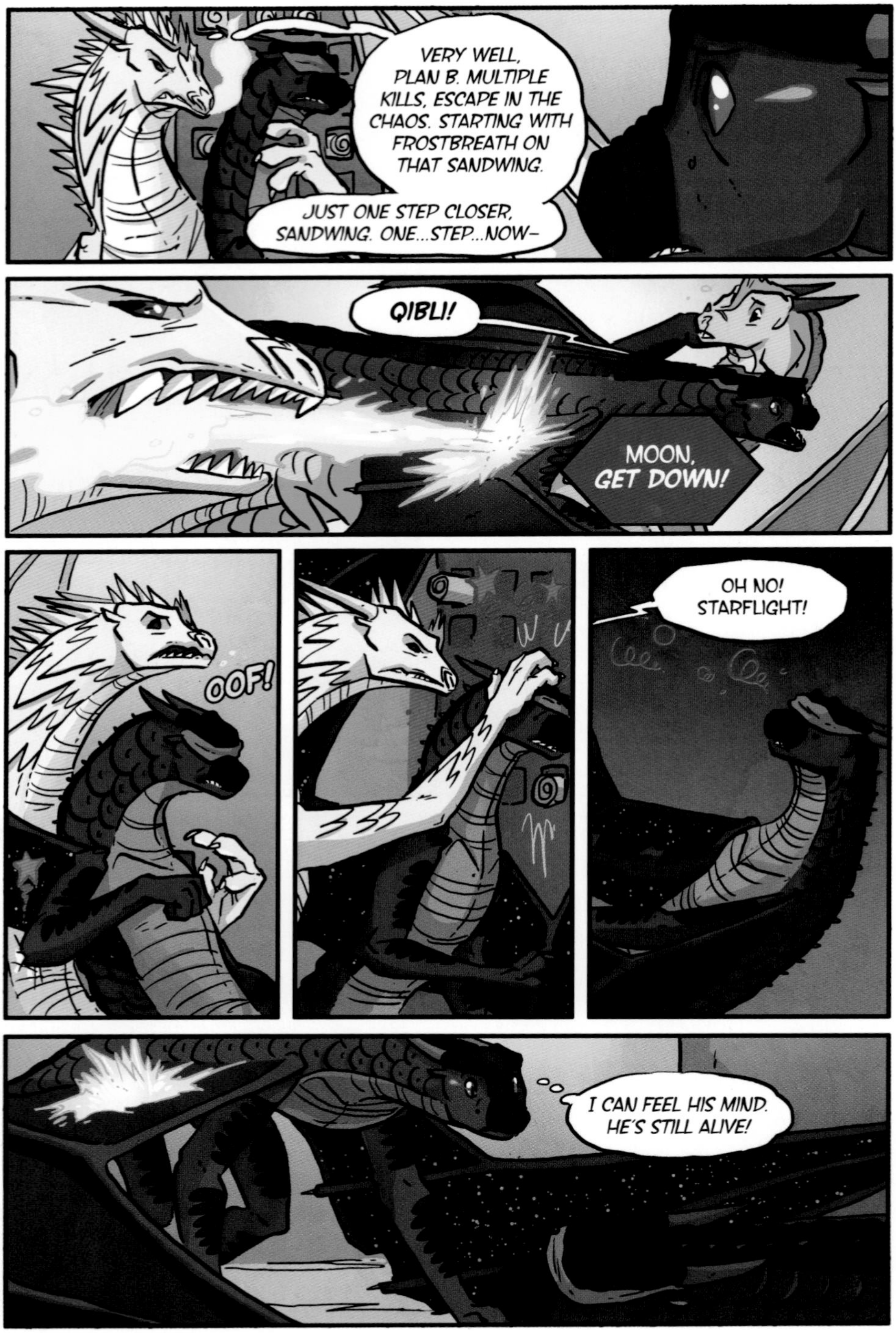
VERY WELL, PLAN B. MULTIPLE KILLS, ESCAPE IN THE CHAOS. STARTING WITH FROSTBREATH ON THAT SANDWING.
JUST ONE STEP CLOSER, SANDWING. ONE...STEP...NOW–
QIBLI!
MOON, GET DOWN!
OOF!
OH NO! STARFLIGHT!
I CAN FEEL HIS MIND. HE'S STILL ALIVE!

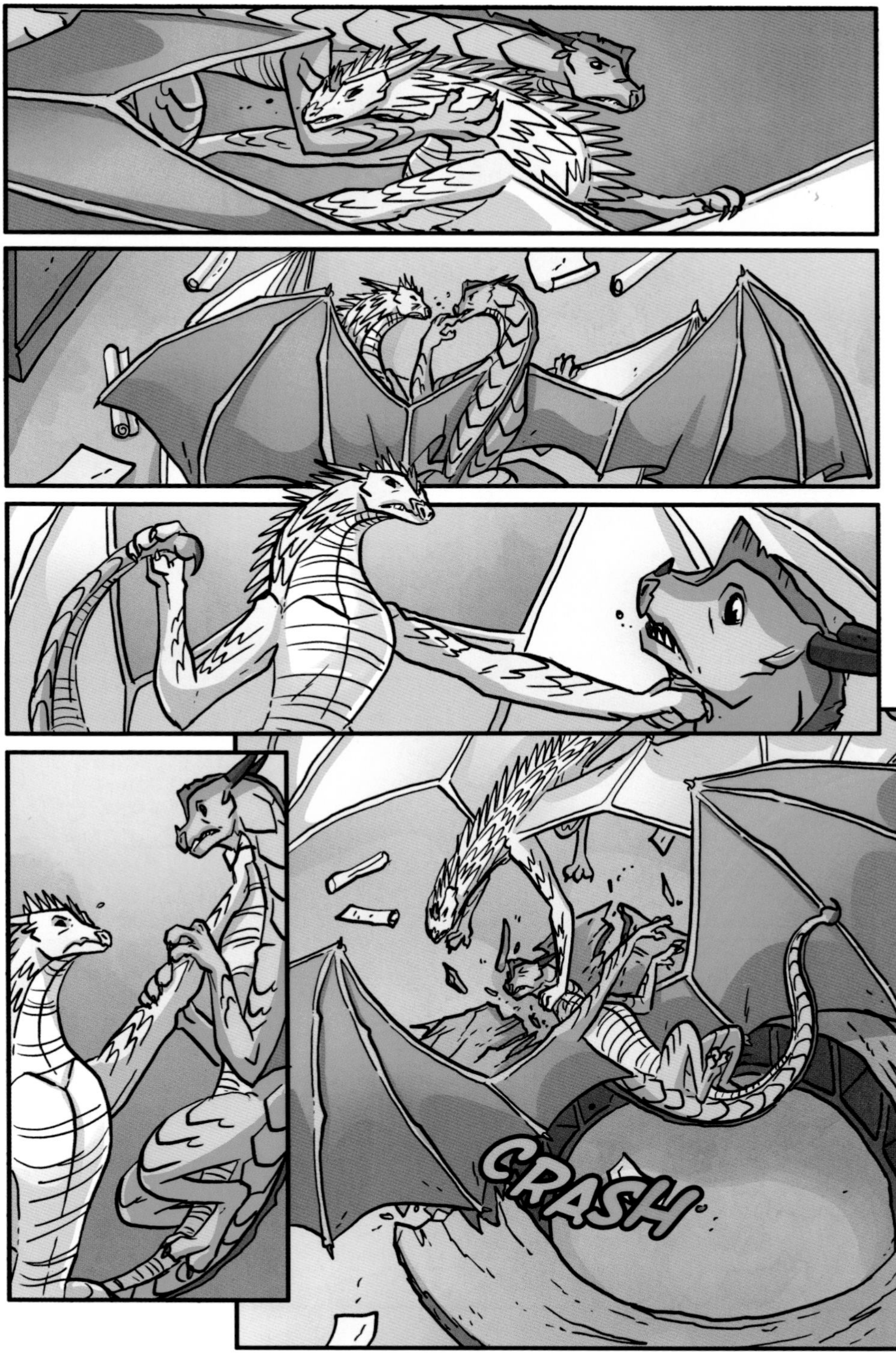
CRASH

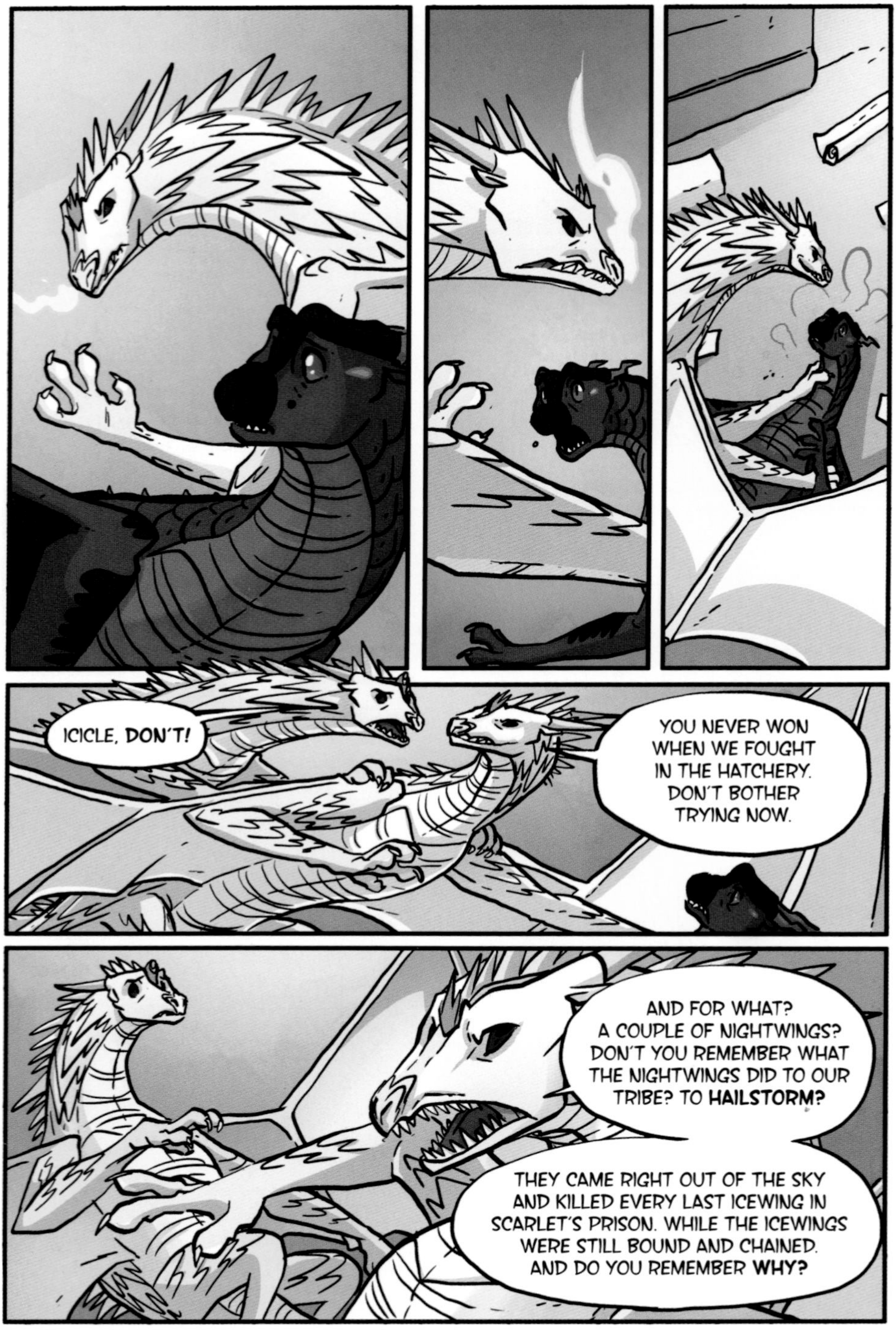
ICICLE, **DON'T!**
YOU NEVER WON WHEN WE FOUGHT IN THE HATCHERY. DON'T BOTHER TRYING NOW.
AND FOR WHAT? A COUPLE OF NIGHTWINGS? DON'T YOU REMEMBER WHAT THE NIGHTWINGS DID TO OUR TRIBE? TO **HAILSTORM?**
THEY CAME RIGHT OUT OF THE SKY AND KILLED EVERY LAST ICEWING IN SCARLET'S PRISON. WHILE THE ICEWINGS WERE STILL BOUND AND CHAINED. AND DO YOU REMEMBER **WHY?**

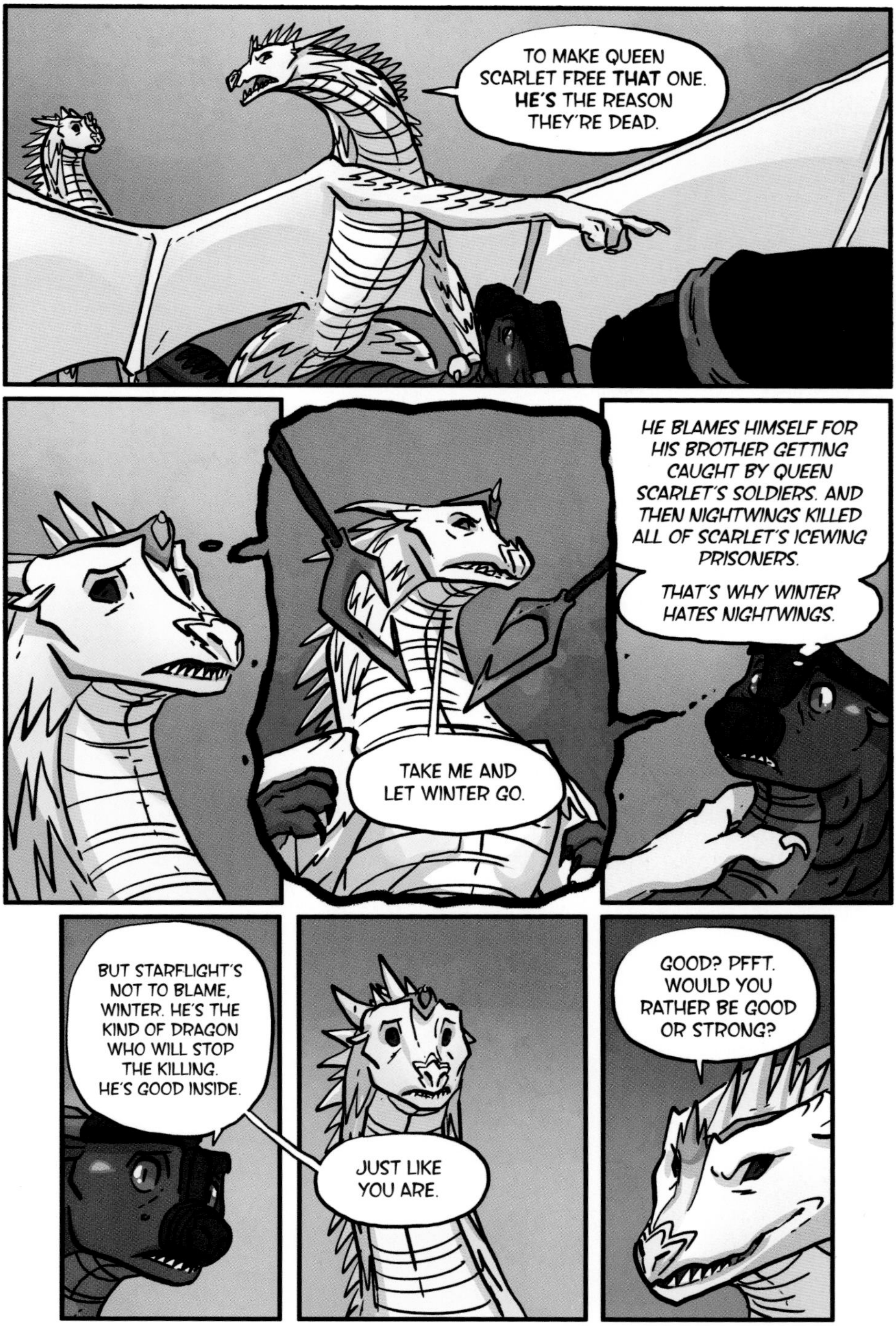
TO MAKE QUEEN SCARLET FREE THAT ONE. HE'S THE REASON THEY'RE DEAD.
HE BLAMES HIMSELF FOR HIS BROTHER GETTING CAUGHT BY QUEEN SCARLET'S SOLDIERS. AND THEN NIGHTWINGS KILLED ALL OF SCARLET'S ICEWING PRISONERS.
THAT'S WHY WINTER HATES NIGHTWINGS.
TAKE ME AND LET WINTER GO.
BUT STARFLIGHT'S NOT TO BLAME, WINTER. HE'S THE KIND OF DRAGON WHO WILL STOP THE KILLING. HE'S GOOD INSIDE.
JUST LIKE YOU ARE.
GOOD? PFFT. WOULD YOU RATHER BE GOOD OR STRONG?

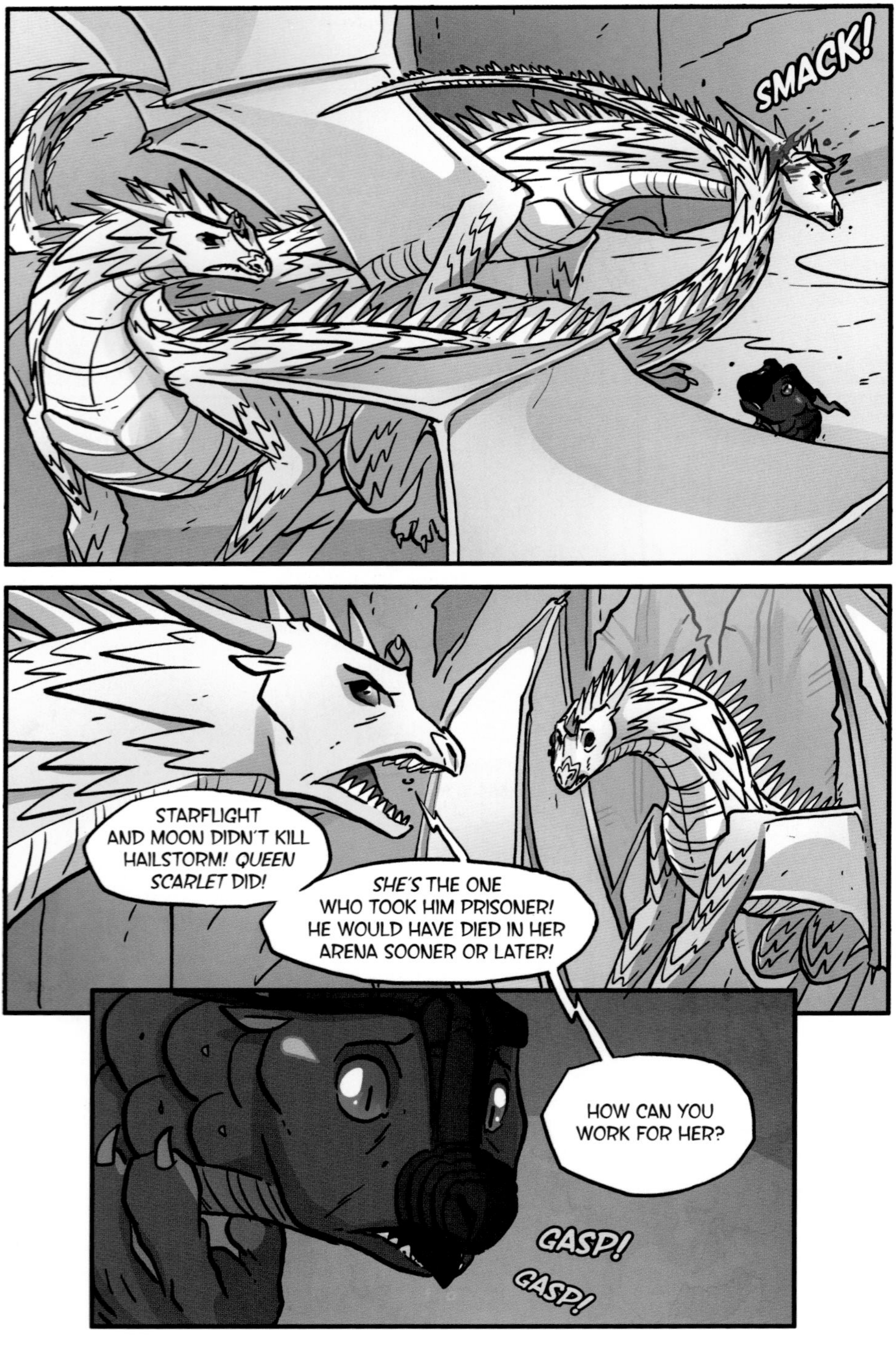
SMACK!
STARFLIGHT AND MOON DIDN'T KILL HAILSTORM! *QUEEN SCARLET* DID!
SHE'S THE ONE WHO TOOK HIM PRISONER! HE WOULD HAVE DIED IN HER ARENA SOONER OR LATER!
HOW CAN YOU WORK FOR HER?
GASP!
GASP!

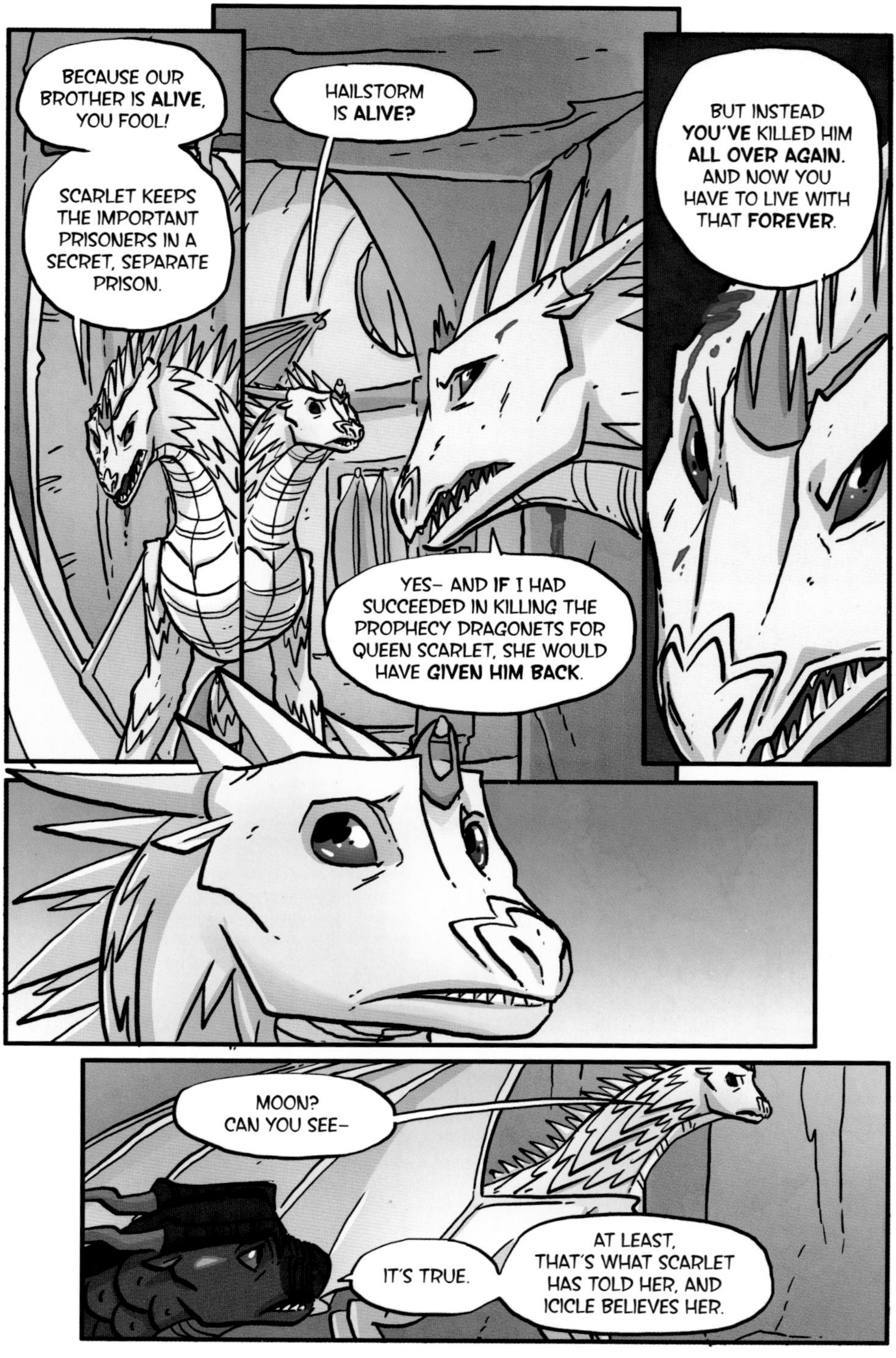
BECAUSE OUR BROTHER IS ALIVE, YOU FOOL!
SCARLET KEEPS THE IMPORTANT PRISONERS IN A SECRET, SEPARATE PRISON.
HAILSTORM IS ALIVE?
YES— AND IF I HAD SUCCEEDED IN KILLING THE PROPHECY DRAGONETS FOR QUEEN SCARLET, SHE WOULD HAVE GIVEN HIM BACK.
BUT INSTEAD YOU'VE KILLED HIM ALL OVER AGAIN. AND NOW YOU HAVE TO LIVE WITH THAT FOREVER.
MOON? CAN YOU SEE—
IT'S TRUE.
AT LEAST, THAT'S WHAT SCARLET HAS TOLD HER, AND ICICLE BELIEVES HER.

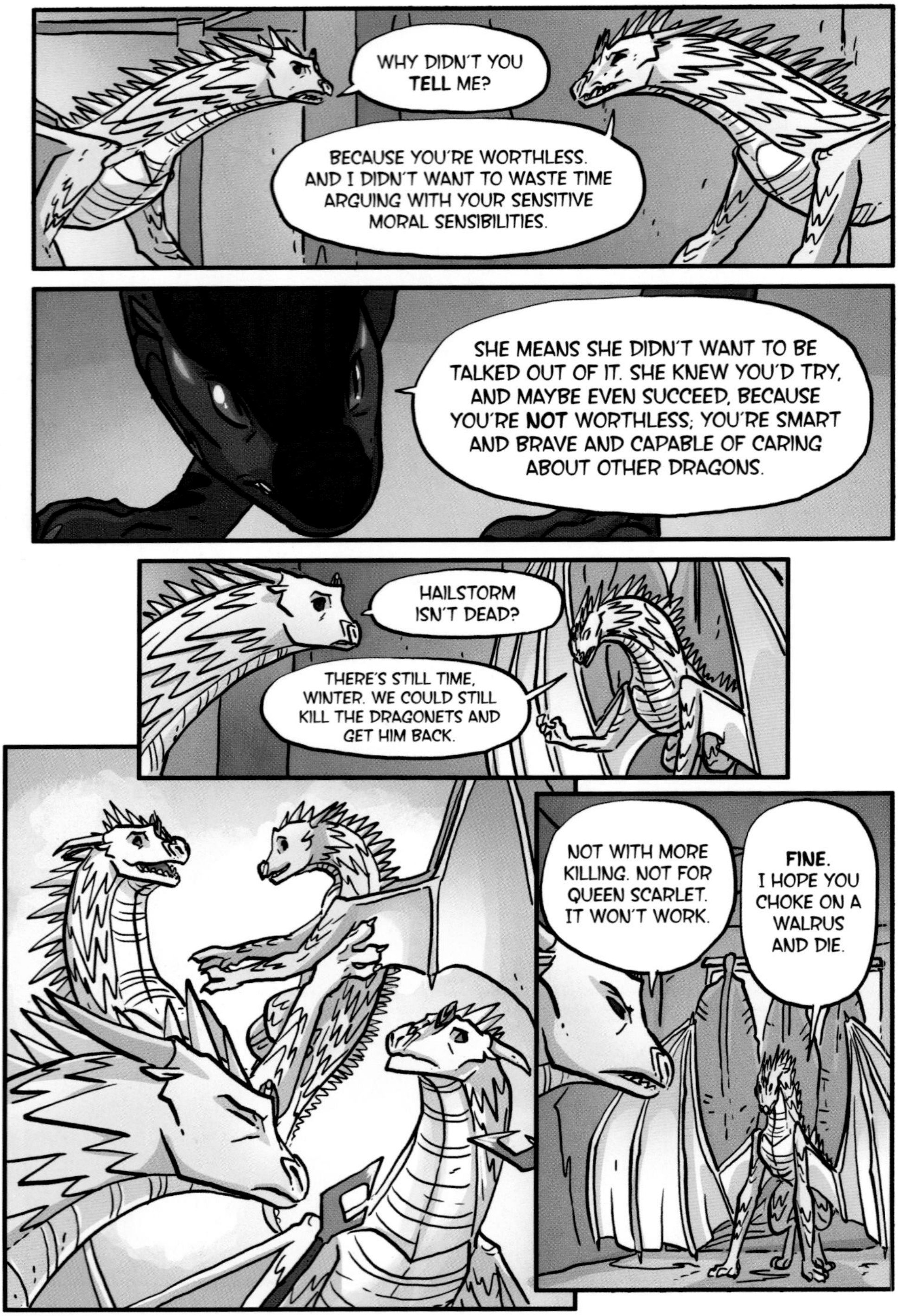
WHY DIDN'T YOU **TELL** ME?
BECAUSE YOU'RE WORTHLESS. AND I DIDN'T WANT TO WASTE TIME ARGUING WITH YOUR SENSITIVE MORAL SENSIBILITIES.
SHE MEANS SHE DIDN'T WANT TO BE TALKED OUT OF IT. SHE KNEW YOU'D TRY, AND MAYBE EVEN SUCCEED, BECAUSE YOU'RE **NOT** WORTHLESS; YOU'RE SMART AND BRAVE AND CAPABLE OF CARING ABOUT OTHER DRAGONS.
HAILSTORM ISN'T DEAD?
THERE'S STILL TIME, WINTER. WE COULD STILL KILL THE DRAGONETS AND GET HIM BACK.
NOT WITH MORE KILLING. NOT FOR QUEEN SCARLET. IT WON'T WORK.
FINE. I HOPE YOU CHOKE ON A WALRUS AND DIE.

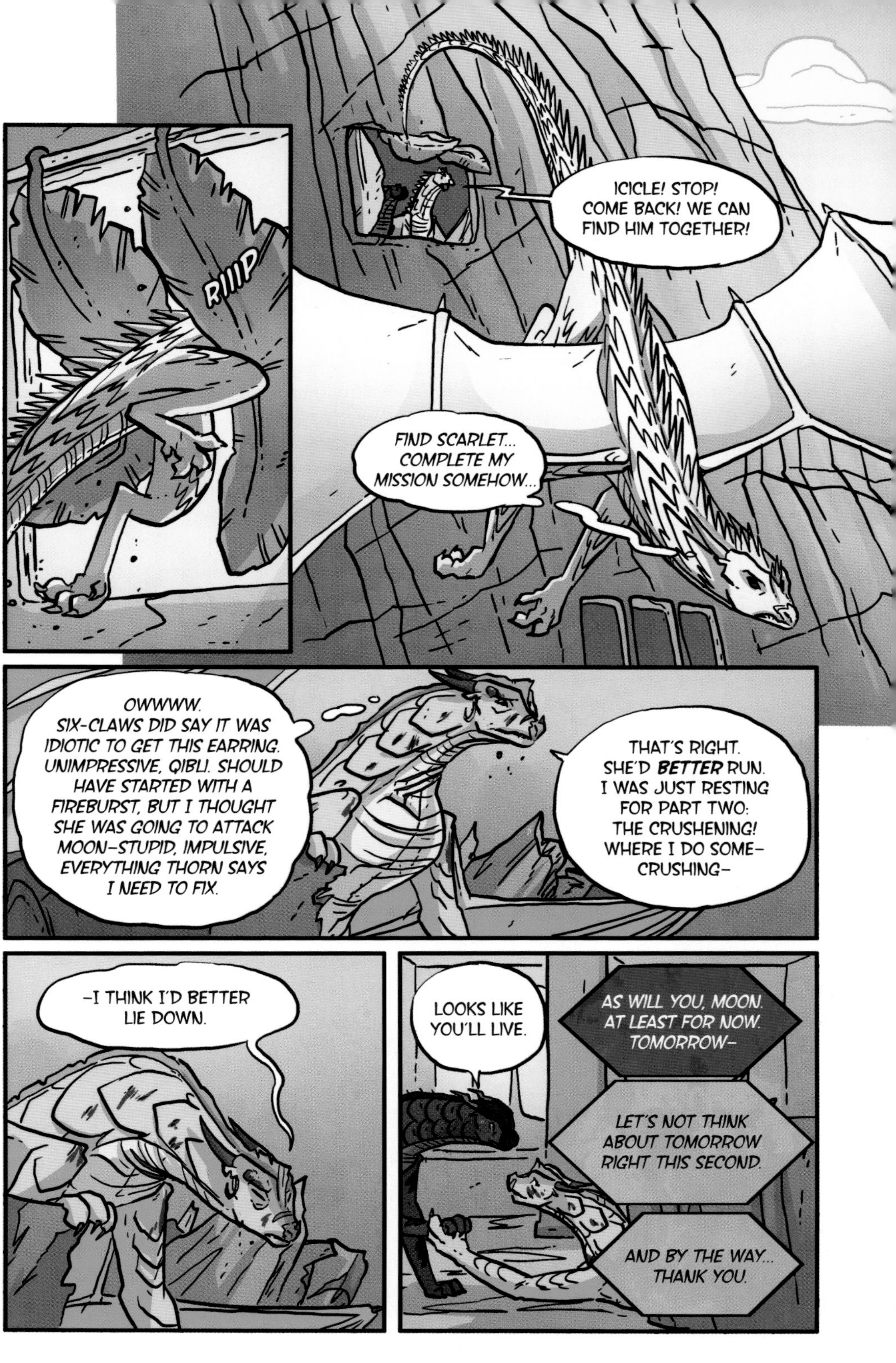
RIIIP
ICICLE! STOP! COME BACK! WE CAN FIND HIM TOGETHER!
FIND SCARLET... COMPLETE MY MISSION SOMEHOW...
OWWWW. SIX-CLAWS DID SAY IT WAS IDIOTIC TO GET THIS EARRING. UNIMPRESSIVE, QIBLI. SHOULD HAVE STARTED WITH A FIREBURST, BUT I THOUGHT SHE WAS GOING TO ATTACK MOON—STUPID, IMPULSIVE, EVERYTHING THORN SAYS I NEED TO FIX.
THAT'S RIGHT. SHE'D BETTER RUN. I WAS JUST RESTING FOR PART TWO: THE CRUSHENING! WHERE I DO SOME—CRUSHING—
—I THINK I'D BETTER LIE DOWN.
LOOKS LIKE YOU'LL LIVE.
AS WILL YOU, MOON. AT LEAST FOR NOW. TOMORROW—
LET'S NOT THINK ABOUT TOMORROW RIGHT THIS SECOND.
AND BY THE WAY... THANK YOU.

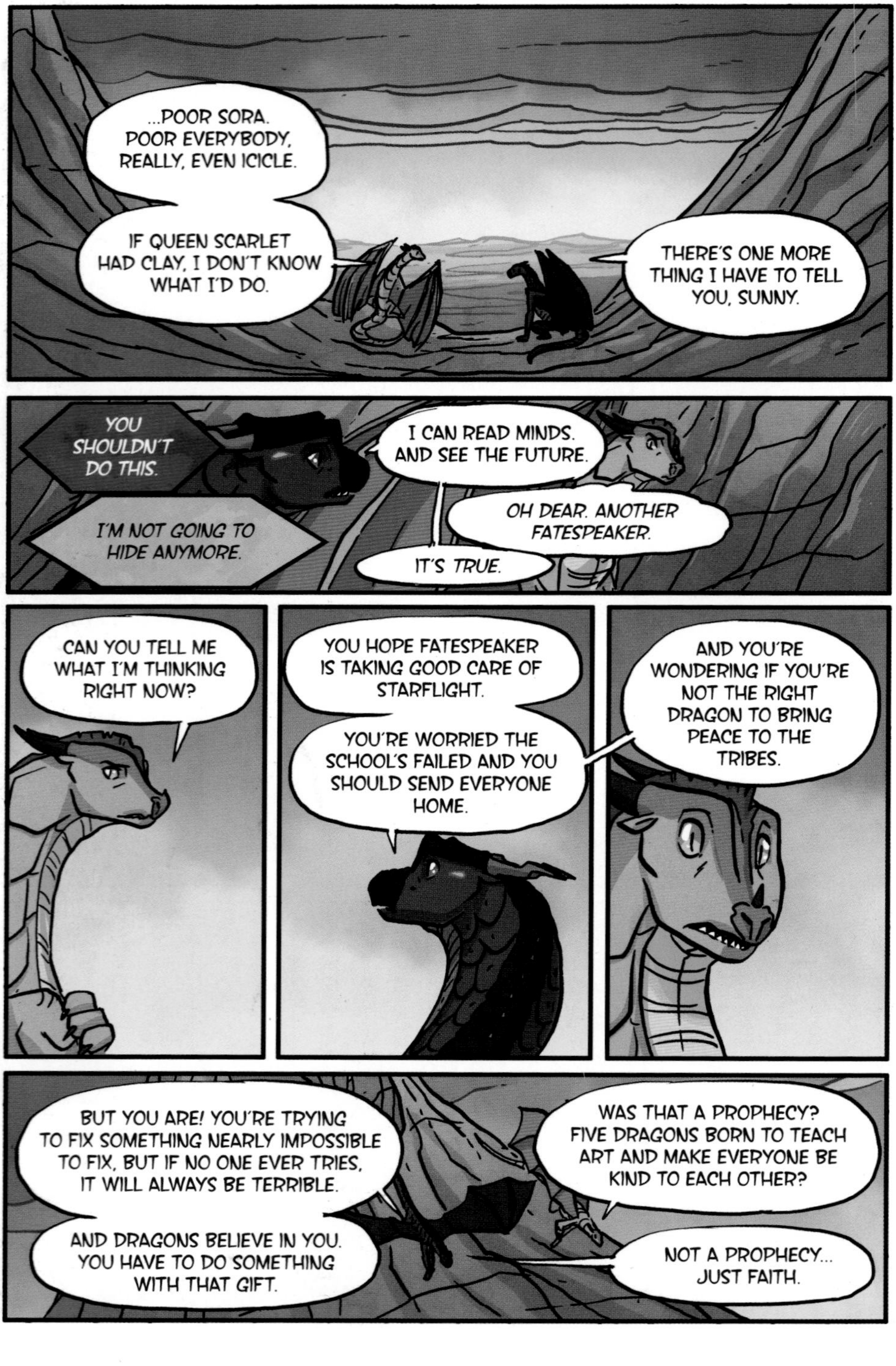
...POOR SORA. POOR EVERYBODY, REALLY, EVEN ICICLE.
IF QUEEN SCARLET HAD CLAY, I DON'T KNOW WHAT I'D DO.
THERE'S ONE MORE THING I HAVE TO TELL YOU, SUNNY.
YOU SHOULDN'T DO THIS.
I'M NOT GOING TO HIDE ANYMORE.
I CAN READ MINDS. AND SEE THE FUTURE.
OH DEAR. ANOTHER FATESPEAKER.
IT'S TRUE.
CAN YOU TELL ME WHAT I'M THINKING RIGHT NOW?
YOU HOPE FATESPEAKER IS TAKING GOOD CARE OF STARFLIGHT.
YOU'RE WORRIED THE SCHOOL'S FAILED AND YOU SHOULD SEND EVERYONE HOME.
AND YOU'RE WONDERING IF YOU'RE NOT THE RIGHT DRAGON TO BRING PEACE TO THE TRIBES.
BUT YOU ARE! YOU'RE TRYING TO FIX SOMETHING NEARLY IMPOSSIBLE TO FIX, BUT IF NO ONE EVER TRIES, IT WILL ALWAYS BE TERRIBLE.
AND DRAGONS BELIEVE IN YOU. YOU HAVE TO DO SOMETHING WITH THAT GIFT.
WAS THAT A PROPHECY? FIVE DRAGONS BORN TO TEACH ART AND MAKE EVERYONE BE KIND TO EACH OTHER?
NOT A PROPHECY... JUST FAITH.

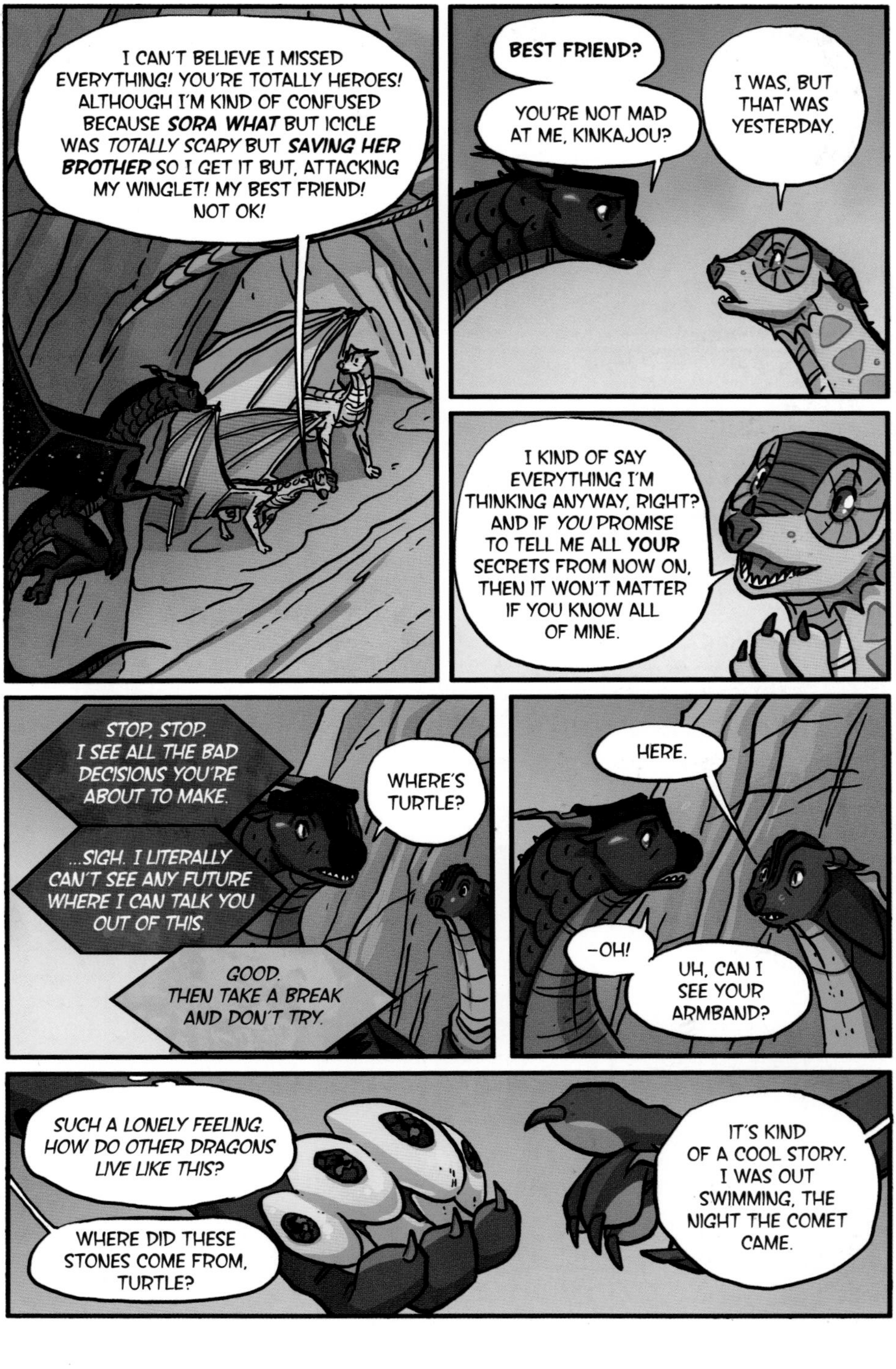
I CAN'T BELIEVE I MISSED EVERYTHING! YOU'RE TOTALLY HEROES! ALTHOUGH I'M KIND OF CONFUSED BECAUSE SORA WHAT BUT ICICLE WAS TOTALLY SCARY BUT SAVING HER BROTHER SO I GET IT BUT, ATTACKING MY WINGLET! MY BEST FRIEND! NOT OK!
BEST FRIEND?
YOU'RE NOT MAD AT ME, KINKAJOU?
I WAS, BUT THAT WAS YESTERDAY.
I KIND OF SAY EVERYTHING I'M THINKING ANYWAY, RIGHT? AND IF YOU PROMISE TO TELL ME ALL YOUR SECRETS FROM NOW ON, THEN IT WON'T MATTER IF YOU KNOW ALL OF MINE.
STOP, STOP. I SEE ALL THE BAD DECISIONS YOU'RE ABOUT TO MAKE.
...SIGH. I LITERALLY CAN'T SEE ANY FUTURE WHERE I CAN TALK YOU OUT OF THIS.
GOOD. THEN TAKE A BREAK AND DON'T TRY.
WHERE'S TURTLE?
HERE.
–OH!
UH, CAN I SEE YOUR ARMBAND?
SUCH A LONELY FEELING. HOW DO OTHER DRAGONS LIVE LIKE THIS?
WHERE DID THESE STONES COME FROM, TURTLE?
IT'S KIND OF A COOL STORY. I WAS OUT SWIMMING, THE NIGHT THE COMET CAME.

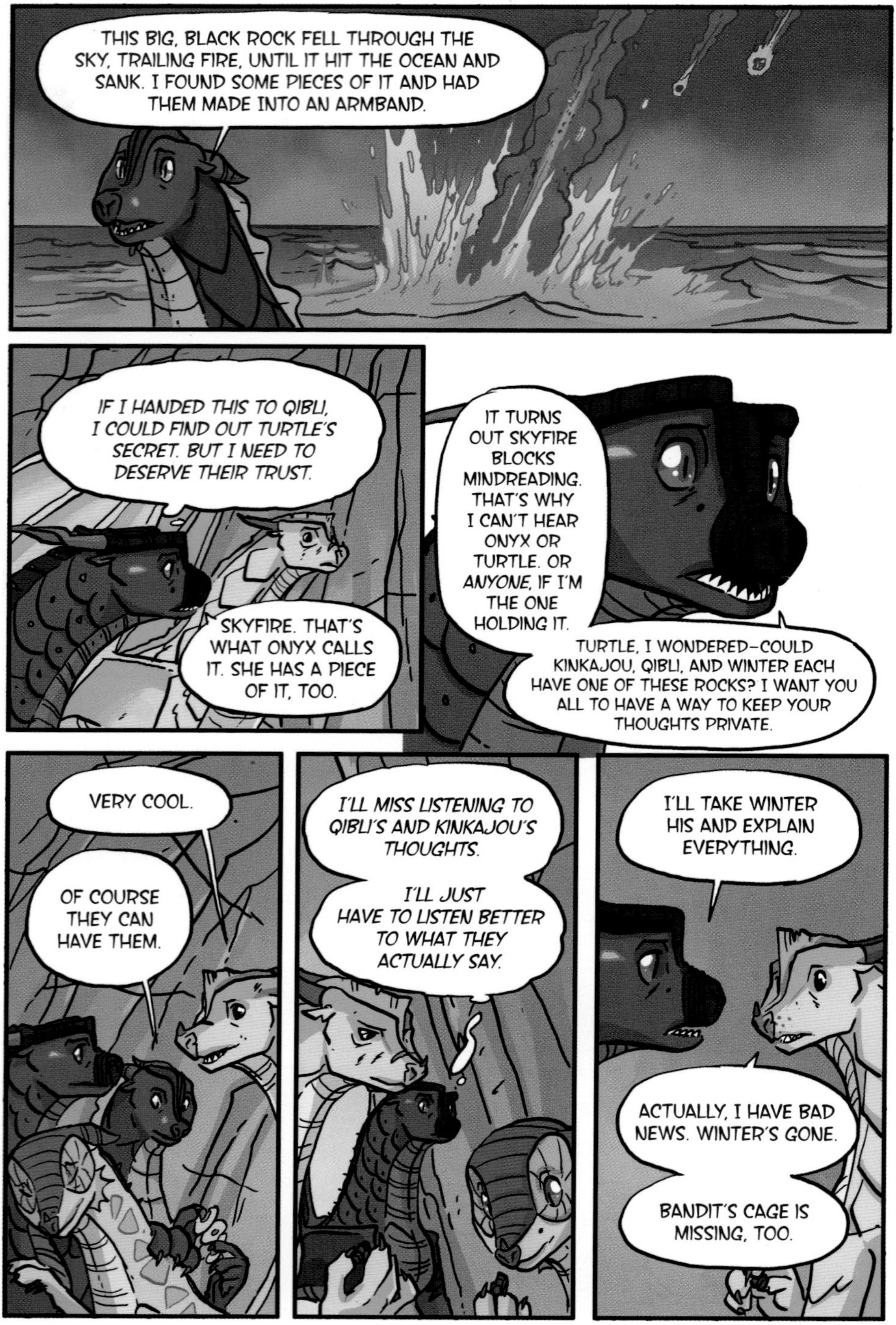
THIS BIG, BLACK ROCK FELL THROUGH THE SKY, TRAILING FIRE, UNTIL IT HIT THE OCEAN AND SANK. I FOUND SOME PIECES OF IT AND HAD THEM MADE INTO AN ARMBAND.
IF I HANDED THIS TO QIBLI, I COULD FIND OUT TURTLE'S SECRET. BUT I NEED TO DESERVE THEIR TRUST.
SKYFIRE. THAT'S WHAT ONYX CALLS IT. SHE HAS A PIECE OF IT, TOO.
IT TURNS OUT SKYFIRE BLOCKS MINDREADING. THAT'S WHY I CAN'T HEAR ONYX OR TURTLE. OR ANYONE, IF I'M THE ONE HOLDING IT.
TURTLE, I WONDERED—COULD KINKAJOU, QIBLI, AND WINTER EACH HAVE ONE OF THESE ROCKS? I WANT YOU ALL TO HAVE A WAY TO KEEP YOUR THOUGHTS PRIVATE.
VERY COOL.
OF COURSE THEY CAN HAVE THEM.
I'LL MISS LISTENING TO QIBLI'S AND KINKAJOU'S THOUGHTS.
I'LL JUST HAVE TO LISTEN BETTER TO WHAT THEY ACTUALLY SAY.
I'LL TAKE WINTER HIS AND EXPLAIN EVERYTHING.
ACTUALLY, I HAVE BAD NEWS. WINTER'S GONE.
BANDIT'S CAGE IS MISSING, TOO.

WHAT? OH NO! WHY? WHERE'D HE GO?

I SAW WINTER HEADING TOWARD THE FOREST, BUT I THOUGHT HE WAS JUST GOING HUNTING.

I'M GOING TO FIND HIM.

OH YAY! ME TOO!

IN THIS WEATHER?

I'M A *RAINWING*. IT RAINS ALL THE *TIME* IN THE *RAINFOREST*. TRUST ME, I CAN HANDLE IT.

I'M NOT SURE I CAN. BUT I'M COMING WITH YOU ANYWAY.

IN THIS WEATHER?

COME ON, TURTLE! WE'RE ALL THAT'S LEFT OF THE JADE WINGLET! PLUS, YOU LIVE IN WATER. YOU CAN BREATHE IT!

BUT LIGHTNING...

BUMP

TURTLE'S COMING, TOO.

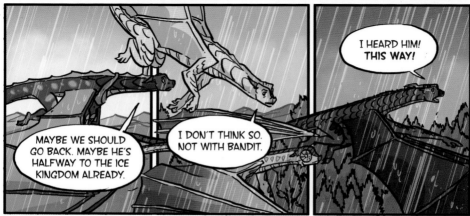

I HEARD HIM! THIS WAY!

MAYBE WE SHOULD GO BACK. MAYBE HE'S HALFWAY TO THE ICE KINGDOM ALREADY.

I DON'T THINK SO. NOT WITH BANDIT.

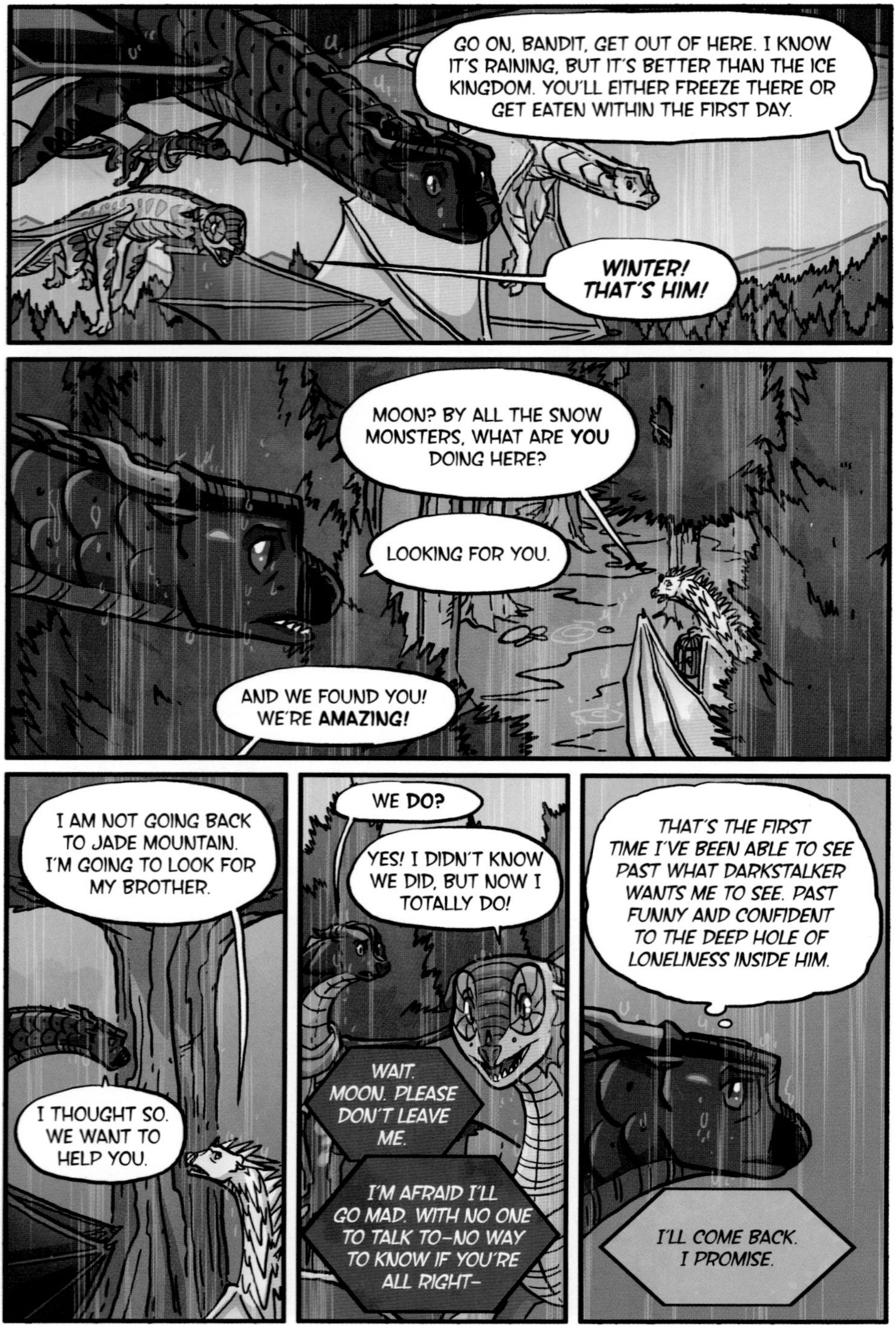
GO ON, BANDIT, GET OUT OF HERE. I KNOW IT'S RAINING, BUT IT'S BETTER THAN THE ICE KINGDOM. YOU'LL EITHER FREEZE THERE OR GET EATEN WITHIN THE FIRST DAY.
WINTER! THAT'S HIM!
MOON? BY ALL THE SNOW MONSTERS, WHAT ARE YOU DOING HERE?
LOOKING FOR YOU.
AND WE FOUND YOU! WE'RE AMAZING!
I AM NOT GOING BACK TO JADE MOUNTAIN. I'M GOING TO LOOK FOR MY BROTHER.
I THOUGHT SO. WE WANT TO HELP YOU.
WE DO?
YES! I DIDN'T KNOW WE DID, BUT NOW I TOTALLY DO!
WAIT. MOON. PLEASE DON'T LEAVE ME.
I'M AFRAID I'LL GO MAD. WITH NO ONE TO TALK TO—NO WAY TO KNOW IF YOU'RE ALL RIGHT—
THAT'S THE FIRST TIME I'VE BEEN ABLE TO SEE PAST WHAT DARKSTALKER WANTS ME TO SEE. PAST FUNNY AND CONFIDENT TO THE DEEP HOLE OF LONELINESS INSIDE HIM.
I'LL COME BACK. I PROMISE.

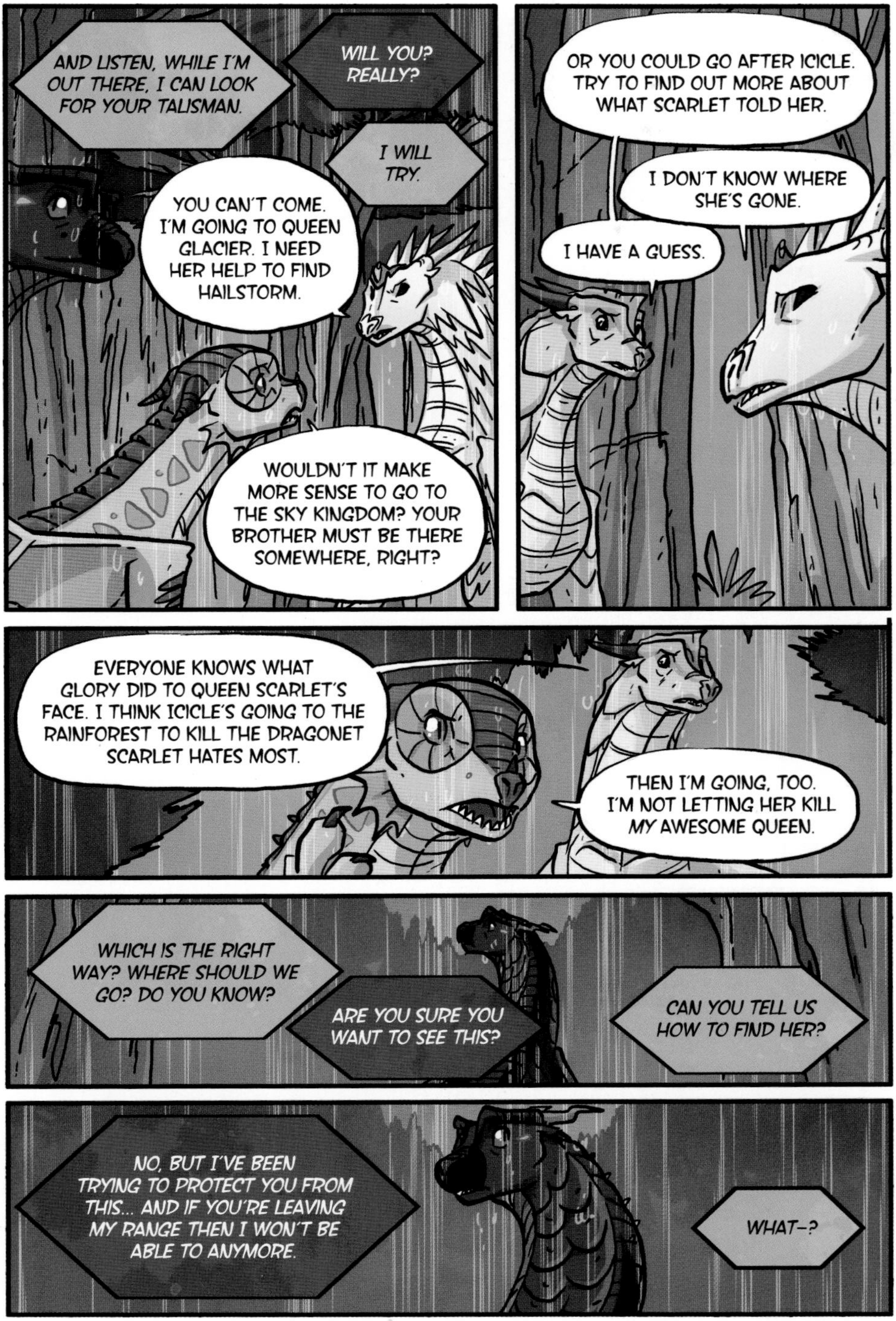
AND LISTEN, WHILE I'M OUT THERE, I CAN LOOK FOR YOUR TALISMAN.
WILL YOU? REALLY?
I WILL TRY.
YOU CAN'T COME. I'M GOING TO QUEEN GLACIER. I NEED HER HELP TO FIND HAILSTORM.
WOULDN'T IT MAKE MORE SENSE TO GO TO THE SKY KINGDOM? YOUR BROTHER MUST BE THERE SOMEWHERE, RIGHT?
OR YOU COULD GO AFTER ICICLE. TRY TO FIND OUT MORE ABOUT WHAT SCARLET TOLD HER.
I DON'T KNOW WHERE SHE'S GONE.
I HAVE A GUESS.
EVERYONE KNOWS WHAT GLORY DID TO QUEEN SCARLET'S FACE. I THINK ICICLE'S GOING TO THE RAINFOREST TO KILL THE DRAGONET SCARLET HATES MOST.
THEN I'M GOING, TOO. I'M NOT LETTING HER KILL *MY* AWESOME QUEEN.
WHICH IS THE RIGHT WAY? WHERE SHOULD WE GO? DO YOU KNOW?
ARE YOU SURE YOU WANT TO SEE THIS?
CAN YOU TELL US HOW TO FIND HER?
NO, BUT I'VE BEEN TRYING TO PROTECT YOU FROM THIS... AND IF YOU'RE LEAVING MY RANGE THEN I WON'T BE ABLE TO ANYMORE.
WHAT–?

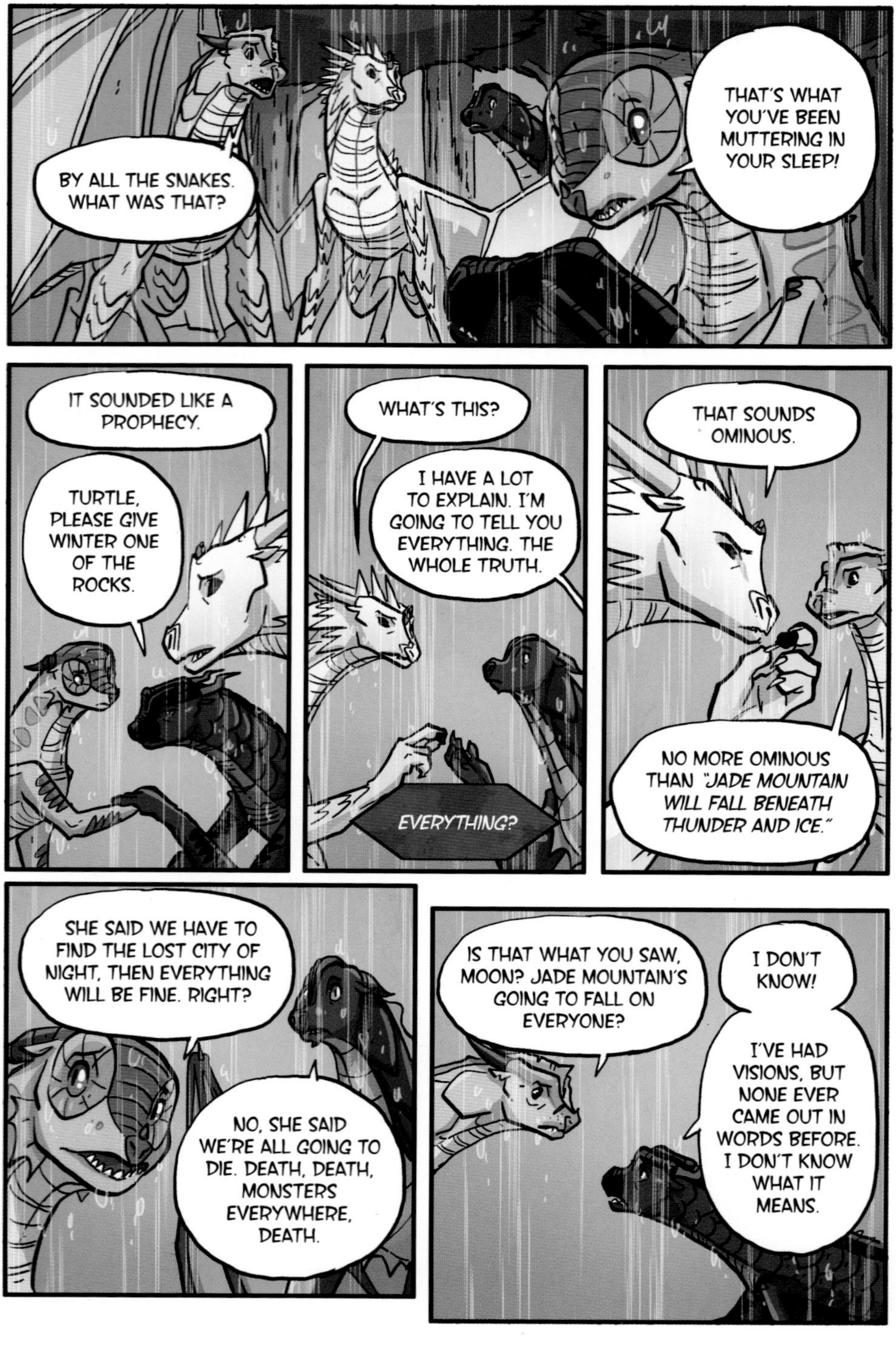
BY ALL THE SNAKES. WHAT WAS THAT?
THAT'S WHAT YOU'VE BEEN MUTTERING IN YOUR SLEEP!
IT SOUNDED LIKE A PROPHECY.
TURTLE, PLEASE GIVE WINTER ONE OF THE ROCKS.
WHAT'S THIS?
I HAVE A LOT TO EXPLAIN. I'M GOING TO TELL YOU EVERYTHING. THE WHOLE TRUTH.
EVERYTHING?
THAT SOUNDS OMINOUS.
NO MORE OMINOUS THAN "JADE MOUNTAIN WILL FALL BENEATH THUNDER AND ICE."
SHE SAID WE HAVE TO FIND THE LOST CITY OF NIGHT, THEN EVERYTHING WILL BE FINE. RIGHT?
NO, SHE SAID WE'RE ALL GOING TO DIE. DEATH, DEATH, MONSTERS EVERYWHERE, DEATH.
IS THAT WHAT YOU SAW, MOON? JADE MOUNTAIN'S GOING TO FALL ON EVERYONE?
I DON'T KNOW!
I'VE HAD VISIONS, BUT NONE EVER CAME OUT IN WORDS BEFORE. I DON'T KNOW WHAT IT MEANS.

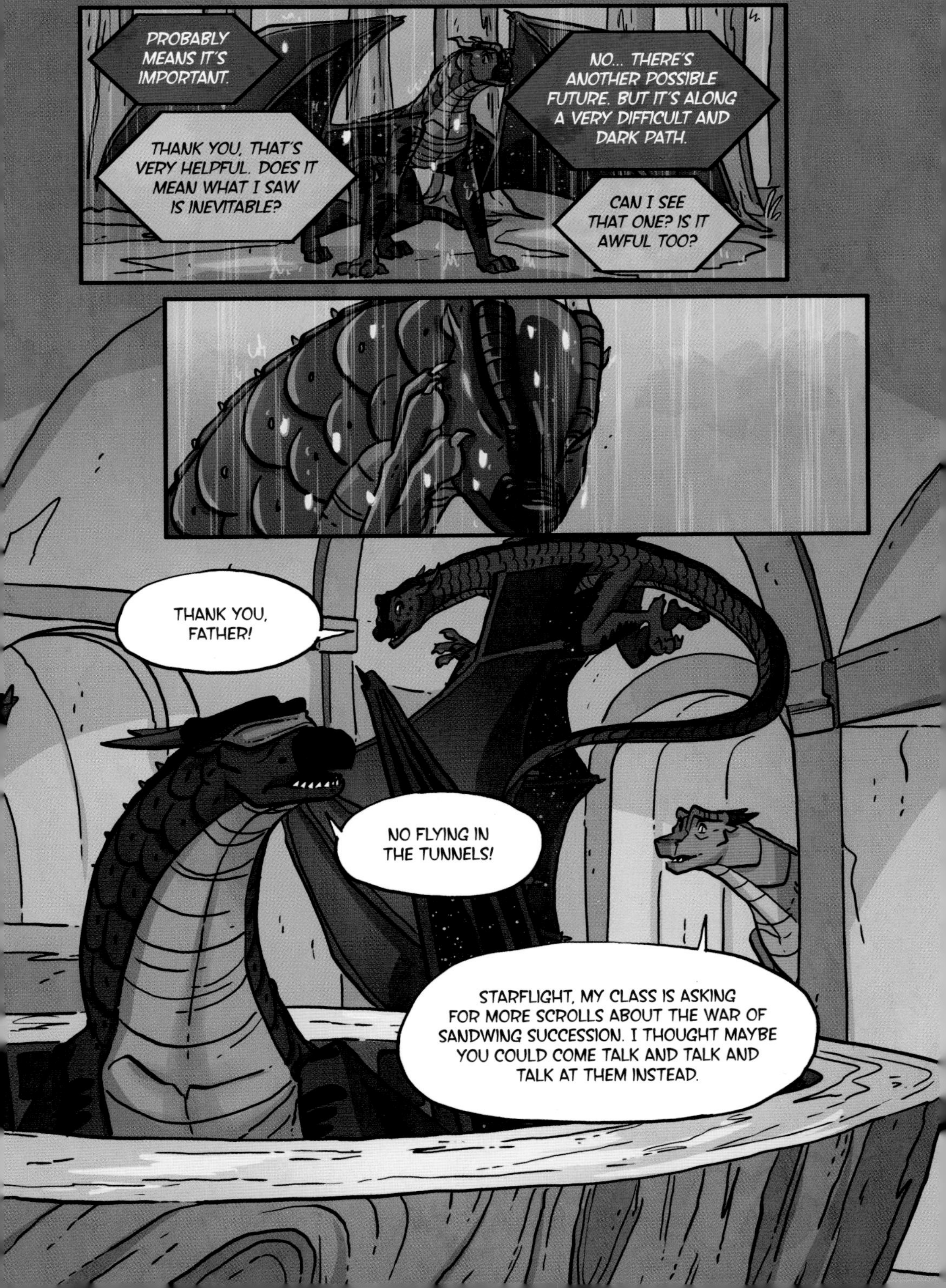
PROBABLY MEANS IT'S IMPORTANT.
THANK YOU, THAT'S VERY HELPFUL. DOES IT MEAN WHAT I SAW IS INEVITABLE?
NO... THERE'S ANOTHER POSSIBLE FUTURE. BUT IT'S ALONG A VERY DIFFICULT AND DARK PATH.
CAN I SEE THAT ONE? IS IT AWFUL TOO?
THANK YOU, FATHER!
NO FLYING IN THE TUNNELS!
STARFLIGHT, MY CLASS IS ASKING FOR MORE SCROLLS ABOUT THE WAR OF SANDWING SUCCESSION. I THOUGHT MAYBE YOU COULD COME TALK AND TALK AND TALK AT THEM INSTEAD.

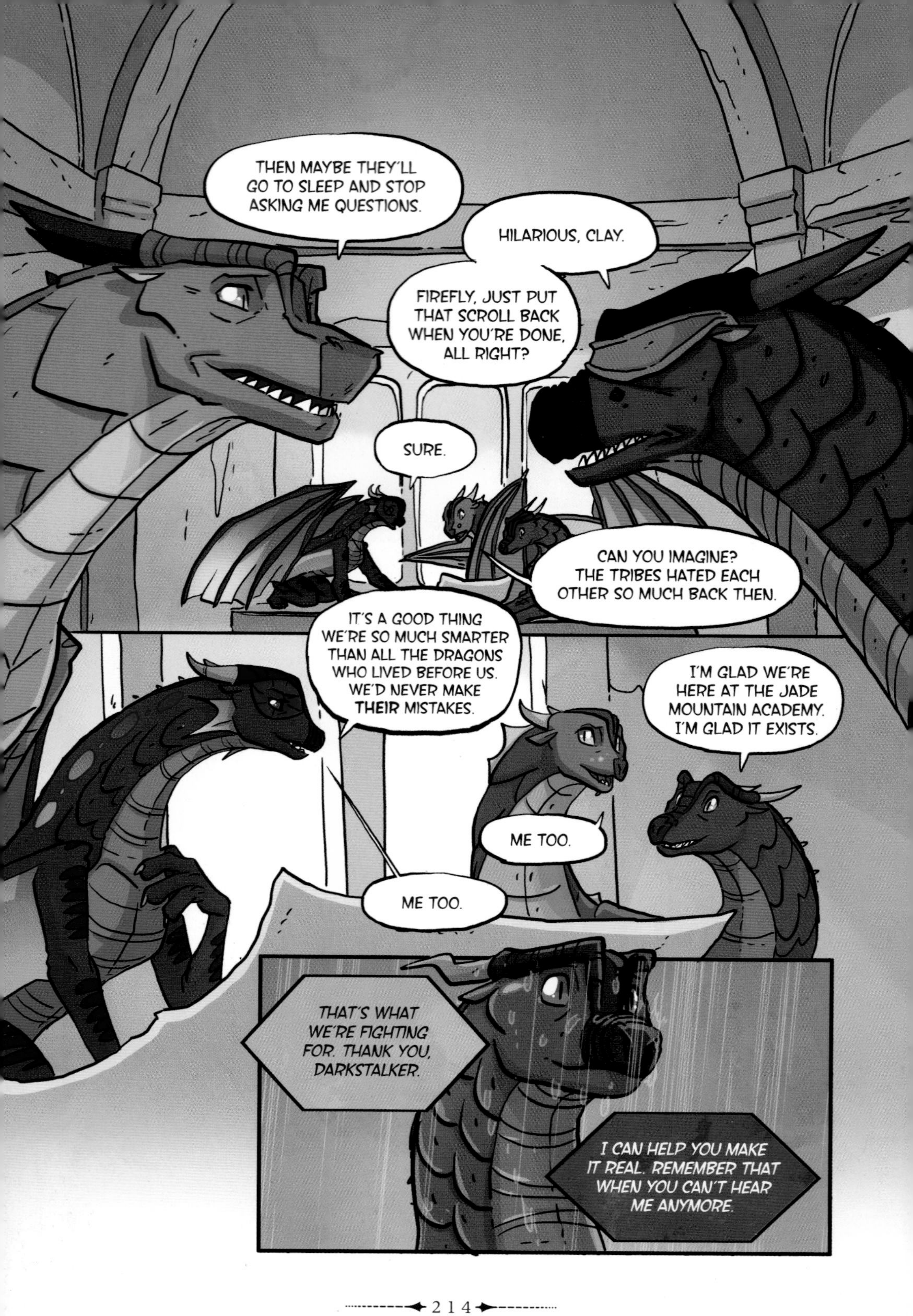
THEN MAYBE THEY'LL GO TO SLEEP AND STOP ASKING ME QUESTIONS.
HILARIOUS, CLAY.
FIREFLY, JUST PUT THAT SCROLL BACK WHEN YOU'RE DONE, ALL RIGHT?
SURE.
CAN YOU IMAGINE? THE TRIBES HATED EACH OTHER SO MUCH BACK THEN.
IT'S A GOOD THING WE'RE SO MUCH SMARTER THAN ALL THE DRAGONS WHO LIVED BEFORE US. WE'D NEVER MAKE **THEIR** MISTAKES.
I'M GLAD WE'RE HERE AT THE JADE MOUNTAIN ACADEMY. I'M GLAD IT EXISTS.
ME TOO.
ME TOO.
THAT'S WHAT WE'RE FIGHTING FOR. THANK YOU, DARKSTALKER.
I CAN HELP YOU MAKE IT REAL. REMEMBER THAT WHEN YOU CAN'T HEAR ME ANYMORE.

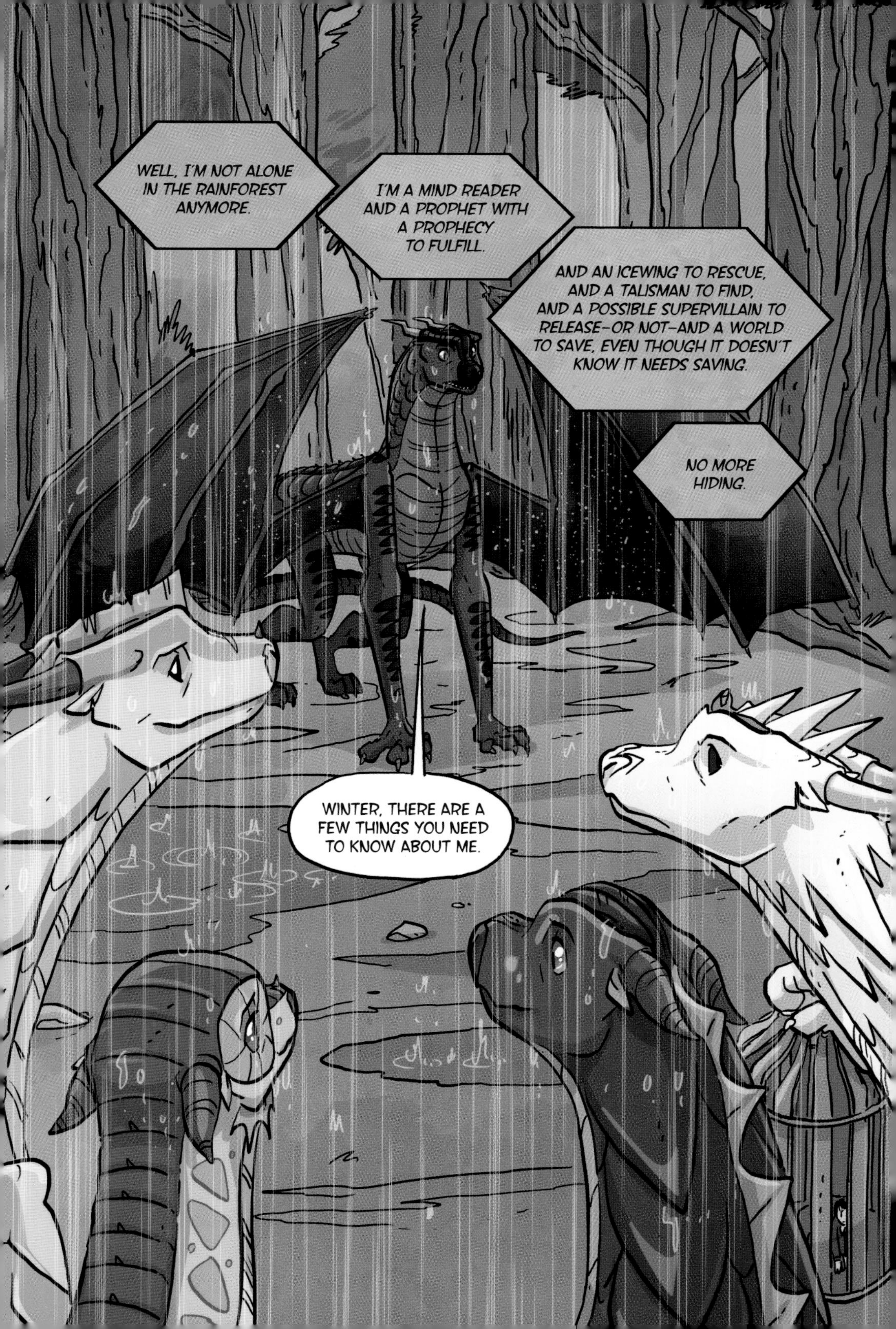
WELL, I'M NOT ALONE IN THE RAINFOREST ANYMORE.
I'M A MIND READER AND A PROPHET WITH A PROPHECY TO FULFILL.
AND AN ICEWING TO RESCUE, AND A TALISMAN TO FIND, AND A POSSIBLE SUPERVILLAIN TO RELEASE—OR NOT—AND A WORLD TO SAVE, EVEN THOUGH IT DOESN'T KNOW IT NEEDS SAVING.
NO MORE HIDING.
WINTER, THERE ARE A FEW THINGS YOU NEED TO KNOW ABOUT ME.

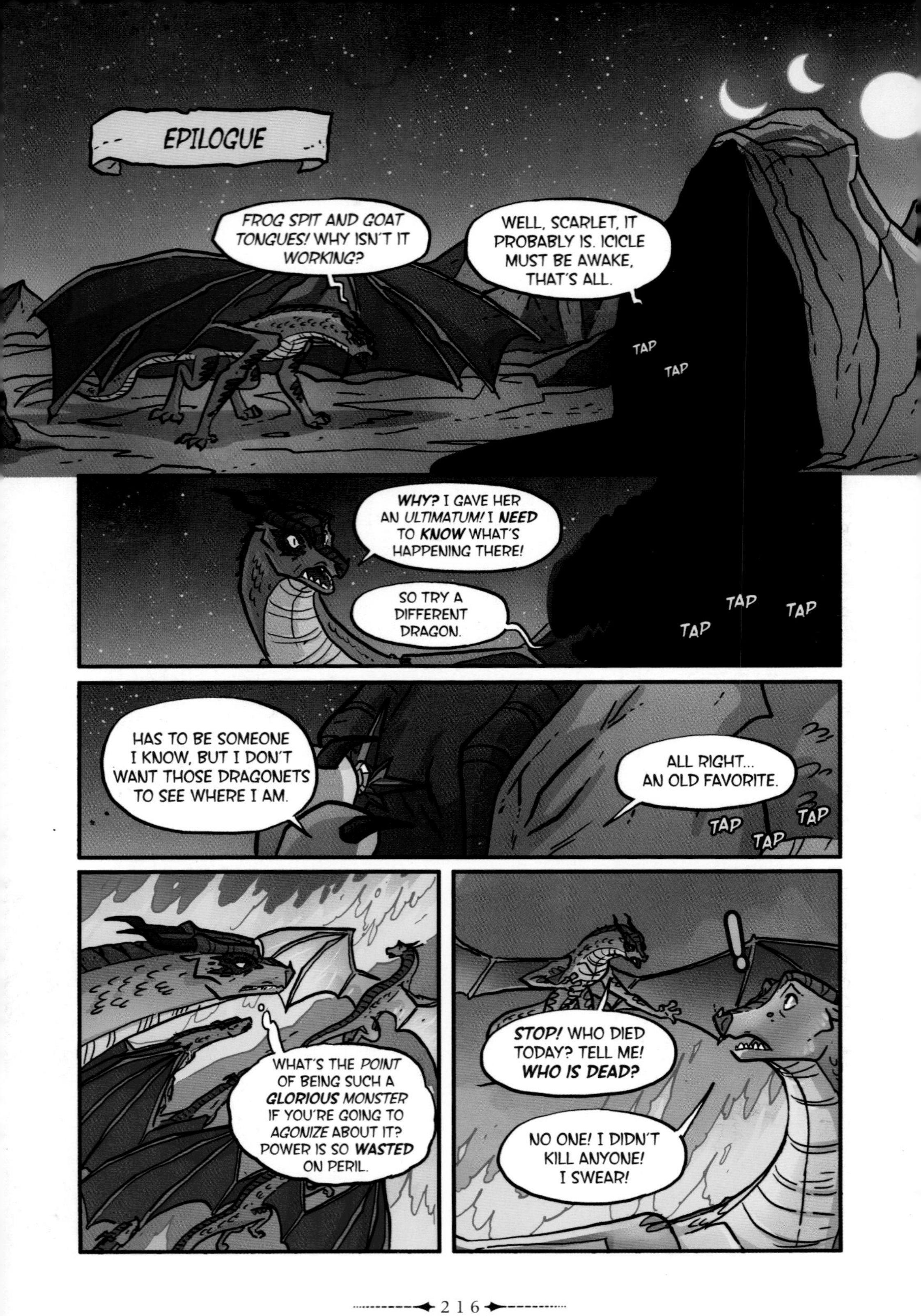
EPILOGUE
FROG SPIT AND GOAT TONGUES! WHY ISN'T IT WORKING?
WELL, SCARLET, IT PROBABLY IS. ICICLE MUST BE AWAKE, THAT'S ALL.
TAP TAP
WHY? I GAVE HER AN ULTIMATUM! I NEED TO KNOW WHAT'S HAPPENING THERE!
SO TRY A DIFFERENT DRAGON.
TAP TAP TAP
HAS TO BE SOMEONE I KNOW, BUT I DON'T WANT THOSE DRAGONETS TO SEE WHERE I AM.
ALL RIGHT... AN OLD FAVORITE.
TAP TAP TAP
WHAT'S THE POINT OF BEING SUCH A GLORIOUS MONSTER IF YOU'RE GOING TO AGONIZE ABOUT IT? POWER IS SO WASTED ON PERIL.
!
STOP! WHO DIED TODAY? TELL ME! WHO IS DEAD?
NO ONE! I DIDN'T KILL ANYONE! I SWEAR!

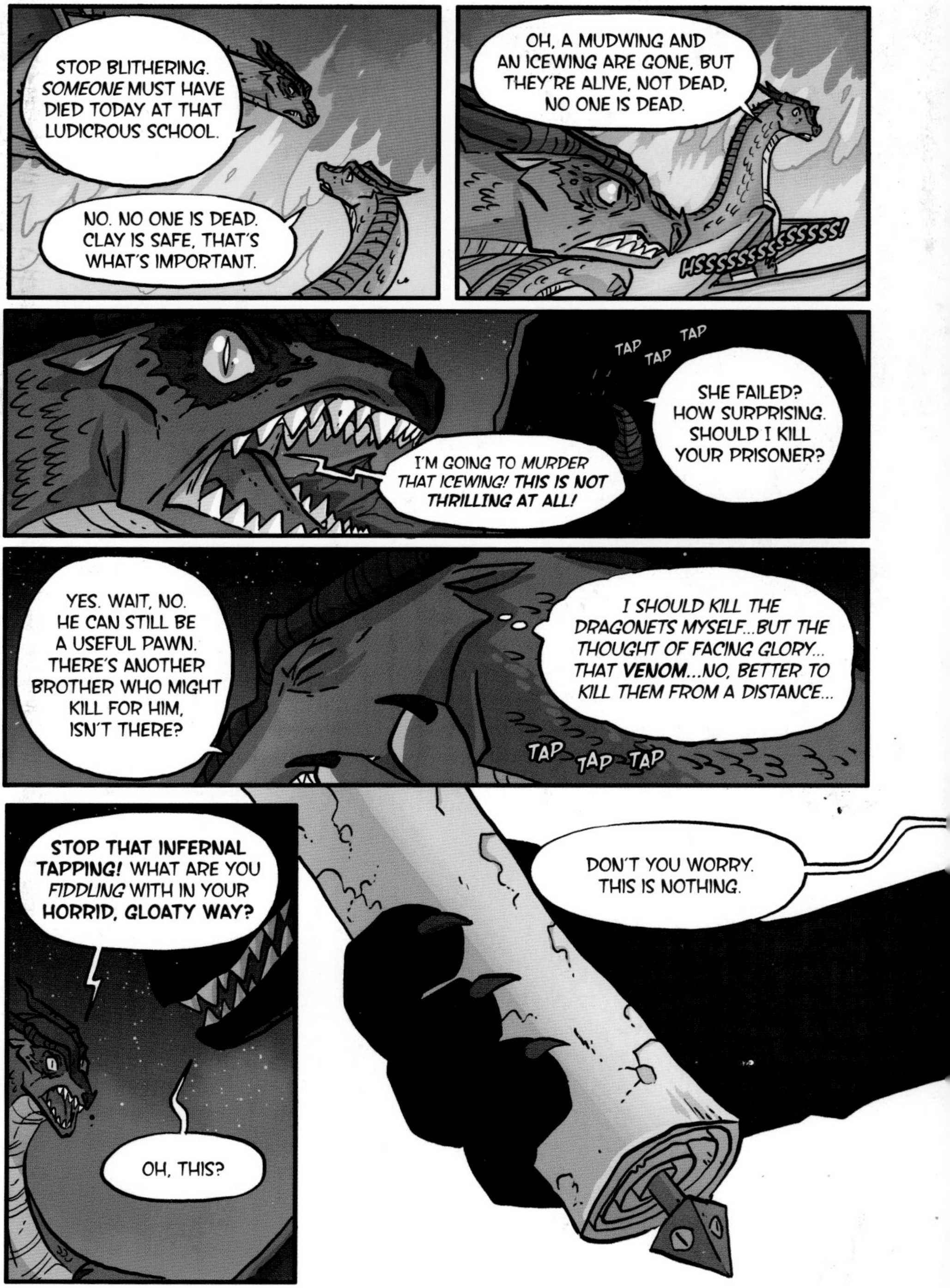
STOP BLITHERING. *SOMEONE* MUST HAVE DIED TODAY AT THAT LUDICROUS SCHOOL.
NO. NO ONE IS DEAD. CLAY IS SAFE, THAT'S WHAT'S IMPORTANT.
OH, A MUDWING AND AN ICEWING ARE GONE, BUT THEY'RE ALIVE, NOT DEAD, NO ONE IS DEAD.
HSSSSSSSSSSSSSSSS!
I'M GOING TO *MURDER* THAT ICEWING! **THIS IS NOT THRILLING AT ALL!**
TAP TAP TAP
SHE FAILED? HOW SURPRISING. SHOULD I KILL YOUR PRISONER?
YES. WAIT, NO. HE CAN STILL BE A USEFUL PAWN. THERE'S ANOTHER BROTHER WHO MIGHT KILL FOR HIM, ISN'T THERE?
I SHOULD KILL THE DRAGONETS MYSELF...BUT THE THOUGHT OF FACING GLORY... THAT ***VENOM***...*NO, BETTER TO KILL THEM FROM A DISTANCE...*
TAP TAP TAP
STOP THAT INFERNAL TAPPING! WHAT ARE YOU *FIDDLING* WITH IN YOUR **HORRID, GLOATY WAY?**
OH, THIS?
DON'T YOU WORRY. THIS IS NOTHING.

TUI T. SUTHERLAND is the author of the #1 *New York Times* and *USA Today* bestselling Wings of Fire series, the Menagerie trilogy, and the Pet Trouble series, as well as a contributing author to the bestselling Spirit Animals and Seekers series (as part of the Erin Hunter team). In 2009, she was a two-day champion on *Jeopardy!* She lives in Massachusetts with her wonderful husband, two awesome sons, and two very patient dogs. To learn more about Tui's books, visit her online at www.tuibooks.com.

BARRY DEUTSCH is an award-winning cartoonist and the creator of the Hereville series of graphic novels, about yet another troll-fighting 11-year-old Orthodox Jewish girl. He lives in Portland, Oregon, with a variable number of cats and fish.

MIKE HOLMES has drawn for the series Secret Coders, Adventure Time, and Bravest Warriors. He created the comic strip True Story, the art project *Mikenesses*, and his work can be seen in *MAD* Magazine. He lives in Philadelphia with his wife Meredith and son Oscar, along with Heidi the dog and Ella the cat.

MAARTA LAIHO spends her days and nights as a comic colorist, where her work includes the comics series Lumberjanes, Adventure Time, and The Mighty Zodiac. When she's not doing that, she can be found hoarding houseplants and talking to her cat. She lives in the woods of Maine.